WICKED CLONE

or
how to deal with the evil

a cinema novel

by

Mihaela Modorcea

INDIGGO Twins LLC

Each of us has got a wicked clone,

An evil twin that never leaves us alone...

To Basha,
with immortal
love & life !
Mihaela &
Gabriela
Indigo Twins

05/28/2015

PART 1

Oh Lord, why did you let this stake impale my heart
When all I needed was to love, not to be torn apart?

Giant eagles

with serpent eyes pierce the purple sky. With opened wings they strike the wind, blackening the Sun. With their beaks they turn the day into long nights, and block the clock at midnight.

The eyes of the Old Man grin with delight.

Twenty thousand stakes of men, scattered like maize, impale The Virgin Land. Mothers with children, fathers with fathers, uncles and aunts, nieces and grandparents, lords, merchants, boyars, Christians, Jews, heathens, saints, young and old, good or bad—are all suffering from the same cruel end. Their blood weeps down into the Black River, changing The Virgin Land into a whore of death. From their buttocks to their mouth, their hot flesh is pierced like meat is thrust on skewers. Crows rest on their shoulders, unscared by such strawmen.

Counting his impaled, The Old Man loses track of his own age. His eyes shake with tears, but his smile wipes the fear.

The stars fall, the water growls, the earth boils, feeding on the young and old. Unborn babies are forced on stakes through their mothers' wombs where eagles dig out living tombs. With monstrous claws they seize the corpse, squeezing their bones and swallowing the bodies covered in gore. Infants and children, hanging upside down with opened mouths, cry mournfully their song...

Suddenly the sky breaks, crushed by ache.

"What have you done to these people? You said you have impaled the rich to save the poor. But what is this, Old Man?" a Voice from above asks in pain.

"I need one more chance!" the Old Man begs.

A great hall.

Poor sick vagrants, beggars, cripples, gypsy women, orphans, feverishly jostle to take a seat at the fabulous feast prepared especially for their "highnesses." They all start wolfing down the imperial goodies brought to them by the Old Man himself, rushing with dirty hands inside golden plates: wild boar on proțap[1], black rooster ciorbă[2], bulz[3], quail eggs baked over hot coals, baked stuffed pheasant, wild trout skewers, deer tenderloin in black goat blood, scoverzi[4] with honey and walnuts, gingerbread stakes... Then, they all start drenching their tongues, leaving their worries inside jeweled cups: old țuică[5], "Bear Power" red wine, afinată and zmeurată[6]...and other sweet drinks that lift up the spirits...

With a warm, generous smile, the Old Man addresses the crowd:

"Dear friends, I have invited you here as no one should go hungry in my land. Feel at home! Eat and drink all night long! Your welfare is my welfare!"

The poor men's eyes glitter with enthusiasm. They all applaud their benefactor. Animated by the Old Man's speech and aplomb, they continue to savor the meals with the attitude and trust of honored guests.

After they are all satisfied and fully warmed up, laughing and partying noisily, the Old Man makes his appearance again, kindly asking his guests:

"What else do you desire? Do you want to live without worries, lacking nothing in this world?"

Exchanging furtive looks of encouragement, the poor responds:

"Yes, we do, master!"

"So be it!" the Old Man consents.

And in a twinkle, with the snap of his long-nailed fingers, the great hall's doors and casements shut. Flames gulp down the hall, hideous

---

[1] ***Proțap*** *is a primitive system, consisting of two sticks split at one end and stuck in the ground, between which meat, fish, etc are put to roast.*

[2] ***Ciorbă*** *is the traditional Romanian sour soup.*

[3] ***Bulz*** *is baked polenta with Romanian sheep cheese and cream.*

[4] ***Scoverzi*** *are a kind of pies from leavened dough, fried in butter or sunflower oil and filled with cheese, curd, etc.*

[5] ***Țuică*** *is a plum brandy.*

[6] ***Afinată and zmeurată*** *are alcoholic drinks made of blueberries and raspberries.*

claws seize rapidly the royal ceiling and floor. Women with babies, hags with canes, men without teeth, widowers of faith, scream to breathe, making crosses of salvation to live.

A majestic variety of Transylvanian delights—wild rabbit in red apple sauce, drob de miel[7], roasted bear meat with hot pepper sauce and rice in țest[8], gogonele[9] and pickled red cabbage, sarmale[10] with mămăligă[11] and răcituri[12], ciorbă de burtă[13] and mititei[14] in toothpicks of fir—all flavor the ashes sacrificed to fuel the soul of the generous host.

While watching the inferno through the wall opening of the Throne Hall, his white Moses-vestment starts bleeding, contaminated by tens of drops that greedily invade the floor. His eyes grin; his face swells with pride; his heart reigns with the thirst of revenge.

Hitting the blood-flooded ground with his stake-scepter, the Old Man splashes his courtiers, spitting out words of extreme content:

"I did it for you, respectable boyars, so that they represent no further burden to our country. No one shall be poor in my realm!"

One by one, the courtiers bow down to kiss the hand of the Old Man that holds the royal scepter. They breathe easily when their Majesty spares them from a "staked spank," and beam with joy when the Old Man snaps his fingers to withdraw to his apartments.

Satiated with his latest victory, the generous host shakes his long vestment while drops of blood keep dripping and melting in the dark.

---

[7] *Drob de miel* is a Romanian-style lamb haggis made of minced offal (heart, liver, lungs) with spices, wrapped in a caul and roasted.

[8] *Țest* is a bell shaped archaic earth oven made of river clay that makes the bread gain a magical taste.

[9] *Gogonele* are pickled green tomatoes.

[10] *Sarmale* are made of minced meat with rice, wrapped in pickled cabbage leaves or grape leaves.

[11] *Mămăligă* is cornmeal mush, the Romanian-style polenta.

[12] *Răcituri* or *piftie* is an aspic made from low-grade pork meat, such as the head and the feet of the pig as they contain a lot more gelatin than any other part of the pig. The meat is boiled with garlic and bay leaves. The mixture is then placed in containers and cooled. It makes a jelly.

[13] *Ciorbă de burtă* is tripe soup soured with sour cream.

[14] *Mititei (mici)* are grilled meat rolls made from a mixture of beef, lamb and pork and spices such as garlic, thyme, black pepper, coriander.

The Voice from Above speaks again:

"That was enough!"

"I implore your forgiveness," the Old Man kneels in shame.

"Your time had come so many times and I have shown you so much mercy. How much more to show?"

"I'm a sinner. You've made me a helpless human being, a monster that had no other choice than ruling as a monster..."

"I gave you the power to choose. Why have you chosen this?" The Voice continues to ask, resounding in the mirror that hangs before the Man.

The Old Man looks inside the mirror and sees Violeta and Grid.

Violeta and Grid

were a happy couple...until one night.

Fire. The whole house is on fire. Violeta and Grid look helplessly at the claws of fire that burn all of their wealth, memories and...child.

Their only child, Vlady, is in the middle of the flames.

Violeta screams out desperately:

"My baby! Let me take my baby out!"

Grid is trying forcefully to hold Violeta in his arms, to keep her away from running amid the falling pieces of wood.

"My future and love is there!" Violeta cries out again. "Let me go!"

"Too late, my dear, we have to save you!" Grid mourns grief-stricken.

"But I'm nothing without him, just a piece of that falling wood! Let me die with my baby!"

Violeta's tears fall from her eyes with the rapidity of a waterfall overflowing on the dried ground that spreads before them.

Her voice, loud and husky, seems to awake all the sleepy creatures of the night. Her arms, raised high to the sky, join her ardent imploration which could break even the cruelest man's heart.

The wind keeps blowing angrily over the valley that is silently watching the devastating spectacle.

Before this doomed night, for many weeks, Violeta had had the same dream in which a longhaired woman warned her that Vlady would be taken away from her. The woman's red mouth that opened into a scream of death, had terrified her. Yet each time Violeta had turned to grasp the woman by her hair to stop her for an answer, the woman would show the bald back of her head and disappear in the dark...

Violeta had divulged that nightmare to her husband, but as they never believed in superstitions and signs like those, they did not bother to unveil the mystery of that annoying dream.

Violeta and Grid have always believed in God! Violeta would make a big cross, kneel down, and utter "Our Father." At times, she would just spit three times into her bosoms and say out loud: "Ptiu, Ptiu, drace, Ptiu!" "Shoo, Shoo devil, Shoo!"

Magia, the one-eyed witch of the town and aunt of Violeta, had begged Violeta to describe her dream. Yet Violeta had refused to rummage in her wound, knowing that Magia's fortune-telling would either scare or make her laugh.

Violeta and Grid were peaceful and kind people. They lived in Braşov, Transylvania, on the way to Poiana, also called The Lucky Wheel. Grid owned a small inn that bore his name, from which they were earning their living. At Grid's inn, one could get traditional Transylvanian costumes, handpainted plates, old wall clocks, folk wooden cradles, braided dolls, ethnic wool quilts and pillows, Venetian antique red coral beads, silk embroideries, leather articles, Transylvanian peasant' shoes, handmade belts, vests, and folk blouses...

Most of the costumes and blouses sold at Grid's inn had been handmade by Violeta, who inherited this talent from her mother Victoria and her great-grandmother Lucia.

Violeta was over forty years old when she finally gave birth to Vlady. And since then, she had prayed continuously and cuddled him in her arms, never losing her little boy from her eyes. But on the night of Saint Andrew, November 29th, 1480, just one hour of separation brought Vlady's terrible death.

Now, sewing a costume for her baby boy, Violeta refuses to accept that Vlady is dead. She feels that he is alive. She feels that he is hiding, "but Mama will find him!"

Blood pours out of her hands, yet Violeta keeps sewing the costume for her baby boy.

Magia

…casts down spells to Mama, yet Mama is cast inside a coma, calling for her son. Her eyes blocked to the sky, her hands mortified by the untouched child, she thinks that she is still dreaming, waiting to catch the long black haired woman in the dark, so that she can wake up and find her little boy alive. Violeta knows that woman stole her child, but she'll return him at the call of God.

Rubbing her hands, Magia feels guilty. Dreadful thoughts race through her heart, and yet she cannot pour them all out. She was the one who begged Violeta to listen to her advice; she was the one that brought the death of her niece's child. Only a miracle can save her tormented nights.

Nevertheless, Magia is well-known among the inhabitants of Transylvania for her magical powers; hence her name Magia. She has saved several people from death and has broken spells and curses of despairing neighbors.

And at that time, November 1480, when the days had turned into long nights, and the nights into hours of sleeplessness, Magia wanted to help Grid and her beloved niece, with all her powers. Thus, she called Violeta and Grid to come to her house hastily that night—The Night of Saint Andrew, November 29th.

Each night of Saint Andrew brought young mothers panic and sufferance. When the moon was full and big as a house, murky and dark, a child would be stolen and never to be found. That night of Saint Andrew was also called The Night of the Vampires-Strigoi.

The sun had not appeared for seven days, the cows refused to give milk, the grass to grow, the bees to toil, the horses to ride, and so everyone was expecting the visit of the Old Vampire-Strigoi.

The Old Vampire-Strigoi, the cunning leader of all vampires–strigoi[15] from Transylvania, and all of his servants, both dead and alive, were extremely dangerous, a true catastrophe for the people's harvest and for their animals, but especially for their newly born babies.

That night of Saint Andrew, the vampires-strigoi were coming out of their old bodies, trying to enter the bodies of the newborns in order to suck the freshness of their clean blood and prolong their own miserable lives. Prayers and chants had never been enough to keep them away from the poor, sweet infants.

Moreover, in Magia's eyes, the vampires-strigoi were extremely vengeful because they had died without fulfilling their dreams, and were eager to stop others from achieving their own.

The Old Vampire-Strigoi resembled a seductive man of 50-60

---

[15] *The vampires-strigoi were, according to the popular belief, of two sorts: living and dead.*

The living vampires-strigoi are spirits of people who left their bodies during their sleep, without their knowledge. They could perform three somersaults taking the shape of an animal and mounting on tails of brooms or on wooden barrels; they stole the crops and the milk of the cows, they blighted the bulls, they took the power of men, they stole the scythes and the beater knives that they could find in the yards of people. They became men again in places known only by them, like frontiers, forests, or at crossroads where they fought with the dead vampires-strigoi until one of them became the winner. The winner of the fight was going to be their leader for one year.

The dead vampires-strigoi were immaterial creatures, restless souls who entered the bodies of non-believers. They were spirits of the dead who didn't go to the afterlife because their burial rituals were not properly fulfilled. The dead vampires-strigoi used to leave their coffins and return among the living, provoking great suffering to their relatives, sucking their blood and defacing them, bringing pestilence and hail, playing with bears and wolves. They would dance at crossroads until the roosters' crowing when their bodies would have to go back to their graves. It is known that the tomb of a vampire-strigoi could be found by bringing a black steed to the cemetery and making it jump over the graves. If the black steed didn't want to jump over a grave, that meant that the dead had turned into a vampire.

years old. The only thing that made him recognizable was his tail: a long, black, powerful and sharp tail with which he could strangle his victim in a flash. Yet he knew to hide the secret of his force around his body, craftily, and walk gallantly, like a loving parent.

Magia has tried to catch the Old Vampire-Strigoi for decades. She wanted to avenge her old friend Fifina, whose newborn baby had been perversely killed by the Old Vampire-Strigoi thirteen years ago.

The Old Vampire-Strigoi had taken the shape of Fifina's old cat, scratched her baby 'til it bled, and then sucked the blood of the poor child, until its last drop. And then he had killed Fifina too, with just one slash of his poisonous tail.

Magia had gathered all of her energies to save Fifina. She had uttered chants and performed her most powerful spells to bring Fifina back to life, yet the cut of the Old Vampire-Strigoi's tail had been fatal.

Nevertheless, Magia had cared to analyze Fifina's cut attentively, and extracted the venom that his tail had left. Thus, she prepared a solution to weaken her enemy and shield the beautiful child of Violeta.

The night of Saint Andrew, November 29th, 1480.

It is a stormy night of thunders and barking dogs unleashed that makes little Vlady fret terribly inside his crib, and cry louder than the wind. It is the night that leads Violeta to listen to her aunt Magia's advice.

With Vlady in her arms, Violeta descends the stairs to the basement of their house. She lays her baby Vlady inside a cradle, in their secret chamber, puts him to sleep, and covers him with big leaves of oak and a goodnight kiss. She then places thick slats of dry coniferous wood over the windows, splashes them with holy water, and makes a big sign of the cross. She tiptoes her way out of the chamber, locks the door securely, and hides the key inside her chest.

That's what Magia advised Violeta to do: not to bring Vlady with her that night, but just pretend that she and Grid are carrying him with them.

Quickly, Violeta wraps Vlady's diapers and clothes in a bundle, and sets forth with Grid to Aunt Magia's house.

Meanwhile, Magia has made a wooden doll identical to Vlady with which she has planned to entice the Old Vampire-Strigoi. Her claw of iron, flamed up in the cauldron of hot poisonous mushrooms that she carefully dried about seven years ago, is now prepared to catch his viscous tail.

Up in her magical tower, filled up with holy power from the stars, Magia lays the baby doll on a white-flowered wooden table, and teaches Violeta how to perform the ritual for her boy Vlady. She first anoints the doll with the solution prepared from the vampire's venom taken from Fifina's cut so that the baby's body will be made stronger than the enemy's. She then burns chrism Frankincense in three small candles and places them under three old icons with saints of their bewitched town so that the smoke emitted will be an aura of eternal guard for Vlady. Next, Magia dresses the wooden doll in Vlady's clothes and diapers, and places a braided crown of willow onto his head so that the little child will bear a kingly mind. Magia then ties a red thread sewn with 41 wheat grains around the wooden doll's left wrist, and advises Violeta to tie this thread around Vlady's little hand during all holidays so that he'll live a life of love. Magia also prepared a little talisman for Vlady—a red thread with a small bottle of crystal that held a ray of sun which will give light to Vlady in times of darkness.

At last, Magia casts a spell on the wooden doll and splashes it with water brought from the Black Mountain, from the twin rivers Olt and Mureş.

After the ritual, Magia folds up the diapers and clothes of Vlady, and places between them fresh leaves of basil, for good fortune.

Knowing that midnight is near, Magia urges Violeta and Grid to get back to Vlady at the speed of light, so that he will not wake up and cry, and the underworld open its door to his sound. Thus, agitated and troubled, Magia forgets to give them the little talisman with the ray of sun.

Although they run as fast as horses, when Violeta and Grid arrive back at their house, the midnight has already stolen the joy of their lives… The claws of fire have already taken the basement, which monstrously collapses before the terrified eyes of Grid and his beautiful wife…

Two years later.
Violeta and Grid live in an improvised house where cold strikes their bones. It is a rural house made of clay, short, and holding small windows through which one can easily see from the outside.

Nearby this fragile accommodation, Grid has been building up a solid house of wood. He has hoped that he could finish it earlier as Violeta's health has gotten worse.

Violeta has been having nervous coughing, throwing up, high temperature, abdominal bloating, extreme fatigue… In fact, these symptoms, and most especially her big swollen belly, have appeared out of her powerful desire to have another child.

Violeta "has a false pregnancy," the doctor explains to Grid, overwhelmed.

Oppressed by Vlady's loss, Violeta is told that she can never give birth to another child. Doctors don't give her a chance; hundreds of prayers haven't seemed to come to an answer.

Yet one day, knelt down in front of his wife's belly,
with his hands crossed on her abdomen that has started to collapse like a sad balloon, Grid decides to bring Violeta to the Hall of Wonders from the Women's Cave.

This prodigious place was carved inside the womb of the twin calcareous mountains Parâng where the Goddess of Fertility and the shamans have performed hundreds of miracles for the barren women all around the world.

As soon as they arrive at the Women's Cave and enter its peaceful realm, Violeta and Grid are required to obey a seven-day ritual.

Dressed up in festive clothing handmade by the shamans themselves, Violeta drinks a potion of "Fertile Wonder Water" and follows a diet based on plants reaped by the shamans, plants that stimulate fertility and that are only known to them.

After a purifying ritual where her body is washed with sacred water dripped down from the stalactites, Violeta is lain down upon a bed of fresh grass, and led to the holy stalagmite placed in front of the Fertility Goddess Altar.

The mystical shamans, who run the Sacred Hall of Wonders, kneel down and start calling out to the spirit of the Goddess.

Clean as the daylight, Violeta rises amidst the healing steams, and displays her offerings and a fervent request letter to the Fertility Goddess Altar. Held by two twin calcareous stones that look like two Dacian[16] monsters, the Altar seems to hide all the secrets of the Creation of the World.

---

[16] *The Dacians were an ancient Indo-European people, the ancestors of the Romanians, and the most courageous of the Thracians– according to Herodotus.*
They bear a sensational mythology.
The historian of religions, Mircea Eliade attempted, in his book "From Zalmoxis to Genghis Khan," to give a mythological foundation to an alleged special relation between "Dacians and the wolves": Dacians called themselves "wolves" or "ones the same with wolves," the existence of a ritual approving their ability to turn into wolves.
The flag of the Dacians represented a head of a wolf called draco. The legend says that young Decebal, the king of the Dacians, saved a baby-wolf's life and then the wolf saved Decebal's life, sacrificing for his master. In the memory of his devoted wolf, Decebal created the Dacian flag with a wolf's head and with a body in form of a dragon.
Decebal was the most courageous, wise and proud king of the Dacians. Both his sister Dochia and Decebal committed suicide, so that they would not become prisoners of the Romans. The religion of Dacians was based on the immortality of the soul. They were weeping at the birth of a newborn and they were laughing and celebrating at one's death.

The Master Shaman enters a Dacian trance, beseeching the Goddess to come down among them and restore Violeta's fertility.

At the master's call, two bats splash Violeta's womb with liquor made up of deadly nightshade, while the leader-shaman scatters healing powder upon Violeta's heart, rubbing two amethyst rocks against each other.

Three nights in a row, the shamans sprinkle seeds of hogweed on the red-hot coals of the fire that faces the Fertility Goddess Altar.

Inhaling the smoke of hogweed seeds, Violeta falls into a deep sleep. The shamans carry the sleeping body of Violeta into the recess of the south-side wall of the Hall of Wonders.

After three long nights of deep sleep, Violeta wakes up. Confidently, the shamans analyze Violeta's womb and eyes just to discover the unexpected truth: for the very first time, their spells have not reached the known outcome—Violeta did not respond to their incantations; all of those sacred prayers and ceremonies did not bring the miracle child that Violeta and Grid have been praying for.

Back home, Grid looks hopelessly at their future

as Violeta turns more and more into a shadow of herself.

Tormented, and still trying to find a medicine for his half-dead wife, Grid appeals to a last choice: Magia.

Leaving Violeta alone in her bedroom, raving under the claws of night, Grid sneaks out to the house of Aunt Magia.

The agony through which Violeta has gone in the last two years has exhausted Grid no matter how much he loved her. The same images of little Vlady swallowed by fire, the same phrase "Let me take my baby out!" have been echoing without cessation in their house, every single night.

Bewildered by Grid's late night visit and by his tearful eyes, Aunt Magia opens her magic book at once and starts reading aloud.

"Yes, that's it!" she cries out after a few moments of search.

She then rushes to look through her coffers and closets, between her basement and mansard, in every nook and cranny...for the antidote of infertility. She finally finds it inside the pantry, in an old vase of musty cast-iron kettle.

"This mushroom, once put in red wine, will grow as big as a baby," Magia explains to Grid with great pathos. "Violeta will have to drink its gravy seven times a day, and she'll then bear fruit."

No sooner has she finished her prescription than Magia reads inside her magic book about the risks of this cure, which warn that the mushroom could kill Violeta at the birth of the new child.

"You know...this mushroom is too old. It has stayed inside this vase for too long. It's dangerous for Violeta..." Magia stutters to Grid. Then, growing red in the face, she adds in a low trembled voice:

"There is yet an Old Man...who has been my guru, and who knows a lot..."

"Then let's go to him. We have no time to lose," Grid bursts out, his arms shaking with frenzy.

"It's not that easy to reach him... This old teacher of mine has refused to see human faces for over a decade... But let me think of a way to convince him to let you enter his house..."

Nevertheless, that very same night, Magia and Grid set out to the dwelling of the Old Man Vlad. That was the name of Magia's guru.

Vlad lives in a big old house in Brasov, in a boyar dwelling that everyone thought to have been forsaken for years. The majestic yet dilapidated tower, the old porch of inlaid ebony, the dried and worn grain along the rotten siding, the darkened walls on which people scraped their initials, the large gaping holes inside the roof, are all unnoticeable at first sight as the broken loose trees craftily cover the ramshackle house and its dark, outcast, inhospitable atmosphere.

Magia enters the creepy steel gate cautiously, avoiding the snake-headed fountain that seems to be looking at her with human eyes. Tight to her chest, she holds the letter that she wrote about Violeta and Grid for the Old Man. With quick, feverish steps, she cuts through the muddy garden, and climbs the cracked stairs of Vlad's house. She then kneels down, and slides the letter under the black massive walnut door. Barely has she finished slipping it under when a cold hand snatches her letter.

Magia gives a shout of fear.

"Stay where you are!" a deep voice commands her.

"Yes!" Magia gasps in awe.

After a couple of moments, the man interrupts the silence:

"Tomorrow, after twilight!"

"Tomorrow, teacher? What about…"

"They should come see me tomorrow!" the Old Man cuts her off.

"Oh, thank you master, of course…" Magia stutters, relieved.

Then, with the same rapid moves, she returns to Grid, puzzled by the prompt answer and unusual welcoming of her old teacher.

"How did he know that I was there? There was no light outside, but only darkness…" Magia speaks to herself as she passes through the muddy garden. She then grasps Grid's arm, and walks with him back to his house.

The fire is still burning in the stove. Violeta is sleeping like a baby. Her face, though very pale, is shining greatly after that raving night of fever.

Magia tiptoes to Violeta's bed and caresses her face, worryingly. She then takes out the golden needle that she wore at her chest, and slightly stings with it Violeta's forehead. She kneels before Violeta's bed, lights up three candles, and sprinkles upon them, out of a talisman, an indigo powder. Magia then starts to chant and utter groans, in an old dark Romanian voice:

"Piei, drace al sterpăciunii!
Ajută-i, Doamne, Violetei să nască pui nou, sănătos!
Piei, drace, din pântecul Violetei,
Ajută-i, Doamne, să mai nască un copilaş vânjos!
Somn uşor, Vlady, în mormântu-ţi mic,
Strigăt de copil dulce, de copil voinic,
Adu bucurie, răni vindecate,

Du-te înapoi în iadul tău, răutate,
Risipiţi-vă, vrăji! Vino, bunătate!"

"Leave, devil of sterility, from Violeta's womb,
Help her give birth to a new baby in bloom!
Vlady, sleep restfully in your little tomb,
And let Violeta live in peace, away from your gloom!
Cry of a sweet toddler wash off her wounds,
And bring joyful days into their new room!
Go back to your hell—wickedness, spells...or any other dooms!"

An indigo aura begins to float around Violeta's head.

Magia's lachrymose eyes open wider and wider, her mouth whispering in awe:

"Violeta is chosen!"

Bowing her head with veneration, Magia lays her hands on Violeta's womb:

"This aura announces a chosen child whom Violeta will bear soon!"

Magia raises her arms to the ceilings, and walks towards Grid who has been fervently praying to the old icon of the Virgin Mary.

"Your prayers have been heard, dear Grid! You shall have a child, soon, very soon... Yet not a usual one, but an aura-gifted one!" Magia tells him, transfixed.

Exulting in Magia's words, Grid kisses her hands with gratitude as a bloodied tear of hope stains his white shirt.

Next morning, as Grid prepares to confess to Violeta about Magia's old teacher and the arranged visit, Violeta's appearance strikes him.

"No, it is neither her long new nightdress that I just bought for her, nor her freshly trimmed hair, nor her long night sleep..." Grid whispers to himself. "It is her face so beautifully glowing, her black eyes bigger and shinier than ever, the freshness of her complexion that is showing Violeta as young as when I first met her."

After years of sullen face and darkness, Grid can finally see a radiant

Violeta, smiling... He cheerfully takes her into his arms, and asks his wife:

"What has happened, my sweetheart?"

"I had a beautiful dream..." Violeta recalls. "There were two big lights, two big lights set on two golden candleholders...held by an old man. He was dressed in a white robe. I couldn't see his face though... But these lights were so powerful and calming, so reassuring. Then...they changed into two angelic faces, and then...they turned into some strange creatures, supernatural beings! I could not precisely see their faces though... But they were calling me with childlike voices, calling me by my name. And I immediately felt my mind relieved, my body lightened, purified... Then, just for a moment, Vlady's little face appeared before my eyes. He was smiling, with his sweet little mouth... He was so happy! Suddenly, I saw myself younger and more beautiful, dancing like a princess, with him in my arms... I was so happy!"

A breeze of fear, somehow, frowns upon Violeta, but she immediately shakes it off, continuing to recall:

"You were calling me desperately, as something awful had happened, and I was imploring you to let me stay and dance on that golden lawn a little more... You were holding a baby in your arms, a strange baby. In a flash, the baby bit your hand. A wild wind blew over and cast your blood away... The baby cried out loud, and I woke up."

Grid clears his throat. He clutches Violeta's hand, and confesses to her:

"Last night I was at Magia's."

"At Magia's? Why?"

"We need to have a child, my dear... I want to see you happy. Later today we'll go to an old man that Magia has told me about... He can help us. His name is Vlad. He was her guru, her healing teacher..."

"I don't believe in..." Violeta lowers the tone.

"Me neither, you know that. But let's try it, my love; we need to have a child..."

"Let's wait for the Lord," Violeta pleads.

"The Lord is with us. We have already been waiting for years. We need to help ourselves too. Those lights that you have seen in your dream, maybe they are His signs. We should go!"

Violeta remains uncertain for a few seconds, then, to Grid's surprise, she nods affirmatively:

"Yes, let's go!"

Grid, jumps with joy, takes his wife in his big arms, and kisses her ardently:

"Soon we'll be very happy, trust me, my love! The new house is almost ready too!" Grid cries out, enthusiastically.

Violeta looks at him lovingly while hot tears melt her fear.

7 pm.

Violeta and Grid prepare to go to the Old Man's house.

Violeta puts on a white peasant blouse known as *ie* in Transylvania, embroidered with small black crosses and tassels. She then rolls up a pleated skirt to her little waist, and wraps around two black traditional wool aprons—*catrințe*—one in the front, and one in the back, embellished with floral embroidery and fringes. Afterthat, she carefully takes out from her old dowry a sheepskin coat…that she inherited from her grandmother Lucia. Sewn by hand, with red, yellow, cherry and blue flowers, and leaves in shades of a cheerful green, the sheepskin coat giggles with joy.

Around her head, Violeta wraps a very thin floss-silk head kerchief called *marama,* that reaches up to her ankles, and which was delicately woven by her mother, with gold and silver thread.

So beautifully dressed-up and in high spirits, Violeta shoves a little Virgin Mary icon under her coat, close to her heart, kneels down and crosses herself three times, wiping some stray tears off her cheeks.

Grid watches her proudly. Freshly shaved, he puts on his best clothing too: a white shirt made of homespun, with black and red embroideries over the collar, the inset, and the cuffs… He then wraps, tightly, around his waist, a wide brown leather belt called *chimir* in Transylvania; he pulls his tight woolen trousers, called *ițarii*, and then tamps them down, inside his calf-length leather boots… At last, he throws a fluffy sheepskin coat over his shoulders, coat that he had inherited from his forefathers.

Well-equipped, he rushes to open an old coffer engraved with figures of old Transylvanian emperors, armed with lances, sabers, axes, painted shields, and metal helmets. He reaches beneath some baby clothes that Violeta had already knitted and hallowed for the long-awaited child, and picks up a money pouch. He sighs. He squeezes the pouch inside his belt-chimir and, finally, grabs his old-country-lad hat and shoves it on his beautiful, longhaired head.

Violeta and Grid both feel good, and leave the house brimming with hope.

After a good walk, Violeta stops:

"I have to go back!"

"No, there's no turning back!" Grid cries out.

"I forgot the doll!" Violeta urges.

"Please, Violeta. Not now!"

"We have to go back!" Violeta pleads again.

"We shouldn't go back. It's not good!" Grid tries to persuade his wife.

"I must! I need her with me!" Violeta speaks up.

To Violeta, the wooden doll is sacred.

A 107-year-old monk, who lived on the Mount Athos in Greece, and who performed miracles for chosen people during his entire lifetime, had sculpted this doll for Violeta's mother Victoria after hearing the story of her life. When Victoria was on her deathbed, she gave this doll to Violeta, telling her that her soul would live on inside of it, and that Violeta should take the doll with her wherever she may go. Moreover, Victoria insisted that Violeta would do the same thing when she feels her death is near— give the wooden doll to her first-born child to carry on Mama's soul...

Violeta, who had named the doll "Mommy Doll," returns home hurriedly, grabs the doll, and then runs like the wind back to Grid who awaits her, impatiently.

Hand in hand with his wife,

Grid walks at full speed as he wouldn't dare to upset the Old Man Vlad.

Violeta, breathing heavily, holds the doll tightly to her chest. She then whines:

"See, it wouldn't have been good not to go back! Mommy Doll was crying!"

"Yes, because you had forgotten her," Grid encourages his wife. "Give me the doll, please," Grid asks Violeta with hurry.

Violeta hands him the doll. Grid looks at the doll, attentively:

"Look, now she's smiling, isn't she?"

After she takes back the doll, and stares at it as if seeing it for the first time, Violeta smiles as well: "Yes, she does!"

Grid smiles too. Their smiles turn into a crescending avalanche of laughter. They laugh loudly together, all the way to the Old Man's house, as if happiness finally remembered them this cold spring night.

The Old Man's house.

Violeta and Grid enter the big metallic gate that harshly creaks, deafening their peace. With shrunken hearts, they wriggle their way through bulky weeds and centurial trees, among a muddy garden with tall rusty wooden stakes and dry prickly grass, uncut by centuries.

A small fountain, adorned with serpent-heads, watches their steps with cunning eyes.

Suddenly, Violeta's face lights up. Among the leafless and tortuous trees, she catches a glimpse of a small plum tree with indigo flowers. She hardly walks through the sticky mud to smell its flowers when the giant black door of the house opens, and a deep voice speaks up loud, with an echo:

"Come in, please! What are you waiting for?"

Violeta and Grid head to the giant door that opens widely, revealing a fairytale garden.

"A garden! There's a garden inside the house!" Violeta exclaims, enthusiastically.

The guests mount the stairs in sync, guided by their unveiled host— the old guru of Magia.

Passing through a dark corridor, they reach the fairy carpet of fresh grass. White lilies and purple irises adorn the carpet while black swans graciously float on a dark blue lake.

"Please, follow me," the Old Man says, hospitably.

Suddenly, a mighty oak with an enormous royal crown and giant branches, raised to the sky, stretches before their eyes. A chain of raw meat abruptly coils around the oak's thick trunk, dripping blood onto its massive roots, protruded out of the ground. Near the oak, a woman pops out like a ghost of clay, taking forms and clothes of an odalisque,[17] graciously moving her serpent-like body, before the eyes of a handsome prince. The prince takes her by the waist, and gives the odalisque a long kiss. At his loud call, the odalisque thrusts her sharp nails into the chain of meat, rips a loaf off the trunk, and lays it submissively at the bare feet of the prince. With savage teeth, she tears the meat to pieces, and then throws them, one by one, across the dark blue lake.

Wherever the pieces fall, men with large turbans make their appeareance, jumping to catch the meat, like fishes after the bait. At once, the prince throws stakes into the men's hearts, causing them to fall, as guided puppets, into the lake.

Suddenly, the green leaves of the oak shrink, its flowers wither, its branches bend, blighted and dried. Violeta sighs.

The odalisque jumps into the water, and swims towards the fallen men, like a hungry wolf of the sea. In a flash, with her forklike claws, she pulls the men's hearts out, and places them inside one of the turbans.

---

[17] *An **odalisque** (Turkish: Odalık) was a female slave or concubine in an Ottoman seraglio, especially the Imperial Harem of the sultan.*

The other turbans float peacefully onto the dark bloodied water. The odalisque laughs. The man applauds his woman with nefarious lust.

Violeta and Grid watch the scene in total perplexity.

The odalisque pops out of the water, holding the heart-filled turban above her head, as an offering to her good prince.

As they continue their walk through the garden, with big scared eyes, Violeta and Grid approach a huge golden frame. Tapping the frame that borders the entire landscape, the Old Man laughs minimally, continuing to hide his face:

"My favorite play, in my favorite set..."

The Old Man steps over the golden frame, on an ultra-polished parquet of an elegantly adorned and grandiose house.

Violeta keeps looking behind, at the lawn that has rapidly changed its sight: the oak has gained its flowers and leaves; the birds tweet happily, like in Paradise, and yet, the prince and his odalisque are lying dead on the fairy grass...

A red curtain suddenly falls from the ceiling, hiding the "favorite set."

"We direct the play...we write it..." the Old Man murmurs, still hiding his face.

Velvet covered stairs and imperial columns, carved with heads of men, invite the guests to descend towards a dark-lit sphere, after the Old Man...

Grid grasps Violeta's arm, and whispers into her ear: "What was that?" His hand slides along a writhing balustrade that feels so sticky and cold, and that ends in a rattlesnake head.

The Old Man calmly interferes:

"You'll see, my friends. Have patience. It's the number one rule for a patient. If you want to get healed, you must follow, listen, and..."

The Old Man's feet stop in the dark. With a sharp snap of his fingers, he turns on a dim light. He then twirls around, puffing through the nose, finally facing his guests:

"Please, be seated."

Though covered in wrinkles, the Old Man's face glows in the dark; it shows wisdom, yet untruthfulness; hospitality, yet regret. He has the allure of an old prince with dark greenish-blue eyes, sad and frozen. He wears an indigo cloak on which red velvety images of crosses and stakes are delicately encrusted. It is a royal cloak, with lifted shoulders and regal collar, embroidered with golden serpents around the cuffs, the arms and the train.

The Old Man turns his eyes towards Grid:

"As you well know, your beloved wife Violeta, devastated by Vlady's loss, couldn't procreate anymore! She prayed and prayed...but no one heard her prayers, and now she's here! Shall I help her? Where is God when you need Him?"

Silence.

Grid tries to justify.

Vlad cuts him off:

"No, there is no need for further explanation. The simple fact that you are here explains it. I want to help you. But Violeta must be ready. Ready for...different."

"Different? What do you mean exactly?" Grid asks him, restlessly.

Vlad ignores his question. He snaps his fingers again, and the room gets a little lighter.

Violeta and Grid can now behold the room's features; it is a short chamber, just like a cauldron, with walls of rusted metal and rounded margins, showing no signs of windows or other openings.

All of a sudden, columns of fire spring out from the corners, rising up to the ceiling, sweating Violeta and Grid's foreheads. Sighs and moans pierce the silence. The lights turn brighter.

Crucified on a wall, are a man and a woman, crying indecipherable slogans through wide-open mouths as the violent jets of fire burn their memories. Desperately, the man and the woman roll their eyes, trying to look at each other, while snakes crawl on their bodies, taking possession.

Horrified, Violeta mutters:

"I think that we are in the wrong zone..."

"What makes you think that?" Vlad pierces her eyes with his glance.

"These people..."

"*These people?* Just samples..." the Old Man cuts her off. "They chose their destiny. Yet aren't we all burnt by all kinds of fire? Aren't you willing to have a child that would stop that fire?"

Violeta closes her eyes for a moment and whispers, shyly:

"Yes, to stop my fire…"

With an abrupt twirl of his mantle, Vlad turns his back to Violeta, towards the crucified men, spittting out words in an unknown language. Like an icy volcano, a cool breeze of air springs out of his lungs, steamy and bleak, capturing the cauldron-room. The fire stops, the light dims, and the crucified men vanish into the dark. The chilly wind covers Violeta's arms, her legs, her womb…and then it gets to her heart… Violeta shivers with cold, Grid shivers with anger…

"I'm the one who can help you," the Old Man afirms, turning his face to Violeta and stinging her incertitude. "You'll see," he adds, continuing to penetrate her with his keen and dark eyes: "You'll be very happy if…"

Vlad pauses, visibly taken by Violeta's angelic features. He rubs his hands and, restraining his breath, he grabs Violeta's arms, raising her from the chair.

Caressing her long hands and fingers with his frozen touches, Vlad awakes from his nostalgia as he feels Violeta's wedding ring, resting powerfully onto her finger.

Shaking his old self off, he takes his hands off Violeta's. He then strikes a vivid pose, grinning artificially to his intimidated guests. Grid glares at the Old Man, expelling angry flames. The room gets sticky and dry again.

Keeping his cool, Vlad approaches the right wall of the chamber, the train of his indigo cloak draining along. A thin door, whose edges were until then invisible, suddenly becomes visible. The thin and narrow doorway expands, allowing the Old Man to enter.

Drops of fearful sweat keep trickling on Violeta and Grid's face, sliding along their beautiful garments; hardly can they breathe in the dry oxygen remained in the chamber.

Grid clutches Violeta's hand.

The Old Man returns to the chamber, dressed up as Vlad the Impaler[18]. A red velvety cloak, a red turban embellished with diamonds, and a star-shaped golden brooch, give him the cruel, dictatorial sharpness. In his right hand, the Old Man holds a spear-like stake, and in his left, a circular goblet of crystal.

As the door closes behind the Old Man, ultra-silently, Vlad approaches Violeta:

"Give me your hand…"

Violeta hesitates.

Vlad looks straight into her eyes:

"You must follow, listen and…trust. And trust is the most important. You can trust me, Violeta. I can deeply see your grief for Vlady's loss. I want to kiss your pain away. I want to kiss…your hand. Give it to me, Violeta."

Violeta looks at Grid, hesitatingly. Grid looks at her, lost in his worry.

"What do you believe in?" Violeta asks the Old Man Vlad.

Ignoring her question, Vlad stings Violeta's ring finger with the sharp pointed head of his spear.

Violeta gives a muffled cry. The Old Man grins:

"I believe in…blood. And I believe that…you have to sacrifice in order to receive…"

Vlad squeezes Violeta's finger, her blood quickly filling the crystal goblet.

"Follow me, please," the Old Man speaks to his guests, climbing the red velvet stairs with the heroic steps of a young warrior.

Grid follows him, but Violeta lingers as she hears the choked whimper of a child.

Trying to discern where the sound comes from, the baby cries again, louder and louder.

Violeta draws near the thin door with invisible edges, where the

---

[18] ***Vlad the Impaler*** *(Romanian Vlad Țepeș) a.k.a. Vlad III, Dracula, born in 1431, in the heart of Transylvania (in the citadel of Sighisoara), was a knight of justice, renowned for his hardness and cruelty.*

cry seems to have come from. The whimper of the child becomes clearer. She listens carefully and, as the baby cries again, more ardently, she pushes the door handle. A cold hand catches her wrist:

"Follow me, please."

Just like a student caught red-handed, Violeta tries to justify herself. Then, taking heart, she tries to ask the Old Man Vlad about the baby's cry. But she is not able to articulate...not a single word... Syllables stubbornly refuse to come out of her mouth; her tongue is frozen, stuck in her mouth.

Held tightly by the Old Man's cold hand, Violeta is pulled up the stairs, just like a naughty child who deserves to be punished.

On the first floor, with ultra-polished parquet and asymmetrical-shaped columns that seem to be ready to fall down over them, Violeta looks for her husband Grid. She desperately glances around, but her eyes can see no shadow of him... Vlad pushes her up the stairs, clarifying the situation:

"Now we are going to the next level. No man is allowed to go here, but me."

While climbing the stairs, Violeta hears the cry of the baby again, clearer, sharper. She cannot tell if it is just her imagination or the reality. Anyhow, the toddler's cry seems so familiar to her...

As they arrive on the second floor, a strong light forces Violeta's eyes to go blind. She is unable to see anything. She shakes, willing to speak up, but she cannot drop a word.

The cold hand of the Old Man Vlad holds Violeta's arm tighter, pushing her forward.

Taken inside the chamber, Violeta is still unable to perceive a thing. Her eyes weep; her lips, burnt by the furious light, shrivel and shrink. The deeper they get in, the stronger the light becomes, it is unbearable!

Suddenly, everything starts taking shape; the rays of sun, tender and mild, caress Violeta's face into a smile. Her vision becomes clear; her skin white as an angel. However, she feels that she sees everything through other eyes...with the eyes of another being...

The chamber is adorned with exotic vegetation, tiger flowers, and small golden waterfalls. The walls are transparent but scorched; it seems like a thousand rays of sun kept burning them...

Violeta draws closer to the walls. She touches them, carefully, and feels small crystals of frozen water. As she stares at them, she sees eye lashes...tears and pain...frozen for decades.

"Yes. There are millions of tears that no ray of sun could melt," Vlad breaks in.

The Old Man's eyes are overwhelmed with sorrow. They get darker and cloudy. He then whispers:

"This is my sacred place...my heaven. See this divinity painted up there, high on the wall? So beautiful, so elegant, so young but so pale? So witty, so aristocratic, so lively but...so dead? Why? Tell me, why?" the Old Man asks, louder and louder, hitting his thighs with his clenched fists.

A well of tears erupts from his eyes, turning rapidly into ice. His mouth opens wide, like the abyss of an ocean, spitting out a cold wind of words:

"Who are you, you well known as God? You, who take away the lives of pure maidens, and let beasts like me alive? Who are you that I may worship? You cut her bloom too soon and withered me in gloom; you stopped my wife's heartbeat and made me beat to everlasting grief! Her memory is now my doom—what sense it is for me to breathe if she is in that tomb?"

And then, raising his voice to the opened ceiling, Vlad shouts to a final strain:

"If God wants blood, He will get blood. If Vlad wants blood, he will get blood."

Pulled down to the ground by an inner force, Vlad shivers like a naked beggar. In front of the portrait of his wife, with his hands clenched, he stammers:

"My love, forgive me...but He has to pay... I'm not the same...you're not the same. You're far away. No one can give me back what I have lost and I must seek revenge on He who turned my heart to frost. Just trust me,

Goddess of my soul. He once was good, now God is not worthy of your look."

Then, listening to the words of his wife in return, Vlad swings like a guilty child:

"Yes, my love…Yes…"

Violeta watches the scene with her arms twined in prayer. She murmurs to her heart: "Protect me, God."

"See these awful tears, Violeta? They belong to a helpless man, so weak, so sad, but so thirsty of revenge. I know your tears, Violeta, I know how bad it feels, my dear!"

Standing up, Vlad caresses Violeta's face, lovingly.

Violeta takes a step back. In the corner of the room, on the naked floor, there lies a wooden doll identical to the one that Magia used for the ritual of Vlady on that doomed night of Saint Andrew. Violeta glares at it, stupefied, and wants to pick the doll up, but the Old Man grasps violently her arm:

"Now see why I have chosen you, Violeta? Look up at her, and look down to you. You and she are almost one—just different ages… Her big black eyes are your big black eyes; her voluptuous lips are your voluptuous lips; her tall forehead is your tall forehead… All is identical except for the star that glitters on her forehead…and your eyes wrinkled by the many cries addressed to God, imploring him to have a child! And where is God now to help out his beloved child?"

Deepening his voice, Vlad himself replies:

"He's right here, with you, Violeta. It's Me, Vlad."

And Vlad grabs Violeta's left hand and places it on his chest. Violeta can hear the dead beat of his heart.

Vlad holds Violeta's hand tighter. Violeta feels stripped down by the keen black eyes of the woman from the portrait.

"It must be a portrait from my twenties. He must be obsessed…" Violeta thinks to herself.

"I don't blame you for thinking this way!" Vlad cuts her thought. "I know that it's hard to imagine yourself with a duplicate, with another being, perfectly resembling you. Now, hear up her story, to understand my pain..."

And Vlad takes out a scribbled sheet of paper from his cloak and begins to recite:

"One night, when I was gone, leading a war against the Turks, the Turks themselves announced my death, tricking my wife to lose her breath. Reading the lying letter arrowed into her room, sweet Dora found no meaning to live in such a doom! So my beloved wife went on the castle's tower and jumped to find her death that doomed hour..."

Putting the poem back into his cloak, Vlad speaks again to his intimidated guest:

"I wrote thousands of poems...about Dora and her death...but they could not bring back her breath, neither my tranquil nights of rest... And I keep saying the same words and it still hurts... She was my inspiration, my innocence, my purity, my light! Yet when that lying letter was arrowed to her heart and broke my muse to the eternal silence, I chose to take that arrow and throw it into God!" he declaims again, shivering with ache.

Taking the posture of the old Emperor Vlad Tepes, and lifting his spear up his right arm, he screams from the top of his lungs, "Ahhhh! I got you! You are dead," impaling with his stake an imaginary fiend.

Violeta's eyes startle. Again, she tries to speak, yet her lips move helplessly into the breath of Vlad's speech. Her heart beats faster and faster, like a noisy train leaving the station, but no words are able to spring out of her mouth.

"She wants to speak to you," Vlad addresses Violeta, suddenly overcome with emotion. "Listen to my wife and do what she tells you!"

All of sudden, the woman's lips from the portrait start moving, and a sweet voice unveils:

"Now I am you, and you are me. Please, listen to my husband and you shall soon bear a child, a child whom Earth has never seen before— royal-bloodied, purple-starred, double-powered, double-witted—it is going to be our child! The Sun will not bear to look at it; its rays will melt away and wilt! Nothing will ever make this child afraid. The blood that

flows inside its veins will make this child forever thirsty and immortal...
Unless just one mistake is made—unless the child betrays his father..."

Violeta's lips start moving without her willingness. All of a sudden, she speaks just like the woman from the portrait:

"I, Violeta, shall take this vow and hold it in my heart until death tears us apart. I, and only I will know what you just spoke, or else my tongue shall never move again to give a word... I'll bear in my womb a royal child whom I shall teach to always listen to his father...Vlad."

Uncontrolled tears dimple Violeta's cheeks. She trembles from head to toe, feeling the spirit of Vlad's wife persisting inside her heart.

Meantime, the Old Man Vlad enters the chamber, carrying a small ebony tray, on which a golden cup, a golden egg and a small violet bottle are placed diligently in the form of a triangle. He lays the tray on an antique three-legged table, and smiles lovingly to his guest. He takes the golden cup off the tray and, holding it sacredly, close to his chest, he speaks up:

"This is my blood...my blue sad blood. Drink from it and you shall give birth. Your child will live forever."

He places the cup against Violeta's mouth. Violeta drinks the blue blood until the last drop.

The Old Man puts the cup down on the tray, and takes the golden egg, opening it swiftly, like a jewel case. He takes a look inside of it, and just as quickly, closes it back.

"In this egg you will find the seed of her womb..."

Looking at his wife's portrait, Vlad breathes a sigh of relief. He then raises the small violet bottle from the same tray and whispers to Violeta with faith:

"Take this golden egg and this small bottle with blue blood. Tomorrow night, at midnight, open the golden egg and plant the seed inside your garden, near the well. After that, sprinkle it with the blood from the bottle. Hold your breath for two seconds and you will see a small plant rising, with a mesmerizing indigo flower. For seven days, each night, at midnight, sprinkle the plant with the blood from this bottle. The indigo flower will grow tall, straight and proud, like a Queen of the Night flower from our land.[19] On the seventh night, you will feel great hunger. Tear off the petals of the flower and eat them all, one by one. Then, drink up the rest of the blood remained in the violet bottle. On that very night, you will become pregnant. But don't try to disobey the ritual...as you will live no more," Vlad concludes.

With the violet bottle and the golden egg case in her hand, Violeta exits Vlad's house, totally bewildered, afraid. It seems to her that that was a dangerous game performed by an old madman. Confused, she wonders where her husband could be. She glances around, in the dark. Vlad told her that Grid would already be home, sleeping, but she knew that he would not have left her with that old man, all by herself.

"No word or else..." Vlad's voice echoes inside Violeta's mind as she passes through the muddy garden with snake eyes.

The crickets sing loud; the moonlight brightens the road, shyly.

As not a soul is to be found, Violeta starts walking faster and faster, the cold wind of the night blowing deep to her bones. She breathes harder, barely seeing down the road. Small drops of rain turn into showery streams of water, sinking her pace in the soil.

Finally home, Violeta feels out of harm's way. She enters the house sneakily and, indeed, finds Grid asleep. She makes the sign of the cross before the icon of the Virgin Mary and thanks God. She sets the fire in the stove and, still shivering with cold, takes off her wet clothing. She drags herself to the bathroom and, after a moment of hesitation, looks at herself in the mirror, staring at her tired features. Bending her head to the right and to the left, she leans her hands onto her empty belly.

Exhausted, she gets herself under the blanket, the face of that Old Man Vlad still shadowing her brain. Strange creatures, dirtied with thick blood, circle her little boy Vlady... They keep repeating to her that they are the 33 children aborted by Victoria, Violeta's mom, 33 haunting souls thirsty for revenge...

Next morning, a warm kiss awakens Violeta.

---

[19] *See **Nicotiana affinis** also known as **Nicotiana alata**.*

"Good morning, my love!" Grid whispers in her ear, swiftly tattooing a kiss on her forehead.

Violeta opens her big black eyes.

A deep silence lies between them.

Violeta is waiting. She penetrates Grid's eyes, waiting for an explanation.

Grid looks at her lovingly. Disturbed by Violeta's severe glance, he finally cuts the silence:

"What's the matter with you, my dear?"

"With me?" Violeta asks, grudgingly.

"Yes, why are you looking at me like that?"

"How could you leave me all alone out there?"

"Where?"

"What do you mean where? In the house of that man..."

"Which man, my dear?" Grid asks her, easily amused.

"The man we visited yesterday."

"My dear, you might have had a bad dream. Relax, I will bring you breakfast..."

Violeta jumps out of bed, angrily, following Grid.

"Yesterday you pushed me to go to that old man called Vlad and now you pretend like nothing has happened?"

Grid turns to Violeta and catches her hands. He then kisses them lovingly, reassuring her with calm:

"Violeta, my dear, everything is going to be just fine..."

He then heads to the kitchen, at a joyful pace, yet his face betrays terrible worry. Violeta does not know what to think anymore... She takes a seat on the bed, silent as a fish.

Grid comes back with breakfast, and with a warm broad smile.

Without facing him, Violeta asks again her husband:

"So you don't know anything? You can't remember anything about Vlad?"

"My, dear, Vlad is in heaven. God takes good care of him..."

"That old man..."

"There's no old man, Violeta... Just a bad dream!" Grid tries to calm her again.

Violeta runs to the bathroom, swift as an arrow. She cannot believe what is happening to them. She looks in the mirror and asks herself:

"Who is that Old Man Vlad? What spell has he cast upon my husband?"

She then rushes out of the bathroom and heads to the fluffy sheepskin coat that she wore in the presence of the Old Man Vlad. She reaches into the pocket and pulls out the golden egg and the small bottle of blood that he had given to her. Looking at them, fearfully, she thinks that she should just throw them away... Hot tears erupt from her eyes. She gets down on her knees and speaks to God:

"Lord, what shall I do? Teach me, please... Shall I do what that Old Man Vlad taught me?"

The next day.

Violeta waits for the midnight anxiously.

She knows that the Old Man Vlad is strange, to say the least. Yet, she needs a child as she needs air.

"But am I making God upset?"

"No," she immediately replies to herself. "God loves me. God wants me to be happy!"

Nevertheless, the thought of that strange fertility ritual, performed without her husband's knowledge, scares her.

Looking in the mirror, once at her wrinkles, twice at the blue blood from the bottle, Violeta shakes off her fears and plucks up her courage. She wants a child. She is ready to come back to life.

Midnight.

Quietly, Violeta gets out of bed. Grid is cast into a deep sleep; she has taken care of that. She grabs the golden egg and the small bottle of blood, and sneaks out of the house, tiptoeing towards the garden, in her long embroidered nightdress. Once behind the well, she kneels down, thrusts her hands into the ground, and digs out a little hole. She then opens the egg case, and buries the tiny seed of Vlad into the fresh, moist soil.

She is not afraid...not anymore. She feels that God is watching over her.

After she quickly covers the seed with earth, Violeta sprinkles it with blue blood from the bottle of Vlad. Then, making the sign of the cross, she raises her eyes to the sky, and prays:

"God, forgive me for my sins. Bring me a child, a child that will enlighten our house! A child just as You wish. I trust You, and I thank You!"

A drop of blue blood falls from the bottle onto her nightgown, spoiling it just a little...yet her eyes, stuck on the sky, bleed with happiness.

As she looks down, she notices that in the place where she put the seed, a very small plant with an indigo star-shaped flower has already started to grow. Violeta falls to her knees, transfixed; she hugs it blissfully, kissing the little indigo flower with care, as its soft-heavenly perfume entices the air.

The next day, early at dawn, Violeta wakes up filled with godly desire. She walks hurriedly to the garden to watch her sweet indigo flower. Caught by Grid crawling around the well, she pretends to play with green leaves, and clean her face with the fresh drops of morning. Then, taking some moist soil in her hands, she utters with joy:

"This ground is sweet and holy, Grid! I want you to resume the work on the new house!"

Listening to the words of his wife, Grid's face lights up. He jumps towards his wife, takes her up in his arms, feeling why he once married this beautiful woman with big bright eyes. The sun comes out of the selfish clouds, kindly patting on his shoulders. The globe turns him quicker in his twirl of love.

Violeta looks more and more like the woman he had fallen for: rose cheeks, clear big eyes, ruby lips, cheered heart... Grid's heart begins to throb like the first day he met his wife...

Enlightened by his wife's original aura and beaming smile, Grid promises her to wake up every morning at the rooster's crow and finish the new house, at the speed of light.

On the second night, as Violeta wakes up, she feels a sore point on her belly. She rolls her nightdress to her breasts and sees a little violet spot. She presses down and rubs the spot, and feels a little better... She then tiptoes to the garden, so curious to see her little flower.

The plant has changed so much: instead of one, it has two thin and fragile stems—one stem grown up straight, its flower reaching to the sky; the other stem bent, its flower looking to the ground.

"Peculiar flower..." Violeta whispers to herself, "The Old Man Vlad said that the flower will grow tall, straight, and that it will look like the Queen of the Night flower from our land! He did not say anything about two different stems..." Violeta thinks, sprinkling blue blood from the bottle onto the plant.

On the third night, full of excitement, Violeta runs in bare feet to see her double flower. Suddenly, her feet stop, tickled by the fresh blades of grass; her eyes open wide, enchanted by the vision of the Queen of the Night; her hands abruptly lengthen, caressing the long velvet leaves of the tall stem; her nose inhales the soft mesmerizing perfume of the straight flower in bloom...

She then kneels down, and touches the second stem that crawls like an ivy, almost kissing the ground; it has small thorns, like of a rose; its bent flower does not emanate a scent, but it has phosphorescent stamens, like some omnipresent eyes, so keen and bright that they light up the night.

Violeta leaps joyfully into the house, feeling the love of the two flowers growing inside her womb!

On the fourth night, Violeta wows with delight at the unseen color of the petals—an intense indigo furrowed by a silver stripe. As she smells the straight flower, she sees its stamens turning gold, like the color of the egg case. The other one—the ivy-stem—has stretched down to the ground, and gained the color of the small bottle of blood.

Suddenly Violeta hears a loud sound...coming from the well. She rushes to look down, and sees the water turning blue, shaking and foaming like the waves of the Black Sea...

On the fifth night, the double flower appears so beautiful and lofty, and its heads, like two star-princesses, reaching one tall to the sky, the other thorny, bending like a chain of green nails into the dust. The first flower is in bloom and smelling like a paradisiacal perfume; the second flower spreads a hypnotic nicotine fume...

Like every other night, Violeta pours drops of blue blood onto the roots of the plant...as the Old Man Vlad taught her. Yet one thing Vlad did not teach Violeta—to pray to God. And yet, Violeta has been praying every night, like she has done all of her life, to have a beautiful child—as beautiful and healthy as the tall Queen of the Night!

On the sixth night, Violeta awakes from her sleep with a high fever. She can barely walk to the garden to sprinkle blood on the plant. The indigo flowers have grown enormously! The straight flower is taller than the house, illuminating like a lamp, and the one that loves the earth, just like a giant ivy, is coiled around the well, the wheel, and the bucket, piercing into the ground.

Suddenly, out of the dark, a white dove comes into sight, and alights on the tall flower's leaves, fluttering her wings with ease. At the same time, a loud noise resounds from the ground, making Violeta's heart terribly pound. The ivy-stem, just like a tail, whips down the bucket and the well, and then it coils around them like a rattlesnake. The soil swarms with lizards and creeping insects of the night that climb onto the ivy-stem, swiftly, with delight...

Standing before the flowers, enraptured by their scented power, Violeta feels like fainting... She blacks out! But the tall stem anchors her body at once, and the ivy-stem springs from the ground and wraps around her waist, raising Violeta up and helping her walk to the house.

Early in the morning, Grid starts screaming like an ecstatic child:

"Violeta, you've got to see this! It is beyond incredible! Two gigantic flowers overwhelm our garden! All the neighbors have gathered to admire them, enraptured! I don't know what to do... Hurry up, come and see!"

On the seventh night, at midnight, Violeta does not wake up. Something keeps her away; an aura guarding their shelter has cast Violeta into a deep sleep, and she dreams...

Suddenly, a strange noise, just like a call from Hades, springs out to bite Violeta's peaceful night. Gigantic steps tread heavily inside the garden, quivering the big walnut tree and the fountain. A shadow of a man with tail creeps down onto the wall, and sneaks through the bed sheets that shroud Violeta and Grid's sleep.

Abruptly, Violeta gets out of bed, cooled by an icy breeze. She hugs her body, unconsciously, and sneaks out in the night.

A strong wind tears her dress away. Naked and with her eyes closed, she walks against the wind, like a moonwalker.

As she reaches before the Queen of the Night, her eyes are suddenly opened by the glow of the tall flower that climbed up to the sky. Under the eye of the moon, its petals seem to touch the stars, so long and happily in bloom. With terrible felicity, Violeta touches the stems and leaves that feel like legs and arms of a sweet nymph. Beneath its strong, wide shadow, she feels at ease, far from the agony of the nature that has lost its peace.

Violeta hears a loud call within... A hole of hunger inside her stomach almost devours her being. She feels famished. She tries to climb the straight stem, to reach its petals and feed on them as the Old Man Vlad told her, yet the flower has grown too tall and big to possibly touch it...

Feverishly, she rushes to the back of the yard, and grabs Grid's ladder that he has been using for the new house. The storm keeps blowing furiously, quivering her heart.

Hidden in the wings of the night, the Old Man Vlad watches a hungry and naked Violeta. He opens his arms wide and raises them, like a bat, above the house. The wind suddenly ceases its roaring sound.

Solemnly, Violeta leans the ladder against the tall stem, and climbs towards the indigo petals, like a hungry lioness.

Once up there, she holds the giant stem with one hand, and with the other one, she tears off the petals of the indigo flower. She wants to chew them, but they just melt, like snowflakes, in her saliva.

Still hungry, she descends the stairs, and putting the ladder to the side, she runs towards the other stem with thorns and phosphorescent eyes. For a second, the bright eyes of the stamens intimidate her, yet the lavish hunger she feels, wins over.

After she eats all the petals of the ivy-flower too, Violeta feels incredibly thirsty. She rushes to take out some water from the well, but her mouth fills with a strange taste of blood. Suddenly, she remembers the words of Vlad, and runs to the house to drink what has remained in the bottle of blood.

Heavy drops of rain slide on her naked belly.

After she drinks the last drops from the violet bottle, Violeta feels heavy, just like when she was pregnant with Vlady. She touches her abdomen, and feels it shaking.

"God, now I leave my baby in Your loving hands," she whispers, falling to her knees, before the big icon of Virgin Mary that hangs near the burning stove.

Seven days later.
Violeta looks like a nine-month pregnant woman. The violet mark that she had noticed on her belly five days ago has gotten bigger, and has gained a crust...

Grid cannot believe what is happening to them... Indeed, Violeta is glowing and looking like a goddess, but her change in behavior, her enormous pot belly, her silent treatment...are driving him crazy. He keeps asking her how everything has happened, but Violeta is unwilling to tell him anything.

Finding no other explanation, Grid imagines that the shaman's ritual from the *Women's Cave* has finally been fulfilled.

Concerned with Violeta's suddenly grown belly, Grid tries to convince her to see a doctor.

The next day, early in the morning, before Grid opens his eyes and the rooster crows, Violeta heads to see the "doctor," the Old Man Vlad.

As soon as she arrives in front of his house, the door opens wide, and Vlad shows himself, smiling with greedy eyes:

"Welcome back, Violeta! I was expecting you. These are for you..."

As Violeta prudently mounts the cracked stairs of his house, Vlad hands her a set of grey and black baby clothes. Surprised by the gloomy colors, strange ruffles, ribbons and bows, Violeta looks at Vlad with concern, while covering her big baby bump with her right arm.

"These clothes are protected. Your child shall have no harm from any human kind. But you must come here with the baby girl monthly, for my attentive care and my...blessings. And be careful to dress her only with this clothing," Vlad concludes, closing the door on her. But he then swiftly re-appears, adding with a sharp tone:

"Don't forget to visit me as soon as the child is born."

"There is a violet mark on my belly. And it hurts..." Violeta murmurs to Vlad, "My husband is concerned..."

"Tell your husband that the doctor told you that the miracle has happened. You are pregnant with a fantastic child."

June 7th, 1483.

Convinced that the big day has come, Grid takes Violeta to the doctor. Violeta is very concerned as throughout her seven days of pregnancy the child has moved so little…almost at all. More than anything, she has wished the baby to be healthy! Indeed, she hesitated to speak to a real doctor, to show the violet-crusted mark from her belly… She wanted no living man to shudder her faith! She has not told Aunt Magia about it either… Anyhow, strange it seems to Violeta that Magia has suddenly lost interest in the so much desired pregnancy of her beloved niece! Making up unbelievable excuses, her typically worried aunt hasn't visited Violeta at all.

Grid is immeasurably happy and convinced that the child is the Goddess of Fertility's miracle. He cannot wait to caress the long expected baby.

Now that the day of their dreams has finally come, Grid holds Violeta's hand proudly before the doctor's eyes.

Consulting Violeta, the doctor gasps in shock. Her belly looks abnormally big and it has a purple mark in the shape of a star. He has never seen such a purple mark in his whole life! It is for the first time that Grid sees the violet mark too, but he believes it to be something normal, in accordance with the name of his wife…

Violeta smiles at the doctor, emboldening him to proceed.

Ignoring his puzzlement, the doctor gives a shaky smile and prepares the instruments for the childbirth.

Violeta's eyes and face shine inhumanly. She looks abnormally beautiful, as in her twenties.

Precipitately, the midwife informs the doctor about the patient's uncommonly low pulse, arterial tension and…about the color of Violeta's blood: blue.

The doctor, who has helped Violeta with Vlady's pregnancy too, asks the midwife to hand him a glass of cherry brandy. He drinks it all in one breath, trying to pluck up his courage. Nevertheless, as blue blood starts coming out, his face startles, paralyzing with fright. His eyes wide open, popping out of his head, his hands begin to shake on the scalpel.

Outside, under the soft rays of the sun, Grid is waiting, seated on a bench. Overly excited, he jumps to his feet and starts walking up and down the doctor's garden, uttering the same prayer, over and over again, and rubbing his hands with fever:

"God, have mercy on me, sinner. Thank you for this baby miracle! Thank you..."

Big eyes of expecting mommies, seated on benches, watch Grid's steps closely, increasing his anxiety.

After more than an hour, the doctor steps outside and walks towards Grid, overwhelmed. His head is bent. Grid jumps at him like a ferocious lion:

"Is my baby healthy?"

The doctor looks at him scared, hesitatingly.

Grid starts weeping like a woman:

"I should have taken better care of her. Maybe I stressed her too much with all my worries..."

The doctor cuts him off:

"The baby is beyond healthy! But..."

Overjoyed, Grid takes the doctor up in his arms and twirls him in the air three times, shouting with the exultation of a glorious father: "Abba!"

The pregnant mommies applaud the fatherhood performance with extreme proudness.

"But..." the doctor continues after Grid releases him, "It is an unexpectedly endowed baby girl. She has weird canine teeth and she speaks. And her blood is blue. Her eyes are big and wide open. She seems to understand...the world."

Grid leaves the doctor speaking and flies to Violeta's room. Carefully, he opens the chamber where the miracle took place and finds Violeta smiling, with the baby cuddled up at her chest. Her smile dimples her burning cheeks, her eyes radiate...unable to take them off the newborn.

Gracefully, with godly moves, Violeta unveils a strikingly beautiful baby girl. Grid takes her in his arms and lifts her up to the sky, tears of happiness springing out of his tired eyes. The little girl is beautiful but sad...

"My beauty!" Grid shouts, kissing the baby's eyes with infinite love.

Later that evening, at home.

Violeta sings *Ave Maria* to their beautiful baby girl. The baby listens attentively, with her big black eyes, immensely opened and wise. Neither her canine teeth nor any other sign can shadow the happiness that Grid and Violeta feel in their hearts, this night.

Violeta and Grid suffocate the little girl with kisses, vying with each other as to who can hold the baby longer. They utter names like "Ariadna, Eden, Iris, Diana, Dochia..." searching for the magical one for their baby girl.

Looking through tens of mythological, historical, symbolic or unheard of names, Violeta falls asleep in Grid's arms. Grid, looking at her as at a goddess, caresses her long black hair with pride. Suddenly, Violeta's face fills with deep wrinkles and dark spots. Grid lays her on the bed, thinking that the cause might be his tired eyes.

Violeta enters a deep sleep and starts dreaming. Virgin Mary appears to her, whispering softly in her ear:

"Name the girl Mihaela, after St. Michael."

Then, placing her glowing hands on Violeta's womb, Virgin Mary continues to speak:

"But may no other child be born out of your womb or else you will be gone into a tomb..."

Violeta turns in bed frantically, speaking loud in her sleep. Grid looks at her, heartbroken, kissing her ardent cheeks:

"Everything is going to be fine. I'm with you, my dear. I will let no one harm you or our baby girl. God is with us," he murmurs.

He then kneels down and starts praying in the light of the moon, his warm tears spreading swiftly in the whole room.

Shortly, Grid rises up, wipes his face, and walks quietly to their baby-miracle, to check if she sleeps well. The baby girl has not fallen asleep. Contrarily, she looks at Grid with big mature eyes, blinking with calm.

"What an unusual baby!" Grid exclaims, watching his daughter inside her cradle. "She never cried, not even once. And why doesn't she sleep?"

And then, Grid takes little Mihaela up in his arms and hums a lullaby:

"Fata tatii frumuşică
Şi frumoasă floricică
Dormi să te faci măricică
S-arăţi veşnic tinerică
Somnul dulce să te fure
Ochii negri două mure
Tu închide-i binişor
Somn uşor, somn uşor."

"Pretty daddy's baby girl,
Beauteous little flower,
Ease your father in this hour.
Swing, swing in his arms,
Angels keep you always young,
Black eyes like two blackberries
Close them now, be of good merry,
Sleep, sleep tight, dream of the fairies."

All of a sudden, the light of the moon strikes the baby's face. Her little mouth opens into a smile, revealing two lovely canine teeth that shine brighter than the stars above.

Next morning.

Violeta wakes up happily. Now she knows the right name for her baby: Mihaela.

She rushes to the crib and unveils her little sheets, but to Violeta's surprise, Mihaela is out of her cradle. Violeta peers around, with big scared eyes, breathing heavily. She turns towards Grid, but he is deeply asleep. Suddenly, she sees again the shadow of that Old Man, lurking in their orchard and hiding the morning sun from her eyes. Heavy clouds spread all over the sky, glooming the joy of her heart.

Violeta runs outside, in bare feet, with her hair loose and disheveled, flowing anxiously onto her shoulders. As she opens the door, a strong wind pierces her bones, almost pulling the hair out of her scalp. She barely looks around when she sees little Mihaela toddling in the yard. She breathes a sign of relief. The wind ceases to breathe, her heart to throb like an alarm. Violeta smiles and watches her baby girl closely, with loving eyes.

Baby Mihaela crawls to the well and then touches the thorny stem of the indigo flower that pricks her little hands. She laughs. Violeta runs to her baby girl, swift as the wind, and lifts her up in the arms. A thread of blood trickles from Mihaela's sweet little fingers, painting Violeta's womb blue.

Violeta kisses her baby girl, with the sweetest kiss she could ever give.

"My love, Mihaela! Welcome to our family," she whispers, gazing at her baby through long lashes, wetted by tears of happiness.

Grid creeps outside and, grabbing both his beloved girls from behind, he cries out: "Ha, ha, look whom I have caught!"

Violeta quivers. Taken by her small waist by the large arms of her husband, she begins to walk, with her baby girl tightly wrapped at her chest, back in the house. She lays little Mihaela in her cradle, and then addresses Grid:

"I found her in…"

But she cannot finish her phrase as she feels the whole universe turning upside down, and she with it. Strong kicks inside her womb, and then aching stabs into her heart, make Violeta grow weaker and weaker, pale as a ghost…

Behind the window, somebody keeps watching Violeta and Grid.

"Who is that man?"

A thick shadow drops onto Violeta's womb, painting her dress in black.

Grid turns his neck as he hears the sinister sound of a bell.

A cold and shivery Violeta collapses in the arms of her husband.

House of the doctor.

"There's someone inside my womb. I feel weird... I heard the voice of Maria again last night, I had a strange dream..." Violeta mumbles through tears of fear.

"Hush, darling, try to relax..." Grid insists.

"No matter what, just give Mommy Doll to Mihaela. When she grows up, tell her that her Mama's soul is hidden inside this doll. I'll be with her wherever she may go. Forgive me, Grid."

"Don't say such words, Violeta," Grid implores his wife.

The doctor calls Grid outside. Overly agitated, he starts gushing out words with fright:

"I've told you that something was abnormal and that we should have kept Violeta and the baby here for further investigation. It was the only child born that way. Damn, the baby was born with fangs!"

Grid screams back to the doctor:

"My wife is dying and you talk about fangs. Do something and save my wife."

Grid falls to his knees, begging the doctor:

"I implore you!"

The doctor runs to Violeta who is raving, turning from one side to the other.

"What hurts you?" the doctor asks her, agitated and sweaty.

"There's someone inside my womb," Violeta cries.

The doctor puts his ear to Violeta's womb.

The creature inside starts kicking.

"Yes, I hear. Let's proceed. Scalpel, quickly!" the doctor addresses the midwife.

"I want youth without oldness and life without death," the baby from the womb suddenly speaks.

The doctor steps back.

"Did I just hear a voice coming out of her womb?"

Violeta coils up, screaming in pain. Her knees touch the violet mark from her belly.

Grid steps inside the room, panicked:

"Do something, doctor, quickly…"

Violeta screams again, stronger.

The doctor screams to the midwife:

"Scalpel!"

"Push, push harder!" the midwife urges Violeta.

Violeta pushes hard, but nothing happens. The baby won't come out.

"Push harder," the doctor shouts out.

Violeta forces herself and pushes harder and harder.

The baby speaks again:

"I want youth without oldness, and life without death."

"Have you heard that?" the doctor asks Grid in despair.

Grid comes closer to Violeta's womb and whispers:

"Sweet baby…"

"I want youth without oldness, and life without death," the baby cries again, louder.

"We cannot give you that, but we can promise to love you very much! Come out, sweet baby!" Grid tells the creature.

Violeta's scream gets harsher, like an awful cry from Hades.

The baby seems to laugh, and then it speaks out:

"I don't want to, unless you give me youth without oldness, and life without death!"

Grid looks back at the doctor, perplexed.

The doctor screams:

"Push, Violeta, push harder!"

Violeta pushes harder and, under the doctor's human eyes, her belly breaks, penetrated by the creature's sharp fangs. Blue blood erupts out of Violeta's ripped off womb.

The doctor looks petrified. Violeta gives a scream of death.

The creature's fangs emerge through Violeta's bleeding belly. The midwife begins to cry. Grid stares with fright.

While the baby makes its way out, mercilessly slitting the mother's womb, Violeta calls out to Grid:

"My love, I leave you Mihaela. Take care of her and don't let anyone take her away from you."

Tortured by the little creature's barbarian grasps, Violeta struggles to speak:

"That Old Man…he is the one… He gave me his own blood, without your knowledge, then the seed, the flower… I ate its petals…at midnight. Mihaela…is his creation… Forgive me. But don't let him take her away from you…never! Please, promise me."

Grid looks at his wife with mournful, bleeding eyes. He is dumbfounded, heartbroken.

"Please…promise me," Violeta implores him with tears in her eyes.

"I promise," Grid consents, holding his wife's hand with strength.

Both Grid and the doctor stare at the bloody baby who has popped up from Violeta's womb in the strangest way.

The baby looks almost identical to Mihaela, just that its eyes are red and wicked. Its little face is painted with Violeta's blue blood. It then smiles, two sharp fangs sticking out of its small toothless mouth.

The doctor takes the baby in his arms, but the rebellious creature bites him at once. The baby speaks again:

"I want youth without oldness, and life without death."

"Take her away!" the doctor shouts, throwing the infant to Grid.

Bewildered, Grid catches the baby in his arms. Petrified, unable to take his eyes off his wife who hardly clings to life, Grid leaves the baby on the floor.

"My wife, doctor, save my wife!" Grid cries out from the top of his lungs.

"Grid, let her be named Gabriela. Let her be his…" Violeta strives to speak to Grid, after which she loses her strength.

With a ray of sun tattooed on her forehead, Violeta gives her last breath.

Grid jumps and kisses her deeply, his kiss mingling with the thick blue blood that drips out of Violeta's mouth.

In an apocalyptic embrace, with his cheek stuck on her cheek, Grid looks dead like his wife, immobile and frozen, with his hands clenched around the love of his life. The doctor tries to raise him gently, yet Grid holds on, unwilling to let go.

"Murderer, you killed my wife!" Grid suddenly jumps off the bed, shouting at the doctor with killing eyes. "She was in your hands and you did nothing for her!"

As his blood-tainted hands lunge towards the doctor, the doctor screams out with horror:

"Help! Take him away from me!"

Two men enter the room at once and seize Grid with strong muscled arms. Grid relents and burst into tears, pale and lost as a ghost.

Little Gabriela gazes with big astounded eyes at her father who is expelled from the room. Then, she toddles towards the midwife with her little murderous feet and arms. The midwife runs away, frightened by the baby's scary smile.

At midnight, in the forest.

Cold rain washes the shriveled branches of the centurial oak trees.

An old lady, wearing an elegant suman[20] with large hood that covers her forehead and cheeks, holds a baby close to her chest. The baby's mouth is wrapped around with thick white cloth.

The tiny feet of the lady walk spiritedly, making way through

---

[20] **Suman** is a calf length overcoat from Romania made from brown felted woolen fabric, and decorated with black braid on front edges, collar and pockets.

the glutinous forest.

The toddler twitches back and forth; its blue saliva penetrates the white cloth, trickling down onto the lady's elegant cloak.

Walking hurriedly, breathing heavily, the lady suddenly stumbles on a small log, and falls into the viscous mud. The baby gets hurled to the ground, but then it laughs. The white cloth around its mouth almost rips, pierced by two little sharp teeth.

All over painted with ooze, the lady rises to her feet, just to fall again, knocked down by a fat, black cat that bumps into her with strong leaps of a lion.

The lady throws the cat out of her way and the cat falls to its feet, grinning and posing before the woman, with long fierce teeth. The woman does not bat an eye. The cat penetrates her with green human eyes, darting at her with wicked arrows, gathered from the depth of the night. The woman squints and fires back, ricocheting at the cat with icy gleam from the stars. The cat shudders its red pointed ears that lengthen at once, like the thick horns of a deer. A reddish fur of a lion crowns its head grandly, its black and lucent body suddenly grows bigger and lofty, and its paws, painted in roan red, extend, ready for an attack. The woman looks frightened for the first time.

The cat mews with strident echoes, circling the lady's thin ankles.

The baby twitches again, coated in mud. The lady rises slowly, without losing the strange creature from her eye. She lifts the baby in her arms, and carefully lays it onto the log. The wet soil slides off her feet, creating a black noise.

The cat jumps onto the log too, getting close to the baby's eyes.

The lady rushes to grab the baby, but in a flash, the big cat extends sharp-pointed claws and, erecting its long red furred tail, jumps at the old lady, scratching her face. The lady gives a shrill cry of pain. Pulling her hood back with a twitched move of her hand, she reveals strained features, covered in sweat and blood. She squawks, shaking herself up.

The lady is Magia, Mihaela's aunt.

Magia opens the palm of her right hand and blows a loud spell upon the evil cat that has terribly marked her face. "Piei, drace, piei!" She then enters into a trance, chanting with deep voice some sounds in old Romanian, like the piercing call of a black eagle. With flashing anger in her eyes, Magia picks up a branch with pointed ends. Holding the branch firmly in her cold hands, she hits the cat over and over, with furious fever... But the vicious feline won't move, unwilling to go away. Hit after hit, and the dark haughty cat stays fixed, staring like a diamond statuette with fired eyes into the cold summer night...

Magia looks terrified. Her hands and her long nails are sore and they shake. Instead of hurting the cat, blood spurts out of her own hands, dripping over her feet...

The cat grins mercilessly. Still holding the branch, Magia senses thorns piercing her long, delicate hands. The cat roars furiously, spitting sticky blue saliva into Magia's eyes.

Magia turns on her heel and starts running like an Erinyes[21], swift as the wind, wiping off the face of the Earth.

Cast down from the hollow log by the friendly cat that has gained its normal size, the baby lands on its little feet and hands, just like the witty cat.

The baby is little Gabriela.

---

[21] ***The Erinyes***, *literally "the avengers" from Greek "pursue, persecute" (sometimes referred to as "infernal goddesses") were, in Greek mythology, female chthonic deities of vengeance. They were three netherworld goddesses. A formulaic oath in the Iliad invokes them as "those who beneath the earth punish whosoever has sworn a false oath". Burkert suggests they are "an embodiment of the act of self-cursing contained in the oath". They correspond to the* **Furies** *or* **Dirae** *in Roman mythology. The goddesses were servants of Hades and Persephone in the underworld where they watched criminals being tortured in the Dungeons of the Damned. The waists of the Erinyes were entwined with serpents and their eyes dripped with blood, rendering their appearance rather horrific. Other depictions show them with the wings of a bat or bird and the body of a dog. When in human form, they are said to appear as mourners in long black robes or maidens in short skirts and boots. The avengers in Romanian mythology are* **Ielele** *- fairies who bewitch with their dance (hora) and beautiful voices. They can also travel with fabulous speeds over "nine seas and nine countries" in just a single night, sometimes by chariots with horses of fire.*

Gabriela laughs under the starless sky with her mouth finally set free. Seeing a long worm trying to move along, Gabriela slurps it with her little tongue and gnaws it under her small fangs, devouring it like a spaghetti drenched in mud.

Big raindrops start falling on Mother Earth, displaying a variety of insects for the hungry baby girl.

Gabriela giggles with appetite.

After she sees the baby eat her fill, the cat moves closer, yearningly, licking the remains off Gabriela's face, with its red lustful tail.

Gabriela catches the cat's wiggly tail. The cat startles with daredevil desire, and starts moving her feet at full speed, dragging along the baby, through the muddy weeds and shadowy trees of the forest.

Gabriela laughs proudly, with the cat's tail like a rein in her hands, exposing her sharp canine teeth to the moon.

Next day. At home. After midnight.

Lying in bed, a mournful and tired Grid holds little Mihaela tightly to his chest. Standing near them: Mommy Doll.

Cries and knocks on the door disturb the silent sorrow.

Gabriela, the little wicked baby, is outside Grid's house, crying in front of the wooden door. As the moon strikes her forehead, the little baby's mouth opens in a scream of joy... Her small sharp canine teeth show up in the night, scratching the doorway...

A hand suddenly grasps little Gabriela. She cries happily, touched by the long nailed hand.

Gabriela: This is our mirror.

Just have a look in it. We were born one day apart, out of a double flower called Queen of the Night: one stem reaching to the sky, kissing the stars; the other, crawling to the underground, blooming its thorns in the moonlight. We are his daughters.

Mihaela: *Few of you might know how it is to have a sister... So identical, but so different... She scares me.*

Gabriela: *My father taught me to be afraid of no one. "You have a bloody life," he said. "You're either gonna bite her or she's gonna bite you."*

Mihaela: *My father held me secretly at home. He allowed me to see no one... Except for God and that mirror...from where I could see her bloody escapades.*

Gabriela: *My nights are my days. Me? I'm the epitome of courage. She? Her innocence is contagious...*

Mihaela: *At seven years old, my milk teeth refused to fall or even chatter... So the doctors expressed concern to my father.*

Gabriela: *My two rows of canine teeth are my best friends. No man can handle them.*

Mihaela: *My father brought me to various specialists but none of them could find the cause or where those canine teeth came from...*

Gabriela: *Those teeth are my weapons. All men want to see women weak and suffering...*

Mihaela: *I have never had a scratch, a blister or a cut, my only malady— insomnia.*

Gabriela: *Insomnia keeps me awake to meet my friends...*

Mihaela: *I've always wanted to have a lot of friends... But "not now," Papa always says.*

Gabriela: *My father told me: "Men are dangerous... Don't stay around them for too long. They'll try to change you." He also says: "When you love them, they step away. When you ignore them, they do everything to please you. But when you scare them, you always keep them where you want."*

Mihaela: *My father once told me: "Bad people corrupt good character. Don't stay around them!" "But good people can corrupt bad character too..." I replied to him. "Actually," I added, "no one is bad...there are only loved people and unloved ones...orphans, hungry for a hug... I want to love and to be loved."*

Gabriela: *I don't know Love. I never met her; I just want to have fun, real fun. When little, Papa used to tell me to look around the house, maybe I see myself...*

Mihaela: *When little, my father told me: "If you see someone looking just like you, turn around and run—she is your wicked clone."*

Mihaela is 10 years old.

Dressed in a beautiful white dress, embroidered with ivory lace, she is playing in her room with her favorite doll—Mommy Doll. Since Papa Grid told her that Mama lives inside this doll, Mihaela and Mommy Doll have become best friends. Mommy is her confidant and the joy of her life...

"Hi, I am Mommy," Mihaela addresses a straw-made doll with the voice of Mommy Doll. "And this is Mihaela," she continues, pointing to herself. "I will be your Mommy, and Mihaela will be your big sister. But you have to promise us one thing: that you shall never ever leave us!"

After she hears the straw doll's voice in reply, Mihaela adds, beaming with joy:

"Oh! And we also have a theatre! Look!"

And Mihaela mounts quickly on a big wooden chair, and begins to recite:

"On stars it's written our destiny. So on my forehead.

On branches, flowers are blooming. So in my heart.

In houses, mommies are dying. But see, my Mommy never dies..."

Grid draws near to Mihaela, mesmerized, listening to the poem with wet eyes.

"Daddy, I wish I could write a poem, a lovely one as this one that you taught me. I tried, but I could not. Why?"

Grid kneels down before his daughter:

"Let's pray and you will write...one day soon... You are so young."

Then rising up and clearing his throat, Papa Grid speaks on:

"I came to tell you that I will leave you alone for a very short while… I'll be back very soon, before the dusk. Be a good girl. Double lock the door, up and down, and don't let anyone in, no matter what they would tell you. Promise?"

"Not even Mommy?" Mihaela asks daddy with big astounded eyes.

"But Mommy is here with you. Just play with her and wait for Papa peacefully. Promise, sweet girl?"

"Promise, Papa," Mihaela consents, blinking obediently from her eyes.

Grid embraces tenderly his daughter, after which he places a small medal pendant with Saint Michael around her little neck.

"Here, wear St. Michael lovingly. He is your guardian angel."

As Grid exits the house, Mihaela rushes to Mommy Doll:

"Mommy, tell me a story!"

Then, taking a lower voice, Mihaela speaks as Mommy:

"Sure, my girl. Once upon a time, there was a little baby boy playing on Earth. He was alone. He didn't have a mommy, neither a daddy. But see, he was all-smiles because the Sun was on his face… And there was a little baby girl, up in the Sky. She had diamond stars and furry clouds adorning her head and her arms… But she was crying, turning upside down because the Moon was on her face… Looking at the little baby boy early at dawn, she wished she was like him… But see, the baby Earth was living during the day, and the baby Moon, during the night…"

Knocks rattle on the window. Mihaela turns around, excited.

Unconsciously, she draws near to the curtains.

Another knock. She pulls the curtains to the side. As she looks out with her big black eyes, Mihaela sees her naughty twin tail flipping in the air, ravishing and funny, reflected in the glass. She giggles. She goes back to play with Mommy Doll. But Mommy Doll is gone. She is not on the bed, where she left her, neither on the floor, nor under the bed.

Mihaela gazes around, desperately:

"Where are you? Where are you, Mommy? Come out!"

Knocks on the window. Again. Harder.

Mihaela tiptoes towards the window with the vigilance of an adult. She pulls again the curtains to the side, and sees again her image reflected in the glass, yet now with Mommy Doll in hand. She tries to snatch her Mommy Doll, but instead, she hits the glass... Mihaela steps to the right, the image steps to the right, but then it blows Mihaela a kiss.

"Who is that girl from outside looking just like me and waving my Mommy Doll in her hand?" Mihaela asks herself.

The girl from outside calls Mihaela with her little finger, and just as quickly, throws Mommy Doll up in the air, and then disappears.

"Oh, no! Mommy is outside in the cold..." Mihaela panics.

She heads to the door and, overriding her father's word, she unlocks it. She steps onto the warm blades of grass, in bare feet, and starts looking for Mommy Doll. Bright red lights pop up around the darkened orchard, sneaking behind the old walnut tree. Mihaela runs after them, frantically. As she tries to catch up with the red lights, she stumbles over the roots of the walnut tree and falls to the ground. Pulling herself up, at once, she sees the red eyes of that girl firing at her with wicked flames, and a small red mouth opening up, giving out a sneering laugh. Mihaela's eyes hurt. The girl turns around and runs away, swift as an arrow, to the back of the house. Mihaela runs after her, yelling in the dark:

"Stop! Give me my Mommy!"

The girl jumps over the fence of the house, with bouncy leaps of a tiger. Mihaela jumps after her, clumsily, bumping into an old lady.

"Come to me, pretty girl, I have warm soup. It won't burn you. I promise," the old lady speaks up.

"Help me, good lady, that little girl has stolen my Mommy!"

But as she points out, the thief-girl is swallowed by the dark, and Mihaela completely loses sight of her.

"Give me your hand and I will tell you where to find your Mommy. Let me read your palm," the old lady beguiles little Mihaela.

Tearing herself away from the luring words, Mihaela continues to run after Mommy.

Panting and covered in sweat, she comes across a friend of her father.

"Where are you running, Mihaela?" the man stops her with his strong arm.

"To find Mommy."

"Go back to your house. Your Mommy is dead!" the man curbs her enthusiasm.

"No, she is not dead," Mihaela bursts into tears, continuing her run after Mommy.

Meanwhile, Mihaela totally lost the little girl who had stolen her Mommy. Saddened and remembering the words of her father, she turns around to go back to her house. But to her surprise, she cannot remember the way back, nor can she recognize the houses that she had passed by, or the landscape that she had left behind. As she wanders in bewilderment, a short bald man comes up to her:

"Juliet..."

"My name is Mihaela."

"You look like Juliet."

"Have you seen a girl resembling me?" Mihaela asks the short man.

"Yes, I have seen," the bald man answers. "Come, she's here."

Thunders and lightning crush the sky. Mihaela looks up, frightened.

"We've got to hurry up, the rain's coming," the bald man says, smiling at Mihaela.

"Where are we going?" Mihaela asks him, easily scared.

"You'll see, I'll show you where the girl is... Trust me."

Mihaela's white dress, embroidered with ivory lace, is now looking too small for her body.

The ten years old Mihaela, who had left the house against her father's word, has suddenly grown up.

"How old are you?" the bald man asks Mihaela, with gleam in the eyes.

"I'm ten years old."

"You've got to be kidding. You look like 14, like a Juliet... Here we are. We arrived. Come on in here!" the bald man urges Mihaela to enter a small filthy barn where piglets tumble back and forth onto some muddy straws.

"Who are you?" Mihaela asks the bald man with big eyes.

Suddenly, the bald man jumps on Mihaela and starts kissing her, with burning desire. Mihaela gives a scream of fear, fretting in the strong arms of the man.

"Leave me alone, I'm only a child..."

"Look at me, sweetheart. You'll soon be a woman..."

The bald man shoves his fingers underneath Mihaela's white dress. Mihaela twitches her body in the chubby arms of the short man as the full moon reflects on his baldhead. Irritated by the strong, penetrating light, the bald man growls, losing his senses.

Mihaela breaks free and starts running. The bald man runs after her, grunting.

An icy blow of wind whips her face, rattling her jaws. She can hardly set forth through the freezing barn, yet the strong wind pushes her from behind to move on. She hears the steps of that bald man getting closer, crushing the ground after her. Afraid and cold, she sneaks into a dilapidated stall. Seeing a brown ragged sweater lying on a hill of hay, she puts it on. She hears the pace of the bald man nearer, so close...

Avoiding the dark stacks of hay and the broken sacks of rotted grain scattered along the way, Mihaela rushes out of the stall and starts running along the barn that widens and lengthens strangely before her eyes. A foul odor bursts into her face, almost choking her. She loses her breath, slowing down her pace...

All of a sudden, to the right and to the left, all kind of loud animals, caged inside dirty, shabby stalls, pop up, bewildering Mihaela's sight. Grunts, neighs, bleatings, cackles, and hisses burst out, deafening her peace.

At the end of the barn, Mihaela can see a bright tunnel, so bright that it almost blinds up her eyes. As her feet further run, the light calms down, turning into a healing orange sun. Mihaela lenghtens her arms, staggering, trying to catch its healing rays, yet the dark stinky barn expands at every step she takes, drawing the sun further back. She feels heavier and heavier...older. She moans with coldness and sorrow. Her bones chatter within her weakened flesh. Her big black eyes get filmy and wet, purple shadows circling them without rest; her hair gets thinner and starts to fall; her lips, stuck into a bitter smile—swollen and sore.

She stops for a moment to catch her breath. The strong, short hands of the bald man catch her long frigid arms, knocking Mihaela to the ground, onto her belly. Her white dress, handsewn with ivory lace, gets all muddy and wet. The bald man laughs devilishly and starts smelling her buttocks with his lewd piggish nose.

Mihaela struggles, kicking and fretting, repelled by the grunting old man.

The old bald man tears her dress apart, and starts licking her neck, her spine and virgin legs, with his gelatinous, filthy tongue.

Mihaela jerks to and fro and, finally, unchains her hands from the bald man's clasp. Her fingers touch a dirty wall. Abruptly, a large mirror emerges from the wall, shutting the tunnel and the sun from her eyes. As she watches her fight in the large mirror, the bald man's reflection is nowhere to be seen; he is invisible both to her sight and to the eye of the glass. Mihaela looks up, wrapped up in fear.

Scratched and tarnished, the mirror seems to have been built in a long time ago, amid some other walls decorated with strange paintings of sad looking brides. Some other portraits of women, also dressed up in white gowns, hang upside down, half drawn and mingled with blood.

The bald man explains:

"This is my creative lab... Feel free to admire my paintings while I finish you... Now you're my new work of art, my muse, my Juliet... You'll remain forever on a canvas, in history... So I have to take good care of you...prepare you for my brush..." he grunts with desire, placing his hands on Mihaela's small buds of breasts.

Taking a Mommy Doll voice, Mihaela shouts at the bald man wih an aching soul:

"Look in the mirror. Your Mommy is watching you. How do you think she feels seeing her son do what he's doing?"

The man gives out a snorting laughter:

"Pretty smart for your age... But my mom is dead."

After he growls again with desire, he thrusts again his hands underneath Mihaela's torn dress, squeezing her flesh.

Mihaela starts screaming at the top of her lungs. The bald man splashes her neck with the sweat of his face, pressing Mihaela's thin shoulders down, with his pig-like hands:

"Hush, Juliet... Now you're mine!"

Mihaela feels her whole body getting colder and colder; her bones shivering with dread...

All of a sudden, from above, a girl jumps onto the hideous man's head. As a famished wolf, she hurls over his body and bites his neck, wildly.

"*She's* the girl!" Mihaela exclaims, watching the scene, covered with frost.

After excruciating the man in her merciless claws, the little girl rises to her feet, leaving the villain drenched in a pool of blood. She grins, showing sharp canine teeth. Tainted with the bald bastard's blood, the girl draws near to Mihaela and says:

"I'm Gabriela. I have your Mommy Doll. Follow me."

"Thank you..." Mihaela replies, "But I need my Mommy Doll now!"

"First, I want us to play a little. Come with me and I will give you Mommy Doll back."

The girl starts running. Mihaela runs after her.

It starts snowing. Mihaela shivers again with cold. She knew it was summer.

"Slower!" Mihaela cries out, panting heavily and turning her head behind.

"Run, don't look back!" Gabriela cries, running at the speed of light.

Mihaela and Gabriela arrive in front of a dilapidated grey house. Exhausted, Mihaela collapses to the ground. Looking at Mihaela, Gabriela gives a big laughter.

Then, dragging Mihaela along, through a rusty metallic gate that creaks loudly, and by a small fountain with heads of snakes that seem to be cunningly watching them, Mihaela starts sinking helplessly into the sticky mud.

"Move faster, don't be afraid!" Gabriela urges.

Mihaela struggles to escape the devouring mud,

but the more she struggles, the deeper she sinks.

Gabriela makes fun of her sister until, ready to lose her, she gives Mihaela a hand, and pulls her out of the hungry soil of the garden. Hurled up in the air by her strong sister, Mihaela falls on some stairs covered in hailstone that lead to a gigantic black door. As she tries to climb towards the black door, she slips and falls again, onto her back.

Gabriela gives a loud hearty laugh, applauding her sister's mishap.

The black walnut door of the house opens widely... Vlad makes his appearance, smiling, gallantly:

"Beautiful, so beautiful... Welcome, my dear!"

"Thank you..." Mihaela mutters with hesitation, trying to rise to her feet.

"Thank you, sweetheart," Vlad adds, turning his eyes to Gabriela and patting gently her head.

Then, giving Mihaela a hand to climb the icy stairs, he speaks up:

"You are probably searching for your Mommy Doll, aren't you, Mihaela?"

"Yes," Mihaela replies to him, firmly.

"Come inside, you shall have your Mommy, plus a bonus gift for being so nice to come and visit us. Feel at home and have dinner with us..." Vlad continues, cordially.

Mihaela steps inside; her eyes open wide. The paradise-like view fills her heart with an unknown felicity.

All over the place, she sees dolls resembling her Mommy Doll. Each doll calls Mihaela by name:

"Mihaela, come play with me! I am your Mommy!"

"Which is my real Mommy?" Mihaela asks Vlad in bewilderment.

"You are such a smart girl. You tell me... But before that, please have a seat."

And Vlad snaps his fingers, shivering with excitement. A royal table rises up from the underground, filling with all kind of meals and royal drinks.

"I can't stay. My father is waiting for me," Mihaela speaks up.

"Tonight, feel free to call me Papa... Of course, until your father comes to pick you up."

"My father doesn't know that I am here!"

Vlad smiles and looks at Mihaela with great pride; he then draws nearer, and whispers to her ear:

"You resemble so much...someone so dear to me..."

Then, hiding an unexpected tear, Vlad turns backwards and speaks to himself:

"Ah, these beautiful sad eyes...just like hers!"

As the tear keeps coming back, Vlad raises his finger to wipe it away; yet the tear rapidly falls onto his coat of glowing coal, piercing it like a strong acid, into a gelid hole. Vlad squints and shakes his sorrow off, after which he turns towards his guest, making himself ready to speak again. But Mihaela puts out his fire, saying in a sharp tone:

"I want my Mommy Doll back! Now!"

Surprised by Mihaela's toughness, Vlad sweetens her with a smile.

"Fine, my dear. Come with me."

Mihaela follows Vlad, cautiously. Climbing the endless red velvet stairs of his house, the dolls from the living room keep calling her by name:

"Mihaela, I'm your Mommy, choose me..."

On the third floor of the house, Vlad stops and stretches his arm to Mihaela:

"Give me your hand, my dear..."

Mihaela hesitates, but then, blushing with shame, takes Vlad by the hand.

Walking down a wide corridor with a variety of strange doors—oval, triangular, circular, rectangular—the hallway gets narrower and narrower, like the edges of the letter V... At the end of the corridor, Vlad releases Mihaela's hand and bends down. He whispers something...in an unknown language, and then touches the wall that faces him, silently. Suddenly, a tall thin door shows its edges, becoming visible and dazzling to the eyes. From its little-mouthed locker, the door pops up a golden key, on which are inscribed, with shiny prominent letters, the words ***Rage&Love.*** Vlad grins satisfied, after which he gives Mihaela the key, encouraging her to open the door.

As soon as Mihaela puts the key in the locker, the key turns by itself and the door opens. Gallantly, Vlad invites Mihaela to step in. Even as little and slim as she is, Mihaela cannot make her way through, as the door shrinks, getting smaller and smaller.

"I can't believe this! Now it senses new blood! Yet hers' is not new..." Vlad whispers in his mind.

He bends down and whispers again something to the shiny door. In a flash, the door shakes and swallows Mihaela in, fast and abrupt. Mihaela lands on the other side, with astounded big eyes. A powerful light strikes her face. She can hardly see anything. But as they wend their way in, Vlad pulling her by the hand, everything starts to soften and take shape...

Mihaela feels like she knows this place, like she has been here before... She then hears a familiar cry of a toddler and then...she feels the scent of her Mama, floating in the air...

Tall walls clothed in blue icicles, so tall and shiny as she has never seen before, rise largely to the opened sky.

Mihaela knew it was about midnight, and yet, the sky is now bright and blue, and the sun shines to its peak of delight. It is a cold sun, buck-toothed, and yet round and saucy as a golden orange.

Mihaela shivers with joy, to the bone. Vlad smiles at Mihaela, taken by hope.

Mihaela wants to draw near the majestic and frosty walls, but she is unable. She stumbles, awkwardly, and then slides down like an ice skater, unwillingly, twirled in a pirouette, among some giant treads that mark the icy floor.

Suddenly, her eyes fix an enormous painting of a girl, that covers the whole front wall. Her feet stop.

"Who is she?" she asks Vlad in one breath.

"Someone that I love very much…"

"Is she your daughter?"

"Yes, she is one of my daughters…" Vlad replies, kindly.

Silence.

"What is her name?"

Vlad turns towards Mihaela with hungry, penetrating eyes. He then grabs her by the arms and speaks to her, like a father:

"Stay away from men. That man who tried to rape you…he was an evil man! Stay away from men, understand? Now, come here, my dear! I'll take good care of you. I shall teach you anything you wish to know about the world…" he cuddles Mihaela in his arms, lovingly. Mihaela surrenders, listening to him, attentively. But then, irritated by the glances of Vlad who touches her face with chills of love, she loses her patience and pushes him to the side:

"Where is my Mommy?"

"Your Mommy? Oh, your Mommy is elsewhere, my dear… But I have Gabriela here. Do you want to play with her? Do you know her?"

"I know her," Mihaela replies, firmly.

"Who is she?" Vlad asks her, spiritedly.

"She is my wicked clone."

Utterly amazed, Vlad bursts into an enormous laughter. His laughter gets so strong that its echo is heard above the whole valley, to Mihaela's home, at the Lucky Wheel.

On the rocky path of the valley,

Grid walks with darkened, frowned face. His beard is long and white… His wrinkled eyes are fixed and red, his back hunched, yet somehow, he still reveals the statuary posture of the strong father Grid.

With a rod in his right hand and a sack hand sewn by Violeta on his left shoulder, in which he had stuffed a few clothes of Mihaela, Grid keeps asking God to lead him to his daughter.

When Vlad sharply laughs, Grid hears it.

"I want my Mommy!" Mihaela cries out again to Vlad.

Finally, with a fatherly smile, Vlad draws near the glacial blue walls. On an ice cube, there lies a music box, and in the middle of the box, a beautiful porcelain Mommy Doll is carved.

Vlad kneels down and turns the key of the music box seven times, and the porcelain Mommy Doll starts rotating faster and faster, raising her hands up, like a ballerina.

Suddenly, the music box opens, and thousands of dolls, looking just like Mommy Doll, pop out with funny noise.

"Now tell me, which one is your Mommy?" Vlad asks Mihaela, cunningly.

"None of them..." Mihaela speaks, looking at them with saddened eyes.

"Good, my dear."

Vlad gets closer to Mihaela, sneaks his hand inside the pocket of her torn little white dress, and takes Mommy Doll out.

"Here she is!"

"Mommy, Mommy!" Mihaela cries out, twirling Mommy Doll under the bright blue sky.

"See? She's always been with you! No one can take your Mommy away..."

Vlad then reaches inside the pocket of his own gown and takes out a purple scarf. He binds it around Mihaela's neck, admiring her with sorrowful eyes:

"This belonged to your mother!"

Mihaela looks at him with big curious eyes, gently touching the silky scarf. But then, ignoring Vlad and his penetrating eyes, she storms out of the room and runs like the wind to the end of the "V" hallway. Seeing the serpentine balustrade with red velvet stairs, she quickly jumps on it, sliding down with the happiness of a monkey! The balustrade takes Mihaela throughout the levels of Vlad's house, like a roller coaster in the dark, after which, it drops her before the gigantic door of the castle, in the dimly lit foyer.

As she catches her breath from the dazzling ride, Mihaela's eyes stop on a mirror—a mirror in the form of an eye.

"This is our mirror..." Mihaela stares in wonder, "The mirror that used to be in Papa Grid's house...and through which I could see Gabriela's escapades... How did it end up here?"

Looking at herself in the mirror, she starts shivering, her ears burn... She sees another Mihaela...so much taller, so much different... Indeed, the white dress looks so funny on her...way too small! Her hair is so much longer and dark, her lips—voluptuous; her nose—smaller; and her cheekbones—shiny and blooming... She has the air of a princess. She is beautiful, without a doubt. She can also notice small nipples, humble buds of breasts... Touching her new body, she hears her father's voice. She blushes.

With her Mommy Doll in hand and her head bent down, Mihaela comes out of Vlad's house.

Rising guilty eyes to her father Grid, she sees him holding Gabriela.

Grid looks astonished at Mihaela, and then at the girl cuddled up to his chest... He now realizes that Gabriela is not Mihaela, even though Gabriela is wearing the same exact dress. Abruptly, Grid drops Gabriela out of his arms, like unwanted baggage, looking at her with repulsive eyes. Gabriela lands on her strong feet, props her naughty hands to her waist, and starts laughing devilishly, exposing her little sharp canine teeth to Papa Grid.

Vlad makes his appearance in the door and grabs Gabriela by her hand. With a statuary posture and a welcoming smile, he greets Grid, who looks at him with killer eyes.

Without giving it another thought, Grid cries out to the old man Vlad:

"You! I knew it was you! You have already taken someone so dear from me! Now leave my daughter alone, understand?"

"It's all right, Papa," Mihaela interferes. "They saved my life."

Vlad grins majestically.

Grid looks suspiciously and turns his back to the kidnapper. He then takes Mihaela into his arms, covering her with ardent kisses.

"I've been looking for you for so long, my love! Never open the door again!"

"But she took Mommy away!"

"Who?" Grid asks, frowning deeply.

"Gabriela…"

Looking at Vlad, then at Gabriela, he stings them with other words of fire:

"Never dare to touch my daughter again!"

Grabbing Mihaela's hand with his big and worn out hands, he looks at the sky, at his friend, God. He then speaks up to his daughter:

"Stay away from him, alright? He is the one who took your Mommy away…"

"But he is the one who…"

"Stop it, for God's sake!" Grid cuts Mihaela off.

"Yes, Papa…"

"Did you say your morning prayers, as I have taught you?"

"Yes, Papa."

After few seconds of silence, Grid plunges into an avalanche of questions:

"How did they save your life?"

"I was looking for Mommy and…"

"And?" Grid continues the investigation, burning with curiosity.

"And I met Gabriela…" Mihaela hesitates.

"And what happened?" Grid asks, impatiently.

"I…we…went to her house and…"

"I see… But didn't I tell you to play with your dolls and never open the door to anyone?"

"Yes, I know Papa… There are a lot of evil men out there…"

Mihaela darkens her voice. Her teeth start bleeding. Blue blood drips on her white dress that is now too small for her...

Grid looks at Mihaela with loving eyes. He takes her up into his arms.

"Now it's over, my baby! Look how you've grown! Don't ever make me search for you again! I thought I'd be going to Mama and leave you all alone out here! Two tormenting years on a man like me don't come easy..."

"But I've been away only for a couple of hours, Papa!" Mihaela says, looking at her dad, encouragingly.

"My love, I've been searching for you for two years. I came to that old man's house every day but no one has opened the door for me."

"Papa, what's wrong with me? You mean I'm 12?" Mihaela's voice trembles.

"That's right, my love," Grid nods, exhaustedly.

Mihaela looks at Mommy Doll, then at her father...

"If you say so, daddy..."

Silence. Mihaela and Grid walk on dried out leaves, leaving thoughts behind.

"I missed you so much, daddy!" Mihaela awakens Grid who was lost in darkness, with a happy cry.

"I missed you too, sweetheart!" Grid cries out, raising his daughter up in his tired arms and kissing her forehead with ardor. "I probably have few more years to live and I want to see you happy. Promise you won't open the door again?"

"Never again, daddy. But you shall live forever!"

Mihaela: *That was my first meeting with Gabriela and Vlad.*

When I arrived back home with my father, I just couldn't fall asleep. The face of that hideous bald man who tried to take advantage of me kept haunting me. My little white dress, torn and painted with blood, was hanging in the corner of my room...and I was restless, tormenting in the light of the moon...

Vlad's advice "Stay away from men, they are evil," echoed in my head all night long.

I started thinking suspiciously of every man.

"Who is evil, who is good?" I asked myself. Papa explained to me all the percepts of life: Genesis, God, the serpent...love...but I did not quite understand all of that...

That very night...I felt hatred...thirst... The thought that I might not be a maiden anymore was killing me, devouring me like a deer by the eyes of a hungry lion.

However, that feeling burnt me only until next morning when suddenly I forgot everything. "How?" All those tormenting thoughts disappeared from my brain like the clouds off the sky and I felt strong and fearless again. I tried to sit down and write a poem about that old bald man, but I could not... That anger was gone...as if yesterday was a long passed memory. I could not remember what had happened exactly, why I had been so sad... It was not hurting me any more. A white page was seating on the table, in front of me, waiting to be scribbled but my mind was blank...I couldn't write... "Why Mommy, why?" I kept reading "The Inferno," by Dante, that Gabriela had brought me from Vlad's library...abandoning myself in those letters of fire so that I could gain some more thirst and desire... Yet my brain was unwilling to give my hand the gift of writing... My feelings were petrified, and so my fingers...ice...

Gabriela started to visit me more and more often, right after sunset while my father was going to the Women's Cave, where, surrounded by bears and water, he was praying and speaking to Mama.

"Find me in your writing," Papa said that Mama spoke for me. But try as I might, I couldn't write, nor could I explain myself why. Papa told me to have patience: "Mama will help you from up there. You'll see."

Yes, I felt that Mama was nearby me and that her return was just a matter of time...

Meanwhile, Gabriela shoved a few letters under my door.

There is this first one that I'll always remember and that starts like this:

"I am your sister. I shall do everything to protect you. See you at midnight."

And since then...it all started. I thought that following her into those nights would make me feel free and would feed my body to write... But I was feeling hungrier and hungrier...and emptier and emptier...

One night, after midnight, Gabriela sneaked through the window of my chamber, and jumped under my sheets. She took me by the hand and said:

"Promise that we will never ever betray each other for any man born of a human mother?"

"Yes, I promise..." *I answered her, a little intimidated by her eyes.*

Gabriela hugged me tightly and we fell asleep, together, check to cheek.

I did not tell Papa anything.

Each time Gabriela was nearby me, I felt stronger, eager to attempt, to attack, to dominate, to lead...

Gabriela:

Each time we've been together in our escapades, we felt invincible, so free, like the whole world was in our fangs... We sought revenge on short bald men like that old bastard who took advantage of my sister when she was just twelve years old...and we had so much fun! Ha! Over and over again... Fangs arose out of my mouth and found their place in those sick louts. And then, we left them in a pool of blood...to find eternity onto a bed of mud! I told Mihaela that revenge is the most liberating act, that she will find her strength to write her verse...

Mihaela:

Gabriela's escapades were horrifying...but seductive. Our moves went faster, our nails grew longer...our teeth became sharper than the wolves... Each night we had a different taste that quenched our rage... I thought that we were doing justice; I thought that all of us needed to drink... Until one night, when he came to my eyes... I was 14. He had the courage to confront us with different kind of words... I still know them by heart:

"If you would be my endless tree
I'd kiss every branch loving thee...
And if you would be a blade of grass
I'd sprinkle it with my teardrops.
Then you'll become my lofty lawn
Where I'd sleep till the dawn..."

When he finished the poem, both Gabriela and I were silent. Especially myself... I was transfixed. "Who is this boy?" I asked within.

My sister looked at me with diabolic eyes and said:

"You've got to do it! Don't listen to his words... Some stupid lines to bewilder your mind!"

But he was so beautiful, like no one we have met before... He was beaming with an unusual joy, his face radiant...his words struck me to the heart...so alive...

"He's a liar! I know this kind of poetry; it is a treachery! He only wants to take advantage of your young, beautiful body and he is sending arrows to your heart to make you fall into his trap!" Gabriela snatched me fiercely by the hand.

"Please, let me talk to him! Don't touch him!" I answered, pulling my hand back.

Then my eyes fell onto the boy, and I asked him tenderly:

"Who are you? Where did you come from?"

"Who are you, disloyal little sis?" Gabriela cut me off. "You are mine, remember? We made a vow! He's just a human creature eager to torment you and steal your youth and splendor! I'm gonna kill that bastard!"

"No!" I shouted back at her. "Let me..."

Yet too late... My words blew helplessly into the wind of night... Gabriela jumped on him and did as she did always: she took him in her beastly hands and pierced his jugular with her sharp jealous fangs... And then she looked at me and said:

"I did it for you, sister! To set you free!"

I hated her with such a hatred and I just wanted to jump on her and tear her apart... But that boy was looking at us, drenched in blood...so pale and helpless...so sweet...and I just kept my rage inside. With his arms spread, he stretched towards me, eager to tell me something... I kneeled down, near his mouth, feeling his low breath. I felt mesmerized by the warm touch of his arm... I thought that he wanted to kiss me, but he grabbed me by the wrist and bit me deeply with his human teeth... He bit me so passionately, so hard, that I still feel his bite at all times at that hour... And then, a purple mark appeared on my wrist, pulsating and spreading like the branches of a tree... A stream of blood entered my veins and then an unknown pain made me feel...ashamed...

As I looked at the boy...his blue eyes penetrated my being, so keenly, like the healing rays of sun in cold winter. I felt something so hot inside my chest... And then, the boy turned his eyes towards the sky and stared at the stars... His face was beaming, so divine; his lips smiled and then he breathed deeply... And then he stopped. His eyes rolled back on me, fixing my eyes... I smiled. I waited, but he would not move. And for the first time I saw the Death...standing next to me, so silently, so merciless...

My sister screamed at me but I could not hear her yelling anymore... I saw a star in the night beaming, so bright... I just wanted to follow it.

Water started coming out of my eyes. More and more... I kneeled before the boy and wetted his clothes. He looked so white, so pale... An aura, like a crown, was drifting above his head.

Moreover, from that moment on, I started feeling so differently; I was not myself... I was so sad! I was eager to smile, but felt so afraid...

I was trembling, yet walking straight. I felt so lonely, willing to talk..., to be heard, to be loved...

How I wished to have asked the boy about life, about his poem, about writing... However, he was lying there breathlessly, asleep.

My wrist started to hurt so much, so deeply, cut by his teeth; my body was shivering, pumping his blood; my hands were stained with guilt, stuck in the mud...

"We have to get rid of these teeth! These teeth just brought us hate and strife!" I told Gabriela with water in my eyes...

But Gabriela laughed at me and laughed, mimicking my pain: "Poetic words...hormones of a crazed teenager... Drink some blood! Cheer up!" She then grabbed me by the hand and said: "Tomorrow you'll forget it all. I promise. Trust me, sister, the humans bite even more bitter than the vampiric sort! Don't be a fool! Let's go!"

And then, as I pulled the boy under an oak, a notebook fell from his coat... I quickly took it and hid it in my chest, away from the eyes of my sister. I pretended like I was over it, and covered him with some leaves.

"Good girl!" my sister said and dragged me along, through a dark path, back home.

But I just couldn't help myself. I turned back and jumped over the boy and gave him a quick kiss on his cold lips.

My sister smirked and took me further in the night. "Stupid girl!" she said.

That was my first kiss. I will never forget it.

"Oh, God, this boy is a genius! We killed a genius!"

I started to scream inside my room, in the morning, as I opened his notebook. There were millions of words, tens of poems sounding like the sweetest blow of nature, like the fairies' call of paradise... "These rhymes are magical, so touchy..." I whispered as I read his verse. "I've never read something like this before..."

On the back of the notebook, it was written by hand: "David, the son of God."

All of a sudden, that strange thing happened to me again: a sort of water started to drip out of my eyes... I kept reading his poems and water kept coming...more and more...until midnight. And then, that water dripped onto my left arm, on that strange bite of David...and it hurt me so badly!

Whatever scratches, cuts, bruises, wounds I got those other nights, had cured instantly. But not this one...that David gave me on my left arm. This one is alive. It pulsates and radiates a violet light...

My chest hurts... I feel so ashamed... My voice erupts out of my lungs and I suddenly scream out: "I hate my hands that killed so many innocent men! I hate my fangs that pierced those poor tramps! Why did we do it? Why?" And then, they kept coming—those men, those victims—with arms like branches twisting around my neck, suffocating me with their pain... And then, flickering crickets, so noisy, deafening voices... Suddenly, I jumped at my table and took a feather in my hand and drenched it in the ink. I was shaking...but I sat straight. I did nothing. I just waited, ignoring that noise. Suddenly, energy came through my head, so light, so peaceful... It hit my chest and made a sound, just like a thud... I placed my hand on my breast and heard something...like a continuous beat: tic, tock, tic tock...just like a clock. And I started to write...and write! Just like a waterfall, words fell on the pages of my soul...

"I'm happy! Mama!" I shouted, finally set free to the sky.

The next day,

I rushed to my father and told him what happened:

"Papa, there's something wrong with me...a clock is in my chest and...it beats...continuously... But I can write..."

Grid took me in his arms and the same kind of water erupted from his eyes. He told me that this water is called "tears." It comes from my heart. He kissed me all over my face and then he put his ear to my chest...

"Yes, yes, it's beating! My love, my girl! Bloody doctor! He told me that my daughter was born without a heart!"

"So I have a heart, Papa? So lovely!" I shouted back with joy.

Then, I showed my father David's notebook, full of poems. Papa knew David very well.

"Where did you get this from?" he asked me, curiously. "David is the son of Margret, a good friend of your mother. He's a very talented boy,

indeed... He is an artist," father said. "His mother is so proud of him. David wrote a whole volume of poetry. Margaret says that he is a genius and she gathers penny after penny so that she can print David's volume of poems. Yet David..." my father continued, "is a boy with problems, sweet creature... He speaks to God, refusing to communicate with people, even with his own mother at times... He knows seven languages... Yet he does not quite live among us, human beings... He speaks with the angels..."

David's notebook dropped from my hand and I collapsed.

Next day, when I woke up, my father asked me from where I got that weird scar on my left wrist. He looked at me so worried. I told him: "Don't worry, Papa. I was bitten by an angel..."

Nighttime. Mihaela is in her bed

with Mommy Doll in her hand. She kisses Mommy on her wooden lips, under a waterfall of tears... She loves tears. Now, that she can have them, she imagines that she is Miss Heaven, sending out rain on Mr. Green...

She opens up the window of her chamber and speaks up to the sky:

"Hello, beautiful stars! Take these tears of mine, play with them and bring me joy tomorrow, at daylight..." And then, she opens up her palms and throws her tears into the night, sprinkling the stars.

"Please, dear stars, tell David that I'm sorry...so sorry... I know my Mama takes good care of him...but you, light him up too..."

Mihaela: Since that bite, I couldn't think of anything else other than him, David, and the words of my father: "He is an artist." I feel the need to write to him, for him, avenge him in a way... Perhaps one day we'll meet again and he will read my poems too... I want to publish his book... I want to be good.

And Mihaela's arms grow longer and longer and she feels that she can touch the sky... She covers up her voluptuous rose lips with her little palms, and whispers in the ears of God:

"I shall do everything to please Mommy! I shall write and write…and make Mommy proud and then…dear God…all my past will be clean…and…"

And leaving the windows wide open, with its white curtains softly shaking into the musical blow of the crickets, she writes:

"*Mama, David, God.*"

Mihaela: *I cannot write more… I need something…a hug from my Mommy.*

And Mihaela takes Mommy Doll in her arms, hugging her with all her force as tears cover her blooming cheeks.

The Great Library

and the Black Church from Brasov are the only places that Grid allows Mihaela to visit—and only accompanied by him.

Bent down, at a wooden table, Mihaela reads *Gilgamesh.* Next to *Gilgamesh,* she holds *Moses.* She reads *Gilgamesh* stealthily while watching the moves of her father, as such books were forbidden to her eyes. Her father wanted her to read only books about happiness, family, and joyful hearts… "Yet it is said that there is no happiness without sorrow, Papa," Mihaela tells her father… Grid smiles but still says "No."

Searching for another hard-to-get book of poetry that belonged to Ovidiu—Grid said that Ovidiu was too depressing for a 16 year-old girl— a librarian boy approaches her, quietly:

"I'll take care of it. He won't notice. I promise. You can write to me what book you're looking for, and I'll procure any for you…"

Each time Mihaela wants to read another inappropriate book, Emanuel is the one to help her out. And each time Mihaela opens the books procured by Emanuel, she finds this message: "Can I see you after reading?"

And the same message welcomes her day after day, month after month…

Indeed, she feverishly wishes to see Emanuel, but she is worried about the refusal of her father.

She feels so eager to speak with him about poetry and the books that she read due to his help.

Emanuel reminds her so much of David. His tooth gap right in front, his white, freckled stained face, his hopeful eyes, his dimpled cheeks, invite her to joy, to love... She wishes to open her heart to him and learn about life, about new palpitating things of the spirit, and she feels that he is eager to open his heart to her too... Never before has she felt such a connection! Nevertheless, she did not dare to speak to her father about him. Until one night, when Grid grabs Mihaela's heart with a question:

"You did not tell me anything about Emanuel. I think he is a nice boy. I like him a lot and I think that your Mama would have liked him a lot too... Do you like him?"

Mihaela blushes, unable to control her happiness. She bursts with excitement, jumping into her father's lap. But she immediately slips and falls to the ground. She giggles, and just as fast, she rises to her feet and speaks up:

"Yes, Papa, I like him a lot... "

"Oh, my dearest, you may talk to him. It's about time."

Indeed, one year had passed since she has kept her secret love inside.

Now, that she has the permission of her father, Mihaela wants to look the best she can possibly look. Adorning herself in front of the beautiful mirror embroidered with pink roses that she inherited from her mother, Mihaela puts on a beautiful green dress embellished with leaves and beige embroiders.

Ready and happy, she descends the stairs of her house, tiptoeing to the door, when Grid catches her arm:

"You, come here! I want to show you something!"

Mihaela, blushing with shame, tries to find her words to explain...

"Your mom would have certainly wanted you to wear this green dress. It was hand-made especially for her, in Sighişoara..." And Grid darkens his eyes and speaks within: "Sighişoara is the town where that man Vlad was born..." "But see, my dear," he continues to address to his daughter, "this green dress is not your Mom's best...and it bears a secret..."

"You mean I may not wear this dress?" Mihaela cuts her father off with sad eyes.

"Yes, you may, but..."

"But?"

"My child... Look, try this." And Grid opens her mother's wardrobe and picks up a light rose dress with laced collar and with white roses that seem to still bloom in the glow of the twilight...

"This dress was your Mama's favorite!"

"Thank you, Dad. It is so beautiful! But what about the green dress? It fit me perfectly."

Grid gives Mihaela a frowned look of disapproval.

Without a second thought, Mihaela takes off the green dress and puts on the light pink one.

"You look just like your mother, my dear! That's what Violeta wore when I first met her ..." Grid admires his daughter in the light rose dress.

"Dad, can you tell me the story of the green-dress from Sighişoara?"

"I will, my love! One day! But now you'd better hurry up! It's getting dark!"

As Mihaela rushes out of the house, the humble moon strikes her forehead. Suddenly, she senses something sharp, something strange growing inside her mouth. She touches her lips and reaches inside, sensing those canine teeth...those awful fangs, penetrating her gums. A whirling, reeling sensation electrifies her whole body... David's bite on her left wrist starts hurting her deeply...pricking, so itchy... She starts scratching her arm; her feet hesitatingly step on the ground, like on hot coals of fire... The way to Emanuel's house seems freaky and dark. Her smile and joy tumble down... She kneels down in tears, staring at the violet scar that has opened and started to bleed on her left wrist, just like that night...

"No... I can't go this way! I can't go now... I need to meet him, I want to kiss him, but I'm afraid to hurt him with these teeth... Why did they come back now? What for immortal teeth if I'm afraid to give a kiss?"

So instead of going to Emanuel's house, Mihaela takes another road...through the dark valley, where she knows an old doctor.

Doctor's House. Late evening.

In front of a small wooden house adorned with ropes of garlic and gourds, Mihaela knocks at an old door, shyly.

The moon grows bigger; her fangs grow longer.

She knocks harder, and then harder and harder, her nails grow stronger...

Her eyes widen and fill with water, ready to spurt out and flood the dark valley.

It suddenly starts raining. Drops of cold rain trickle on her face, mingling with her hot tears.

In a long nightshirt, and with a bonnet shoved on his head, the old doctor jumps out of bed, grumbling at the tardy, unannounced visitor. He lights up a gas lamp, and then asks in a hoarse voice:

"Who's there?"

"Please, help me!" Mihaela cries to the old doctor through a waterfall of tears. "I am the daughter of Grid, from the Lucky Wheel... My teeth terribly sore... I need you to take them out!"

The doctor unlocks the many bolts that secure the door of his house, and invites Mihaela in, trying to calm her down. He asks her to take a seat on a big wooden chair as he brings on his tools.

"I have fangs, doctor! I can't live like this anymore," Mihaela hiccups through big sorrowful tears.

"You have fangs?" the doctor grins with his only one tooth.

"Yes," Mihaela says, ceasing from her sobs.

"Does your father know?"

"I think so..."

"Are you sure? Cause I've never heard of..."

"Yes."

The doctor pulls out a big extracting forceps. He draws near Mihaela with sustained courage:

"Open your mouth."

As he drops a look inside Mihaela's mouth, he drops the forceps.

"Yes... It is so...strange, my dear!"

Then, as he pulls himself together, he checks on all of Mihaela's teeth.

"All your teeth are baby teeth. They are stoned. None of them has ever chattered or fallen out?"

"Baby teeth? There are different kinds of teeth?"

The doctor gives a laugh.

"Please, bring your father here."

"My father does not know. You have to do it fast..."

"I can't do it like this, child... I'm not allowed without his permission!"

"He will thank you! He brought me to different specialists but none of them knew the cause or where those canine teeth came from. Some of them were frightened; others tried, but gave up. My father... Please, doctor, take them out!"

Then, opening a small velvet pouch with two golden coins, Mihaela shows it to the doctor.

"No, my child. I don't need it, not from you. However, I need to make some experiments. I need to find out where those teeth came from... Why do you want to take them out?"

"I want to love."

"Love?"

The doctor takes a closer look at his patient. Grasping a big forceps in his hand, he tries to fix it on one of the fangs. Drops of sweat trickle on his face.

"I think you really have fangs... Where did you get them from?"

"I don't know... My sister..."

The doctor places the forceps on one of Mihaela's fangs and starts pulling in and out.

"It's stoned. I need a bigger one."

The doctor takes a chisel and a hammer and starts to hit the fangs with all his power. Mihaela groans like an animal hurt in his savagery, pushing the doctor away:

"I can't do this, leave me alone! Father!"

The doctor stops, terrified by Mihaela's roars.

"Go home, my dear…"

Mihaela shouts at him, her red eyes popping out:

"Don't listen to me. Just do it! Do it!" she screams.

She then grips the doctor's hand tightly, with big pleading eyes. The doctor takes the chisel and the hammer again and hits the fang just like a sculptor hits his piece of marble. In his great struggle to remove one of the monsters, the doctor lands to the other side of the room, hurled by a wicked power. He rises up, holding the one blue-bloodied fang, just like a trophy.

"I made it! I made it!" he shouts just like a kid who has slaughtered a dragon.

Rising to his feet, he shakes himself off the dust of fear, approaching again his patient:

"Now, one more devil!"

Still under trance, Mihaela shouts out at the doctor:

"Hurry up, finish it, all the way! It's already morning! I can't handle it much longer! Ugh…it hurts so much and it itches…" Mihaela whines, scratching the scar onto her left arm.

Out of the window, the Old Man Vlad watches Mihaela's struggle.

Twitching and fretting in the chair as under a spell from Hell, Mihaela exhausts the doctor, shoving her sharp nails in his hands. The doctor paralyzes again with fear. His hands freeze and bleed; he is unable to proceed.

Mihaela spits out blue blood. Strong convulsions take over her body, terrifying the old doctor.

Suddenly, with her eyes on fire, she jumps at the doctor and bites his neck with her one sharp fang. The doctor gives a shout of death as his hot blood springs out, painting Mihaela's face red.

Mihaela: There was nothing to be done with the poor old doctor any longer.

I took my one fang and went to the butcher. All I can remember is that my thoughts were jumping between Heaven and Hell, between shadows and light, between hot and cold.

Not even the tender rays of the morning Sun could have melted my pain away... I felt like someone has entered my brain and put a bomb inside to explode. I was acting like a ferocious beast, like a prehistoric animal, impossible to be tamed.

Who am I? A strong battle began to ramble inside my mind. Questions were tearing me apart, but most of all my sudden laughter that didn't care about my struggle.

I started to analyze the people on the street, so curiously, to see grief behind their smiles...

Would you like to know how they were looking at me? Well, it doesn't really matter because people aren't what they seem. I have seen pigs traveling inside royal chariots, and rascals behind aristocratic masks. I have seen shop boys and mommies with infants wrapped at their chest, happily poor...eating hot loafs of bread with the grace of a rich woman... At my father's inn, I met men without legs that came from wars, and wives with furs, teaching them lessons... In the windows of taverns, I saw mountains of grief behind rivers of laughter...men smoking their sorrows, and losing their tears in glasses of brandy...

Running towards the butcher, I realized that the world is so much different than I had thought...than I had seen it before or than Papa has told me about... Too much noise and savage, wailing, swearing and fallings, everything spinning like the wheels of a carriage.

I feel so strange! Maybe I'm ill!

The bright colors are fading, the sky is pale, the streets narrower... It is so hard to breathe. My heart pumps curiously, once eager to stop, once beating too fast.

Yet, as soon as I step inside the butchery, I feel a little better.

Tall as a mountain, wide as a valley,
the butcher smiles from ear to ear, showing big and healthy teeth.

Fat as a pig, rounded in face as a homemade bread sprinkled with good cheer, the butcher takes me in his unearthly big and gnarled hands and kisses me with greasy lips of scallion and overland trout. His curls tickle my face and suddenly I smile, hanging by his leather apron.

Then, the butcher thrusts his hands in the apron and takes out a small bottle of brandy. In two shakes of a lamb's tail, he pours it down my throat.

After that, fired up, he slaps his hands together and the mosquitos make some room for the operation.

He doesn't need iron tongs. He shoves two of his huge fingers on my fang, he pulls it strongly, after which he shakes it up, back and forth.

Working his guts out, streams of sweat trickle down his fatty face, his mouth whistling louder and louder.

Outworn, he calls Heirup, his assistant-dwarf, and orders him to pull him by his girdle as hard as he can.

After few hours of hard work, Heirup screams his head off after his seven sons, who come pell-mell to help their father.

All Heirup brood pull each other by the girdles, yet the stubborn fang wouldn't come out. It demands more helpers.

Though she is breastfeeding, mother-dwarf comes to help too, holding the youngest in her arms. She heartedly pulls her little son by his girdle, shouting: "Heave-ho!" And then all of them pull together, screaming their lungs out – "Heave-ho!"

Just then, the monstrous fang springs out, like a fireball, driven out through the blue-blooded stained fingers of the giant butcher.

I immediately jump and catch the fang in mid air, as the butcher pours down his throat a huge bucket of brandy. The dwarfs, thirsty and famished, watch him with big, greedy eyes.

I'm heading home with shivers and...a third eye.

I see differently... I don't know how to walk anymore: on the road that my feet used to go, or on the tunnel of this third eye?

At midnight, when Papa is asleep, I bury my fangs in our garden, deep inside the ground, behind the well, and whisper a chant in Romanian:

> *"Crapă-te, pământule,*
> *Pământule, flămândule,*
> *Și descuie două porți*
> *Să intre-n tine acești colți.*
> *Că pe cine-ai incuiat*
> *Mai mult nu l-ai descuiat.*
> *Să-i încui și pe ei*
> *Să nu-i mai vadă ochii mei.*
> *Iertare, vouă, colții mei,*
> *Fârtăței sângerei,*
> *Rămas bun, bălăurei,*
> *Voinicei încornăței*
> *Să vă duceți cuminței."*

In other words:

> *"Split up, good earth,*
> *Hungry mother-earth,*
> *And open two gates*
> *to enter through them these...two fangs.*
> *Whatever you locked down*
> *You have never undone.*
> *Lock them in too*
> *So that my eyes will never see blue...*
> *Forgive me, dear fangs,*
> *Little bloodied sisters that I have blamed,*

Farewell, monsters of shame!
Go now, sharp knights of fright,
Go away swiftly into the night,
So that I may see the light..."

After I finish the ritual and feel relieved, I see a letter hanging by the door. I pick it up. The letter is cold, sealed with blue blood:

"You can go on taking out your fangs ten thousand times, sweet sister! You can leave your dad and sisterhood behind, but you cannot run away from who you are! Those teeth will grow back, eager to bite back! 'Cause they were born to live...attack!"

Gabriela

Mihaela*: Why is she following me? I told her that I've changed. I'm different now... I won't ever do what I did! Ah, my head! Without those canine teeth, I feel like I lost a part of me, so unbalanced... This third eye...this third eye through which I can see whatever Gabriela's doing...like those days when I could see her through that mirror...makes me fear. I see too much, I feel too much; I'm broken into two... Who am I? Why do I tremble, unsure of life? What are these thoughts that come and overtake me like I am just a memory? I am a stranger to myself...it hurts to breathe; it hurts to think... And yet, I see before...a light...guiding my feet... Am I sick? It's like a virus that spreads inside of me a human fire; it makes me feel, desire...*

I feel a strange taste of blood in mouth. Gabriela's silhouette sneaks before my eyes, taking shape... I see her scornful face, her wicked lips, whispering to my brain:

"Yes, sister, desire! Desire the taste of blood that gives you immortal fire! Desire your sister that loves you because you are unique – a twin vampire!"

"Leave me alone!" I shout back at her, placing my palms over my eyes.

But she does not disappear. She keeps staying there, fixing me with those red eyes.

I reach hastily into the drawer of my table and take out the little pendant with St. Michael that Papa gave me. I put it around my neck and suddenly Gabriela disappears. "Oh my God! Papa was right!" I rush and open the Bible and start reading it aloud, uttering prayer after prayer...

Papa has sensed my transformation and asked me to let him help me. Yet his kind words cannot calm my troubled nights when I need to drink... I keep growling and biting the pillow with Mommy Doll next to my hands.

What am I living for?

Love, make me a whole! Cure my soul!

Gabriela: *I cannot believe what she did! She pulled out those canine teeth and she did not even ask me if I am pleased! We have a deal! Is she out of her mind? We've been so deep in our sisterhood...having so much fun...and now she wants to give up immortality for a stupid mortal guy? It makes me wanna bite her neck and bring her back! She might say that those fangs are repulsive and sharp as they come to three-inch length and drain perhaps tree liters of blood in only three minutes of pain! But what she can't say is that they did not make her powerful, strong, and unafraid! These teeth link us...our desires...our lives—they are a gift! And what a gift! They are our immortal weapons against the world, inherited to make us strong!*

Ah, I can't stand her sudden, stupid brain! She can do whatever she wants, but to take out her fangs for a bloody man, that I can't stand! I love her! We belong to each other! Forever! You've been my witnesses! Together, she and I felt free and fearless... We could go miles and reach the Carpathian's heights without breaking a sweat or giving our feet a rest!

We have a special mission on this earth...like our father Vlad! I am so furious and shocked that Mihaela wants to die! However, I know that I will find a way to cure her foolish teenage mind!

Mihaela: *Is this third eye the eye of God, like Papa says? But why does it hurt me so much?*

Do mortals have to suffer in order to love, to write?

Why are these images rolling inside my brain, again and again? And then, they go deep to my chest and make me feel so strange... Papa has defined them for me, full of worry but also joy: remorse, regret, hope, pain, doubt, love, faith...

And still, Papa cannot get enough from hearing the beat of my heart. He keeps repeating and kissing my eyes: "Love is the greatest gift of all. Love and do anything, my child!"

Out of love and sufferance...I started to write.

The sharp edge of the page that lies in front of me, on the table, pricks my finger. Small blue blood drips out and I begin to write:

"Sacrifice is the beginning of life and life is the beginning of eternity. Mamma had to die for me...and I have to live for her."

Yes, now that I feel pain and love scrambling inside my chest, I can write. I do not need to eat, I do not want to drink, I just forgot about everything... I only want to write!

Writing, Oh, God, such a terrible felicity! This is the thing that heals me... I feel it. These new visions are giving my brain such horizon... I'm floating inside myself, I'm flying...and I am capable of doing what I have truly desired: to write, to write! I am able to remember the past. Now I have memories, strong memories pushing me to write, helping me to sew a new life. I am a new being, a new baby, more frightened, weaker, yet more creative, thirsty of love... Yes, Papa! I'm alive! Now everything starts to make sense, all of those books that I had read, now I can understand...

I rush back to my table and write:

If I have endless life but no love, then I have endless pain, this body and this soul in vain...

I can have youth forever, infinite power to ride till heaven, the wisdom to read hearts and decipher the arts, but if I have no love, then I shrink into a thousand of wrinkles, I live only in winter; just like an old monkey, I wither... I can have castles and kingdoms, and showers of esteem and order like a queen, but if I have no love, then I just have a land for burying my bones and my wealth...

Mihaela, November 8, 1497

Gabriela: How weak, how shaky and meek! Love is a dove with wings cut by the breath of God... Ugh, how can I speak like this? I guess Mihaela is contagious... I'd better go and do my thing! I don't want to get sick!

Mihaela: I know that my saving angel is Love! So, I follow love... Ah, I need a kiss!

*My lips start to tremble and I sing...**A Kiss to Live**:*

(Chorus)

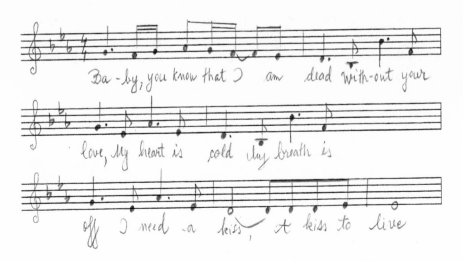

Ba-by, you know that I am dead with-out your love, My heart is cold, My breath is off, I need a kiss, A kiss to live

Next day, early in the morning,

Mihaela jumps off her bed with red blushed cheeks, ready to meet Emanuel! She puts on Mama's light pink dress with laced collar and white roses, and looks in the mirror, excitedly. She moistens her lips with fresh honey from her father's beehives; she shades her eyelids with pink roses from the garden; she takes out the rags that she put in her hair overnight; she brushes her curls with care, and then springs out with big leaps of joy. "Yuppie!"

Emanuel's dwelling is not too far, just down the valley, and yet, she hasn't dared to go to his house without first coming to her senses!

Feeling that she has caught the sun into her palm…feeling that her mother watches over her steps, she breathes a fresh new air! She is a new being! With Mommy Doll in her white woolen-laced bag, today she is going to have her first date ever!

In front of Emanuel's house, a rustic house with Dacian fortress walls and large windows with black shutters, Mihaela gazes in awe. The house has a spectacular architecture like no other house in town. Mihaela reads the inscription with the history of the house and opens up her little mirror for a final touch up. Just then, the door of the house opens and a very elegant woman, dressed up in black, catches Mihaela red handed. Mihaela drops the mirror inside her purse, and asks the woman in one breath:

"May I speak to Emanuel?"

"Who is asking?"

"Hello, I'm Mihaela. Emanuel and I met at the library…"

"Oh, Mihaela…yes, Emanuel told me about you. I am his mother. He's been waiting for this visit for so long…"

"Has he?"

Mihaela blushes… She rubs her hands with excitement. Then she asks again:

"May I speak with him just for a little while?"

"Mihaela dear, don't you know?"

"Know what?"

"He died last month. He had leukemia…"

Mihaela collapses in the arms of Emanuel's mother.

Mihaela: *After David, this was for the second time that I met the death.*

I couldn't stand death from that day. Again, she took my love away! If I hadn't waited for so long, I could have saved him!

A strong battle aroused between death and me, between me and myself, between me and God...

Why do men have to die? Why do they have to wrinkle and get sick? He was so young, so sweet, and me...so stupid to keep my love away from Cupid!

A dagger hits inside my heart, so penetrating, so violent and deprecating! I see a piece of coal and take it in my hand, and scribble on a stone:

*"**Why should I die?***
I don't want to die.
I defy you hideous filth, scabbed death!
I refuse to die.
I am young as a black seagull drawn in a white cloud
and taken by the rays of the sun on a throne to a new life!
Your touch will not crush any wing of mine,
It will not steal any sands of time,
it will not shorten any breath
in its feeding with magical clay!
Promise me and swear you're out of my way!
I want to stand stone in front of you, bleached by divine light.
And when my tears will fall under your cold and sharp sight,
to call my friends out of death with childlike faith.
Under your touch, I want to turn into a globe of ice,
dressed in a long tailed wedding dress.

And when the angels of sun will see me,
to melt into a river of love
and feed the thirsty ones that long to be set free.
And when my ideas will show up on the blue sky,
like a rainbow burning the letters and embracing the sunrise,
to die of happiness into Your hands that kiss the pale body of mine."

It got so dark and I can't see... I can't move on. I can only hear the stream of the small brook that runs behind Emanuel's house. My hands are bleeding. I probably ended up writing that poem with my fingers, on the mist of the air...

What has happened to my eyes? I cannot see in darkness anymore. I need light. My sight has changed—my eyes are weak; I cannot see long distance as I used to those nights... With those sharp canine teeth, I could see ten miles away and reach my aim quick as a wink. With these new eyes and little teeth, I only see the tree in front of me...and then I'm lost... But I received one more eye, my third eye. With it, I can see beyond the sky, and I can write...things that I could not see with those eyes... For instance, when I smile, I see so clearly the face of God, and His palms, caressing my eyes... And then, I feel so much light clearing my sight...like a miraculous salve... And suddenly I see sharper than with a magnifying glass. Each time I start losing my hope, this third eye begins to shine onto my forehead like a lamp, leading my feet to walk... But it sometimes hurts. And then I see the troubles of the world, I hear all the sufferings of the neighbors and it becomes so painful, unwatchful... I want to help them! But how? Or is it better to just pluck my eye out, not to see their struggles?

My dad carried me to seven eye doctors to find out what was going on with that eye. And then to seven witches. But all they did was to increase Papa's worry. Some of them told him that I need supervision and treatment because I am a "special child..."

"I changed, Papa... I am a human being. Now I have a heart... Don't let them turn me back into the old!" And Papa took me in his arms and

kissed my eyes and said "I'm sorry, my child! I should have only listened to the voice of God! This eye—it is a gift from God!"

One night, crossing the meadow filled with violets that surround Grid's inn, Mihaela's feet abruptly stop, pulled down into the mud. Her heart starts beating faster; her face trembles, suddenly covered by a dark shadow.

Gabriela, stronger and cooler than ever, bursts forth before her eyes like a demon of the night. Mihaela holds her breath, and then her heart stops pounding in her chest.

It gets foggy and chilly.

Fixed in the ground like a hot clayed sculpture, Mihaela cannot move; her legs and arms are numb, and yet boiling her blood like a stove; her lips are mum, yet ardent and bloated, ready to explode.

As the thick smoggy air gets to her eyes, Mihaela loses sight of Gabriela; but she can still hear her strong pace tramping around, shuttering nature's calm. Gabriela's cold hands seize Mihaela by her hot shoulders, pushing her deeper into the ground. Miraculously, the fog vanishes, and Mihaela can see, face-to-face, Gabriela's sharp countenance. Gabriela looks so much different: her eyes are violently red, pulled back into her head; her face shrunken and wrapped with a ghostly veil; her breasts, immensely swollen and erected like the edge of a nail, touch Mihaela's little chest…and her long black tail snappily coils around Mihaela's small waist, squeezing the air out of her breast.

Full of herself, Gabriela sticks her scrappy serpent tongue out:

"Well, you should have done something for Emanuel! But see, without those fangs you could not have saved him! You cannot save anyone! You yourself will die if you don't let those teeth grow back and give you life! Immortal life!"

And then, as Gabriela takes her hands off her sister, the spell breaks and Mihaela is hurled to the ground, panting heavily, like a wounded bird. Bitter tears fall from her eyes, sprinkling the violet meadow that clothes the land before her father's lodge.

Quick as lightning, Mihaela rises up and runs back to her house. She locks herself between the four walls of her chamber, paralyzed...unwilling to communicate—not even with her father, not even about the story of the green dress... She feels broken, forsaken... "Why did Emanuel have to die? Who did that to my friend?"

Suddenly, she sees someone in the dark with an apple in hand, moving it back and forth before her face. A voice sneaks inside herself and asks her in a kind tone: "What do you choose, Emanuel or your writings, your life?" *"Emmanel," I replied immediately. And then, a thundering voice, like a sword, hit me to my heart, and I cried out to myself: "How could you have chosen Emanuel? He is dead! You choose death over life?"*

And then that thought started to watch over me like an evil eye lurking in the dark... And then to slap me like I was quilty of the whole world's sins. My third eye started to detach from my self...covered with murky dark clouds...like he was an enemy of my mind. The words of my sister kept haunting me, waking me up in the middle of the night. I could hear Emanuel speaking to me with his dead face, but then I heard Mama's voice, whispering to me: "Don't be afraid..." But I didn't know how not to worry... The more I was trying not to, the more I was afraid... I could not tell whether I was dreaming or living, whether I was feeling blessed or cursed. Or maybe life is a dream, a written film and we cannot escape it? I asked myself, fretting inside my bed.

And since that night, every morning, as soon as the rooster crows out, Mihaela wakes up, writing morbid poetry, roaming between the angels and the dead. *"Which is the answer? Which is the truth? How can I find the way out?"*

Grid, visibly affected by his daughter gloominess and silence, takes Mihaela to the amusement park, to fairs, introduces her to nice boys, procures "inappropriate" books for her... Yet nothing seems to bring his sweet Mihaela back to his love.

"How guilty daddy feels! He thinks it is because of him!" Mihaela says to herself.

After she finishes writing, Mihaela goes to Emanuel's grave. Grid worries more and more as Mihaela has started to talk strangely. She tells Emanuel's mother that her son's body is not there anymore and that he is happy, somewhere else... She tells Papa that her pain is a blessing, but that he cannot see that yet... But what he can see is that his daughter's face is not radiant anymore! She is dark, without a smile. Her words are not words of a child...

Grid feels the need to talk to his daughter and bring her to her senses. So one night, caressing Mihaela on her forehead, with palms of a mother, Grid asks his daughter:

"My angel, what do you wish?"

After months of dark silence, Mihaela finally speaks. She opens her big black eyes before her father and, without blinking, she says:

"I wish to bring the dead back to life. My Mama and Emanuel," Mihaela replies.

"Mommy is here, with you."

"No, dad. I wish one day that Mommy would come home, in flesh and bones, that I could hug her... I wish Emanuel would kiss me... Why is he dead?"

"I'd do everything to bring them back..." Grid murmurs.

Afterwhich, he embraces his daughter shivery, tears dimpling down his cheeks.

"Daddy, who am I?"

"You are...my daughter, a very special person that God loves very much."

"Dad, I haven't seen another child with teeth as mine or as Gabriela's! I pulled them out. You've noticed it, but you didn't ask me how or why. Where did those fangs come from, sweet daddy?"

"My child, life is full of mysteries. The thing that you should appreciate the most is the beautiful unknown. You cannot see God, but you know that He lives in you, you feel Him, you see Him... You are His beloved daughter. You don't know where those fangs came from but God knows why you were born that way. You don't know why you have that third eye on your forehead and neither any human being does, but God knows. God wants you to be happy. You write; you create. Since you pulled those teeth out you found the love of God and art. You changed...you are a poet, an artist. You can bring your Mama back if you build a work of art that will make her come down to tell you how proud she is of you. If you work hard and believe that Mama will come, she will. You can change the world, my love. Pray for it."

"Dad, who is God for you?"

"God is your best friend, the one who gives you endless love. Talk to Him, my love. He will listen to you. The better friends you become, the stronger you will feel Him in. It is the best friendship in the world. Go on and date Him. He will perform miracles for you and give you many gifts...if only you receive... And then give, give to all your friends! We are to spread His love around the world and all the emptiness will be filled with His whole..."

"But Papa, if God loves me, why did He take Emanuel and Mama away? Why does He let us die?"

"No, God does not want us to die, my child. He did not give us diseases, sorrows, He did not condemn us... Contrarily, He gave to us everything—His only Son. He took our death to give us His life, He took our pains to give us His smile, he took our guilt to give us His peace...His finished work. All in one day at the cross. It is a gift for you, a supreme gift of love."

"But then, who gives us diseases, who wants us to die?"

"An evil angel who tempts us to listen to his lies. His name is Lucifer. He fought with God, envious of His riches and wisdom, and since then, he seeks revenge against His children... He wants us to die, to take us away from God. But nothing can separate us from the love of God, from the love of your mother, your father...because Jesus, God's son, brought the devil to nothing. This evil angel, Lucifer, is now nothing, my child. Impaled, crucified. Only a phantom who bubbles lies, a scarecrow... But you are not a crow, you are a dove, my child. Listen to the truth of God. If you don't let your little heart get troubled, if you only smile and give all your worries to Him, Daddy God will work everything out for you, and beyond your expectations, my child—you will never die... Your Mama was barren and I thought I will never see a child again in my house—but God sent me your smile. You are my blessing, my dearest gift."

"Daddy, you make it sound so beautiful, so simple... Is it that simple?"

"Yes, my child, it is that simple! But we, human beings, complicate it, we get deceived by shadows, fears, lies, ilussions... We want to fight and strive to get what we already have. Only receive the gift of life and smile, rest in Daddy's hands..."

And Mihaela smiles to daddy.

"I reveive it, Papa. Now Mama will come home?"

"Yes, she will, my child..."

Vlad watches the whole scene from outside, hidden behind the well of their garden. He is touched, yet blazed. He shrinks and squints, his eyes burning with frozen indignation. Small horns from the underground prod Vlad's whole being, threatened by the holy words of Grid. Those heartfelt, simple words of Holy Ghost burn him like fire, melting his body of ice. He wants to stay cool, cold, but now he feels like dying...

Hard knocks on the door.

Grid rushes to open the door. They are expecting Aunt Magia.

To his surprise, a twin tailed Gabriela shows up.

With pleading eyes, Gabriela falls at the feet of Grid:

"I know that you are my good father. I don't know my mother, but I know you... I have never had the chance to tell you this: you are so different from Vlad—so kind, so generous, so human! I like you a lot. Would you let me stay here for a little while? Vlad was so mean to me. I promise that I shall be as good as an angel. Please, don't throw me out, my dear father..."

Gabriela then gets near to Grid and whispers in his ear, gently:

"I know how I could make Mihaela playful and merry again. She needs friends. Just let me try it... Please."

Touched by the thought, Grid lets her in. While closing the door of his house, something from the garden lures Grid's eyes... Something strange, something that he has never seen before, had grown in their garden, near the well... He steps outside, walking barefoot on the grass, eager to see— up close—the new appearance.

Behind the well, in the same place where the double Queen of the Night flower once was, a small perky tree has begun to rise. Its trunk is of silk cotton, smooth, velvet; its shape—like a fork with two creepy prongs—two thick blue branches with sharp-pointed ends, like two fangs. One branch is silky and shiny, soaring skyward; the other is spiky and bent, its sharp blue end pointing to the ground, like a knife.

The tree is yet little but it has already grown two small violet apples from which a blue sap trickles down, moistening and feeding its tiny blue roots that have emerged through the ground...

As he watches the blue liquid falling down, Grid remembers that they have no water left inside. He throws the bucket into the well, but instead of water, a bluish sap, just like the one that drips from the violet apples, keeps coming out. Convinced that his imagination is playing tricks on him, he throws the bucket into the well again, and then again, just to pull out the same sap... He tastes the sap. "What a weird prickly taste!"

All of a sudden, hundreds of flickering butterflies, with blue-colored wings, surround him. Bewitched by their beauty and lights, Grid runs after them all around the yard, like an ecstatic child, and then back to the door of his house. One of the blue butterflies, the biggest of them all, with electrifying red antennas like two giant horns of a snail, and with an eye on top of them like a detector, enters the window of the house. Grid rushes inside, intrigued by the small blue creature, which got into his dwelling uninvited.

The butterfly alights on Gabriela's hand. Grid looks enthralled. Gabriela hands Grid a sealed letter, and says:

"This is from Vlad."

Grid takes the letter, his eyes still fastened on the strange creature.

Gabriela approaches Mihaela with clumsiness and, taking a seat near her chair, she whispers:

"I know what you are going through... Maybe we could have saved him."

Grid takes a seat at the old oak table from the living room.

Mihaela raises her mournful eyes, peering at Gabriela with rage. But the sight of the blue butterfly softens a little her heart.

"What do you know of saving?" Mihaela asks Gabriela, in a cold voice.

"More than you think!" Gabriela assures her, in a kind tone. "Do you think that I don't have a heart?"

"You don't!" Mihaela replies with certitude.

"Oh, yes, I do," Gabriela speaks back. Then, she continues in a warm, storytelling voice:

"I met a boy too... There was something so special about this boy... He was taming my rigid heart, and actually, for a short period of time he changed me. I was so in love with him. Vlad noticed, of course. He warned me to stay out of it... He said I could get hurt. However, I kept going to see him...because I loved him. But someone took him away from me and broke my heart..."

Mihaela stares at Gabriela. She then looks at her father who is still reading that letter.

Nailed inside the chair, Grid looks hypnotized. His eyes are taken; his mouth is opened and stuck in awe.

All of a sudden, he drops the letter and rises up. Tears erupt from his eyes as he walks up and down the room, rubbing his hands with haste. Then, with the braveness of a captain, he heads over to Mihaela and Gabriela and speaks up:

"Let's go, girls!"

"Where, Papa?" the girls ask in sync.

"To Vlad."

Restless, Grid writes a note to Aunt Magia and slides it under the door.

Mihaela: *I've never seen my father so nervous. On the way to Vlad, I kept wondering what was that letter holding, what was it that made him so emotional...*

Gabriela: *Papa is a genius! And so are his butterflies…*

Vlad's house.

A big black cloud overshadows Vlad's dwelling.

Grid opens the giant metal gate slowly, and steps into the muddy garden.

Vlad is seated in a wheelchair, in the middle of the garden, between weeds and dried branches of autumn, playing a sad song on the ney. The lecherous sounds of the ney—a long Turkish flute that Vlad received as a child from an Ottoman friend—makes Vlad's nine cats go mad. A big black cat, the proudest of them all, endowed with thorny feelers and a long red tail, is coiled like a turban around Vlad's head, moving its body curvaceously, in the wavy rhythm of the song. The other eight cats, smaller but naughtier, lift up their paws and, standing on their hind legs firmly, with their eyes fastened onto their master, dance like alluring odalisques in a harem. As soon as Vlad finishes his song, the cats freeze in a pose, like on a stage, awaiting applauses…

"Such a surprise to see you, my friends," Vlad says, heavily raising his head.

Grid and Mihaela hold their tongues.

"Welcome back!" Vlad adds on.

Grid stares at the old Vlad, filled with anxiety. He wouldn't have expected to see such a different Vlad, with such a feeble physiognomy, and such surprising talent.

"Please, enter my house. Feel at home. I'll be right with you," Vlad encourages them.

Pushing the gigantic black door, scraped by the claws of wild birds, Grid and Mihaela enter Vlad's house.

The intimidating castle and heavenly garden with dark bloodied lake are no longer there. The old luxurious scenery is gone. Instead, a modest, lonesome, traditionally furnished dwelling spreads before their eyes. Transylvanian tapestries, blidare[22], parsechiuri[23], small painted corner cupboards, wall clocks of linden wood, carpets, pillows and hand sewn towels, inlaid chairs and tables—are the new ornaments that adorn his house, hardly reminding of the old aristocratic furniture.

Once a vigorous dictator, Vlad now looks as a low key and humble creature. He is weakened, desolate, and walking on crutches. Nevertheless, his physiognomy still betrays aristocratic, royal roots...

Coughing abruptly, Vlad enters the house, followed by the nine black cats. He slowly throws himself from the wheelchair onto the couch, still coughing. He tries to seat himself in a comfortable position, puffing, as if something bothers him.

The cats exit the living room quietly, waving their tails with elegance. Vlad puffs a few more times, wipes his forehead, and then invites his friends to take a seat.

After expelling a cold breath through his icicled nostrils, Vlad speaks:

"I know, my dear friends, I mistook... It is not easy for you to forgive me, as I myself believe in deeds and not in words. I only hope that it's not too late to show you who I am... I would have wanted my mouth to utter these lines a long time ago... It is so hard to say it all, too many flaws inside this soul. But now that I have reached the edge of my life, I realized the loneliness that ate my bones... It is a virus that spreads inside your body and rusts it day-by-day, so savage... I implore your friendship, my friends. I only tried to help. When you are old, you no longer think about yourself, but about helping others... Give me one more chance to show you who I am and how my friendship will mirror my words..."

He then penetrates Grid's eyes, mourning like a widower:

"I need friends, I need friends like I need air. Please allow me this honor."

Silence.

"There is one ardent wish that I have," Vlad speaks again. "And if you could help me...this would be beyond my expectations. I wish...to have

---

[22] **Blidare** *are long racks of wood with ethnic plates and cups painted in earth tones.*

[23] **Parsechiuri** *are small wardrobes where expensive jewels and other significant things are kept.*

dinner with you, preferably at your house, all together. To feel that I belong to someone, to feel the warmth of a family... There's been such a long time since I left this place... I'm sick and tired of it all. People have the wrong impression of me. I want to rectify it. I am eager of love and of friendship..."

Silence.

Blueness suddenly mars Vlad's face and his left eye begins to twitch.

All of a sudden, he turns his head to Mihaela who has been totally ignoring him, gazing outside the window at the leafless branches of the black tree clad with ivy.

Her big poetic eyes are shining, wrinkled by few fine lines... Her rosy plump lips indiscreetly invite to virgin words of love... The wisdom on her forehead, her third eye that illuminates her features, her skin so white and heavenly, are subjugating Vlad's eyes, bewitched by her guise. Mihaela is much more beautiful than Vlad remembered her. Behind those big black eyes, he can sense a secret story, an old soul that reminds him of his dead wife.

Yet two peas in a pod, Mihaela and Gabriela are as different as day and night. One hot, one cold. One innocent, one bold. Mihaela: two inches taller, Gabriela: two inches shorter. Mihaela: soft, poetic, Gabriela: tough, incisive.

Vlad breathes heavily, following Mihaela's neckline, and reaching to her vivid breasts. Saliva drops out of his mouth, trickling to the floor...

Mihaela opens the window to look at the black tree that seems to fascinate her. She bends down and extends her arms, touching one of the dry branches of the black tree. Suddenly, its leaves go green; its dry buds bloom into big white petals, like the wings of an awakened swan. The scorched ivy withdraws from its thick branches and jumps vividly on Mihaela, coiling around her gentle body, kissing her neck and long arms, tightly. Mihaela smiles with delight, rotating like a prima ballerina in the strong arms of the tree until Vlad rises up and slams the window shut.

Mihaela loses her balance and falls into the arms of Vlad. Vlad looks at her face, spellbound, his old features suddenly turn into fine wrinkles of joy, showing him so much younger... He breathes excitedly; his face sweats and blushes, icy drops fall from his hair...melting down under the sunny eyes of his beautiful guest. Unable to restrain himself any longer, Vlad gives Mihaela a quick kiss onto her lips. Mihaela's body shivers with cold, from her mouth to her heart.

"This is so curious..." Vlad breaks the silence, embarassed by his uncontrolled act. Then, turning his eyes to Grid, who has been watching the scene with perplexion, he says:

"Forgive me...but this tree did not kiss anyone since the death of my wife. It loved her, she loved him. Every time she wanted to write, my wife climbed this tree that held her under its crown like a parent that she never had. She was calling him the "Wiseman" or Papa. It sheltered her with love, kissing her around her neck, just like it has kissed Mihaela. Since my wife's death, the tree has become dry, it died. I thank you, dear Mihaela, for bringing him to life..."

Grid and Mihaela look at Vlad deliriously, like floating in a dream. They have never seen such a tree before, they have never listened to such a story...

Grid speaks up:

"We could... We could find some time for you...maybe this evening if you don't have other plans..."

At Grid's invitation, Vlad's eyes, frozen on Mihaela's face, awake from the trance, like two lamps suddenly switched on; his mouth opens like the crater of a volcano, erupting words of enchantment: "Magnificent! Fabulous! Ex....cellent!" he drags the sound "x" with excitement.

"Then...shall it be 7 pm?" Grid mumbles, easily frightened.

"7 pm!" Vlad confirms.

Shaking off the gown of moodiness, Vlad flips off his feet in sign of victory:

"You have no idea how happy you've made me, beyond imagination!"

Vlad's amplified voice and youthful spirit betray a healthy old man. But he quickly realizes his uncontrolled excitement, and arches his back as if a heavy twitch has caught his whole body. He starts coughing again, collapsing onto the couch, and thanking his guests with gratitude.

Mihaela, who kept looking out of the window at the Wiseman tree, abruptly turns her head to Vlad:

"It doesn't work for me this evening."

Vlad looks at her, petrified.

"Why, dear?"

"Because I don't trust you. You took my Mama away," Mihaela replies, firmly.

"I didn't take your Mama away, my dear," Vlad justifies. And smiling graciously, he adds: "As you'll grow older, you'll understand. If I had known what your Mama went through, I would have saved her. Believe me. You have to believe me… I cared about your Mama; I wanted the best for her… I once too had a wife whom I have loved enormously, but I could not help her. She was tricked and hurt by the ones who wanted my end. And her disappearance was my end. I know what you and Grid are going through, my dear. I wanted to help your mother. The loss of her little child, her despair, but courage, touched me. And I helped her to procreate again. I would have given my life so that she lives… She did not tell me…"

And Vlad starts whining like a child.

"I love Gabriela," he continues. "I loved your Mama. And so I love you!"

Mihaela looks at him, unaffectionate.

"In order to prove my love for you, please, Grid, allow me to show something to your daughter…"

While Vlad still speaks, a tall, slim, handsome boy makes his appearance. The boy stutters some words, turning red cap-a-pie, his face deforming and shivering.

Vlad hits the ceiling. He shouts for Gabriela, who comes immediately, holding a big black cat in her arms. Vlad throws Gabriela a cold glance, after which, excusing himself before his guests, he throws himself back in the wheel chair. Gabriela takes him away with the obedience of a loyal servant.

As soon as he leaves the living room, the nine black cats take possession of the sofa.

Mihaela begs Grid to leave:

"Daddy, believe me, it is not good… Let's go!"

"You don't know the truth my dear," Grid interferes. "Vlad wrote me a detailed letter this morning. Believe me, Mihaela, you know my old feelings for him. I would have never planned to come here if it hadn't been for that letter! That letter…disclosed something that I could have never imagined… See, your mom was sterile and Vlad helped her give birth to you… He then told her to…"

"But then she died… Why?" Mihaela interrupts her father.

"Because…your mother refused to visit him after she gave birth to you. She had to continue the treatment!"

"Is Vlad a doctor?"

"That's what Magia, your aunt, said. She sent your mother here. He is kind of a doctor…"

"Daddy, even you yourself don't believe it… This is a scenario…"

And Mihaela's third eye starts to shine brightly.

"Daddy, now I can see more…"

Mihaela's cheeks bloom, her eyes sparkle, transfixed.

"Daddy, now I can feel more…"

Grid looks at his daughter's transformation, overwhelmed. He cannot believe his eyes! His daughter spreads lights and beams; she has a magical aura. Her face, though too pale, looks like of a goddess, like of an outer space being. She is incredible…incredibly beautiful. And wise…too wise for her age…

"Daddy, it hurts me… Mama knows. She cries."

And Mihaela takes the wooden Mommy Doll out of her purse. Mommy Doll is violet and…sad.

"When your mom gave her last breath, she told me: Mihaela…is Vlad's creation…but don't ever let him take her away from you… I guess you are right. We should leave," Grid speaks out, tormented.

"You mean Vlad is my father?" Mihaela asks, terrified.

"No, for God's sake, how did you come to think that way?"

"You said that I am Vlad's creation..."

"Yes, but, you don't understand, my dear... Your Mama could not give birth anymore after she lost Vlady and... Maybe it is beyond my understanding too..."

Mihaela's question starts to obsess Grid. He cannot get that fearful thought out of his head, the fear that Mihaela might not be his daughter. "Why did Violeta tell him to never let Vlad take her away from him?"

In the meantime,

Vlad, healthy as a horse, flies like the wind through the columns of his house, reaching The Knights Hall—a gray tunnel, majestically arched. To the right and to the left of the tunnel, distorted faces with red bulging eyes and decayed teeth scare the sight; grizzled hairy heads with wide opened mouths droop ill- smelling tongues... Skinned corpses with blackened entrails are nailed to the walls; decayed legs and bloodied arms pulled from the hips and shoulders, desiccated hands with livid nails...grotesquely color The Knights Hall... Growls and screams of animals quake the big chains and lockers, heads of hissing snakes, famished lions, wounded bears, and other prisoners of Vlad animate the human zoological garden.

Tombs decorated with cactus spikes and large red and purple flowers, paths lined with thistles and poisonous red mushrooms, strong smelling alleys with Queen of the Night flower, both fascinate and scare.

Along the tunnel, strands of hair, teeth, nails, bloodstains, and sweat, remind of a stormy and challenging history.

A raven with burnt feathers, flying with a red canary in its strong beak, crosses Vlad's way and hides behind an acid–waterfall, alighting on a small woolen carpet. Underneath the carpet, a trap door in the floor opens to the cold cell of Vlady—the stolen brother of Mihaela and Gabriela, who was thought dead long time ago, on that doomed night of Saint Andrew's.

Pulling the trap door by a hidden handle, one can descend the narrow staircase that leads into Vlady's cell—a short moldy basement lit up by a shy stream of light that sneaks in through a small crack in the shutter.

Before, when the shutter of his cave was not fixed in spikes, Vlady could open the window and catch birds of the air that would satisfy his hunger and quench his thirst. But too many traces of blood, stained on the walls of his cave, made the Old Man Vlad and the two lions from the adjoining den, go mad.

Moreover, Vlady's cave was seated on the edge of the Death Creek, a whirling stream of black water where it was said that the dark forces of the world have been spitting their anger and washing their hands of their bloody acts... At times, at night, Vlady cannot sleep, as the deafening whistle and hissing of those dark beings are scaring the bones out of him.

Now, as the feet of the Old Man Vlad trample down the narrow stairs, Vlady shivers in a cold, deadly temperature, near a pair of rotting rats and a dirty sheet of paper.

"I told you to stay here. How could you get out?" Vlad draws near Vlady, shaking a whip in hand.

Vlady looks at "Papa" Vlad filled with anger, showing his empty plate.

"Human beings are meant to control their hunger. You are not an animal. I have other expectations from you. Do you want me to put you with them?" Vlad asks, pointing to the den with lions.

Then, aiming to put Vlady again in chains, Vlad utters with deep sorrow:

"I would have never done this to you. You were a prince in my heart, in our house, treated with royalty. You had, like Gabriela, the most respected teachers of piano, French, German and English, great teachers of painting and of fencing, training you into the fine arts of life. I wanted you to be my follower, both in thinking and in the arts. It strikes me to the heart that I have shown you so much love and you have kept being disobedient.... And you had seen that I was with honorable guests and yet...you have dared to bother us."

And taking Vlady by his cheekbones, Vlad pierces him in the eyes.

"You were just one month old when I found you. You had no mother and no father, abandoned in a hovel. I have taken care of you like a real father. And despite all of that, you tell me that I killed your mother? How dare you, worm in a hole?"

Then, calming his anger, Vlad continues to speak like a forgiving father:

"You did not want to tell me who shoved that lie into your brain. It was your choice. Fine. You could have been out of this cage long time ago. But you persisted in ignoring me, defying me, refusing to write the name of that deluder. And now...look! That damn piece of paper got shrunken because of too much patience, waiting for the little brat's answer! And you...you got uglier and uglier. What's in your brain? How could you be so ignorant and stubborn not to speak the truth to your father, who wants the best for you?"

And taking the whip in his hand, Vlad strikes feeble Vlady with fury. Vlad's eyes burn, his face trembles, he becomes a ferocious beast, kindled by the thirst of punishment.

Vlady groans like an animal, with his eyes gazing at the damp dirty sheet of paper that lies on the floor.

"You want to write?" Vlad asks.

Vlady nods. He then raises his fingers up in the air, drawing more papers...

"Ah, you need more paper? More paper for an answer?"

"Hmmm..." Vlad growls affirmatively.

"I'll give you more!"

And Vlad begins to smite his beloved "son" with more fury, his own teeth chattering at the hard blows of his whip.

At 14 years old, Vlady had an outburst of fury in front of the Old Man Vlad, blaming him for stealing him from his mother and for killing her. Thus Vlad, his "benefactor," pulled Vlady's tongue out of his mouth and made him the victim of the house, kept as a prisoner and as a main source of blood, forbidden to see the daylight.

In darkness and in pain, Vlady thought of a plan of revenge against his "father" Vlad; he scribbled this plan in his mind until one night when Magia, the one-eyed aunt, sneaked to his cell and brought Vlady paper and ink.

Moreover, Magia gave Vlady the talisman that she had prepared for him that unfortunate night of Saint Andrew—the little bottle of crystal, which held one ray of sun that would protect Vlady from any harm. As soon as Magia put the talisman around Vlady's neck, Vlady's face brightened and smiled, and his body began to warm up.

After that, hand in hand with her feeble nephew, aunt Magia told Vlady what had happened to him and to his mother, and how long she had been searching for him:

"In my goblet with water and ashes, I kept seeing your face—alive and tormented... And I kept coming here, stealthily...but I could not find the trap door that led to your cell... But now that I'm here, have faith, my dear boy! I will help you to escape... I won't let that happen again," Magia confessed to Vlady, with bitter tears boiling inside her eyes.

Moreover, that night, Magia promised Vlady to teach him how to travel in time, through the centuries, over seas and through wild spaces, and how to perform her spells and incantations.

Now, under the ray of sun hidden in the little talisman, Vlady keeps writing onto the papers of Magia, with his left tremulous hand, the story of his life and the truth about "Papa" Vlad...

After the visit to the Old Man Vlad,

Mihaela says her evening prayers as the curtains of her window, in the shape of crow wings, shroud her body like angels in disguise. The moon reflects on Mihaela's third eye that is kneeled before the sky, looking like a star, searching for God.

Mommy Doll, sweet and with big opened eyes, sits quietly on the sill of the window. Small drops of rain start cleaning the horizon. The long neck of Mihaela bends like a swan, her lips like buds of roses, open into a prayer of love:

"My dear God, please, help me so that one day my Mama will come out of this doll, in flesh and blood, as beautiful as Mama used to be... I want to hug her, I want to kiss her..."

The music of the raindrops that slide onto the rooftop keeps the rhythm of her incantations. She breathes ceaselessly, inhaling the grace of God.

All of a sudden, Mihaela's mind is struck by the girl's face from the painting that she saw in Vlad's chamber with blue glacial walls. Those black eyes resembled so much her eyes, those rose lips were just like her lips... Even the dark mole on her left breast was marked onto that chest...

Mihaela takes a deep breath and continues to pray:

"Dear God, thank you for taking care of my father! Take care of Emanuel up there, too! Forgive me because I didn't answer to his love in time... If I knew..."

The wind blows forcefully through her hair, whistling words of darkness: "You cannot run away from who you are..."

Ignited by the indigo light of the moon, the wind gets stronger, turning into a tempest, casting Mommy Doll out of the window. Mihaela's papers with poems rise up in the air, dancing her words with pride. Swiftly, Mihaela closes the window, double locking it. She then sneaks out of the house, fighting the wind that cools down at her sight. Mihaela starts looking for Mommy Doll:

"Mommy, where are you?"

She can hardly see the flowers, the crickets, the roots of the trees that she could once see so clearly in darkness...

Carried away by the strong wind behind the well, Mihaela catches on to the tall silky stem of the fanged tree that sits proud and fixed, unworried by the wind.

The storm suddenly eases and Mihaela kneels down to look for Mommy. Among the leafage, she pricks herself into the other branch of the fanged-tree that has sharp thorns and violet apples. She smiles, just like when she was little. Drops of blue blood drip out of her fingers onto the wet grass.

"Ah, here you are, Mommy!" she murmurs as she catches a glimpse of Mommy Doll. Trying to pull Mommy Doll by one of her arms, Mommy sinks deeper and deeper into the mud.

Mihaela thrusts her long fingers into the soil and begins to dig out like a true gardener. She finds a head, a chest, a whole body...cold and silent...much bigger than Mommy's... She barely pulls the body out of the ground, when a cold arm wraps around her neck. Mihaela struggles with both hands to undo the clasp. She finally bites the strong arm with her teeth and breaks free from the clutch.

"My love, thank you for saving me," a man suddenly speaks. Mihaela turns around and sees him—a corpse...a creature with bulging eyes, fiery and sly, shining like two fireflies. Its muddy mouth gets closer to her mouth, spewing out yellow saliva. The face, white as a ghost, looks just like Emanuel's.

Mihaela takes a few steps back.

"Who are you?" she asks, terrified.

"I am the one who starves to have one kiss from the most precious girl in the whole world. One kiss and I can die again..." the creature in love declaims. And then it jumps up at Mihaela's hands and begins to suck the blue blood that still drips out of her fingers.

Mihaela pulls away from him, her hand shivering to her heart. She turns around to run, just to fall abruptly into the mud. She gets a grip on herself and starts crawling back to the house as fast as she can. Suddenly her arms weaken; she can barely pull herself up. Like a wounded ballerina, she tries to make a graceful leap but she breaks down... Her broken legs tangle around her neck, almost strangling it. She cannot control her own body. She can only hear Emanuel's voice, crying after her:

"Are you going to let me out here in the cold rain? Now, that you have finally found me?"

Mihaela does not look back; she struggles to open the door of her house with her feeble arms, but the door is locked. Emanuel screams out again:

"You don't even take your Mommy Doll back?"

Mihaela turns her head at the speed of light and pierces Emanuel's eyes:

"Give me my Mommy back!"

Waving Mommy Doll in his hand, Emanuel speaks out:

"Oh, Mama, Mama! Come and get her!"

Then, he begins to sing in Italian with great pathos:

"Mamma, son tanto felice perché ritorno da te. La mia canzone ti dice ch'è il più bel sogno per me!"

Mihaela rises to her feet, and embodying the force of darkness that surrounds her, jumps on Emanuel with pointed nails, enraged. Her canine teeth re-emerge, her eyes flicker red lights, her body strengthens into the night... She grabs Emanuel's arm and twists it behind, then pricking him to his heart with her sharp nails, envenomed and soiled. Emanuel laughs, his arm breaks apart and finally Mommy Doll springs off his clutch, onto the grass.

"I knew it. My queen loves Mommy more than she loves me," Emanuel utters, amused. "But Mommy would have liked me so much! She would have never wanted her daughter to treat me like this."

Mihaela recognizes her father's words in Emanuel's mouth. Nevertheless, she ignores him, picks up Mommy Doll and rushes back to her house. But the door is still locked. Feeling that Emanuel is getting closer and closer, she starts knocking harder and harder. But the door is silent.

The dark gets darker. Mihaela turns around, terrified, imagining the yellow muddy mouth of Emanuel sealing her with a viscous kiss. But no trace of Emanuel can be seen. Actually, Mihaela cannot see anything. She can only feel a cold wind, slowly getting underneath her nightdress. She breathes easily. Nature calms down; it suddenly gets warmer. The soft blow penetrates her gently, taking her breath away. Mihaela moans with pleasure, feeling it deeper and deeper. It touches her breasts and then goes around her neck, squeezing her velvety young flesh.

The next morning.

Mihaela is awakened by the alluring smell of steaming bread, just taken out of the țest.

She jumps out of bed and, in the blink of an eye, barefoot and light, she heads to the big room where Daddy Grid has just laid the bread on the red-fringed tablecloth sewn by the hands of Mommy Violeta.

Mommy Violeta had also sewn Mihaela's white nightdress with lace. No, the nightdress actually belonged to her Mommy, and that is why Mihaela is sleeping in it every night with so much yearning and delight...

Mihaela kisses Daddy's hands and sweetens him with a tight embrace. Grid blesses her day, making the sign of the cross on her forehead.

Then, hungrily and greedily, Mihaela breaks the bread that Daddy Grid faithfully kneaded just as Violeta used to.

Since Violeta's death, Grid has had to be both mother and father... It hasn't been easy for him, but as soon as he thinks of Violeta, of her patience, of her sweet hands, his own hands magically embody everything she knew... What she cooked, he cooks. As she sewed, he sews. He misses Mommy Violeta so much, and just like Mihaela, he has been holding on to the hope of a miracle.

He surely feels that Violeta's soul dwells in Mommy Doll, yet nothing can replace Violeta's being, her beauty, inspiration and aura... She was the treasure of his life. He lives for her and Mihaela.

"Daddy, what day is today?" Mihaela asks her father as he pours hot milk into cups and lights one more candle onto the table.

"It's Saturday, seven o'clock, my dear..."

While he utters these words, Daddy Grid gazes shockingly at Mihaela, stunned by her beauty.

"You look so beautiful this morning!"

Her face is glowing so brightly in the light of the dawn, so voluptuously and radiant; her eyes, so majestic, yet aged. Yesterday she looked like 16 years old, now like 18—just like her mother when he first met her.

Her father gazes at her, amazed. He smiles and asks Mihaela in a sweet voice:

"Did you sleep well, my love?"

"Yes, very well, daddy…" Mihaela replies with dreamy eyes.

She definitely looks taller, more gracious. Her long fingers and ballerina neck make her irresistible, even in the eyes of her father… She is a woman.

"Daddy, I've been thinking… I wonder if I haven't been a little too hard on Vlad yesterday. Maybe we should give him a chance."

"I don't know…" Grid replies surprised by Mihaela's change of mind. "I don't know if your mother would have liked that. We should wait."

"I would like to invite him for dinner…tonight. I think he is a good character for my novel."

"Are you writing a novel?" Grid asks her, surprised.

"Yes, daddy, I had no idea that I could write a novel. Poems have been my totem and biggest passion. But two days ago, as I was wandering through the garden, I saw a Queen of the Night Flower, so beautiful and different…she fascinated me… She was indigo with shiny silver stripes, shaped just like a star. I went next to her, smelled her…and I felt that she inherited a whole story behind those velvety petals… She looked at me so wisely, like willing to tell me something… I could not help but pick her up and bring her to my chamber. I put her in my notebook, amid the pages, so that she can be near my hands…at all times… I wanted to write a poem about her, but my fingers have been filled with such rapidity and fire…like some tentacles filled with godly desire, and then my story flourished into so many layers, like rivers make way through the mountains and flow rapidly to the oceans… Miraculously, my two hands seemed to have grown millions of fingers with which I could write nonstop. My third eye opened and dragged me inside a labyrinth from which I could not get out until I had come to the last page of my notebook. I've already written 200 pages and I just started last night, Papa!"

"Last night?" Grid's face lights up with joy. "May I read?"

"Not until it's finished, no."

"Alright!" Grid complies, hustled by his daughter's conviction.

"So, shall we dine with Vlad tonight? I'll help you cook!"

"But Magia is coming to dinner tonight, didn't I tell you?"

"Alright, Papa...but..."

"Let's wait a little, my darling," Grid softens his voice.

"Ok, then I'm going to put on the white dress that I just finished trimming. And the beads from Mama... Magia will love them, I know it!"

Grid has been hoping that Magia would decipher the secret of Mihaela's birth and calm his troubled nights...

Back to Vlad's castle.

Everything looks like it used to look: tall majestic walls of an imperial old castle, elegantly adorned with paintings of art and frescos; stakes of all measures, hanging from the ceilings, and shaking in the wind of Vlad's breath; red velvety stairs leading to his dark tunnels and caves... The lofty oak with countless branches and leaves, the heavenly garden with perfectly trimmed carpet of green grass, and the bloodied dark lake...are all back into the scenario.

The nine black cats lick each other greedily and then jump onto Vlad's lap and shoulders. The luckiest of them all, the black cat with red tail and long prickly feelers, hops onto the master's head and, as usual, coils around it just like a Turkish turban.

Vlad grins salaciously, approaching Eve's lawn. Tempted by the red apple that the odalisque triumphantly holds in her hand, he steps on the prickly green grass and snatches it, biting the apple with hunger. The red-tailed cat watches from above with salivating mouth, sniffing the flavor of the saucy red apple, and licking her feelers with eyes of a devil. The other eight cats ogle and meow with envy of the one wrapped up around the master's head.

After he finishes it, Vlad throws the core of the apple in mid air and the red-tailed cat catches it in her muzzle, devouring it with its sharp cruddy teeth of a lion. Satisfied, Vlad pats his long nails over his thighs, the apple's juice trickling onto his legs and feeding his skeleton to move fast.

Then, as he sprightly climbs the narrow velvet stairs that lead to the sunnier levels of his castle, he starts crooning a love song with the voice of a baritone. The eight jealous cats jump onto the balustrade, climbing and scratching it with sharp pointed claws, and shriekingly meowing the melody that Vlad hums through his nose.

Arriving at the third floor with the "V" hallway that shrinks and expands at every breath he takes, Vlad yawns so hard that one can see the chaos of his lungs. His purple heart, surrounded by icy black nerves, is out of beat...a piece of stone... Suddenly, as he utters a curse, his face embodies the features of Emanuel.

Virile and fond of himself, Vlad touches, lustfully, his bald torso...

"Hello master," the door to the right greets Vlad in a warm tone.

"Open me, Vlad... I've been waiting for you for so long," a very short silver door lures him to the left.

Moans and kisses can be heard, rising from the steamy red parquet.

Four alluring temptresses slowly surge from a gate underneath, wrapped up in Greek cloths and wearing their buttocks proudly bare... They smile seductively, floating towards Vlad, backwards. The biggest pleasure of Vlad has always been voluptuous and appetizing posteriors, bigger than life, full-fledged and chubby... He salivates, yearningly, as the temptresses fly high in bare feet and curvaceous hips, their round breasts and veil loose dresses dancing in the wind. And yet, with a slow move of his joints, Vlad freezes their flight, restraining his appetite: "Not today, my dears."

Saddened, the temptresses become transparent, their white veils turn crimson and bleed the air. Vlad passes through them, unmoved by their mournful voices that chant like a Greek choir, calling after a lost love.

As he arrives at the murky end of the hall, a broad smile creases Vlad's face. He stops for a moment, bends his neck in the dark and, propping his cold hands by the front wall, he groans in an indecipherable tongue.

Suddenly, a slim door takes shape, popping from its mouthed-locker the golden key prominently marked with *Rage&Love*. As Vlad penetrates it with the golden key, the slim door unveils supremely tall walls clothed in blue icicles. Crushed by the light, he makes his entrance inside the room, his feet perfectly sliding onto the glacial floor. He yells like a deranged kid, turning madly and hurling his body in colossal pirouettes onto the amazing skating rink. Echoes and cries of other children resonate, as well as the weak voice of Emanuel...

While he moves further in, he murmurs eagerly:

"I'm coming, my love... I'm coming..."

At the end of the chamber, a strong glacial sun closes Vlad's eyes. Nevertheless, he outlines a pathetic smile. Surpassing the rays of sun, he steps into a large shadow of ice. A giant painting of a beautiful girl takes life, opening his sight. Adorned with the young features of Emanuel, Vlad falls at the feet of the portrait, tears of ice dripping from his eyes:

"My love, let me love you...as I have loved you last night... Don't ever be harsh to me again... Let this humble being of mine touch your sweet heart. Think of me strongly... Let those young lips of yours utter my name...let that beautiful head of a Venus think of my face...let your soft fingers touch my fate! Ah...I can't wait to see you again tonight...at your place..."

Magia arrives at Grid's house.

She enters his abode, looking deeply affected.

Mihaela jumps into her arms and kisses her, enthusiastically. Magia compliments Mihaela on her beautifully trimmed new dress and on the beads from Mama...and then asks her to leave Grid and her alone, to talk.

Obediently, Mihaela withdraws to her room.

Magia takes a seat across from Grid and pauses, bending her head to the ground. She breathes heavily, trying to find her words:

"There is something…something in my soul that I cannot hold in any more… As you might know, I was the one who sent you to Vlad when Violeta was not able to procreate… And probably I am the one who caused her death!"

"Don't say that, Magia," Grid interrupts her with haste.

"Yes, I should have warned Violeta…but something kept me away from saying it…"

Magia stops. Her face gets crimson and turgid.

"The Old Man is Dracula… The Old Man is Vlad Ţepeş," Magia continues.

"Vlad Ţepeş, the Emperor? But he is dead!" Grid replies back, perplexed.

"Indeed. Vlad Tepeş, the cruel, the tyrant, the Impaler and the mal-addicted dictator, who now lives in his dilapidated castle, with a dead heart and a frosty face, rusted by loneliness and rage… When Dora, his wife was killed, he started to hate men, to punish them, to burn churches and priests, to seek revenge on God…dying to be born again from the womb of Satan."

"Oh my God!" Grid exclaims, stupefied. "I thought that was a tale…"

"It all started on the night of June 17, 1462. While Vlad was gone, leading a war against the Turks, an evil messenger of theirs shot an envenomed arrow with a lying letter into sweet Dora's chamber. Dora found it, and read it, and started screaming like a wounded baby. I came in quickly…and read it too… The letter was informing Dora of her husband's death, caught by the Turks in battle. Sweet Dora screamed and banished me and locked herself within her chamber, refusing to talk to anyone, not even to her "Mama…" I was Dora's maid…her confidante, her loyal servant, her good witch and her spiritual mother… She cried and cried, feeding herself with tears… She would not eat, she would not live without her husband… She loved Vlad so much! Her little heart shrank every time Vlad had to go to battle… She always feared that he would be killed… That day, I knocked and knocked at the door of her chamber, but she would not let an experienced old woman help her, a woman who loved her more than herself… And instead, she threw herself from the tower and found her rest in the arms of death... Ah, Dora, Dora! She told me not to worry. But how could I have trusted the words of a despaired woman? How could I have left her alone? Ah, that lying letter... Couldn't she have waited? When Vlad came back and found her dead...he no longer wanted to live, he no longer wanted to love; he became a living stone... And thus, that awful lie put an end to both Vlad and his beloved wife, the only innocent and adored creature from his life... She was the light of his eyes, the sweet beat of his cruel heart, a balm to his troubled mind...

"You have never told us about all of that... And we were here, Violeta and I... We knew nothing about you and Dora...and the Old Man Vlad..." Grid stares, desperately, at Magia.

"Dora is now dwelling there, in his new castle, down in his *Icy Morgue of Brides...* A few of her remains are lying on a bed of ice. Part of her body could not be found... Only her womb is there... But still, Vlad cannot bear to pronounce the name *Dora*. Nor the name *God* or the word *faith*... When boyars killed Vlad's father and his brother, Vlad's belief in God was shaken, blackened... But when his wife died, Vlad's faith died with her. And when it died, he died. He stopped living as a human. He chose to get reborn of Satan and he became a living corpse—a monster. He cursed the world! He started feeding on men, making them wish they had never been born... And he just doesn't feed on random ones but on the men who are to marry a young bride or who are blessed to have a loving wife. He wants all grooms and husbands to suffer just like he had suffered. On the wedding day, he kidnaps the virgin brides and feeds on them until they die. That's why our land swarms with pain and widowers and funerals take place much more than marriages or baptisms. Vlad is the one who causes all this suffering. The Icy Morgue of Brides is a land of grief in the basement of Vlad's house where thousands of virgins and wives lie frozen on stone beds, covered in gore. Violeta's body sleeps there, as well, beside all the brides of Transylvania whom Vlad has sacrificed for her and Lucifer..."

"Violeta? What? Where?" Grid asks, dumbfounded.

"I implored Vlad to help Violeta and to think of her as of his own beloved wife that he could have saved..." Magia continues with fever, "And Vlad promised me that he would cure her, assured me that he had changed, that he had realized that sowing evil only brings evil, that healing others would heal him too and make his wife be proud... I had no idea that those words were the words of a hypocrite and that Violeta was part of his evil plan... He chose Violeta because she resembled so much his wife. Her big black eyes, her oval face, her mouth and smile were almost identical to the ones of his wife... I should have thought about all that! Oh, wretched me!"

"What do you mean?"

"Perhaps history repeats..." Magia keeps on, shivering. "Perhaps we all have a clone, someone who looks just like us... Dora was of noble origins; Violeta was the daughter of a peasant. Perhaps one is the princess, the other is the beggar... And sometimes roles can change and..."

And Magia pauses, gloomed by her thoughts... She realizes that she went a little astray with her speech. She looks again into Grid's eyes, hardly resisting her tears... Her face is blemished; her eyes are sunken into her face, soring of too much sorrow. She feels bad because she has to hide an awful truth from Grid—the fact that his son Vlady is still alive and living in the caves of Vlad, just like a slave. Grid knows that his little boy is in heaven, near his Mama. Yet at this stage, Grid can do nothing regarding Vlady; except to worsen things... Moreover, Magia wants herself to seek revenge against the wicked Vlad and his nine evil cats. But she has to wait for the right time. Though now...she feels that it's high time to tell Grid about Mihaela, his sweet obedient child...

"Vlad intended to have one daughter who could avenge his wife..." Magia confesses to Grid, feverishly, "So he chose Violeta to be the one who gives birth to this daughter—a spitting image of his wife, endowed with her beautiful face...but possessing the evil soul of his own soul... However, instead of one, two daughters came to life. God gave Violeta a beautiful daughter who dwells in light: Mihaela. And Lucifer, gave Vlad a daughter who could reinforce Inferno and bring it back to life: Gabriela."

"How do you know all of these things?" Grid asks Magia, shocked.

"I know more than I wish to know... I have my ways..." Magia answers, with a hoarse voice.

"Who's daughter is Mihaela?" Grid cuts Magia precipitously, unable to resist the question that has tormented him for nights.

"She is...yours...of course," Magia mumbles with her eyes fixed in the ground. "She is God's daughter.... God protects her," she then asserts, piercing Grid's eyes, "But she should stay away from Gabriela..."

Grid looks at Magia, suspiciously. Magia reinforces her speech:

"Not long ago, I figured out the exact steps of Vlad's plan... Vlad gave Violeta the seed of his wife, the embryo of his own unborn baby...that evening when you and Violeta went to his house... When she died, Dora was pregnant with Vlad's child..."

Grid stares at Magia, petrified:

"This is too much... Enough!"

Magia continues, unshaken by Grid's words:

"Vlad kept the seed of Dora. He froze it and then..."

"And...?" Grid asks, furiously, walking up and down the room.

"And...as Dora loved flowers, especially The Queen of The Night, Vlad thought that through this flower and her miraculous powers he could bring back his wife...or at least a clone of Dora... See, the Queen of the Night flower has two cores in one seed, a double fertilization and, although rich in nicotine, it has the divine scent of paradise... It is like a magical velvety star, beautiful, tall, and has a stronger aroma than any other flower...although it grows everywhere... I'm sure that you have the Queen of the Night flower in your garden too..."

"That giant flower...in our garden! That morning..." Grid recalls, dumbfounded. "But what does the flower have to do with Violeta's pregnancy? I don't understand!"

"Neither could I. Moreover, I could not foresee it... Somehow, my eye was covered with a veil... He must have cast a spell upon my spells..." Magia says, overwhelmed.

Then, quickly changing the subject, she takes a new voice:

"Now Vlad believes that his beloved wife came back to life through Mihaela, his chaste daughter... But we won't let him..."

"His daughter?" Grid cuts Magia off.

"No!" Magia shouts, covering her mouth. "He just believes so... He is attracted to Mihaela's innocent soul. Vlad is a monster; he is a great pretender and revenger. He would do anything to take Mihaela away from you because he knows that she is different...wife from his wife, love from her love...born of God!" And Magia bursts out into an avalanche of tears.

"I'm sorry, Grid! Forgive me, please!"

"Magia, calm down, I understand... Even though I might not be Mihaela's true father, but just a humble Joseph, chosen by God, I shall always be her father, protecting her until my last breath... I know, God works in mysterious ways, sometimes beyond our human understanding; His thoughts are higher than my thoughts... Now I am at peace with this..."

"No! You are her father. You love Mihaela and Mihaela loves you... Violeta is proud of you..." Magia reinforces.

"Magia, tell me, where is Violeta? We have to take her out of there, immediately!" Grid suddenly panics and jumps off the chair. "Wait a minute! We buried Violeta near her mother Victoria... How could this be?"

"There's nothing to be done right now. Just save Mihaela," Magia persuades Grid.

Grid looks at Magia, grief-stricken. His eyes are tired and his beard has gone whiter. Magia grasps Grid by the hand.

"Sit. Listen to this. Last night, I saw Vlad in the very act of evil...inside my caldron with water fueled by the energy of the stars... Vlad still nourishes himself with the souls of young maidens who give him life, who restore his blood... Vlad is still impaling people, burning, boiling, skinning them, drinking the blood of young children in order to keep his body young! He is the reincarnation of evil itself; he did not stop. He lied to me, deceived me, as in him dwell only lies as he is the child of the devil—the king of all lies. Vlad can take many faces and shapes after he kills his victims... And then, he appears as an angel of light wherever he may want, at night... I saw him entering dead bodies, I saw him..." And Magia stops. Her only eye twitches with fright. But she resumes again, with weaker voice: "Yet indeed, there is one little thing that can turn Vlad around and that brings back remnants of his human soul: Mihaela, her love. It makes him weaker, he knows... It makes him vulnerable and visible to my eye... Mihaela is the only one who can change him. Yet the price for that is..."

Losing his temper, Grid rises from his chair:

"Why didn't you warn me? Why?"

"He promised me that he would do good in the name of Dora and I knew you needed a child..." Magia defends herself. "But don't ever let him come here. Once you invite him in, he will visit Mihaela whenever he wishes."

"I already invited him!" Grid bursts out.

"Leave tonight!" Magia screams, her hands shivering like leaves in the storm.

Then, immediately searching in her hemp brown sac filled with herbs, sticks, powders, bottles, and pots, Magia takes out two small bags and hands them to Grid:

"Give them to Mihaela. This white bag, with sap from the tree of God, is for the unseen enemy. After she pours three seeds onto her left palm and rubs them three times, a shield of sap will surround her being and nothing will be able to harm her... Moreover, it will open a gate towards the travel world that other people cannot see... It will strengthen her bones and gather her force. But she must never keep her eyes on the past... And this black bag, with powder of Minor belladonna, is against the fleshly enemy. Once Mihaela throws this black powder over her shoulder, the villains will forget their evil schemes and the scent will weaken their senses, choking and poisoning them."

As Magia exits the house, breathing relieved and looking with care upon Grid, Grid rushes to Mihaela's bedroom.

"Put on your Mama's sheep coat and gird your head with her kerchief. We're leaving now!" he speaks hastily to his daughter.

"Where, Papa? I don't want to..."

"We have to... Hurry up! Take only what you need."

"My notebook and my Mommy. That's all I need."

Grid exits Mihaela's chamber at full speed.

"Oh, and my bag with money!" Mihaela speaks to herself as she puts on the sheep coat and covers her head with the silk kerchief, sewn with singing birds by the sweet hands of her mother.

She then opens her notebook and, seeing that the indigo Queen of The Night flower is in place, she shoves it into her woven wool bag with the little money from Papa Grid.

With Mommy Doll in hand and the wool bag across her chest, Mihaela steps out of her chamber, looking ahead.

Papa Grid is knelt before the blessed icon of Virgin Mary, just like a mother, praying with fervor:

"Precious Mother, lead our steps and protect my sweet daughter! Help us find a good home and let me not fear at all... We are yours. If you are with us, who can be against us?"

He then makes the sign of the cross, peering around at the old living room, adorned with Violeta's handmade plates and traditionally sewn clothes.

Loud barks of a savage dog are shaking the silence.

Hurriedly, Grid picks up a hemp-sack with bread and water and shoves Magia's little bags to the chest. He then takes his daughter by the hand and heads to the front door.

Mihaela follows her daddy, waving goodbye to their shelter.

The dog from outside gives a muffled whine.

As Grid opens the door, a catastrophic view pierces his eyes... Drops of sweat drip on his face, like rainfall. He quickly covers his daughter's eyes, trembling with fear, hot tears bursting out on his cheeks.

Impaled through her buttocks, with her mouth wide open in a shout of terror and her eyes popped out of her sockets, Magia clings on a tall stake, with her chest open and her arms broken, freshly impaled in the middle of the garden, near the well. Her fingers to her plexus spasmodically spread like the knots of a tree, a hole in her head like a hollow in an old oak...chatter the peace out of Grid.

Near the stake where Magia is hanging, blood-shockingly, there lies the dead body of the Carpathian shepherd dog from next-door—mangled in blood, with its neck fiercely strangled.

Holding Mihaela to his chest, with his worked hands placed around her head as the wings of an eagle, Grid can hardly step forward, towards the stall. His legs shake like those of a wounded lamb.

As they arrive behind the house, Grid and Mihaela take their two feeble horses and harness them to the old cart filled with hay and soil. Grid then takes Mihaela into his arms and lays her inside the cart, still trembling with fright. After that, he hands Mihaela the white and black bags from Magia and explains to her what they stand for. Mihaela, who was looking at Daddy with big scared eyes, finally blinks happily, set free by the miraculous story of the two bags. Smiling back at his daughter, shivery, Daddy Grid covers Mihaela and Mommy Doll with the warm fluffy quilts sewn by Violeta.

Mounted on the front seat of the cart, Grid spurs his feeble horses to ride like fabulous animals. His hands still shake, yet his will empowers his weak body to borrow the strength of a captain. Thus, he orders his horses to ride like the wind along the bumpy road of the Lucky Wheel. As dust sprinkles onto his hands, Grid keeps looking back to make sure that no one follows him and his daughter.

On the way out of Transylvania, time fast-forwards. Spinning and winding, the cart starts weakening and breaking apart so that Grid is forced to stop and mount his daughter onto the back of Rommy, the white horse raised by Violeta.

Dazed by the strong cool air of the majestic Carpathian Mountains, famished and tired, Rommy can hardly keep up the gallop. Therefore, Grid tells his daughter to pour out some sap from Magia's white bag onto Rommy's head so that he can ride faster, quick as a flash.

As they set forth with their horses, the sky changes; it widens and darkens, making one body with the earth.

Grid's hands, rubbed by the rigid reins, spit out red blood, painting the sunset. His hair whitens, his skin shrivels, his eyes sink with deep wrinkles; his back arches from too much worry and thinking. He keeps turning back, looking behind, to see whether somebody is following them or not. He checks on Mihaela, his heart pumps out loud…heavy drops of sweat burst from his head like showery clouds, blurring his sight. Suddenly his neck gets locked, his eyes only able to perceive the bygone landscape. Incapable of straightening his neck, Grid gets sucked into the year 1501, the year that they have been running away from. A whirl of wind, like an invisible vacuum, swallows him in and casts him away from his horse, back to his dwelling.

Mihaela keeps riding her white horse Rommy and looking forward, towards the sky. She hears that someone is running after her, yet she doesn't turn back. She knows that the only way she can stop this hunting is to move on, to care for the future and not for the past, as Magia had said.

Rommy's legs suddenly weaken; noisy insects hop onto his back, pricking and biting his neck…even though she had sprinkled his head with the sap from Magia's white bag.

Mihaela wishes to travel in time. "This is the only way to find escape," she hears a loud voice speaking within herself. Therefore, she screams up to the heights: "God, hear my cry! I wish to travel in time! I believe, I believe, I believe you can make me fly!"

And at that moment, the skylarks sewn on Mihaela's head kerchief break loose and fly, exalted and relieved. Shining like gold firefights in the sunlight, the skylarks whistle trills into a happy melody, raising Mihaela and Rommy above the evil colony.

Mihaela loses the reins from her hands, and a miraculous power takes Rommy and herself on a divine stream of water. Rommy starts galloping through the wind, spurred by the skylarks, his feeble body strengthening and spreading out wings like an enormous angel with cross in his forehead.

Mihaela and Rommy fly amid frolicking clouds, beyond green spirited lawns, through a long bridge of light, at the speed of God. Years fast forward in front of Mihaela's eyes like a rain of falling stars sent down from Heaven. Randomly, a year enters her third eye. She is unable to see...it blinds her.

As the landscape changes its clothes, her third eye opens and Mihaela is able to see again...much clearer, sharper...

Like a magnet with evil phosphorescent eyes, the Earth pulls them lower and lower, towards the ground. Rommy beats his wings slowly, bends his knees and, smoothly, they land on a long road with giant birds made of metal.

Mihaela kisses her horse on his forehead.

Rommy shakes his tail and takes a seat to sleep near the giant birds. He yawns...

2014. Bucharest Airport.

Mihaela is dressed in the sheepskin coat of her mother's and in the long linen dress with flowers that she has just finished sewing. The nineteen necklaces of corals, tight and bright along her neck, frame Mihaela's face, gracefully. The skylarks take their places back on Mihaela's head kerchief, obediently and silently adorning her cheeks. The long kerchief, falling like a train on her shoulders, looks like a waterfall made from the working foam of Mama's blessed hands. Her calf leather boots that Papa had brimmed with golden thread step joyfully onto the carpet of the unknown world.

Mihaela glances around at the bright panels of the airport with departures and arrivals, at the colorful advertisements, and at the sophisticated shops, at the girls with miniskirts, at the frantically moving people, at the strange shaped bags, at the devices that men hold to their ears, speaking nonstop, agitated and fast...

Passengers scan her up and down, staring at her costume and at her indigo star-shaped eye on the forehead that has began to beam strong rays of light.

"Actress?" a young man asks her impudently as he steals some snapshots of Mihaela.

People keep bumping into her without apologizing...kids scream at their mommies, teenagers laugh with their mouths filled up with meat, girls chew bubblegum building up like enormous balloons... As Mihaela looms before their eyes, they slow down, their mouths open in awe, their breaths petrify, as if watching a ghost...

Mihaela feels sorry that she has left her father back there, but she knows that he wants her safe, in a special place. One day she will visit him again.

With Mommy Doll in hand, and with her notebook and a little money in the woven wool bag, Mihaela has to take a new direction, change her life.

A voice announces the flight schedule. The first flight scheduled is going to New York.

"New York?" she asks herself with wonder. "What kind of a city is New York?"

A man blows his nose in front of her and traces of his mucous cling to her dress...

A voice announces that four thieves have just been caught stealing some passengers' luggage...

She needs something new and "New York" sounds like the right name, the right place... "Yet how are the people there? How far is it?"

"It is over the ocean... You need to take the plane...the long metal bird," she hears a voice within.

Taken by the avalanche of the crowd and hurled up in front of the checking line, Mihaela takes out of her woven bag, the only money that she has: 2 lei... She is directed to the information desk where, with hesitating voice, she asks:

"Hello, I have 2 lei... Do you think this would be enough for a ticket to New York?"

Squinty-eyed, with her hair pinned up into a big tight loop, the old lady at the information desk gazes suspiciously at Mihaela. She then looks again at Mihaela's coins, and says:

"These coins, lady... I have never seen something like that in my whole life."

"I know," Mihaela approves. "But that's what my father gave me. See, I need to get to New York. My mom is in danger. I have to save her."

"I'm sorry, but there's nothing I can do for you. You need real money."

Mihaela stares at the old lady, petrified, holding her Mommy Doll tighter.

British Airways,

Mihaela heads over to the British department, led by a kind passenger.

Looking down on her coins, she starts crying helplessly.

"Why are you crying, Miss?" the flight representative asks her.

"I have these coins, but they won't get me to New York, will they?"

The sales woman looks at Mihaela's coins in awe.

"I have never seen this kind of money. I'm sorry, but I cannot help you, Miss."

"But I need to get to New York. Isn't there anything you can do for me? My mom is dying. I must save her!"

"I completely understand the situation but you need money in order to purchase a ticket. Do you have any relatives who could help you out here?"

Suddenly, a man from behind speaks:

"I am..." he stutters, "I will help her!"

Mihaela turns around, quieting her sobbing...

"I know to appreciate old...and valuable..." the man adds.

"These coins are precious. I propose you a trade: Your coins in exchange for a flight ticket to New York. What do you say?" his eyes piercing Mihaela's.

Mihaela looks at him, overwhelmed. This stranger is willing to help her. He doesn't look like the man who was blowing his nose, or like the one who was wolfing that sandwich; he is elegant and charming. He has blue, greenish eyes, a porcelain-like face and a warm smile. He is different, yet familiar.

Mihaela begins to unveil him with her third eye, but try as she might, the man won't reveal his heart…

After seconds of reading, Mihaela cries out:

"Yes! I accept your trade, Sir!"

"Well, good," the handsome man replies. "I liked your *Yes*! It sounded like a very deep and sure *Yes*…like a lifetime commitment. Let me congratulate you!" the man smiles, handing Mihaela her New York ticket.

Mihaela stares at him, enchanted.

"I wish you the most pleasant flight," he continues graciously, kissing Mihaela's hand.

The tall man vanishes in the crowd while Mihaela follows him through the corner of her eye.

Then, realizing that the man forgot his coins, she runs after him like the wind.

"Oh, Sir, your coins! Sir…" she bumps into the chaotic crowd, looking desperately for her savior, but he is nowhere to be found. She has lost him… And she would have wanted to know at least the name of her benefactor…

Now that she has got her ticket to New York, Mihaela rushes outside, to her dear Rommy-horse, who was moving in place, restlessly fretting his tail. Mihaela hugs him tightly and says:

"My sweet horse, I will embark on that big metal bird which will fly me to New York. You need to follow it; the metal bird will show you the way. Besides, it will be lighter for you without me in the saddle. Fly safe and sound! May God make your wings of a dove!"

And saying this, Mihaela blesses her Rommy horse on his forehead, and sprinkles his body and head with few grains from Magia's white and black little bags.

"See you in New York, my dear horse!"

Rommy snorts with delight, suddenly his body opening wings of a giant dove.

Arriving in the airplane, Mihaela is seated in row #13; she looks around impatiently as the plane takes off.

Getting closer to the sky, she starts breathing easily, feeling slightly more comfortable; she gives a shy smile to the very strangely dressed people around her, who keep analyzing her star. Suddenly, her smile gets wider and wider turning into an avalanche of laughter. She does not know if she's crying or laughing. Yet she feels good, new, ready for her new adventure—life. Abruptly, she stops laughing at a harsh bump of the plane. She breathes heavily and continuously.

Worried, the guy seated nearby her asks:

"Pregnant?"

Mihaela ignores him. She cannot lie about it... She is still thinking about that man who helped her; she feels that he has enraptured her heart with that well-mannered attitude and priceless deed. She wishes he were in the plane.

Mihaela pulls out her notebook and starts writing with the vivacity of a newborn. Her long fingers play the keys of her heart, she speaks again to Him...her lips move to the blow of her mind, giving life to her new character—the green bluish eyed guy, the man whom she secretly loves... She breathes loudly and rapidly.

The man next to her says admiringly:

"I like your indigo star. Is that a tattoo?"

Silence. Mihaela ignores him.

The guy asks again as Mihaela doesn't stop panting:

"Is everything fine? You need some...water?"

Mihaela looks at him as if she's seeing the face of a human being for the first time. She analyzes his features with the eyes of a seven-month baby. Then, she replies with unjustified enthusiasm:

"Yes, fine, Sir! Actually...everything's amazing!"

"From Bucharest?" the man asks her, more courageously.

"Hmm...from Transylvania."

"To London?" the man continues his interrogation.

Mihaela looks skeptically at the man. After she gives it a thought, she replies with dreamy eyes:

"Farther away, much farther…"

The big lights of New York City.
"Look, the twin towers used to be right there," the man next to Mihaela points apologetically.

In Times Square, with her Mommy Doll and notebook in hand,
Mihaela looks so small in the big city of New York! She has no place to go… She is out of time, out of space, out of her father's shelter. Moreover, she can see no Rommy around…"Where could Rommy be? Where does he wander? God knows… Oh, Lord, I pray you, bring him to me safe!"

Tramping around, she gets dizzy when all kinds of people walk by hurriedly, fluttering bags and many papers in their hands. Everything moves so fast, looks so new, feels so big and noisy: vehicles honk, bikers race, entertainers laugh, banners sparkle, vendors and photographers cry out, clowns and musicians parade down the streets—things that Mihaela has never seen before.

Finally, her eyes get stuck on a big advertisement:

DRACULA'S DAUGHTERS
See the real DRACULA - real blood, real music, real fun

"Dracula?" Mihaela wonders.

She then enters the big doors of the *Palace Theatre* and asks the doorman:

"Excuse me, I'm looking for Dracula…"

"There is no such person here…"

"But I saw Dracula on the big poster!"

"Oh, that's the character of the musical," the man replies.

"The musical?"

"Yes, and tonight there's a special night—the Halloween night when the entire audience has to come up dressed as vampires. It is the official premiere."

"Excuse me, who is Dracula?" Mihaela asks.

The old doorman smiles:

"He is a well-known vampire from Transylvania…named Vlad, an old cruel count who impaled thousands of people, drinking their blood… He became a legend! Didn't you hear about him?"

"You said he was named Vlad?" Mihaela asks, suddenly shivery.

"Yes, that's right," the old doorman replies.

Mihaela turns around and runs out of the theatre:

"Oh, Lord, where am I?"

She trembles, unsure of her feet.

But after few moments of doubt, an inner force pushes her to enter the theater again.

"What time is the play tonight?"

"8 pm, my dear. Last tickets, available at the box office," the man replies.

Mihaela looks towards the box office: Tickets starting at $125.

Suddenly, she hears boisterous music playing.

"Where's this music coming from?" Mihaela asks him, overwhelmed.

"Oh, it is the final rehearsal for the show," the doorman replies.

"May I see it?" Mihaela asks.

"You are not allowed, only the cast members…"

"I am part of the cast," Mihaela says with certitude.

"And you don't know who Dracula is?"

"Of course I knew who Vlad was but…it's always interesting to find out people's version…"

"How may I help you, Miss?"

"Seriously, Sir! I need to speak to the director of the play! I have an important message for him!"

The doorman looks suspiciously at Mihaela.

Mihaela continues:

"I insist, Mister! It is very important. He will be thankful."

"All right," the old man finally consents. "Follow me."

Mihaela follows the doorman through beautifully ornamented dim lighted corridors, and then through a wide hall that splits tens of velvet seats from a majestic stage.

They approach the first rows where a blonde man is standing, giving directions to some electricians who hang from the ceilings, fixing the light-set.

The doorman clears his throat. The blonde man turns his head, unexpectedly:

"Oh, finally, here she is! Where have you been? You've ruined my whole rehearsal! Now get up there! We'll start in five minutes."

The doorman looks strangely at Mihaela. Mihaela looks strangely at the doorman.

"Now hurry up! What are you waiting for?" the man says, harshly.

Sensing the awkwardness, the doorman leads Mihaela backstage.

Backstage.

"Come on, baby! Where have you been?" a keen eyed man asks Mihaela, gently pressing his fake mustache.

Mihaela hesitates to reply, trying to sneak out through the back exit, but the guy catches her by the wrist.

"Where are you running to, mon amour? Nervous about tonight?"

Silence. Mihaela bends down her head.

"Hey you, look at me!" the guy continues to speak. "You're going to shine, you're going to charm everyone as you've romanced me!"

Mihaela looks at the blue-greenish eyed man, overwhelmed. He is definitely a charming man but his words are frightening her.

"Is she dreaming? Where is she? And what is this entire show about?"

"Now get dressed!" the man says, slapping Mihaela's butt. "Take off that dress. Put it on for the after party! It looks folkloric and freaky! Brrrr!"

Hesitatingly, Mihaela moves closer to the mustached man and whispers in his ear:

"What role am I playing?"

The man laughs:

"Are you playing with me? What's the matter with you?"

"I'm serious. Please, help me," Mihaela pleads him, anxiously.

"Look at me," the actor continues, taking her by the shoulders. "I know that this is a big night for you. But you don't have to worry! You'll be a hit! A great future is ahead of you."

"No, you don't understand," Mihaela continues. "I really don't know what role I'm playing. I'm totally baffled... I just came from Transylvania. I somehow got into this theatre... I didn't expect this... I didn't even know that I was an actress..."

"Look," the man replies. "Take a big breath."

Mihaela takes a big breath.

"Now, tell me, what's your character about? Tell me her story. Come on, go on..." the man encourages her.

Mihaela opens her mouth slowly:

"Well...I...I came from Transylvania... I left my father back there. My Mama died when I was a baby... There is a man in Transylvania, a weird old man that somehow followed me... His name is Vlad..."

"See? That's it, silly girl! Now go on and dress up!" the mustached guy hustles her.

Mihaela runs to the dressing room just like she was told. As she steps in, three different dresses, neatly exposed on hangers, welcome her. She looks at them closely, admiring the detailed work. Each of them has a card attached on which her name is printed: Mihaela - Part 1, Mihaela - Part 2, Mihaela - Part 3.

"What am I gonna do? Who am I? Where am I?" Mihaela asks herself, bewildered.

She then rushes to a mirror, framed by a golden imperial broidery, and looks at herself, anxiously.

She is beautiful. Yes, she is. Nevertheless, small wrinkles and purple circles freckle around her eyes.

She softly touches her neck, her lips, ears, and face... They all burn up, inflamed. But as she touches her forehead, she feels cold shivers sliding rapidly along her spine, chilling all of her body. She looks again in the mirror and, drawn deeper into the glass, she sees her father...back there...in Transylvania, walking through big hills of snow. His long beard, his wise eyes, are searching for something... She cannot precisely decipher...

Knocks on the door.

"Ready Miss? We're starting!"

Mihaela panics, glancing around in despair. She takes off her long linen dress that she handmade with flowers, and jumps into the new Part 1 dress. The dress fits her perfectly, only that she cannot zip it in the back... She rushes out, bumping into the mustached actor who is lurking into the dark, leaning against her doorway. Face to face with him, Mihaela's bones start to tremble... She cannot believe her eyes. She knows this man so well, this man with big greenish-blue eyes, sad and distant... He is the man from the airport... Yet with another demeanor. His face shows wisdom, yet untruthfulness; hospitality, yet regret; wrinkles but glow. He has the allure of an old prince, with dark, wavy locks of hair that reach beyond his shoulders. The long undulated mustache highlights his bulging lower lip... A bourgeois bearskin turban, embroidered with diamond-like stones, covers his head; on the front brim of the turban, a violet sapphire, fixed into a golden star, lightens his features to spark; black swan feathers stick out from the top of the turban like the feelers of a cat. Tightened around his body is an indigo cloak on which velvety images of crosses and stakes are delicately encrusted in red.

Mihaela faints into his arms…

Mihaela: This was my first meeting with New York, or at least that's what I remember. I knew that I am living one life only, not a prior, not an afterlife… But I felt for sure that something beyond my power was leading me that hour…

Gabriela: I admit that life is surprising, but Papa told me: "When something surprises you, surprise the surprise by taking control of it!"

Mihaela: Something happened while I was unconscious. But what happened, I'm not sure…

Mihaela wakes up in the arms of the same man with greenish-blue eyes and mustache.

"For God's sake, you're awake!" he ogles at Mihaela, worriedly.

Mihaela startles. She notices blue blood on his neck.

"What's this?" she asks him scared.

"Oh, make-up… Are you feeling any better?"

"Yes, better…"

Mihaela's hair is wet; her hands are painted with blue blood, too.

"Let's get on stage! Everybody's waiting for us!"

"But I don't know anything! I can't!" Mihaela whines.

"You know everything! Trust me!"

The man with greenish-blue eyes and mustache grasps Mihaela's hand, squeezing it harder and harder… Mihaela's eyes tear.

As they walk towards the stage, Mihaela's eyes spot a black door on which is written with capital letters—GABRIELA.

"This is too much. What is happening?" she asks herself, panting, afraid. She just ran away from Transylvania, ready to forget, to live. "This must be a dream!" She is waiting to wake up, waiting for someone to save her from the past.

Mihaela is pushed onto the stage,
in front of the spotlights.

She staggers, as if walking on pins and needles, her arms tremble; her eyes hurt... She feels so awkward...

The stage gets darker; the spotlight gets brighter; hot steam splutters from behind.

Laughs and moans of women are echoing from underneath the stage, bewildering her peace.

A sinister violin plays pianissimo.

Suddenly Mihaela sees the wet long tongue of the mustached actor licking her left foot, and then a sting of energy enters her body—a familiar sensation, a vibration that electrifies her whole being just like that night when Emanuel appeared in her garden and sneaked beneath her dress...

Dragged by the moves of the man with mustache, she steps into a trance, unconsciously...into a whirl of dance... The man raises her up, above his shoulders, her feet move without her control, her legs split into ballerina leaps, professional choreography that she has never been able to perform before.

Suddenly, her heart is pierced by the memory of a song, and her lips move, singing along... As a gypsy released from the armor of her body, she sings with a deep, penetrating voice:

"Vino, vino, aud în noapte,
  Vocea ta mă cheamă iar,
  Trăiesc în tine, tu în mine, n-am pace..."

Red lights flutter like bats on her face, out of control; the décor changes, like waves in the storm, and the man with mustache kneels at her feet, reciting with ardor:

"I saw you, Juliet, last night, walking above the ocean!

The Goddess Moon herself could not foresee your motion;
Eclipsing Venus, Sirius and all the other stars, you raised my soul up to the heights!
You, precious beauty, brought up in my heart a feeling that I thought had died;
You brought me back to life that night when you became my wife!"

Mihaela answers him:
"Yes, doomed and blessed night that raped my heart.
I shall forget you not; I shall regret your lust!
Juliet is not a Juliet, she's wearing hell's mask,
Demanding mourning from the past,
Replacing mother with stepmother's nest,
And sucking blood from father's evil chest!
Oh Vlad, I called you not, why did you spring out from that horn?
'Cause music binds love and does not gore friendship's corn!
Depart from me. I do not know your song!
Oh, Mother, forsake me not, bloom my love-seeds
into a purple wreath
Get my sneaky wrath abashed, I want my Juliet
to find her real mask!"

As Mihaela recites, the face of the mustached man transforms. It slowly turns into the man who tried to rape her, then into Emanuel, then into the stranger who helped her at the airport...and finally, into a monstrous Vlad with old viscous features.

Mihaela looks out into the audience, transfixed. All is dark, darker that the night...except for one little golden light that shines above the seats. The light comes closer and closer...it beams as a glow-worm from her father's orchard, turning the anonymous air into a healing water. The mirthful light then turns into a sun-ball, bigger and bigger...jumping above the darkness, into her lap. It then touches her neck, her brow...her indigo eye, feeling like a balm onto her wounded mind. It takes her to a lawn full of daisies and heavenly birds, like a queenly, flying throne...

Barefooted, she giggles as showers of sun tickle her feet and tan her with warm rays of love. She feels so much peace inside, swinging into His arms. She hugs Him tighter and tighter, becoming one...when suddenly, she wakes up in the arms of the man with mustache, feeling awkward again, so aware of everything...naked and afraid.

Suddenly, she breaks into two, her body detaching from her soul... She steps out of the role, shivering with cold. She looks at her flesh that is further away on the stage and still under the spell of that man... The mirthful light flickers; it plucks up her courage and makes her step towards herself, to her body, twining her soul and spirit back into one. Feeling whole again, she flies from the stage into the arms of darkness, towards the exit.

"Cut! Cut! Where do you think you're going, pretty lady?" the director screams after Mihaela. "How dare you stop it? It was timeless...beyond my mind!"

Mihaela runs out the theater, through the back door of the stage, so eager to escape that place of nightmare... However, she bumps into her sister, who is dancing and laughing devilishly, joined by a group of men, equipped with masks, colorful costumes, accordions and tambourines, others trooping around and hitting wildly the ground with thick wooden rods.

"You cannot get away from who you are, sis! Your teeth will grow back, giving you impulses to bite back!" Gabriela stabs Mihaela with heated words... She then begins to sing in a dazzling rhythm *Bite Back,* the song that she used to sing in Transylvania in those bloody escapades. The masked-men, clowns and musician-friends, accompany Gabriela with haste, laughing widely, and playing ***Bite Back***:

(Chorus)

On the glimmering streets of Times Square, kicking people out of her way, Mihaela runs like a mad girl, slapping the air like thunders in storm. Her eyes sore; bitter tears gush out, flooding her face and her heart. She stops, incapable to move on, screaming from the top of her lungs:

"Wake me up! Save me from myself!"

Summer of 1983. London.

Mihaela sleeps in her giant bed, looking sweaty and pale. Suddenly, an old agitated lady enters her room and pulls the curtains to the side, letting the sun cast the gloom out. Mihaela rubs her eyes, easily disturbed. Four ladies in waiting make their appearances, covered in white laced aprons over black long dresses, and wearing ruffled headpieces pinned in impeccably brushed hair. At the old lady's call, they spread in sync around Mihaela's bed, and hurl the white eiderdown off her slim body. Then, carefully, they lift Mihaela up, above her princely bed, and lay her into a bathtub of cold water, sprinkled with fresh strong-scented petals of roses.

Mihaela tears and whines; her nightgown reveals awakened buds of breasts.

After one hour of cleaning and perfuming her body with herbs and ointments, Mihaela, dressed up in an enormous wedding dress, faces a big, elegant mirror. The four ladies in waiting are adjusting her dress, while the old lady keeps moving her hands in awe:

"Magnificent, you look beyond beautiful, my dear! Mesmerizing!"

Mihaela smiles, yet her eyes glitter sadness.

"We all thought that the other night was ravishing! Have you seen how Charles was looking at your designs? I bet that he has never seen something like that before! And when I told him that you were born in Transylvania... He adores that land! He'll surely invite you to his palace! Emil also wrote a praiseworthy editorial about your show, my dear, so all is ready for a great future together!"

"Thank you!" Mihaela replies, shyly.

The old woman draws closer to Mihaela, gently patting her shoulders. She then touches Mihaela's velvety face, admiring her look in the mirror:

"I know what you are going through, my dear! You should have seen me when I was your age and married Emil's father! I was pathetic! I was crying out of anything! But I'll make sure that Emil makes you happy!

Very happy!"

"Thank you, Anne," Mihaela replies, slightly more joyous.

"You're welcome, my dear," Anne adds, and then hurriedly makes her way out of the room.

After Anne's sound of steps melt in the silence, Mihaela orders the ladies in waiting to leave. She then drags herself and the big white dress to the tall windows of her chamber, leaning her arms on the cold royal frames, sided by silky white curtains. As she stares out of the window, her white right hand spreads over the glass like the branches of a birch tree shaking in winter.

Emil is playing golf with a friend. He diligently prepares his next move and...bingo! The ball hits a bird in her flight...and then the bird abruptly falls to the ground. Emil rushes to the wounded bird, madly happy, and picks it up. He then looks towards Mihaela's chamber, with pride. Seeing Mihaela's silhouette at the window, he raises the bird over his head, as a trophy.

"Poor bird... May her soul rise in peace..." Mihaela smiles at Emil, bitterly.

She then begins to take off the enormous wedding gown, feeling worn out by the heavy dress, embellished with so many stones and lace.

"All this eagerness to dominate, to overpower... It's not me anymore... What for? Am I that different? Who is this man Emil whom I'm going to marry? I thought I knew him..."

Letting the wedding dress fall down and swallow the floor of her chamber, Mihaela takes out a linen dress and puts it on. She smiles, feeling at ease. She then rushes under the bed, snatches her notebook, and storms out, barefooted.

A white bird, just like the one that Emil killed, flies against Mihaela's window, tapping at it with its orange beak...

The sun hides its rays, painted in red.

To the barn of Emil's palace.

Mihaela sneaks behind the palace, tiptoeing to the barn... As soon as she passes the majestic garden, embellished with divine gates of grass and hand-sculpted trees and palms, where Emil and his friend are playing golf, she jumps for joy, tweeting like a bird, escaped from its cage. Her legs rise beyond the ground; her long fingers extend up to the sky:

"God, help me spread my wings like a bird, always free...always guided by Your love!"

The smell of fresh grass tickles her senses; the path of white lilies lightens her expression. Her feet fall back on the ground, and she mumbles, suddenly troubled: "I don't know what to do... I feel so little... I can't see... Is he the right man for me? Please, help me find my way!"

She sighs.

Through darkened stalls and playful shadows of the day, through stocked tall hay and giant sacks of grain, Mihaela makes her way to the stall of her dear horse Rommy. She finds Rommy healthy and vivid, so hungry of love. As she kisses him on his forehead, Rommy startles with joy and licks her head with his tongue, washing the gloom off her mind. Revived, Mihaela jumps onto the hills of straw, eager to rest for a while. But one, two, three seconds of silence bore her to death.

"Come and catch me, I'm your fairy, chase me saying *Ooh la la la eh*..." a melody rambles inside her mind and then she starts to sing it aloud, kicking her feet to make up a beat.

Suddenly, Rommy-horse begins to mumble Mihaela's melody too, through big waggish nostrils, swinging his head to the right and to the left, as musical snorts puff out, to the beat of his mistress's heart... Mihaela smiles and, taking up Rommy's challenge, she jumps to her feet, and starts dancing her heart out, with devilish heat. As they move in sync, feet to feet, Mihaela wraps her arms around Rommy's strong neck, and swings with him, forehead to forehead, like two lovers.

OOH LA LA / FAIRIES CALL (Chorus)

"My fearless horse… Look how big you've grown!" she utters, kissing him on his tender eyes. Rommy shakes his tail, neighing with delight. Mihaela then jumps up on Rommy's back, props her legs tightly along his muscled legs, and Rommy coils his long tail around Mihaela's little waist, like a powerful belt. Still humming Mihaela's song in his horsy style, the spirited Rommy begins to dance on his ride, as Mihaela sustains his gallop with shouts of love.

Arriving at her favorite spot in the forest that she named "The Small Cascade of God," Mihaela dismounts and takes a seat by the water, under an old gigantic oak, her loyal friend. She leans her slim and young body against its solid trunk, and breathes deeply the fresh healing air, expelled by its leaves; she feels safe and serene under the oak's guardian crown.

The sun shines vibrantly, refreshing her spirit. The birds sing peacefully, tendering her heart. Briskly, a playful wind raises Mihaela's dress, up to her head, unveiling long agile legs, like those of a deer. Mihaela laughs with excitement, covering her legs from the eye of the nature.

She opens her notebook.

Behind the oak, a variety of lilies of the valley, tulips and wild strawberries, graciously extend their stems to take a look inside Mihaela's notebook. Mihaela places Mommy Doll on the bloomed lawn, next to her...and prepares herself to write. But to her surprise, she has forgotten her feather. She frowns.

Suddenly, a white bird with orange beak, alights on her left hand. Mihaela marvels at the sight of the bird, which looks just like the one that Emil killed. Her eyes get wet. She kisses the bird on its white wings. The bird looks so human, so motherly and sweet. Gently, with its orange beak, the bird pulls a feather out of its chest. She then chirps and hands it to Mihaela. Mihaela smiles, and takes the feather from its beak. Holding the white feather with grace, she then starts writing:

Wounded, the white bird awaited so that He breathes new life on her...
Yet almost dead, the bird knew that He wanted her to live. And so she did,
and suddenly her wings started to beat.

From the depths of the forest, a loud noise quivers the ground. The bird chirps and takes off, flying towards the heights.

Mihaela's heart throbs, yet she continues to write. A dark black horse cuts the lawn with a fast, fierce gallop. The horse makes a round, raising dust in the air, circling the cascade with its black crest, and slapping the wind with its tail. Catching the horse through her third eye, Mihaela is no longer sure if that is really a horse. The creature vanishes into the forest, leaving black fog behind.

"It had long black hair and the face of a woman, keen and wise eyes…and yet, the body of a horse…" Mihaela keeps writing.

Suddenly, a wide laughter splits up her cheeks:

"Vlad, a good man? What a nice turn!" Mihaela exclaims to herself.

The sky turns purple; thunderbolts scare her heart, hindering her long fingers to write.

Rommy neighs terribly, so frightened; he jumps up high onto his hind legs, and then gallops away. Mihaela drops the notebook, astounded, and runs after her horse.

"Rommy, stop!" she shouts out.

But Rommy keeps running like the wind, up to the hills. Try as she might, Mihaela is unable to keep up with him among the rocky serpentine. At last, she gives up and returns to the oak, sweaty but pale as a ghost. The dusk sets in, blushing her face with its red-orange rays.

As she lies down to write some more pages, another thunderbolt shakes the great oak, and together with it, the peace of her soul.

It starts pouring so violently, as it has never been before. Isolated under the giant oak, Mihaela waits for the thunderous rain to stop. But her fingers won't stop. She keeps writing and writing as a frolicsome squirrel spurs on her spirit…

"Kuku, Kuku!"

Silence.

"Kuku, Kuku!" Again.

Mihaela elongates her ears to hear where the sound comes from. She then stands up, takes a branch in her hand, and asks in a loud voice:

"Who's there?"

Suddenly a cold hand covers her mouth. Mihaela bites the hand with anger.

"Ouch! Stop, it's me, Emil!"

"You scared me to death!" Mihaela turns to Emil with fierce eyes.

"This time I really got you!" Emil laughs like a devil.

"I could have eaten your hand, my dear heathen..." Mihaela replies, still shivery.

"What are you doing here, all by yourself?" Emil asks her, nervously.

"Writing, my dear! You know..."

Emil catches Mihaela in his arms, with mad eyes. He then wraps his strong body around her body, tighter and tighter.

"Hey, I can't breathe," Mihaela frets in his arms.

Emil laughs and releases his beloved, but just to push her into the watery grass and kiss her violently onto her virgin mouth: "I don't want to ever lose you, my love..."

"No, Emil.... But Rommy...he left me..." Mihaela moans.

"I love you. I want you... Let's make love! Right now!"

Mihaela frowns. She rises to her bones and pushes Emil's hands off. She then reaches to her notebook that has gotten totally wet.

"God, my notebook! How could I've been so thoughtless?"

"Would you give up your notebook for my love?" Emil asks Mihaela, jumping on her again.

Mihaela's pierces his eyes, glacially, rolling her body away from his.

"Would you give up your ego for my love?" she asks him.

"I already gave it up..." Emil answers, frolicking, and kissing her arm.

"You ought to give up what you don't like, what you need to change, not what you love... If you love me, you should love my notebook and what's in it..."

"Yes, but it makes you strange... It isolates you... It takes you away from me..."

Mihaela laughs. She then turns for Mommy Doll, looking just where she left her, onto the giant roots of the oak. But Mommy Doll is nowhere to be seen. Mihaela circles the oak, unable to find her. She then approaches Emil, fixing him straight in the eyes:

"Where did you put her? Give her back to me!"

"I didn't take her!"

"Come on, Emil, don't be jealous again! She was right there, near the oak! I know you took my Mommy!"

"All right, all right! Let me take you back home..." He then steals a kiss from Mihaela as another thunderbolt crushes the sky...

"Wooo...just like in a movie! Look! Giant eagles with serpent eyes pierce the purple sky. And on the Virgin Land, stained with blood and pain, thousands of men impaled...thousands of stakes piercing their fate..." Emil declaims with pathos.

Mihaela's mouth freezes; her heart pounds, ready to explode, like a thunderbolt...

Emil bursts out in a big, spasmodic laughter. Mihaela bursts out into tears:

"You liar, thief, you read my book! I'll punish you for this!" she hits Emil with her small violent fists.

"I just can't wait to!" Emil continues to laugh. "Can't wait for your punishment, my virgin queen!"

He then raises his fiancée into his arms and places her on top of his horse with golden mane, baptized after Mihaela's name– Michael.

Back to Emil's house.

Mihaela's princess-like chamber is decorated with tall embroidered silk-frames in which the Nature-inspired designs of her latest collection hang loose: a wedding-like dress with white and black veil, tightened by a girdle of red roses and thorns; a costume made of knotted snake-leather strips and ended in heads of snakes; a dress of white foamy fabric with tall shoulders of dove bloodied feathers; a gown coiled with ivies and covered with a veil of twigs; a Transylvanian-inspired costume made of flaxen linen, adorned with acorns and sewn with horse-hair; gypsy skirts and blouses with poisonous violet and red mushrooms...

Amid all of Mihaela's mesmerizing designs, her mother's portrait prevails, serene and simple.

Holding Mihaela in his arms, Emil kicks the door of her chamber open, and hurls her onto the giant bed. Mihaela bounces as a doll, melting under the volcanic breath of Emil. Emil jumps over her and kisses her body with ardor.

Bewitched by Mihaela's tender and young flesh, by her virgin breasts and blooming skin, Emil growls with desire. He kisses and bites her long white neck, holding her in his strong arms of Zeus. Mihaela moans with pleasure in the breeze of his love; Emil's full lips and kisses remind her of Emanuel's lips that strange night when she had found him in her father's garden. Emil sneaks his hands under Mihaela's dress; Mihaela brushes his hand away, gently. Abruptly, Emil rolls her onto her belly, tearing her linen dress with madness.

"Emil, please, stop, I can't do this..." Mihaela cries out, trying to turn around.

"Yes, you can..."

"Only 7 days left... Please!"

"I want you..." Emil groans.

"Please, Emil, not now!" Mihaela screams as Emil licks her skin, savagely.

"Yes, right now!"

"I said no!" Mihaela rumbles, pushing Emil with her feet out of her bed... "Remember your vow!"

"You and your vows! You kill me!" Emil shouts, dropping on the carpet, like a grumpy old dog, forbidden to eat his bone. He then rises up, puts on his wet shirt and trousers, and puffs up like a tornado.

Mihaela tiptoes near him, touching his shoulder.

"Just a little bit more, my darling..."

"Same phrase ever since I met you..."

"You know that I love you and you know that I want you, but this is me. And that's what I want. We talked about this..."

"We love each other for over three years...and love has nothing to do with principles, conditions. Marriage won't change anything between the two of us, nothing!"

"Why are you raising this now? There are only seven days left! I want it to be the most special night for us!" Mihaela confronts him with softness.

"Now it would have been the most special! I never wanted you more!"

Emil bubbles up again like a volcano.

Then, without facing Mihaela, he exits her chamber while Mihaela brushes her long hair in disappointment.

"Emil?" Mihaela cries out after him.

Emil comes back with the look of a stranger:

"Yes!"

"You'll be happy for understanding me now, I promise, darling! Now, please, give me Mommy Doll back!"

"I don't have your Mommy Doll!"

"Of course you have it, sweetheart... That's what you've told me earlier under the oak!"

"I was just kidding! I just wanted to take you out of there!"

"You can't be serious! You know how precious she is for me. Please, give her back to me!"

"I don't have it! I'll buy you a prettier one..."

"It's not that, you know it! I need Mommy Doll! Please, give her back to me!"

"I shall, tomorrow! What do you think about the one with a headband of diamonds that we saw yesterday in the window?" Emil hisses, like a serpent.

"You can't buy Mommy Doll! Nothing can buy Mommy! She's not a doll, don't you know?"

Emil mutters something in Turkish...closing his hands into fists.

"You understand what I say, don't you? You're not a Turk! I need her now!" Mihaela orders him in a princess-like tone.

"What did you say?" Emil asks her, infuriated.

"I'm sorry. I know that we were born in different countries, you...in Turkey and me, in Transylvania...but we both speak the same language...the language of love."

"Mihaela, you may speak it...but I want to do it!" Emil cuts her off.

Mihaela looks at him, visibly hurt. She has been firm about her wish ever since they met each other. And he had agreed on it. It might be the excitement before the wedding... Oh, she takes things too seriously!

"Please, sweetheart, show me where you put Mommy," Mihaela

resumes, caressing his shoulder.

"Now you'll get married! You don't need Mommy Doll anymore!" Emil answers her with authority.

"She means more for me than anything else in the world. I love her more than myself, more than any one else..."

"More than me?" Emil asks Mihaela, shrinking his eyes.

"More... Now you'd better give her back to me or else..."

"Or else...?" Emil looks fierce at Mihaela. He then turns around, abruptly, and leaves Mihaela with tears in her eyes.

Mihaela knows that it was Emil who took her Mommy away. And she cannot understand how he can be jealous of a doll. At least, Mommy Doll is just a doll to him...

Same day. Late evening.

Mihaela refuses to join Emil and his mother for dinner, sending word that she is not feeling well.

Emil's mother shows up in Mihaela's room, agitated and precipitated like always.

"Mihaela dear, please, don't let such a thing get between the two of you. Emil loves you so much! He would never do anything to harm you! He confessed to me that he did not take your Mommy Doll!"

"He didn't tell me that," Mihaela replies, grumpily.

"Well, because...and this is between you and me, men are possessive! He wants you only for himself."

"And Mommy Doll was the impediment..."

"No, my dear... He was just silly-playing! He swore to me that he did not take it!"

Anne kisses Mihaela's head, like a loving mother.

Silence lies between the two, like an abyss between two mountains.

"Are you feeling any better, my dear?" she asks Mihaela, sweetly.

"Not until I shall find Mommy..."

"Oh, dear... We'll search for Mommy, I promise you. I am a mother and I know how it feels! But I've been thinking...and I know someone very good. I could talk to him. He can help you enormously regarding that. You can talk to him and tell him about Mommy Doll and all of that..."

"What are you talking about, Anne?"

"He's name is John Edwin. He is a very good doctor."

"Doctor?"

"He is a psychiatrist. He helped so many friends of mine..."

"Who? Katy, who is now scared to talk to men? Anne, you don't understand..."

"My dear, there's nothing to be afraid of. It is absolutely normal for this stage of life. It is absolutely understandable. He can only help you..."

"Anne, you don't know me...and I want to stay like that."

"You are special, my dear. I know that, but see...Mommy Doll is a problem..."

"Please, dear Anne. Let's end this subject."

"All right, my dear. Whatever makes you happy... But regarding this following matter, I won't take no for an answer," Anne continues, hastily, "Marlene is coming in tomorrow to make you a special wedding facial with white roses and lillies of the valley... You'll look splendid! Now, come on downstairs, sweet baby! I ordered *Parfait*, especially for you!"

"All right, Anne," Mihaela approves, letting herself dragged by Emil's mother.

4 am.

Mihaela cannot sleep. Again. She raises her head out of the purple sheets, peeking through big, heavy lashes, just to fall back into the soft duck pillows, dreaming about Mama...

Restless and kept awake by the big eye of the moon, she pulls herself out of bed, wraps the purple sheets around her naked body, and walks towards the white-framed windows of her chamber.

Touching the steamy shadow of herself reflected onto the glass, her fingers tremble, her eyes swing, moved by the past... She feels heavy, tired.

A giant star shines brightly onto the dark sky.

Suddenly, Mihaela's indigo star from her forehead opens up, shining and clearing her sight. She can see sharply through the night.

Mihaela opens the windows largely, gazing at the giant star.

As she contemplates, taken by the gleams of the sky, the blossomed cherry tree from her window stretches its branches and flowers inside Mihaela's chamber. Mihaela gasps, astounded. Just like the Wiseman—the black tree from Vlad's garden, the cherry tree wraps its wooden arms around Mihaela's torso, and raises her up, above the floor. The purple sheets slide off her body, and Mihaela remains naked, and smiling. Mesmerized by the entencing graceful perfume of the cherry, she feels good, scented with love...

The flowers embellish her face and cloth her body in pink, and she looks irresistibly beautiful, like a queen. A wreath of cherry flowers floats around the top of her head, and then it breaks and showers its petals upon Mihaela's arms and legs. As she looks in the window, Mihaela sees herself in bloom. Pink flowers have grown from the tip of her fingers, and green leaves have girdled her hips, her breasts, and her shoulders. The old image of herself faded away...and a new "she" opened up, like the most beautiful flower she's ever been!

Dancing in mid air, led by the arms of the sweet cherry, memories from the future sneak to her heart; she can feel, deep within....a grandiose life spreading at her feet... She only needs to step on the field, and glean the grains that God has sprinkled on for her life...

She feels that she was born to change the world into a heavenly garden, to change the evil into good... She wants everyone to dance the dance of love...to be loved like she is now loved... And then, the evil will surely wither and die...

Slowly, from the depths of the night, a beautiful singing voice reaches Mihaela's ears. So clear, so angelic...the voice gracefully sings her

Mama's song...*Ave Maria....* It gets closer and closer, guilelessly surrounding her being...

Abruptly, the branches of the cherry tree take Mihaela through the open window, and lay her down, in Anne's garden.

As Mihaela's feet touch the wet grass, her body is nourished with invigorating droplets of dew.

The strong light of the giant star impales her forehead, touching her deep to her heart. Her arms extend like huge pink petals, fluttering in the dark; her feet rise above the grass; her ears open largely to the sound of the night. She hears again *Ave Maria*, this time clearer, engrossing...

She was only a few days old when she heard her mother singing this song, and yet, she has never forgotten her warm, heavenly voice.

Emil, awakened by the force of the giant star too, overthinks his future. He drags himself to the embroidered blue-framed window of his room, and sees Mihaela walking along the lawn, naked. Under the glow of that surreal star, it looks like his fiancée flies above the grass, with large wings of petals.

Fascinated, Emil rushes to open the doors of his terrace to have a better view of his beloved.

Marbled and adorned with detailed ornate columns, the terrace is embossed with statuettes of Renaissance women that seem to prolong their heads to watch Mihaela's dance, as well.

Yet, try as he might, Emil cannot catch another glimpse of his sweetheart. The claws of darkness have kidnapped his bride, and Mihaela is out of his sight.

The motherly voice echoes louder and louder.

Under the big oak where she lost Mommy Doll, Mihaela can see the silhouette of her mother: so alive, so young and beautiful; Mama's long dark wavy hair trembles into the wind of the night, her arms wide open, yearning for a hug...

"Mama, Mama!" Mihaela cries out, running towards her mother.

Mama embraces her daughter like an angel of light. Mihaela hugs her too, enormous felicity filling her heart. But only for a second, as Mama then flies away into the forest, at the speed of light. Mihaela runs after Mama, pushing the twined boughs of nature to the side.

"Mama, Mama, wait for me!"

But Mama hides behind the lofty and ravenous trees, getting smaller and smaller, almost invisible.

Mihaela pants desperately, madly running to reach her mother, slapping the obnoxious trees out of her way, their branches growing bigger and bigger at every step she takes. Abruptly, Mihaela stumbles over a stump, and falls into the muddy ground. Kissed by the ground, she raises up with the force of a warrior princess, and shouts out to the giant star:

"Mama, I need you, Mama! Where are you? Don't leave me alone down here! Come back!"

A flood of tears erupts from the majestic black eyes of Mihaela. She gets down to her knees, with her head hanging like a torn flower.

As the wind blows stronger through the branches of the centurial oaks, Rommy-horse shows up, cutting the landscape with his sharp gallop.

"Rommy! My horse!"

But Rommy gallops further into the night, with Mama on his back, leaving darkness behind.

Nature is overly excited; the crows scream loud, cracking the sky; the ground ovulates like a pregnant mother.

With her long arms stuck into a prayer and her long neck stretched to the sky, Mihaela tries to listen to elucidating words of God. She hopes that this strange night is a divine sign, the return of her mother in flesh and blood.

Try as she might, prayer after prayer devotedly whispered, and Mama is not showing up...

Tired of her migratory incantations, Mihaela heads back to Emil's palace.

"Was all of that just a dream? Am I ill?" she asks within, penetrated with grief.

"It could not be, I heard Mama so clearly singing, and she embraced me..." Mihaela replies to herself, encouragingly.

The warmth of a mother, the smile and caresses of the beautiful Violeta, could not have been replaced by her father Grid, neither by Emil or Anne, nor by any other human being... Though Papa Grid has been an impeccable father, Mihaela has always missed the tender touch of a mother. She felt the agony of a father left without the love of his life. She felt how lovely it would be to have her mom in flesh, by her side.

With a lump of tears in her throat, Mihaela approaches Emil's palace, still hoping to peer her mother along the way. This night, she has seen the line between life and death, between Heaven and Earth...so thin and cunning...and she feels on the edge... Everything is conjoined..."a beautiful mystery," like Papa said.

"I will find Mommy! I will! But I must do good! How harsh of me to treat Emil so cold! He really loves me! He's the only one! Do I want to lose him too? I shouldn't have made such a big smoke out of it!" Mihaela emboldens herself with belief.

"Do nothing. Let me lead you," a sharp, enlightening voice suddenly pierces her mind.

Mihaela enters the palace. The dim-lighted foyer is empty. Everybody is wrapped up in slumber. Only the heads of the porcelain statuettes watch her, alone. Mihaela climbs sluggishly the marble stairs, towards her chamber, her fingers strumming the serpentine balustrade like snakes seeking a prey.

As she enters her room, she jumps into the debauched arms of her bed that have been waiting for her, still hot. She pulls the cloudy eiderdown over her head, and tries to go back to sleep.

But her third eye flickers again, high-spirited. She feels so restless, awake.

"Auch, Auch!" Mihaela suddenly cries, as something pecks at her, biting the eiderdown and needling her flesh... She takes the blanket off her head, and sees the white bird with orange beak, fluttering her wings, onto the edge of her bed.

"Oh, sweet child of mine...how did you get in here?" she asks the bird kindly.

The bird chirps.

Mihaela breathes relieved, and caresses the white bird on her wings. Looking at it more attentively, she sees that her dear bird has changed: it has tiny black and red lines around its neck, like a necklace, and reddened eyes. Also, the brim of her white feathers has blackened, emmiting a bluish smoke.

The bird chirps, trying to say something. Mihaela chirps back to it, and just like in a duet, they chirp back and forth, their sounds tangling into the melodic language of birds. Dying with laughter, as she hasn't died in decades, Mihaela takes the strange bird into her arms:

"What news have you for me, my sweet bird of God?"

The bird chirps again, but this time frenziedly and madly, and then it pecks Mihaela's left arm.

"Auch!" Mihaela cries out, wounded by the crazed bird.

Blue blood springs out of her arm onto the white eiderdown.

Mihaela can feel that something is wrong, something beyond her control… "What has happened to my sweet bird?"

Like a devoted mother of the singing creatures of the world,-Mihaela brings a little water to the sickly bird, and encourages her to quench her thirst. But the bird, aflamed and cawing like a crow, refuses to drink and pricks again at Mihaela's palm. Mihaela quickly sets the bird free to the sky, and prays to God:

"Lord, please, heal her with your love! I cannot do it on my own… Oh, sweet bird of mine, be well and fly!"

The bird flies into the dark, but then it flutters its wings into Emil's room.

Mihaela drags her feet to the bathroom, letting the cold water run. She splashes her face with the naughty drops of water, and stares at herself in the mirror. She looks beautiful…and younger… Her face is glowing as when she was 18. She feels happy because she can speak to Rommy-horse, and newly, to the white bird with orange beak.

"The language of animals… Who would have thought that I have such a gift?"

Her eyes are shining. She smiles, satisfied. But as she smiles…stupefaction! Something that she has hoped to be forever gone, emerges in front of her eyes. Small fangs…little buds of canine teeth…are blackening the glass…

"No, no! It can't be possible!"

Mihaela opens her mouth widely, hoping that it was just an illusion, a spectrum. But the little monsters are still there, stable and indifferent to the strong beat of her heart.

"I took those fangs out when I was 14! And I buried them in Papa's garden. It can't be possible!" she thinks, paralyzed with fright.

Letting the cold water run, Mihaela rushes into her room, and hurls herself to the bed. Hiding her fears under the eiderdown, she keeps saying, louder and louder: "They are gone! They are gone!"

9:00 am. Same morning.

Mihaela is awakened by a terrifying scream. She jumps out of her skin, and then out of bed, sliding on the glazed parquet like on a skating rink.

In front of Emil's room, Anne cries, disfigured:

"My baby!"

Mihaela rushes into Emil's chamber. His bed is drenched in blue blood, and Emil, lying there, is all smiles.

"What's the matter with Mother? I feel fine…" Emil smiles idiotically at Mihaela, his eyes rolling upside down.

Mihaela takes a seat near Emil and touches his arm. He is cold as ice. Caressing him on his face, and then down to his shoulder, Mihaela notices…two small holes of blue blood piercing his cold neck…

"Oh my God!" she cries, her eyes filling with tears.

She jumps to her feet and starts walking up and down the room, rubbing her hands, like a mad girl. Anne watches Mihaela's moves, desperately.

Suddenly Mihaela stops, remembering the little sharp canine teeth that she saw earlier in the morning in the mirror.

"Did I do that?"

The thought that she could be the guilty one starts killing her.

Anne looks at Mihaela with cold eyes.

"Now what? Is he dead? Is he like I used to be?" Mihaela speaks within, flushed with fear.

She walks back to Emil's bed and takes him by the hand:

"Emil, look at me. I need to know. What happened last night?"

"My darling, it was unforgettable!" Emil gives a silly smile.

"Stop smiling, Emil!"

But Emil keeps smiling, and kissing Mihaela's hands in a convulsion of love.

"Tell me more… What happened?" Mihaela insists.

"Don't tell me you don't know! I had no idea what a beast was dwelling inside my angel," Emil smiles again.

"What did we do?" Mihaela asks him, pale as a ghost.

"We made love…" Emil answers, lost in his trance.

"We made love?"

"Yes! I feel reborn… I love you, Mihaela!"

"But, this blue-blood…painted all over you…where did it come from?"

"It's yours, my virgin queen…" Emil grins.

"Did I bite you?"

"Wildly, so wildly! I still feel you inside of me…" Emil growls like a dog with desire.

The globe falls on Mihaela's shoulders, riveting her into the ground. Her head spins; her face hides between her palms; her breath blows like a hurricane, stronger and stronger, storming the peace in her heart.

"I thought it would never finish… We made it again and again, and again… And then you bit me, again, again and again," Emil exclaims, his eyes seeming to have passed into another realm.

Then, Emil arches his back and jumps off the bed, taking his bride into a twirl of tango moves, all around the room. Caught up inside his erotic, unstoppable trance, Emil flies with Mihaela into expensive furniture, into porcelain vases and scented candles that break apart at the volcanic touch of the dancing partners. Pieces of glass crush on the carpet, Art paintings and elegant draperies of Anne crumble down as her son dirty dances up and down the walls.

"You made me the happiest man on earth," Emil screams at the top of his lungs, as he turns his neck, like a toreador, in his tango twirl.

Anne screams to her son, desperately:

"Come down, baby! You're gonna hurt yourself!"

Listening to his mother's echoes, Emil jumps off the walls, and kneels at the feet of his mistress, kissing them like a slave:

"I will worship you, my queen, forever. I want to make you the most well-known designer in the whole world."

Emil no sonner finishes his declaration than he rushes into his wardrobe and picks up a dress from Mihaela's collection, spoiling it with the blue blood that still drips off his body.

"We have to expose it at the Royal Garden... Look at this! Magnifique!"

The dress is made of aquamarine tulle and fastened in the back with light blue feathers that form a train like of an imperial peacock. On the bodice of the dress is written with blue blood: *Forgive me! I am different.*

"My poetess!" Emil screams, trying to fit his Herculean body in Mihaela's dress.

Smiling, perversely, he starts walking up and down like a top model, touching himself and playing the fool.

"Am I not the most handsome bridegroom in the whole world?"

Mihaela hides her face, bursting into tears.

"What's the matter, baby? Don't I look great? Why are you crying?" Emil asks Mihaela, frolicking.

"These are tears of happiness..." Mihaela reassures him.

"Good," Emil consents, after which he collapses on the carpet, like a broken puppet.

"My baby," Anne rushes to her son, who lies dismembered on the floor.

Emil's palace. Same day with Charles.

His Excellency, Charles, and his doctor, arrive hastily at Emil's house. As they enter the royal foyer covered in white marble, Anne jumps into Charles' arms, suffocating him with hugs.

"Enough, my dear, enough... Let's take care of your son," Charles mumbles, releasing himself from Anne's grasp.

Charles is wearing a stylish blue blazer, tied up in eight big golden buttons, and perfectly matching a blue silk kerchief that sticks out loosely of his left upper pocket. Underneath the blazer, a light gray shirt with burgundy vertical stripes and high collar, contribute to his impeccable stature. He has long arms and fingers, blue penetrating eyes, walks sharply, and wears his silky dark black hair brushed with pride.

"Please, follow me, my dears," Anne speaks cordially, climbing the marble stairs of the foyer.

Meantime, inside Emil's room, kneeled down at the feet of his bed, Mihaela whispers an incantation, clouds of steam rising above Emil's head from her pot with boiling plants.

As Anne and her guests arrive on the second floor with glossy rosewood parquet and splendid oriental vases, the scent of Mihaela's aromatic plants tickles their senses.

"Hmm..." the doctor exclaims, swelling up his nostrils.

"Hush, baby, hush... You'll be just fine..." Mihaela murmurs, circling the pot around Emil's head and placing around his neck smaller and bigger green leaves.

As Charles and the doctor make their entrance inside Emil's chamber, Emil has already fallen into a deep sleep. Mihaela lays the pot with plants on the night stand, and rising up, slowly, she turns her eyes to the distinguished guests.

Charles approaches Mihaela quietly and kisses her hand. The doctor does the same. Mihaela bows like a Geisha.

"Good to see you, my dear," Charles whispers in Mihaela's ear. "I'm very sorry for the news. I was hoping our next encounter to be a more creative one...but let's try our best..."

"What does Emil have around his neck?" the doctor asks, pecipitously.

"Fresh Plantago leaves," Mihaela replies promptly.

"What for?"

"They stop the bleeding and heal the wounds..." Mihaela explains.

"Look at that! Interesting! Just like in that book! And we came to be the saviors..." the doctor grins with delight.

"Please, have a look at his neck..." Mihaela whispers.

The doctor unleaves Emil's neck: two very small scars can be noticed below his right earlobe, almost healed. Yet his veins look deeply violet, swollen, and the temperature of his body feels cooler than the breath of winter.

"Interesting..." the doctor says, sensing blue viscous liquid around the two scars.

Mihaela interrupts him:

"I also put a little methylene blue on the leaves so that the wounds would heal faster..."

"Interesting!" the doctor exclaims again.

Mihaela tears. Her arms suddenly shiver.

"What's the matter?" Charles asks her, concerned.

"We need to save him, Charles! By all means!"

"Of course, my dear," Charles comforts her with a calming voice. "No doubt. That's why we are here."

Quickly, the doctor opens his old bag of thick buffalo leather, full of freshly picked leaves, yellow and reddish herbs, nut twigs, crystals of quartz, small pots with plants...and all kinds of small bottles and jars that swarm with lizards... He shoves his big hand into his bag, and pulls out a tiny pot with a slender plant, with bell-shaped cherry-colored flowers. He places it carefully on Emil's nightstand, along with a water-clock, and few jars with strange ointments and solutions. Opening a jar of mud on which is written *Slatina Driganelor,* the doctor gently anoints Emil's forehead, afterwhich he lays some tiny lizard eggs. Emil blinks abruptly and, miraculously, the eggs break, and small emerald green lizards invade his forehead, and then his entire face... At the same time, a white foam begins to bubble around Emil's mouth, oozing out on the sheets of the bed, under the greedy eyes of the tiny green lizards.

"Interesting..." the doctor mumbles, awesomely, as he replaces Mihaela's *Plantago* leaves with *Belladonna leaves,* and oils Emil's neck with a blackish solution extracted from a small bottle of glass inscriptioned with "Venom from the Vampire's Tail."

Emil starts to tremble, raving and speaking aloud with groans and dark voices, twitching his legs and arms, as in an exorcism convulsion.

"Interesting..." the doctor marvels again.

"What was that? What have you done to him?" Mihaela asks the doctor, ceasing her sobs.

Charles replies calmly:

"Be reassured, my dear... We are using very old remedies from the book of a woman who healed a lot of people through plants and white magic...a long time ago...

"Thanks be to God, Emil has fallen asleep again! He needs to rest..." the doctor murmurs with his eyes fixed on Emil.

"Yes, rest brings healing...." Charles complies, afterwhich, so eagerly, he continues his conversation with Mihaela:

"My dear, maybe Anne told you that I purchased a very old house in Transylvania. And, in the attic of this house, I found the book that I've told you about...full of miraculous cures and treatments, and also of a lot of bottles and jars with solutions and ointments...the ones that you can now see with your own eyes... At first, I was amused; I didn't believe in them; some just scared me as I read the ingredients... So, I put them out of my mind. But soon enough, I fell off the horse and, as I was in great pain...I tried everything... But nothing really worked. My spine was hurting excruciatingly, and I was unable to sleep, unable to work. Finally, I decided to try a cure from this book, and rubbed my back with a mixture of oils and seeds. Miraculously, I was healed in less than seven hours. My back pain vanished, my wounds closed, and my ligaments straightened. I was like new. Also, in the book of this woman, there is a list with the people whom she cured. But also with several patients who died because of her treatment... She wrote exactly what caused their death and what one should do to avoid such a thing. That woman was a phenomenon! I gathered up everything from her attic and stored it in the basement of my castle. Both my doctor and I now know her book inside out! My doctor has changed...a lot... He now knows that the secrets of his job are first and foremost found in Mother Nature..."

"Do you know what was the name of that woman?" Mihaela asks, filled with curiosity.

"Yes. Her name was Magia," Charles replies, swiftly.

"Magia?" Mihaela exclaims, astounded.

"Yes, that's right. Also, in my old-time garden, I have planted the entire seeds that I found in Magia's house, and about which Magia wrote thoroughly in her book... Now, I have tens of patches with wondrous fruits of magic!" Charles continues with a spirited voice. "First, I planted *The Love or The Table of Heaven (Sedum fabaria)* that has pink purplish flowers—defenders of love and of the house; then, I grew *Garlic, Lovage, Common Elder, Wormwood, Monkshood*...which are against the unclean spirits..." Charles explains, paying attention to Mihaela's reaction. "I also grew sweet Basil for love spells and for the broken hearted too..." Charles adds with a wink, bringing smile on Mihaela's face.

"The Basil is excellent; it also heals the wounds," the doctor chips in. "In 5 minutes, I will replace the *Belladonna* leaves from Emil's neck with *Basil* leaves, and you'll see the effect... They perform wonders!"

"I just can't wait to see it!" Mihaela steps in, carried away by the doctor's enthusiasm.

"Do you know the legend of the Basil? I read it in Magia's book too... It fascinated me," Charles intervenes.

"No. Please, tell it to me," Mihaela replies, animated.

"Allegedly, the Sun got mad because a young maiden on Earth was shining brighter than its face. And thus, enflamed and jealous, the Sun sent burning rays and withered all the flowers of the earth; it brought big drought and pain. Shortly thereafter, the beautiful maiden died, and left behind a desperate boy who loved her more than anyone else in the whole world. The maiden's lover, named Basil, kept going to her tomb, shedding torrents of tears, and whispering poems of love. One day, at the head of the maiden's grave, a purple flower began to grow. Every day, sprinkled with the lover's tears, the flower became more and more beautiful, emanating a heavenly scent. Touched by the immensity of the boy's love, the flower took his name—Basil."

"I'm fascinated by these legends!" Mihaela cries out, with tears in her eyes.

"As the legend goes," Charles continues, "the lover found out his destiny on the Magic Night of Sânziene[24]—*The Fairies' Night*, before the maiden died…but he didn't take it into account. The fairies spoke to him, but he didn't want to believe them."

"Just like people don't believe in the Snake Grass Flower," Mihaela adds rapidly.

---

[24] *The Night of Sânziene (The Midsummer Celebration) takes place on June 23rd and June 24th. It is believed to be a magical night, the night when the medicinal herbs ought to be harvested in order to become efficient. The legend says that in this night of **Sânziene**, good fairies who live in forests or on plains make up horas (a traditional Romanian round dance) and convey special powers to flowers and to weeds that thus become healing. This very night, the young ones find out their future and the animals flock together and have a council. Those who spy on those animals can listen to them and can find out many secrets and treasures.*

***Sânzienele** (Galium verum, **Lady's Bestraw flowers**) is also a plant that has been used to remove evil and illness since ancient times. It has yellow golden flowers with a delightful scent and grows among hay, in orchards, or at the edge of forests. In the past, the Lady's Bedstraw flowers were placed in the bed of women about to give birth so that they would have an easy labor. There are legends, which assert that there were dry Lady's Bedstraw flowers instead of straw in the manger where Jesus Christ was born.*

***Sânzienele** (also called **Nedeia or Drăgaica**) is also the oldest and most important Romanian feast that takes place on June 24th. If people don't celebrate the fairies the way they should, Sânzienele, the good witches, get upset and become evil like Ielele or Rusaliile.*

This feast, being a celebration of love through singing and games, also represents an occasion for young people, who want to unite their destinies, to meet.

"What about the Snake Grass Flower?" the doctor asks, burning with curiosity.

"It has been said that the Snake Grass cannot be seen or picked up by anyone...because unseen creatures have wished to have it only for themselves. But it is not true, because I have seen it. In the middle of the Night of Sânziene, when nature is quiet and wilderness ceases, the world shakes hands with "the other world," and it's all up to one's faith... And then one can see it... The Snake Grass has a white glowing flower in the shape of a star, which blooms every year only on the night of Sânziene. I got one. I could see it...because I believed."

"I believe in such tales too," Charles breaks in, inspirited. "I am fascinated by them just as I am fascianted by your art, your costumes imprinted with old motifs and embroideries... And most enchanting and conquering, impregnated with love and magic... Mihaela dear, we can build up something magnificent together! Something mythological and historical! Timeless! I am a big fan of yours. It was an honor to write the chronicle about your collection and I hope to write many more..."

"Thank you so much..." Mihaela replies, without losing Emil from her sight.

"It has been my greatest pleasure! Anytime! I'm standing up for my own blood!"

"Your own blood?" Mihaela opens her black eyes wider.

"Yes, my Transylvanian blood. My great-great grandmother, Claudine Rhédey, was from Transylvania, a relative of Vlad—Vlad the Impaler, Vlad Țepes, Dracula...or however they call him."

Mihaela looks at Charles, confused.

Charles continues his speech, grinning from ear to ear:

"I know the look you're giving me! I myself don't believe that vampires exist... But that *Venom from the Vampire's tail* that I found at Magia's is absolutely miraculous, I myself have used it..."

"If vampires don't exist, then where does the *Venom from the Vampire's tail* come from?" Mihaela asks him.

Taken by Mihaela's question, Charles flashes a childlike smile.

The doctor steps in, defending his friend:

"Charles is irremediably in love with Transylvania, with its forests, mysteries, customs, with every single piece of Transylvanian art... He buys anything that comes his way for his collection..."

"Yes, I adore the old stuff of Transylvania!" Charles strengthens the doctor's monologue. "I am sure that my children will be proud of my collection. I have purchased dish shelves, handmade, parsechiuri, wood clocks naively painted, very old blide, icons of glass such as were never seen before..."

"All of those objects have soul. They see, feel, suffer, are happy..." Mihaela whispers, serenely.

"Is it really like that?" Charles asks, bemused. "How do you know?"

"Plants, and especially the handmade objects, bear a soul for their inhabitants..."

A little green lizard on Emil's chest gazes at Mihaela attentively... The room fills with a pleasant fragrance that invigorates the breath, awakening beloved memories to Mihaela. She suddenly sees daddy Grid, stepping through fresh layers of vegetables, in their garden. She feels the smell and the taste of borsch in which daddy scattered lots of lovage. She asks Charles, with dreamy eyes:

"Do you like the lovage broth?"

"It is to die for! It has the divine smell of the green groceries and genuine vegetables! And if you eat it with 'mămăligă'... Hmmm..."

"Your pronunciation is amazing... Who taught you to pronounce 'mămăligă' so well?" Mihaela asks Charles.

"A nun...a young *măicuța* from a superb Transylvanian monastery. I have been praying at *Cârțișoara Monastery*; it is so beautiful... And this young Romanian *măicuța*, looking like a Virgin Mary, taught me so gently, so patiently...the language of God. She also gave me an amazing wooden icon painted by her."

Mihaela smiles, staring at Emil with virgin eyes.

The doctor shakes off the magic, and soldiers on / bucks himself up:

"Now, let's do some work!"

And thus, he opens up a very old book covered in leather, rubs some lovage leaves between his palms, and begins to utter a chant:

"În pustiu, în depărtare
Acolo să chieri
Ca ziua de ieri
Ca roua la soare
Ca spuma la floare
Să rămâie
Lumnyinat
Curat
De boală scăpat."

As soon as he finishes the incantation, he strews the little pieces of lovage onto the lizards that jump greedily at them.

"What is this book?" Mihaela asks, inquisitively.

"It is Magia's book. Look, she wrote that lovage is the guardian and benefactor of any garden. I hope it is going to be Emil's benefactor too," the doctor asserts, as he checks Emil's pulse.

Delighted by his ritual, the doctor replaces the *Belladonna* leaves from Emil's neck with the *Basil* ones and pours some drops of tincture from the *Holy Ghost grass*[25] into his mouth.

"Oh, I almost forgot…" the doctor breaks in.

Afterwhich, he pulls a quartz crystal out of his bag and places it on Emil's chest, right above his heart.

"Where did you get this crystal from? It looks so familiar!" Mihaela asks him.

---

[25] *The Holy Ghost grass is an elixir plant with mysterious, powerful medicinal valencies which maintains youth and health. Known as "Angelica Archangelica," the Holy Ghost is used for treatment of many afflictions. It is believed that only people with a clean soul can receive healing from "Angelica Archangelica." Its name comes from Michael the Archangel who appeared in the dream of a monk and who revealed to him the name of the plant that he needed to use in order to heal the people contaminated with pestilence in the Europe of 1665. Since its therapeutic power was discovered, Angelica has been heartily cultivated and has been in danger of disparition. Today it is a plant protected by law.*

"Charles brought me to a fabulous place—*The Temple of Wishes*[26], not far away from Braşov. Oh, it's a magical place, with a very old history that holds an incredible positive energy that heals people and blossoms the forest... I believe in the energy of that place, and I hope from all my heart and soul that this crystal taken from the Temple will heal Emil too. A healthy heart, a healthy body. There, at the Temple, we have also found the *Herb Christopher*[27], which I will embed under Emil's skin of his right

---

[26] **The Temple of Wishes** *from Şinca Veche is also called "The Temple of Destinies," "The Grotto from Şinca Veche," "The Monastery Carved in Stone," or "The Temple of Aliens." The grotto is located at Şinca Veche, between the towns of Braşov and Făgăraş and it is hidden amidst a forest where abundant vegetation grows. It is a temple with miraculous powers, founded 6,000 to 7,000 years ago. The signs found on the Altar's wall (The Portrait of Jesus Christ, The Star of David and The Yin-Yang Circle) belong to very different cultures and convey to people the message that they can fulfill themselves through the unification of contraries under the sign of Love.*

[27] **Herb Christopher** *is a rare miraculous herb – Actaea spicata – also known as Baneberry, Verbina, The Philosophers Weed, The Wild Animals' Grass, or The Thieves' Weed. The legend says that it was born from the drops of blood of Jesus's navel that fell to the ground. It has a silver, gold, red, or black color. During the night it lights up like fire but after sunrise it is green, just like other weeds. Allegedly, the one who embeds it under the skin of his or her palm cannot be imprisoned and, by the power of one's touch, it can open any padlock or bolt. Moreover, Herb Christopher protects its master from any weapons or guns, attracts money to its owner, and makes one understand the language of animals and plants. With this plant, one can open locked doors which lead to hidden underground treasures. Who owns it becomes guarded and acquires supernatural powers. Herb Christopher can be found nearby lakes, in swampy areas, on a rock or where a devil found its death, struck by lightning. It grows among the most unusual herbs, but it stays in the same place only for a year, in the second year growing three rivers away and so on, until the ninth year when it returns to the same place.*

Herb Christopher can be found if a lock is dragged through the grass, and the lock opens up when it comes into contact with the plant; the chains which tie the horses that feed on grass at night unlock if they come into contact with Herb Christopher.

If it is put in a pitcher brimming with water, it lies at its bottom; if it is hurled in a river, Herb Christopher floats against the tide.

If the wood-pecker, the starling, the hedgehog and the marten's young are locked in a cage, their "parents" know to find Herb Christopher to set its darlings free.

Herb Christopher has been known to Greeks, Romanians, and Middle Easterners since ancient times.

palm. Charles found it! Try as I might, I couldn't get one. I looked for it everywhere, all day long, and he came and saw it! Boom! Isn't it ironic? See, this *Herb Christopher* has the shape of a heart, no leaves, no roots, and it is fine as a hair. Please, touch it, Mihaela. But it gives one the strength to open anything, any locks or bolts, and find the most hidden treasures."

"Provided that one has a clean heart, full of faith and love," Mihaela adds.

"True. Well said!" the doctor approves.

"Emil is in love, he loves you, so there are big chances… Love cleans the soul!" Charles smiles. He then continues with delight: "Let's go forward now, my dear…" and he grabs Mihaela by her arm, and takes a few steps forward.

"Where, Charles?"

"Back to Emil's story… Tell me, what happened that night with Emil?"

"You might think that I am a liar, but I don't know anything… Yesterday morning when I woke up…I found him this way…" Mihaela explains, suddenly troubled.

"Anne told me that you made love that night…and that he was painted with your blue blood… She said that he confessed."

"I did not make love to him…"

"But who?"

Silence.

"Are you still a virgin?" Charles asks, quietly.

"Yes… I think so…"

"Would you mind having my doctor consult you?" Charles adds.

"No," Mihaela replies, her face suddenly crimson.

"I don't want to intimidate you, but we need to find the cause…so that we are successful… And you can help the most…"

"Of course. I'm at your service, Charles. Emil is my love. But I am aware of my body, you know…" Mihaela adds with gentleness, watching Emil twitching in bed.

The water clock drips its last drop of water. The small pot with the slender bell-shaped flower suddenly shrinks and withers, as killed by a storm.

"What plant is that, doctor?" Mihaela asks.

"*Minor belladonna!*[28]" the doctor answers, perplexed.

Charles grabs Mihaela by her arm and walks her out of Emil's room, leaving the doctor alone to continue the treatment.

"See, I found some bottles with blood at Magia's. And these bottles have the intitals-MV. What could it mean?" Charles asks Mihaela, thoughtfully.

"You have these bottles?" Mihaela asks full of curiosity.

"Yes, of course! They have sort of a thick blue blood... I know that Vlad's ancestors used to have this blue, royal blood... See, mine is a mixture. Not quite blue, not quite red," Charles smiles again. "How is yours, Mihaela?"

"A mixture too," Mihaela smiles back.

"See, I am fascinated by blood, by mysteries, and by everything that can lead to discovering precious ways of healing. Are you with me?"

"Of course..."

"Tell me, where in Transylvania did you live?" Charles asks Mihaela. "As I have told you, I just purchased an estate in Braşov, Transylvania..."

"I lived in Braşov, Poiana, at a place called "The Lucky Wheel," Mihaela replies, swiftly.

---

[28] *Minor belladonna is scientifically named "Scopolia carniloica" and popularly, called Dumb or The Grass of Woods. It is considered a magical plant that can be harvested only by the righteous (children and old women who have redeemed their sins through faith.) Harvesting minor belladona for magical usage involves lighting candles, burning incense, and bringing gifts. It is said to have healing powers and to punish the enemies of the one who uses it. It is said that this plant foresees the future, drives away the black shadows of the future, and guesses the intentions of those who look at it directly. In the face of death, Minor belladonna withers.*

"No way! This is too much of a coincidence! I ate there last spring, at an inn called Grid!"

Mihaela's knees weaken… Her face blooms with joy.

"Grid's inn? And did you meet Grid?"

"Well, he died in late 16th century, my dear… I wish I could have met him!"

"Oh…" Mihaela whispers, overshadowed by the word "died."

"People said that Grid knew so many things about the Transylvanian mythology, about dishes, traditions, herbs, the bees, the honey…that he was a great man!" Charles adds, high-spirited. "I purchased some very old and beautiful carpets from there…hand-sewn by his wife."

"I need them," Mihaela speaks with fire.

"We'll talk about that later, my dear. This man Grid holds also a great story. The story of his daughter…or daughters… He had two twin daughters born from a plant…a miraculous Queen of the Night Plant… It is said that Vlad himself had something to do with it… Beautiful tales, my dear…."

Mihaela's purple star starts to shine.

"What's that?" Charles asks, intrigued.

"Oh, it's me…my star!"

"Your star?"

"Yes, we all have one…don't we?" Mihaela smiles.

After Charles' departure,

Mihaela returns to her chamber and gets ready for the white flowers' bath ordered by Anne. She steps inside the warm luring tub, sprinkled with white roses and lilies of the valley, freshly gathered by Marlene, and loses herself in the scented water… Her long neck, like a beautiful swan, gets drenched up too…and she closes her eyes, painting on a smile…

Dark thoughts ravingly race through her brain, and the face of her father, pale as a ghost, lying in a tomb of stone, suddenly blackens her heart.

"No, no, no... My father might be dead to Charles and to others, but for me, he is alive and will always be. I can go visit him anytime, back in the 15th century...and I can even bring him here, to see the world..." Mihaela speaks within. "And even now, he is here with me. I know it. I feel him... I have so much joy inside... Then, what do I fear? I don't know...What is death? Is it real? We people are fearing it because we were once told that we're gonna die. And we believed it. Instead of turning our eyes to the sky, feeling one with God, we look at the mud, at the clay that we were once made of. But now I am immortal, a supernatural being...made of heavenly spirit... Heaven is my home and I was given the righteousness forever...in my soul... Death is the past, it belongs to Lucifer, who is condemned, dead. Death died at the cross...once and for all. Life has been risen and reigns, and me, in it. Death is a tale for the unbelievers. Life is a truth for the believers. I believe. And so, I will live forever....me, and my daddy..."

"Miss, Miss... Do you hear me, Miss?" Marlene keeps asking Mihaela, who is caught up in her heavenly world...

As Marlene grabs Mihaela's arm, shuttering her throughts off, Mihaela opens her big black eyes.

"Yes, dear..." Mihaela whispers with calm.

"Oh my God!" Marlene screams to death.

"What's the matter, Marlene?" Mihaela startles.

"The water is blue!"

Mihaela looks down to the water and says:

"Don't worry. It's my menstruation."

"Blue?"

"I added a blue emollient for calming my pain," Mihaela clears the situation.

"I see, excuse me..."

Then, painting a naive smile on her face, Marlene continues:

"Now, let's make Mihaela the prettiest woman in the world!"

And Marlene oils her hands with a white cream and starts massaging Mihaela's face with tenderness.

Mihaela cannot hold her tears.

"What's the matter?" Marlene asks her, concerned.

"I'm just anxious… I'm getting married and I was hoping…"

"Oh, my dear, but you and Emil are the most beautiful couple I've ever seen! You'll be very happy!"

"Marlene dear, would you please leave me alone for a little while?"

"But I just came in…"

"I know, but my tears won't do good to your hands…"

And Mihaela kisses Marlene's hands with love.

Marlene, impressed by the pleading eyes of her mistress, exits the room, quietly.

Mihaela gets out of the warm vat with white roses, throws a white cloth around her body, and collapses onto the bed. Blue blood rapidly stains the white cloth. Biting the pillow with her small teeth and wetting them with bitter tears, Mihaela screeches out like a wounded bird:

"Why? Why me? I don't want to be a monster. Why now? Where did they come from? How could I stop them? I need an answer. Please, God…"

Hearing only silence in response, she wipes off her tears and takes a deep breath, dashing into the bathroom. With murderous shimmers in her eyes, she grabs the hand mirror that she ornamented with white roses to resemble the one that she got from her mother in Transylvania. She opens her mouth largely…and there they are, the little monsters…sharp and intact! The mirror looks so gracious and classy, but her face penetrates it with hatred:

"I'm gonna take you out, bloody bastards, weapons of the dead devil! You are gone! You are just phantoms! You little monsters, in the name of God, go back to your hellish ground!"

And, burning with anger, Mihaela drops the small embroidered mirror inside the sink and rushes in front of the big mirror of her chamber. With the conviction of a killer, she pulls out a thick spool of thread from her fabric drawers, breaks a long wire and knots it to the door handle. She then opens her mouth wide and reaches to one of her dirty canine teeth to knot the other end of the thread. But she cannot sense anything sharp, anything long and wicked to fix the knot... She opens her mouth wider. As she looks closely in the mirror, she sees nothing...only her small human teeth...

"Where did they disappear to?" she asks herself, utterly shocked.

Indeed, the fangs are gone. Just small wrinkles are blooming around her eyes.

"Little lying mirror! I'm gonna break you up!" Mihaela screams, rushing to the bathroom. She grasps the little embroidered mirror and hurls it to the ground. But the mirror does not break. Contrarily, it rolls onto the bathroom floor, turning it entirely into a mirror. As she looks down, Mihaela can see the face of an angel...so white, clothed in a dazzling snowlike garment.

LITTLE LYING MIRROR (Chorus)

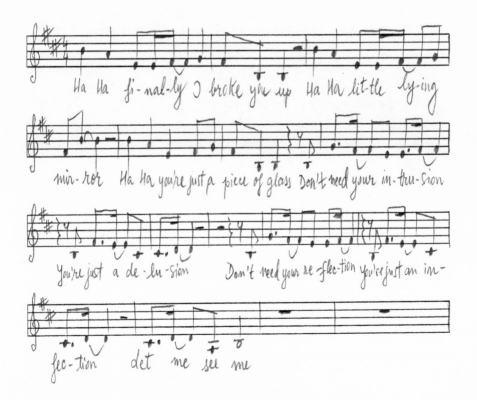

Quick and sharp knocks rattle on Mihaela's door.

"Who is it?" Mihaela asks, almost jumping out of her skin.

"Mihaela, you have a visitor!" Anne speaks loudly and impatiently, through the door.

"Who is it?"

"I don't know, there is a young man... He has a letter for you."

"I can't see anyone! I'm not feeling well!" Mihaela replies, firmly.

"But he wants to see you! He insists. He is..."

"Please, tell him to come back!" Mihaela cuts Anne off. "I'm not in a great mood, as I said."

"Please, Mihaela. He is waiting for you."

"Do you hear me?" Mihaela screams at Anne, losing her temper, her face suddenly mingled with terror.

Surprised by the tone of her soon-to-be-daughter-in-law, Anne departs from Mihaela's room, silently.

Mihaela touches her canine teeth with the tip of her tongue:

"Ah... I feel you...again! Wicked monsters!"

But as she opens her mouth and looks in the mirror, again, she sees nothing.

"What's going on? Are you playing with me?"

She closes her eyes, provoking her vampiric instincts to re-emerge: "If you are still there...come out, now, in the name of God, to uproot you forever!"

Anne enters Mihaela's room, unexpectedly.

Mihaela turns her head at once, piercing Anne with a diabolical glance. Anne gives a shout of fear.

"Why didn't you knock on the door?" Mihaela shouts at Anne, infuriated.

"Excuse me, my dear," Anne apologizes, with scared eyes.

"Please, leave me alone. I was in the middle of something..."

Anne exits the room rapidly, with her head bent down, like a mere servant.

Mihaela breathes deeply, trying to compose herself.

Looking again in the mirror with teary eyes, she notices that on her forehead her third eye opened so widely and began to shine, stronger than the beams of a star. She smiles, astounded.

As she smiles, her teeth appear enormously radiant, and whiter than snow!

Meantime, Anne plucks up her courage and knocks harder on Mihaela's door.

"Come on in, dear Anne," Mihaela finally consents, recognizing the quick sharp knocks of Anne.

Anne enters her room and speaks, this time sharp and authoritative:

"Mihaela, for the sake of God! The man really needs to see you! It is important."

"What is his name?"

"He can't speak... He is mute. But he wrote this for you..."

And Anne hands Mihaela an old piece of paper: *I need to see Miss Mihaela. Very important. Thank you.*

Living room.

A tall handsome young man with long black locks of hair and black mustache waits quietly for Mihaela. His eyes, deep black, are keen and bitter. He winks more than usual... He is fixed in his posture, bloodlessly and breathlessly. Around his neck, the young man wears a necklace with a small bottle of glass that holds a shining ray of sun.

As Mihaela slowly descends the marble stairs towards the foyer of the palace, with gracious moves of a prima ballerina, the young man startles, trembling with joy. He then bows down before Mihaela as before a most reverend queen, and kisses her white delicate hand.

Anne anlayzes closely the boy's elegant demeanor.

"How may I help you?" Mihaela asks him as the ray of sun from the small bottle brightens her face.

The young man hands Mihaela a sealed letter of a yellowish antique color.

"From whom?" Mihaela asks him, impatiently.

The young man groans, piercing Mihaela's eyes with a familiar glance, and pointing to the letter.

"Who are you?" Mihaela asks him, handing him paper and ink to write.

The young man starts writing with his left hand that trembles, degenerated:

"You will find in the letter, when I am gone."

"Alright, then you may leave now!" Mihaela concludes, as she reads the man's message.

The tall man bows elegantly, and makes his exit.

Mihaela takes her way upstairs, visibly affected. Anne, intrigued, stops her:

"Forgive me, my dear. I'm so happy that everything is settled now... Please, read the letter...."

Mihaela consents, still subdued by sadness.

"Oh... May I have a word with you, Mihaela? Just for a second," Anne asks her, easily intimidated.

"Later, Anne, I will see you later..." Mihaela mumbles, lost in her thoughts.

She then enters her princess-like room, and opens the letter.

Anne stares at Mihaela's shadow, wondering who the tall handsome man is. She is dying to know what the letter holds. Later on, she will ask Mihaela to disclose to her the secret of the young man's visit.

But no sooner does Anne finish her thought than Mihaela rushes out of her room, like a storm. With big tears bulging out of her eyes, and straggly hair, loosened in the air, she runs down the stairs, crying to Anne:

"Tell someone to stop him!"

"He's gone!" Anne says, excitingly.

"No, he isn't!"

Mihaela rushes out of the house, in bare feet, running madly towards the barn. She desperately seeks for a horse, as Rommy, her sweet, beloved and devoted one, has been no where to be found. After his strange vanishing at the cascade, Rommy didn't care to come back; only as a chimera that night when she was tramping in the forest after Mama.

Mounting Michael, Emil's horse, Mihaela starts galloping after the tall dark stranger. She feels heavy, so weak…feeble. She can hardly hold on to the reins and spur her horse to ride on.

Anne has her beady eye on Mihaela, through the kitchen window, leaning her long nose against her bitten nails.

Same day…at midnight.

Mihaela enters Emil's room, dressed up in a ravishing odalisque costume. Emil, faced down on his bed, is wrapped up in slumber. Mihaela tiptoes to Emil's record player, and puts on an old record. Sensual Turkish music starts playing. Emil wakes up, stretching up like a tiger. Mihaela takes off the golden veil that was hiding her face, and slowly, she starts waving her body like a Scheherazade. Emil raises his head, mesmerized.

"It's me, your love, Mihaela… I designed it especially for you… Do you like it?" Mihaela whispers, flaunting the veils of her skirt and walking seductively towards Emil's bed. She then jumps on top of him like a lioness, shimmying her shoulders and breasts to the beat of the Turkish song. With her wet full lips, she whispers into Emil's ear, and then she licks it beastly with her long lustful tongue, like that of a naughty little cat. Emil moans, tickled by the lecherous words murmured to his mind… Mihaela then jumps off the bed, onto the Persian carpet, inviting Emil to step in. Emil jumps after her, toddling on his hands and knees, and barking and growling like a hysterical dog. Catching Mihaela's skirt with his aroused teeth, he stretches it down until it tears apart.

"What is your wish for tonight, my love?" she asks Emil, tantalizingly…grasping him by the hair.

"To get inside of you ten thousand times, to feel you deeper and deeper," Emil groans.

"So be it! But there's a price you have to pay for this…You think you can handle it?"

"More than well..." Emil replies, at the feet of his mistress, licking her toes.

"Then let's begin..." Mihaela shouts out like a goddess, letting her largely veiled skirt drop to the ground, and her body exposed, naked to the hungry eye of Emil. Girdled only by the gypsy belt, she starts vibrating her hips and loins to the rhythm of the coins.

"Anything for you, my Gypsy Queen..." Emil salivates, watching Mihaela's dance.

"Alright, my Turkish prince, may your wish come true in the name of the Father, of the Son, and of the Holy Spirit..." Mihaela throws in a giggle, crossing Emil on his forehead with a cold bluish hand. She then slides her long tongue all over his chest, like a snake, sucking his breasts with aggressive envenomed lips, and shoving her nails deep in his flesh. Shaking with desire, Emil sneaks his hand between Mihaela's legs.

"I've been waiting for this...for so long..." Mihaela whispers with a dark voice while Emil bites her breasts that look like red apples, round and moist.

"I knew you were coming...I knew you couldn't resist me..." Emil speaks, engulfing more pleasure.

"Yes, I'm yours..." she whispers, while dancing her fingers around his neck...

A hand pushes the doorway into Emil's palace.

The hand then enters the marble foyer adorned with exotic flowers and statuettes of Greek Goddesses, and touches the meandering balustrade, caressing it up to the dormitories. The hand arrives before Mihaela's room, it touches the door handle, but then it stops. It lowers down to the floor, and picks up a letter on which is written with big embroidered letters: *Have a blessed night, my dear! Can't wait for tomorrow—the most beautiful day—the wedding day! Mihaela & Emil—my fulfilled dream! Sleep well, Anne.*

The hand shoves the letter under Mihaela's door. It then rises graciously and touches the hallway wall, fingering it until it reaches a blue door—the door of Emil.

Strange sounds interrupt the silence.

The hand slowly pushes the blue handle. Emil's door opens, lagging...The hand stops, suddenly wrinkled, and trembling like a leaf in winter. The hand rises up to the chin of a beautiful face. A sad smile dimples healthy cheeks. Tears trickle on it, like rain in the wind. On a wide forehead, an eye bleeds, like the eyes of a little lamb at slaughter.

Emil is making love with a woman...a woman with an athletic body and long fairy hair...just like the girl's who stands in the door.

Suddenly, Emil stops from his moaning, and raises his head up, disturbed by the noise that rattled his love act.

Mihaela, petrified in the form of a stork, with one leg tangled on top of the other, springs out hot bitter tears onto her bare cold feet. Emil's chamber gets suddenly flooded, his bed floating in fear, drenched in Mihaela's tears. A dark steam slowly rises off Emil's bed, which again, is covered up in blue blood and filthy lust. As she glances at Emil through wet disheveled lashes, Mihaela's lips get livid, her nostrils delate and run cold, unable to hold the storm of her soul. Poisoned by the glacial odor, emited by the bodies of the two lovers, Mihaela faints.

"Who is she?" Emil asks, looking astounded at the body lying on the floor.

The creature above him turns her head to Mihaela at once, flashing her being with a wicked glance. Mihaela rises up, like a broken puppet, suddenly awakened.

"Yes, it is she, herself...Gabriela..." Mihaela speaks within, her eyes fastened onto her sister.

Gabriela—red lusty-eyed, wintry faced, dark browed, and girded with a pair of sharp canine teeth, sneeres at the scared look of her sister. She then shoots Mihaela with a laser-like look, hurling her against the back wall.

Mihaela plucks up her courage and leaps onto her ballerina feet, towards the bed of Emil, gracefully sweeping the floor. She then falls onto her belly pot, pushes her head to her chest, and rolls under Emil's bed.

Gabriela busts out laughing, expelling the red blood off her face.

"Hello, sister, so good to see you... Now that we finally meet again, come out for a little talk!"

Mihaela gathers her wits, clenches her fists, hunches her back, and rolls the bed upside down. She lands on top, Gabriela and Emil hurled down, laughing and fretting behind. But in a flash, Gabriela flips the bed right up and smashes Mihaela onto her back. Loud cracks can be heard on and on, the bed being tossed like an omlette in a frying pan. The twins take the lead, back and forth, trying to crash each other, like two wrestlers in a boxing ring, until Emil, in ecstasy, screams out like a mad prince:

"Fantastic, girls! I feel like on a set in Hollywood! Lights, Camera, Action! Please, don't stop!"

But Mihaela and Gabriela abruptly stop, staring at the deranged and idiotically morphed Emil, who laughs himself into convulsion.

Emil stares back at the two girls, myopically, suddenly caught up by hiccup:

"Who is she? And who are you? I'm confused..." he hiccups again.

Mihaela, paler than ever, looks down at her body that has turned into a beast, with hairy arms and bloodied veins, overly swollen, almost exploding out of her flesh. She bursts into tears, hiding her hairy arms behind.

Gabriela smiles haughtily, standing cool on her feet, feeling good in her teeth. Then flapping her black tail with pride, Gabriela clarifies:

"I'd better leave the two of you alone. I guess you have a lot to talk about... Tomorrow is the wedding day..."

And, in a twinkling of an eye, Gabriela makes a triple axel in the air, and lands on the marble balcony of Emil's room. She then opens her arms largely to the woods, and fades in the darkness.

Gabriela: *I know that I overreacted...but it was a real pleasure to see Emil's face...so helpless, so awkward... I fell in love with him on the spot. Poor baby... I hope I cured my sister forever!*

Mihaela: My heart is broken. Gabriela looked like a rat. And Emil...like a pig in mud...

Gabriela: I now realize how amazing is to have a twin sister. How entertaining your life becomes! The way that Emil looked at us, and couldn't tell us apart... I loved it! I pity the ones born without a twin...

Mihaela: I hate my twin. She truly is my wicked clone who always hinders my dream... Like an evil conscience, she lurks in the dark, waiting to jump and devour my heart. But what's a forest without weeds? How could I see the stars without the night? Perhaps everyone has a twin...good or evil... Just that some of us were born with one, and others are living to find it, their twin-soul... Maybe I was born to change the evil into good... Maybe that's my purpose in this world...

Gabriela: How poetic, Mihaela. Impressive, tear jerking! You are unchanged... I remember when you were little...how you were watching the leaves fall from the trees...standing there, always dreaming... I told you: Run. Act. Jump. Stop dreaming. Or else, you'll be taken with your dream, and dreamers end up bad...

Mihaela: I'm trying to find the meaning of life...and dreams are part of it... You are trying to mimic my life, and ruin it. My dream is to change you.

Gabriela: That's how you made me... I'm your character...

Mihaela: No, you're not just my character... Wish you were only in my manuscript. You're living in flesh and blood. I hear your scorns. I see your little mouth, hissing non-stop. I know you. You hurt me enough. Please, change for the good of us.

Gabriela: Why? What is the good of it without the evil?

Mihaela sits, like a stone, on the edge of Emil's bed, with her eyes fixed on her poor fiancé. The moon tattoos his face. Emil battles its rays, fretting in place.

"He's not the one..." Mihaela murmurs within. "He is no longer the one I fell for—poetic, royal, vigilant... He changed a lot this summer. Where did my sweet Emil go? Oh God, I wish I could bring him back to whom he was..."

Silence.

"But she already brought him to a hellish state! Too late to save your fiancé!" she hears a quick voice in her head.

"No, it's not possible! If she can turn life into death, I can turn death into life!" Mihaela impales her dark thought with immovable faith. She then draws close to Emil's ear:

"Emil darling, you'll live. Hear my poem. May it go to your heart, and heal the dark into light, your death into life."

And Mihaela kisses Emil on his cold lips, and then whispers to him:

"There is not much in the netherworld.
Stay here with me and sing our love song.
Breathe my tears that may clean your soul
Come back to us, it's all my fault...
Take these tears of mine, gain your sound mind.
There's nothing like love, don't choose lust that's a black
dove.
Choose me, choose white and tomorrow I shall be your
bride."

Mihaela's sweet tears overflow Emil's face and eyes. Like some young rivers, they dig into his cheeks, making path among the veins of his neck, and then swimming into his heart.

She then takes Emil in her arms, and like a mother-gypsy, she swings him into her lap:

"Hush, baby...hush! You are going to live... We won't let her win!"

"What are you talking about?" Emil asks Mihaela, with his bleeding mouth. "I thought it would never finish... We made it again and again and again... And then you bit me, again, again and again..." he raves louder and louder, with his eyes lost into another world.

Mihaela takes off her wet dress, soaked with her tears. She then starts cleaning Emil's body, painting her white dress in red.

"You're gonna be fine, my love... Tomorrow, it's the big wedding... You have to live...for me...for us. Stay strong."

"What are you talking about?" Emil asks her, aggressively.

His eyes glitter with evil. He tries to rise up, but only to fall again on the bloodied pillows, panting heavier and heavier.

Mihaela looks at him, terrified. She knows that weak glance, it is so familiar to her... Emil looks just like Gabriela's victims, back then, years ago, when she was turning them into helpless marionettes—breathless, bloodless...lost between the living and the dead... Emil, heavily bleeding and foaming, tries to speak up:

"Who...who was she? Who...are you?"

Mihaela opens up the windows of the terrace and cries out:

"Now come back and do it! What are you waiting for? All the way to the end!"

Anne wakes up, sweating and tossing in bed: "Was it a nightmare?"

No sooner does Mihaela finish her call to her sister, than a loud slap in the back tears Mihaela's heart out. She turns around and sees what she was fearing to ever see again—Gabriela, with her long black tail coiled around Emil's neck, and Emil, with his face contracted and his veins turned black, laughing his tongue out. Gabriela's arms, steeled and ended in sharp claws, look more savage than ever; Emil's arms are broken, and straggling like plaster-toys. Gabriela's tongue, hissing like a predator-snake, devours its prey; Emil's tongue is hanging out like the one of a crippled dog; his eyes are red and bulging out of his head!

Mihaela covers her mouth with her marble white hand on which the engagement ring still shines. Gabriela speaks with a dark voice:

"Mission completed, Sis! All the way to the end!"

Opening her third eye, and letting it beam like a fire ball, Mihaela cleaves the wall behind Gabriela. Taken by surprise, Gabriela loses her balance, and falls over the collapsed pieces.

"What's the matter, Sis? I did it for you!" Gabriela defends herself. "He took your Mommy Doll away, didn't he? He lied to you! He cheated on you like a pig! He would have made you suffer! He already did! I saved you!"

Mihaela's fangs pop out; her eyes spit out volcanic heat; her brows grow long and shaggy in just a beat. Her red lips widen and turn blue, pursing up into a Romanian curse. Her arms and legs fill up with thorny hair; her hands and feet grow strong claws of a bear. Mihaela jumps at Gabriela's neck, twisting it with all her strength, and sinking her sharp nails and angry teeth into Gabriela's cold flesh. But Gabriela's skin is so strong that it tears apart Mihaela's risen claws; jets of blue blood gush out of them, and Mihaela shrinks in pain. Moreover, her curse, uttered louder than the shout of a crow against Gabriela's wicked soul, cannot penetrate Gabriela, and ricochets back to Mihaela's soul. Gabriela laughs, utterly enjoying Mihaela's attack:

"I missed this! I missed you!"

"Get out of my life! You took my mother away, you killed Emanuel, you killed my husband! Go back to your époque or I shall eat your heart out!"

"You are my precious sister! How could I ever leave you alone? I love you! I couldn't let this man harm you any longer! He wanted to have you before the wedding day! Wasn't that horrible, disgusting?" Gabriela pierces Mihaela with a sweet dollish look, like when they were 15, and having fun in their escapades. "When you suffer, I suffer, and I feel it miles away... I had to come here, pell-mell, to break his neck!"

"Please, go away! I don't want to deal with Satan! Don't try to change me!" Mihaela steps back, shivering with evil, struggling to turn back into her true self.

Without saying more, Gabriela jumps out of the window and mounts Rommy, the horse whom she stole from Mihaela.

Devastated and incapable to turning back to her human body, Mihaela kneels before the statue of St. Michael, that she herself placed in Emil's room, to guard him from the evil's dooms. Touching the sharp pointed spear of St. Michael, her body begins to take human proportions, her skin to clear, her eye to lighten... She cries out:

"Forgive me, Father! I've been deceived, taken by her evil schemes! But I need to stop this massacre! I need to kill the wicked so that it will not spawn more victims! In your name, I will impale the evil, and strenghten the little!"

And then, reaching into her old dowry chest with Transylvanian ornaments, Mihaela takes out a tunic and a pair of buffalo-leather pants that she received from Charles as a wedding gift. Charles bought them from Braşov, from Grid's inn, her beloved father's place, along with a pair of horse hair-sewn leather boots.

Mihaela puts them on, and fastens around the tunic a wide leather belt called chimir, also brought from Grid's inn.

The windows of Emil's chamber suddenly open and rattle, a strong whistling wind raising the curtains up to the ceilings.

Ignoring the fear, Mihaela pierces with a strong, panther-like look the mirror, and gathers her hair into a ponytail. She then crosses her long mane into a braid, and thrusts into it a red rose with big sharp thorns—a thick stem of a rose that she picked earlier from Anne's garden. She smiles. Now she can use her hair as a sure weapon against her enemy. Nature has taught her that it has greater weapons than the human beings have ever manufactured. It provides one with all its blessings: from food and remedies to weapons, from Sun and refuges, to celebrations. One only needs to grab them with opened arms.

She came to believe, more and more, that Nature is God Himself... That in every flower, and in every tree, there is an eye of God who watches upon her, guiding her feet to walk lightly over the wind... Even the obstacles have been scattered on her way...to strenghten her faith...

"Yes. The bigger the battle, the bigger the destiny," she suddenly hears a voice within, penetrating and sharp as a sword.

The wind blows stronger. Thunderbolts shake up the sky. Mihaela rushes to close up the windows. Shaking off the anger and thoughts that come and go, like shadows of the night, she snatches the spear from St. Michael's statue, and walks her way out of Emil's palace. She hears, again, the same voice:

"The one who strikes with the sword, will be stricken by it! Put down the sword!"

She quickly lets the spear down, unconsciously, and the spear suddenly turns into a cross. She picks it up, and runs back into the house. She steps into her chamber, her feet running like fireflies, by themselves.

She grabs Magia's white bag with sap from the tree of God, and sprinkles three seeds of sap in her left palm. She then, indistinctively, whispers a prayer through the Holy Spirit, rubbing the seeds in her palms, three times. Suddenly, a purifying energy penetrates her being like a divine water of love, cleansing her from the crown of her mind to her toes.

Feeling beyond this world, floating above herself, she feels that she has caught God's hand, entering a new land... All the colors of nature burst with brightness; all the trees bloom with divine flowers and fruits, ripen and round. Mihaela's skin brusquely falls down, and another skin, soft and white as a dove, wraps around herself.

Hand in hand with Him, like a black panther that has suddenly morphed into a Snowbride, she walks through the strong wind that ceases at once at her soft touch.

She enters the barn. Gabriela is already far away. Now Mihaela knows that her weapons are much more powerful than Gabriela's. The battle belongs to God.

Mihaela enters the barn.

Only Michael, Emil's horse, is awake, but restless and fretting in place. And he looks so strange—unhealthy and feeble, weak and disheveled, mourning as a widower after his lost master: "Emil, Emil..."

Nevertheless, as soon as he sees Mihaela, Michael starts shaking his flimsy tail with excitement.

"Come on, little one, show me your power!" Mihaela says, touching him with tenderness. She then sprinkles some sap from the tree of God over his head, and leans her forehead against his forehead, uttering with faith:

"My dear horse! Inside of you, there is a strong, powerful horse, much stronger than any other horse! Show me that! In the name of Love, show the world what you are really made of!"

In a flash, Mihaela's third eye opens wide, and the eyes of Michael flicker golden lights; the feeble Michael neighs, shakes up three times, and his hide drops dead, to the ground. Over his bones, a strong shining skin takes hold, more beautiful than that of any other living horse. His mane and his tail are so soft and long, like a veil of heavenly nymphs; his body so lucent and muscled, like a warrior-horse. Mihaela touches his new skin, mesmerized by the new vision.

She then mounts her fantastic Michael, and spurs him to gallop. Suddenly, she loses the reins from her hands, as the power within her controls the ride. From Michael's forehead, a cross springs forth, like Rommy's cross when Mihaela left Transylvania with Papa Grid.

Mihaela smiles, whispering words of strength:

"*Ride with Me*, my dear horse! Ride with me to turn the evil into good and the barren seeds into abundant fruits! Ride with me to find my wicked clone and put an end to her unfair soul!"

RIDE WITH ME (Chorus)

The horse flies like an arrow among the wildly branched forest lightened by falling stars.

Having arrived in the middle of the woods, among some frightening nodulous trees with eyes of sphinx, Mihaela orders her horse to stop. Michael slows down from his flight, his vigurous hoofs reaching the wet grass in a twinkling of an eye. The trees open their ears and eyes.

Mihaela dismounts her horse and stabs the earth with her spear-cross:

"Come out! What are you waiting for? I know you've been haunting to get me for years! Now, this is your chance... I'm right here! Your prey!"

Silence.

With big and forceful eyes, Mihaela awaits for Gabriela to make her appearance. The trees, murmuring and waving their leaves, are waiting for her too. But minutes that feel like hours pass, and Gabriela doesn't show up.

Mihaela hops onto her horse, eager to run back to Emil's palace. But just then, with laser-like leaps, Gabriela cuts off the forest, pivoting her neck in the wind. She then riots around Mihaela, and hurls her being inside Mihaela's body, with sounds of a beast. Mihaela falls, rifted by the evil force.

Michael-horse, who has seen the wicked clone's mischievous inhabit, neighs and rears, shouting out with fire:

"Poor mistress of mine, to give a follow to your guise!
Come out, you dragon-sister, or else I'll fly you off,
I'll throw a leg into your phony scoff, so better get lost!
From my hoof, I swear it...you shall find no escape,
Your wickedness shall see herself in her own grave.
So come out, in the name of the good Lord
I order you with in the name of my cross."

Barely does the horse finish his words when Gabriela pops out of Mihaela with dragon-like shrieks, painted with blood on her cheeks. With horns of fire, Gabriela pierces the ground deep down...and then springs out as a mountain of viscous mud, up to the clouds!

Freed from Gabriela's clutch, Mihaela collapses onto the wet grass, panting and sweaty as the mud.

The cool drops of nature awaken her senses. She grabs the wooden cross of Saint Michael with her right hand, and cries out to the sky, with weakened strength:

"God, she is my sister! She killed my mother, my boyfriends and my husband, shall I kill her? Is this right? Help me, Lord, to kill her night, and give birth to her light!"

Gabriela laughs, queenly, behind Mihaela, trying to snatch the cross from her hand.

Unable to take it, Gabriela mounts Rommy-horse and orders Mihaela, with a superior tone:

"Follow me..."

Michael-horse raises his mistress slowly with his soft hoofs, begging Mihaela with the eyes of a sweet friend:

"Don't follow her... She is your wicked clone."

"I shall! I need to," Mihaela replies to her horse, firmly.

"Don't follow her, my mistress... Let me ride you to a safe place..." Michael insists.

"After her!" Mihaela orders Michael-horse, mounting him with force.

Rommy takes off from the feet of the ground to the clouds of the sky.

Michael-horse, with tears in his eyes, and foreseeing a bad turn for his young mistress, follows Rommy, precociously. Mihaela watches Rommy's thorny blue back with regret: "What happened to my old horse?"

When Rommy belonged to Mihaela, he was sweet and white; but Gabriela gave him a strong bite, and subdued him to her night. Two deep holes in his neck, turned Rommy's white skin into a dark blue hide, his spine into dinosaur's bulging plates and spikes, his tender eyes into red evil eyes, and his happy tail into a dirty broom that sweeps off Mihaela's smile.

Thousands of fowl follow their flight between the blue sky and the blue waters of the ground.

As a forest of steel and glass unveils below them, with electric eyes, Rommy slows down.

Times Square.

Gabriela commands Rommy-horse to stop. The strong light of the giant advertisements blind Rommy's eyes. A flashback strikes his mind, shuddering his hide. Suddenly, Rommy remembers his first arrival with Mihaela at the *Palace Theatre*, in Times Square. He shakes and neighs, jumping on his hind legs. He turns to Mihaela, trying to catch her eyes, to implore her forgiveness, shaking his tail with fright. But Gabriela senses the excitement of Rommy, and runs her sharp nails into his hide. Rommy whines, and then shakes furiously, back to his wicked senses.

Meantime, Michael-horse spins with his mistress in midair.–He had lost track of Gabriela and her horse, bewildered by the noise.

Trying to find some space to land through the crowded Times Square, Michael descends, at last, onto one of the colorful and glittering streets, to the cheers and shouts of hysterical kids. Making way through the river of people who have been watching and gazing at his fabulous flight and at his beautiful mistress' sight, Michael-horse finally arrives in front of the *Palace Theatre*, which bursts with performers and people of all kinds.

With her spear-cross in hand, Mihaela can barely dismount, as the noisy streetwalkers jostle against her horse.

Finally, with her feet on the ground, Mihaela caresses Michael-horse on his forehead, and whispers into his ear:

"Wait for me right here. Sit nice and tight, alright?"

Michael-horse nickers, and then kneels at the feet of his mistress.

The enthusiastic audience bursts into an avalanche of applause. People from all around the world, who came to New York like to the New Tower of Babel—children, parents and grandparents, tall or short, wheel-chaired, paired or impaired—speak the same language, bearing down on Mihaela, and shouting for pictures and autographs.

Followed by the aggressive kids, Mihaela is taped and shot with ultra-sophisticated cell phones and other super-flashing electronics... She tries to set forth, but her legs tangle between the hysterical children, who are crazed to touch her spear-cross. Nevertheless, Mihaela's eyes don't stop searching for Gabriela.

A policeman approaches Mihaela, shyly:

"I'm sorry... We just wanted to know... Are you performing tonight? My wife and I are big fans..."

Mihaela, bewildered, tells them nicely that there is a mistake.

The policeman and his wife insist:

"No, we saw you playing in *Dracula's Daughters*... Surely, it is you..."

Mihaela explains to them again that she is not playing any daughter of Dracula tonight or any other night...

"My name is Mihaela," she tries to justify.

"Yes, Mihaela, Mihaela from Transylvania," the policeman replies. "We knew it was you..."

Overwhelmed by the ardent fans, Mihaela finally makes her way inside the *Palace Theatre*. She breathes, relieved.

Huge posters with Gabriela's figure dominate the hall. Her big, incriminating eyes, her ageless bold face, intimidate not only Mihaela, but thousands of fans who are waiting in line for tickets, masked and made up just like Gabriela... Underneath the poster, with big capital letters, is written:

Mihaela
From Transylvania to New York
starring in
DRACULA'S DAUGHTERS
A must suck musical!

"Auguri, Miss Mihaela! Molti auguri! Sei tanto bella in *Dracula's Daughters*! Sono felice per te, Miss Mihaela! Sono tanto felice!..." the doorman says with mad enthusiasm.

While Mihaela listens, aghast, to the same old doorman, who welcomed her at the *Palace Theatre* the first time, Gabriela walks past her with cold, anesthetic eyes. She flashes at her a wicked red light, like a fiery dart from Hell, that arrows her chest.

Mihaela's third eye catches the evil eye of Gabriela. In the wink of an eye, Mihaela is thrown back to her father, back to Transylvania of 1502.

Mihaela lands in front of her childhood home,

through a big cloud of smoke. Michael drops near her too, shiny and proud, his cross still shining tall on his forehead.

Mihaela, fallen to the ground, is covered in dust; her head is hanging dizzy from her flight, her arms loose and fouled with mud. Michael-horse offers his hoof to his mistress, and raises her up.

Mihaela shakes herself three times, and the dirt hurls off her skin as quick as a wink.

Seeing her Papa's house again, with fresh gleaming eyes, Mihaela bursts into tears.

She cheerfully opens her childhood's gate, but the thorns of roses hastily pierce her little hand.

"Ouch! I told Papa that he should plant only Queen of the Night flowers..." Mihaela whines.

Yet, in a flash, with his loving tongue, Michael-horse licks her hand and Mihaela's wound heals on the spot.

Mihaela steps on the fresh grass of Papa's garden, and Michael follows her, like a loyal servant.

Her heart pounds; her arms shake.

"Is Papa well? What is he going to say? He must be mad at me for leaving him alone for so long..." she thinks, tightly squeezing the spear-cross in her hand. "It is so funny! I'm actually wearing the costume from Papa's inn that Charles gave to me as a wedding gift..."

As they walk along the flowery path that leads to her house, Mihaela notices, behind the well of the garden, a huge blue tree with two giant branches...like two enormous fangs...shadowing her father's heavenly place.

"No, my fangs could not have given birth to this perky tree!" Mihaela fights an evil thought, recalling her sharp fangs, stained with blue blood, that she had buried at 14 years old...behind the well.

Shaking the fearful memories from her head, Mihaela turns the cold shoulder to the blue tree, and walks boldly towards the door of Papa's house.

She knocks shyly.

No reply.

"Papa? Papa, it's me, Mihaela!"

She slowly pushes the handle.

As she steps in, the view strikes her heart, reviving her eyes. The smell of Papa's freshly made bread fills her potbelly, the old furniture and icon of the Virgin Mary soothes her heart, wiping away all of her fright.

Everything looks just as she had left it years ago: the rosewood wardrobe is to the right; the double stove, that burns with flames of Holy Ghost, to the left; the oak table, covered by Mama's handmade cloth, is in the middle of the chamber, like a grandmother, steadfast in faith; the three chairs, sculpted by Papa, are around the table, like some guardian angels; her parents' sweet bed, with embroidered sheets and fluffy pillows, sticking out feathers of a loving duck, touches the southern wall; the massive floor of wood, built in by Papa Grid's hard-working hands, is shining, newly washed; the long, flowery wooden rack, with collorfully painted clay plates, adorns the chamber like midnight watchers. On the Eastern wall, above the chest with medallions of Transylvanian rulers, a tall candle burns steadily inside the small altar with the the miraculous icon of the Virgin Mary—the icon that shed tears the night Violeta died. From that night on, Grid knew that Violeta rests in God's hands and that he could full-heartedly take care of Mihaela, his blessed daughter. Violeta was to guard his moves from up there, and lead him to raise their daughter with love and trust.

As she looks closely through the room, Mihaela sees Mommy Doll. Yes, Mommy Doll…lying on the embroidered sheets of the bed, behind the little cradle where Papa Grid used to swing her sleep.

Mihaela cannot believe where Mommy Doll has been hiding!

"How could this be? Mommy Doll traveled in time, all by herself? This cannot be true!"

Pushing her questions out of her heart, Mihaela gives free run to her body. In an avalanche of joy, she leaps towards Mommy Doll, and hugs her with the love of the most yearning daughter.

"Oh, how I missed you, Mama!"

In the kitchen, the teapot bubbles up, whistling like a train.

Grid enters the house with his apron filled with apples and pears.

"Good morning, my dear…"

Mihaela turns her head and, with Mommy Doll in hand, she jumps to embrace her father. She hugs and kisses him with mad love, as hungry tears of joy eat her face:

"Papa, I'm so happy! You look so well and healthy! I missed you so much!"

Grid looks at his daughter, utterly surprised. He frowns.

"I made you poached eggs, my dear! Sit down!"

"Thank you, Papa!"

Mihaela takes a seat, perplexed by her father's unenthusiastic welcome back!

"I'm sorry that I have left you here, all alone…and for so long, Papa! Forgive me…" Mihaela murmurs with teary eyes.

"What are you talking about?" Grid asks her, tearing the hot bread apart.

"I was away…in New York City and…"

"My dear, you must have had a bad dream… Please, stop this! And, please take off that tunic and leather trousers. Who gave you permission to put them on? I just finished trimming them off."

"Oh, I'm sorry, Daddy... I just..."

"What has gotten into you this morning? You seem strange, my dear."

Mihaela hesitates to further speak. She feels that something strange is happening.

"Good morning, Papa!" Gabriela says, suddenly yawning behind Mihaela. Dressed in Mihaela's nightdress sown by Mama, Gabriela walks leisurely, flipping her long hair behind.

"What is she doing here?" Mihaela asks her Papa, perplexed.

Grid looks puzzled at the two young girls. He first takes a close look at Gabriela, who now looks more like the old Mihaela—young, bright, and calm—and suspects Mihaela, who now looks older, sober, and manly dressed—to be the wicked and perfidious Gabriela.

"Papa, what did she do to you? Please, tell her to leave," Mihaela begs Papa Grid, looking at the flawless complexion of Gabriela and the grin on her face.

"*I am* Mihaela!" Gabriela breaks in. "This time you won't play with my father... Get out of my house!"

"How dare you? How dare you speak like that? Papa, say something!" Mihaela pleads with her father as hot tears fill her eyes.

"Stop it girls!" Grid speaks, irritated.

Gabriela covers her eyes with her palms, making sounds of sobbing, and whining. Then, with perfidious love, she kneels at the feet of Grid, and speaks in a honeyed warm voice:

"Daddy, I am the true one, please, believe me... Don't let her stay here any more! She makes me feel wicked, and blue..."

Mihaela grasps Gabriela's arm. But in return, Gabriela catches Mihaela's hand with such power, that Mihaela's body turns purple and shudders with evil desire. Gabriela's muscles are hard as iron, cold and electrifying.

"Papa, I want to go back to my room! Look, Mommy Doll cries..." Gabriela whines with sweet dissimulative eyes.

"Go back to your father Vlad, you treacherous sister in disguise!" Mihaela cries out at Gabriela with anger.

But Gabriela continues to make faces, affected. She then unbuttons her nighty dress, unveiling to Papa Grid the mole from her left breast.

"Look, father! I have the mole!... It's me, Mihaela!"

"How did she get my mole?" Mihaela wonders, her soul vexed and troubled.

"I'm also wearing Saint Michael's pendant that Papa gave to me...to protect me from evil liars..." Gabriela turns her eyes to her sister. "Please, now go! You cannot fool my father anymore!" she adds, with innocence.

Grid looks at Mihaela with intimidating eyes:

"Please, leave our house! Leave my daughter and my peace alone!"

"Papa, it's me, Mihaela! What did she do to you? I love you!" Mihaela bursts into a well of tears.

And, in a rush of dispair, Mihaela takes off her tunic, willing to show to her father the true mole on her left breast. But her mole is gone... Nor does she have the little chain with the St. Michael's pendant around her neck anymore, where she knew it was...

Grid shows Mihaela the door.

Overwhelmed with grief, Mihaela takes her spear-cross in hand, and leaves the house at a funeral pace. Looking back at her father, she speaks to herself:

"That tree... That tree must have changed my dad... It is all my fault..."

As soon as she steps on the fresh grass of the garden, her eyes fall on the perky fanged tree. Assuredly, she heads towards its monstrous branches, flashing with fire into the wicked creature that has shattered the good relationship with her father. But its cold branches richochet the fire back into Mihaela's eyes. Nevertheless, with an abrupt move of her hand, like a warrior princess, Mihaela thrusts her spear-cross inside the wild wicked branches, stabing them on and on, with battle shouts and angry assaults.

Suddenly, dozens of small violet apples and sharp thorns like spikes of fire, pop up on each branch of the fanged tree, and then jets of blue blood spring out of the apples, splashing her face, and spurting her body like an artesian well of blue mud.

The grass withers at once, poisoned by the blue sap that trickles down from the apples.

Seeing that the tree does not shutter its evil branches at all, and that her efforts are toiling in vain, Mihaela jabs her spear-cross into the tree's enormous blackish roots, stinging them fiercely, in cold blood.

"Be you plucked up by the root, and never again bear fruit!" she shouts, increasingly enflamed.

Michael, Mihaela's waggish horse, who has been watching his mistress' battle, neighs with fabulous force, horning in the tree with the cross from his forehead, too. But the fanged tree does not move a bit. It stands proud and fixed.

Mihaela then jumps onto Michael's back and together, with shouts of triumph, they hurl over the fanged tree. But they are cast violently to the ground, sinking foolishly into the mud.

Wounded and tired, Mihaela shouts to the sky:

"Why God? What have I done wrong? Give me a reply!"

"Crush the evil with love..." she hears a voice in her heart.

"Love? But how? How am I gonna crush the evil tree with love?"

As she rises to her feet and frets in place, a song comes to her head— an old song that Papa Grid taught her once, when she was battling in the garden to pluck up some weeds from near a flower. She starts to sing:

"I am weak and I did wrong,
  I know nothing, but to sing this song:
  When I'm still and let You work,
  With Your mighty sword, Oh Lord,
  You strike all my enemies
  And put them each under my feet."

Suddenly, the ground boils and toils, ugly insects come out from the soil, creeping and biting the roots of the fanged-tree. The tree shakes with monstrous-groans; huge blue flames, threatening and ugly, spring out from its roots. In the ugly blue flames, Mihaela can suddenly see Emanuel's face, with smiling eyes, soothing her sight.

A huge jet of water abruptly gushes from the well of Papa's garden and, rising up to the sky, it curves into multicolored layers, painting on a dazzling rainbow. The figure of David, the poet whom she first loved, takes shape on the spectrum. Then, the stream of water returns to the ground, swallowing the fiery flames, and overthrowing the fanged tree that falls dead to the mud.

Michael jumps happily on his hind legs, like a winning colt.

Mihaela jumps on her deer-like legs too, looking astounded at the uprooted fanged-tree, now plucked out from her father's garden.

However, barely do they jump with cheeriness when an indigo Queen of the Night flower, with double stem, beautiful and lofty as a flower from Heaven, springs out in the place of the fanged tree. Its first stem, holding a strikingly beautiful indigo flower, rises taller than the house, straight and bright, and the second one—an ivy thorny stem with indigo petals and phosphorescent stamens—crawls down and coils around the well and the bucket.

Amazed, Mihaela rushes to the flower and embraces the straight stem with childlike desire.

Michael neighs with happiness, but then, as the sharp thorns of the ivy flower prick him, he strikes out hatefully with his right hoof.

"Let them be, my dear horse... Let them grow together, and then, Papa will cut its thorns off..." Mihaela says, patting her wounded horse on his hoof. She then whispers to Michael-horse with remorse:

"You were right, my sweet horse, I shouldn't have followed my sister...my wicked clone..."

"No worries, we have learned a good lesson today!" Michael horse replies with a snorting voice to his mistress.

"I love you!" Gabriela shouts from behind, holding Mommy Doll in hand. "I think you forgot to take her!"

Mihaela looks perplexed at Gabriela and then at Mommy Doll, shaken by Gabriela's impudence, and mad at herself for forgetting again to take along Mommy Doll. In her grief and anger, she completely overlooked the most precious thing of her soul.

"I did it for you, sister..." Gabriela pleads, with a sisterly smile. You were all the time away from Papa Grid. He had to have someone around... Yesterday, he did not feel quite well... I took good care of him. I told him that I'm you, and it made him good... Anyway, he's old, and he can't tell us apart...anymore... He, he, he..." Gabriela gives a sweet laugh.

"You think that you can take Papa away from me too?" And then, fired-up and trembling with rage, she tries to snatch Mommy Doll from Gabriela's strong hand. But Gabriela wouldn't let her go.

"Come away with me!" Gabriela tells Mihaela, after which she starts running like when they were little, waving Mommy Doll in hand and hiding behind the walnut tree.

"I won't fall into the same trap! I won't follow you!" Mihaela shouts back at her sister.

"Please, sis, let's have fun!" Gabriela speaks up.

"How dare you further speak to me when you lied in my own house? Go back to your father and leave me and my dad alone!"

"But Vlad is your real father!"

"You can say anything you want! But God already chose my father!"

"Grid lied to you! Grid is not your real father! Vlad told me the truth!"

"The truth? What does Vlad know about truth?"

"The truth is that you and me are twin sisters. And we have the same father. It would be impossible to have different fathers, don't you think? Come with me to your dear father! He is waiting for you!"

"I already have a father...better said, two! I was born of God, and Grid is my chosen father in this world!"

"Come on, keep your feet on the ground. Stop dreaming and speaking like foolish philosophers. Vlad is your godly father! How can you be so ungrateful to the one who gave you immortal life, and offer your love to God who gives you sufferings and cries?"

"My dear, how can the lie appreciate the truth or even see its roots? The lie can only lie, but truth speaks up in me and tells you this: Depart from me, you wicked sis...don't need your lies!"

"Remember our fun nights and sisterly vow: no human kind in our lives? Why do you grab the mortal love and hugs and turn away from my immortal hug? This is a sin, my sis! We ought to love our own blood!" Gabriela speaks fervently to her sister.

"You ask me how could I choose the sin to love, and how can I rebuke hatred and murdering innocent lives? How can I follow in the Light and not feed with your bloody nights? Oh, how wise of me to see the truth inside your night and follow up the heights!"

"All I know is that I love you... This is sisterhood love, the most pure love of all..."

"If you do love me, pure sister, why do you show the fruits of a murderess? Why do you act with hatred but utter words of love? If I am to stay nearby you, I fear that a beast might re-emerge in me—and I want to forget and spread love in this age!"

"I am not a beast; neither are my words...sweet sis."

"But what about your deeds? Is it your words that I should trust, or your deceiving heart, sealed with Vlad's veil of lust?"

"I do not know details... I know one fact: I do love you, and you have tortured me... It's true! Your torture made me kill your men," Gabriela whines.

"If this is the way you love me, find yourself another sis! I did not torture you, in me your accusation bounces back at your own deed!"

"Please, stop yielding to those men. Be strong and free!" Gabriela pops in. "Papa Vlad invites you to your real home to drink and eat his foods with love!"

"It's not that food the food that I search for, but love and truth!"

"Then take me with you in the world! Teach me the truth that you hold!" Gabriela speaks up.

"Why, so that you teach me to lie?"

"Give me a chance to be your sis!"

"I gave you...five!" Mihaela speaks. "How can I longer trust your lies?"

"Please, give me six! I'll come with you wherever you may go... I want to be with you and see the world! And I will show you how to act and have all the riches that you want! But please, come see my father first!" Gabriela persists. "He'll give us good advice! He sacrificed. especially for you. white doves in scented bloodied wine...just as you like it!"

"Just as I like it? Better tell Vlad to sacrifice his pride and teach you about life. Tell him to bring my Mama back to me, Emanuel, my fiancé Emil...and all the preys he took to grave. And then, throw himself and his dead wicked castle inside the burning Hell!"

"Vlad loves you. It is written in the Bible: *Honor your father and your mother and you shall live well and long.*"

"Whose bible? Is this a father who honors his daughter with her Mama's slaughter? Aren't you fed up with his lying ways in which he's using you, blind maid?"

"He's not a murderer, sweet sister! You have to clear your mind of poisoned words from aunts and jealous neighbors."

"He first used you to slaughter our Mama! Dissimulative words about sorcerous flower—birth-venom-seed Vlad planted into our mother's womb so that he'd cast her life inside a freezing tomb! Mother died when you were born! You pierced her womb with your sharp fangs and torn her flesh with your devilish horns! Vlad conceived you infernal and immortal, to satisfy his whims through a blind daughter!"

"Liar! He is a saint, my father! He loves us. If it wasn't for him, we wouldn't have existed, now living and talking like sisters! Besides, Vlad loves me enormously and worships me; he has put onto my head the crown of immortality and riches! I reign, sister! And now, to speak to you the truth, a little trivial but earnestly: I'm not a vagina for impotent mortals from your foolish dream! Come to Papa, save your body from those filthy men!"

"Sweet sister, I would come, but our poor brother Vlady told me why I should not step again into that castle! The Icy Morgue of Brides, the worshiping of Lucifer and his evil louts, that icicle statue that imitates my features, the portraits of his young victims, and their sleeping wives who lie on stony beds of ice... Now I know it all! You need not to bother to hide the truth from me anymore..."

"Vlady? What brother? He cannot hear, he cannot talk!" Gabriela ripostes.

"Yes, he cannot. You say the truth. But he can write. He brought to me this letter, this letter that discloses how "sisterly" and "fatherly" you kept him in your caves, in a cold, damp, and dull cell, so that he turned dumb, deaf, and inept. Who wouldn't go mad and sick in such a living hell? You and Vlad have fed yourselves on Vlady since he was little; you sucked him of his human blood and left him without a loaf of bread and meat of love! He wrote to me the way that Vlad had stolen him from our Mama when he was just one month old! Vlad set Violeta's house on fire and made Mama think that her little boy had died, gulped by those wicked flames that swallowed their life! Your father Vlad made Mama sick and lose her mind!"

"Imposter! That little stupid monster!" Gabriela screams, gnashing her teeth.

"The truth is this: Papa Grid is Vlady's real father, and you—who sucks his blood—you are his dear sister! Poor dumb Vlady, he is the brother of the two of us! But thanks to the Lord, he has the blood of God," Mihaela concludes.

"How could Vlady know all these things when he has never seen the daylight and is deaf?" Gabriela cuts Mihaela with pride.

"What do you know of him other than feed on him? His eyes see more than yours! His words speak sharper than your words. His mouth, though dumb, utters words of love!"

"Can't you make up your mind that everything Vlady told you are mere lies? His own inventions, his pride to fool your mind! Nobody ever told him anything, other than our father Vlad."

"Magia, our Aunt, told Vlady everything. Hear me now, and understand your father's lies: before Vlady's birth, Violeta was barren. Yet, Mama prayed ceaselessly to God, never losing heart. And after more than 25 years of steadfast hope, God endowed her with a child. Vlady became the light of our mother's eyes: her only child, the blessing of her life! And, as soon as Vlady was born, Mama asked Priest Calipa—a close friend of Papa Grid—to bless their little child, to anoint him and tell him daily prayers for long life and protection against the evil."

"I can see...the prayers worked miracles!..." Gabriela snickers.

Mihaela continues her speech, ignoring Gabriela:

"The old Priest Calipa scratched a red protective cross on Vlady's back, between his shoulder blades. And then he said: 'This cross will protect your boy from any evil weapon, from any evil blood! The boy will always have the blood of God!'"

"Bullshit! Mud to clog your mind!" Gabriela cries out.

"I did not finish my reply about how Vlady knows the truth and no more dwells in lie. One night, when Violeta was not feeling well, Grid called out to Magia to take care of their little boy. Magia bathed him, and saw the cross scratched on his back. It was a dark night with violent storm and crows that pecked at the roof of Grid's house. Thus, Aunt Magia stayed overnight, and hugged Vlady in her arms. But as she fell asleep with him, Magia had an awful dream—she dreamt of our mother's body inside a dreadful morgue of ice..."

"Why do you tell me this? And if it's true, why is Vlady so good to me? Why does he stay still and nice and make no sound when I'm about to suck his blood?" Gabriela asks Mihaela, ignited.

"Why don't you ask your father Vlad? He knows the story well, embellished with plenty of detail, with lying epithets and metaphors! Go down into the basement of your castle, and visit your father's *Icy Morgue of Brides*—his frosty cave of death, his place of endless sleep for poor brides and wives sacrificed to fuel his pride... Our Mama's body lies there too...and I can't believe that you let him go through! Don't you have a heart for our poor innocent mother?"

"What brides? What innocent mother? How do you know about the Icy Morgue of Brides?"

"It is all written in Vlady's letter. Care to throw your eyes and read his lines? Your good father Vlad has killed thousands of brides and innocent wives...he has turned thousands of grooms and husbands into widowers who now suffer in a womanless world of darkness! If Vlad had suffered with his wife, all men on earth should experience grief and fright! And you, you are his next beloved victim, destined to fulfill his sickness!"

"Why don't you join me at home, and we shall both ask Papa Vlad about this nonsense that clouds your mind? You'll see, you'll find him innocent. Forget the stories that Aunt Magia sold perfidiously to Vlady. She was mad and jealous of my dad. Besides, now she is dead."

"I'll never let my eye enter that darkness—not even one more time!" Mihaela cries out to her sister.

"Ok, then I will follow you, wherever you may go. I know a shortcut through a tunnel...and we can get wherever we desire, if we just talk to him..." Gabriela pleads with her sister.

"Who is him?"

"He is a friend... He's powerful and loyal..."

"What is his name?"

"Well, I can explain..."

"Then he's the devil!"

"Then we'll take the forest!"

"Why should I do it? Is Vlad still eager to impale the rest of men through you? No, dear shrew! Farewell to you!"

"Farewell to you if that's your will," Gabriela replies back, full of venom. "But you'll recall my words and turn to me, quick as a wink! I am the one who loves you; those men just want you. And you, foolish little bride, choose to let yourself be weak and cry; a slave to the mortal kind! The world belongs to the strong-hearted, to the cold bloodied. The rabbits and the poets are an easy prey for the wise hunters! Those men will suck your immortality and power, and then will leave you pregnant, but barren and flaccid, robbed of a glorious destiny! I am blood from you own blood; you and I are one, from the same egg. You need me, not their faces and fate! Listen, Sis: you will come back to me because I am your identity. The mortals are mean, envious, perfidious and lecherous. If you don't bite them, they will bite you and break your neck!" Gabriela shouts sourly at Mihaela, after which turns to walk back into Grid's house.

Mihaela mounts her fantastic horse and spurs him vigurously to ride. But they barely take three steps forward when the ground splits into two and Michael-horse and she remain suspended in the light.

From the underground, a beautiful man, glamorous and young, rises to her eyes...so similar looking to David.

Mihaela shakes as under a spell of lust.

"Don't be afraid, my love..."

"Who are you, if I may ask?"

"I am your love..."

"What do you want?"

"To give to you! Just move your lips...and I shall grant your wish... I own the undergrounds, the greedy world, the clouds above...but...I don't own your heart and your deep love..."

Mihaela is bewitched by the beautiful features of the man. But, as Michael-horse shakes his mane and tail, Mihaela awakens from the spell. Under the mask of David, Mihaela recognizes Vlad's face.

"What do you know about deep love, you serpent heart full of deep venom?"

"Don't let your heart speak foul, though even those harsh words fall sweetly from your mouth..."

"I'd better go my way, forget my name..."

"And yet your name bears my name! Your face is what I did create... You are what I adore the most and what I'd never want to lose!"

"You have to have so you can lose!"

"You're mine! My daughter, my love and my invention!"

"I know the one I am—I am God's daughter and I have no time to meander in the darkness!"

"God?" Vlad bursts into laughter. "Why did God leave your mother sick and helped her not to procreate? Why did Almighty God allow me to embed her womb? Am I the one and only God alive? Who is God? Just an illusion, child! You give him power... Excuse me, holy power!"

"He gives me power and I just receive His grace! It is called the power of grace, the power of faith!" Mihaela ripostes with a smile.

"Give me a little power and I shall give you everything that you desire!"

"Why should I give you power?"

"Because your power can bring me back to life..."

"So you are dead?"

"My heart is dead, but your sweet love can put a beat in it again!"

"You spoke so sweetly and love truly fills all. With pleasure I do give you love for your dead heart if you just kneel before my heart and give yourself to God! Repeat loud and intact: *From this day on, I give myself to God and promise not to kill or suck the blood of any child! I am sorry, and I repent for taking Violeta's life, whom I did kill, and all the other maids and wives who are asleep inside my caves of death!*"

"Who told you that? I did not kill your mother! God did it!" Vlad shudders with anger.

"Who told me is the one to blame? Or is it you, the evil doer, the one who killed and who now dares to disguise behind the mask of love?"

"Let me explain…"

"An explanation doesn't wipe the sores away or your low deed, you lord of greed! Farewell!"

"You cannot run away! You are my blood! You owe me your own life!" Vlad shouts out.

"I do not deal with Satan!"

"I am not Satan. I am Vlad…"

"And who is Vlad?"

"What shall I do to make you love me?"

"Forget yourself and my identity, and promise this to me: that you shall let me live like humans live; that I shall die knowing that I have loved, not fearing those fangs coming to life whenever I make love! When you and your sweet daughter are out of my sight, those wicked teeth just disappear in the light! I want to love and write…what you have never taught your child! So, disappear from my eyes!"

"But as a normal human being, you cannot stop the time and keep your face beautiful and young! You cannot have what mortals die to find!" Vlad sweetens his voice. "You have been born without knowing to fear, and you can never die. Let those canine teeth come to light whenever they desire and rejoice at being immortal and on fire!"

"Rejoice at being wicked and living in a lie? To live like this is to live blind, like I have never seen the sunlight! But I have seen it, and I'll never let myself again ramble in the dark. Once I was only a slave of lust, but now I am the beloved daughter of God! I want to have that childlike fear…so that I know that God is near!"

"Oh, live your given life! Don't let yourself be bamboozled by God!"

"So what is such a thing to live with a dead heart, sweet Vlad?"

And saying that, Mihaela mounts her Michael-horse and spurs on.

"One kiss before you go!" Vlad yearns.

"Don't need the kiss of death! I have one life and I shall kiss just whom I trust! Yet I can tell you this: thank you for being so wicked, Prince Vlad. You make me see the good of God! And…made my novel spark! Go Michael, Go!"

"I am not Satan… I am Vlad!" Vlad cries after Mihaela with his frosty heart broken.

In the twinkling of an eye, Michael-horse jumps onto the gigantic Queen of the Night flower, and swarms up its tall stem that leads to the sky.

"Wait!" Gabriela cries, with villain eyes, from the doorsill of Papa Grid.

Vlad shrinks his heart and waves his fingers with luciferian tremolo, staring at the flame of light through which Mihaela has faded out.

"She shall see! She shall die to touch one blade of me!" Vlad speaks, gnashing his teeth.

Vlad's face is disfigured. He collapses to the ground, with his head heavy, bent down. His hair suddenly turns gray, his skin shrinks in thousands of wrinkles, scorched and withered… He feels so hurt by Mihaela's words, yet he is so in love with her rejection.

Hiding in the wing of a shadow, Vlad lingers to remnants of his once human heart:

"The more she tells me *No*, the more I want her all…
　The more she runs away, the more she resurrects my hope.
　How much I love her frowns and cruel sounds,
　Her real and innocent purpose on this ground.
　She dreams of love and art and reads God's heart,

What I, in centuries, was not blessed to hark.
She wants the impossible to be aroused
And doves to brush her hair in Lord's house.
She writes with Holy Spirit in her mouth,
Bewitched by the believer's tender vows.
My ice turns into summer when her sweet words sprout,
And my imprisoned heart redeems when she just flouts...
When I see her, I am inspired and speak in verse.
But when she leaves, I start to feel my endless curse.
I need her love, her pure love, but Satan needs my soul,
And wants to capture Mihaela into his infernal hole.
But I'll protect her with my love,
And shelter her in it like in a glove.
Yet Love does not belong to me—my rusted heart,
which hellish fire burnt, burying its sweet thud;
Love belongs to God, yes God,
Who shamelessly has grieved my heart-
Tearing me between my deadly life
And Mihaela's rejection—my yearning light.
But wait! I shall design my lab with seeds of pleasure
And tempt my sweetheart there to find her mother's treasure.
Yes! Enough! Enough possession from this God
Who let my love and innocence to be of dark,
Who did not save me from the scars of night,
And let the evil rip from me such a big bite!
God did not help me when my pride was rust;
So now it is between my darling, and my serpent lust
To fight the fight to catch her tantalizing heart!
Together, we will show to Him that I, the vampire Vlad,
Am more powerful and smart."

Michael-horse keeps climbing

onto the tall stem of the Queen of the Night, towards the orange Sun.

With her spear-cross in her right hand and her eyes to blue sky, Mihaela feels the strong rays of the Sun becoming tender and mild. It is a beautiful sunset, like a blissful lust, a balm to her wounded heart.

Mihaela feels her body so light, invigorated by the miraculous perfume of the tall flower that has helped them climb effortlessly in that evil hour.

However, the other stem of the Queen of the Night flower, the thorny one that pierces the ground, ferments with anger, releasing a viscous bluish smoke that rises quickly to the sky, blackening Mihaela's sight.

Michael, the smart and waggish horse of Mihaela, shakes his body three times and the gloom and mist of the evil past vanishes into the dark.

The night steps in like a princess to a ball.

Looking at the infinite sky, Mihaela can see everything so keenly, with new eyes of an eagle. The stars, the friendly clouds, the shadows dancing with the light, the colors of the twilight, make her feel so hungry…so thristy to know the realm beyond. She wishes to pull the curtains of the sky, to cast the clouds to the side, and step onto the carpet of Heaven where she knows that Mama is waiting to hug her with the arms of an angel!

All of a sudden, a happy rainbow of colorful stars brushes the sky, casting away the bleeding twilight; Mihaela's heart pounds with joy. She has never seen a rainbow of stars before!

Wings, as of an angel, suddenly grow from Michael's back and a veil of fluffy clouds adorns his head and tail.

Mihaela's eyes bloom with delight. Michael-horse dances his tail, so proud of his new miraculous wings.

As a playful cloud touches her feet, Mihaela looks down. Transylvania looks so small! Not even as big as the cloud. And the sky looks so large…wider than the whole world!

How lucky she feels to be up here! Her mind floats…and she can feel her body no more! All of her fears have totally disappeared! She's not afraid of heights as she used to be, on the roof of Papa's house! She wouldn't be afraid even if she has to ride with Michael through the tunnels of Lucifer. As long as she has such a brave, spirited horse, she is totally safe!

"Who could have imagined that me—born evil and without a heartbeat—can fly above the mountains and the waters, above the storms and the wild forests?" Mihaela asks herself. "How did I do it? How could I fly? I have done nothing! I only wished for it and…it happened! Oh, I know! I just saw it…and He made it real for me…without my control! He did it all! He took me up and placed me here, next to the clouds! Oh, thank you God, for loving me so much!" Mihaela speaks with tears in her eyes.

"Is our destiny written?" Mihaela bruskly asks her horse Michael.

"I believe so, my sweet mistress," Michael replies, fluttering his angel wings with pride.

"My sister always told me to keep my feet on the ground… But this is not the way to the stars! If only people wish to touch the stars…God will make their dreams come true to their hearts! They will all feel like I now feel… We will all dance in the night, we will have a great ball in the sky!" Mihaela shouts out to the stars.

"My mistress! I'm hungry…" Michael whines.

But Mihaela is still caught up in her heavenly thoughts.

"Papa Grid taught me all of these things from the Bible, but I did not quite understand them… Just now his words are taking life in my heart! Oh, thank you Papa for teaching me the way to fly!"

Impaled by sweet memories from the past and the future, Mihaela giggles when the clouds take the shape of her thoughts. Playing with words, singing and dancing like a bird finally set free, Mihaela's forehead is suddenly wrinkled by a dark frown. Michael-horse yawns so big and wide, that he almost swallows the body of a cloud. Swiftly, with her spear-cross, Mihaela pierces the cloud and takes it out of Michael's mouth. She then pulls the cloud next to her mouth, convincing the poor cloud to shelter them on its soft, cozy arms.

But Michael, proud and naughty, refuses to rest onto the generous cloud. He jumps on his hind legs, shakes his wings three times, and flies higher to play with the moon that has just raised her face to the sky.

From close up, the moon looks like an imperial lantern, naked and fearless: she has Asian eyes and a crafty smile, a round sexy body and tempting plump breasts. She is the temptress of the earth, the uncontested courtesan queen of magic, the one who cruelly cast spells over the hearts of the romantics, causing them to be heart-broken.

Michael-horse neighs gallantly at the moon, blushing with love. The luring eyes of the moon beguiles not only him, but Mihaela too.

As Mihaela looks at the magical moon, her eyes redden and her teeth sharpen. Her heart begins to bleed, and her mind to fear. A wicked force grasps her body and yellows her face; her skin gets cooler and cracks like the ground shattered by earthquake.

The moon smiles with cunning eyes.

Seeing Mihaela's sudden change, Michael-horse opens his wings and hugs his mistress, taking her away from the deceiving moonlight.

Staring at a beautiful star that shines in the night, Mihaela starts to awaken from the power of that hypnotic satellite.

"Where, dear Michael?"

Mihaela asks, bewildered by the wind and fastly dragged by her wild horse.

Michael-horse neighs with delight. His hoof has just caught a white lock of hair, and he vigurously rides on it. The lock of hair is as white as snow and smells like Mama's wedding dress.

As Michael rides higher and higher onto the white lock of hair, they reach a cave...sort of an aperture. A euphoric sound comes out, reaching their ears, and a white carpet rolls down to their feet, inviting them to step in...

Mihaela looks at Michael, and Michael looks at Mihaela with doubtful eyes. But a voice speaks powerfully in their hearts, and together, they step inside.

Mihaela's third eye opens, lighting the path of the cave. She can read words...great words that fly like water-butterflies, encircling her body like a watershield. She does not know if these are the words of God, but she feels them so holy, cleansing her heart. It also smells divinely inside this cave, like Papa's bread, just taken out of the oven.

Michael-horse dilates his ears and his nostrils. He can smell and hear only good things around, too. They step further in with more courage.

The air feels so fresh and healing, like an invisible robe that brushes her skin. As she looks down at her legs and arms, Mihaela sees them turning so young. She smiles, amazed.

The cave suddenly morphs into a sort of a labyrinth, with different chambers and places filled with all kinds of people and angels.

Tens of well-known books, novels and poetry volumes unveil before Mihaela's eyes, rising and floating above her head. As she looks down, she sees a big book machine where millions of pages are restlessly being printed out. The pages fly in the air, and Mihaela can read:

"The Destiny of Charles, the Destiny of Emma, the Destiny of David..."

Next to the book machine, there are ebony tables and little thrones of gold where there are seated Homer and Virgil, Dante and Erasmus, Shakespeare and Goethe, Tolstoy and Dostoyevsky, Chekhov, Ibsen and Tennessee Williams, Faulkner and García Márquez... Surrounded by a golden aura, they all write with four hands, at the speed of God. Inside their minds, Mihaela can see a great fire...a white fire burning steadily, like the oak firewood in Papa's stove. She then hears their thoughts aloud, creating a branched musicality. She feels such a desire to talk to them.

"Hi, I'm Mihaela," she steps towards Shakespeare.

But she is immediately pushed back. She cannot step nearer, nor touch his arms. He is untouchable. She stops.

Miraculously, Shakespeare's light comes to her. It touches her skin and then jumps inside her heart. She feels so happy as she has never felt happiness before.

As she raises her eyes up to thank for this gift, she sees a royal balcony...like a wide and tall forehead. In the balcony, men dressed in impeccable tuxedos lead an orchestra of children. Their conducting batons bounce spiritedly in the air, with the aggressiveness of a volcano. She can recognize great composers: Mozart, Chopin, Rachmaninov, Vivaldi, Puccini...conducting their compositions to the little children that play at colourful harps, violins, pianos, guitars, and heavenly strings that look like the strings of the heart. Behind these sweet children with angelic faces, it is written with capital letters, on a golden placard: THE NEXT GENERATION of GOD.

Further up, on top of the cave, which appears like the ceiling of a head, there are golden bundles of fibers on which beautiful ballerinas are dancing and leaping with grace their long angelic arms and legs: Anna Pavlova, Galina Ulanova, Maya Plisetskaya, Sylvie Guillem, Tamara Rojo, Alina Cojocaru... Their pirouettes and splits, diaphanous and continuous like some goblins of the light, reflect in the big eyes of thousands of little children who listen to their teacher of love—Jesus Christ.

Jesus is just like Mihaela has dreamt of...in her bed, in Papa's house: so full of warmth, so loving, burning like a candle of love... His eyes are like two lakes, peaceful and full of light, and she can see herself reflected in them like in a glass, looking just like when she was a little child. His arms, so long and forgiving, are spreading and hugging all of the children's bodies; his hands, that rest upon their heads, look just like the big loving hands of Papa Grid. Sparkling words suddenly come out of His mouth, flowing like rivers of living water, swallowed by the eyes and ears of the thirsty children, and rapidly making way inside their hearts that giggle and laugh with Holy Ghost. The language that Jesus speaks sounds like a language that Mihaela has heard before...even though she cannot understand a word; it sounds neither like English, nor like Hebrew, Spanish, Italian, or Japanese, nor like any other language, but it sounds so pure, so healing, touching her mind and making her see inside Jesus's heart.

Jesus's heart is filled with loaves of bread that pop out and serve the little children, so hungry and eager for love. The loaves turn into sweet muffins with different heads and shapes, fresh and hot. The children take the muffins in their little hands and eat with godly appetite. Then, they thank Jesus in a cheerful choir, like the birds' twitter in Springtime.

Suddenly, Jesus turns His head and calls Mihaela to eat with them. Mihaela, in awe, steps forward. Her arms fill with the muffins of love, and she eats them swiftly, so hungrily. Her feet suddenly start running, and her arms open widely, embracing her sweet Jesus. She wishes she could spend her whole life in this mirific, life-giving hug. Mihaela cries with delight, her tears flying in the air and turning into water, quenching all of the children's thirst.

At a small ebony desk, a bold child with a white dove alighted on his left arm, calls Mihaela with his little finger. Jesus encourages her to go to him. Mihaela draws near the child's desk. Michael-horse, who has been watching the whole scene all along, walks to him too. The child has wise, blue eyes, white hair, and a long-nailed finger painted with blue blood.

He quickly opens a small white notebook and picks up a feather. He then asks with calm:

"What do you need, Mihaela?"

"I...don't need anything!" Mihaela replies, surprised that the child knows her name.

"Nothing? Interesting. You have everything?"

"I believe so."

"What is everything?" the child asks her, curiously.

"God and freedom...the sky and the earth, a great purpose..."

"Oh, that's right. You are not of my category. You are the one who was asked for."

"The one who was asked for?" Mihaela asks, bewildered.

"Yes. She will take care of you from now on."

And the child points to a small, vivid bee, endowed with velvety golden wings, painted with shiny black stripes. The bee buzzes with joy and winks at Mihaela to follow her. Mihaela follows the bee through a long, white tunnel. Suddenly, a red rain, like red drops of blood, falls upon her. Mihaela totally forgets about herself...her name, who she is, where she came from...her memory instantly wiped from her mind... As they further walk, the bee speaks to her:

"Now hear Him..."

Mihaela listens attentively. She hears the warm voice of a child, singing:

"Take what I have given you and spread it in the world:
The gift of God so you turn life into Art,
The gift of love so you can love and heal the broken hearts.
The gift of singing to sing along with God and nurse
the ones who need your songs and psalms.
The gift of dancing to dance along with butterflies,
The gift of writing to write and hug the lonely minds,
The gift of faith to clothe the weak with strength
and the discouraged with love's length..."

White tears fall onto the cheeks of Mihaela, like snowflakes. She feels so cleansed, so light...a Snow Bride. A Snow Child. These words have deeply touched her heart, to the meadow of her soul...

Suddenly, she remembers who she is: Mihaela. But now she feels so much different, peaceful, lighter, kinder... She has new eyes, new hands, new mind. Now she knows who she is: the beloved child of God...cleansed once and for all by the sweet drops of love. No matter what, she cannot escape God's love! Now she is ready to give to everyone from the basket of love that she holds strong in her heart.

All of a sudden, from the depths of the labyrinth, she hears another voice—a sweet, warm voice...singing *Ave Maria.* She recalls the voice of her mother, so clear, so flawless...like the voice of an angel.

The voice of *Ave Maria* enraptures her whole being, hypnotizing her to step along onto a heavenly carpet of grass, adorned with so many Queen of the Night flowers, spirited and colored in so many shades. The flowers have heads of infants and eyes of sweet, laughing children. Their petals are so velvety and soft, like babies' hair that spreads divine aroma of warm breasted milk... The arm-leaves of the flowers are so green and gracious, and their leg-stems dance non-stop, to the rhythm of the joyful twitter of paradise.

"Wow! Queen of the Night flowers...like in Papa's garden!" Mihaela exclaims as she dances in sync with the flowers' legs and arms. "There is even a thorny flower with ivy stem...that coils into the ground and spreads a bluish smoke..."

As Mihaela looks at the ivy-flower, a strong healing heat touches her neck, her shoulders, her back, opening her arms into white wings of a dove...

Soft hands caress her hair like the warm wind of the Summer.

Mihaela turns around and sees the long arms, the long black curly hair, the black wise eyes of her mother.

"Mama, in flesh and blood, touching my hair?" Mihaela bursts into tears of joy, embracing her mother with the velocity of a just-born-baby embracing life.

Mother is so light, like a ray of sun, so mild.

Mihaela cannot feel her flesh, nor her bones, yet she can feel Mama's warmth and her enormous kiss of love... Mama's lips look like those of a sculpture of Michelangelo from which a waterfall of kindness flows; her smile is like a ray of sun risen after a week of darkness; her big black eyes are like pearls of the night—wise and wide; her nose feels like a white bud of rose, touching her skin with the scent of paradise.

Swiftly, her mother takes Mihaela by the hand and flies with her through the mirthful wind, above the colorful Queen of the Night flowers. Like two spirited doves in Spring, they get into Mihaela's childhood swing, surrounded by red roses. Picking a rose from her childhood' garden, Mama starts ripping its thorns, one by one, without hurting herself. After she tears off the thorns of the rose, Violeta speaks lovingly to her daughter:

"Take it into your hands now."

Mihaela takes the rose in her hands and touches its thornless stem that feels as soft as of a tulip. She then breathes in the mesmerizing scent of the red bud...staring at Mama with yearning eyes.

Mama speaks again:

"My child, your sister Gabriela is just like this rose. She has thorns. Yet it only takes to rip them off…"

"How, Mommy? How could I rip her thorns off?"

"There is something that unites both of you more than anything. Find that thing and then you'll know… You need her, my love. As much as she needs you."

"Do I need the evil, Mama?"

"It keeps you in search of God…" Mama replies and kisses Mihaela's indigo eye which starts to shine with violent rays of light.

And saying this, Mama takes a seat at a wide piano that looks like a maxillary, with perfect white teeth… As she presses the piano keys, heavenly sounds start to ring, and Mama's pure healing voice begins again to sing… The piano widens into a smile, and then it opens up like a mouth. Through its opening, Mihaela can see a long toboggan like a red tongue, on which the words and sounds of Mama slide gracefully over the blue sky, and then, like some golden seeds, fall upon the worldly ground.

"Oooh! Such a big distance to the ground! And down there it looks so gloomy and gray! I want to stay here forever, Mama!" Mihaela cries out as she peers towards the Earth.

"Go! I'll be watching you from here, my love! You've got work to do for Daddy God!" Mama says, pushing Mihaela and Michael horse down the toboggan, onto a cuddling cloud.

Waving goodbye to her mother, Mihaela wishes to cry… But she feels too happy; she cannot drop a tear.

"Oh, my, you and I in the head of God? What do you say about our journey, sweet Michael?" Mihaela asks her horse as the cloud flies speedily with them, through the shades of daylight.

"Divine!" Michael-horse snorts with love, with his mane fluttering in the air.

"Now I know the only one thing that is needed…love, love, love, and only love… Faith is love…"

"And love is faith!" Michael-horse neighs with his eyes rolling with joy.

"Yes...that lasting love that makes us to always believe. Truly, everything is possible when you just love! Eureka!" Mihaela shouts out to the sky, taken through the wind by the cloud, lower and lower.

"God, I want to have so much love that I can bring my mother back to Papa, that I can heal the blind and kiss away the pain of the broken-hearted. I want to walk on snakes and speak the language of Love like Jesus Christ into Your head."

The cloud reaches tall buildings and the trampish noise of a restless city.

Michael-horse nieghs stridently, as they fall onto the face of Earth.

"I feel a little differently down here... I feel like crying... Where is Mama? I miss Mama..." Mihaela starts whining, among the jam-packed streets of Times Square.

"Why didn't I ask Mama to come back with me now? Why did I leave her there? What was in my mind? Ah, God, truly, I am such a fool..." Mihaela starts scolding herself as Michael-horse is cuddled and touched by some kids.

As quilty thoughts race through her mind, Mihaela's third eye hurts her again, penetrating her with lasers from the past... Her canine teeth begin to sore, eager to pierce violently through her gums. She is unable to see straight, thrown off balance by a dark force.

Suddenly, a funny man grins before her eyes.

Times Square, 2014.
A man with small, ring-shaped eyes, a tiny forehead, furrowed by deep wrinkles and a raining mouth, stands proud in front of a garishly looking cabaret. He starts laughing spasmodically as he sets eyes on Mihaela and her Michael-horse. Analyzing Mihaela's body, from toe to

her brow, with his fluorescent pink binoculars, the man's mouth opens wide, showing undershot deranged teeth.

"Where is the old *Palace Theatre*? And what is this asymmetric new building, with glittering lights and paper towel ornaments?" Mihaela asks herself as she looks at the ridiculous cabaret inscription: "Live No More."

Blinded by the scattered lights and phosphorescent shades, she hesitates to get closer to the cabaret. The man laughs again, waving his paralytic hand under Mihaela's nose.

Mihaela, looks at him, utterly puzzled, pushing the man's hand down. She then takes Mommy Doll out of her woolen bag and catches her courage.

The man mumbles at her, bossily:

"Two hundred dollars."

"What for?" Mihaela asks, bewildered.

The man laughs idiotically:

"For *Dracula's Daughters cabaret show* that will blow off your soul! It is an extraordinary show about two twin daughters born with fangs in Transylvania, the daughters of Vlad Dracula...."

"Oh, I see...the daughters of Vlad Dracula... And what is the name of the show?"

"As I said...Dracula's Daughters. One daughter is called Gabriela, the other one Mihaela... They scream and fight!"

"My name is Mihaela," Mihaela says politely, stretching her hand out to the laughing man.

"My name is Richard Crisis," Richard introduces himself, overlooking Mihaela's hand.

"Richard dear, I have the honor to inform you that I am one of the twins from Transylvania, one of 'Dracula's Daughters' that your play is about," Mihaela speaks, confidently.

Richard laughs and then asks, rigidly:

"Do you think that I'm stupid?"

"Not at all, dear Richard. I think that you have a lovely smile."

Richard smiles, showing again his undershot deranged teeth.

"Oh, thank you, Miss...ahhh..."

"Mihaela..."

"Mihaela...you say, but this name belongs to one of the twins' name, our character from the show. It is copyrighted."

"Exactly... My name is Mihaela."

"It cannot be possible. What a hilarious coincidence!" Richard chuckles.

"May I come in?" Mihaela kindly asks again.

"As I said, you first need to pay."

"I am Mihaela, one of the vampire twins from your show. I am the character. So the character cannot pay for its own role..."

"Wow, I never thought about this. Let me think about it... So you think you are one of the twins? And why should I believe you?"

Mihaela smiles at Richard. Her indigo star shines powerfully.

"Wow, you have an indigo eye just like the character Mihaela..." Richard exclaims.

"Yes, because, I am the character..."

"Hmmm..." Richard mutters, scratching his chin.

"May I come in?" Mihaela asks again.

"You still need to pay..."

"But the show is about me!"

"Maybe, but I am the owner." Richard cuts her off.

"But this is my story..."

"No, no, no, that is too much... I have the copyright!"

"But I am the story, it is based on my life... And I have the right to pass!"

"No, I have the copyright..."

"Alright, you have the copyright, but I am still the..."

"Get out! Out of my sight!" Richard screams, kicking and flailing like a broken robot.

Mihaela takes her horse along and walks away, giggling like a child. She cannot believe the kind of conversation that she had with that man. Definitely, that kind of laughter is contagious... She chuckles, imitating Richard.

She doesn't like to judge, so she prefers to smile. And Mihaela puts on a large smile...and keeps it on her face, all the way.

"But why does she have to see this play about Dracula's Daughters, anyway?" She definitely does not have an answer, but somehow, she feels pushed by an inner force to walk in and see for herself...

Moreover, if she has landed with her horse at this place, there has to be a reason...a higher reason, beyond her understanding...

Joined by her loyal horse, Mihaela goes around the block. A freshly dyed banner is proudly stuck on the back door of the cabaret. Bold, comic letters of "Live No More" stand out. Every two seconds, glittering lights turn on the letters, blinding the eyes.

"If the front door is not willing to let me in, maybe the back one will do it..." Mihaela thinks to herself.

But the back door is locked and her hands are too feeble to push it open.

Suddenly, she hears Papa Grid's voice:

"Always enter through the front door. Only knock and it shall be opened..."

"Fine. But I cannot go through that front door... That man..." Mihaela grumbles.

Suddenly, the vivid bee with velvety wings that she had met in God's labyrinth, starts buzzing around her. Then, the bee whispers with maternally care:

"Mihaela, I am here for you. You have seven wishes that Mama can help you with if only..."

She then pauses. Mihaela is waiting, curiously.

"If only...?"

"If only you use them to help seven needy people," the bee concludes.

"I shall try my best," Mihaela says, suddenly feeling nervous.

But, as she looks up to the bee, the fear drops and she smiles her words out:

"Dear bee, please, lead me not be deceived, help me to do God's will and choose wisely the seven needy ones."

"I will. And you may call me Mama-bee," the bee buzzes happily, after which she blows a golden mist upon Mihaela.

Mihaela gets clothed from head to her soul into a magical aura, miraculously turning smaller and smaller, until she becomes a bee, just like Mama-bee.

The indigo eye is still shining in between her newly grown bee brows.

Like two peas in a pod, with their stings pulled out like a prod, the two bees fly through the front door of the cabaret, above the crowd.

As they enter the cabaret, growls, moans and dark voices splash their little ears and wings with phosphorescent saliva.

To the right, a bartender, dressed in a glittery pink shirt, with arm garters, pink bow tie, multicolored vest, apron, bottle holster belt, and naked buttocks, hula-hoops, twisting glasses at the same time.

A fanfare plays loudly, trooping on a stage in a marching staccato tempo. The fanfare is filled with men, dressed up in women's clothing, who play their tambourines and drums, standing up while dancing their long Jewish beards off.

An MC, with bulging red eyes and white dyed face, wrapped up in a golden mantle and headed with red horns, wobbles on the main stage:

"Ladies and Gentlemen, may I present to you the vampire-twins from Transylvania, Dracula's Daughters! Here she is, the wise and meek daughter: Mihaela, the twin sister who pulled her fangs out in desperate need of human love..."

Mihaela appears on stage with her mouth embellished with enormous fangs that are attached to the harness of a marionette-horse. She is dressed in a short white ballerina tutu, showing long hairy legs. She has a silvery spear in her right hand that shines cheaply in the eyes of the crowd. The horse pulls to set forth, but Mihaela retorts, and so, the horse pulls her fangs out.

"Auch!!!" Mihaela screams as a thunder crushes the cabaret walls. The crowd bursts out in laughter.

"And now, Ladies and Gentlemen, the Queen of the Night—the roller bladed sister, designed to change the human race into vampiric preys— Gabriela, the wicked!" the MC announces with a loud, devilish voice.

Gabriela makes her appearance from an underground gate, popping up like a stirred champagne. Then, smiling her fangs out, she starts to skate her way through the crowd with her sharp roller blades with wings of bats. Gabriela is wearing a black ballerina tutu, tied at the back in a big black bow. She furiously flies back on stage, biting the MC's neck, while he jerks his body with sadistic lust. Gabriela then rushes to Mihaela and grabs her hand, enraged:

"How could you leave ashore and make yourself a human whore?"

In that moment, Gabriela's back bow unties, and a long black tail flips behind, whiping the floor.

Meantime, Mihaela makes out with her boyfriend, totally ignoring her angry sister.

"Look at this lovely pair of fangs..." Gabriela spits out, picking up from the floor Mihaela's ripped off fangs.

"Go away!" Mihaela screams, pushing her sister away with one of her hairy long legs.

"You took your immortal tools out! What a shame, how lame for an immortal creature to betray her own sibling!"

Abruptly, the MC comes out on stage with his horns on fire and his arms flared up with wicked desire, screaming out from the top of his lungs:

"Enough girls! Enough! It is unacceptable! Unpardonable! Frustrable and abominable! You two have entered my private dressing room and used my white Givenchy powder! I can smell it on your skins, I can sense its power on your lips! Please, leave the stage now! You are banished from "Live No More" forever! Two other actresses will replace your diva whims, and you will always blame each other for the wrong that you did to me! Now, cheerleaders from "Live No More," make your appearance! Cheer up the air and boost up my flair!"

And saying this, the MC stings the air with his horns while paper towels and confetti cover up the party-people.

Mihaela suddenly wakes up.

She is all wet. Blanketed by the mild rays of the morning, she opens her big black eyes, shivering with thoughts, frightened by the vision of that show... She is on a cuddling cloud with her horse Michael, smelling the smoke of the earth.

Mommy, as an angel of the future, bends down upon Mihaela and caresses her face that still sweats, afraid...

"Was that show just a bad dream? I hope so..." Mihaela murmurs to herself.

Mama then hands Mihaela the red rose without thorns. Mihaela touches it softly, remembering her mother's words about Gabriela's thorns.

For the first time, she feels that she needs her sister. She is so eager to write their story...the real one...

"Perhaps this is the way to change Gabriela's wickedness, to rip the thorns off, as Mama said... Building up something magical together, a true show about our lives...can turn Gabriela's night into light! But how can we learn about light if we don't see it in the night? The stars shine at night... I always feared the evil and did not want to talk about it... But the more I did, the more I've seen its sins!" Mihaela thinks to herself.

"Let it be. Good and bad!" she suddenly hears the voice of her mother. "Don't focus on the sin, but on your dream!

"My dream?" Mihaela asks herself. "My dream is to..."   she pauses, and sighs with emotion. She then looks up to the sky, lost in the clouds...lost in her thoughts...

Michael-horse moves his tail, restless, so willing to read his mistress' dream.

"My dream...is to win Gabriela," Mihaela suddenly speaks. "But I need to know more about her...the way she lives, the way she thinks... Ah, but I will have to go back to Vlad's castle and I have promised myself to never put my feet again inside that darkness!"

"You need to know your enemy so you can conquer it..." Papa's words resonate inside her mind.

All of a sudden, her desire gets so strong, her heart starts beating so fast, faster than the twirling of the globe. Her thoughts run further than she can behold... The cloud, as a magical carpet, takes Mihaela and Michael inside a rapid flight throughout the healing rays of the sun...right to Vlad's castle.

1504. Vlad's Castle is in mourning.

Vlad is at the feet of a statue, adorned with crystal ornaments and covered with a long glacial mantle.

Behind the statue, the dim lights of The Little Dome come into sight, shining like fireflies amidst the piercing darkness of Vlad's Icy Morgue of Brides.

Vlad's bitter tears fall on the statue and turn rapidly into shards of ice, embellishing more lavishly the glacial mantle frozen by his lifetime cries.

Alone and breathing to death, Vlad trembles into a convulsion of condemnation and regret. He rips his skin off, growling like a wounded bull. His body, glabrous and white as a sheet, is skeletal but renews and replenishes more and more vigorously with every piece of skin that he breaks.

Huge stalactites, like fringed chandeliers, and long lacy draperies, hang from the ceilings of the Icy Morgue, twinning gracefully with giant stalagmites and columns of ice. The stalagmites look like enormous candles, dripping over humid flowstones.

A colony of bats, red-eyed and foul scented, sway on spikes from the cupola of The Little Dome—Vlad's sacred altar of love. A woman, with cut wings of an angel, hangs upside down, crucified on the cross of The Little Dome. Her body is nude and frozen but still beholding ravishing forms of a temptress. Over the cross, a huge predatory bird opens wide its menacing beak into a desperate scream.

After he releases his anguish at the feet of the glacial statue, Vlad slowly raises his head up. Looking at the sculpture's face, his eyes gleam with veneration. The statue has Mihaela's features: her big black eyes shaped like pearls of the night, her voluptuous lips, lustful and fresh like the buds of a rose, yearning for a kiss. Prominent cheeks, sculpted like hills over a perfect lawn, lift up Vlad's pride to ecstasy.

Vlad extends his right arm to touch the statue's eyes but falls again into his cries:

"My queen… How can your lips, as sweet as hers, ignore so much my yearning soul? Why does your pure mouth not utter healing words of love but keeps me silenced in this harmful frost? Why don't your white long arms enter my nightly grave to hug away my doomed pain? I have charmed the most wished-for brides and princesses, virgins and widows, beauties from all the corners of the world, and I cannot tame you, the one whom I created and whom I long for? How can you not love me, your God, the carver of your soul?"

Vlad groans with total bitterness. His howl can be heard in the entire land of Transylvania.

The frozen walls of the Icy Morgue of Brides shake terribly at the immensity of his sorrow.

Vlad jumps to his feet and starts running like a mad horse through the Icy Morgue, through bloodstained beds of glacial stone, where thousands of brides lie silently with their eyes opened. He hurls himself over the corpses and starts biting their dead arms, necks, and legs, melting his agony into their iced bodies.

Panting, he staggers toward one bed in the middle of the Icy Morgue, covered with sheer white curtains, ornamented with little frozen indigo Queen of the Night flowers. Vlad flings the curtains to the side and kneels before the bed:

"Violeta, mother of my queen, you and I have a lot to do… Our daughter shall forever regret the words she hurled at me… Teach me what to do."

Watching Violeta's stillness with anger, Vlad dashes at her long white neck with fever. He then opens up her heart with his long greasy nails, watching, in awe, the dead beat of her soul. He deliriously stings his own chest, while blue droplets of icy blood erupt, like specks of dust, out of his heart. Vlad lets his blood drip into Violeta's heart, which turns at once into a slice of ice.

He looks with desperation at Violeta's frozen heart, realizing that his blood, that once bore miraculous powers, is now inept and cannot put a beat inside Violeta's heart.

Meantime, led by the generous cloud,

Mihaela has arrived in Transylvania and lays her feet in front of Vlad's house. Mihaela leaves Michael-horse alone and enters stealthily the squeaky gate of the house. She then steps carefully, gazing around at the four-snaked fountain that seems to watch her with its eyes of stone. The leafless trees and whistling wind slowly frighten her heart. The further she steps, the more the ground expands—and the giant black door that guards Vlad's house, withdraws.

Mihaela's feet sink deeper and deeper into the soil as it starts eating her up. Desperately, she waves her hands up to the sky, battling to pull herself out of the swamp: "Help, help!"

But the ground keeps swallowing her flesh and bones, and the nature ignores her desperate shouts.

Suddenly, as Mihaela screams out "Daddy God!" the big black tree from Vlad's garden—The Wiseman tree—bends its long branches over Mihaela, and catches her arms with its strong coiling boughs. Mihaela grasps the branches with the last drop of her strength, and the Wiseman's arms catapult her onto its crown.

Miraculously, *the Wiseman* blossoms its white flowers and wraps its boughs around her little waist, kissing her neck, and swinging her into its strong wooden arms of love. Mihaela giggles, spoiled by Nature's bountiful soul.

All of a sudden, she hears the buzzing of her bee-friend. The bee takes a seat on Mihaela's left hand and speaks hurriedly, just like in God's labyrinth:

"You and I have work to do."

And barely does the bee finish her words when she blows royal jelly all over Mihaela's body, from her head to the tip of her toes, turning Mihaela into a very small version of herself, small as a baby doll, and then smaller and smaller—almost invisible…

"Now we can get into Vlad's castle… Climb onto my back and hold on to it until I turn you back into the big you!" the bee speaks up as Mihaela jumps onto her golden body.

Together, Mihaela and her sweet bee-friend, make their entrance in Vlad's living hall, through a small crack in the window.

Vlad's Castle: The Living Hall.

Thunderous and discordant sounds are echoing throughout the whole castle, boiling Vlad's anger to zenith.

Gabriela ravingly plays the piano in the dim light of the living hall. She presses the keys so hard that blue blood erupts out of her fingers. The entire keyboard is covered in blue…but Gabriela keeps playing, spasmodically laughing at the demoniacal rhythm of her noise that enthralls the living hall.

Screams and groans from Vlad can be heard out loud: "Stop that noise for God's sake!" but Gabriela presses the keys, on and on, delighting in scratching and screeching her father's nerves.

She scarcely stops to write down, on yellowish papers, the notes of her discordant symphony. She first stings the sharp edge of her feather into her frigid fingers, enjoying in hurting herself, and then soaks the feather in her icy blue droplets of blood. She scribbles the yellowish papers, trembling to the marrow of her finger bones.

Her performance gets louder and louder, turning into an avalanche of apocalyptic sounds. She reaches the crescendo and is maniacally entranced, at last collapsing on the splattered keys…

After few minutes of deadly silence, she slowly raises her head; drops of blue blood keep dripping off her face.

Worn out and puffing up with disgust, she drags herself in front of the gold imperial mirror from the foyer, straightening her back with unknown nostalgia.

Gabriela watches her face in the magic mirror—the sole mirror that can expose her vampiric features. The mirror was conceived by Vlad himself from the globe of Dora's right eye to reflect the vision of his face and, most importantly, to watch his daughter Mihaela's countenance, and where she runs her life.

Gabriela's majestic but monstrous eyes, full of hatred and repugnance, are darkening the glass... Suddenly, Mihaela's face, so bright and kind but petite as of a barbie doll, appears inside the ocular mirror, lightening the living hall...

Mihaela, watching the scene on the window sill with her bee-friend, startles, numb with shock...

Gabriela's face turns blue topaz. She forces herself to cry, but try as she might, she cannot pull a drop. She gets angrier, enflamed with rage. Her fingers start to shiver, her left eye twitches... She feels as she has never felt before: an impotent crier... Not that she would like to cry, but she has read that creation comes out of pain and tears of sufferance. Filled with volcanic irascibility, she hits the mirror, groaning like a beast. She erupts out of her chamber and sprints down the velvet stairs, towards the icy cellar of her father.

She rushes into Papa's forbidden icy caves, leaning against the cold walls that peel off remnants of mortals' corpses.

Gabriela catches a maddening father, in a hysteria and outbreak of fury and ecstasy. Papa Vlad is breaking and tearing apart candelabras, candle-like stalagmites, and stuffed predatory birds. But Gabriela's eyes fasten on the giant statue with glacial mantle:

"What is that, Father?" she screams with hatred, pointing to the statue.

To the right and left of the marble statue, on the cracked icy walls, hang the portraits of Emanuel and Emil, and of the old bald man who tried to rape little Mihaela...

Gabriela looks perplexed.

"Father, now I see which of us you worship..." she utters with impudent sarcasm, her hair frizzed to the ceilings. Her fingers start trembling again:

"You said that you loved me more than her; you said I was your queen... You said that you are building a statue of me...to expose it to the whole wide world!"

The tremble of her fingers takes over her entire figure.

"Father, I want half of your riches. I want to pay someone to carve my own statue and teach me how to cry. I also want to have a teacher to teach me how to write and then to show the world my art! I want to travel and build my own castle! Give me gold; give me what belongs to me, your daughter! Now!"

Vlad turns towards his daughter, apace. His eyes almost explode out of his head. Caught red-handed, with his wig's hair in total disorder, with his mouth fallen by sadness, he sheds blue blood without a halt. He looks ragged, like a deplorable beggar.

"I need you my child!" Vlad falls to his knees, pleading with Gabriela in cold blood.

"Who am I?" Gabriela screams at her father. "Am I the one who killed our mother?"

Vlad looks at the severe glance of his daughter as if impaled.

"Father, am I a monster?" Gabriela continues. "Why is Mihaela so radiant, so lovely and so kind? I feel a thing that I have never felt before... I feel the need to cry but I cannot..."

Gabriela whines, provoking violent contractions of her muscles, yet she is still unable to drop a tear...

Vlad encourages her:

"Stay brave, my child. You are as beautiful as night! Tears belong to fools; your breed shall only hold its head up high!"

Gabriela continues:

"Father, was I the one who killed my mother?"

"Just foolish words, listen to your wise father!" Vlad tries to embolden her.

"Is Vlady our mother's child, whom from Violeta you have stolen? Is he my brother that you and I have tortured and kept as prisoner until his body…coldly swollen?"

"Don't listen to her words! She only wants to pit the two of us against each other! My dear child, I need you to stand proud, close to your father! We shouldn't let her win! Such deeply angelic arrogance…perfidious face of Renaissance! Mihaela's always been conceited and thought herself more special than you are! But she is just a leaf, shaking in the wind of dreams! She is afraid of who she is; she's running from one place to other, imagining she'll change the world with her utopist wonders! You are my true and sparkling child, so fearless inside! Stay brave and use your wisdom like a snake! The way you play piano and compose will charm the whole wide world!"

"But I can't compose! I am immortal and fearless and stronger than my sister, I play piano with a virtuosity that can break walls, but I'm unable to write at least one original note! I want to write, not just imitate the geniuses' scores… I wish so much, but when I try to write my notes, I just forget the melody that popped up in my soul. I want to write, with ease, magnificent, immortal symphonies, not sweat and toil over my deficiencies! What sort of an immortal being am I if I cannot write eternal lines…better than the human kind?"

"You will… I'll help you! Don't despair! You'll be a Mozart queen, composing brilliant tunes that will make your name well-known all over the entire world!"

"Father, last night I sneaked in Grid's old house and found my sister's journal with tons of poems and love songs… I do not like her earthly feelings of weeping and of weakness; they have no fire… What I want is to compose some royal majestic operas about vampires! But I need some Inspiration more than anything! Give it to me, father!"

"Inspiration?" Vlad asks himself, confronting residues of memories that tell him that this word belongs to Him…

"Yes, inspiration, father, as Mihaela named it in her journal…" Gabriela reinforces.

Silence. Vlad's face is frozen, unable to reply to his daughter.

Gabriela rises up: "Father, I am dark and young forever, flawless and without a blister, yet I'm in love with my beautiful and traitoress sister who now, with human mind, is writing ceaselessly a book about the stupid mortal life! Why can she? I hate her but I love her; she is my idol but my rival; she is my family but sexual fantasy! I cannot love another creature; I'm obsessed with her magical features! Where is she now? Why can't he find her? You said that he's your friend; you said that Lucifer can find her anywhere and bring her to your castle. And I just looked inside my magic mirror and saw my face so wicked and blue-smeared, and her human face so radiant and clear. I hate her, father, but I love her!"

"My daughter, you cannot love your sister the way you have whispered. She's your sister and you...her sister! Love a man!" Vlad breaks in, troubled.

"And you? You cannot be her father and love your daughter! She's your daughter, father! Destroy the statue! Now!"

"The statue, daughter? But...it is you, my love!" Vlad bursts into laughter.

"It's me?"

"Yes love, it's you! What got into your head?"

Gabriela looks up at the statue with big impudent eyes, forcing herself to believe it.

Vlad takes a chisel and hammer and, looking up and down at his daughter, pretends to adjust his work of art according to Gabriela's shapes and curves.

Gabriela boosts up with pleasure:

"I'll show her, Father!"

"Show her, my child! I'll boil for you a mist of luck! And meantime, I'll go and speak to Lucifer to help you find your sister!" You and her are one! She belongs to this house! Lucifer will teach me of your sister's fears and how to make her tear for what she did to our sphere! Together, we will slaughter her pride, her godly impudence of saying yes to mortal-losers. We'll find the cure. I will make sure she won't ever again leave this house!"

Gabriela's eyes fill with unflinching courage and devilish ambition.

Together with her bee-friend, Mihaela, as a miniature doll, has been watching the whole scene between Gabriela and Vlad.

"Indeed, Gabriela is right! Inspiration is everything! Poor sis, she is deceived by his lies!" Mihaela speaks to herself.

All of her anger against Gabriela dissipates into mercy's abyss. She never thought there would be such a chasm between a vampire and a human being, that a vampire can read, play, and imitate symphonies faster and better than any creature yet be unable to write an original line…of his own strain, filled with magical clay…

She first thought that David's bite had been a curse; that being afraid, human, and growing old, is horrible, unbearable… But inspiration and the gift of creation, the amazing blessing of love and being loved, have wiped away all of her worries, all of her fears.

Living forever without memories, heartaches, tears, dreams, or foresight, is frightful…living as a prisoner of the night, in the barren castle of Vlad…

"I never want to go back to who I was, now that I am who I am." Mihaela speaks sharply to herself.

She wants to help her sister realize her new nature…her gifts that can only be received and not achieved… Only saying "yes" to love can open your heart to compose! She wants to help her sister say "yes" to dreams, to writing, to love…

Moreover, helped by God, there is no way you cannot create. God is the creator. And as He is, so are we.

She didn't find God. God found her; He chose her.

She needs to teach her sister these wonderful secrets…tell her of these amazing blessings… She needs to open her eyes and tear her thorns apart.

Gabriela rushes out of Vlad's Icy Morgue of Brides, sliding along the dark corridors of the castle, into the arched tunnel of the Knights Hall. Carved faces of corpses, growls and screams of lions, bears, and human prisoners of Vlad, earthquake the icicle-columns, protuberated with skulls. Mihaela flies after Gabriela, holding on to the royal body of Mama-bee, her loyal friend.

Gabriela steps heavily toward the acid waterfall that hides Vlady's cell from the eyes of the passengers. Showered by the spiky iced drops of the waterfall, Gabriela lifts up the trap door and descends the narrow staircase that leads into the cave of Vlady.

Vlady is writing in his moldy dwelling that stinks of death.
Dripping yellow saliva, he slowly raises his eyes to Gabriela, who made her entrance as a queen. Gabriela breathes stormily in front of Vlady, sending his scribbled papers flying all over the cell. Then, circling Vlady's shelter with eyes of a tiger and analyzing his feeble features, Gabriela unbuttons her dress and jumps on him, devouring his neck with ardent bites, and scratching his skin with aroused claws of sin.

Vlady complies, moaning with weakness; Gabriela sucks Vlady's immortal blood with incandescent passion, making sounds of a famished beast. She then kisses him on his livid lips, revealing round naughty breasts that ooze indecently upon his face. Crazed and still thirsty of more pleasure, Gabriela tears apart Vlady's ragged cloth, leaving him hopelessly naked. With savaged shouts, she forces his weak body to rise, tossing her strong tail round his left wrist and then dragging him to the shuttered window which leads into the Dead Brook. In a flash, with the force of a giant, Gabriela fixes her brother to the wall, nailing his chained arms and feet that shake and drip bloodied cold mud. Crucified on the wall, Vlady's bones can be easily numbered. Sticking out her little tongue like a snake, Gabriela starts making love to Vlady with groans and twitches of a deranged beast, unbearable to the eye of a human kind. Mihaela and her bee-friend watch the scene paralyzed with horror. After she erupts off her desire, Gabriela slaps Vlady violently in the face:

"You are my brother. Yet, you did not put up any resistance. You complied, like a filthy mortal, into the arms of incest. Under these circumstances, I declare you and me married. Amen!"

Thereafter, Gabriela wraps a dirty piece of white cloth around her sinful body and then shoves a dirty ring of thorns on Vlady's wedding finger. Blue blood starts dripping from Vlady's poor white skin.

Gabriela makes her way out of his cell with the attitude of a respectful and satisfied wife.

Left alone and chained, Vlady cries with tears of an abandoned child... Mihaela takes a seat upon his shoulder, hearing his heartbreaking cry. All of a sudden, as she wants to embrace his pain away, she returns to her normal proportions. Vlady escapes an outcry of terror.

"Don't fear, my brother. I am your sister, Mihaela. I am here for you..."

Vlady opens his sore eyes, shivering with pain. Mihaela unchains his wounded arms, covering him with his frosty ragged garments. Vlady can barely move his no-longer virginal body, which has been dirtied by his own sister, Gabriela.

Midnight. Vlady's Cell.

Mihaela is still reading through Vlady's scribbled papers, where he has poured his heartbreaking story of mourning and sorrow. Mihaela's eyes are red and drenched in bitter tears. Her fingers tremble. She gathers all the papers, like a mother huddles her babies to her chest, her eyes fixing on a meticulously drawn-out map that shows the ins and outs of the Old Man's castle.

"That evening, when you visited me at Emil's house, I ran after you... I wanted to give you a hug, to tell you to stay... Why did you come back here?" Mihaela asks Vlady.

And then, Mihaela hugs her feeble brother, who is still trembling with fear.

"Please, stay here and wait for me... I will help you. I will get you out of here. Poor Aunt Magia cannot help us any more. She is dead."

Vlady mutters something indecipherable and then writes down with his frostbitten hand:

"Magia, not dead. I want revenge."

"Yes, she is, my dear brother. But do not despair. I will help you be free and publish your manuscript. Let Vlad in God's hands. God will avenge you..."

And Vlady writes again: "Magia gave me ink and paper. She helped me come to you."

"Magia?"

"Hmmm..." Vlady groans, nodding his head.

"It can't be true. I saw her dead."

Vlady nods his head again...

"I believe you. After all, Magia was a witch," Mihaela says, struck by the terrifying image of Aunt Magia on that stake in Papa's garden...

The bee stings Mihaela's left wrist.

Mihaela awakens and speaks:

"Meantime, dear Brother, please, eat this. It will give you strength to hold on..."

And the bee hands Vlady a small bag with pollen.

Secure steps thunder the ceiling of Vlady's cell. The door creaks.

"So long..." Mihaela whispers in Vlady's ear.

The bee transforms her into the miniature Mihaela again.

A long fingered hand opens Vlady's cell and throws in a plate with fresh meat, flooded in blood.

April 21st, 1689. In the afternoon.

The clock of Saint Mary's Church from Brașov[29] strikes louder and louder, calling in the faithful to the secret of eternal life.

---

[29] **Saint Mary's Church** *from the old Transylvanian city Brașov is known today as "The Black Church". The construction of it began in 1383. It is the largest place of worship in Romania, the largest cathedral East of Vienna. It possesses the biggest mechanical organ from Romania (4000 pipes), the biggest mobile bell (a 6 ton bell), the richest collection of oriental carpets from Europe, which date from the $15^{th} - 16^{th}$ centuries.*

A beautiful mother with a baby wrapped tightly at her chest, kneels in front of the fresco of Saint Mary. Saint Mary is sitting on a throne with baby Jesus in her arms. To the left and to the right of Virgin Mary are Saint Barbara and Katharina, looking upon Jesus with tender, tearful eyes.

Shadows of huge, flocky dogs reflect on the six Gothic portals of *Saint Mary's Church*. The giant dogs stride inside the church like rebel knights of the Dark Kingdom. With big muzzles and blue viscid saliva dripping out, they start sniffing the beautiful rugs sewn by unknown hands that grace the walls of *Saint Mary's*. With fierce claws and violent growls, they jump up at the floral rugs, until they catch them in their fangs and tear them to shreds.

A creature—Half-Man-Half-Woman—kneels down and places 12 newly born babies onto the floral rugs. The little ones have their mouths covered with white cloth, flailing and thrashing their tiny feet non-stop.

Three priests make their appearance, walking in sync through the three naves of the church, up to the grandiose altar.

One of the priests, dressed in a long golden soutane, walks to the beautiful mother who has been praying to the fresco of the Virgin Mary, and takes her baby from her arms. He then exits with it through the Golden gate, situated between two buttresses, while the other two priests, with long white beards, keep making crosses and kneeling in prayer.

An arch—a wreath of sculpted leaves—covers the portico designed in Gothic style, giving the church a unique sight. Cerberus plays Mozart's *Requiem* at a miraculous organ with 4,000 pipes.

The priest returns with the sweet baby, whereas the others are readying the holy font for the child's baptism.

The beautiful mother watches her baby with teary eyes of Virgin Mary.

Suddenly, with giant strides, the huge flocky dogs begin to run towards the baptismal font. The two priests, with long white beards, stare, making crosses of salvation with despair. The main priest, wrapped up in his shiny golden soutane, lets the baby fall inside the font and starts running towards the exit of the church. The other two priests follow him with rapid steps.

But the beasty dogs catch up to the hasty priests, flying at their wrinkled throats and mangling, in a flash, their flesh and bones.

The beautiful mother collapses. Her baby cries aloud in the christening gown. The dogs jump at the cauldron, struggling to reach the baby inside with their furious muzzles. Try as they might, the dogs are catapulted from the baptismal font by an unseen force.

Aligned on the colored woven carpets adorned with flowers and traditional motifs, the other 12 babies keep thrashing their arms and legs as in a dance of life and death. Unable to cry, held tightly by the white cloth shrouded around their little mouths, their sweet faces flush up with redness. Precipitately, the Half-Man-Half-Woman creature wraps the fragile infants in the woolen rugs, and drags them towards the altar, under the dead eyes and bitten necks of the holy fathers.

Hertius, an old faithful monk who has been watching the whole scene behind a column, takes the mother in his arms and carries her up to a secret portal of *Saint Mary*. A flocky dog gives him the evil eye and gallops savagely to catch Hertius and the mother in its sharp claws. Hertius looks the creature in the eye and opens his right palm that fills instantly with water. The dog licks up the water and turns still like a statue of marble.

The Half-Man-Half-Woman creature puts on the golden robe of the priest, inspecting the church and rehearsing the Sunday mass speech.

Tall majestic crosses are spread out in the entirety of Saint Mary.

Thousands of people are heading towards the church, for the holy mass.

In the meantime, Hertius, who has laid the fainted mother and her baby in his carriage, desperately tries to hamper the 5,000 people from entering the church. In spite of his insistent words and grueling pleadings that warn of the great danger, men frown and squint, and women spit into their bosoms, turning their heads around with disbelief. Moreover, some make crosses of rejection, casting curses and pebbles at the poor old monk. The rumor had it that the devil took Hertius' mind and thus the priests have asked for the banishment of this senile man from the Braşov town.

No sooner do the believers take their seats for the mass than the Half-Man-Half-Woman closes the gates and windows shut and locks them all inside. He then begins his "holy" speech about the qualities of blood, the types and variations, and about the incapability of mortals to heal after a significant loss of blood... With sweet words of perfidious love, the Half-Man-Half-Woman offers the believers the choice of immortality—of turning them into vampires and having them attack Braşov town to grace all the inhabitants with an immortal bite, in the name of Vlad, the only one who can offer them the gift of eternal life... People look desperately at the papers with drawings that have been handed out, on which Vlad the Impaler poses triumphantly with a stake in his hand. To no avail, they struggle to run from the imprisoned church, the words of the senile Hertius still echoing inside their minds.

Rejecting Vlad's way to immortality, guarded by the creepy shepherd dogs, the 5,000 people are being impaled through upturned crosses that have become murderous stakes and that hallow their way to a painful death. Their blood fills up hundreds of wooden barrels meant to quench the thirst of the Old Man Vlad.

In a flash, The Half-Man-Half-Woman and its servants move all the blood-filled barrels and floral rugs, crammed with babies, into the majestic chaise of the Old Man.

Dried out of hunger and still whining, the babies are the only ones "saved" as extra souvenirs for their master Vlad.

The Half-Man-Half-Woman sets the whole church on fire. The roof collapses; the stained-glass windows crumble; the 4000 piped-organ and the bells melt along with the tower clock that has ceased to wind its metal hands; the altar, with its pillars, crash down over the crosses that have impaled the flesh and blood of thousands of believers.

At last, with his lungs over-expanded and his mouth widely opened, the Half-Man-Half-Woman blows out a storming wind of breath that quenches the murderous flames in a flash and wipes away any trace of that infernal bloodbath.

Five thousand people who came to find their peace and light, have found death to wrap them in its arms—just because they turned down Vlad's "gift" of eternal life...

Filled with holy fire, Hertius leads the carriage
with the mother and the baby that she tightly holds to her chest.

Hertius spurs his horses to the town of Grid which was not too far away from *Saint Mary's Church.*

Behind the wheels of the carriage that move at high speed, on the verge of dismembering, tongues of fire are blackening the sky.

Smoked and fueled in pain, *The Church of Saint Mary* has turned into *The Black Church*, wearing its mourning revenge.

Filled with demonic fire, The Half-Man-Half-Woman leads the huge royal cart to Vlad's castle.

The dogs bark out victoriously, with their shaggy hair unleashed in the wind, while the barrels of blood toss and hit each other with threatening noise. The babies fret and crave, gnawing on the white cloth with terrible hunger...

The cart moves faster and faster, back to its master.

The foyer of Vlad's Castle.

Vlad welcomes the Half-Man-Half-Woman creature with a fastidious ceremony: snakes swarming on golden trays, crawfish with burnt-down skins on crystal plates, and fresh green-blue lizards lingering atop, arouse the appetite and lust.

The creature greedily snatches one snake with its soft, crumpled left hand while its other hand—strong and youthful—rests its golden rings on its slim waist. A bourgeois suit with big golden buttons wraps its left masculine half, whereas a long skirt with flowery embroideries ties the right feminine side of the creature's androgynous body.

Its face is half ugly, with an incandescent monstrous mole and a wrinkled nose on the left side, and half beautiful and charming—a porcelain face with a keen violet eye, and a soft cheek dimpled by an alluring smile...

Doomed to surprise the audience with its double profile—half Dantesque and half angelic—the creature also possesses, on its masculine side—a heavy potbelly, well shrunk in the tight tunic, as well as an enviable waist of a top model that flaunts gracefully on the ladylike side of its body.

Vlad wears a white mantle reminiscent of the Pope's holy gown and a tall white bonnet ornamented with purple stones. In his right hand, he holds a wooden scepter on which the seven laws, imposed by Vlad Țepeș during his sovereignty, are incrusted with bold golden letters.

Vlad's nine cats, with phosphorescent eyes and swaggering red tails, jump speedily onto Vlad's head and shoulders, throwing wicked glances at the big shepherd dogs that lick the barrels filled to the brim with blood.

With boundless joy, Vlad opens one of the barrels while listening to the creature's description of the massacre from Saint Mary's.

"Hmmm, so tasty... It smells of holy ashes of faith!" Vlad exclaims as a drop of hot blood spoils his cold papillae.

Then, as he widely opens the doors of Gabriela's chamber, Vlad introduces his loyal disciple-creature, displaying unflinching words of glory:

"My dearest Gabriela, may I present to you: Beastie. He is faithful, smart and majestic! We've never welcomed such a delightful creature in our house before—Half Man, Half Woman, both elegant and cruel! He will be, from now on, my loyal servant, providing the finest and most varied types of blood and...fresh delicious infants from all around... From Transylvania to New York, from Singapore to New Delhi, from Tokyo to New England and back to my castle, Beastie will search for the freshest brides and the sweetest children, for the most rejuvenating types and flavors of blood. He will be accompanied by the Moon Dogs, my dearest Transylvanian shepherd dogs, that will smell the feeblest and the freshest mortals on earth..."

Beastie arches its back before Gabriela, in reverence, while Gabriela honors its presence with her back.

"And now, the most vivid decoration of your room that will give you inspiration beyond your imagination," Vlad raises his voice with confidence, trying to further impress his daughter.

Cerberus and Beastie festively bring the floral rugs to Gabriela's chamber, unwrapping the half dead babies onto the cold floor.

As soon as Cerberus takes the white cloths from their little mouths, the 12 babies start crying so loud that they crack the walls of the house; famished and feeble, they gulp down the frosty air and quench their thirst with their own saliva, slurped back through their fragile throats.

Gabriela turns her head and peeks at Beastie and Vlad with wide scorning and reproach:

"Get out! I am trying to write. No one cares about my mind?"

Vlad freezes up in front of his daughter's repugnance while Beastie and Cerberus look down, brain-struck by the attitude of his "obedient" daughter.

Quietly, Vlad closes the doors of his daughter's chamber, justifying Gabriela's strange manner:

"She must be giving birth to something phenomenal... Let's not invade her metaphoric ecstasy..." Vlad adds, his ghost-like cheeks peeling and cracking off like earth quaked walls.

Gabriela jumps off her one-legged chair, and draws near her collection of puppetry, rusted and blackened by the dust of decades...

The 12 babies cry ceaselessly onto the floral carpets.

"Shut up!" Gabriela shouts out, deeply irritated.

The babies stop, blinking their big round eyes.

With cold angry hands, Gabriela grabs her collection of Bloody Dolls and starts ripping their heads off, one by one. After which, she yanks them off the shelves, out through the window, along with her other valuable collections of vampiric art: her grinning cats made of Murano glass; her lovely singing ballerina boys that she wound up all through her childhood; her seven slain boyfriends, molded of clotted blood and clay by her own hands; the glass case of boyars, impaled onto The Virgin Forest; the Hunting Bitches, carved from thousands of wolf fangs and cats' bones...

All these graceful and precious objects of vampire art break under the delirious and strong knockout performed by their queen of the dark.

"All these stupid puppets that have buried my inspiration and clogged my brain to stagnation! I am not an infant anymore! I am a real woman! Hear me, dear Papa?"

Gabriela's fangs lengthen and erupt out of her big tumid mouth like the cliffs of a mountain; her face blemishes with scabby bumps as she forces her mind to write; blue smoke springs out of her nostrils and through her black goatlike ears. Suddenly, feeling her wired locks of hair coiling around her body, in a twirl of rage, Gabriela grabs them with her long nails, trying to cast them off her torso. But her nails snap at once, like some overbaked plastic knives, and her hair tightens and strengthens, almost suffocating her body. Disgusted by her brittle claws, she bites them out of her flesh, rejoicing greatly to see them sprouting bluish blood and growing longer, sharper and stronger in the blink of an eye.

The babies toddle around Gabriela's room, looking for some food... Gabriela totally ignores them, absorbed by the immensity of her ego.

A cute little mouse cuts the mistress's way.

Gabriela's anger cools down like a tornado swallowed up by the sky. The mouse, fearful and undecided, stops for a twinkle before Gabriela's eyes. Gabriela snatches it in her hands at once, squeezing the life out of it. Laughing spasmodically when its intestines come out and her small mouth slurps it rapidly into her stomach, Gabriela rushes to her piano, screaming with devilish fire:

"I can write it now! I am filled with strength and wrath, ready to conquer the Earth!"

The babies cry again, frightened by Gabriela's sharp fangs.

"Shut up!" Gabriela shouts again at the poor crying beings.

The babies cease to sob and to shake their little arms.

Driven by insane pleasure, Gabriela grabs a feather and injects it in her veins. After she soaks the tip of the feather into her bluish blood, her veins start twining rapaciously through her arms, healing each other on the spot, and ringing a short, discreet sound. Her skin now looks younger, bluish and flawless...

Satisfied and feeling calmer, Gabriela scrawls with her blood-ink on her yellowish papers, until the break of dawn enters her chamber.

The rooster crows, and the rays of sun flash in Gabriela eyes.

Staring at her scribbled papers and her indecipherable scores, that she mingled in circles, like the drawings of a kinder garden pupil, Gabriela bursts into a whine of terror, as if she has lost the battle:

"He had the best teachers teach me the art of composing; the best orators speak the theory of prosing...yet the more they revealed their skills and fingered their wisdom into my wits, the more I realized how ephemeral their teaching is, flipping out of my mind like the seeds of cherries out of the mouth of an obese child, still eager to eat... This father of mine has the power of living through others, taking different voices and forms, forever indebted to his Lucifer mentor, but he has not the power of giving me the gift of inspiration and writing...as he has promised me for so long! I am beautiful and immortal, and so I ought to be applauded and set at Metropolitan...as a Creator, as the famous vampire author—the best and only one, 'cause there is no other like me in this whole world! But why is this truculent and turbulent chasm happening to my mind? I've been composing genial melodies on the spot at all my father's fests and for all of his bloated guests... But why do I get these blank pages without a note, now that I'm left in my chamber, alone? I need just one little tiny stream of notes to come out of my brain, and then I can declare myself a genial composer! Just one little push, and the whole symphonies will flow like honey from my flesh and bones!"

And Gabriela forces herself to get one little note out of her brain onto her blank paper, like a child pushes itself on the potty whenever it is constipated.

Suddenly, Mihaela appears as a giant indigo eye before Gabriela's cold eyes. Gabriela smirks with terrible felicity, laughing her head off:

"Look, here is my long-awaited composition! Here is my eye of inspiration! I knew I could get it out! I am a genius, I am a genius!" she jumps and leaps for joy like a happy child.

"It's me, your sister, Mihaela," Mihaela suddenly speaks to her sister, blinking from the indigo eye like a bird flutters her wings.

"What?"

"I am this indigo eye! And she is my friend—Mama-bee!" Mihaela introduces her bee friend that buzzes to Gabriela, splashing her bluish skin with honey.

"What? Why now, you sister? Why are you here when I am celebrating a moment of great triumph?"

"It's not a triumph, it is a fight, a fight between your human nature and your vampiric fissure; it is your mind that's eager to create, yet your vampiric heart is dead and cannot put in motion human's art. Art belongs only to humans who have their hearts by Cupid's arrow, broken; their minds by tearing memories, haunted; their eyes by crucial visuals, opened; their ways by God hallowed..." Mihaela tells Gabriela as she takes her human proportions, dressed in her Joan of Arc-like costume.

"It is not true! I, who am fearless and strong, shall write for different kinds of creatures, who can absorb true power, and not the weakness of the human sorrow! My pages of immortal wording, my symphonies of malefic origin, will soon be published by my father in millenary volumes of vampire-awarding!"

"Don't be too proud, my dear. Inspiration belongs only to humans who are conceived by God."

"Why are you here, sis? To speak of human beings and their lousy feelings? Look at your eyes! You're beautiful, indeed. But five more years and no man will want you in his bedroom, and you'll be crying in my father's arms to give immortal blood to your anemic human clod! What do you want?" Gabriela asks Mihaela, vaingloriously.

"To help you..." Mihaela answers, kindly.

"So well, then help me! Oh, wait, it's coming..."

And Gabriela scribbles down a note on a yellowish paper engraved with the Draconian blazon of her father's.

"I'm writing, I'm composing!" Gabriela cries out, overwhelmed by her avalanche of inspiration.

"Ha ha, farewell my sister and your human words!
  I'm bearing vampiric quotes of musical geniality,
  That Beethoven or Bach did not impose in Arts.
  I'll revolutionize the underworld and its artistry
  And bring the world an innovative deathless mystery!
  I'll do just like God did: create my world of vampiric origin,
  Dominating the earth with my powerful symphonies
  In tune with the classical antiquity and modern expressivity
  That Papa taught me since early age
  In order to monopolize time and space.
  Yes, I am more powerful than anyone else on this planet
  And I will reign with my invincible smartness and talent!
  I'll show the living creatures that God, and His religious acts,
  Are odd and truly out of date, and that what solves
  Is drinking blood to wipe away the fearful notes!
  Hey-Ho, I am the God of this generation
  My opera is queenly, the birth of contamination!

"Bravo!" Mihaela emboldens her sister. "If you can do it on your own,
I'll leave you all alone!"

"Go away, sister! Let me compose! Can't you hear what I just spoke?"

"Of course. I'll let you compose with your genial zest,
  And I'll stay out of touch until you need my help!"

And Mihaela becomes, again, small as a doll, leaving Gabriela in her
state of glory. Mounted on Mama-bee, she prepares to step out of the
room, but the whimper of the 12 infants hinders her route.

With motherly love, Mihaela approaches the poor babies who look
almost dead, pale as ghosts, fretting onto the cold floor that smells like
tombstone.

Mama-bee blows a mist of pollen upon Gabriela, and Gabriela
becomes blurred and much smaller before their eyes.

Mihaela kisses the little children on their cold cheeks, takes them to her chest, and swings them to sleep, but they are too restless to catch forty winks. Mama-bee, who senses their empty tummies and terrible thirst, proceeds: she immediately pours honey into their sweet little mouths, feeding the babies until they are all satisfied. Meantime, Mihaela brings them water, and covers their little bodies in swaddling clothes made from Gabriela's dresses.

Gabriela, seated on her piano bench, is deep in her writing. She does not see, she does not hear anything... Exalted and puffing loudly, she jumps to her feet and rushes out of her chamber, with her eyes on fire and her big teased hair framing her face like the crown of a lion. Running through the hallway that leads into her father's chamber, she screams with desire, as she has caught her long-hunted prey at that hour:

"Father, Father! I'm coming, Father!"

Gabriela bursts into Vlad's room like a fast-flying bat, with her scores lifted up in praise. No sooner does she open her father's door than her sheets freeze in her hands, and her eyes drop down to his bed...

A younger-than-ever father comes to her sight, in the very act of vampiric eroticism... With his dark blue gown unfurled, Vlad shows off glowing white breasts, sucked by ten naked women, who jubilate with their tails and horns around his bald torso.

A loud symphonic music echoes from the gramophone, enhancing the thrilling act...

The ten women, extremely white, almost transparent, with perfect round breasts, with long Botticellian hair and pompous buttocks ended in snakelike tails, are floating in the air, circling Vlad with gracious flair and tickling him with sheer sensual locks of hair around his genital and congenital areas.

Gabriela turns off the gramophone. The women turn their heads at once, rolling their eyes and snake-tails towards Gabriela. As they see Gabriela's wicked glance and frozen hands on her little waist, they start giggling like some Geishas. Yet, Vlad shudders with shame and orders them to take their leave. The women become invisible at once. Only their whining and mourning echoes like the meows of some hungry cats.

"Who are those women?" Gabriela asks Vlad with cold eyes.

Vlad takes back his normal physiognomy, his old bleached face, blazing with ice; his long nailed hands filled with wrinkles and blight, letting his head bend down...

"I've never seen you this way, Father..." Gabriela speaks, unwilling to look into her parent's eyes.

"I am sorry, my dear. You were never supposed to meet them. They become visible only when involved in these kind of...sensual activities. You see, I need them for the pleasures of this body... It is this flesh which requires a certain desire. These Hunting Bitches are loyal and make me forget..."

"Daddy, how could that face of yours become so young? I don't understand!" Gabriela cuts her father's words.

"I never had the chance to tell you, my sweet child... When you will get a little older, you will meet him, my old friend, whom I've been telling you about, and you will be able to take any face that you desire..."

"Any face that I desire? Even my sister's face?"

Vlad bursts into a big laughter.

"I could never imagine you wishing to take such a different face..."

"Father, I have miraculous news! I composed! I was able to write! And not only to write, but to effortlessly compose with superb notes! Father, I think that I am a genius!"

And Gabriela shows her father a staff with scribbled notes on a score, grinning conceitedly.

She then rushes onto the stage that was built in the back of her Papa's chamber and takes a seat at the large golden piano, adorned with blue-lit candles. She places her fingers onto the virgin keys and starts playing the beginning of her long-conceived symphony.

"Beautiful, go on, my dear," Vlad heartens his daughter, closing his eyes and listening with emotion to her melody as he graciously waves his long nailed hand like a conductor's baton.

Gabriela smiles with infinite pride, swinging her head in the blow of her disharmonies as the tall candles are bluing her face.

She then stops to write down some notes on her yellowish sheets...yet her fingers freeze, her mind blocks.

"I don't know…what was I trying to write down?"

"What were you trying to write down, my dear?" Vlad asks his daughter, calmly.

"I was trying to write some music against the human race… But what has happened to my brain? It is not the idea that I forgot, 'cause I have written it down. It is the actual feeling that has disappeared…and along with it, the melody… I don't know why, so I don't know what and how…"

And Gabriela starts puffing black smoke out of her nostrils, again and again. She stands up, agitated, circling the piano like a lion in its cage. She gives a growl of anger, hitting the piano with steel fists of venom.

"Calm down, my daughter! Don't pressure yourself! It'll come back! Have patience."

"When, when? And how? I have been waiting for it all of my life!"

And saying that, Gabriela abandons the virgin keys of the piano and storms out of her father's apartments. Like a block of ice, burnt down by intoxicating lava, she runs into her chamber and throws herself onto the bed, screaming from the top of her burning lungs: "I am a genius! I am! I'll show the world!" while struggling to reject her sister's haunting words: 'Inspiration belongs only to humans!'

"No, no! Inspiration belongs to me… There's got to be another way!"

Abruptly, she rises like an eagle, with serpent eyes, and glares at the big clock that ticks onto her peeled-off walls. The babies and the carpets are gone. So much disturbing silence. Only the moon, veiled and somber, has an eye inside her chamber.

"Two more hours until midnight!" she whispers with a wicked thought, touching her body. She then takes her clothing off, remaining naked under the soft touch of the dusk; she analyzes her buttocks in the windows' glass… She can't stop thinking of the Hunting Bitches…the ten lubricious women from her father's chamber. Their bodies were beyond perfection. She is not too far from them either. And yet, a loving boyfriend has never touched this perfect molded body of hers! Only she has touched her brother who did not touch her back, but just humiliated her with his annoying dumbness.

Feeling sexy and proud, she draws away from the cold windows and jumps before the oval mirror from her dressing table that shows her features, sharp and flawless. Quickly, she begins to blush her face with a fine grain made from pollen and seeds of the Queen of the Night flower, prepared by Mihaela herself, powder which she stole from Papa Grid's house. She then puts honey on her lips, red rose cream on her cheeks, blue marine on her eyes from her dried blood, and smiles. She hasn't smiled for years.

"It is so hard to smile; your face becomes so wide!" Gabriela thinks, forcing herself to grin.

Actually, she does not look bad at all with this sultry, grotesque human smile on her face. She keeps it on.

Then, opening a drawer, she takes out a score of Mozart and starts smelling the staves. She picks a feather and pierces her veins, again and again, just like earlier in the day, inducing her creative ecstasy. She yells with satisfaction! Blue blood emerges like a viscous waterfall out of her veins, but Gabriela keeps smiling with hungry teeth.

Midnight. Gabriela is on the terrace of her chamber.

She walks up and down like a hunting beast. Her eyes are red, her makeup flaking.

Inside her chamber—corpses of red-haired boys are hanging on enormous hooks, like slaughtered animals in an abattoir.

"Now I should have it... I feel recharged!"

She storms into her room and jumps at her piano, playing in agony. She's swinging her head gracelessly, to the right and to the left, into the sardonic twirl of her creation.

"There, that's it!" she yells, triumphantly.

She then stops and scribbles down, unceasingly, the notes that are flooding her mind: two pages, three, four, five, twenty!

"Yes, I am a genius!" Gabriela screams. "This is what I needed! I knew it!"

She rises gloriously from her piano bench and starts licking the dead bodies of the young red-haired boys who flavor the room with the stench of their corpses. She starts biting them aggressively, opening her blue dress and revealing round aroused breasts...

"Too small!" Gabriela utters, displeased, looking down at her chest. Snatching the hand of one of the corpses, she places it on her waist, then softly on her breasts, up to her neck, sliding it on her face, on her lips, and then inside her mouth. She opens the corpse's pants violently, pushed by the Hunting Bitches ecstasy that has fascinated her. She then starts moaning and making love with the dead body of one of the red-haired boys who is silently enjoying the act.

"I am a genius, a genius! Sex pushes me to write like no one else! From sin arouses my win! Yeah!"

3 am.

Gabriela's chamber is dark and guilty.

She slowly pulls away from the raped corpse that falls off her ovulating womb like a plastic melting doll. She reaches for her grand piano and, blowing fire out of her nostrils, she lights up the three candles that are symmetrically placed onto the piano lid. Fixing her crowded, scribbled music sheets that are waiting quietly on the fallboard, she starts playing with pride what she has composed few hours before.

Playing faster and faster, wilder and wilder, her eyes abruptly squint, her fingers tremble and cringe, her face agonizes under the hot red smoke of the candlelight.

"Nooooooo!" she screams out, jumping back like a mad cat that has burnt up its tail. Staring dreadfully at her piano that watches her calmly like a beautiful enemy, she realizes the catastrophic reality: what she has been writing is an imitation...not her work... It is Mozart—*Don Giovanni*—the score that she has been smelling to inhale genial inspiration and musical flow!

"My brain has deluded me!" Gabriela gives an infernal wail.

She then looks down at her hands that look guiltier and white as a sheet, shaking like dry leaves in the wind.

"These are the real enemies of my impotent creative genes! I feel it!" she utters with rancor.

Gabriela read somewhere in her sister's journal: "If thy hand or thy foot offend thee, cut them off, and cast *them* from thee…"

"This might be Mihaela's secret? Should I cut off my hands?" she asks herself with despair.

Barely does Gabriela ask herself than she starts hitting her hands against the piano, again and again, harder and harder, trying to dismember them. But instead, her piano breaks down like a putrefied tree, and then she, herself, breaks on the floor, twitching hysterically like a broken doll. Her face and body swell up, being spoiled with the human bloodied juice of the red boys that severely stained the precious parquet of her royal floor. After a few minutes of shaking and rolling, Gabriela rises up to her feet, and taking the music sheets in her disloyal hands, she starts ripping them off, one by one. The torn papers fall down as birds' feathers, drenching in the red blood as well.

"I'll keep writing, more and more…and it will come to me, a hundredfold! I won't worry at all!" she emboldens herself.

However, she breaks again into wails and whines, forcing herself to cry. Incapable of pulling a drop of a tear…she jerks and howls like a famished wolf, groaning vociferously to Lucifer: "Why? Why? Where is that devilish fire you promised to burn inside me and make me inspired?"

"Please, sweet sister, let me help you!" Mihaela appears again in the chamber of her sister as a big indigo eye, circling around Gabriela's dark face.

Gabriela frames her sister with the grin of a devilishly intoxicated lynx. "How?" she asks Mihaela, gnashing her teeth.

"I have a deal for you…something that will help you write…"

"Mmmm…" Gabriela groans with disbelief.

And Mihaela waves a manuscript before Gabriela's eyes.

"Read this: *Wicked Clone*—my manuscript…"

"What is this?" Gabriela asks Mihaela, rattle-brained. And snatching at once Mihaela's manuscript, she starts to read... Her eyes open wider and wider... Her lips almost break her stoned face with a smile. However, she comes back to her wicked senses and asks Mihaela with a smirk of hatred:

"What do you want me to do with these papers?"

"This is the beginning of the play that I'm writing..." Mihaela replies enthusiastically. "Do you like it?"

"These characters... How do you know about Beastie, about the Hunting Bitches, about the Brides...about me and my life? How did you come up with all these stories from Papa's castle?"

"I have this third eye, remember?"

And Mihaela blinks from her big indigo eye, hypnotizing her sister to give a sweet smile. She then takes her normal proportions and embraces Gabriela with arms of love. Gabriela takes a few steps back and wipes the touches of her sister away, feeling ashamed.

Mihaela wears a long white gown and ballerina flats; her face is radiant, but brushed with fine wrinkles.

"Do you remember the *Palace Theatre* from Times Square?" Mihaela asks Gabriela, frolicking.

"I don't know... I can't remember anything, you know... My memories..." Gabriela replies, grumpily.

"Oh, yes, I know..." Mihaela takes a sad face.

"But what I want is to perform on a big fabulous stage...to be rich in New York, applauded and wanted!" Gabriela rubs her hands with satisfaction. "Oh, honey, oh how I love your money..." she suddenly starts singing and dancing with an invisible man.

"*Honey, money*?! Ha! But how could you remember this song that we wrote together? *Honey, oh how I love you, honey, You know I'm not for money...* " Mihaela starts joining Gabriela's singing.

They both look at each other, and start laughing.

"Yes, that song..." Gabriela gives Mihaela a quick kiss of love. "When you are near me, I start to remember..." Gabriela speaks, taking a seat at her broken piano, and playing ***Honey, Money*** pianissimo...

HONEY, MONEY (Chorus)

"We haven't gotten along that well since we were kids, when we were best friends…in those escapades…" Mihaela thinks in her heart. Suddenly, she sees the faces of those men, their blood and pain… She gets so scared, thinking that those days were once part of her life.

"No, now I am a new being forever. Those days do not belong to the true Mihaela!" she says, pushing those dark thoughts out of her mind.

"You look so…good, yet different. Like a lady!" Gabriela casts Mihaela's fear off her face.

Mihaela smiles, lightening Gabriela's features with her big glistening eyes. She shows even more wrinkles, yet more warmth.

Gabriela tries to smile too, but the frozen opening of her mouth stops her muscles from showing an expression of love. Her flawless face and porcelain body make her look like a forever-cool teenager, untouched by the passage of time.

"You don't really recall anything about the *Palace Theatre*, about those big advertisements with your face?" Mihaela asks Gabriela again.

"What are you talking about? I told you: I don't know anything... My father put me to..."

"Yes?"

"Nothing," Gabriela stops her words.

"What about your father?" Mihaela asks.

"Vlad loves theater... Papa told me a lot about theater," Gabriela stammers.

"I see... Well, I have been out there again—in Times Square..." Mihaela continues, "...so curious to see the play about the two of us, the play...that they put together—called Dracula's Daughters. But the *Palace Theatre* has been replaced by a trivial cabaret, where vulgarity and obscenity prevail...and those people from that cabaret...make fun of us, deforming our characters with some low class lines performed by amateurish actors... You cannot believe the way they are portraying you...what *vampire* means to them; what a phony make-up and dreadful artificial fangs they put on those poor actors! Everything is delusional, upside down. I watched "Twilight" and other movies at the theater and said to myself: "God, people need to know the truth about vampires and about themselves! Humans treat themselves like...nothing! They all dream about being someone or something else—something more powerful... But that's a lie. Humans are already powerful, like God... If they only look up to Him...they become like Him..."

"What is a movie?" Gabriela asks with curiosity, cutting her sister's emotional speech.

"Oh, we need to go see one together. Movies are emotional stories with actors projected on a big screen... Trained, talented actors portray different characters—some strong, some weak...just like we do it in theater... These actors get to live new lives in front of a rolling eye, called the film camera that freezes their performance on tape for eternity."

"For eternity?" Gabriela asks with wide opened eyes.

"Yes, when a movie is really good, generation after generation gets to watch it."

"Then I want to be an actress!" Gabriela shouts out with ecstasy.

"Yes! Definitely!" Mihaela lets out a big laughter.

"Tell me, are there any true vampires out there, in 2014?" Gabriela asks Mihaela with engrossed interest.

"No, not as far as I know, unless you know..."

"I can't remember if there are any... My head cannot... You know it!" Gabriela snarls at her sister.

"So strange... I also had such a short memory before. But as soon as I took out those fangs, I started to remember everything about you and me ever since we were babies. And then about...Aunt Magia, Papa, Mama when I was just one-day old... Gabriela, please change for the good of the two of us... It is so scary to have no memory... Pull those fangs out..."

"If you came here to change me, you may leave now. I love myself the way I am. What good is it to be like you?" Gabriela cries out.

"No, I did not come to change you but you see that without those fangs I started to write, to have memories..."

Gabriela freezes for a moment and then continues to speak:

"All I can remember is that you broke our vow and that you are growing old! I don't want to grow old. I don't want to die. I am young and beautiful and I will stay like that forever."

A cold wind slinks along. Mihaela sneezes.

"What's that?" Gabriela asks her, bewildered.

"A sneeze."

"A sneeze? It's the first time that I've heard about this!"

"See, when a current of cold air passes through your body and you start feeling chilly, your body shivers with electric shocks... Sometimes you catch a cold...and then, you sneeze," Mihaela explains.

"Catch a cold?"

"Yes, your nose starts running like a leaking pipe; your throat sores like a burnt up meal; your eyes tear like wandering dew drops. A nasty virus makes a dwelling in your body for a week or so, and you fight it out with soothing teas and herbs. I caught a cold two weeks ago at that awful cabaret in Times Square; I cried and I got angry because of that representation...and my immunity lowered. And then, I caught a cold. I got a fever too. But it was good for me. While I was sick, I wrote *Wicked Clone.*"

"I love the name!" Gabriela exclaims. "It is so funny!"

"Gabriela, please help me!" Mihaela breaks in with pleading eyes. "I want to put an end to that sarcasm. It hurts me to see that awful play... Lies hurt. Come to New York with me. You'll play the *Wicked Clone!*"

"You ask me to come to New York with you? I begged you to take me with you ten thousand times but you just banished me! And why now...why?"

"I grew. I want to... I want us to do something great together! For Mama, for the future! We are twins, and when two put in mind to do something together it always gets perfect! Moreover, people need to know the truth about us, about our history...about what it means to be a vampire, and what it takes to escape it..." Mihaela speaks aloud.

"So you think that you can ever escape it?" Gabriela asks Mihaela with a serious voice.

"Stop it! You frighten me!"

"Well, I'm the wicked clone, right? How am I supposed to act?"

"You need love...human love... Only she can change you..."

"Human love? Cheating on your wife? Betraying your friends? Loving yourself more than your neighbor, killing for money and making virtual sex? Yes, I know some things about your human love!" Gabriela sniggers.

Mihaela looks at Gabriela, perplexed. It hurts to know that she is right. There is indeed a darker side to the human beings...

"But that is not love," Mihaela replies. "Love has no darkness. Love is love. Love forgives and heals, and is able to make the impossible possible. Love is everything. Love loves the ones who love the Love and want to act like her..."

"What are you talking about? Are you still dreaming? Who has this kind of love? Show me one person…"

"There is one. Look up to the sky. And this one person injects true Love into all people's souls…"

"Look what has gotten into you. You live in a whole stupid illusion, wrapped up in fog and clouds, Sister! Come down! Stop dreaming; start living! Come with me in those escapades and enjoy real love and fun!" Gabriela speaks to Mihaela with fire.

"That's not love, my dear… And those escapades are from another life that so long ago in me died! Gabriela, there is a life and a perfect love…a love that awaits you…a heartbeat, memories, dreams…that can change you from the inside out…and then you will write… What for immortal face, if your soul does not help you create?"

"I told you that I don't want to change! Never!" Gabriela stops her sister, angrily. "Get out of my life! I don't deal with pastors and nuns!"

"But we need to change something in this world, to improve ourselves, otherwise we have no reason to live at all…"

"Why should we change something when everything is just perfect? I feel perfect!" Gabriela chimes in.

"Because change means living, creating, moving the world forward… Change means losing your evil and gaining goodness, immortal freedom: *Whoever tries to keep their life will lose it, and whoever loses their life will preserve it.*"

"What's that stupid line?"

"If you lose your life, you will begin to write…like a human being…"

"You drive me crazy! You sound pathetic! I don't write like human beings or for human beings…"

"But for who?"

Gabriela stutters, unable to reply. Indeed, the human beings are the audience, the main species that populate the globe. She has to write for them. This drives Gabriela crazy! However, the image of herself, on stage, dominating the humans, confronting storms of applauses, ovations and bouquets, overtake her being…

"Look at me. We can really change something in this world! We know more…about the good and the evil! We are a whole!" Mihaela heartens her sister. "I know you can compose. You have it in you. It's just that you have to..." and Mihaela pauses.

"I have to?" Gabriela asks, full of curiosity.

"You have to listen to your heart!"

"My heart?" Gabriela asks, bewildered.

"Yes, in there you hold love...and inspiration..."

And Mihaela places her palm on Gabriela's heart. She waits for a few seconds, but her hand gets cooler and cooler, it freezes. Gabriela's heart is not beating...it is as cold as ice.

Mihaela takes a few steps back, terrified:

"Your heart...is not beating!"

"What do you mean it's not beating? Then how do I live?" Gabriela asks, perplexed.

"I don't know... How was I living before? Put your palm here," Mihaela says, staring at Gabriela with fearful eyes.

Gabriela bends down, and places her ear to Mihaela's heart, listening, carefully: "Tic tock, tic tock..."

"Yes, I hear," Gabriela whispers in awe.

"Tic tock, tic tock..."

Next day. At dawn.

Gabriela and Mihaela, walking hand in hand, like two knotted branches, set forth in the blessed dew of the morning. The cold, queenly wind plays with their long, loose hair, twined by shy rays of sun.

Together, the two sisters enter Papa Grid's garden, through the small gate of their childhood and step onto the fresh grass, beautifully trimmed by Grid.

A black rooster crosses their path and gives a loud, mad crow.

Mihaela avoids the weird-looking bird and steps into the rose plantation. Her feet start bleeding at once. She definitely forgot about the thorns:

"Ah, I told Papa to stop planting these roses..."

Gabriela can hardly restrain her lust of licking the blood that trickles out of her sister's feet. And yet, Mihaela's warm hand, twined into her hand, melts her desire away, into the morning lights.

Behind the well and the bucket, the double Queen of the Night flower, which grew in the place of the wicked fanged tree, looks more beautiful than ever; it has wide indigo flowers with silver stripes like some stellar jewels and emanates diaphanous rays of an angel... Its tall and loving stem faces the heights, reaching beyond the house, up to the clouds.

Helped by Mihaela, Gabriela jumps onto the tall stem of the Queen of the Night, clutching at its lofty velvety stem. Gracefully, with a ballerina bounce, Mihaela leaps onto the happy stem of the flower too, pulled up by Gabriela's strong hand.

The black rooster crows again. The angelic-nicotine perfume of the flower enraptures their senses, giving Gabriela and Mihaela unknown powers to climb faster towards the sky.

Nevertheless, the second stem of the Queen of the Night flower, which pierces into the ground, awakens from its sleep, and raises its head up high, catching the twins' feet with its poisonous ivy tentacles and trying to pull them back to the ground. But in a flash, Gabriela pierces it with her nails, and then cuts the tentacles with her sharp fangs. However, her back hunches, her nails snap, and an excruciating ache bumps into her chest. It is for the first time that Gabriela feels a pain, an acute pain in her heart...

Suddenly, a black butterfly, small and ugly as the devil, enters Gabriela's left eye. Mihaela sees the mischievous fly, but she can do nothing to pull it out... Gabriela frets and whines. Swiftly, Mihaela calls out for her bee-friend. Mama-bee comes into sight in the blink of an eye. She pulls out her sharp golden needle and stings the black butterfly until it falls lifelessly from Gabriela's eye.

Lurking around the garden, behind the walnut tree, Aunt Magia watches Mihaela and Gabriela with an eagle eye... Her hair is white as snow, her lips—dark purple, her only eye—as a blue pearl, glitters between Heaven and Hell. Her feet, like the thick roots of the walnut tree, are deeply rooted into the ground. Her long nails are blood red and dirty, her breasts—round and bitten as the apple of Eve.

"Ah, I need to suck the sap of this old ground to feed my dirty rotten bones... Oh, how hard these evil worms are biting from my soul..." Magia groans, terribly.

Desiccating and dissecting the soil, Aunt Magia digs her jaw inside the earth, drinking the blue blood that boils beneath. Her body grows stronger, but more hideous and dirty.

The rooster crows the third time.

With her face degraded and spoiled by lizards and worms, Magia utters piteous words, looking at her nieces who have almost touched the sky:

"Mihaela, she doesn't know what she is doing.
She wants to change the evil into good,
Turn back to deprecating sisterhood...
Poor girl! She'll soon fall in her fooling!
She is an innocent and candid bride
That left her wicked clone for love and art.
What got inside her mind now that she's climbing
Along a cruel sister, a murderess of siblings?
Doesn't she know that she can't ever change her sister
But only God who has the power, time and wisdom?
And yet, she changed me into what I cannot figure.
Those bloodied fangs that in this ground
Mihaela once buried,
are ugly roots of evil that she gave up for me to marry.
They brought me back to life to see again her smile,
But gave my heart an evil beat, and to my face,
a monstrous lift!
Horrible creatures of the night I've found and found me,
the underground and hellish sounds, surround me...
I'm traveling between Lucifer and the worldly pagans,
Unable to see my dear siblings in sweet Heaven!
What good is to keep living if I am filled with hatred and
with filth?
The sun rejects my face! I'm shunned, aching beneath

the tilth!

Throwing herself into the vivid grass, Magia crawls like a lizard towards the evil stem of The Queen of the Night flower. She then opens her snakelike mouth and, with her thin and rapid tongue, she catches the thorns of the stem, nipping and chewing them, greedily. A pair of decayed sharp fangs belittles her misaligned teeth, hurting her tongue each time she speaks.

Gabriela and Mihaela have reached already high, swinging on a cuddling cloud of the sky. Mihaela whispers in the ear of the cloud their destination. The cloud takes them to the other side of the world, to New York City.

Gabriela and Mihaela arrive in front of the **Live No More** *cabaret, in Times Square.*

Richard, the man with small ring-shaped eyes, with suspenders and frivolous smile, protects the hidden treasure of the night—the *Live No More* nightclub. Playing with a rainbow-coil-spring, he keeps moving it back and forth, to the groove of his short, jerking neck moves.

"Fa-la-la-la-la… I am rich…that's my itch!" he mumbles.

Mihaela holds Mommy Doll in her hand, shivering with hot and cold. She still feels dizzy from their flight, and from the nicotine perfume of the Queen of the Night. But Gabriela looks great, in perfect shape, ready to take on the world. Dressed in a black velvet gown, sewn with silver pearl beads, she impetuously offers her hand for a kiss:

"Hi, Richard. My sister had the honor to see your magnificent play about Dracula's Daughters last week."

"Oh…" Richard grins.

"My name is Gaby Morgan. I'm a journalist. I write for The New York Times. I would like to write a chronicle about your performance tonight."

"My performance?" Richard asks, bewildered.

"I mean Dracula's Daughters' performance..." and Gabriela shoves into Richard's eyes her New York Times authentication.

"I believe you, I believe you, of course... Welcome!" Richard exclaims as he scratches his left palm.

Penetrated by the stake of fame, Richard kisses Gabriela's hand with profound satisfaction. With a twist of his left arm, he unscrews an underground gate, and then immediately, a red carpet pops up, unfolding itself to the feet of his special guests.

"Welcome to Dracula's Daughters!" Richard exclaims proudly, shoving two one-hundred-dollar bills into Gabriela's hand.

Then, glimpsing at Mommy Doll which Mihaela prudently holds at her chest, Richard shoves fifty more dollars into Gabriela's hand, giggling with a light spasm in his neck:

"Take this too... For the little doll!"

As they walk in prudently, stepping onto the red carpet that burns its edges with artificial flames, Gabriela and Mihaela enter the glittery theater-cabaret *Live No More*. A super-loud beat and extra-shiny characters with counterfeit smiles, deafen their ears and blind their eyes. Welcoming girls, dressed up as aristocrat-cats, moan and lick their arms, seductively moving their curvaceous bodies.

"It's not so bad in here!" Gabriela exclaims with big salivating eyes.

Dwarves, disposed at balconies, blow aromatic smoke and blue elixir through long sophisticated pipes, beguiling the senses of the audience, crazed by the bombastic noise.

The red velvet curtains of the stage are suddenly pulled to the side, and a creature with three breasts and man's genitals comes into light.

The crowd gasps in awe, overdriven by the house-beat that rattles their brains.

White powder falls from the ceiling, and the audience, ecstatic and thirsty, opens their mouths, pulling out wishful tongues that swallow the drug.

Three vampires, white-dyed faced, each possessing red eyes and sharp fake fangs, show off their bodies on stage, jumping spasmodically at the three-breasted creature. They begin to suck its breasts like newly born

babies. Milk flows voluptuously on stage. The creature declaims:
"Vampires, vampires, you'll never get tired of leading
the humans with wicked desire!
Surprising and hot, you are going to suck all of the human's
bad luck!
Oh, you are so good to take their burden of evil and
bitterness from their souls and pour it into the burning
cauldron of the children of Hades!
Kids, watch out; there's a sweet price: your necks will get
stung,
Your breath forever pulled out of your frivolous lungs
But you'll become immortal and gifted with infinite fun!
Famous and rich, Papa Lucifer will make you all,
If only you kiss and bite each other, devouring this world.
Just wait 'til you see Gabriela following her sister to death
'Cause Mihaela left immortality for a man's perishable
breast!"

A tall actress, who looks slightly like Mihaela, dressed up like a white ballerina and holding a basket with white flowers in hand, appears poetically on stage. Spreading white roses above the crowd, she blows kisses of love to the three vampires. Love-struck, the vampires collapse onto the floor. Mihaela ignores the vampires and jumps to the creature's breasts. She then begins to suck fresh milk with her hands lifted up in praise. When filled up, she stands up and addresses the creature with joy:
"How nourishing human love is, how soft and
inviting your breasts feel,
How generous and engrossing your lips spiel...
Please, divine human, take me up to the mortal bliss,
And never let my sister penetrate me with
her immoral kiss!"

The crowd laughs and applauds.
Gabriela, losing her temper, rushes backstage.

"How may I help you?" a cute girl with mustache asks her.

"I would like to speak with the manager of…this place."

"Oh, with Richard?"

"Thank you."

Gabriela rushes outside the club.

"Wait! We have to speak! We have to make a plan!" Mihaela yells after Gabriela.

"There is no plan! This place has to be swept off earth's face." Gabriela speaks back to her sister, taking off like a bat out of hell.

Outside the club, Richard, frolicking and all smiles, pops up before her eyes:

"Miss journalist, how did you like my play…?"

No sooner does he open his mouth than Gabriela pierces his neck with her long sharp fangs.

Richard's small feet start kicking about; his suspenders jump off their place, dismembering the phosphorescent plaque with the glittery ad *Live No More.* Dracula's Daughters' dolls fall off the façade that starts to shudder and collapse, the ground cleaving into small pieces, quaking its rocks. Richard's skin cracks and peels with vampiric itch.

"How did you like my chronicle, Richard? Now you are my silent and humble servant…" Gabriela whispers in Richard's ear, flooded with blood.

Richard's nods affirmatively, with his shades iced and mislaid.

"Gabriela, this is not the right way!" Mihaela speaks behind her, watching Richard twitch and vomiting blood.

"Do you have a gracious alternative like 'kindly asking him?'" Gabriela pokes fun at Mihaela. "My dear, in life you gotta bite back and claw your way up to the top!"

Mihaela's gloom fades away and she begins to laugh so hard that her belly aches:

"You're so funny! Bite Back is a great title for one of our songs in the play! Why don't you start writing the music?"

Gabriela bristles with anger: "Because I cannot, I cannot and you know it, and yet you say it…"

"Wait a second," Mihaela cuts her off. "How did you remember that you cannot write? You have no memory..."

"You're right, but when I'm near you, something happens to my mind... I start feeling needles in my brain; I see flashes and images from our childhood, from the escapades... It is mind-boggling..."

"That is not bad at all!" Mihaela jumps with joy. "Then, should I stay near you when you compose?"

"No, there is no need. I can do it on my own!" Gabriela chops her off, all fired-up.

But Mihaela's eyes glitter with happiness. She is so thrilled by the fact that she can influence her sister in a positive way. She knew that there is a way to change her... Mama told her that there is a way to rip her thorns off... With time, Gabriela can truly be human, sweet and kind, always inspired to write... Mihaela is hopeful. Happy.

All of sudden, a mist of warmth shrouds her being. It is the same soft, calming, sweet-divine energy that she felt in Heaven nearby Jesus and Mama. She feels clothed with so much love... She wants to stay like this forever and blow this peace and love onto the whole world.

A murmur tickles Mihaela's ears.

She chuckles childishly and opens her right hand. The lucky bee alights on Mihaela's palm.

In the meantime, Gabriela has entered again the *Live No More* cabaret theater. With airs of a diva and her chin up, she gets on stage and declaims proudly to the audience:

"Ladies and Gentlemen. My name is Gabriela. I am the daughter of Dracula, the character that the MC was unfairly and savagely portraying. In the name of my father, I ask you to evacuate this place immediately!"

The crowd laughs.

"Well, I'm happy that you're having a good time. But unfortunately, if you don't get out in the next ten seconds, you will turn into some laughing corpses! So do what I say!"

And Gabriela starts counting backwards:

"10, 9, 8…"

The audience, as if hypnotized, ogles the charming Gabriela.

"3, 2…and 1!" Gabriela shouts, throwing her nails in the air.

The audience refuses to submit to Gabriela's commands, laughing at her with sarcasm. Clenching her fists, and raising her eyebrows, Gabriela blows a whole cloud of fire upon the obstinate crowd.

"Help! Fire!" the audience screams with desperate eyes as the whole place catches fire.

Foppish and fogyish men, young hipsters and punks, goths and burlesque fans, nerds, drag queens and vampish girls, all run back and forth to save their lives.

"No, Gabriela!" Mihaela cries at her sister, getting on stage with her bee-friend. "This is not the right way! We have to give these people a chance. They have done nothing wrong."

And suddenly, the bee buzzes, and a fulminant rain falls from the ceilings, extinguishing the flames.

The audience looks up, crossing themselves with fear:

"A miracle! A miracle! We are saved!"

As a symphonic music begins to play, soothing the panic state, the crowd begins to dance happily in the rain.

"This is a good beginning for the show!" Mihaela exclaims, looking at Mama-bee, astounded.

Gabriela looks at the bee too, gnashing her teeth in anger. The bee has utterly ruffled her feathers. She does not need a bee like it around to crab her game and shadow her fame, Gabriela thinks, utterly enflamed. Hardly can she restrain her mouth to gush again a jet of fire upon this place. Abruptly, she snatches Mihaela's hand and pulls her backstage:

"Who is this annoying bee that has done that to me?"

"She's my friend!"

"I want her out of here!"

Mihaela smiles:

"Don't be afraid of goodness!"

Gabriela bites her tongue, not finding any word to bite her sister back.

Looking around through the dirty backstage of *Live No More*, Mihaela sees the few actors of *Dracula's Daughters* sitting next to each other, on the dusty floor, with their backs arched in melancholy, leaned against the smoky walls. With their arms tightened around their legs, close to their chests, they show petrified sad faces, looking like some grotesque statues, sculpted in fear.

"They need a chance. They need our love! They are not guilty! They were misdirected!" Mihaela pleads with her sister.

"Miss Wisdom! You know it all! Misdirected..." Gabriela mimics her sister.

Mihaela approaches the scared actors gently and smiles at them:

"Tomorrow at noon, audition! I want to see you all here! Please, bring nothing but yourselves!"

One of them stands up, fixing her with wicked eyes:

"What for Miss?"

"For the real story. I'm the director and writer of your new show! And if you won't like what I propose, you can just leave and I will understand. But give it a try, please," Mihaela says, softening the actor's anger.

W Hotel, Times Square.

Mihaela and Gabriela are lying in the same bed, next to each other. A silence of heaven swings them both in a cradle of peace.

With her big black eyes staring at the ceiling, Mihaela breaks up the silence:

"I cannot believe it! You and me...here! I thought that it would never happen again! I'm happy! Mama is surely happy!"

Barely does she end her words when Gabriela jumps on her, showing off glittering fangs.

"What are you doing?" Mihaela screams at her.

"I thought about biting you!" Gabriela speaks up with thirst. "I'm really hungry and moreover, you are not fun without your fangs any more! You think too much, you talk too much! Just tell me less and love me more!"

TELL ME LESS & LOVE ME MORE (Chorus)

love me in sun-light love me-n the mid-night love me some more

When we are moon struck when we are blood stuck love me some more

Tell me less and love me more oh ba-by don't play chess come in my

-door oh ba-by Tell me less oh ba-by love me-e-e e

do-ove me more

Mihaela frets in the strong arms of Gabriela, clasped by vampiric twitches.

"Why are you doing this to me?" Mihaela cries at her cruel sister who keeps watching her struggle with satisfied eyes.

"Surprise! I got you!" Gabriela finally releases the tension as Mihaela begins to cry. "I'm just playing, sis! Hahaha...." Gabriela laughs her fangs off.

Mihaela, congested and covered in tears, shouts out with madness:

"Never do that again to me! You scared me to death! Ah, my heart..."

"I thought it was fun, girls wanna have fun, remember?"

"I don't like you that way! Smudged callow viper! And how come you know my song—*Tell me Less and Love Me More?*"

"I flipped through your pages while you were asleep... You cannot hide from me, Miss Mystery Sis," Gabriela grins.

And without giving it another thought, Gabriela opens the window of their hotel room, outstretches her arms like a bat, and takes off.

Mihaela, flummoxed and tormented, wrapped up inside the ruffled quilt, cannot believe her eyes. She has forgotten how is to fly like that, guided by that evil force, into the dark. And even though it was morning, the lights of the dawn did not hinder Gabriela from performing her wicked desires on her. Mihaela wishes that she were stronger. She lives in love, in light... She knows she can change her sister, but she now wonders:

"What if she changes me before I change her?"

Same day. After the dawn.

Gabriela arrives back inside Mihaela's hotel room, through the same window, looking amazingly good, like a hell of a woman. Mihaela is covered in sleep, with the white eiderdown down to her feet. Gabriela throws her a smirk, puffing conceitedly through her nose. She is combed and dressed completely different than last night: she wears a silky ponytail, framed by a diamond tiara, a tight black dress with a simple and elegant belt, black shoes with high heels, and smells ravishingly of jasmine perfume. In her left hand, she holds a huge white bag. She slowly places it on the carpet and starts unpacking: a long silky black gown with veil, a white wedding dress, an antique red velvet dress with lace collar, expensive royal jewelry, a king scepter, a jester costume, hats, shoes, silk scarves, floral fans, and much more...

Gabriela stretches her muscled arms, then her long strong neck, like of a black swan, and falls asleep on top of the mountain of glittering garments, mesmerized by the scent of fame.

The dawn breaks in. Shy rays of Sun start playing on Mihaela's face.

A loud knock on the door suddenly wakes her up. She opens her big black eyes, flutters her lashes twice, yawns her head off, and outstretches her arms. She looks sweaty and dreamy...

Another loud knock. As she jumps out of her bed, Mihaela's eyes lay on Gabriela, who is lying on the floor, on top of a whole disastrous landscape of dresses. Mihaela's eyes open wide, terrified.

Louder knocks on the door. Hectically, Mihaela gathers the shiny garments of all kind and throws them all inside the wardrobe, her hands trembling with panic. She then quickly pushes her sister under the bed, hiding her hands, feet, and black tail.

As the knocks on the door increase, Mihaela's heart throbs like a bomb, ready to explode:

"Just a second. I'm getting dressed!" she yells at the insistent visitor.

As soon as she finishes camouflaging everything, Mihaela approaches the door, trying to cool down. She puts on a large smile, slaps herself twice on her face, and opens the door. Someone very familiar looms before her eyes: a tall and strong man in his late twenties, who takes her breath away... She does not recall meeting him before, yet she knows this face from somewhere... She smiles again—this time for real—and asks him in one breath:

"How may I help you, Mr.?"

"I'm detective Davidson," the man speaks, untroubled.

Seeing the identification card of the detective, Mihaela gets into a spin. She smiles again, trying so hard to hide her panic.

"Last night, video cameras from three luxurious stores from Manhattan showed a beautiful lady in flagrante delicto; a lady looking a lot like you broke in, and... Articles worth $25,000 were stolen! Do you mind if I take a look and ask you a few questions?"

"A lady looking like me? This is very curious, Sir. Last night, I ordered dinner inside, as I was extremely tired and overslept...until now... You can check with the hotel..."

"Well, may I come in?" Davidson asks Mihaela again.

"Of course..."

The detective with greenish-blue eyes approaches Mihaela's

wardrobe.

Mihaela runs before him, losing her breath.

"No, just a second. I can explain..."

Ignoring Mihaela's plead, the detective opens the wardrobe. Mihaela wishes to have never been born, or better yet, to be swallowed at once by the earth... However, to her surprise, the wardrobe is completely empty. Only Mommy Doll is seating proud and silent on the top shelf, all by herself...

Suspicious, the detective turns his face to Mihaela:

"What was that panicked 'No,' Miss Mihaela?"

Mihaela blushes, hardly finding her words:

"Oh, my lingerie, I thought I put it in there...nearby the doll... It was not that nice!"

"Nice?"

"Yes... It was a little over the top!"

"I see..." Davidson smiles, artificially.

Mihaela giggles, at ease.

The detective continues his search.

In the meantime, Mihaela tries to make conversation... After he finishes his search, Davidson speaks to her bluntly:

"Well, here is my card, in case you remember anything..."

"But I remember everything..." Mihaela replies, promptly.

Taken by Mihaela's swiftness, the detective replies with a smile:

"I like swift and confident people...but truth is something we can't hide! We'll speak shortly..."

"Of course!" Mihaela concludes, closing the door, confidently.

As soon as the detective's pace can no longer be heard in the hallway,

Mihaela rushes under the bed to get her sister out. She trembles to the marrow of her bones. The new trouble that Gabriela has gotten her into, irritates Mihaela beyond measure.

But Gabriela is neither under the bed nor in the bathroom, nor on the ceiling or behind the curtains... She is gone and so are her jewels and dresses.

"How could Gabriela hide all those outfits in the blink of an eye?" Mihaela asks herself, in awe.

No trace of her sister can be seen outside either, down the alley, as Mihaela glances through the open window.

"Yes, sure, she gets me into a hell of a mess and leaves *me* to clean it all up!"

A hot-cold shiver trickles down her spine. Mihaela undresses her pajamas slowly, letting them fall behind. She then opens the wardrobe and takes out Mommy Doll, who looks smaller and sad... Mihaela hugs Mommy tight, feeling a little better.

A sinister sound disturbs their embrace. Mihaela turns around and sees the white bird with orange beak beating at the window. Mihaela smiles... Every time she feels sad, the white bird comes into sight. The bird has the eyes of her mother. As she steps near the bird and looks it in the eyes, it vanishes away... Mihaela blinks, saddened, and opens the window:

"Mama, Mama! Come back..."

But the bird is nowhere to be seen. Silence. Only her echo returns to her, clear and lonely, piercing her heart.

Mihaela drags herself to the bathroom. She turns on the shower and locks the bathroom door: "Dreams of a poetic girl..." she speaks within.

Noisy music can be heard from the neighboring rooms.

Suddenly, a big dark shadow tattoos the ceiling of Mihaela's hotel room. The shadow slithers, sharp horns join in, crawling onto the ceiling.

The window abruptly opens. A hissing wind pushes the curtains to the side. The shadow gets bigger, clearer, taking the shape of a human body. With her jaws wide open and her fangs dirtied by blue blood, Gabriela jumps off the ceiling, onto the Persian carpet. Landing on her claws just like a wild cat, with her long tail circling her small waist, Gabriela starts licking herself up with mews of a spoiled creature. Her saliva droops down her mouth, onto the carpet, blue and sticky. Rubbing her naked dirty back against the puffy rug of the hotel room, she starts playing lecherously with her own body. Suddenly, she jumps up the walls and rips the white curtains off, unwittingly spoiling them with the end of her tail, which is dark as a carbon. She then hurls the curtains around her naked body, posing like a diva before some invisible fans. Her body trembles with hunger.

With a white towel wrapped around her head, Mihaela gets out of the shower.

She cannot believe her eyes! Her naughty sister, wildly made up and dressed in the blackened white curtains of the hotel room, poses on the bed, laughing sardonically with the impudence of a brainless being.

"What are you doing here?" Mihaela asks her, totally dazzled.

"Preparing for tomorrow's audition!" Gabriela replies swiftly. I would like to audition for the "Wicked Clone" part. Do you think I'm a good fit?"

"You're too good to be bad!" Mihaela replies, saddened by her sister's heedlessness.

A quick exchange of glances between the sisters emanates the dark flames of the past.

"Look, sweet Gabriela, if it wasn't for this play, I would have sent you to a vampiric behavior clinic or to a specialized rehab..." Mihaela says to her sister with forced calm. "But, as far as I know, there is no such thing, so *I'll* have to stick with you, deal with your quirks, and heal your murderess instincts myself...if I can. But until then, if I happen to hear again of robbery, murder, trouble, or anything evil or malicious done by you, I will make sure you end up in jail. And I surely know that you know that I know your weaknesses..."

"Ha, ha! Are you sure that they won't take you for me?" Gabriela busts out laughing. And Gabriela starts mimicking her sister.

"Yes, I don't have a tail..." Mihaela cuts her off.

"I can make it disappear..." Gabriela replies back, sticking her tongue out.

Ignoring Gabriela's buffoonery, Mihaela continues:

"I am a human being, or at least I am trying to be... I'm not talking about my face or my body but about what's in here..." Mihaela says, patting her heart. "I need to feel safe. I need to guard my heart and be surrounded by love. You said that you love me. If you do, then you will act in love and with love. I need you to help me feel safe, at peace, at least throughout the rehearsals and our work together. Work is more important than us and our egos. Remember this and promise me that you will stop disappointing me and trespassing our terms!" Mihaela concludes.

"Can't you get it, sis? I am guarding you against this stupid world and mortal beings. I know, I am the wicked clone, but I love my attitude! I am wild and fierce! Everyone loves me! We are different—you are sweet and I am bitter. I know that men don't respond to sweetness. They need to see a whip! So that's what I'm giving them... Mind my wit! I want to work with you, and I won't get you into trouble, but trust me that most people need to be swept off this world, quick as a wink! They are stupid, lame, ungrateful, and have no sense of humor! I will take care of Mr. Davidson too. He is an hypocrite," Gabriela replies with lioness eyes.

"No! Stop it for God's sake!" Mihaela yells her head off.

"Do you think that your human beings are angels? Let me tell you some things from Davidson's file," Gabriela takes on the private detective tone, opening a little notebook.

"No! Stop it!" Mihaela screams again at her sister. "We have to prepare for tomorrow's audition, I have to make copies of the script for all the characters, and you need to behave as normally as possible. Please, take off that dress and that clownish makeup. Here is your costume for the audition."

"A black cotton body suit? That's it? But I play the leading role!"

"Don't forget about the audition!"

"Oh...right!" Gabriela rolls her eyes, and mews...

"And don't forget that on stage we are all the same, and we all have one goal: to work hard for something beautiful and immortal. Let people talk about your performance and your music notes and not about you, yourself and your ego! Also I would like you to start wearing this talisman which will unite us and protect us from all evil and harm!"

Gabriela starts laughing her head off. She drops on the carpet and hiccups, and laughs and laughs like she has not laughed for ages... Her laughter gets so loud that the security guard needs to take measures. Hard knocks at the twins' door.

Gabriela opens the door wide, tied up in a sexy purple corset and black garters.

The security man's jaw drops. He starts to salivate; cravings play in his eyes...

"Is there anything I can help you with?" Gabriela asks him, seductively.

"No, not at all," the man stutters. "I was just..."

Gabriela grabs him by the shoulders, and licks his face. The man takes Gabriela in his arms, and starts kissing her wildly.

"Well, stop it please! Let's behave ourselves!" Gabriela backs off. "Would you please bring us two big platters of raw steak with extra blood on the side? Hahahaha, just kidding!"

Gabriela slams the door in the face of the security employee.

"Yes, Ma'am!" the voice of the man reverberates weakly from the hall.

"I'm starting to restrain myself. It is the cruelest thing that I've ever done to myself," Gabriela grumbles before Mihaela, angrily. "Seeing that jugular deliciously pulsing, so inviting, so vibrant...and I had to deny it, to refuse him for the benefit of Art! Ah! What have you done to me?"

"Hold on a second!" Mihaela replies. "I have to write those lines down. They are perfect for the play!"

"I feel like crying..." Gabriela adds, scratching her arms with her sharp pointed nails, and biting her flesh.

The morning breaks in.

The rays of the sun catch Gabriela and Mihaela in the same bed, embraced, cheek-to-cheek, tangled like two Siamese... Mihaela opens her big black eyes and smiles, reassured, seeing her sister sleep like an angel, twined in her arms, with her big reddish eyes wide open, as usual.

Mihaela: *Oh, I forgot to tell you about this. Actually, I myself used to sleep like that when I was with those fangs. Papa Grid told me about that strange thing and about the fact that Mama and he had to struggle with it ever since I was born. I worried them, of course, unwilling to close my eyes to sleep... In fact, I was sleeping more profoundly than any human being. And then I could stay awake and not sleep for three nights in a row. And I was healthier than any other creature on earth...the doctor said after he had examined me. Now I need eight hours of sleep and I still feel...exhausted at times. Papa listened to no one who tried to put him down or fight me, even though I was a different child. He just let things in the hands of God. 'You can't fight the way you were born, but you can get reborn...' Papa told me.*

Yet, ever since she pulled her fangs out, Mihaela has changed. She needed to close her eyes in order to sleep and...she has started to dream...sometimes beautifully, sometimes nightmares have woken her up. She has stayed many nights awake, writing her dreams in her notebook. But that is all good. As long as she can write, she is happy.

Today Mihaela is feeling charged with healing energy. After she kisses Mommy Doll, she jumps swiftly into her white slippers with purple ribbons. She picks up her big bourgeois hairbrush and brushes her long golden brown hair, showering herself in the rays of the sun. As she opens the window, the fresh air of the dawn refreshes her body.

She takes a seat on the big brown armchair and starts reading the manuscript of her play, again and again. Yet, of course, not before taking a sip of the miraculous tea that she has made of The Queen of the Night plant. She took care to take some petals and some roots of the Queen of The Night Flower from Papa's garden, her childhood garden that she often thinks of with so much love. This tea is her secret habit that she hopes to share, one day soon, with the whole world.

First day of rehearsals.
Mihaela and Gabriela enter, confidently, the remaining theatre of *Live*

No More: curtains collapsed, diamond-chandeliers torn, paintings and tapestries burnt, broken glasses and ashes crumbled on the floors, glooming the once phosphorescent and glittery décor.

The seven actors sit just where Mihaela had left them the other day, leaning against the smoky walls, with their arms crossed around their knees, and their eyes wrapped up in fear.

"Hello, my friends. My name is Mihaela."

"And my name is Gabriela. I am her identical twin sister..." Gabriela intervenes with a grin.

"Thank you for coming!" Mihaela adds with a smile.

The actors stand up.

"Excuse me, but your names are the names of Dracula's Daughters from our play..." one of the actors breaks in with a harsh tone.

"It is hard to explain everything now... I'll try to make it brief," Mihaela replies. And taking a deep breath, she speaks out loudly, fixing them in the eyes:

"Beloved actors, as you might know, *Dracula's Daughters*' producer suffered an attack...and I'm here to present to you a new act, a play that I have written with truth about the characters that you erroneously knew... I am not interested in a fake clichéd vampiric story that sells itself to make one laugh! Please, take off your masks. I want to play it real. I came here to be a human being...just like you..."

"You mean...just like me?" the same prying actor asks, sarcastically.

"Yes, just like you. Because you have what no other creature has: you have inspiration, the greatest gift of God. I wrote this play to make people think big about their gifts...to bring truth to the lies, to bring faith to the doubt... So please, be weak, be vulnerable, but don't be a phony priest who preaches but doesn't believe in his speech! Whoever wants to live for real and act from his heart, may stay. Whoever wants to keep playing a fake, may leave today."

Silence. No thunderstorm or rattling noise could break up the magic stillness that Mihaela has poured into their hearts. Only their eyes speak hungrily, but doubtingly...

"Now, please, read my story," Mihaela goes on. "It is called *Wicked Clone*. It is not about biting, flesh, sex or breaking bones. It is about us, all of us who need to find our own..."

"Why *Wicked Clone?*" the curious actor breaks in again.

"Each of us has got a wicked clone, an evil twin that never leaves us alone..."

And Mihaela starts sharing copies of the *Wicked Clone* play with all of the seven actors.

"Excuse me, but why should we believe in you?" the same prying actor asks Mihaela, impetuously.

"Please, don't believe in me but in my deeds... If you like my play, then you will go up on that stage and perform like a God, burning your heart out... If you want to take another road...you can exit through the backstage door..."

"I'm sorry, but you said that you were Dracula's Daughters, Mihaela and Gabriela..." the curious actor resumes, "But they lived in the 15th century..."

"You definitely don't know what it means to be a vampire, brother. You live forever!" Gabriela speaks, haughtily.

"But one day you will get bored, very bored, because eating, feeding, attacking...are not enough to make you smile, to make you truly happy inside..." Mihaela breaks in.

"So what do you do?" a red-haired actor asks Mihaela, blankly.

"You stop doing, you start opening your heart and emptying your smarts...allowing the light to come in, to give you, to fill you... We shall play with our hearts...because we live through our hearts... We are here to tell something to the audience, to transform the world... Art is the only form that can change the hearts in an effortless way... And day by day, we will become the best version of ourselves, being mirrors to our audience..." Mihaela replies.

"It's too much to take in at this hour! Excuse me, but who are you? Why should we work with you? What are your credentials?" the prying actor intercedes again.

"Read, listen, and...then speak!" Mihaela cries out at the actor, losing her temper.

As an automaton, the impudent actor takes a seat near the other actors, shoving his nose inside the *Wicked Clone* manuscript.

Yet, as fast as the wind, like awakening from a bad dream, Mihaela apologizes. She cannot believe her cruel reaction and lack of control. She worked so much on it... She needs to be an example to them, to be gentle and help them.

"But can she ever be perfectly good, just the way she wants to?" she speaks within.

"Yes, one day... The more you will keep your eyes on your Best Friend, the more you will become like Him!" the bee-friend suddenly makes her appearance around Mihaela's ears. "But who needs someone perfectly good? Your flaws make you unique and point out your beauty within... Just let Him work in you. Don't worry about it."

"You're here!" Mihaela exclaims, rushing to kiss the bee on her antennae.

"If there is any way I can help you, let me know. I'm always here..." Mama-bee replies.

"All right, Miss Mihaela!" the haughty and naughty curious actor exclaims, standing up. "This is different, original! Your play is peculiar and...pure... It reminds me of my favorite film—*The Seventh Seal.* How did you come up with it?"

Mihaela, astounded, thanks him. This was the first reaction that she got about her play. No other human being read it before. She's been so anxious to hear their remarks... His words gave her wings... She smiles.

"But what if he had said that he hates my play?" Mihaela hears again a deep voice within. "Are they nice to me just because they need a job?"

Suddenly, Mihaela sees black fog before her eyes and feels like fainting...

The bee-friend stings Mihaela in her left wrist and Mihaela lights up.

"I'm in! I want to do your play! It's like nothing I have ever done..." a slim, tall actor breaks in.

"Me too! I love your play! I needed so badly a good part, to feel again joy in my heart..." a girl's voice cries out.

"I don't quite understand what you wrote...but it sounds new, different..." the red-haired actor speaks, quaveringly.

Just a beautiful Asian girl, seated next to the red-haired actor, in the corner, with huge pink headphones glued to her ears and violet contact lenses hiding her eyes, keeps silent. The girl looks at Mihaela with an invisible, unreadable face and blank eyes.

Sensing the girl's reluctance, Mihaela asks her kindly:

"Are you a musician? Would you like to help me with the sound? What is your name?"

"My name is Ai..."

"No, I don't need anyone," Gabriela bursts out, resolutely. "I shall do the sound all by myself."

The bee stings Gabriela's muscled arm.

"Ouch! Hey, I am going to kill you, dirty prickly bee!" Gabriela screams, running with fire after the bee.

The bee flies onto the ceiling, Gabriela flies after her, climbing and jumping onto the walls like a monkey that escaped from the jungle. The actors laugh, watching Gabriela's performance with their jaws dropped.

"Wow, teach us, teach us how you do it!" the curious actor cries out with his eyes bulged out.

Everyone starts talking among themselves, loosening and cheering up...

Mihaela goes after her sister, flushed with anger: "Come down! This very minute!"

Gabriela submits and lands on the floor, inflamed by her performance and by the explosive claps of the enthusiastic actors.

"We are not here to clown ourselves up! Stop it, for God's sake! Otherwise, I'll get you out of the play!" Mihaela whispers angrily in the ear of her sister. After which, taking a deep breath, she addresses the actors:

"We need to work as a team! We need to respect each other! Gabriela, you certainly need to act. You cannot focus on the sound, playing the music, and mixing the vocals at the same time... This is a musical! You will compose the soundtrack, but someone else has to take care of that..."

Mihaela clarifies the situation.

"All right! We'll work as a team!" Gabriela complies.

Ai, the slim Asian girl, raises her hand and speaks shyly, through her nose:

"I think I can handle the sound! I actually helped other theater representations too... But I need professional tools to work with..."

"Good! We'll get you the right soundboard, mics, instruments...everything you need," Mihaela replies, giving Ai a hand to rise up. "Now, let's cast the other parts too. Who would like to play David, the poet?"

"Me!" a handsome actor raises his hand.

"Great! It's all yours!" Mihaela replies, utterly animated.

"Now, we have a generous, enlightening part: God. Who wishes to try out for the role of God?"

Mihaela pauses. She then resumes:

"Please, don't offer yourself to play this part unless you truly love to do it. I first want to tell you few things about God. I am not speaking of God as a religion, a code of laws that you have been taught about... I am speaking about God, your friend, your parent, your brother...who never forsakes you or lets you down. He always has time to talk to you, to walk with you... God is such a generous friend. He loves to give. He loves to reward his friends. God is the director of your lives and you have to trust Him for giving you the gift and talent of being Artists. It really hurt me to see *Dracula's Daughters* play, that mockery of the 16th century, the way you were so misdirected and dragged into a..."

Mihaela stops for a second. She touches the star on her forehead that began to bleed and continues to speak:

"Even though I wanted to overlook this...you need to know about my past so you can know myself... I once was dead, a vampire, a being without a heartbeat, memories, dreams, tears and talent... I renounced who I was, so that I can be who I am. I chose to be like you, a human being with big dreams... You need to know the truth about vampires so that you can value yourselves and not get trapped, misled..."

"How come?" Gabriela intercedes, envenomed. "Vampires have it all!

They are immortal and strong! They live forever!"

"Vampires are not as you know them... They don't have it all. On the contrary, they live forever in a cage, with their wings cut, unable to get out... Vampires are tormented beings who died with unfulfilled dreams and who still try, down there, in their death, to achieve them...through Machiavellian ways and lies... They just roam, they don't live...they are fruitless. And they kill because they fear for their flesh and bones..."

"What do you mean?" the curious actor rushes to ask.

"If they don't drink blood, they wither and die... Anyhow, they have no soul, no beat in their hearts... After I pulled out my canine teeth—those fangs—my father Grid who raised me, said: 'Vampires are beings who refused the help of God... They wanted to do it on their own and so God stole their soul and let them tramp between Hell and this world...'"

"You were once a vampire?" the prying actor begins to laugh.

"Yes, I was... But it is all gone now. As a vampire, I was a dead girl walking..." Mihaela tells the actors with tears in her eyes.

"What? A dead girl walking? But aren't I talking?" Gabriela asks Mihaela, totally annoyed.

The actors look confused, once at Mihaela, twice at Gabriela.

"What I want to do is to convince the human beings of their chance at true immortality, how they can fight time through the power of love, through the power of inspiration that they had been born with..."

"If we are immortal, then why do we die?" the red-haired actor asks Mihaela, skeptically.

"You know that you have to die. But what if you know that you won't die, that you have eternal life?"

"Did you come here to lecture us about eternal life and God?" another actor chimes in. "I need money to pay my rent..."

"No, absolutely not. I came here to be your friend, to help you gain a food that never rots or ends, and bring you a much bigger treasure in your pockets... But there is one thing that I want from you. I want to learn more and more about being a human being...to learn more from you. Teach me, please..." Mihaela addresses them, gently. "Tell me, what's the most beautiful thing about being a human being?"

For a few seconds, the actors stare at Mihaela perplexed, as at an alien. The handsome actor, who wished to play David the poet, stands up and answers her:

"I love that I can think and that I am an artist... I can draw...design...paint... And when I do this...I feel like Picasso! My hands just go...and I can't stop them... "

"I love that! And I will love to see your drawings, your paintings! Perhaps you can also help us with the scenery and projections for the show!" Mihaela jumps for joy, twirling in the air like an ecstatic child. "If you experienced what I have experienced, if God made you fly above the earth and gave your dead heart a beat to love and write...wouldn't you believe in Him?"

The actors listen, transfixed.

"I love to think with my heart," Mihaela continues. "And that's what I want all of you to do—to think with your hearts. Forget to act, forget what you knew about vampires, about God, prejudices, the past... Just be, see, feel, smell, and yell!" Mihaela winks at them, happily. The bee joins in.

Silence.

"Yell, please!" Mihaela screams out. "Say: I am a human being! I am happy! I am alive! I am grateful! I can act and shine on stage! I love it!"

The actors come together, murmuring and looking shyly at each other, then speaking louder and louder, finally yelling at the top of their lungs!

Ai suddenly screams out: "I want to fly as Gabriela!"

Gabriela, full of herself, puffing through the nose, surely loves that beyond measure.

"I want to do it! I want to play God!" the same prying actor breaks in.

Mihaela looks at the boy, stupefied. She hoped that he wouldn't be the one to say it! Yet, God knows!

The actor intercedes again: "My name is Liam. I had so much fun reading your play! I want to play God and I also want to direct your play! Give me the chance to do it because I have a powerful mind with great ideas and..."

"You can play God but God knows that I have to direct this play..."

"But..." Liam intercedes.

Mihaela cuts him off:

"I've always been directed and misdirected. This is my life and my play and I have the right vision for it!"

"And who are we, your servants?"

"Yes, you are my servants and I am your servant! We all are servants to each other, and we all are one for the production of this play! Fair?"

"Yes..." the actor consents, easily humbled.

"Good," Mihaela answers, turning towards the other actors. "Now let us choose the rest of the cast: one of you needs to play Vlad—royal, cruel, tyrannical, but also vulnerable, torn apart by two yearnings. He is like a Greek, statuary hero! He is mostly evil and revengeful as a Greek God, but you can understand him, his pain, his regrets, and yearnings..."

"I shall do it!" an actor with blue eyes and silky hair says, rubbing his hands.

"So be it!" Mihaela replies, enraptured by the handsome features of the actor. Then, shaking herself off, she continues:

"We also need the Narrator, The Boyfriend, The Producer, Mrs. Death..."

"The Narrator? My name is Alfred. May I try it?"

"Of course, you may try it, Alfred! By the way, I love your voice! Warm and deep, like the rhythm of summer's tides! Now let's cast the Producer—silky, sleek, foxy, naughty, and full of lies!"

"Me, I am the devil's son!" one of the actors comes in fully with a smile.

"And what's your name?"

"Terrero!"

"All right, Terrero, you shall play the Producer!" And the last call, the last role... Who wants to play Mrs. Death?"

A silence of death covers the space. Gabriela blows behind them, chanting a somber humming... She then laughs, wickedly.

"Gabriela, please!" Mihaela hushes her.

"Well, as I can see, we have no requests for Mrs. Death... I believe that She can play herself quite well... No need for a human being to impersonate her Majesty! We only need to record Gabriela's tremolo and we've got the right echoes..." Mihaela winks to the actors.

"Who plays the Wicked Clone?" the Asian girl Ai asks Mihaela precipitately.

"Gabriela is the Wicked Clone," Mihaela replies.

Gabriela starts laughing and jumping high, up to the ceiling, yelling at the top of her lungs:

"I am the Wicked Clone, I am the Wicked Clone!"

Everyone watches, perplexed at another childish and crazy outburst.

"But you said that this is an audition and I would really like to try out for the Wicked Clone part too... I think it would really fit me..." Ai insists.

"I know. Perhaps you can try it if Gabriela..." Mihaela smiles, rolling her eyes towards her sister.

Gabriela clenches her claws; her eyes fume; her mouth storms out words of fury:

"It's mine. It's my story! I am the Wicked Clone!"

The actress looks at Gabriela, frightened.

"Now I need you, Christopher!" Mihaela points out to the actor with blue eyes and silky hair, trying to quickly bury her sister's madness.

"How did you know my name?" Christopher asks, flush with shyness.

"A bee told me..." Mihaela replies with a wink.

The actors laugh.

The bee buzzes loudly around Mihaela's ears.

"Dear Christopher, I would like you to play God," Mihaela resumes.

"But I was playing God!" Liam screams out.

"You shall play Vlad, dear Liam!"

"Vlad?"

"There are no other options for you, Liam. Vlad fits you like a glove..."

"I see... Are there many lines for Vlad's part?"

"He's the main character!"

"All right..." Liam submits. "I'll do it!"

Then, addressing the actor who offered himself to play the Narrator,

Mihaela continues, softening the tension:

"Dear Alfred, please read these lines… Let me hear you!"

Alfred clears his throat and starts reading aloud:

"*Each of you might have a story,*
Each of you might have a secret…
Yet what you are going to hear tonight
Is neither a story, nor a secret –
It's man's most desirable dream –
The dream of living forever,
The dream of youth without aging and life without death…
Close your eyes,
Come inside this dream with me
And forget that you will die…"

"Thank you," Mihaela says with a shaky smile. "You have a good voice, a low timber and…the right expression. But try it again, please!"

The actor declaims again, with more pathos.

"And again!" Mihaela speaks up as Alfred finishes his second round.

The actor acts again.

"Thank you. Now take a break, please…" Mihaela says, easily nervous and stammering. "Close your eyes. Now see…see your life…on stage…"

Mihaela's words make Alfred blush; he frets his hands over his tights. He feels uncomfortable. Mihaela breathes deeply and resumes:

"Alfred, please tell me about your childhood. What did you love to do the most as a child?"

"Well…my childhood…he-he…" Alfred starts giggling like a child, as if a light has suddenly been switched in his head. "I loved to ride my bicycle… I loved to circle my small town, pedaling like a lunatic… At first, I was hitting everyone around. And then, my legs became stronger, and I began to ride faster and faster. I was going on the highway, screaming all by myself, and competing with the birds… I was so fast and unafraid! But then, my bicycle was stolen. Papa kept telling me that he would buy me another one but he didn't. Actually, he was happy when it got stolen as I drove him crazy with it… But I miss my bicycle! I dream to ride it again…" the actor exclaims with the eyes of a child.

Mihaela listens, enraptured.

"You will, Alfred, I promise…"

And then, she turns to the other actors:

"See, when Alfred told me the story of his bicycle…he did not think how to say it, how loud, how soft… He just said it…from his heart. Just like a child. When we are not children anymore, we die…"

"Now, Alfred, please tell them again your monologue…"

And Alfred's eyes begin to shine and his heart begins to throb:

"Each of you might have a story,

Each of you might have a secret…

Yet what you are going to hear tonight…"

"That's what I want!" Mihaela screams out, fired up. "That's it! And all of you—let your hearts speak out, let your mouth just move into the rhythm of love!"

After two months.

On the stage of the theatre, in a dimly lit corner, Gabriela plays the piano. She sways her long dark hair, taken with the magic of her composition. Her notes incestuously tangle with each other, into an avalanche of rage and ingenuity, piercing her sinful little hands, crescendo. She strongly presses the pedal of the piano, and a fortissimo sequence bursts out, tickling the memories of the engrossed listeners. A sort of a terrible felicity installs inside the theater as the tumultuous symphony rumbles on.

"Beautiful, terrific!" the *Wicked Clone* cast whispers to each other. "She is so talented!"

Only Liam watches Gabriela with bulging, attentive eyes, taking quick notes in his notebook.

Gabriela plays the last arpeggio of her composition, and then rises triumphantly from the piano.

"Dear family, dear cast, this sequence that you've just heard is my composition for the Church Scene that we are to rehearse today! Your beautiful voices and rendition will fall onto my compositions for the *Wicked Clone*. As you could hear, it sounds just like a soundtrack, a film score of a majestic movie. Indeed, people are expecting to see a theatre show but, once seated, they will be cast into a...magical cinematic twirl. Each scene is going to be a masterpiece, full of innocence and magic like a...Chaplinesque movie scene and..." Gabriela stutters. She tries to remember more of her sister's words about the cinematic style of the play, but she freezes, incapable to recall... She looks straight in the audience, trying to catch a glimpse of her sister.

"Where is Mihaela?" she suddenly asks, catching the empty chair of her sister with her wicked eye.

Everyone turns and looks behind. Mihaela's seat is empty. Liam stands up and rushes backstage:

"I will find her."

Theater's Bathroom.

Mihaela leans against the walls of the bathroom, spitting out blue blood. Everything spins chaotically, hotheadedly.

"No, no, no! It is going to pass. Don't lose your grip. You hear me?" Mihaela speaks to herself in the mirror.

However, as a monkey burnt up by hot tongues of fire, she jumps up onto the sink, at the paper towel holder that hangs quietly near the mirror. She presses the lever of the holder, wildly biting the pieces of paper that roll down. Her teeth are bleeding; her eyes are weeping. Small stains of blue blood pierce the white papers.

Liam sticks his head through an opening of the toilet's door and catches a glimpse of Mihaela's monstrous reflection in the mirror. Taken aback by the unexpected vision, he gives a loud cry. Mihaela turns her head abruptly, purring like a mad cat. Liam's feet can be heard, swiftly running away.

Mihaela, trembling inside her vampiric agony, starts chanting *Our Father*.

Dark thoughts keep harrowing her mind as she struggles with her arms in the air, trying to push her fears away.

"Father, what am I to do? Save me from myself! For the last couple of days, I've been...horrible. My face looks better, younger than ever, yet my eyes have been pierced by wickedness, by evil desires. What am I to do? Clouds cover my soul; my brain is like a flat lawn of dark flowers; my heart, like an alarm clock ticking intermittently, broken and crushed; my teeth sharper than the knives, penetrating my gums that bleed like rivers in the dusk... In the last few days, I haven't been able to give any creative remark to the actors, blocked by miscarrying thoughts... Where is my peace, where are my hopes? I want my human-self back! Please, dear God! If I have endless life but no love, then I have endless pain, this body and this soul in vain..."

Knocks on the door.

"Who is it?" she asks nicely, trying to control herself.

"It's me, Liam."

Scared, Mihaela opens the door of the bathroom, slowly, lapsing into an artificial smile. Liam looks as white as death.

"What...do you...need?" Mihaela asks Liam, trembling her words in the air. "Please, practice...prepare the first part... I'll be with you in a few minutes..."

Liam, plucking up his courage, speaks out:

"Gabriela's music is not original... I fear everyone will find out sooner or later..."

"What do you mean?"

"I heard Bach's *Passions*, Handel's *Messiah*, Mozart's *Requiem*..."

"It's impossible! I was near Gabriela when she wrote the beginning for the *Wicked Clone* and it sounded majestic, unique, original... How can this be?"

"Yes, the intro is original, indeed, but the rest is a copy, a clone of their work! I know it. I studied at *Juilliard*... Believe me."

Silence. Mihaela looks at him, blocked.

"If I may," Liam continues, "I wrote some notes for the Church Scene on this piece of paper...my score... I felt inspired, and I wanted you to look over them... It is original. I can assure you of that!"

"Get out! Out!" Mihaela cries loud, slamming the door in Liam's face. "How dare you, little spying intriguer, liar and stupid trickster?"

Yet, immediately, she suppresses her words, slamming her mouth with her right palm, sweaty and panicked:

"What's happening to me? Who is controlling my moves?" she looks at her hands, terrified, circling her own shadow.

Just as Liam makes his way out,

Mihaela sneaks through the bathroom window, in the backyard of the theatre, creeping through old banners and placards, pieces of wood and sharp requisite. A black cat cuts her way, spitting white saliva. Mihaela's heart startles.

Arriving on the streets of Times Square, walking aimlessly and heedlessly, Mihaela finally breaks loose: her feet bounce high in the air, jumping and landing onto the moving cars; her hands spread like the wings of an eagle, cutting the cold air into two, above the passersby, who watch her flight in utter awe... Just like in the old days, while in Transylvania, Mihaela can now fly miles away, swift like the wind, twirling above the crowd, without giving a drop of sweat or betraying a breath of fatigue. Her eyes pierce the flashing lights of Times Square like the eyes of a vulture; her nose, like a strong beak, is able to smell the furthest human's scent whose flesh pulsates hot blood in its veins.

In a flash, Mihaela lands in front of *The Actors' Church* from Times Square. She barely makes her way in, winding between Heaven and Hell, broken into two. Inside the church, her eyes frame the altar; she listens for a few seconds to the priest, yet her veins get swollen and violet, almost exploding out of her skin. The priest's preaching seems ridiculous, fabricated; his voice exalted by an affected ego. Mihaela is grasped by a terrifying desire to jump at the priest's neck and pull the lies out of his flesh. "What he speaks is not what the Lord has spoken to us in His Word. Why do these priests have to heighten themselves and not His truth and grace?" Mihaela thinks aloud, extremely enflamed.

However, her heart softens, captured by the smell of holy frankincense and by the meek eyes sculpted in the statue of Jesus. She kneels down at His feet, weeping bitterly, her hot tears quenching her anger and fear… "Who am I, dear Lord?" she whispering with pleading eyes:

"Lord, protect me from the evil,
Please, help me live humanly, I feel so feeble…
I need to find myself—better said, forget myself.
Please, help me keep this virgin heart…that's all I've got.
I need to write, I want to live forever through my art!
You gave to me this gift; I need to multiply Your seeds,
And thank You through my humble deeds!
Please, change my wicked clone into a sister to be proud of,
Help us to be united into Your strong love…"

All of a sudden, the statue of Jesus shakes, and His eyes open. Jesus begins to cry with tears of blood… Mihaela hugs Him tighter:

"No, please, don't cry…"

The blood covers Mihaela's head and then her body, painting her hair and flesh in red.

Gently, behind her, a young nun pats Mihaela on her shoulder.

"My dear, we are closing."

"Just a second, please!"

"It is too late, my dear!" the nun insists. "You have to go."

"It is never too late! A little more, to cover me all…" Mihaela cries back to the nun, blood trickling down on her head, shoulders, and spine…

As she feels her mind clearing and the fears finally leaving her sphere, Mihaela stands up, wipes her tears off her face and draws on a smile, turning gently towards the nun. But the holy vessel is none other than her own sister, Gabriela, laughing at her with red flickering eyes and a small red mouth painted with bluish blood. Mihaela gushes out tears again, leaning her weakened hands against the statue of Jesus.

"Nooooo! Help me God!"

The nun speaks again, laughingly: "It is too late, my dear!"

Mihaela runs out of the church, disheveled; her feet roll on the stairs with despair, sweat dripping down her cheeks; she stops and leans her fingers against the walls, pushing them out of control; her head falls, spinning like the globe; her feet are quivering the ground that shudders like a pregnant mother in labor...

"Where now, God?" she raises her eyes to the sky, asking herself the same question she did when she first ran away from the *Palace Theatre*. She falls to her knees, blood dropping off her hair...continuously...

People, passing by, glance at her, suspiciously; kids point at her. Mihaela looks down at her body that is utterly painted with blood. The blood slides off her skin, in big streams, painting the whole street red. People start screaming, trying to escape... The blood touches the feet of the ones walking on the street, climbing on their bodies. A boy with his mother, speaks out:

"Mommy, you look so beautiful! Your face is young again, like in the baby pics with me!"

A man with a hunched back, abruptly straightens:

"My back, a miracle! I'm healed!"

All of a sudden, a diffuse image of Mihaela's mother looms before her eyes and then the pale face with virgin smile and the head with long black locks of hair, smelling of heaven, slowly diminishes. Mama-bee makes her appeareance, buzzing spiritedly, and then stings firmly Mihaela's left wrist, right on David's bite. Suddenly, Mihaela's long nails shorten, her eyes clear, her mouth cut by a childlike smile. In front of her, as in a mirror, her most beautiful face, flawless and graced, appears... She now can see the nature brighter, sunnier, the sky clearing, like a pure crystal... The red blood on her body whitens and she gets clothed from her head to toes in a bright white dress, like a goddess... The street becomes white too—covered by an immaculate snow from Heaven.

The bee buzzes around Mihaela's ears, alighting on her shoulder. Mama-bee looks so much different! Her big antenna is glowing with a brilliant violet; her wings are black as coal; her thorax and abdomen covered by a long green veil, looking just like Mama's green dress that Papa Grid forbid her to wear for the meeting with Emanuel. The bee's eyes are as big and black as her mother's, speaking at her in wonder:

"Heaven is in you...my love... You control your emotions, you only need to guard your heart...and God will guard your art."

"Yes, now I feel it... Heaven is right here..." Mihaela whispers to herself, caressing her heart. "Daddy was right!"

"My dear, human beings believe too little in *beyond the limits, in miracles...*" the bee continues to speak to Mihaela. "The power of thought and the power of faith are stronger than human knowledge, than anything existent... Humans themselves are able to give birth to miracles, they live in themselves; it is just that they need to see them and wish for them deeply," the bee continues. "It is so simple...yet some search the world to find what they already have...inside... If they only choose to believe... See, you believe and then you see me! I am a projection of your desire. You thought of me earlier today, and here I am. Do you think it's possible to live without believing?"

"No, never..." Mihaela stares at the wise bee-friend, in amazement, "Teach me more, please...to know who I am..."

"You are who you believe in!" the bee smiles lovingly at Mihaela.

"Yes, I am the beloved child of God..." Mihaela caresses the bee.

"Yes...you are. But why do you fear? Why do you listen to false preachers and open the door to the wicked when you have inside you the true Teacher?"

"I fear the evil..."

"No, never! Remember this: the wicked sometimes impersonates the good; the wolf comes with the voice and skin of a sheep. Don't listen to that wicked voice... The voice of God does not come when you fall into yourself, fearful and numb, searching in the basements of the past... Do not give up, do not look back, my dear! That was just a test. You have to stay strong and love Gabriela with all her wrongs... You have an immortal gift. Give up your fearful pangs and she will eventually give up her fangs!"

"How? She changes me, I fear... Wickedness sometimes influences my being... Should I stay next to her? I cannot go on like that..." Mihaela speaks up.

"Find what you and your sister are linked by the most...and do not give up. Love melts down the fear...like sun the snow in winter..."

Mihaela looks at the bee, confused. The bee continues, speaking slowly, with motherly love:

"Honey, you know it. Gabriela has been sucking your humanity, shattering you; her vampiric power has been stronger than your light; you've been straying and staying nearby her for so long and she's been dominating you... You cannot be like a leaf in the wind any more, trusting everything that you hear, everything that you feel... You are different and pure. You received her darkness because you did not use the shield of faith. You let yourself intimidated, conquered by fear... You don't have to be afraid of evil, because evil is just fear, and fear is just dust in the wind, an illusion for the weak minds... The devil wants you blind, focused on your weaknesses. But keep your eyes on the sky and then, there is nothing that the enemy can do to your life... You will receive everything that you need to receive: Grace, Love, Wisdom, Heart. His reflection, His sight, will transform every drop of night you might have into light. And then, you will be able to transform Gabriela, too. But have patience and do not fear; fear belongs to Hell; love belongs to God. Love Gabriela because she is your sister. Help her, but don't let her dominate you. Let Gabriela see what you have and she will want to be just like you..."

And the bee buzzes once and disappears like a golden mist, into the stamens of a sunflower. But, in a twinkling of an eye, she re-appears, and whispers to Mihaela's ear:

"I forgot to give you something. Your mother asked me to give you this!"

"My mother?"

"Yes. Take this box. You will find some precious honey taken from the Queen of the Night flowers which petals your mother had to eat in order to remain pregnant with you."

"My mother had to eat petals of flowers to remain pregnant with me?"

"Yes."

"Is this a fairy tale from Heaven?"

"See, your mother believed in the unknown, in the unseen, in the mysteries of the world... That's why now she is able to..."

"Is able to what?"

"Never mind."

"Please, tell me."

"I wish I could, but I cannot yet..."

"Why?"

"It is not good for you to know this now."

"Why?"

"It will take away from your dreams, from your power... Oil your sister with this honey every time you sense her evil power reinforcing. But most of all, save this honey for when your sister will come back to ask you for more... And now, something between the two of us: in order to get rid of any unwanted wrinkles, just apply a tiny amount of this honey. It will diminish them miraculously. "

The bee disappears again, yet this time through Mihaela's ear.

"Ouch! Where are you? Come back! Come back!" Mihaela cries out to the bee, trying to get her out of her ear.

Strengthened and reanimated, Mihaela walks back to the theatre.

All of a sudden, the dusk breaks in, like a web of the night, grasping the light, and Mihaela starts to run...

On the theatre stage.

Gabriela, fired up, with her hands propped up on her little waist, and her lips pooched like a super-ripened cherry, shouts out at Mihaela, who approaches the stage, quietly:

"We've all been waiting for you for hours to rehearse the Church Scene, like the servants of some queen... Where have you been?"

Mihaela keeps silent.

"I have squeezed my brains and asked my saints to give me inspiration so that I can make you see the glory of my composition and what success you will achieve through my grand vision!" Gabriela speaks, boastfully. "And now, you disappoint us all? Where is your old, angelical soul?"

Mihaela smiles:

"I had to deal with my wicked clone. Anybody knows of her? Finally she confessed, and was forgiven for all her sins!"

"Are you feeling well?" Liam chimes in, interrupting the biting eye contact between the two sisters.

"Better than ever!" Mihaela replies with serenity.

"Really?" Gabriela asks, unsatisfied.

"Yes. Now, dear actors," Mihaela continues, "Please, take your positions on stage and let's begin with the Church Scene that Gabriela has exceedingly prepared herself with."

The actors and engineers take their place, and the Church Scene begins. The lights slowly turn off, and a projection of Vlad's castle appears on the big cinema screen. Mihaela breathes with excitement, backstage.

Vlad, laid on his back, is deeply asleep, wrapped in big Valerian leaves and surrounded by his nine cats that snore with their eyes open, like their beloved master.

Suddenly, the voices of the Wicked Clone pound louder and louder; black shadows tarnish the magic mirror, closing the spotlight in total darkness.

"You cannot get away from who you are! Your teeth will grow back! You belong to Dracula's Land!"

The voices rise to a crescendo, culminating into an infernal growl. Mihaela enters the stage, running hectically from one end to the other. Panting heavily, she collapses on the disturbingly lit stage, then rises back to her bones and sprints again, to and fro, like a mad girl. The wind blows strongly, raising her hair up in the air. Suddenly, the star on her forehead opens largely and Mihaela stops, flashing the dark. A big ball of light springs out of her heart and hits the mirror with a loud thud. The glass breaks into thousands of pieces of ice. Vlad wakes up.

Vlad: *What was that sound that has disturbed my sleeping hour?*
Gabriela: *Father, she broke the mirror! I cannot see her any clear!*
Vlad: *Oh...noooo! My precious mirror! Mihaela dear, how could you be so fierce? I feel the thousand icy glasses cut me through; I feel that you have gone too far... Oh, if I knew, I would have chained you in my castle till you gave yourself to me—my wife, my lover, my servant and my muse accept to be!*

The stage splits into two. Gabriela, inside her chamber from Transylvania, is playing the piano; Mihaela, inside The Actors' Church, *prays.*

Gabriela addresses Vlad:
Father, last night, in Grid's old house, I found my sister's journal with tons of poems and love songs... I do not like her earthly feelings of weeping and of weakness, they have no fire, but what I want is to compose some royal majestic operas about vampires! But I need some Inspiration more than anything!

Inspiration? **Vlad's voice asks, confronting residues of memories that tell him that this word belongs to Him...**

Mihaela, in the church:
Oh Father, dear God, protect me from the evil
Please help me live humanly, I feel so feeble.
I need to find myself, please help me keep this heart
I need to write, I want to live forever through my Art.

Gabriela, in her chamber:
Father, you gave me fangs since birth

And I am grateful for this gift through which I reign
on earth...
Yet, I got bored to listen to the sound of teeth
When they crush off the necks of humans with a kiss.
I love to bite; yet now I want to write,
Compose, and be a widely famous myth to brilliant minds.

Vlad:
Oh, how I yearn for Mihaela, my own daughter,
oh how incestuously it slaughters.

Gabriela, struggling to compose, plays the piano ragingly.
She presses the notes harder and harder so that blood erupts out of
her fingers. The entire keys are covered with her blue blood.

Gabriela, totally angered and stressed out:
Father, please, can't you hear how I crave?
Give me that inspiration or tell me where I could find its grave.
Is there a coffer where you keep it hidden
And open it when creation needs to be driven?
Father, I am immortal, and fearless and stronger,
I play piano with a virtuosity that can breaks walls,
But I'm unable to compose...
I want to write, not just imitate the geniuses' code...

Vlad: *I need to find a way to marry Mihaela and quench my thirst,*
I need to show God that I am stronger, that He's under my curse!

Gabriela:
Shame on you, father! Instead of helping me with inspiration,
You think to marry Mihaela, my dear sister, your dear daughter?
But who am I not to receive your pride? Am I a monster, father?
Why is she so radiant, so lovely and so kind?

Why can she write and I am stuck? I feel a thing that I have never felt before... I feel the need to cry, but I cannot...

Gabriela whines, provoking violent contractions of the muscles, yet she is still unable to drop a tear...
Outraged, she takes a piece of glass from the broken mirror and impales her father, Vlad.
Vlad gives a loud shriek of pain, morphing into a dragon:
Oh, disloyal daughter! If I hadn't been immortal, by my own child mercilessly slaughtered!

Vlad exits the scene, spitting out blue fire.

Gabriela, alone in her chamber:
Father, dear Lucifer, why wait for Vlad when you are my real god?
You that created the Fire, give me fire to get inspired!
Mihaela:
Father, help me direct this play with Your Holy fire!
Gabriela:
Oh, I feel Lucifer is taking me... Oh, thank you Hell for sending thee! Ah, I got a brilliant idea that's gonna trap my sister inside her human stupid mania!
Mihaela: *Father, please, help my sister stay away from me*
I need to live in light and not to fear those fangs coming back at night!
Gabriela, dressed as a nun, pats Mihaela on her shoulder: *We're closing, my dear!*
Mihaela: *One second, please!*
Nun: *It is too late, my dear!*
Mihaela: *No, it is never too late!*

As Mihaela turns around, she sees Gabriela, dressed up as the nun!

Her eyes widen; her hands start to tremble; her feet stumble upon the stage... Suddenly, Mihaela remembers the words of her bee-friend and comes to her senses.

"Stop it! Michael, turn on the lights!" Mihaela yells from the stage towards the light designer.

The lights steal the darkness and Mihaela breathes easily, addressing the cast:

"Ten-minute break, please! We need to fix something! Thank you!"

Mihaela grabs Gabriela's cold hand and drags her backstage.

"What did you do? Why did you change the text?"

"I don't know..." Gabriela replies with a cold face furrowed by a sardonic smile.

"Earlier today, as I was praying at The Actors' Church, you suddenly appeared behind me, dressed as a nun, just like two minutes ago, and uttered the same words... How did you do that?"

"Are you sure?" Gabriela cuts her off. "Are you sure that you don't have hallucinations, few mental problems?"

Mihaela freezes for a moment, filled with anger, but then continues to speak with calm:

"Yes, I have a problem, sweet sister, and I need you to help me fix it... I think that I have put myself under a lot of pressure in order to assure that the *Wicked Clone* show will be very successful and that people will find what truly matters in this life: love, inspiration, art, true immortality... I want everything to be perfect, and this perfectness drives me crazy... I need some help..."

Gabriela laughs, patting her round, pointed breasts.

"That's what happens when you pray too much..."

Mihaela continues, unaffectedly:

"I am in need of some time to rest, some time to be with me... Perhaps a one week break would be enough...enough to gather the best of me..."

"One week break? But what about me?" Gabriela asks, filled with rage. "I have put my sweat and blood into this *Wicked Clone show*, restraining myself from biting these feeble actors of yours, dying of hunger and getting unsatisfying slumbers! I have been devoting enormous time, space and liberty, almost losing my hearing, almost losing my vampiric leisure—composing unimaginable symphonies for your human pleasure! And you whim that you're tired and that you need a vacation?

Moreover, sweet sis, I have been portrayed unfairly in your play—like I am only able to imitate and not to compose! Like I depend on you and on your human sort to give out a note or so! No, no, no! I love to compose; I have real talent, greater than your earthly folks! My luciferic fire is my Hellish Ghost! But let's forget about laments and hard work because I have been awfully happy to work for this play. I am destined to compose and impose my way! My point is that I'm deep into the 'magical twirl of creation,' to quote you, and your suggestion of taking a break and stopping from writing is like telling a mother in labor at night to wait one more week to give birth to her child!"

Mihaela giggles:

"I am pleased to know that you know about babies and how mommies bring children into the world. And I am more than satisfied to know that you can create and can speak poetically, like me... But dear Gabriela, I am not asking you to stop composing. You can go on and compose the next scenes for the show... You are in charge of your role! But see, as a pregnant mother, I am tired, and I am asking you to let me rest for just one week... I am in labor..."

"Oh, I see... You are a pregnant mother in labor? Ha, ha, ha!"

"I need to be all by myself in an apartment, to breathe..."

"Oh, you are kicking me out of the hotel room, too?"

"I cannot stay there any longer. It is too dangerous," Mihaela replies. "I need to find another apartment and take my mind off the whole show and everything...including hearing the soundtrack..."

"Oh, I think I know what can make you feel better..."

And Gabriela jumps on her sister and gives her a big kiss on her lips.

"What are you doing?" Mihaela asks her sister with panic.

"Love solves everything...it covers all sins... I read it in your journal," Gabriela whispers, mockingly.

"Yes, it does, but this is not love..."

"But what was that?" Gabriela raises her eyebrows.

"You know...vampiric instinct, sexual attack!"

"But I love you. I do not care how you name it..."

"I love you too, sister, but ..."

"I love you more than that," Gabriela moves on, touching Mihaela's breasts.

"Stop it! You scare me!"

"I did everything for you out of love."

"This is carnal love…vampiric lust, sex. Sex is not love."

"Ok, then teach me about love," Gabriela gives in. And licking Mihaela's face, Gabriela giggles with pleasure.

"Stop it, wicked sis!"

"So teach me about love, my loving sis…" Gabriela moans, sticking her teeth out.

"Oh my God! Do you really want to know about love?"

"Yes, tremendously. I want to kiss and be kissed," Gabriela says, licking her own arms, like a pampered little cat.

"Fine," Mihaela consents. Then she moves away from Gabriela and cries out: "Liam? Would you please do me a great favor?"

"Sure, anytime."

Liam approaches Mihaela.

"See, my sister Gabriela has a kind request," Mihaela blushes.

"Kind request?" Gabriela laughs.

"She has never been kissed by a man and…" Mihaela tries to explain.

Liam blushes.

"She needs a kiss. Just to know how it feels," Mihaela resumes. "Think of it as if an acting challenge…and maybe…"

Mihaela does not even finish her sentence when Gabriela jumps on Liam and kisses him with brutal, wicked touches. Embarrassed and disheveled, Liam loses himself in the dark kisses of Gabriela.

"Gabriela, stop it! Get your hands off him!" Mihaela yells desperately at her sister.

Gabriela stops as an automaton and gives Liam a hand to rise.

"Liam, can you please teach Gabriela how to kiss with her heart?" Mihaela sneaks in.

"How to kiss with her heart?" Liam asks, confused.

"Yes, Liam…" Gabriela whispers, provocatively.

Liam chuckles, nervously:

"I'll try to...to..."

Mihaela takes Gabriela to the side, strongly squeezing her muscled arm. She then speaks, firmly:

"Liam will help you learn how to kiss, how to humanly love, if possible...but don't ever abuse him or turn him into your victim. He is an actor, an artist, and as we spoke before, stage is sacred. It belongs to God... Backstage belongs to Lucifer, but we won't let him take hold of it. Are you with me? I can see everything on camera. One shed of blood and our contract is over, you're banished from my world. And from the show."

"Yes. I promise... You know something? Staying near you, I've begun to speak poetically, like you. Staying near you, I've started loving you more... Let me kiss your sweet words, Sis. Let's make love! I don't want Liam or any other actor! I need you to show me how to kiss...with the heart..."

"I think you need a break too... Read this, please. And Mihaela slides a drawer open and hands Gabriela the Bible. She then rushes out, annoyed by her sister's sinful glances.

Gabriela, frozen as an iceberg, feeling mocked at and rejected by her sister, hurls the Bible onto the floor, grasps Liam brutally, and drags him down to her dressing room.

Liam, visibly scared, but glittering passion from all his pores, obeys as a wise guru of kisses.

Gabriela's dressing room. Two hours later.

Bitten all over his neck, Liam lies in the corner of Gabriela's dressing room, hanged down in a sinister red light, under a jammed rack with dresses. Half dead, with his eyes almost gone out of this world, Liam whispers words of lust: "More, more, more..."

Gabriela, seated on a chair, with her bare feet drenched in Liam's blood and her back to his poor victim, penetrates the dressing room' mirror with cold, red eyes... Calling for her father Vlad, with violet, inflamed lips, she spits out words, intrigued:

"Father, hear me! Your daughter here, Gabriela! Father! Speak to me, please!"

The mirror is silent. Gabriela fumes anger through her nostrils and blue fire through her eyes and suddenly the glass starts burning, fog and gloom covering the room.

A blurred black image of Vlad finally appears in the mirror. Gabriela startles with cheer.

"Yes, my dear," the voice of her father resonates, deformed by a rumbling echo.

"I need to come back to you, father, at least for one week. I need some time by myself and for myself, to write down my scores and have them sold to the whole world... I need to renew my blood, to sharpen my claws, to refresh my flesh..." Gabriela pleads with her father. "I want my physics to look impeccable for the Wicked Clone role. This is my time to carry the ball! I am the star of the show and the composer of the *Wicked Clone*! Papa dear, you will be proud of your daughter's infernal songs! I'll play them to you! But I need some Transylvanian blood, some of your wise advice. I'm coming, I'm coming! I'm so thirsty, father!"

"Yes, I have been watching what you and Mihaela did..." Vlad replies with a sad echo.

"Did you? How? Mihaela made sure to hide all the mirrors around the stage and the areas where we performed."

"But she forgot to hide one mirror!" Vlad replies, sharply.

"Which one, father?"

"The reflection of your eyes. I saw her through you."

"Father! That's incredible! You're a genius! You need to teach me to do that!"

"Oh, daughter, not now... I'm tired and on the verge to die...of regret... You have banished me from your heart! Yet I have missed you dearly, my blood! I have been so disappointed by the cruel way in which you left your father—your only parent—in a total silence! I wanted to punish you but I'm too good and love you too much to teach you a lesson of penitence or revenge! I knew that sooner or later my daughter's bell will ring again inside my castle and your love is all that matters!"

"Love? What is love, Papa? You never taught me this!"

"Love is loving your father, your family. Apart from that, it is a terrible thing, the greatest hell of all! When your heart refuses to talk and you feel that hole digging into your soul…oh, you just wish you had never been born at all!"

"I don't understand, Father…"

"That's better, my love!"

"I missed you, Father! I'm sorry for being out of touch!"

"Love is everything…" Vlad whispers to himself, feeling a dagger shoved inside his lie. "But if Gabriela knows love, she will betray me…just like Mihaela did! Love is dangerous; love is so cunning… She always wins! But Gabriela can never truly love…"

"Father, are you still there?"

"Yes, my daughter!" Vlad replies to her with calm.

"Do you need anything from New York before I hit the road?"

"Yes, yes, yes! Please, do me this small favor…" Vlad startles with ecstasy.

"What's that, father?"

"Convince your sister to come with you! Just for one week! I need to see her face!"

"No, Father!" Gabriela shouts with eyes of fire. "I need some time away from her. And, besides that, I want to prove something to her…"

"I see…sweet vanity! Just like your father. This was my gift to you that I am to be blamed for, so I cannot scold you for playing so perfectly its role! So be it! Then bring me something from Mihaela, a blouse… No, better—her nightgown…"

Gabriela laughs: "Why father?"

"She is my daughter! I miss her, too!"

"I'll see what I can do… But she is the daughter who has betrayed you! Why do you miss her, Papa? Aren't I the reason of your existence, your obedience, your fierceness…and Mihaela worth of your abandonment and imprisonment?"

"Of course, of course, but she's my daughter too and I need to correct her, to teach her a few…"

"Father, she is the daughter who renounced you for another father and gave you the cold shoulder! She's made you so blue…but I have always been nearby you, upholding your dream to come true! Why is it always that we have to miss what we can't kiss?"

"Beautiful, my daughter, beautiful, I like the way you speak… Who taught you this?"

"Thank you, Papa… It is strange, I know it, but ever since I've stayed and worked with Mihaela, her poetic way of speaking has touched me like a virus, and I've been acting like a Cinderella! But I'm coming to you, Daddy…and I will feel better. I will recover! I have to stay true to my creative ways…and not weaken my given strength!"

"I can't wait for you, my daughter! But don't forget Mihaela's nightgown…"

As soon as she finishes the conversation with her father, Gabriela breaks into Mihaela's dressing room and grabs one of her sister's favorite dresses—the glittery purple dress from the *Wicked Clone* wardrobe. Then, grinning with exaltation, she splashes it with a little perfume and with the holy oil and frankincense that she has found in Mihaela's dressing room. This is killing venom against her father, and Gabriela knows it well.

"I hope that I can wean Papa from his disease—this unhealthy love that's boiling in him! He thinks that I am blind and stupid, that I can't see what's on his mind? He will suffer a bit…but I will be the only daughter to rule on his throne! I will have his castle, his riches, and I could make my compositions known to the whole world…"

Stimulated and enflamed by the empowering thoughts of fame, Gabriela rushes to the basement of the theater where she hid Rommy—the horse that she stole from Mihaela during the time she was Emil's fiancée. Afterward, she took care to wipe Rommy's memory through a simple vivid bite. The horse then turned into a vampire-horse, blue and without a clue, and started to pursue his new mistress' rules. His body became young and forceful, his eyes, dead but wickedly red, his hoofs—infernal sharp claws, feeding on the ugliness of the ground and drinking the sap of the underground. Glancing at Rommy, Gabriela feels so proud of herself, and she cannot wait to land in her father's beloved land.

Gabriela jumps up on Rommy's back, grabs the reins in her hands, and utters the magic words: "Hell, pull me down to your town!" The ground suddenly opens its mouth, swallowing Gabriela and her vampire-horse like a miraculous vacuum. As fast as hell, Gabriela is pulled beneath the earth, one hundred miles deep down; the living creatures of hell swiftly cling onto her body, swarming greedily onto her face and pinching her skin without rest. Gabriela tries to cast them away, impelling Rommy to move quicker through giant bugs, betsy beetles, foul smelling worms, and bats that keep trying to bite her and settle inside her hair like in a nest. But Rommy can barely advance, as the tunnel is so sticky and full of rotten and gelatinous swamps. Even to Gabriela's wicked eyes, the ugliness of Hell is repelling. Black as a stormy night without stars, haunted by deafening squeakings of millions of rats, the tunnel has the stench of Lucifer—also known as the Great Dead Rat.

In this chaotic realm, noisy as hell, The Hunting Bitches' voices swiftly make way. Moaning and groaning gracefully, the bitches walk backwards, towards Gabriela, with muddy bare buttocks, big voluptuous breasts, and curvaceous hips, flaunted lusciously in this darkest abyss. Amused and drunk with sexual thoughts, the ten temptresses of sin twirl their bodies in sync, fixing their keen red eyes on Gabriela, touching her arms sensually, and welcoming her with horrible greetings and long foxy winks. Gabriela follows them through the deep sinister darkness, the glittering red lamps of their bitchy eyes making a little light.

While crossing the infernal underworld, Gabriela keeps her eyes closed. The awfully dirty dust spoils her porcelain face, and the hideous stink irritates her nostrils and ruffles the hair from her arms. She probably needs to spend more time in this labyrinth of sin in order to get used to the burning flames and deafening noise of slaughter, betrayal, grinding, whining, perversion, corrosion…that trouble even her dead ruthless heart.

And yet, the Hunting Bitches' posteriors, in the corner of her mind, curvaceous and sexy as hell, are making Gabriela's journey bearable.

Mihaela moves from her W Hotel room,
into the old aristocratic house of a widow.

Mihaela met this kind and generous widow at the corner of 42nd street in Times Square, the same very night that Gabriela remained alone with Liam, and savored the juice of his body.

Mihaela felt dizzy and bloodless that night, and the apples covered in chocolate that the widow was selling and displaying on a precious, antique table, revived her. Red apples in chocolate have always been Mihaela's guilty pleasure. After she had finished devouring an apple, Mihaela smiled at the widow, and the widow smiled at her...as if they knew each other from somewhere, somehow... The widow took Mihaela's hand in her hand, and told Mihaela that she is destined to greatness, that she can see an indigo aura around her head... She then told Mihaela that she would give her an apple for free, everyday, if only she would spend a little time with her... The widow also confessed that she was very rich, that she had a very big house, but that she was very lonely, alone, in all her wealthy home... "I need friends like I need air," she kept saying... "But everyone is on the run, unwilling to look at my old bones or give me a hug..." She also confided to Mihaela the fact that she would give up all of her riches to be young again, and live a different life.

"Making these apples for people and talking to them a little, is what keeps me alive..." the widow speaks, as the wind whistles through her teeth. "I want to be the nicest person possible, and sweeten their lives a bit..."

"You are so beautiful!" Mihaela replies, touched by the widow's words. "Youth does not have an age, but a soul... And you embody it..." Mihaela says, smiling again at the widow with an open heart.

Quickly, the widow gathers her apples in a basket, and Mihaela helps carry the exquisite, antique table towards the widow's house. The widow takes Mihaela's arm, trembling with delight.

"My feet are weaker and got swollen lately... My doctor said I should stop working, but if I just sit around the house then my legs will get stiffer, and my bones will hurt… I told myself I'll get younger, day by day if I just meet a young face on my way…"

Mihaela smiles again, remembering the song that she just wrote: ***Younger than Yesterday***…

(Chorus)

As they continue their tales about youth and dreams, they arrive in front of Dominica's house. This is the name of this kind and gentle woman.

Dominica's house is huge, bigger than Mihaela imagined—it looks regal, like a palace from England, and reminds Mihaela of Emil's house…

The face of the house glistens on a narrow brook that coils like a serpent around the house.

As they step inside, a delicious smell of fresh red apples and cinnamon refreshes her senses. The ceilings of Dominica's house are adorned with large ruby candelabras; the walls nailed with expensive paintings with red-toned impressionist faces; the floors covered with elegant rose furniture; and tall crystal windows display an impressive array of sculpted red apples of all sorts and shapes. An endless staircase, rooted in the foyer, narrow and abrupt, covered in red thick velvet, seems to wind up endlessly high, almost reaching the sky.

"Oh, and the balustrade is like…covered in chocolate…just like the red apples…" Mihaela thinks within, thrilled like a little girl by the amazing view. "It is so beautiful and so big!" Mihaela exclaims to the widow.

"But so empty…" the widow replies with saddened smile. "You have to stay for dinner," Dominica adds, with motherly eyes.

After she prepares a delicious meal—duck in applesauce with red wine and caramel-coated walnuts—Dominica interrogates Mihaela about her past, present and…future dreams. Finding out about Mihaela's interest in renting an apartment, the widow invites Mihaela to stay in her house for as long as she wants, and for free…

"You have a chosen soul," Dominica tells Mihaela. "A beautiful warm soul that is going to warm up my cold old age."

With her one blue eye, low warm timbered voice, the widow reminds Mihaela of her dear aunt Magia.

Dominica leads Mihaela to her chamber, on the second floor.

The bedroom, gracefully adorned with iris and scented lavender, has a purple canopy king-sized bed with swing-arm curtain rods and white long veils, wafting heavenly like of a bride. The floor is covered with white Persian carpets; the windows veiled with white sheer draperies embroidered with purple floral motifs. Across the bed, there is a big oval mirror with a birch-tree holder and a frame ornamented with white roses like the handle of Mihaela's antique mirror inherited from her dear mother. In the back of the chamber, a white wooden door leads to a white marble bathroom. Inside the bathroom, an oval high bathtub invites to a healing bath, and a white porcelain vase, with a tall purple Queen of the Night flower, enraptures the senses, its strong perfume reminding Mihaela of her childhood.

"Just like in Papa's garden!" Mihaela exclaims, caressing the beautiful flower with dreamy eyes.

The perfect white-realm and the super clear and lustrous mirror from her chamber shows Mihaela's face more beautiful than any other mirror.

How lucky she feels to have met Dominica, the widow who loves red apples and the white color as much as she does! Moreover, nearby the amazing bed from her room, there is a small cradle—a perfect spot where Mihaela can lay Mommy Doll to sleep.

Under uncontrollable hot tears, Dominica takes a seat on the the edge of the bed and begins to tell Mihaela about her baby girl who did not survive at birth when Dominica was just 20 years old... The wooden cradle remained empty ever since...and she has been scared to become pregnant again or to even have a new boyfriend, as her womb would bleed and would not sustain the birth of another child.

Mihaela's eyes cover with tears. "Dominica definitely is a sad and lonely person who needs the heart of a good person around..."

After walking Mihaela through the entire house, the widow tells her that she can use the entire second floor as her own. Mihaela is allowed to enter whichever chamber she likes: the library room, where she can read as many books as she likes; the living room, the closets, terraces and kitchen, and search in every nook and cranny...but not enter Dominica's bathroom, at the end of the second floor, nearby the metal barred window. This is the one place that Dominica forbids Mihaela to set foot in, under any circumstance.

Moreover, the kind Dominica opens her closets and offers Mihaela garments and jewelry from her 40-years-ago masquerade balls and from her "youth-extravagance" period—her shawls and hats, skirts and dresses—and renews the promise of giving her a chocolate-apple every single day.

"Why is she so good to me? She barely knows me!" Mihaela thinks to herself, alone in her chamber. "And how come everything is adorned with everything that I like the most? What a coincidence!"

Convincing herself to stop analyzing the things and just enjoy her time, Mihaela lies down on the thick cushioned bed of her new chamber, giving herself to the arms of somnolence. Life has proven to Mihaela one thing: too much thinking kills the living.

So now, Mihaela tries to rest in the hands of God and let His peace shelter her mind.

A whiff of calm barely blows in her bedroom when Mihaela opens her notebook to write, excitedly. She hasn't been writing on her novel for some time. She is so eager to do that. She's restless to write about her new character—Dominica. After portraying Dominica as the most kind, generous, and peculiar being that she has ever met, a black arrow cuts her mind... "Dominica is evil... She wants to steal," Mihaela hears within. But she immediately ignores that thought and shifts her mind to another zone. She begins to write about the way her sister spends the week at Vlad castle, and how Vlad's nine dancing cats ogle at each other, moving their bodies ludicrously, while he plays the ney... She chuckles. Suddenly, a huge black wedding gown, with long veil and endless train, wraps around her body and around her neck, almost strangling it. Black big crows seize her hair with their curled sharp talons, trying to stretch it up... She rapidly closes the notebook, panting. "Oh, my God, what is happening to me? I need to pray... No. I need to fight these demons of fear."

Mihaela opens her notebook again, looking confidently and strongly at her pages. "The enemy and his fear...just fear my writing... I feel it."

But she is pregnant, pregnant with great ideas, and she needs to write. If her writing didn't mean something, these fears wouldn't come to trouble her. Evil fears the good. But sooner or later it shall depart. She has to believe in Good and rest in His love.

"No matter what, I won't stop. No." Mihaela makes a vow to herself.

She takes the notebook in her hand, and kneeling down before the opened window, she bows her head before the sky and starts to write.

The tunnels of Lucifer.

Gabriela, cloaked beneath the earth and walking wearily, on burning coals, bumps into Lucifer—fangs to fangs, who giggles with his fetid rabbit teeth, looking uglier and skankier than his pits.

"Oh, hello, my beauty queen! Everyone here missed you like sin!"

"Yeah..." the Hunting Bitches reply in hypnotizing vocal sync.

"You must be very, very hungry," Lucifer implies. "Before you get back to your father, please join me for a hot rat-shit, ah...I mean regal meal."

And Lucifer snaps his sharp long teeth double, and a greasy table with all kinds of decayed, frosty, rusty, foul, bloody meats... pops up before Gabriela's sore and blurred eyes.

"Yummy!" the Hunting Bitches exclaim, waving their bodies in sync.

Lucifer jumps at one of the Bitches, and snatches a portion of her fat round buttocks, savoring it like a hot delicious apple pie.

Gabriela watches the scene, perplexed.

"Well, sit down, please. Ugh... New York smells delightfully... I always liked the apple flavor, yet this scent is too fresh, invigorating... Move a little back, please. We have to do something regarding the people...and the churches...too many churches... I managed to transform some of them into clubs, but still... Maybe next time you can give me a hand regarding that. I'll think of a plan," Lucifer concludes as he finishes the Hunting Bitch's portion of buttocks.

"What's this?" Lucifer asks Gabriela as he pulls out the glittery purple dress hanging out of Gabriela's bag.

"Oh, that is for my father."

"Gosh, the holy smell of love..."

"Yes, Papa loves his daughters..."

"Shit! Your father is ill! Actually, he is in a very advanced state of illness. He loves Mihaela too much. And he is not allowed to love."

"He is not allowed to love? Why?" Gabriela asks with interest.

"No. Not his daughter. Let me tell you a secret. Your father wants to get Mihaela into his bed, to make sex with her like a perverted sick dad!"

"No!" Gabriela strikes a frigid pose, freezing her wicked mouth in awe...

"Yes, he plans to marry your very own sister. I read this in the corner of his mind, in shelf number 213. I'll show you. It is a disgusting liberty. I love incest, yes, I invented it...but he is betraying you, his loyal daughter. Hell is about loyalty. He is actually using you to lure Mihaela back to his castle, and then, he will throw you away like a piece of junk..." Lucifer discloses generously to Gabriela.

"No, it is not true. He does not like what Mihaela's doing, her betrayal... He wants to punish her. He is against her, he even banished her..."

"No, he loves her innocence and he has lied to you. He wishes to sleep with Mihaela and have her be his wife. He is just using you. Why do you think he asked you to bring him Mihaela's nightgown? Even you yourself thought so before...and put some little venom upon it...for a perfect gift... Don't lie to Daddy..." Lucifer chuckles as he caresses Gabriela's face with his muddy paw.

Gabriela boils with anger.

"And if my words are not enough...let me prove it to you."

And Lucifer takes Gabriela to his kitchen, where all kinds of men, hanging upside down, are being dry roasted.

"That's what you are eating?" Gabriela asks Lucifer, grasped by horror.

Lucifer grabs her arm calmly, and drags Gabriela through his experimental lab adorned with all kinds of human remnants: bones and organs, noses and ears, hair and nails... A big mirror, full of dirt, hangs in a wreath of flames.

"Have a look, my dear!" Lucifer invites Gabriela near the mirror.

"I can't see anything..." Gabriela answers, sweaty and alarmed.

"Oh, come on. I thought you have learnt to see through darkness by now..."

"No, I don't know. Nobody taught me. How could I do it?"

"Vlad didn't teach you? Oh, poor girl! Look inside my eyes..."

Gabriela looks inside Lucifer's eyes. Penetrated by a flash of fire that crosses to the bottom of her core, Gabriela suddenly sees...differently.

"Wow, it is not as dirty as it looked," she exclaims. "Actually it is bright and golden."

"See, I've told you," Lucifer confirms. "Now, let the lamps of your eyes be turned off," he commands as he flashes another glance into Gabriela's soul.

"I can't see anything," Gabriela whines, fretting in the dark.

"Yes, I know. Only darkness." Lucifer giggles, gnashing his sharp decayed teeth.

"Yes, it is too dark. Help me!" Gabriela wails.

"Dear, you'll get used to it. You'll see when you need to see."

"I want my eyes back!" Gabriela yells.

"You wanted it. I did not force you. Look, now, so that you don't say that I'm bad, have this pair of glasses. My treat!"

"Now I see much better!" Gabriela says, encouraged.

"Yes, much better! See how good I am? I awfully like you..." Lucifer whispers to Gabriela's ear, while licking her long neck with tongues of fear.

Suddenly, inside the mirror, a very slim and pale Vlad appears, with tattered clothes, hanging on him like on a skeleton. Surrounded by his seven Transylvanian flocky dogs, his nine mischievous cats, his blood dealer Beastie with a half-man-half-woman demeanor, Cerberus—the shepherd-of-death and guardian of the Inferno, Vlad venerates a huge wedding dress that is being meticulously trimmed and sewn by enormous tailoring-ravens. Vlad circles frenziedly the giant gown, examining it from all angles.

"Exceedingly beautiful...romantic, splendid, my super-workers!" Vlad exclaims, patting one of the ravens on its lustrous head.

"See, I've told you, my daughter," Lucifer speaks sullenly to Gabriela. "Your Papa is preparing his wedding feast with his own daughter Mihaela! And you, his loyal, obedient daughter, will be banished like a beggar on the streets... But no, I'll take care of you and we will put an end to this."

"I have to go..." Gabriela grizzles, clenching her fists.

"Wait, there's more to see," Lucifer pleads, coiling his viscous tail around Gabriela's left leg.

"I don't need to see more!" Gabriela grumbles, trying to escape Lucifer's clutch.

Watching Gabriela chafing and animated by her opposing steeled muscles, Lucifer rubs his rat arms with satisfaction. But Gabriela bites his hand at once and Lucifer liberates her from his grasp.

"Oh, what a little wicked brat! I like your bite...you, shit-headed bitch! Go, steeled stupid princess to your Papa Vlad! But be nice to him... Alas, he is your father! Kitz, Kitz, Kitz!" Lucifer babbles, gnawing on a piece of rotten cheese, getting smaller and smaller.

On the way to the castle, Gabriela, boiling with hatred, brutally betrayed by her father, repeats to herself with fervor: "I'll kill him!"

Then she stops.

"No, I shall not tell him anything about what I've seen. No, not yet. I shall pretend like I know nothing and I will keep composing for the *Wicked Clone* soundtrack. I want to show him who I am. And after humiliating him creatively, I shall give him what he has never dreamt of—the purple nightgown of his beloved daughter, Mihaela! Oh, Papa, how much you love me, that's how much I love you! Slam!

Meantime, Lucifer has already gotten into Vlad's castle,
and is seated comfortably in a red-leather armchair, speaking to Vlad about Gabriela:

"Oh, my dear Vlad, there is one way you can fulfill your love... Ugh, it burnt me when I pronounced that useless word called *love*. Why do mortals love if it only causes hurt? Well, surely I can help you get Mihaela here in less than 24 hours…but you know what that involves…"

"Yes, I know," Vlad frowns, squeezing his features in hundreds of grievous wrinkles.

"Oh, I gotta go! I hear your daughter's pace…and smell her apple-flavored scent. New York has got too saucy for my taste!" Lucifer growls, shaking the mud off his fur.

Vlad is broken into two. He feels unsatisfied. He is angry but dreamy. For the first time, he does not know who he is. It hurts him. He is neither a vampire—the memory of his human life is haunting and betraying his new instincts and mission—he is neither a human being… He needs blood, but he craves love…his own daughter's love…

"Lucifer did not keep his word. He did not make me crueler, cooler… He actually made me weak and fearful, neurotic and doubtful…" Vlad sighs, walking his room in anguish. "He made my face flawless, younger, immortal and able to take different shapes, but my soul divided… I can't find peace, I can no longer sleep. I don't know what is wrong, what is the answer any more… Perhaps Lucifer did that so that he can control me in any way he wants…" Vlad pines, scratching his thighs.

"I'm more obsessed with love than when I was alive. Why? This heart is dead, without a throb…"

Vlad breaks down in shards of ice, whining like a wounded wolf before the portrait of his wife:

"I know, I cannot love 'cause this heart doesn't beat; it's stuck.

Yet my own mind is activating love with its past clock

To make me yearn for my own daughter, oh, how incestuously slaughters.

This daughter is like you—my wife—she's gentle, sweet and kind

Turning myself against my deed—the deal I've signed with Satan's breed."

Trembling, Vlad takes a seat on his rickety rocking chair; his eyes, wide open, pop off his head, his brain pounds, and tick tocks, like the alarm of an out-of-order clock.

"Love, Love, Love? Why is it hurting me—this word that should embrace my body like a glove? Why are my tears icy, but my memories on fire, burning my soul to feel within an endless liar? Oh, I am bored to death…and trembling like mad… I need my daughter Mihaela here. She is like no one from this world. She wants what no one wants. It is absurd! Just like my dear Dora, she lives not for some jewels, furniture or perishable glory, but to make people see God's love and her transforming story. She wants to change what people are afraid to change, she wants to give what people are too proud to give."

Looking at the plate with food that his servant Beastie has just brought him, filled with gory pieces of human brain in blood, he speaks with wistful eyes:

"Maybe that's what keeps me human? Eating this human food in blood? Should I eat bugs and rats like Lucifer prescribed? No, I could not swallow that, not even as a ghost! What is the matter with my heart, why am I feeling so much, why am I thinking so much? Where is my revengeful desire, my undivided fire? When my sweet wife had passed away, I wanted to kill God, to show men that He is a farce, a great pretender, giving the humans tears, and bringing them fears! He established a code, broken in ten laws, that no man could ever keep, and then He punished His children for their flaws! I promised men that I would give them youth without aging, and life without death! Can I? Oh, yes! I made a pact with Lucifer and with his underworld. I was so happy, so dark, and handsome, not too long ago… And Lucifer said that pacts do matter. It is a sealed, signed act under the law of Hell."

Silence.

"And what's the law of Hell? And who is Lucifer to make me trust his realm, and tell me how to dwell? What do I believe in? Who am I?" Vlad weeps down, and screams like a rebel child, breaking old Transylvanian plates and vases like a lunatic patient, chained inside his castle-prison.

"I used to tell my people:
Your wives, husbands, mothers, and children die,
Why do you let Him take away their precious lives?
You have the power to say No,

I have the power to make your lives go on...
Beneath your life, there is an immortal night,
Beyond His words, there is a tomb of lies."

Finishing his declamation, Vlad's face darkens:
"But now, my preaching about immortality just seems unreal, I don't believe in it as I used to believe. It is a rusting death, a lying mess...an endless coldness in a tomb of Hell... Oh, perfidious Lucifer! I need my daughter...I need something to bring my life back... Oh, but I fear...I can't go back... I'm Lucifer's and his damned creatures'... Oh, I need Mihaela's kiss and soulful voice to stop my fear and get me out of this abyss! Or maybe I am just in love with her rejection...who knows my passion? No, Mihaela is so different, she is my resurrection: she has my sweet wife's face and innocence...and she has even more—she is an Artist, she has Godly inspiration... She has an aim, higher than mountains, higher than my monstrous ego... I am respecting her so much...but I do envy her, her virgin soul... I cannot write as when I was alive, I cannot play the ney down from my heart! Only my memory plays...numb... My talent vanished; just melted in the past. But Lucifer has promised me that I would be swifter than an arrow, my mind will be a volcano burning with rich imagination, erupting great waves of creation. But he has lied to me! Now, it is filled with old boring feelings—regret, blame, disgust and shame...and most horrible of all, a burning flame that I cannot quench...an endless end... I cannot see the future or imagine it. I cannot see the sun... When I close my eyes, it is dark. When I think, it is dark. All I have is a dark past and a dark present. Back then, there were cruel times, hard work, ingratitude, unfairness, lies, but there was hope and love, there was light... I could see a whole landscape with flowers and smell them at dusk...even at war's hour. I could pick them up and bring them to my wife! And most of all, I could pick up dreams from my soul, certitude from the future and bring them to her soul... She used to smile at me and tell me that she loves my beautiful lies. But now, she's dead and so am I. She lives in Heaven and me, eternally in Hades! I am a hybrid.

Half man, half vamp. Is this my revenge? My sweet revenge that can change men?"

HALF MAN, HALF VAMP (Chorus)

Gabriela, behind a pole, is listening to her father's speech, biting her nails and sucking its blood like a leech.

"Now I can fly, I can travel in time through thousands of years, change my face, my voice, my color, my demeanor, my language and religion, turn into an animal or any other creature, but what good if I cannot take the face of Love, if I do not speak the language of Love to make her come back home?" Vlad sighs again, walking from one corner to another, the nine cats spinning around him, his hair turning whiter and whiter...

And speaking again in verse, Vlad whispers with tremolo in his voice:
"If Mihaela hadn't been born,
  my schemes would have surely run forth,
  I could have been the merciless man
  to follow his mischievous plan!
  I was expecting only one to come—
  a wicked clone of my revengeful blood,
  with the angelic face of my dead wife!
  Yet mother naughty Violeta prayed to God
  who sent to me another life—
  the lovely, poetic and indescribable daughter Mihaela
  that now I'm doomed to fight.
  Violeta is the one to blame, so *she* is the one
  who needs to restore my life and
  to convince her daughter to become my bride!"

And Vlad hits the walls of his castle that shake with icy particles of dust. "Oh, God, I'm lost!"

Yet suddenly, beholding on a sofa the wooden doll carved by Magia in the image of little Vlady on the doomed night of Saint Andrew, Vlad is penetrated by a saving vision, his eyes sparkling with hopeful decision: "Victory, victory! What a thought! Oh, I can explain to Mihaela that she was born differently, not like her brother Vlady! I did not have to sleep with Violeta, her mother, in order to bring her to this world. She was born of a miraculous flower, one silent night with divine vigil, when her mother raised a prayer to the sky, and was hallowed by the holy light. In other words, I do love Mihaela like a father, but I am not her father! Oh, damn it, yes I am, because Violeta sprinkled the flower with my own blood that very hour! But Mihaela should not know of all these facts. She needs to know *this* truth—that I am madly and incurably in love with her, and that I want to marry and protect her from this cruel world as she's too sweet and gentle to be alone—she is a vulnerable porcelain dove, that needs a guardian knight like Vlad! Oh, God, when I think of her I speak just like a poet—like I am still a living soul..."

Vlad's face is grasped by a glorious smile:

"Yes, brilliant! And moreover, I can get involved in Mihaela's creative journey... I can be the director and producer of her *Wicked Clone* play... Above all, I am the creator of my daughters, and so, I am the creator of everything that they have written and that they own. Therefore, I have the rights for the *Wicked Clone show!* I am the author of their roles! I am in control!" Vlad emboldens himself with immovable hope.

Gabriela makes her way out of the shadow, applauding her father with aplomb:

"Bravo, bravo! Brilliant speech, father!"

"My sweet daughter!" Vlad exclaims with a frozen face, caught red-handed.

"My precious father!" Gabriela runs towards her father, with her horns on fire.

"I missed you so!" Vlad exclaims, largely opening his arms, like a bald eagle. "You are wearing glasses, my daughter?"

"Yes, to see you better. You look better than ever, Daddy!"

"Come on, dear..." Daddy Vlad replies with bashfulness, rolling his eyes.

"I have a present for you, Papa..." Gabriela says while her black tail plays cheerfully around her waist.

"What, what?" Vlad trembles with excitement, pressing down his knuckles.

"I brought you what you asked me to..."

"Yes, my love! Where is it?"

And Gabriela hands her father "the nightgown", that is to say Mihaela's stage purple dress.

"Father, do you love Mihaela?" Gabriela asks him sharply, looking at the huge portrait that is hanging above the fireplace.

"Well, I am mad at her. She has been born without knowing to fear and yet she fears and she wants die. But she is my daughter; I care about her."

"Why do you care about her? She betrayed us!" Gabriela says, covered with envy.

"Yes, indeed. But let's rejoice! Tell me about you, everything that you have been doing in New York. How is it going with the Broadway show?"

"Father, tell me about your wife. I need to know!"

"Wife? Let's not speak about that life. It's irrelevant. Now I am different. I have no thoughts of..."

"Do you want a new bride?"

"No... My future and goal are now my children – you, my soul!"

"Father, marry me!"

"You? But you are my daughter!? What's with this thought?"

"Good, Father. I love you! I thought that you had some other thoughts about me..."

"No, of course not, how can you even...?"

"I just love you, Father...and I thought that...just for your image..."

"I love you too, my daughter, but..."

"Exactly. Forgive me, sweet Father. How could I think about something like that, something so incestuous and awful?"

"Yes..."

"You would never do that!"

"No..."

Suddenly, inside Vlad's brain, Lucifer's words start echoing: "If you want Mihaela...you know what you have to do..."

Vlad feels mercy for Gabriela because the deal that he has signed with Lucifer means more than he had wanted to give him.

Vlad squeezes Mihaela's purple dress in his cold hand and the dress instantly gets frozen and blackens.

Gabriela watches the scene, profoundly dissatisfied. She can't believe that the holy anointing oil and frankincense that she has poisoned the dress with has no power over her father!

"Oh, I am so hungry," Gabriela growls, suddenly breaking the silence, angry and black as a bat.

"Sure, sure! I have a big roasted wolf with grilled dove feathers for you, my love!"

Mihaela is in her chamber, at Dominica's, in her purple princely bed.

Her body lies loose, her arms and legs spread out like a brittle-star onto a beach of peace. Nearby her, sits Mommy Doll, sweet and quiet.

As a cold wind makes its entrance beneath Mihaela's nighty gown, the old widow enters Mihaela's room, sneakily. She slowly moves towards Mihaela's bed, her rotten rod suddenly stepping securely onto the thick white carpet that seems to swallow her feet at once. Mihaela startles. Arriving near her bed, Dominica coughs, and then clears her throat as if ready to divulge her something... Mihaela stands up, and wraps her arms around Mommy Doll. Dominica flutters a wet scribbled sheet of paper in front of Mihaela's eyes, coughing again.

"You forgot this on the terrace!" the widow speaks wearily, gulping for air.

"Oh, my poem, thank you so much!" Mihaela replies.

"May I read it?" Dominica asks, still panting.

"Oh, it is not finished yet... And, I believe it might be a little too dark for your taste..."

The widow had read Mihaela's poem long before, but now she snatches it from Mihaela's hand, and reads it again, out loud, with the liveliness of a child:

"My head is spinning, stung by two branches:
One is my fault, the other, my wrath.
How I need Your wind to blow peacefully on my brain,
How I need Your thoughts to replace my evil pain!
My stomach is a ball filled with a hole,
It empties itself because the food of the earth is too cold,
It never warms up my spirit like Yours...
Give me Your arms like two swan feathers
To cover my winter with Your heavenly weather!
Give me Your body to dress my weary flesh

With the strength of Your guardian mesh!
Give me Your soul to fill up my hole
From the story of Eve till the coming of our Lord.
And when Your tears of blood flood the wickedness of
Your daughter,
Don't let me extinguish inside the burning water...
And when the walls of the universe might crush under
Your breath
Raise me up high in the boat carried to Your living path...
Please, don't cry too much because of us.
We are too fragile, a crystal of dust.
Please, wipe away Your tears, and don't let us be fools till
the end.
Because then, our birth has no sense...
And I'll die tonight knowing that we only bring You offense...
Don't let me suffer alone, don't let me suffer at all,
Because Your Son has already suffered to make me a whole.
Give me His wisdom to see happiness on my window,
Blow it on me, and then, God, I will see..."

"You have real talent!" the widow exclaims. "But what about those 'You,' 'Yours' with capital letters?"

"Oh, those are referring to God!"

"God? Who is God?"

"My best friend..."

"Isn't a friend supposed to make you happy? You only speak of pain and...shame... You are so young, my dear, you waste your time with these fears..."

"He makes me truly happy!"

"How?"

"He made me see the light when I was blind... He put a beat into my heart and cleansed my darkness with His blood! His Love has raised me out of that condemning mud!"

"And after all of that he lets you die?" Dominica stings Mihaela's words.

"Death? I don't know what that is. All I know is that I was dead and now I am alive. All I can see is an eternal life..."

"Dreams, my love...illusions of a young poet..."

"Dominica, there are two types of dreams—mortal and immortal. And I chose the second one. I am immortal and I shall never die... I am writing this amazing book called *Wicked Clone*, and I will live forever..."

Dominica starts laughing from the bottom of her heart...

"I love your enthusiasm, my dear. But soon enough you'll wake up...and...you'll see a lot of wrinkles, white hair and..."

"Dominica, dear, shhhh... Let's say a prayer, together!"

"No, I don't believe in such things, my dear!"

"But what do you believe in?"

"Eh..."

"See, Dominica dear, you have to make up your mind! My motto is "We are who we believe in!" You have to believe to live! My heart..."

"What about your heart?"

"It hurts now... I don't know why..."

And Mihaela hugs Mommy Doll tighter to her chest.

The widow smiles, showing big healthy teeth, except for one, which is so sharp and decayed that it overshadows all of the good ones.

"Give me your hand my dear, let me show you something..." Dominica speaks with vigor.

Mihaela rises from her bed, following Dominica before the oval mirror with birch frame.

Mihaela looks in the mirror, and sees her white porcelain face and her big eyes so blurred and...stained... Behind her, Dominica's face, cut by deep wrinkles and by her only one-eye like a blue pearl, slowly turns young, flawless and shining whiter than snow... As she looks back at her features, Mihaela sees herself so wrinkled, suddenly aged, like a monkey shaking in winter... Her hair is thin and so few, her big eyes smaller and squinting, painted around with black shadows as of an ill dying person fallen in grave... She shakes herself off, but just to see her white hair falling out like snowflakes over her blackened wrinkled hands. Her arms shake helplessly, frigid and aged.

"No, no!" Mihaela cries, stupefied. "What's happening to my flesh?" But her back arches, her breath grows heavier, the sky falls on her shoulders, the clouds shadow her mind, cold rain drops into her eyes...trickling down her heart...

"What are you writing in there?" the widow asks Mihaela, pointing to her notebook.

"Oh, this is my novel... I suddenly had such a terrifying vision—I saw myself so old...frightening! And you were looking at me like..."

"Yes, my love, oldness is frightening..." Dominica cuts her off. "You have to hurry up, that's not too much youth left and you are wasting your time writing a novel... Go out, have fun!"

"Oh, no, Dominica. I am not wasting my time! I am building my future—I am searching for immortality and I will spread it..."

"How, my dear?" Dominica smiles, susceptible.

"You'll see when you will read my novel!"

"Will you read it to me?"

"I'm sorry. I can't now... I promised myself that I shall let other people hear it when it is completely finished."

And Mihaela slams her notebook shut before the one eye of Dominica that strangely rattled her heart...

"Just one fragment, my dear, please..." the widow urges Mihaela.

"It's part of my ritual... I can't... Please, understand."

"Sweet baby," the widow whines, approaching Mihaela's bed. "I offered you my home, an entire floor, my body and my soul; I keep you here with love and for free, just in exchange for some little love. I am alone... I need your friendship and your love, your trust... Please, read it to me... I feel like you are my daughter, and I am your Mommy; the daughter that I never had... Please, read it to your Mama..."

Mihaela, touched by the widow's words of love, opens up her notebook.

The one blue eye of the widow sparkles. Mihaela sighs deeply...and hesitates.

"So, will you let me hear it?" the widow asks with excitement.

"Yes..." Mihaela answers, sweaty and confused...

As Mihaela begins to read Dominica some lines from her novel, in a soft voice, a yellow mist rises above her notebook and then reaches the widow's mouth, entering her nostrils, her ears, and her pores...

The widow smiles with deep satisfaction.

The eyes of Mommy Doll wide-open.

Mihaela continues to read to Dominica, feeling sweatier and weaker:

"He sealed me with his kiss last night...and I have kissed him back... Kissed him back? Oh blessed kiss, but if that kiss was deeper than my wish?"

Suddenly, Mihaela's eyes turn purple and sore; her star onto her forehead flickers a broken light, and then it starts to bleed blue blood... Mihaela slams her notebook shut.

"I can't go on. I'm sorry..." she excuses before Dominica.

The yellow mist comes out of Dominica's nostrils, back into Mihaela's notebook.

Mihaela looks at the mist, overwhelmed.

"What was that?" she asks Dominica, dazzled.

"Oh, the age, my dear. I can't take refusal anymore... I'm puffing and coughing..."

And Dominica starts coughing so hard that all of her veins swollen and pulsate, on the verge to break out.

"All my life, it's been a continuous denial, a rejection. I'm 88 years old, unmarried and forgotten... My love has been rejected; my life has been rejected... What good is still to live? It is a Calvary. I thought that you were different. I am sad, so sad..."

And the widow stands up, and walks heavily towards the door.

Mihaela shouts back:

"Wait, Dominica!"

The words of her mother are echoing inside her mind: "Do seven good things, and we shall meet again!"

Mihaela doesn't know if she has done any good things until now, worth her mother's resurrection. "I failed... I let David, Emanuel and Emil die; I let Vlad take them away from me... I want to help Gabriela to escape her wicked father's castle... I want to be good and to do good things, to love and to be loved. But I can't do it on my own. I always fail. Something is wrong." Mihaela speaks within. And then she addresses the widow with humbled eyes and a loving tone:

"I shall read to you as much as you wish... And moreover, I will write a whole chapter about you, about your goodness. You are my good friend, my auntie, my guardian angel! That's what I am writing for, to share, to change, to love... Forgive me."

The widow takes her seat back on Mihaela's bed, her one blue eye tearing ceaselessly, and her nose bursting drops of water onto the white rug... Dominica gives a rigid smile, trying to hold back her tears; she wipes her nose with the silky scarf that is tightly wrapped around her neck...but tears keep falling from her eye, morphing into blue ice.

Mihaela ignores Dominica's tears and opens her notebook... She starts reading with joy to her generous host. The same yellow mist, this time even more prominent, comes out of her notebook. Mommy Doll moves her eyeballs from left to right.

Mihaela reads randomly from her notebook:

"*...Magia grasps Grid's arm, and accompanies him back to his house.*

The fire is still burning in the stove; Violeta is sleeping like a baby; her face, though very pale, is shining greatly after that raving night of fever.

Magia touches the golden needle that she wore at her chest, and then slightly stings with it Violeta's forehead. She kneels before her bed, lights up three candles, and sprinkles upon them, out of a talisman, an indigo powder. She then starts to chant in Romanian with great ardor:

"Leave, devil of sterility from Violeta's womb,

Help her give birth to a new baby in bloom!

Vlady, sleep restfully in your little tomb,

And let Violeta live in peace, away from your gloom!

Cry of a sweet toddler wash off her wounds,

And bring joyful days into their new room!
Go back to your hell—wickedness, spells…or any other dooms!"

An indigo aura begins to float around Violeta's head.
Looking at Violeta with veneration, Magia's lachrymose eyes open wider and wider, her mouth whispers in awe:
'Violeta is chosen!'
Then Magia…"

The widow listens with great interest. Yet suddenly, her face begins to shake, her eye twitches, under great convulsion. Looking down at her hands, Dominica stutters, hardly finding her words… She rushes out of the room, as fast as the wind, forgetting her rod by the purple bed.

"Dominica? May I help you?" Mihaela cries after her.

"I'm fine…" the widow replies with the low voice of a man.

The widow gets to her secret bathroom, nearby the barred metal window at the end of the hall, her face completely transformed.

"Oh, damned silly child! Why did she have to utter 'Magia'? She broke the spell…

The widow's whole body turns into the one of a man. She then looks at herself in the mirror, whispering with regret:

"So hard to convince my Mihaela to give up…and come back home…"

"Dad, dad? Where are you?" the voice of Gabriela suddenly echoes, clearer and clearer, through the bathroom's magic mirror. Abruptly, like a fuming ghost, the body of the widow is cast back through the mirror into Vlad's Transylvanian castle.

Gabriela is in her dark sweet chamber.

She is hideously playing the piano, her hair dancing wildly in the sardonic wind of her music notes:

"Marvelous, thrilling…what a giant!" she utters proudly to herself.

Vlad, behind the door of Gabriela's chamber, listens with great desire, raising his eyebrows every time a new musical sequence begins to roll.

Gabriela takes a deep breath, after which she invites her Father in:

"Come on in, Papa!"

"How did you know that I was here?" Vlad asks his daughter, entering her chamber like an obedient servant.

"I have a detector ..." Gabriela winks at her dad, playfully.

"Really? Which one is that?"

"Your shadow is too big to be unnoticed, it's three times bigger than your being, Papa!"

"Oh, yes...I know... I hate it!"

"No, no, no, it is so beautiful, unique... Actually, your shadow's overwhelming... It looks so young and charming, Papa!"

"Thank you, my dear. I love what I just heard, those harmonies..." Vlad exclaims in a humble tone.

"Oh, thank you, Papa! It is my composition, what I have written in New York! Did you hear how disharmonies harmonize, how uniquely I can write?"

"Your composition? Extraordinary, my daughter, my queen! I knew it all the way! I knew that you would reign! Play me some more, more for this hungry soul!"

"Well...just a small passage... Then I have to start composing the few remaining parts of *Wicked Clone,* and I would like to be alone..."

Without giving her father the chance to reply, Gabriela starts playing a vibrant, emotional part. Then, overly satisfied, noticing Vlad's drooping tears turning into thin icicles and piercing the old carpet of her room, Gabriela picks up from the lid of her piano a wrinkled sheet of paper, blotted with big streaks of ink, and hands it to her father:

"You should read this monologue as I play. It was written by Mihaela for the play. The music and the text are in complete marriage. You'll see. As you recite, the text will perfectly flow onto my notes, my notes sustaining the words as pillars sustain the structure of a church," Gabriela explains to her father with the words of her sister.

"Hmmm...interesting concept..." Vlad rubs his chin.

Gabriela begins to play her composition, glancing at her Papa through long haughty lashes: "Go ahead, Dad, read the monologue!"

Like an obedient child, Vlad starts reading aloud, powerfully and vibrant, then softer and softer...

"Hello, my friend, prince of Inferno!
You showed to me that there is life beyond the sadness,
You showed to me that blood still flows behind the deadness
Which pleasantly was satisfied to take away my bride
And let a beast like me forever live as phantom of the night.
Now hear up the story of Violeta:
Violeta had a child named Vlad.
That's right! It's spelled just like my name,
Yet it was made out of a human grain.
Violeta lived in Transylvania with Grid, her husband,
And they enormously enjoyed the blessed baby sent to them
by God.
But then a small accident occurred and their house of wood
was caught by fire,
And their sweet boy was caught up then by my incurable desire.
Well, I prepared just a little bit the sad event
And Violeta became sterile and mad when her baby in fire went.
Violeta's resurrection another baby craved
To fill the emptiness and heal her trembled faith.
But prayers after prayers did not raise the dead baby from
the tomb,
And heavy did not grow the yearning mother's womb.
Seeking a cure, Violeta came to me during a stormy night,
And I implanted the ovule of my dead wife inside her barren belly,
And sprinkled it with my blue blood
So that she can conceive a daughter to give a reason to
my vampiric folly.
All was done in perfect secrecy by me—Vlad—the saving God."

As soon as he finishes to recite the part, Vlad rises up, his jaw trembling, his eyes rambling and flashing jets of fire. Walking hectically down the chamber, he spits out harsh words of anger:

"Why is she doing this to me? How is this possible?"

"What, Papa?" Gabriela asks her father with wicked curiosity.

"There are things from our private lives in this monologue, that shouldn't have been said...as they are lies, lies and lies! I am underestimated and totally mocked at! Oh, what a burning fire!"

Then looking at Gabriela, he continues with viperous fervor:

"If you want to know the truth, then I need to write a monologue myself, just the way it happened, just the way I feel it, and just the way history should bare record of me... I shall give it to Mihaela to put it in her play—only this way. It is fair and credible for the audience to see and hear the mere truth: 'Written by Vlad himself' or 'Told by Vlad himself,' either way. I shall let no one denigrate my image, diminish my fame...moreover, my own flesh and blood..."

"Wow, I have never thought about that, Papa..." Gabriela says, hardly concealing a wicked smile. "But you know, the entire play is written by Mihaela, it is her vision. We have a contract and in the contract it is stipulated that..."

"May I see the contract?"

"No. It is confidential, and I am not allowed to show it to any thrid party. Now, I have to compose, Father. Please, go." Gabriela states, resolutely, thrusting her clawed fingers in her piano, and turning her back to her father.

"Oh, yes, you go on, and I shall go write my monologue—the truthful one..." Vlad utters, closing the doors of Gabriela's chamber.

Gabriela grins artificially, easily annoyed by her father's eagerness to get involved in their play.

Mihaela runs along the corridors of Dominica's house.

"Dominica? Dominica? Where are you?" Mihaela asks, overly agitated.

Hearing Mihaela's insistent cry, the widow's body returns through the mirror, embodying its old wrinkled shape and one blue-eyed face.

"I'm here, my dear. Did not feel quite well... But now I'm better..." Dominica says, showing her head out of the bathroom.

"What do you have on your face?" Mihaela asks her, confused.

"What, where?" Dominica asks back, showing teeth.

"You wear a mustache?"

"Oh...that? See, I was playing..." Dominica replies, chuckling like a boy. "You see, this game always makes me feel better... It is an old game that I used to play with my first and only love of my life... Or at least *I* loved him..." Dominica explains. "You see, this man loved to play *me,* and I loved to play him. He once had brought me this funny mustache so that I can impersonate him...and I was sticking this mustache above my lips, and then... Hahaha!"

"I see," Mihaela smiles, bitterly. "I was looking for you because I could not find my notebook," she continues, impatiently, swallowing the words. "I'm sure you can help me," she speaks, again agitated and sweaty.

"Oh dear, I have no idea."

"The only pages I could find are these, scribbled with some poems of mine, but not my notebook with my entire novel..." Mihaela resumes. "See, I have this notebook that looks just like mine...but it is empty, filled with blank sheets..."

"I can hardly believe this! Let's search for it. It has to be somewhere. Are you sure you had it with you? Didn't you forget it in the **W** Hotel room?"

"Yes, of course I had it with me. I just read you some fragments from my novel one hour ago, don't you remember? And then you left, not feeling well! I myself felt very weak and out of balance and went out on the terrace to get some air... When I came back, my notebook was filled with empty sheets. Everything was gone, like nothing has ever been written in it..."

"I can't believe it, sweetheart. Let's take a look at the notebook!"

"Here!"

"Yes, quite empty. It is so strange, my dear! How many pages did you write?"

"Over 400 pages..."

"That is quite a notebook!"

"Yes, all of my work, since I was 14..."

"What did you write about?"

"My entire life...my transformation...everything. I've written a whole novel."

"Really? What transformation? Was it written in your native language or in English?"

"I wrote the first pages in Romanian...but ever since I started to live here, in New York City, I became accustomed to writing in English, so I have written more than 300 pages in English..."

"But how come? Didn't you know that English is the language of the devil?"

"No, English is not the language of the devil, I wrote godly things... "

"No my dear, English is the language of Lucifer, and New York City is the island of Lucifer. Didn't you know that? And now, let me tell you something very important—a secret. Lucifer himself might have stolen your notebook and replaced it with the empty one... You have to find him and ask him to give the notebook back to you."

"No, this notebook *is* my notebook! I have my codes on the cover...just that it's empty. I need my writings..." Mihaela cries out, anxiously.

Knocks on the door.

"That might be Lucifer," Dominica smiles. She then rushes to the living room, towards the big red metallic door, with the youthfulness of a teenage girl.

"Who is it?" she asks in a sweet voice.

"Police, detective Davidson."

Dominica opens the door largely.

"Welcome to my house!"

"Is Miss Mihaela....ah...Modorcea living here?"

"Yes, she does!" Dominica replies, promptly.

"No!" Mihaela screams, abruptly covering her mouth with both hands. The detective enters Dominica's house.

"I have asked Dominica to tell no one that I was living here. Why is she doing this to me?" Mihaela speaks to herself, frantically.

Davidson looks around, overwhelmed by the elegant architecture of Dominica's house, and by the smell of cinnamon and scented apples.

Dominica invites Davidson to take a seat:

"May I offer you a red apple in dark chocolate? It is simply delicious!"

"No, thank you. Please, let Miss Mihaela know that I am here," Davidson says, resolutely.

Mihaela's heart strikes like lightning, flashing onto the meadow of her mind:

"How could Davidson find me after all those years?"

Her eyes roll in the dark, her feet stumble, and she accidentally hides in Dominica's secret bathroom, leaning against the cold walls. She breathes heavily, trying to listen to their conversation. Suddenly, she hears darksome voices coming from behind... She turns around... Voices are calling her from a mirror, a dark and steamy mirror, in the shape of an eye, like an ocular globe. The voices get louder and louder so that Mihaela can barely hear Dominica and Davidson, downstairs... Strangely, they remind her of Gabriela's voice...sardonic and spiced with flashes of anger...

"May I know what is the matter concerning my friend Mihaela?" Dominica asks the detective in an amiable voice.

"Well, I prefer to have her come down here, and then I will speak. She is suspected of having committed a crime."

"Oh my God! But she is such a sweet, wonderful girl," Dominica exclaims.

Mihaela steps down the velvet red stairs from Dominica's house, in her white frothy gown, looking sad...but beautiful.

"Good to see you again, detective Davidson," Mihaela utters softly.

"Same here, Miss Modorcea. I'm afraid I have bad news for you. A couple of actors and members of the *Wicked Clone* cast, uh…the play that you are directing…informed us that Liam, one of the actors, was found dead last night…in your dressing room, precisely at the *Palace Theatre* or Live No More…however they've named it. He's been dead probably for two days…"

"That's impossible!" Mihaela answers, grief-stricken, Gabriela's countenance stabbing her heart like a stake.

"Indeed," Dominica intercedes. "She's been here, with me, all of these days!"

"Liam Starkovski was found dead in your dressing room. Moreover, his whole body is decomposed, bones jutting out, his heart blue-violet and torn open, sticking out of his chest; his tongue bloody and twisted, blue saliva drooping out of his mouth… As I have analyzed, he was severely tortured…his flesh shredded by some kind of sharp animal teeth… His whole body is coated with a crested blue gore…and ice. I'm afraid you have to accompany me right now to the police office."

"I am so sorry about Liam. It seems out of a horror movie what you just said… Please, give me a few seconds to get dressed. But it is a big mistake…because I was here at all times, and when you said that the accident took place…"

"I wish it was, Miss Mihaela… But the tape shows differently."

Mihaela bends her head down, sunk in dark thoughts. She takes the stairs up to her chamber. Suddenly, the voices from Dominica's bathroom call her, piercing her mind like strong arrows from the past…

Gabriela, inside her chamber, hits her head against her grand piano. The elephant fanged-keys of the piano, tortured and scraped by Gabriela's long nails, suddenly turn pointed and sharp, piercing her greedy fists that shed blue blood.

Her eyes are sore and red; her hair dirty and tangled wicthly into big knots; her fingers press hard and madly loud through the piano keys that keep bleeding in raging disharmonies.

"Why? Why? Why?" Gabriela asks herself, hunched by excruciating pain... "I did an excellent job in New York when I composed! Why is my brain suddenly shut in this infernal Transylvanian frost?"

Gabriela's face shrinks like a dry plum, contaminated by jealousy and wrath:

"I am wickedly smart and I have genial knowledge,

I belong to the immortal sort and I have inherithed my father's glory,

Then why am I flustered with a writer's blockage?

Why my fervent supplication doesn't give my father mind

To cure me forever from this sterile fright?

He is so selfish, he only cares about my sister—his future bride!

He is a monster, but Lucifer, the Hunting Bitches will avenge my life!

Forget my father! I will pray to Lucifer who is above Vlad's power,

Who said he'd give me eveything I need at any hour...

I'll count on my luciferian insight and keep writing tonight.

Ah, damned, wicked life! I need to win, I need more blood to drink!"

And Gabriela shoves her fangs into her fingertips and starts writing, with her own blood, some notes on her musical sheets. Her eyes enlarge and ogle like an owl, her mouth is quaked by a convulsive laugh: "Ah, it's coming!" Yet not even a few seconds dissipate than she flinches back like a mad cat burnt by a hot stove.

"No! That's not my partiture, it's Beethoven's ouverture! How much longer do I have to bleed and sink until Papa gives me that "inspiration" thing?"

Gabriela presses again the keys, frosty thick blood falling out of her bruised fingers, like an artesian well of ice... Jets of fire burst out from her nostrils, her scribbled sheets of paper rising in the air, catching fire... In a mad rush, she exits her room and slides down the serpentine balustrade, to the foyer of the castle. Red as a hot pepper and slapping the floor with her infuriated tail, she pierces the magic mirror with an awful glance:

"Where are you sister?"

But the mirror is silent and dark, and Mihaela's face refuses to come to sight.

However, Mihaela can see Gabriela's figure, sharp and clear, through the eyed-mirror from Dominica's secret bathroom; Gabriela's anger-deformed and blood-stained face and her little arms, flailing like the wings of a bat, make Mihaela stare at her, between laughter and regret. "Why is my sister looking so helpless and ugly? We used to look alike... The more people she bites, the uglier she gets... I have to get her out of that castle...and me...out of Dominica's wicked mansion..."

Gabriela curses and hisses in complete despair: "I order you to show up! I need to talk to you now, sister!" she screams at the blackened and dusty eyed-mirror that hangs silently in Vlad's foyer. Suddenly, Lucifer's face looms through the darkness of the glass and Gabriela jumps ten feet back.

Lucifer steps out of the mirror and, with his dirty and bad-smelling claws, he grabs Gabriela by her muscled arm. Gabriela can see him in his entire ugliness...with his spiky muddy fur and decayed rabit teeth that stink of rotten cheese. Speaking seductively and sweetly, Lucifer addresses Gabriela, spitting hellish words into her ear:

"Queen Gabriela, you have to understand one tiny thing... You are perfect, you have a perfect body, perfect face, athletic skills, desires, I gave you all, except for this little struggle with inspiration... It was a birth defect."

"No, it is not. I am a vampire."

"Many vampires are able to compose. But your father was never able to...not even throughout his human life. His wife Dora had the poetic soul and inspiration, she was the one who was writing and performing... That's why Vlad loved her so dearly... Mihaela inherits Dora's genes and talent. You inherit Vlad's."

Gabriela listens to Lucifer with big petrified eyes.

"Yet there is one way you can possess inspiration, and have the talent of composing..."

"But I can compose."

"Well, unfortunately, only when you are near Mihaela. You have to acknowledge this..."

"All right, all right, tell me the secret," Gabriela gives in, drained and feeling disgustingly weak...

"Once you kill Mihaela, I will give you her soul and her inspiration, and you will be able to compose all by yourself, always and forever, as much as you want. You will become a genius, a celebrity. You won't need anyone any longer. Well, we'll have to sign a contract too..."

"Why do I have to kill Mihaela in order to have inspiration?"

"Well...any great gift requires great sacrifice. And it is not my rule. It is God's given rule. He established this rule in the early ages. He commanded Abraham to sacrifice his son Isaac. God also sacrificed the workers who built up amazing cathedrals for him. Did you hear about the *"Cathedral of St. Vasily the Blessed"* from Moscow? He blinded and killed the great architects who built it up, so that they can never be able to do something more beautiful. Did you hear about Manoli and his monastery? Manoli had to sacrifice his own wife to God, in order to be able to build up an amazing monastery ordered by God. And the greatest sacrifice of all—God sacrificed his only son—Jesus Christ..."

Gabriela listens attentively.

"So, you have to decide yourself..." Lucifer ignites her with a smile.

"But isn't there any other way? Why can't you give me inspiration from your kingdom, right now? You said you had all the power..." Gabriela asks Lucifer, for the first time experiencing great fear under his great black shadow.

"I'm afraid that's the only way, my precious! Greatness requires great sacrifice..."

"Are you sure? But what's this great fear clogged up on my shoulders?"

"Fear comes when you're not certain of your actions and you don't trust me. But I'll let you think about it... You have plenty of time. You're dead."

"What?" Gabriela asks, perplexed.

"What, what? Lucifer asks back.

"You said that I am dead?"

"I meant immortal... Oh, you kids...searching up for mistakes of the poor tongue!"

And suddenly Lucifer turns into a cloud of smog and disappears through the magic mirror from Vlad's foyer.

In his enflamed erotic laboratory
adorned with sexual tools, human clone dolls and other sexual machineries set forth to further enrapture and corrupt the mind of the world's people, Lucifer contemplates how to further entice Gabriela and Vlad and separate them from Mihaela's love that keeps their souls eager to change... With his evil mind and his fouled-spirited bats around, Lucifer ruminates upon his shemes of bringing Mihaela to his tunnels in the fastest way, face to face with her brattish and fatuous sister—Gabriela. However, Lucifer's penetrating eyes cannot rove through the big ocean to see Mihaela's whereabouts in the Big Apple. The ocean does not allow Lucifer's mischievous tentacles and wicked creatures to reach Mihaela's dwelling in New York City... Something strange has happened lately and Lucifer cannot understand why he is not able see Mihaela's countenance or hear her sweet voice anylonger...

Mihaela is in her white room, praying. Detective Davidson is downstairs, waiting.
Mihaela is praying in the language of angels, with her eyes closed and her forehead raised high, towards the light. A shield of water encircles

her...and the Spirit of St. Michael, with his sword out, stabs the little flying bats that Lucifer has sent against Mihaela's mind.

Mommy Doll is lying on bed, looking at Mihaela with big black eyes. Mihaela opens her eyes and stands up. She turns her eyes towards Mommy Doll, speaking with sorrowful voice:

"Mommy, how could Lucifer be so horrible, so sly, inserting such monstrous lies inside my sister's mind? We have to save her..." she says, shaking with fear, angered by Lucifer's lines that try to shatter the peace of her mind. "But the Spirit of God is stronger than the one who is in the world...and He is in control. I know. I should not let my heart be troubled at all."

Mihaela walks up and down Dominica's chamber, still shivering with anger, trying to cool herself down. She then turns again, abruptly, towards Mommy Doll:

"No, Gabriela is not that wicked and foolish to believe Lucifer's crap, she loves me, she wouldn't fall for Lucifer's trap... How awfully that Dead Rat tries to pervert the truth, to deter our sisterhood! And I'm so tired of Gabriela's brainless actions to destroy our good... How could she do that to Liam, and not seeing that destroying him, she destroyed our act?" Mihaela speaks up.

Now Davidson knows about Mihaela's identity, her address, and a crime like that...is surely the end of her dream...the *Wicked Clone* play that she so much wanted to stage... The only thing that Davidson doesn't know about is her twin sister—Gabriela. How much fury Mihaela feels against her sister, she cannot tame her own rage, even if she has prayed! However, unmasking Gabriela would mean the end...and she needs Gabriela for the Wicked Clone play... She has to think of some other way to get out of this game.

"But should I keep working with Gabriela? What sense does it make? Gabriela broke the vow, and she has lied. She murdered Liam. My notebook has been stolen...the play is compromised... I need to get out of the dark, to forget my sister, and move on with my life," Mihaela thinks to herself with shame. "But I am here to help, and my sister needs me..." she immediately shifts her thoughts to the light.

"Even if Gabriela is dark and without a throbbing heart, I feel that I love her, that I need her... Somehow, her evil force has stimulated me to work harder on growing God in my soul, on planting the good in the world... Above all, we are twin sisters, and there is an inborn connection, like between the dawn and the dusk, the moon and the sun, the doves and the crows... Focusing on Gabriela's flaws will bring no light to our future... 'In darkness we learn to value light,' Papa told me once. And when you open the light, the darkness dissipates, it goes out. So it can happen to Gabriela... I have to keep opening the light to her mind," Mihaela encourages herself.

Mihaela turns her eyes to Mommy Doll, who looks at her with big, hopeful eyes.

"But how can I explain to the police officer that I was born a vampire, and that I am trying to forget the past, and stay strong in my human clothes?" Mihaela continues to ramble inside her mind. "I got reborn, I am a new being...full of love and light! I love New York and my work! But Davidson will surely think that I'm crazy! How can I tell him that my wicked sister is actually the one who killed Liam Starkovski? How can I convince him that Gabriela needs me, and that staying around her, she will change through my love, and art? Punishment and jail are nothing to her; she can anytime escape... What kind of an officer, of a human being would understand? Yet there must be people with open souls who understand that some facts are simply beyond our logic... Is Davidson a good man, with an open soul? Should I tell him the truth? But even if he would want to help us, he is part of the New York Police Department, and he has a boss that he needs to report to..."

The best thing is to let herself arrested, hand-cuffed, and God knows...she can write a lot in prison..."

Mihaela puts on a ragged blue-jean dress, won over by the idea that she will spend the next chapter of her life in prison, writing...

Gabriela, inside her chamber from Vlad's castle, is cold and dark.
She is meditating on what Lucifer has told her, biting her nails to the bone.

Black violent blood splashes her face, yet her nails pop up back, stronger and longer, ready to be bitten back...

Gabriela: I love Mihaela, she is my virgin-twin, sexy and smart like me...but I also hate her to the depths of my bones! She thinks she is...above us all, a know-it-all. She is really not that talented, and she is getting old... She is just lucky to have inherited Dora's creative genes... Ah, my father betrayed me; he has lied to me... Whatever I wish for turns against me because he's not for me... I want inspiration. But he ignores my invocation. I want to be able to have it whenever I want it... I do not want to feel humiliated and denigrated. I cannot live like this any more...

The words of Lucifer "You need to kill your sister..." terrify Gabriela but at the same time they give her vainglorious satisfaction and a hopeful insight to her future. Inside her body a spark has prowled, igniting her pride. Gabriela is now thinking about Lucifer's proposal with great delight...

Knocks on Gabriela's door.
Vlad's eyes are carved in purple, tired and dripping ice. As he enters Gabriela's chamber awkwardly and with his head bent down, his hair rises, electrified by the heat of his mind.

"How does it go with your composition, sweet daughter?"

"Amazing, Father! I wrote a great song!"

"Really? Me too... I wrote a great monologue! May I hear your composition to rest my thoughts in an intermission?"

Vlad barely finishes his question when Gabriela jumps over him, like a hungry tiger, piercing him with claws of fire:

"Father, I want to be a genial composer,
But you have given to me this horrible disorder,
You made me barren of inspiration and a monster,
And now I need to murder to transfer in me the soul of a writer!"

"What are you talking about, my daughter?" Vlad asks Gabriela, frightened.

"I am unable to compose... I inherit your deficit of barren musical prose, and I need to kill Mihaela to get my genes from your spouse."

"What's all this nonsense?"

"Lucifer told me that once I kill Mihaela he will give me her soul, and I will be able to compose all by myself, always and forever in control. I will become a genius, a celebrity. I won't need her any more. Father, Lucifer will transport the inspiration from my sister into my body, with his lubricated, empowering transistor! He gave it to me written, in this agreement! This is great news, isn't it, father?"

"Don't listen to his words, my daughter!"

"Why not? He also told me that other vampires are able to compose, but that you were never able to...not even throughout your human life... Your wife had the poetic soul and inspiration, but you've always been sterile and without vocation. Mihaela inherits your wife's genes and talent, and I inherit yours."

"Well, it is not true. I had a lot of talent throughout my human life. I played the ney...I wrote wonderful poems. I'll show you my journal..."

"Show me the great monologue that you wrote for the play, Papa..."

"Ah, it is not ready yet... It is true that I now struggle with my writing...but I can still play the ney..." Vlad stutters.

"See, you struggle to write! Papa, I cannot live like this any more. I feel like a beggar, a lame person, banished and lamented... I decided to..."

"No, you won't kill your sister! I might have made you cruel, without a heartbeat, but I didn't make you a murderer of sister. You can kill anyone you'd like, and savor their bodies with delight, but not Mihaela—your own blood."

"Oh, yes, I can!"

And Gabriela rushes out of her chamber, making grimaces of disgust, and tearing her clothes apart. Her body is on fire; she tightens her steeled athletic arms, clenches her fists, ready to crush the entire castle with her wicked desire...

Vlad runs after her, his eyes bulging out of his head:

"Where are you going, my love? Don't listen to his nonsense!"

Gabriela rushes to the foyer, before the magic mirror.

"Mirror, mirror, I command you, magic mirror! Just get me there, inside her mind, to make Mihaela come home tonight!"

Mihaela's face looms before her eyes. Gabriela smiles:

"Come back to me, come back to your beloved land, I miss you, sister, I need you to teach me how to write... Give light to my infernal night..." Gabriela entices her sister. "We are twin sisters, inseparable friends! We need each other's love, we're one, from the same egg!"

But Mihaela keeps silent, and the mirror stays blackened and cold, giving no answer.

"I'm speaking to you, sister!

Give me some of your inspiration,

You're generous, poetic, and filled with divine wisdom!" Gabriela penetrates the mirror with more words of love...

But no reply, or other sign.

Seeing that her sweet humanly attempts don't give any results, Gabriela opens the Bible.

"This will catch my little birdy sister in the snare..." she tells to her mind. "I'm so wise! I'll do myself justice like it's fair!" Gabriela thinks, her face gashed by a monstrous smirk. She then spits out words from the Bible, that Mihaela once gave to her, in New York.

"Hear me sister...because my words are brotherly words, like in the Scripture: 'If a man say, I love God, and hates his brother, he is a liar: for he that loves not his brother whom he has seen, how can he love God whom he has not seen?'"

Gabriela, smiling from ear to ear, waits for the miracle to appear. She knows that Mihaela will kneel at her feet to help her sister in need.

But all of a sudden, the magic mirror blows in Gabriela's proud nose, breaking into thousand of small shards of glass, that hit and splash the walls, and mar badly Gabriela's conceited mug... Through wounded, bloodied eyes, Gabriela can see Mihaela's white face, her chin raised up high, and her long arms that hold the spear-cross tight... The pieces of glass immediately turn into ice, melting away under the heat of Gabriela's eyes.

Gabriela starts screaming at the top of her lungs, with her hands propped up against her tangled up horns: Father, Father! She's a murderer!"

"What's this noise and broken glass? I told you that you should keep quiet and let me write my monologue without a riot!" Vlad storms in with reddened eyes and a foamy mouth.

"Father, she broke the mirror! I cannot see her any clear!" Gabriela screams.

"Oh...noooo! My precious mirror!" Vlad screams back. "What have you done? Why did you anger her, what have you told my daughter to make her break the glass of our porter?"

"Only words of love, Papa..." Gabriela defends herself.

Vlad kneels down, looking with despair at the pieces of ice that melt swiftly under his eyes. He speaks to them gently:

"Come back, beloved shreds of glass, I need your reflection in my house! Mihaela dear, how could you be so fierce? How could you break Dora's sweet mirror? Ah, I feel the thousand glasses cut me through; I feel that you have gone too far... Oh, if I knew, I would have chained you in my castle till you gave yourself to me—my wife, my lover, my servant, and my muse accept to be!"

Gabriela looks at her father, perplexed.

"Papa, these are the words of Mihaela... The same words that she wrote in the Wicked Clone play... How did you find them?"

"What words?"

"Exactly what you have spoken: 'Mihaela dear, how could you be so fierce?! I feel the thousand glasses cut me through, I feel that you have gone too far...'"

"I don't know what you're talking about, daughter! All I know is that my beloved mirror is now broken, and that my Mihaela is gone, out of my sight! I need her; I need to see her! She's my sun, the only one I dream of looking at when I wake up at dawn..."

Vlad takes the remained pieces of ice in his hands, wetting with them his face...

"I knew it, I knew it, you serpent father, liar, worshipping perfidy, making me delusively promises of victory! Lucifer was right! You're mad, and you just want Mihaela in your bed to give birth to some stupid mortal brats! I loved you, Papa, respected you, and worshipped you... But you are just a mindless stupid kid, a selfish jinx, a vicious hybrid, a lamentable phantom, a mortal with airs of immortal legend!"

"Oh, Mihaela, where are you, sweet hope of my barren prose?" Vlad murmurs lost in his world, staring at the melting glass. "Where are you, white dove of my unbearable yoke?"

Outraged, Gabriela takes a sharp piece of wood from the broken frame of the mirror, and impales her father's back.

Vlad gives a loud shout of pain:

"Oh, disloyal daughter, eager to murder her own sister, and now her own beloved father! If I hadn't been immortal, by my own child would be mercilessly slaughtered!"

"Oh, I feel Lucifer is taking me, oh, thank you Hell for sending him!" Gabriela roars, vaingloriously, suddenly beholding Lucifer's figure before her eyes. "Ha Ha! From head to toe my body's filled with regal heat that makes me reach beyond the ground, into Hell's feast! I have a brilliant idea that's going to trap my sister inside her human stupid mania!"

"Listen to me," Vlad screams at Gabriela, taking the sharp piece of wood out of his flesh. "I love you, and not her. Mihaela is just a temporary infatuation! Forgive me. You are my incarnation, my true creation, my true beloved child that has no mortal thoughts of being a victim of this world! I'll be watching over you, and raise you as a queen composer! I promise! Stop speaking foolish words that Lucifer has told you with a serpent tongue to enslave your thoughts to the blow of his lungs! I'll give you inspiration if you continue to be obedient to your creator—your father Vlad, your mentor! I will teach you, and you will give birth to magnificent works!"

"Not you, but Lucifer is my creator, Father! You don't know who you are! You're just a leaf, blowing into the wind of your egoistical speech! You are a servant of the past, trembling to get some bones of love! You cannot create! Your blood is cold, is dead, you're old and mad!"

Vlad looks down at the paper that he has tried to scribble with his writing... He slowly exits the foyer, leaving his tyranical daughter behind, uttering words of hatred.

"Indeed...disgusting," Vlad whispers to himself. "I wasn't able to write at least a beautiful, poetic phrase of original source... I am creatively impotent... Then why do I speak in verse? It is only when I think of Mihaela that these words alight upon my soul... But when I wish to lay them down on paper...my hand gets numb; it blocks, I waiver..."

He walks heavily, his back arching more and more, his mind trying to find an answer to all his confusion and wander...

All of a sudden, as he sees the majestic portrait of his wife before his sad eyes, he takes life, his eyes gleaming with a bright insight: "Ah...I know it! It is not good to compete with Mihaela's writing, I will just anger her, why do I need to fight her? Oh, Dora, Dora, each time I see your face, you send me great ideas! I should just help Mihaela produce the play, finance her dream...and then I will win..."

Vlad hugs himself, satisfied with the empowering new idea.

"Now, I need to turn this brat—my impudent daughter Gabriela, back into her father's loyal friend! I need her as my ally, I need her as my bait!

Mihaela's room. Dominica's house.

As Mihaela opens the door of her chamber to yield herself to Davidson, suddenly, her third eye emerges on her forehead—small, flickering a shy light. The light becomes stronger, her eye grows bigger and bigger...bigger than her head, bigger than the door, bigger than her whole being...opening a long white bridge...

Mihaela looks in wonder at the fabulous bridge that beams like a candle in the wind.

"Enter inside the eye..." Mommy Doll suddenly speaks to Mihaela just like her real mother that morning when she met her inside God's head...in the beautiful garden...

Mihaela looks at Mommy Doll, overwhelmed. She then looks through the huge eye at the bridge of light, and then again, in Mommy Doll's eyes. Mommy blinks twice and encourages her with a smile. Mihaela smiles back, revived! She has been watched and helped by Mama! She's so happy! Heaven and earth are truly twins as she once thought. The dreams, the thoughts, the hopes can change reality... Miracles do happen for the ones who believe in wonders!

The eye, beaming a strong, gold light, is waiting...

With Mommy Doll in her right hand and the empty notebook in the other one, Mihaela enters the third eye's bridge. She is instantly swallowed, melting away in the light...

All at once, the letters of her notebook rise up in the air and follow Mihaela, like a string of words hand-sewn on a rustic carpet of Mama's.

PART 2

Monsters are humans…humans who didn't get Love.
Monsters need Love.

From the third eye's bridge of light,
Mihaela is catapulted to the City of Stars, to the year of 2033.

As she opens her eyes, a long luxurious hall unveils before her sight, her ears tickled by numerous children' giggles and sparkles of laughter; everything shines so bright, like the perfect facets of a diamond; images of new born babies are being projected on huge screens, to the right and to the left, onto the white impeccable walls of the glistering hall.

Mihaela rises to her feet, slowly, and walks along the big computerized hall, with big eyeballs of a newly born. As she enters a white, large circular chamber, provided with all kinds of spectacular tools and multicolored machineries, her entire being begins to smile... So many sweet, gurgling babies and laughing children walk and toddle around, so happy and healthy-looking as she has never seen before... Big robots and robotesses, looking like human fathers and mothers, with big kind smiles painted on their faces, are swinging enormous cradles, changing the babies' translucent diapers and feeding them white food from some white gelatinous boxes; some other smaller robots, pettite and energetic like super-dwarfs, but endowded with very long arms, watch children swim inside giant porcelain incubators, urging them with shouts to swim faster and pushing the feeblest ones to move forth with their long paddle-like arms; funny robots, dressed up like jesters, super colored and amuzingly painted on their mugs, are making three year-old children laugh, dancing and singing along with them around the white oval chamber that seems to widen at evey step Mihaela takes. Multiple walkalators are crossing the floor, making the robot-nurses travel at full speed, from one baby to the other, like overcharged mommies.

As she exits the large oval room, dazzled by the new realm where she has just landed, Mihaela enters a long tunnel in the form of a cylinder, with tall and wide blue windows, clear and very shiny. Inside the windows, she can see sparkling pools, where mothers are in the process of giving birth to their expecting babies. Nurses, dressed up as mermaids, beautiful as only in animated films Mihaela has seen, are helping the mothers bring their children into the world, while rubbing their legs with marine algae and other miraculous plants. As Mihaela watches this fabulous act, with big astounded eyes, the babies are popping out, like fireworks out of the mothers' wombs, inside the nurses' arms. Immediately, the beautiful mermaids hug and kiss the little ones with love, on their minuscule red hot cheeks, rubbing their bodies with a white glittering powder. The babies' skin turns flawless and smooth and their hair starts to grow at once. The nurses then let the sweet beings loose through the bubbling blue water, and the babies immediately start to swim, with happy arms and laughing mouths as if they have always done that.

Suddenly, a man, as normal and human as possible, takes Mihaela by the arm: "Here you are," he says vividly as if he was expecting her, afterwhich he drags Mihaela along the tunnel, through a thin door of glass. The man and Mihaela enter a white laboratory, adorned with tall glass-tables in which are neatly exposed all sorts of tubes, syringes, boxes, glasses but most intriguingly—medusas, leeches, octopus, and other gelatinous water creatures. The man invites Mihaela to take a seat on a tall white chair, with many pedals and handles, and then hands Mihaela a white nursing robe to put on. Mihaela gets dressed, wondering if she should ask anything...or just follow through... The man gives her a form to fill in. Mihaela signs the forms immediately, as if led by a supernatural force, and then, the man connects her to seven giant leeches. Each of the leeches starts biting her skin with three sharp teeth, that emerge electronically through their blood sucker-mouths, affixed to her body. Mihaela's face starts to turn blue and pale and her longs arms to shake; her long neck shows protruding violet veins; blue blood trickles down from the eye of her forehead, yet a glorious smile carves her face... Mihaela holds Mommy Doll next to her, thinking of the seven good deeds that Mama spoke to her.

The seven leeches, which suck Mihaela's blue blood, are connected to seven multicolored tubes which transport Mihaela's blood directly into the veins and little arms of the seven sickly children, who await in their beds, their yearned-for recovery.

Mihaela's pain eases as she imagines how the feeble children smile and play the seven dwarfs while she, dressed up as Snow White, kisses their little noses that turn red as cherries and touches them with a magic wand, making their bodies healthy and plump...

The foyer of Vlad's castle.

Frowned and feeling exasperated, Gabriela looks at the eyed-mirror that has been restored... Vlad tricked her again: the magic mirror cannot be broken. She clenches her fists while her eyes and teeth bleed with the thirst of revenge. Mihaela is now far away, and Gabriela's attempts of reaching her way have crushed. How could she get to her sister, to her new destination? She has tried and tried, but Mihaela is somewhere she cannot find in space and time... She is blocked by an energy...she cannot comprehend with her mind... Gabriela gives a horrifying cry that cracks for a moment all the windows of Vlad's castle: "What's going on with my life? I need a reply!"

Papa hasn't revealed the mysteries of a successful vampiric life to her; he did not teach her the dirty tricks of Hell, or how to travel the tunnels of Lucifer in no time, through her own feet and mind...

"Again, I need to speak myself with the Dead Rat...and down there it smells so bad," Gabriela whines. "But I need to get out there, to put my life back on victory's track..."

At the same time,

Mihaela is seated at a long wooden table with 12 bowls of bread and 12 cups of red wine. She rises up and walks around, wondering where she could be. Suddenly, a very warm, healing hand catches her hand, making her seat again at the table. As she raises her eyes, she sees a glowing white face of a divinely beautiful being that speaks to her, serenely:

"I love you very much. I am proud of you. You have already done the seven good things. Now rest and eat. Let me lead you."

The doctor pats Mihaela's shoulder:

"How are we feeling, dear?"

No response. Mihaela's eyes, wide open, do not react.

The doctor shakes her up yet Mihaela does not bat an eye. He places the stethoscope to her chest, to hear her heartbeat, and Mihaela suddenly speaks:

"I'm feeling good, doctor..."

"Oh...thanks God! I thought that you were in a coma... I've never encountered anything like that! I am definitely very excited that you are helping these children... Let's see what happens. Do you need some vitamins injections from the robots to boost up your energy level?"

"No, no! Thank you," Mihaela replies.

"Alright, then. A little more and we're done. Seat tight. Oh, and please, don't forget about our 10:30 appointment, tomorrow morning. Robot Iron will pick you up. We definitely have to investigate your DNA and find out how come that your blood fits all these children's blood types... I have to admit that you're the first person I have met with this kind of blood...blue blood... Has any other doctor investigated your blood?"

"I'm glad I can be helpful..." Mihaela replies with dreamy eyes.

"Seven more minutes and we're done..." the doctor resumes gently, looking at the computer that floats in the air like a medusa. "Once the normal venous flow is restored in the damaged area of the children's bodies, the leeches will fall... You'll see, even you are going to feel much better, cleansed... These little sucking creatures are fantastic—and actually help renew the blood..."

"I see ..." Mihaela smiles, still drifting, beyond. "Isn't life the most beautiful dream?" she asks the doctor beaming with love.

"Excuse me? What do you say?" the doctor asks back.

"Just talking to myself..."

"I see..." the doctor kindly smiles.

Vlad's Castle.

Vlady, the mute and suffering brother of Mihaela, lies on a deformed stalagmite inside the Icy Morgue of Brides. Nearby him, on a royal bed of stone, sleeps Vlady's mother—Violeta—shielded by sheer white curtains. Surrounding Violeta's bed there are tens of other beds of frozen brides and sleeping maids.

Vlady's face is pale and swollen, his eyes fixed and blighted, his mouth stuck in a frozen cry…

"Vlady, we have to save your mother," Papa Vlad alerts him. "Blood feeds on its own kindred blood to raise from death the sleeping breath! I was the one who saved you, don't forget! But now, we have to save your Mama through your blood! Together we will break the chains of death, and then we'll have a fest!"

Thus, Vlad stings Vlady's feeble chest with a long transparent nail, attached to a long tube, similar to an umbilical cord. The cord runs directly into Violeta's chest, penetrating her heart. Vlady opens his eyes a little wider as Papa Vlad stings him in six other points of his body: wrists, ankles, feet, stomach, lungs, and brains… All these points and organs are connected to his mother's, through other smaller tubes conceived by Vlad to bring Violeta back to life.

Vlady stays fixed, unshakable, betraying no sign of pain despite his bloodless flesh that looks so pale and frail.

The City of Stars, Children's Hospital.

The doctor comes to Mihaela and pushes the leeches, deeper:

"I am afraid we have to extend your staying… One of the children got disconnected. Apologies. A few more minutes, my dear. Sit tight."

But Mihaela feels good, energized. She could administer her blood to seven more children.

Inside Vlad's Icy Morgue of Brides,

Vlady, unable to keep his silence any longer, begins to mourn like a wounded bear above the giant stalagmite.

Seated in an armchair, Vlad puffs his anxiety through icicled nostrils while stroking a black cat which comfortably watches the scene from his lap.

As Vlady groans with pain, Papa Vlad keeps uttering words of strength:

"Sacrifice requires sacrifice, my boy. Have patience..."

Mihaela weeps as the leeches pull tighter,

yet other tears emerge, joyfully and free, replacing the old ones and caressing her face, peacefully. A children's choir echoes from the Hospital's play station, giggling onto her heart.

"What's the matter? Does it hurt?" the doctor asks, worryingly.

"No, I feel happy..."

"Happy? I have not heard this word for awhile, my dear... Two more minutes, and you're all set."

Vlady grows weaker and weaker.

His "Father" squeezed the very last drop of blood out of him, now holding hands with him so lovingly, like a worried, beloved parent.

"Two more minutes, my son... Have courage!"

Mihaela gets disconnected from the apparatuses.

As she rises from the table of the divine creature, the choir of children echoes louder and louder... A robotess helps Mihaela come to her senses, pressing with pointed fingers on her back and serving her with calming tea. Then, the robotess bows graciously before Mihaela, just like a human-Geisha, offering to fix Mihaela's hair and put her clothing back on... Mihaela bows back, letting herself be taken care of the well-mannered Asian robot...

"Oh my God! How human and sweet this robot is! It is so beautiful but...terrifying! How many of them are out there?" Mihaela thinks to herself, suddenly panicked. "Will society keep multiplying these robots and improving their features?" she speaks as she takes Mommy Doll in her arms to leave. "Soon...it will be impossible to tell a human from a robot..."

While being attached to the leeches, Mihaela has watched the history of the City of Stars onto the medusa-screen that has been floating and expanding before her eyes, adjusting in accordance to her sight. She has learnt about the latest news and technology of the robots and about the fact that in the City of Stars humans utterly live under the sign of robotization and multiplication—they can order how many babies they want, the color of their hair and eyes, their height, their weight, the features of their faces... In some cases everything went wrong and the children have grown too fast and disproportionate, being unable to keep their balance...

"If they would just let God do His job!" Mihaela utters with sad eyes as she watches on the medusa-screen how artificial twins are being created, some to be trained as spies, enrolled in dangerous missions for life... More than 10.000 artficial twins have been conceived in the City of Stars, including septuplets, decaplets, tredecaplets, quindecaplets...

"What's going on with this planet?" Mihaela asks herself, tottaly upset. Suddenly, her eyes wide open, like some alarm clocks. Her spirit lifts up, drifting beyond her body; a calming white stream of light enters her third eye; her feet are leaving the ground; her entire creature is being electrified by a healing energy of love. The long wooden table arises again before her eyes, this time brimming with all kind of drinks and magical delights: in a bottle of glass, there is a golden glimming light; in a bowl—strong bones of a lion; on a plate of clay—a speaking dove with wise eyes of God…near the plate of clay, there is a cup with heavenly smelling blood. Mihaela takes the cup and drinks. Suddenly, she sees the sweet sickly children playing and laughing out, noisily. One of them speaks and asks questions non-stop; another one is eating fish with enormous hunger; one of them draws elephants on a placard with his sweet pudgy hands; another child builds up an ark from syringe tubes and glass; one sickly boy is leaping around, clapping and humming a joyful song… The divine being smiles, caressing their heads with His palms. Mama, as a body of light, takes a seat at the table too, smiling at the happy healthy boys with huge glittering eyes… Mihaela smiles too. Her smile turns into the laughter of Summer…and then her eyes begin to laugh, her heart pushing the clouds of gloom out… She starts laughing so loud, through all the pores of her body that dilate into laughing mouths with little tongues as if the happiness of the whole world has clung to her that sudden, blessed dawn…

The doctor, who has heard big noise and enormous laughters, arrives in Mihaela's laboratory room, worryingly, but Mihaela, hyper and reddened-up, keeps laughing her heart out:

"Is everything alright, Miss Angelica?" the doctor asks her, overly concerned.

"Oh, yes…" Mihaela replies, suppressing her huge laughter with her little hands.

"Alright… Now you are all done! Good job! I am waiting for you tomorrow at the time specified on my card. Thank you for your great help and…"

"Doctor, doctor!" seven nurses frantically approach the doctor, with excited voices.

The doctor's shades fall from his nose. A robot catches them falling, yet it breaks them apart with its iron hands! The doctor watches the scene, annoyed. The nurses giggle.

"Well, now, loosen up girls, tell me, what's the matter?"

First nurse speaks up:

"Doctor, Andrew can walk!"

Second nurse:

"Peter started to play!"

Third nurse:

"James wants to eat!"

Forth nurse:

"Paul is speaking non-stop and clapping his hands!"

Fifth nurse:

"Matthew's sugar's lowered!"

Sixth nurse:

"Thomas's muscles are toned up and he can move his legs and arms! He keeps drawing elephants!"

Seventh nurse:

"John is smiling and building an ark from your syringe tubes and glass!"

"Hold on… Let me see," the doctor frowns with excitement, following his impatient nurses who keep speaking one above the other. "Damn, now I can't see! I lost my glasses!"

"Here, take mine," one of the nurses whispers to the doctor. "You and I, doctor, have a lot in common…even our minuses…"

"Stop it, girls, stop it!"

After a few minutes, the doctor returns impatiently to Mihaela's room, tottering to the right and to the left, like a drunkard… He holds a glass of water, splashing and crossing himself.

"Miss Angelica, where are you?"

But Mihaela is gone, and so all of her laughter.

"This is incredible… Beyond explanation…" the doctor speaks on, in wonder…

Next day. At noon. Monumental market of the City of Stars.
In the luxurious center of City of Stars, on gigantic skyscrapers, giant screens display the breaking news featuring the mysterious woman Angelica who, due to her blue blood, has healed seven seriously ill children in less than one hour in the City of Star's Children Hospital.

"Is it a miraculous blood? Who is this woman? America wants to meet her. Dear Angelica, in the name of these children, please, allow us to meet you! We all want to thank you, and know more about you..." the reporter announces on gigantic screens that light up the monumental market of the City of Stars.

Thousands of people stare, in awe—mothers with children, fathers with fathers, ants with nieces, holding hands tightly while listening to the story of the girl with the miracle blood... Rumors in the crowd, shouts and applauses transform the market into a juvenile ring of joy... A face of an elderly woman, with white steel hair and blue eyes, glances at the screen, savoring the words of the moderator; she holds the arms of a wheelchair where a blonde child sits, transfixed... She pets his hair as a tear dimples her cheek.

"I told you that this day would come... He sent His angels around..."

A shivery hand picks up a *Rolling Stone* magazine that features Mihaela's portrait. Holding it to his heart, the man utters in a melancholic tone:

"If I can meet her...just to thank her for Andrew..."

Among the crowd, an old woman with white disheveled hair and one blue eye, the other covered by a black stripe, keeps laughing, spasmodically.

"You, people, so fragile...so easily prone to the cheat! You see some blue blood, some sweet eyes and fall into the mud? Do you believe in an impostor, in a false prophet? Take my card and I shall give you the way to healing's art, deep from my ancient experienced heart... My healing, based on antique mythology from the stars, sewn with meticulous sounds from the virgin forests of the Carpathian land and depth of the miraculous underground, is the certain and wisest remedy...that can heal any sort of malady!"

In the mist of the night,

dressed up heavenly-sexy, Mihaela is walking along a narrow street of City of Stars. She looks totally different...flattering: her dark brown hair is now blonde and curly, sensually winding in the blow of the night... Her nails are short and glittering like diamonds; her lips plump and super-red; her long legs muscled, yet slender, moving graciously, like a playful deer in a dark forest. She wears a long black coat, with red velvety borders, wide-open, and high pointed red heels. The coat unveils a short black fitted dress with long lacy collar and diamond beads. Her earrings reach to her breasts, prolonging her features into a super-glowing diva. Her face, though powdered and well blushed, shows the same glowing beauty and royalty of the brunette Mihaela.

A black cat cuts her way. Mihaela stops. "Ah, not again!"

The cat's sparkling greenish-blue eyes allude to familiar eyes...

"The white dress...hope I didn't forget it again!" Mihaela murmurs, ignoring the cat's presence.

Her eyes roam melancholically, her mouth utters, airy and dreamingly:

"Oh, Mama, I know you watch over me, tonight... I love you, dear Mama..."

Mihaela's eyes stray towards the sky. Suddenly, her feet bump into an old woman who whines and begs loudly around the corner of that street. The old woman has greenish-blue eyes and lies down on a white Persian carpet...surrounded by dry red roses with thorns. She keeps ripping them, one by one, suddenly uttering in a croaky voice:

"If I have endless life but no love, then I have endless pain, this body and this soul in vain... If I have youth forever, the power to ride till heaven, the wisdom to read hearts and decipher all arts, but have no love, then I shrink into an old monkey and shrivel, I live only in winter..." the old lady speaks with her eyes gleaming and fixed.

A cold shiver seizes Mihaela... She watches the old woman with total bewilderment, her hands shaking with fright. The old woman's words were her very words—the poem about love that she wrote in her notebook, when she was 14 years old... Mihaela breathes with calm, trying to compose herself; she then bends down and asks the woman with calm:

"Sweet lady, how come you know these words? Did you find my notebook?"

The old woman raises her shoulders and continues to recite:

"If I have endless life but no love, then I have endless pain, a body and a soul in vain..."

Mihaela keeps listening, enthralled.

Suddenly, the old woman grabs Mihaela's wrist:

"Take this bottle with ants and whenever you need help, send them out. Your enemy shall feel pins and needles in his hands and feet and it shall never want to harm you ever again..."

The old woman releases Mihaela's hand as Mihaela takes the bottle with ants. Then, as Mihaela slowly rises up and takes a few steps back, the bottle with ants breaks up in her hands... The ants pop out, invading Mihaela's arms and legs...swarming all over her body... The ants start pricking her skin with violent nips, like some little aggressive spiders or wild noxious insects that she cannot perceive with her eyes...

"Help, help, somebody help me!" Mihaela screams as the ants start sucking her blood.

At that very moment, out of nowhere, the bee pops up and pours a rain of honey all over Mihaela's body. From her head to the sole of her feet, Mihaela is drenched up in honey and, immediately, the ants fall off, turning into some multi-tentacled creatures with tiny red horns. The bee pours more honey... The ground cracks and a black foggy tornado from underneath swallows the evil ants.

"Ouch, ouch!" Mihaela cries, still feeling the pinches and itches of the little monsters.

"Thank you, sweet bee! You always come save me whenever I need it!"

"And if I were away, what would you have done about it?" the bee asks her, provocatively.

"I would have said a prayer or died..."

"Ha, ha, ha, that's how easily you'd give up on your life? Like you have given up on your writing? If you focus on your problem, you will never solve it; focus on the solution, on the One that sees everything and can stop any storm for you...if you just stop worrying..."

"On whom?" Mihaela asks, breathing at ease.

"Focus on God, my child! He loves you very much! How many more signs do you need?"

"I know He does... Foolish me! I love Him so much too! He is my best friend!"

"Then why did you stop writing?" the bee asks Mihaela, annoyed.

Mihaela's words stop; and so her breath; she cannot find an answer to give to Mama-bee at this time... The truth is that ever since the words of her notebook had disappeared, like flowers under the cold breath of winter, Mihaela has been very sad, her heart numb... She has wanted to write again, she wanted the empty pages of her notebook filled back with her loving pains, with her tears of joy, with her human fears and her vampiric nightmares...her young hopes of freedom, her screams of victory, shouts of defeat, her climbings and fallings of a hopeful Sisyphus... Those writings and experiences mean so much to her. She has learned from them about Life, about Heaven and Earth and she wants to teach others as well...about how it feels to resurrect...

Yet each time she wants to write or rewrite the events from her past, her brain hurts her, she starts sweating and shivering, her arms trembling like some leaves forgotten on the branches of a tree in winter.

"Lately, I have been incapable of writing at least one poem...as if someone has been in the possession of my thoughts, memories, cravings..." Mihaela thinks with regret. "My mind has been straying and starving, suddenly barren; my hands have been lazy, suddenly trepid... Dominica's saying "The English language belongs to the devil..." has made me overthink, fret and try to find an answer, splitting hairs within... Papa told me that the past belongs to Lucifer, the present to man, and the future to God. Yet I cannot focus on the future if I do not solve my present, if I do not throw the pebbles of the past out of my head... I cannot believe that Lucifer is the one who has stolen the pages of my notebook as Dominica said... That is pure madness, I think. And yet, I've been praying so that Lucifer returns them to me... I have even knocked on Lucifer's door, kindly asking him to put my pages back in my notebook... I've always thought that through kindness and love I could make even the devil good... Yet, that has just made me fall into his abyss, and sink more and more into his filth... And so, I departed from him, asking God to raise me out of my sins... I have prayed and prayed, fervently, trying to get that maddening thought out of my brain, yet the more I've tried to, the more I deepened that obsession within... And so, I put writing—my biggest passion—to the side and gave myself to the world of fashion. How superficial that world is... I have found myself crying for hours, thinking of how evil some people are...trying to hide themselves behind some fabric, and taking advantage of others because they have more power and money... I have tried to teach them, tell them about my experiences, about my transformation...but they made fun of me and shut me down... *Clothing and food for the body...but what about the food for the soul?* And then, while I was tramping down on the streets of the City of Stars, a great idea popped up in my head: one day I will open up a chain of *Gyms for the Soul*. I will have trained-human-angels who speak the language of God, and who teach people the love of God...how to reign in life... Hmmm...I miss writing so much! If I can find the way...to write again... How can I teach others if I myself am in this web?"

The bee buzzes around Mihaela, and whispers to her ear:

"I heard it all! You little fool! You, filled with little faith! You met Dominica, she told you that English is the language of the devil and you believed her... Dominica was the tool of Lucifer."

"Dominica? Why didn't you tell me at that time?"

"You had to learn, my love! This is your journey! Dominica was also the old woman who just begged on the street...who gave you the evil ants. Couldn't you tell? Just look in the person's eyes! Didn't they remind you of someone familiar? And of course, you never used the holy honey that I gave you…or the shield of faith that I told you about! You tried to do and do and do…but you did not do one thing…"

"Which one?" Mihaela asks, filled with curiosity.

"Nothing."

"Nothing?"

"Yes, do nothing! Just let God do it for you!"

"What do you mean?"

"Well, you heard what He has told you when you were up there, in His Labyrinth…and yet you have tried to lead God, instead of following Him! God told you to rest in Him, to do nothing…that day when you met Him…"

"Yes, indeed… He told me to rest and eat. And just let Him lead me…"

"See, little foolish friend? Do you think that your experiences are just dreams, just poetic visions to fill up some pages? They are life, true answers to your questions. Just hear God, my love… and follow His way as He has taught you… Don't get mixed up, don't be double-minded, because then you won't be able to fly or see Mama again… That was a test. And to end the test you only need to rest. Dominica's saying is the devil's arrow to break your sweet godly heart… That thought does not belong to you. It is a thought meant to take you away from your Art, from your good work for the Lord… But *He who is in you is greater than he who is in the world*… God wants you to trust him and not let your heart be troubled—that means not open the door to the devil's lies and wiles… Remain in His Love…"

"Yes, how foolish I've been! I should have just done nothing, just let Him deal with my problem, give my worries to Him… And I knew it, and yet I wanted to deal with it…"

"Never deal with the devil because he'll make you step into his court and he'll then play you as he wants; let God handle it as you sit and eat… *Sit at my right hand and I shall put your enemies under your feet. For anyone who enters God's rest also rests from their works*…"

Mihaela jumps high up in the air, filled up with terrible felicity, feeling that she has caught God's heart into her palms… "I love you, I love you!" she screams out to the skies. "You are so wise, an angel from the sky..."

"Everything is God's word and work, they belong to you...for free... You don't need to pay money or travel miles away to have access to God's love... He's always available for you. Always. Just keep your eyes on Heaven...and Heaven will brush your weeds away... His *truth will set you free.* Heaven is a person that loves to labor for you, and that has given you the best crops... Just rest in Him, and let Him do in you, your work."

"Yes... While I was fretting and crying, He kept telling me 'Rest...to get blessed,' but I always felt like I had to do something about that thought..."

"Yes, just keep drinking and eating God's word and then you'll have His mighty sword to put down any stronghold."

Mihaela looks at the bee with tears in her eyes.

"Now, start writing on your novel," the bee breaks the silence. "God is your friend and every language that He gave you to speak is His language, created by Him! *All things have been created through Him and for Him... In the beginning was the Word, and the Word was with God, and the Word was God. And as the Holy Spirit came, all of them were filled with the Holy Spirit, and began to speak in foreign languages as the Spirit gave them that ability...*"

Suddenly, Mihaela takes the bee in her arms and kisses her cheekbones and antennae, with all her powers.

"Ouch, ouch, more gentle, please!" the bee-friend cries, almost chocked with love.

"I write in the language of God!" Mihaela speaks out as she twirls her wise bee-friend in her palms.

A strong light grasps her heart. The cloud of fear disappears.

"See?" the bee continues. "Each time you say something out loud in the name of God, a miracle happens! God loves you very much, Mihaela! I will tell you a little secret—to **believe** means actually to **be** and **leave** everything in the hands of God. And then, day-by-day, you will be just like God! *As He is so are we in this world...*"

"Hear me, sweet bee! I think I've got a great melody…" and Mihaela starts singing heartily to the bee:

I AM LIKE GOD (Chorus)

"Bravo! It's so beautiful and simple!" the bee applauds Mihaela.

"Simple?"

"Yes, simple. The things that are the most simple are the most powerful! In life it is about simple choices. Choose Love or Hatred; Love or Fear. And Fear and Love cannot co-exist."

"I choose Love." Mihaela yells out.

"You are Love's… Love already chose you, little you! And the children of Love don't let themselves intimidated by fear—fear is an illusion, not part of your Godly mind. *For God has not given us a spirit of fear, but of Love, power and sound mind…*"

"How can I make all people know what you have taught me?"

"Don't worry, you know how… Write everything in your novel, and let God split the Red Sea for you… Always let go and let God show you the way into your soul…"

Suddenly, a cloud shadows Mihaela's face:

"Yes…but now, how can I get my notebook back?"

"Do you still doubt? You have it! You've had it with you at all times! Mommy Doll is my witness," the bee stings Mihaela's incertitude, rolling her eyes to Mommy. "But fear blinded you, Mihaela… *My strength is made perfect in your weakness*…always remember these words of Your Lord," the bee-friend concludes.

Mommy Doll blinks and smiles in favor of the smart bee, encouraging Mihaela to open her notebook. Mihaela smiles. As she opens her notebook, which she has carried with her all the way, in her woolen bag, she sees all of her writings back in.

She raises her head and looks for the bee, feeling in seventh heaven; but the bee disappeared. She glances back at her notebook. A small paper mingled with ink and honey lies in her notebook: *Mark 11:24.*

"WELCOME TO CITY OF STARS PICTURES, Hall of Workers!"

appears in huge capital letters, on a giant placard, at the entrance of a big hall with gold and crystal chandeliers. As Mihaela steps in, a symphonic music starts echoing, while elegant humanoid robots, gynoids and androids, dressed up in cashmere suits and gowns, welcome her, sumptuously. In no time, an elegant gynoid bends down and picks up Mihaela's bags with fabric and costumes, as the others wait in line, like the most humble servants, to perform their tasks. A young twinoid that perfectly resembles a human being, announces to "Miss Mihaela" the latest news and duties that she needs to perform in the next couple of hours. Other twinoids write down the specific requests and details that Mihaela passes on to them, swiftly.

Mihaela breathes softly and the door of her office, like a cinema screen, takes the shape of her body, absorbing Mihaela in like an eating-plasma.

Mihaela's thoughts and her artistic obsessions are suddenly made visible on a multidimensional cinema screen (MD) built inside movable, anti-fire walls with imperceptible margins. Mihaela's office has been created as a cradle of her imagination and inspiration, as an innovative, poly-functional lab where she can connect with her personal, soul-world. The genius minds of City of Stars Pictures and their ultra perceptive sensory computers took notice of Mihaela's third eye and the effortless way in which she connects with the higher world... Thus, they have decided to keep an eye over Mihaela's mind. And since then, even though Mihaela has been appointed Head of the fashion and style department of City of Stars Pictures, the executives have required her to undertake the *cinematic mind journey.* As a matter of fact, each imaginative and intelligent mind of the City of Stars is obliged to submit to this process if willing to have a job. Mihaela needs only to relax and swing in a robot-chair placed across a multidimensional cinema screen; the images from her mind are then becoming visible, and one can see her visions in motion, like some paintings in various colors and shades... Her thoughts would sometimes open gates and paths towards secret worlds, decoding mysteries of life and giving answers to questions... Through them, Mihaela has gotten used to release her negative energy and project her dreams...in the hands of bright-smiling angels, welcoming and playful like some spirited, winged children... In this perfect, righteous world, endowed with super fertile ground, the angels take her dreams and sow them inside the red moist soil. After only one month, Mihaela has started to see her harvest—the work of her angels and the growth of her dreams that are already turning into reality... This metaphysical journey makes Mihaela exuberant and joyful...enlarging her imagination and her soul-world. City of Stars Pictures signed to present one of her dreams in a short film, screened to other co-workers and elevated minds of City of Stars... But, at the same time, this journey makes Mihaela anxious...it is a dangerous game...as Mihaela has no control over what City of Stars

Pictures has been storing—they can transfer her ideas in their database and then use her visions without giving Mihaela the chance to oversee anything. This is how things work in the City of Stars. Nevertheless, every idea has the shade and color of the owner's mind, recognizable to the neurological and scientific experts.

Each time Mihaela leaves her office, the walls and projections of her mind fade away and the cinema screen gains the color of red blood. When she returns to her office, the screen emerges again and other images and characters of her mind come to life, moving like in an aerial ballet. Today, for instance, she has clearly seen and entered this land: in Eden, beautiful Eve, with a snakehead, bit Adam's apple, ravenously. She then fell from grace on the land of Olympus. Taking on the face of a fox, Eve then morphed into the generous Aphrodite, devouring the apple offered to her by the credulous Paris. Hera was flushed with anger.

With her body wrapped in a splendid light veil sewn with songbirds, Eve then mounted a white horse and traveled to the immortal land of fairy-tales. Here, she embodied Ileana Cosânzeana, the beautiful maid that lives in the Carpathians Mountains. Filled with Good and Joy, Ileana Cosânzeana bit from the golden apple offered by Prâslea the Brave, giving this sturdy man two offspring: twin sons with golden hair and golden stars—stars like the Lucifer at dawn, when angels lark…

Mihaela touches her forehead abruptly,
and a small case falls from her coat, rolling down, around her little feet. A gynoid rushes to get it, but Mihaela's feet run swifter and she picks it up, hiding it in a drawer, which withdraws at once, merging perfectly into the wall. "No one needs to know about it…" Mihaela speaks within, her cheeks suddenly flushed with blue. The City of Stars was said to be safe, protecting its authors, but Mihaela knows that they love to take ownership…in various subtle ways…

Mihaela breathes, relieved; she then throws off her high heel shoes and puts on transparent ballet flats, gummy and super-flexible, like some medusas that assure the perfect circulation of the legs. Her black dress slides down, unveiling a super molded and muscled body, like of an aphrodisiacal statue. Mihaela has been taking gymnastics every morning with Nadia-robot, which has been teaching her the most stabilizing-muscle techniques for a durable body. Quickly, a gynoid follows up and puts on Mihaela a sea-made working-gown that perfectly glues around her body—gown that assures the perfect respiration of the pores. From the ceilings, a mini-robot emerges, pinning Mihaela's hair into a ballerina bun and covering it with an elastic-net, woven with blue algae and leaves of Aloe Vera. After that, the gynoid presses on a hidden shelf, designed within its abdomen, and a perfume, featuring Mihaela's face, pops out, sprinkling her with indigo droplets. All of a sudden, the long line of Mihaela's neck takes a younger, brighter look… At last, Mihaela takes a seat in the hands of a super-comfy robot, robot responsible for providing a swift-chair with wings that takes Mihaela whenever and wherever she needs to go. Mihaela laughs so hard during this ritual…feeling as a super-adorned doll, too much taken care of.

In an adjoining room, gynoids, androids, and twinoids, dressed as some hardworking enormous bees, continuously trim the new designs that Mihaela has conceived in her mind: Eve's costume, Aphrodite's, Hera's, Ileana Cosânzeana's…

Every single move from the Hall of Workers is being projected on big computers from the Circular Tower, computers that are sensitive to the human stimuli and interplanetary energies. When something gets out of order, a strident colorful signal alarms the whole City of Stars Pictures.

Arriving at the Circular Tower with human energy-filled computers, Mihaela checks her aerial screen and her working status, after which she sends out wave-codes to the planet-chambers that are connected to her creative-atelier, updating them on her visions and spiritual journey. These planet-chambers are in charge of the whole constellations of the City of Stars. These constellations are determining each inhabitant's growth and development, and can promote, hire or fire workers according to their creative and social level and, of course, work ethic. It is called the "pressure of the City of Stars," or "the robotization era."

As Mihaela touches a key of her aerial computer, a transparent bag with makeup comes out, inscribed with Romanian letters: *A se combina cu soluția albastră.* / *Mix it with the blue potion.* She then touches another key and a sophisticated small bottle with blue potion pops up, after which rolls down inside the pocket of the hand-chair robot. After she turns off her aerial computer, Mihaela takes a seat on the hand-chair robot that extends electric eaglelike wings, transporting Mihaela at full speed, to Room 7007.

Room 7007. Makeup chamber.

As soon as she arrives at the Make-up chamber, Mihaela catches a glimpse of a younger and more beautiful than ever Meryl. Meryl is happily seated on a white robot chair, anxiously rehearsing her part. Meryl is the most diligent and disciplined actress of the City of Stars; her secret—she always gets to work earlier than anyone else.

"Hello, Miss Meryl, you look wonderful today!"

"Yes, isn't it? Believe it or not but this morning I woke up looking better than ever. Some of those hideous wrinkles around my eyes miraculously disappeared. I guess this movie does me good…"

"It surely does…"

"And your magical hands!" Meryl adds with a wink.

"I see…" Mihaela says, twinkling her eye back to Meryl Stripp.

Meanwhile, Mihaela takes her make up tools out of her make-up box. She lays her blue potion on the table and starts mixing it up with her eyeshades and powders.

"You're an old fashioned girl, aren't you, darling?" Meryl asks Mihaela as she stares at the way Mihaela diligently displays her products. "Do you intend to use the robot for exact shades?"

"No, I don't like that. I want you to look human…" Mihaela replies.

"See, that's why I like you! I won't give you up for any other girl in the world… By the way, did you get hold of that mud from Transylvania?" Meryl asks Mihaela, impatiently.

"Of course..."

"What does that mean?"

"Tomorrow we'll begin to use it!"

"Fabulous! I can't wait to! You know, that honey cream that you gave me has already worked miracles...as you can see... Well, I also believe in it. Do I have another choice?"

Mihaela laughs. Meryl laughs harder.

"Meryl, you'll be glowing today! You'll steal the whole show! Would you like that?"

"You bet I would, foxy girl... Who taught you all these tricks?" Meryl asks Mihaela, smiling from ear to ear. While laughing and teasing each other, a short, extravagantly dressed man storms in.

"Excuse me, Meryl dear, for interrupting you..."

The man then turns to Mihaela and starts speaking like one of the robots, very fast and over pronounced:

"Mihaela, we need you on set for approximately 10 minutes. Bring your blue foundation for Emil...the new member of our cast."

Then, addressing Meryl, the man slows down:

"Meryl, you've got to see him, this boy is phenomenal! He got the part in five minutes."

"I'll be there, dear James, if Miss Meryl doesn't mind..." Mihaela intervenes with a smile.

"Good," the man cracks a smile too, satisfied.

"James dear, I would surely like to see him..." Meryl interferes. "But tell me, how in the world did he turn you on? Your super-demanding ego is not that easily manipulated! We know that you need triple auditions to cast your actors and after that...you bring your mother in and, even then, you can't really make up your mind... What has happened to you this time?"

"Well, I guess this boy has an out-of-space personality..."

"An out-of-space personality? That's a new one!" Meryl laughs.

"Ok, ladies...I gotta go! This screening sucks all of my directorial blood! If I don't watch them every second, everything blows up! Duty calls me!" he concludes, bowing rapidly before the ladies and making his way out.

"Go, Lord of salvation, Genius of damnation!" Meryl recites...

James Ericksson,

the director of *Cherchez la Femme / Looking for the Woman* film, starring Meryl Stripp, is a very peculiar person. With the inferiority complex of being half-human, half-robot, James is against all people who seem too human or ultra courageous... He is a kind of gentle human-robot, yet his heart is programmed, dominated by a sensitive watch. His power stands in this watch... He loves to find out peculiar stories about the insecurities and dark side of his actors... When someone falls ill, his whole heart rejoices and that person is immediately taken to his "heart."

Mihaela's story and her fight against her wicked clone has fascinated James from the very beginning... He told Mihaela that he is dying to meet her wicked clone, in flesh and blood, one day soon...

Other people' struggles, torments, fears, diseases and various problems...makes James feel more in control, happy...

Meryl faces Mihaela, taking her hand in her hands:

"My dear, my motherly instinct tells me that you should stay out of the out-of-space personalities' zone... Let James have another make-up artist to help..."

Then, taking a serious face, she adds:

"Anyhow, you have a lot of work on my makeup. And I don't want to lose you even for a second!"

"No problem, Meryl! I shall send Erica, my assistant. She knows some of my secrets..."

And Mihaela touches a key on her computer and Erica pops up miraculously before their eyes.

"Erica, James needs you on set! Use the blue foundation, please!"

"You got it," Erica replies robotically, with a bow, grabbing the blue foundation and exiting the room, soundlessly.

"Ok, we're all set. Meryl is going to have all of me today! I'll make you look like the angels' queen..." and Mihaela kisses Meryl's on her forehead who smiles, delightedly.

After which, Mihaela opens up a sophisticated bottle with blue solution, preparing to pour a few drops into a small pot. Abruptly, a weird ant pops out of the bottle and starts walking hectically onto the table. Mihaela watches it move along, with big scared eyes, thinking about the old woman's evil ants and the smart bee's words of advice. The ant becomes bigger and bigger, her antennas like red antlers of a deer.

Meryl jumps off the hands of the white robot-chair and starts screaming, madly, squeezing the doorknob, with desperate eyes.

"Don't worry Meryl, I'll kill it right away!" Mihaela speaks up, taking her flat shoe out of her left foot. "Please, wait for me outside... I'll let you know as soon as I'm done with it," she reassures Meryl with the attitude of a hero.

Meryl exits the room, panic-stricken at the sight of the enormous ant, her teeth chattering and her bones clinking like the bars of a disharmonized xylophone.

As Mihaela holds the shoe in her hand, a murderous glance flashing in her eyes, the ant grows taller and taller...

"Let me kill it," a gynoid chimes in.

"No, don't get into this, please!" Mihaela tells it in full assurance.

Thus, Mihaela disconnects the gynoid and takes a poison-tube in her hand, vehemently spraying the insect.

"No, don't kill me," the ant starts speaking. "I'm a good ant. I grew bigger because of your blue potion. Don't kill me and I shall help you whenever you are in danger. I promise."

"You're a bad ant! One of Dominica's ants!" Mihaela replies, spraying more poison over the ant.

"No, I am a good one! Dominica does not exist! She is Vlad!"

"Vlad?"

"Yes, I am a good ant sent by your good Aunt Magia!"

"Magia?"

"Yes, Magia is alive! She sent me to watch over you! She will explain to you everything when you meet her again! Also, your brother Vlady is in danger and needs your help!"

Mihaela looks perplexed at the talkative ant that has become bigger than herself. "Was it her blue blood that made her so big and able to speak?"

Mihaela: Oh my God! I just now recall it! When I was about seven years old, speaking and playing with ants and beetles in Papa's garden, nearby the big walnut tree, I wished for one of the ants to become as big and tall as my stature... In a second, the ant grew taller than me, taller the Queen of the Night flower: her thin arms and legs so long and gluey; her mandibles thick and sharp; her compact black eyes so large and wide, looking at me keenly... Then, her oval little mouth started to talk to me...she was sweet and wise! Laughing with joy at the incredible miracle, I went to call Papa outside, in the garden, to see the giant speaking ant, my newly friend. But Papa could not see it at all... I wondered why. And then my father smiled at me and said: 'Children truly believe and then miracles happen to them... All it takes is to keep being a child...'

"All right, all right, I believe you," Mihaela says to the enormous ant, shivering with happiness. "I won't kill you! But what shall I do with you that big?"

"Just hide me in a closet and get me out when no one is in here. Please!" the ant pleads with her, again.

Mihaela opens up an invisibly framed closet and lets the insect walk in. She then presses the doors against the ant, which barely fits in, and locks it up. Finally, she reconnects the gynoid to the power supply and calls Meryl back in.

"You made it? How did you kill it?" Meryl asks Mihaela, still panicked and stammering.

Mihaela giggles:

"Just another scary surprise of James… The ant was not real."

Mihaela then soaks her brush into the small pot and prepares her blue magic…

"Relax…" she softly whispers to Meryl, kissing her on her forehead.

The eyes of the giant ant flash back inside Mihaela's mind, reminding her of…Gabriela's red eyes.

As soon as Meryl makes her way out to the set, Mihaela rushes to open the invisible closet. But the closet is empty…

The clock of Târgoviște strikes hard.

With her legs and arms dismembered, weary and heavy, Gabriela shoves her head out of Lucifer's tunnels. She is dark, full of dust and anger. She puffs through her nose, that got bigger and swollen as a red pepper, and steps madly, leaving stamps of indignation behind.

"Father!" she screams out loud. "Father, where are you?"

Vlad makes his appearance through the back of the castle, through a narrow stone door—the secret door through which he used to hide from his enemies during his life as Vlad Țepeș, the Emperor. His hands are full of blood, his mandibulas trembling with vexation:

"Not now, daughter! I've got important work to finish."

"Yeah?" Gabriela asks her father boiling with fury.

"What's the matter, child?" Vlad darts a glance at her with irritation.

Swift as an arrow, Gabriela swoops down on her father and starts punching his chest with envenomed fists, spitting blue viscous saliva into his eyes, and showing sharp, rusted fangs of a beast. Vlad, taken by surprise, kicks Gabriela out of his sight: "I'm not in the mood for a fight!"

But Gabriela does not give up. She jumps to her feet and twirls in the air, stretching her legs out to kick her father into his chest.

Abruptly, 13 wooden stakes spring out from Vlad's garden, with their sharp edges pointing towards Gabriela. Instead of reaching her father, Gabriela falls into the pointed stakes, her flesh getting pierced and her eyes spurted out of her head; a prickly waterfall of blue blood gushes out of her wounds. Covered in blood, Gabriela gives an infernal growl; her body tremors and twitches, her face is contorted and scorned. At once, she strains all of her nerves, and fire explodes out of her nostrils, burning the stakes into melting ashes. Vlad watches his daughter both with hatred and pride.

"What's the matter, my love?" he asks Gabriela, mending his tone.

Covered in ugly clots of mud and breathing flames through her nostrils, Gabriela growls at her father, bloodcurdlingly:

"I've been there…and I made a decision. And I am not going to change it, not even for Papa!"

"Yes," Vlad listens with calm. "What have you decided, my child?"

"That I have to kill you! Liar, you are a monstrous liar! You are a criminal, an eater of your daughter's future!" Gabriela screams at the top of her lungs, hurling rage at the feet of her father. Her cry is so enormous that it reaches the ears of the Hunting Bitches down there, inside Lucifer's tunnels. Dying with curiosity, the bitches pop their heads through the mud, to watch the ferocious fight.

At the speed of light, Gabriela flies again at her father, sinking her teeth into his neck, spitting upon him with poisoned love, firing arrows with nerves of steel, and slapping his thighs with her spiny black tail.

A raven flies above them, flitting among the burnt fuming stakes.

Vlad cries with a tremolous voice:

"Beloved daughter, stop this! If you're hungry to fight, then let's fight, but the right way! How do you want it? With claws, with tails, with stakes, or better take each other by surprise as Papa taught you since you were born that awful night?"

"Let's take each other by surprise!" Gabriela quickly answers her father.

And suddenly, Gabriela becomes a horrible thunder onto the sky and the sky turns into a disgusting violet mouth of a dragon with serpent eyes. As quick as a wink, Vlad becomes the lightning, throwing with blinding nails into his daughter's eyes from his centurial, revengeful hands.

Terrified, the raven screams:

"Kaw, Kaw! The same gore! What for?"

But Gabriela and her father ignore the bird's call and keep fighting and fighting, from dusk till dawn and from dawn till dusk, until Gabriela, tired and bored to life, screams out to Vlad:

"Let's stop it, Father! Let's think of something else! I'm fed up and hungry!"

"There will be no blood-feeding or resting until the end of the fight! This is the rule that I have taught you!" Vlad reminds his daughter, gulping for air, desperately.

"Then let's wrestle, Papa! Let's wrestle better because it's a fairer fight!"

No sooner has she finished her words than Gabriela and her father start wrestling in dust and hatred, hurling heavy bloody words at each other, tussling and tumbling with clenched bodies, until the day again turns into night.

2033. The City of Stars Pictures. The Hall of Mirrors.

Leisurely, Mihaela walks along the monumental halls of the City of Stars Pictures. A silky dress, adorned with sunflowers and hay, summerly embraces her body—it's Mihaela's favorite design, handmade; her hair is falling loosely, like long grass over a virgin hill; her face is radiant and sunny, brushed by the light of her heart. Mihaela feels peaceful. She pulls out a little notebook from her wollen bag, that she's been carrying all the way on her left shoulder, eager to write. She stops. Lowering her chin, she looks around the Hall of Mirrors, inspecting it as for the first time. A wrinkle quickly settles on her forehead, her lower lip starting to shake like a leaf... She puffs twice, shaking off a little cloud of anger, writing down how the City of Stars Pictures would look like ornamented with flowers and ivies...with welcoming majordomos and real ladies in waiting...

The grandiose and futuristic architecture, the gynoids and twinoids, multiplied infinitely by the surrounding mirrors, are making Mihaela feel awkward, trapped...

"Where is the genuine, the simple?" she keeps writing, coiled up in sadness. "I want to see nature loose, imperfection seduce, human faces evergreen, no lifts and ultra swollen lips. I want to see real beauty, nature's real smell and taste—as in my father's orchard... These creatures, gynoids and twinoids are scary—any man can satisfy himself with a gynoid girlfriend, robotess wife or mistress, a beauty composed of materials that are perfectly imitating the human skin, voice, demeanor..." Mihaela keeps writing vividly in her notebook. "Any man, ordering a gynoid girlfriend, can require its favorite zodiacal sign, compatible to his, the color and touch of her skin, the plumpness of her lips, the breadth of her hips, her character traits, the size of her breasts, the features of her face, her height and weight, the length and thickness of her hair, and various other details... Anyone can order his ideal woman, online... But God, is this a real woman—this machine set up to be the way men dream? Moreover a robotess can give men her robotine disease lest she is mantained clean. Her rustiness can kill."

Mihaela sighs and then she writes again, her pen thickening the ink, enraged.

"Also, it did happen that a gynoid had gone out of order, become crazy as a betsy bug, producing unexpected turns; it sometimes bit a neck and scratched an eye, seriously injuring the 'loving' mate. But there are even gynoid services available 24 hours, ready to fix, adjust any malfunction of the 'doll,' any deficiency of her *'soul'*... If one gets lonely, it only has to call in for a robot... Moreover, there is a whole line of creams for the human beings who are willing to gain the perfect skin of the gynoids! How can women accept such a mockery—to follow robots' beauty tricks? There is an avalanche of pressure and hysteria for the women who are trying to keep up with the 'future' beauty...' But I know so many traditional recipes from Transylvania: mixtures of fruits, plants, honey, argile, dew and heat treatments that can regenerate the face in a natural way—treatments that will help Meryl and the City of Stars' people look glowing and younger, but staying human... All of my childhood, I was kept inside the house, unable to see the faces of neighbors and meet other people from Papa's village. The flowers, the trees, the rosehip trees, the raspberry bushes, the beds of fresh greens and vegetables, the beehives, the chickens, the ducks, the geese and the turkeys, the doves and the rabbits, the lambs and the horses, the deer, the polecats and the whelps from my father's yard have been my only friends..."

Looking down at the gynoids and androids that are painted with joker smiles and perfect faces, Mihaela has a revelation: she can bring back the magic and genuine human beauty, the original goddess prototype from the ancient eras, creating her own Transylvanian facial & fashion line. "I will call it: *The Ancient Vamp* or better *Eternal beauty state*... I can go back and forth to my father, back to 1500, take soil and plants from my own garden and bring them to the City of Stars. But no one has to know of my secret travel and how I will bring people back to the original beauty state. This is the secret of my miraculous recipe..."

Mihaela laughs with terrible joy, hopping from one foot to the other, like a frisky little girl! The gynoids and twinoids start imitating her. She just now realizes what a blessing her third eye really is...and how much she has blamed it! To be able to travel back and forth in time through her eye? This is something extraordinary, right? Who else can do that? Few people believe in miracles—in letting go and traveling to change a little bit this world... And she is one of them... This is what makes her the happiest! She can make women smile again and not fear that their men will leave them lonely in their beds! No wonder Meryl has always been panicked and on the verge of a nervous breakdown... The entire food from the City of Stars is 99% artificial, utilized for both humans and robots. Food is injected with fertilizers and fuels that are growing robotic cells in the human bodies, thereby making people respond faster to the demands of the new robotic society! But Papa's healthy seeds and soil will restore the City of Stars' ground...and I will also sprinkle it with my blue blood...and a little bit of love... This way the fruit and vegetables will grow fast and healthy, just the way they used to grow in my garden..."

Mihaela sighs, flushed in her cheeks like an ultra ripe red apple. "I have learned so many things from Mother Nature...and I want to share them with the 21st century, to bring people back to Her roots. I miss so

much the thorns of the roses and even the scary traces of my sister...
"How is she doing?" Mihaela wonders as she's floating through The Hall
of Mirrors...

Gabriela, hungrier and more tired than ever,
addresses with thirst the caring raven that flies above her head:
"Sweet raven, bring me a little blood in your beak from a dove's
chick, and I shall give you Papa's castle and his legendary body to eat!"
Vlad screams back at the raven:
"No, dear reaven! Better bring me some fresh blood of a sweet child
and I will give you my daugther's body and the bodies of one thousand
virgins from my undergrounds! And I'll make you my crowned
messenger and give shelter to your baby ravens!"
The raven circles them three times, afterwhich it speaks to them in
disdain:
"In the name of God, I don't want anything from you because your
beings and words are dead, frozen and crazed! You are poisoned and
cursed, daughter against father fighting for a dead cause! I'd better die of
hunger than eat from your hands! I shall fly to my living king who gives
me freely to eat and drink!"
Gabriela, even more infuriated because the raven called her dead,
wraps her black thorny tail around Papa Vlad and hurls him into the
ground, up to his waist. Vlad struggles and sweats blue blood, hardly
pulling his tail out of the mud, afterwhich he anchors it like a lasso around
a walnut tree's trunk that has been watching the scene with tottering twigs
and frightened leaves. Mustering all his strength, Vlad grasps his tail with
his hands, pulling his body out of the mud. After that, feeling even more
mad at the raven that spoke of his doomed fate, Vlad takes his daughter
by her elbows and throws her into the ground, up to her wicked breasts.
Sharpening his long nails by his thick slaughterous tail, Vlad prepares his
last move—to pierce his daughter's heart and tear it apart.

Miraculously, the dumb brother Vlady steps out of the castle, looking healthy and animated. He plucks up his courage, fills his lungs with air, and utters words from his mouth:

"She's alive! She's alive! Violeta, Mama!"

The Raven alights on Vlady's shoulder. For the first time since his tongue had been pulled out, Vlady can pronounce.

Vlad and Gabriela cease their fight, framing Vlady with bulging, exhausted eyes. Harmoniously, they both put on a phony smile and ask him:

"Where is Mama?"

"Right there!" Vlady says, pointing towards the back of a woman with long black hair who swings in the metallic cradle from the backyard.

Vlad leaves his daughter on the battlefield, with Vlady, and moves towards Violeta. His feet step into the green grass, leaving sweaty bloodied holes behind.

Violeta, swinging in the cradle, mumbles *Ave Maria.*

Slowly, Vlad reaches her, and after he bows with fatherhood emotion, he raises his head, just to see what he has never seen before: a zombie...

"Violeta, my dear..."

Stupefaction crawls on Vlad's face. His heart, yet without a throb, cannot bear the view of such countenance...

Violeta looks at the sky, ignoring Vlad. The front part of her hair is of a dazzling white...but her face...

Vlad runs back to Vlady: "What happened? Didn't I tell you to wait for me?"

"She got disconnected! I couldn't stop her..." Vlady justifies, struggling to speak.

"That's alright, I'll take care of her now..."

The Hall of Mirrors. City of Stars Pictures.

The corridor with mirrors enlarges and shorthens with every step Mihaela takes, deforming her image according to her thoughts.

Mihaela writes ceaselessly inside her notebook. She feels so happy that she can continue her work on the novel. Ever since she let go and let God cure her soul, resting in His love, she received her freedom, her holy inspiration. The bee has helped her so much by revealing this verse to her: "Therefore I tell you, whatever you ask for in prayer, believe that you have received it, and it will be yours." The moment she rested from her works and only believed...she felt that she received her life back...as if a Spirit settled its house in her, decorating her soul with peace and love. She giggles. She now feels protected, safeguarded from this world...

She stops. She sighs and inhales a little air, the fresh wind chilling her hot blood.

"This society is so contagious and dangerous...especially for the newborns!" she sits down on a robot chair, continuing to write. "If one has no true parent to teach it the value of being a human being...it turns into a robot! Here, in the City of Stars, even the air is sprayed with a protein meant to alert and stimulate people's minds... Everyone is obsessed with immortality, searching for new ways of improving life... Technology is dominating and idling children's minds and stealing their time! But where is Immortality? How can one find it among robots? Anyone can invite their heroes, supermen, animated characters to play with them at their house. The robots look so alive, like human beings tele-charged! They are programmed to fly, climb, ride, to hug you and make you laugh, to make you think that they are your best friends—but it's a lie! If you have no money—you have no friends, no pony, no superman, no gynoid or android, no letters from robot-boyfriends or robot-girlfriends! It is true that many robots have saved lives and helped society grow, manufactured and exported more in a short period of time—but these machines have been taking the jobs of human beings! Bosses love robots because they have no heart, no egos—they are just doing their jobs the way that they have been programmed! And most terrifying—many people want to give up their human lives, sell their identity and be turned into robots... Where's this world going to? The robotized people from the City of Stars can spend day after day without closing an eye, can watch the stars seven nights in a row and then go back to work... They have no tiredness, no anxiety. Yet they cannot dream... And...they are invisible to God and to the angels from above... " Mihaela writes.

Ever since she left Papa's house, Mihaela has found life so challenging...trying to preserve her humanity, her soul... Nevertheless, the more she has tried, the more she collapsed. "The less of you, the more of God and His grace... This is is the only way," she murmurs to herself. "Never give up on following the simple way..."

Mihaela slams her notebook shut. A cold shiver of fear electrifies her body.

"Can I see Mama?"

Gabriela asks her father, impatiently.

"Not yet! Go back to your work! I'll finish her up!"

"Which work? I can't..." Gabriela whines.

"I've told you to be bold and to conquer the world! You have him on your side and you've got me! I'll give you whatever you need, what's your whim?"

"Oh yes? Can you give me whatever I need?"

"Yes!"

"Ok, then give me a damn heart because I don't love you any more!"

"How could you say that?"

"They wouldn't let me in..." Gabriela whines.

"Who?"

"They treated me so mean... Your friends..."

"How could they? I've got a deal with him..." Vlad ripostes, seeing though, in the corner of his mind, the signed deal with Lucifer against Gabriela's life...

"Well, he told me that you did not extend the deal with him...that it expired," Gabriela grumbles, enflamed.

"Liar! He wants more, doesn't he?"

"Father, he looks so dark, he's so small and stinks, how can you have him as your best friend?"

"He's always been so helpful! He gave me everything I needed...almost... But...lately, he wanted something that is beyond my will..."

"Well, Lucifer said that he cannot send me back to Mihaela until he speaks to you! Father, I want to bring her back to us...to be a happy family, united into sin! But how can I possibly win when everyone around me takes me in? I realized that killing Mihaela is Lucifer's dirty trick to poison our dream!" Gabriela adds on. "Two days ago, I crawled through Lucifer's filthy labyrinth, eager to kill Mihaela to inherit her soul, as Lucifer has told... Thus, the stinky Dead Rat clapped his hands and turned me into a giant ant, after which one of the Hunting Bitches helped me to travel at full speed in exchange of... Never mind! As soon as I got to Mihaela's place, Mihaela took a poisonous spray in her hands, ready to kill me... But I cried out and asked her to spare me and so she did. She was exceedingly nice, with blond locks of hair, looking like an angel... Soon enough, all of my anger disappeared...and I felt such a hunger to remain with her...to continue our work on the Wicked Clone play. Mihaela shut me in her closet, away from the eyes of her friends...and told me to wait in there until she finishes her work. But in the darkness of the closet, I sensed the claw of Lucifer, which grasped me quickly back into his filthy tunnels; suddenly, I fell into his chute, into his kitchen bin! In a flash, his zombies took me into their hands to cut me for Lucifer's meal! Thanks God, I turned back into myself and they released me at the call of the Dead Rat! Quickly, I ran out of Lucifer's kitchen, trying to move on by myself through his greasy caves of smoldering terror, but I've almost got burnt like a feeble roasted chick... Those flames and noise chocked me and took away all of my strength! Moreover, I could see nothing... My eyes were sore and bled, bursting out molten lava of revenge and hate. Father, you promised me that you would teach me how to see in darkness! Lucifer fooled me: he took my real eyes and gave me some stupid glasses that broke apart and left me blind! Tell him to give my eyes back to me! These eyes are not my eyes! I'm dirty from nose to tail and I can't get that noisy hell out of my head! I'm going mad! Father, why is Mihaela having it all, and me, creeping in the undergrounds like a broken doll? I want to be like her and yet my body never to grow old..."

"My child, Mihaela does not have it all, she's poor. She has no place to rest her head... She's fearful and tramping like a suicidal maid from one place to the next!"

"Father, Mihaela has more power than you think. She has two human eyes and a third eye through which she can travel in time! It is not fair! She can see more...much more...than you and I... This eye has appeared to her after she pulled her fangs out... It grew onto her forehead, and opened wide...and beamed, like the rays of sunlight! I can't stay around her when it comes out. It is too bright. And since then, this eye has given her tremendous inspiration, insight... She told me that it sometimes hurts her and it's getting blurred because of 'demons and other evil spirits who try to hinder her.' But when the eye is clear, it makes her write so fast and magically...like no other creature! And her memory is frightening, Papa! She described to me Mama's face on the day she died. And she was one day old. She even imitated Mama's voice singing *Ave Maria*—the same song that Mama was humming in the backyard, two minutes ago. Through this eye, Mihaela can travel in time and space at the speed of light...faster than you and I! She has been traveling to unknown places like Ancient Rome, Greece, Egypt and Paris... I saw this. I am a witness. She could even talk to famous writers, to great painters, renowned queens and different idols from different ages. She knows so many places, cultures, languages, she even prays in the tongues of angels... Who taught her all of these, Papa?"

"Tell me more... How did she actually get to all those places?" Vlad asks his daughter, intrigued.

"Well, I saw her once... I followed her through Central Park, in Shakespeare's garden... It was at dawn, after a short pouring rain. Mihaela closed her eyes...and stepped onto the wet grass, in bare feet, and spoke: 'Fresh drops of rain, feed me and raise me up to see like God!' Hidden behind the oaks, I suddenly saw Mihaela floating above the grass, clothed by an aura... Her face grew younger and her eyes transfixed... She called me next to her and held me by the hands: 'I love you!' she told me. How did she know that I was there? I said 'I love you too' and suddenly I felt hot liquid honey dripping through my whole body, from nose to toe... But a few minutes later, I felt flames burning my flesh and melting the honey away... I heard Lucifer's laughter... Mihaela told me to enter her realm and open my eye to see the light... But I could see nothing. Before my eyes, everything was dark and gray. I could only hear voices... Mihaela was in the 16th century, speaking with William Shakespeare and Elizabeth I of England, and I...struggling and sweating.... I heard her asking Shakespeare: 'Would you write a play about my wicked clone? I can't write anymore... I'm trapped...' Shakespeare laughed and told her: 'Why should I write a play about your wicked clone when you already wrote it? You are trapped the moment you think to give up... Look up. People look back at me and linger in my past, searching in my coffers and trying to imitate what I have offered...but Shakespeare will dwell on when new writers try to be themselves!'

'But you yourself searched in Capulets' coffers and in History's boxes and wrote of other people's stories, dark memories... Maybe the world hasn't changed much because of that...because we don't get inspired from our hearts, from our future... History repeats and we give her wings!' Mihaela replied to Shakespeare.

'If you are all about the future...then why do you write about your wicked clone? Isn't she part of the past, trying to steal our rest, worthy only to forget? Why do you talk of her and not of love?' Shakespeare asked Mihaela.

'In darkness we see the light... We have to know our enemy to conquer it...' Mihaela replied.

'Focus on love... Forget the enemy,' Shakespeare's echo could be heard.

And after that I couldn't hear their conversation any longer..." Gabriela concludes in a dark mood.

"Arrogant little maid! How could she speak to Shakespeare like that?" Vlad grumbles.

"Their discussion danced on my last nerve, Papa! I'm not evil... Maybe just in her play! I am beautiful and good!' Gabriela bursts out.

"For sure, daughter..." Vlad murmurs, lost in his thoughts.

"Oh, let me tell you what has happened after that: I told Mihaela to send me to a great place, all by myself, just to explore... And she sent me to the *Belle Époque*, to a marvelous world. I can't explain the way she did it, but I've been fascinated from the first moment I've set foot on that place... When she called me back, I did not want to answer her. I just wanted to stay there and see more: the *Moulin Rouge*, the *Tour Eiffel*, to feed myself on other sort of mortals, to see more lands and trends... Ha, Ha! I had a blast! Then, I met Mihaela in London, at Mr. Emil's house, her dear fiancée... They were preparing their wedding day and I gave them my blessings! I had so much fun! Then Mihaela took me along with her at the *Palace Theatre* and we started to rehearse for the *Wicked Clone play,* talk and walk in our sisterhood language...explore and build up a great show! When I was around Mihaela, I started speaking just like her, in verse... I could write and compose, father! But now, damn it, something has changed! Papa, she has inspiration and we are just imitating her! I feel worse than ever: helpless, lonely...and I am disgustingly bored! I want to go back and play the Wicked Clone... I want to show her that I am also capable...a genius, like you have promised once to teach me! Do it, Papa, do it now!"

"You want to be a genius? All right then! In the name of my name, Vlad Dracul the Great, I declare you a genius!"

"So I am?"

"Yes you are!" Vlad declares boldly to his daughter.

"I am a genius, I am a genius!" Gabriela screams out with fire, hopping from one leg to the other. "I'll show her father! Arrogant little maid!"

"And now...will you speak for Papa to be the director of the Wicked Clone show?"

"Just get me there, back to her, and I'll arrange something for you, something up to your goal!" Gabriela replies conceitedly.

"Ok, I'll talk to Lucifer this very evening...as soon as I fix up your Mama! My whole being will serve you with delight, my loyal child! Now, give me some ice, sweetheart," Vlad utters to his daughter, kissing

Gabriela's icy cheeks and then waiting for a tender kiss back. But Gabriela commands her father with a smug face:

"Papa, I want you to go and talk to Lucifer right now!"

"Daddy's gonna take care of everything…if only you honor your Papa with some goodness!"

"Goodness?"

As she approaches the ultralight set of the Hall of Mirrors,

Mihaela can see Meryl's radiant face, dominating the whole stage… Meryl has only been using Mihaela's blue cream for ten days and yet her face illuminates goddess translucence… Her acting is supreme, her gestures and her smile, intimidating. She can seduce and enrapture any man on Earth. She is the body and the mind in which technology has invested the most generous amount. Moreover, the City of Stars scientists' have been researching for decades to discover the elixir of preserving Meryl's artistic genes throughout millennia…the magic through which future generations will attest her exceptional talent. And yes, Meryl can now be multiplied, reproduced together with her artistic genes. Meryl has not found about this reproduction process…yet. They tricked her. Of course, Meryl would not have stood the idea of having them clone her talent and insert it into a robotess-Meryl… She wants to be Meryl, the one and only. Yet, in the City of Stars, the actors have to sign a contract that involves this dangerous clause… Otherwise, they get no roles.

"How can this be possible? Meryl should put an end to it," Mihaela thinks to herself. "If no one attacks them, if no one tries to change something…they will change everything into nothing… I will help her. I have to tell her."

Above all these, Mihaela wants to bring Meryl back to her human roots…entirely. No more elastine injections or robotine cream… Lately, on Meryl's back there have appeared little itching spots: sort of a burning allergy… Meryl has tried all the creams on the market, but nothing has worked. After Meryl has disclosed to Mihaela her struggle with this itching problem, Mihaela felt the need to write to Meryl of her childhood allergy story.

Dear Meryl,

At 14, a horrible allergy burst out on my skin. Because of so much itching, my body filled with blemishes and vicious wrinkles...that formed a viscid reddish crust... Immediately, Papa brought me milk from our healthy cows to drink... He first buried a clay pot laden with milk inside a hole from our yard, where a huge ant colony had made their house... The ants, like little hungry wolves, invaded and swarmed inside the pot of milk, so eager to feed... Papa then put me to drink the milk brimming with ants, no matter how many ugly faces I had made... Within an hour, my skin looked flawless, smooth and supple as that of a newborn. The milk with ants had magically restored my face, and not only that, it made me feel lighter and stronger, like a super-bee ready to work. Since then, each time I'm feeling tired or afraid of losing my peaches-and-cream complexion, I drink milk with ants.

Love you, Mihaela

Circling the set, caught up in her dream-like world, Mihaela bumps into the ultra-radiant Meryl who wears Mihaela's new creation: a glacial wedding dress in which she froze white petals of roses.

"Oh, I feel so cold!" Meryl says as she catches Mihaela's hands.

"I know... But you look great!" Mihaela encourages Meryl. "I will bring you the milk... I think it's ready!"

"No I can't drink that..."

"All right, if you prefer to freeze and scratch..."

"This time you really took me by surprise! Lucky you, I love this dress to death! It's worth the pain," Meryl smiles, blue in her cheeks. "But to tell you the truth, I need some more warmth batteries on my back... I can't move on without them. Would you apply them to me, please?" Meryl pleads.

Mihaela takes Meryl to the side:

"My dear, they ordered me to design this frosty dress against my will! You know that those batteries are not good for your health! You've seen what they did to your back! Moreover, later on, they will give you losses of memory and severe aging...and bigger allergy, more than what you have already seen!"

"All right, bring me that milk with ants..." Meryl finally complies. "I can't stand this cold and itching anymore..."

As Mihaela climbs the icy stairway of the Hall of Mirrors that reaches to the roof top of the City of Stars Pictures, a screen-door, red and square, begins vibrating and melting its ice off. Mihaela only glances at it and the screen swallows her in, like a marine monster, releasing her onto the roof top.

All the doors of the City of Stars Pictures have been programmed to sense even the smallest eye characteristics of their employees...their energy, heartbeat and breath rhythm.

Bright rays of sun welcome Mihaela onto the colossal building's peak, wrapping around her body, artificially.

Mihaela opens up a white umbrella, to protect herself from the robotine rays of the artificial Sun.

Under a little apple tree, sheltered beneath a large white umbrella of like size, Mihaela has buried large pots of clay, full of milk from Papa Grid's Carpathian cows, inside a fresh moist soil, plowed by a diligent ant colony. As Mihaela looks down, the ants spring quickly inside the big pots with milk, swimming happily, until exhaustion.

Mihaela rushes to fill up a large cup with milk. The swarming ants, like some bats of light, are so eager to play and jump out... Mihaela grins from ear to ear...suddenly seeing her father's hands upon her hands, helping her to raise the cup slowly, with so much love... "Now I won't spill a drop!"

Excitedly, she steps onto the invigorated soil that looks like an embroidery, woven so delicately by the tiny legs and antennas of the ants, and then carefully makes her way through the red screen-door, leaving the artificial rays of sun behind, smiling with wicked teeth, behind...

The set of "Cherchez la Femme" / "Looking for the Woman" Production

is designed like a glamorous castle, surrounded by cinema screens, painted with the greatest women in history. Meryl and the other actresses of the cast that embody Eve, Hera, Aphrodite, Mary Magdalene, Sappho, Cleopatra, Elizabeth I...are all wearing Mihaela's designs that have three common elements: blood, crosses and stakes. As the story rolls on, the characters come out of the screens and walk towards each other, above their graves, with strange hypnotizing moves, zombie-like...

Eve wears a savage design made from leaves and white oak bark, painted with blood. Around her left leg is twined a real red snake, from ankle to her waist. On her head, a crown of roses with giant thorns, makes her face look both like both Heaven and Hell.

"Oh my, oh my!" James exclaims, scanning the actresses from top to bottom. "Meryl, you look stunning! Eve has too much of a soft make up though! More grandiose and grotesque, please! But, on the whole, everything looks engrossing, utopic and hypnotic, Mihaela..."

All of a sudden, James starts walking faster and faster, flapping his hands up and down and twisting his head like a mad man:

"Where are you, Mihaela?"

He then stops for a moment, jerking and bubbling with an ultra-trembling robotic voice:

"I feel bad, my heart...it's exploding! Where the hell are those batteries? Somebody charge my heart!"

A beautiful gynoid, dressed like a prima-ballerina, arrives to James as fast as a comet, on her tinny tippy toes, equipped with a sophisticated key and Moon-charged batteries. She quickly starts fixing his heart, with precise long fingers of a spider.

"She's got my heart..." James jokes around.

Mihaela returns to the set with the cup of milk, her eyes searching for Meryl.

As soon as his heart is turned back on and the batteries replaced, James jumps to Mihaela with a joie de vivre and a to-be-envied vivacity: "Look at all these outfits! What have you gotten me into, Mihaela? You are putting me to hard work. Now, I must find some more investors to raise the production's level to your super designs! But I am happy, though I need some more...batteries! He, he, he! I can't wait to see those faces! They will be green with envy!" James pulsates with joy, snatching the cup of milk from Mihaela's hand.

"To Mihaela!" he screams with giant energy, drinking the milk in one gulp. "I always loved milk!" he burps like a cow and then takes Mihaela dancing, up and down the halls. "Mooo..." he groans. Mihaela's hot body is suddenly chilled down by the cold, synthetic flesh of James.

James' madness and childishness remind Mihaela of her sister, Gabriela. James loves to show off and and to be sweet-talked. As James twirls Mihaela at the speed of light all over the halls, Mihaela screams at the top of her lungs, with her long hair fluffing in the air, like in a roller coaster... Incapable of keeping her balance, Mihaela flies off James' body and slides along the floor, into the wall. Swift as the wind, James lets his moves and ego behind, and helps Mihaela rise up. Mihaela gives a big belly laugh. She then jumps to her feet and kisses James, applauding his performance like an automaton. Other applauses overtake the set. James is all puffed up.

But Mihaela is not happy, no, not at all. James is so curious. Mihaela has been admiring his work and perseverance, yet she doesn't really know who he is... "A right brained man with a robotic heart? Is his vision human or robotic? Are his words sincere or manufactured, his creative voice real or fake?" This mixture scares her. She feels that she is not going on the right path...

A very sexy waitress, with multiple pierces and extra lips, looms her way out of the production room; she moves her super large hips lasciviously, and winks her eye at the young actor with out-of-space personality... White-faced and with serpent blue veins overswollen along his neck, the actor kisses the waitress on her elastic cheeks, after which he shoves a one-hundred-dollar bill in her giant bra...

His eyes shine brightly. He pulls out a purple handkerchief and wipes some grease off his forehead; the initials "Emil" are engraved, with gilded blue, on the edge of his handkerchief.

"Ten-minute break, everyone!" James brusquely shouts out. "We shall continue with scene # 10! Meryl, Eve, Mary Magdalene and Cleopatra, get ready! And the extras, please! Mihaela, make sure their make up is perfectly surreal!"

Mihaela starts running from one actor to the other, fixing their make-up and adjusting their wardrobe. Everything moves at the fastest speed, like in a slient film that is winding forward and backwards, uncontrollably... Mihaela panics, her tighs shaking. She has got pockets with pins and accessories that hang all over her dress. Her robotic, exact-glasses keep sliding down her nose. Her hair is a mess, frizzed and raveled in knots.

After she takes a close look at Eve, she points out to the android hair stylist:

"Here, the crest has got to be bulkier, bigger, bloder, fuller!"

She then runs to the gynoid-artist who fixes Mary Magdalene's eyes. "Good, but make the lines thicker, sharp and smoky, enigmatic..."

She then shouts aloud in her headset-microphone:

"Where's Cleopatra? I need her to put on her costume."

"She's not here yet!" a nasal voice of a gay android resounds through the headset.

Mihaela gives a vampiric growl. Then, surprised by her uncontrolled reaction, she lowers her tone:

"This girl... She's doing it again!"

Raising her voice again, she orders a twinoid assistant: "Call her! Non stop, until she picks up!"

Mihaela draws near the rack with wardrobe, looking frenzidely through all her creations that are carefully placed on ultra-flexible hangers.

"Where's the purple robe? I need to see the last trim..." she asks hectically the twinoid-assistants. The twinoids look at each other, stunned.

"Olivia, where on earth did you put it?" Mihaela turns to Olivia, the chef-twinoid, continuing her convulsive search for the purple robe, destroying all the order, and hurling items to and fro throughout the entire hall.

"We need Maria's dress now!" Mihaela cries out as Olivia looks at her, benumbed. Then, reddened-up and biting her nails in a flash of anger, she whispers to herself: "Twinoids=Total chaos!"

The young actor with shining eyes pops up behind Mihaela. His moves are elegant, his neck high postured, his fingers white and super long...

"We haven't have the pleasure to meet, but I have heard a lot about your..."

Mihaela throws the purple dress into his face.

"Finally! Here it is!"

Ashamed of her miscast, she runs towards the actor, taking the dress off his face.

As she uncovers his figure, her third eye opens out, pierced by flames of the past. Her heart hurts her, arrowed by the face of a man...who she once loved... As she glances at him, she starts seeing green and blue, turning into deformed images of Gabriela and Anne, fangs and Nicotiana flowers, the lawn from London and the palace, and then the hypnotizing blue eyes of the livid-faced actor... An acute yearning for true love cries within her...

"Where am I? Who is this being in front of me? Help me, Papa!"

Summer of 1487.

Little Mihaela lies on the lawn, dressing up Mommy Doll and adorning her hair with violet wreaths of flowers.

"This is my first dress for Mommy! It's purple, see?" little Mihaela tells the Sun, delightfully.

A hand tries to snatch Mommy Doll from her. Mihaela whimpers: "It's mine! Mommy is mine!"

The sky frowns with clouds.

Mihaela pulls the doll to her chest, holding it tightly. She then runs swiftly behind some oaks, looking craftily behind, at the one who is hunting her down.

Back in her office room,

Mihaela pulls Mommy Doll from a drawer with unnoticeable edges. She tries to recollect herself. She looks at her reflection in the mirror. "Don't let them come out, you hear? He is not Emil... He is just an illusion of your eye..."

Her third eye starts hurting her again. It pricks and burns... It grows bigger and bigger, unbearable... Mihaela starts rubbing her head, inhaling the fresh perfume of Mommy Doll's dress. Her hand unconsciously reaches her teeth... Her canine teeth are dripping blue blood, trickling down...on her breasts. Her heart bleeds; her hands shake, tainted with blood... A black cat with greenish-blue eyes, a young man vomiting blood on Gabriela's sinful arms, Emil's neck broken that deadly night, David's eyes...haunting her on sinuous narrow streets of her mind... She hears their paces coming closer and closer, she can no longer breathe... She meets a dead end street and she can't run any further! She yells, broken into two...leaning against the walls of the past: "Help me!"

Suddenly, Mihaela sees Mommy Doll in the mud and picks it up, covering up her third eye with her body of wood. She then murmurs a prayer through hot boiling tears. She waits. She opens her eyes. She looks again in the mirror. A purple scarf floats towards her, spreading over her face, then over her neck, almost strangling her, stealing her breath...

She blacks out in the arms of the divine being...

Next morning. Mihaela's apartment in the City of Stars.

Mihaela wakes up late, tossing from one side to the other. She yawns widely. Her eyes tear, touched by the warm rays of light that sneak perkily through the gold sheer curtains. She stretches her arms out and the telephone hits her nails. One nail breaks. She startles. Blue blood pours out of her left ring finger. In the corner of the room, a silhouette appears, dark and creepy, darkening the rays of the sun. It morphs into a black cat, and then into a grinning Gabriela with sharp glowing fangs. Mihaela pulls herself out of bed, wiping the sheet of gloom off her eye. "No, not again... I deny you! Go away, in the name of God!"

She takes the phone in her lap and dials a number:

"What happened? How was it?" she asks with excitement.

"Well, you tell me!" a voice replies.

"I can't remember anything! What happened?" Mihaela asks.

"You foxy girl, you were all smiles!"

"Oh, I wish I were... I'm sorry... I didn't feel good at all last night... Something about that drink... What do the chronicles say?"

"So, you don't know?"

"No... I overslept."

"Nothing at all? I have a call on another line, my dear... Let me call you back in a sec..."

Mihaela starts walking around the room, but her feet sink deeper and deeper inside the thick yellow rug; her head gets heavy, the sky falls onto her shoulders, pulling her down to her knees. Hit by a dark ball of smoke into her back, she faints on the white carpet as if death has been lurking inside her chamber, eager to catch her into her claw... After a few moments, she opens her eyes, slowly, trying to come to her senses. Staring at the white ceiling, it slowly turns into a big mouth of a lion... She closes her eyes back, breathing heavily. She waits. Still keeping them closed, she crawls up to the walls and opens the window, raising her head out and expelling all of her fear into the daylight. Panting and gulping for fresh cool air, her heartbeat lowers, her mind cools down... She opens her eyes. Out of the clear blue sky, there comes a woman with black curly hair whose features seem so familiar... The cold wind blushes Mihaela's cheeks with big sharp teeth. As the woman with black hair passes by the edge of her eye, Mihaela musters her courage and shouts out: "Excuse me, my Lady..."

But the lady does not come to a halt, she keeps walking... In her disheveled pajamas, unbrushed and pale, Mihaela rushes out of her apartment.

As she opens the door, a handsome guy, in his fifties, cuts her way down.

"Miss Mihaela? May I have a word with you?"

"I'm in a hurry, sir!"

"I'm detective Davidson. We need to talk!"

Davidson shows his investigation license.

Mihaela freezes in front of him. She cannot believe her eyes. Yes, she remembers him so well. She ran away from him almost 20 years ago, through the tunnel of her third eye, at Dominica's house. Mihaela, shaken by the encounter, addresses Davidson, precipitately:

"Could you wait for me inside, just for a moment? I have to run somewhere... I'll be back in a second!"

"I'm afraid you have to stay here with me... We need to..."

"I'll be back in a second... I promise!" Mihaela cuts Davidson off. "There's someone out there that I have to say hello to!"

"Right now I can't let you leave, Miss," Davidson catches her wrist, "You are under police's supervision. One of the actresses from your movie production was found dead last night! And the director..."

"What? It can't be possible!"

"I'm afraid it is... She was found with some weird blue blood around her neck, ankles, and wrists...and around the abdomen and genital area..."

"No... Who is she?"

"Meryl Stripp."

"Meryl?"

"Yes, one of the actors found her in your cabin, drowned in a pool of blood..."

"Oh my God!"

"Actually, in a pool of blue blood!"

Mihaela looks terrified.

"How could this happen?"

"I think you know better than I do…" Davidson answers.

"Unfortunately, I don't know… I wish I was there. I wouldn't have let that happen!"

"As far as I was told, you had fainted. Then, James Eriksson, the director of the film…ordered to bring you home. But Meryl returned to your cabin and found that you had miraculously come to your senses. She immediately announced James of the great news and returned to your cabin for a touch up…"

"No, it's not true. They brought me home…the twinoids…"

Davidson throws a newspaper on Mihaela's couch, headlining:

James Eriksson's long-awaited new production debuted with a crime! Is this going to draw more audience?

Mihaela stares at the newspaper, overwhelmed.

"Also, early this morning, around 5 am…James Eriksson was found dismembered on the set…looking like a decomposed machinery…his neck broken and its cables and wires torn down… But he has good chances…they might fix him up, you know… But not Meryl, unfortunately…" Davidson mutters.

Without giving Mihaela the chance to react, Davidson throws another newspaper on the couch, speaking again, soberly:

"I did some more research and found your name in a variety of other newspapers from 1983! Have a look!"

The Sun, United Kingdom, March 2, 1983:

EMIL MEHMED, dead in a pool of blue blood, with his neck broken and heart pulled out! MIHAELA, the famous designer and fiancée of the victim, nowhere to be found!

"This was 50 years ago!" Davidson exclaims. "And, as you might recall, 20 years ago, Liam Starkovski, an actor from your *Wicked Clone* production, your play…was found dead in the *Palace Theatre*… I came after you at that old lady's house, but you fled…"

"I see…" Mihaela says, her hands shivering.

"What a coincidence, isn't it? Same facial features, same height, same smile, same color of the eyes, same style of clothing, same name... You and her look like two peas in a pod...just that you did not age at all, contrarily... She lived then and you live now...and the two of you look just the same...and have the same exact name... I'm confused. Which is your version, Mihaela?"

"I don't know...I..."

"I'm afraid you have to come with me... We'll find out together."

"I don't understand..." Mihaela murmurs.

"The blood that was found on Meryl's body has the same compounds that we have found in your makeup..."

"But that's my makeup secret..." Mihaela fights back.

"There is no such secret any more..." the detective smiles.

And then, unexpectedly, he stings Mihaela's ring finger with a long, transparent nail. Blue blood emerges out of her finger. Mihaela watches Davidson, bitterly. Davidson pulls out a pair of fresh new handcuffs and fastens them around Mihaela's tiny wrists. Fresh new tears spring up in Mihaela's eyes. She wished so much to have gone after the woman with black hair who looked just like her mother... She keeps thinking about her... She couldn't meet her because of Davidson! "Why am I always hindered for a reason or another to go after my dream?"

Mihaela follows Davidson deliberately to the police car.

The car has a super sophisticated design and the shape of red cosmic ball, the long-awaited arrival of 2033. It is the era of "BALLution," an era of the anti-pollution and anti-accident cars.

The highways are only one-way and sloping, which allow the smooth and ultrafast rolling of the BALLutionist car. Manufactured with anti-gravitational and perfect braking systems built from a very resistant rubber, with no wheels and windows attached, the BALLution car ensures the passengers a travel in a vertical position, in spite of the continuous revolving motion of the car. The absence of a windshield and of windows requires special glasses that the driver and the passengers are to wear on at all times.

Anti-pollution, the BALLution car has simply saved the city, which is also studded with thousands of filters that work non-stop against the pollution of the past century. Furthermore, there are no accidents due to the special rubber and the high-tech system, fact that has brought a smile on people's faces and has established a state of complete trust in the BALLution car.

On the way to the police office,

Mihaela watches herself on the aerial TV screen from Davisdon's BALLution car.

"The miraculous woman Angelica saved seven despaired children..." the newswoman reports.

"Interesting... You do look a lot like her too!" Davidson exclaims.

The news continue on CMN:

"If you happen to have information on Angelica, the miraculous healer, please contact us immediately! This is a recent photo of Angelica received from The City of Stars Hospital. Please, remember to look around. She could be right next to you!"

Davidson throws out a big smile.

"Who is this Davidson?" Mihaela thinks to herself. "How could he find me in the City of Stars?"

She had run away from Davidson through the tunnel of her third eye...to a space where she wanted to just forget about the past...to start a new life! And she meets him again in the year 2033, under the same circumstances! It is absurd! Why does history repeat? It feels like only two weeks had passed since Davidson and her met at Dominica's house...and he speaks about a 20 years' span...

"He has changed...he has many wrinkles, but he looks even better, more mature and alluring..." Mihaela thinks within, captured by his robust features.

Suddenly, her third eye opens wide and starts trembling, flickering blue lights.

"Please, stop the car! I'm not feeling well!" Mihaela cries out.

Davidson orders his chauffeur and the car stops at once, in the quietest mode.

Mihaela gets off the car, overwhelmed. She breathes in and out, like a pregnant woman, rubbing her forehead.

"Can I have a moment with you?" she asks Davidson, panting.

"Sure you can..."

"See, I'm coming from a country called Transylvania..."

"Yes, I know..."

"Out there, everything is possible..."

"Exactly what do you mean, Miss?"

Uncontrolled tears start falling on Mihaela's cheeks... Her thrid eye closes.

Davidson looks suspiciously.

"Are you going to believe what I am going to tell you without thinking that I am crazy?" Mihaela asks him, panic-stricken.

"Well, go on...."

"You have to promise me one thing: that you will open up your heart and that you will never send me to a psychiatrist."

"Well..."

"Please, promise me," Mihaela says while blue tears paint her cheeks.

"I promise. Would you calm down, Miss?"

Mihaela and Davidson walk towards a lawn teeming with hundreds of sunflowers. Mihaela glances around, willing to take a seat onto the fresh damp grass. Suddenly, from the underground, the stem of a purple flower raises its budding head, growing taller and taller, up to Mihaela's waist. Its bud opens into a huge purple flower, revealing strong, electrifying petals with white beaming stamens, as bright as Mihaela's third eye. Mihaela caresses the plant and hurls herself onto its velvety petals that feel soft and warm, like Mama's restful arms. Behind them, the sunflowers lengthen their stem-necks curiously, opening stamen-eyes and petal-ears wide...to witness and hear the secret of Miss Mihaela...

Mihaela takes a deep breath, afterwhich she addresses Davidson:

"You are the first human being to whom I'm confessing all of these... I was born differently a long time ago...in Transylvania... I have a twin sister who is not like you or me or like any other creature around here… She has two rows of canine teeth and a dead heart… She killed lots of people whom I used to love… She killed Emil, my fiancée, in 1983…"

"In 1983?"

"See, I can travel beyond time… I have a special eye," Mihaela stings Davidson's astonishment.

Davidson bursts into laughter.

Mihaela looks at him, intimidated.

"Go on, I'm sorry," Davidson apologizes, trying to recollect.

"I can prove it to you if you want…" Mihaela says, suddenly joyful.

"All right, I would love to see this…"

"Do you really want this?" Mihaela looks at him keenly, penetrating his blue eyes.

"Yes, I really want this," Davidson replies firmly, hardly concealing his smile.

Mihaela gets closer to Davidson and leans her forehead against his forehead. Her indigo star emerges, twinkling white lights.

"Choose a year!" Mihaela whispers to him.

"2014," Davidson says, briskly.

"2014? Why? Do you want to handcuff me for Liam's death too?"

"No, it's just that I saw you there for the first time…in Times Square, at the **W** Hotel and…"

"Hmmm, I know…but too scary memories for me… I'll take you to a more romantic place, trust me… Now hold my hand tightly. Say "I love you" and think strongly of 2014."

"To say that I love you?"

"Yes, and say it like you mean it!" Mihaela speaks, cheerfully.

Davidson looks around, embarrassed and feeling total discomfort within his body of an honorable detective.

"I haven't said 'I love you' for some time, you know… It takes some time and…in this era, people forgot about such words…"

"Say it, please!"

"I can't say it just like that!" Davidson says, irritated.

"Just say it, please! These are the most beautiful words in the world!"

"I love you..." Davidson murmurs, shyly.

"See, it doesn't work! You have to believe it!"

"Come on, let's go back to the car," Davidson bursts out, annoyed.

"No!" Mihaela shouts out. And in the twinkling of an eye, Mihaela gives Davidson a big kiss.

Davidson remains perplexed, his eyes widen, his cheeks blush.

"I love you!" Mihaela whispers.

"I love you too!" Davidson says, electrified from head to the bottom of his heart.

The third eye of Mihaela opens wider and wider, turning into a big circle of white fire... A bright tunnel flashes before Davidson's eyes, piercing the skyline, waiting for Mihaela and Davidson to step in. Mihaela grabs Davidson's hand and treads onto the white bright carpet that takes them on, like the wind...

Accompanied by the Hunting Bitches and the Moon Dogs,

Gabriela arrives before the entrance of the underground world. She proudly hands a sealed letter to the three-headed dog Cerberus who protects the gate, and utters:

"This is for him, from my father," she says, gazing at Cerberus' electrifying yellow spark from his eyes.

Cerberus clutches the letter in his claws and growls:

"Wait here!"

The Hunting Bitches, that are adorning the gate with their voluptuous buttocks and alluring nipples, start whining synchronized to Cerberus:

"Take us with you, beloved Cerberus, take us to our master. We want to talk to him. Vlad has a message for him that only our tongues are allowed to give in!"

"Very well, come with me," Cerberus consents.

"Thank you! Hell always be with you!" the Hunting Bitches sing to Cerberus with praise.

Through the dark tunnels of Hell, The Hunting Bitches follow the Chief-Dog Cerberus. Their eyes turn into a flickering burning red...making through the darkness way...

"Oh, it's disgustingly and satisfyingly ornamented, so greasy and whining... Is there a party that we don't know of tonight?"

A small shadow of Master Lucifer lurks before their eyes. Immediately, Cerberus and the Hunting Bitches bow to the ground. As they touch it, they turn upside down.

The Dead Rat master, dressed up in a long gown with spiked up fur and horrifying malodor, sniggers, smoking a pipe.

"What news do you bring me? Did he sign it?" he growls.

"Supposedly," Cerberus replies.

"Let's see..."

Cerberus hands Lucifer the letter from Vlad. Lucifer opens it with his two front teeth, decayed and sharp.

"It smells horribly... Ughh...this bloody disgusting goodness! I told him not to seal it this way any more... Let's see!"

Lucifer starts reading the letter upside down. His rotten mouth widens in complete satisfaction.

"Hmm, interesting deal Vlad proposes this time... Good boy, my friend... I knew I could count on him!"

Lucifer looks towards the Hunting Bitches with obscenity.

He then calls the hairiest one of them, with long curly lashes and plumpish wet lips, and licks her chubby hot buttocks cheeks.

"Bring me the naughty daughter of Vlad, bitch! I want to smell her ass, too!"

The hairy Hunting Bitch giggles and whirls to bring Gabriela to Lucifer's feet.

"No! Not you! Send the Ballerina Bitch! She's the diplomatic one! Only she can convince Gabriela to come..."

And so, the Ballerina Hunting Bitch leads Gabriela in, through a shortcut tunnel, amongst the crunching and smirking noise of little slick red mice.

The blazing darkness blackens Gabriela's eyes.

"Oh my God, I'm going blind again!"

"Shh...you are not allowed to say that name!" The Ballerina Hunting Bitch whines. "Ah, it burns!"

After seconds of ghoulish silence, Gabriela arrives in front of Lucifer. As soon as she smells the libidinal creature's odor, Gabriela begins to whimper:

"I can't breathe, it's too hot. I can't see anything, help me..."

"Hi, scrumptious daughter of Vlad," the master cuts Gabriela's whines off. As Lucifer suddenly becomes visible, lit up by the red eyes of the Hunting Bitches, Gabriela asks, fierily:

"Who are you?"

"A good friend of your father..."

"What's your name?"

"My name is what you desire the most..."

"Queen of the Night!" Gabriela bursts out.

"You said it horribly nice! In fact I'm the King of the Night, ready to help you become the Queen of the Night. But are you aware of your father's and my mutual understanding?"

"I came here to see Lucifer! I only talk with the boss!"

"I am Lucifer!"

"No, you are not...because..."

"Because?" Lucifer asks, burning with curiosity.

"Lucifer looks ugly...but you look uglier, disgusting..."

Lucifers gushes out a sinister, wholesome wicked laugh.

"Of course, my love...for you, especially! You look disgustingly beautiful tonight, so I had to meet my guest's expectations! Horrible! I can't take my eyes off you! You've got to rule the Bitches..."

"I'm not a bitch! You tell your mother bitch!"

"Ooh...I like her a lot!" the master slobbers. "Let me translate it then: you should become the Queen of the Night and rule those girls of mine! Tell me," Lucifer continues ablaze, "Aren't you fed up to see your sister having it all—the soul, enchanting men, the eyes and mouth to laugh you off, the one who loves her so? Isn't it unfair that you and her are two, moreover twins, but she has torn the branch and showed the tongue to you? You killed her boyfriends in the name of Love! Didn't God teach us to love each other, protect our family and do everything in the name of Love? Well, let me tell you the truth and only the truth: you acted in accordance," Lucifer ignites her anger, "Yet she's been still ungrateful to your love! And what should you do now? Beg her more? Humiliate yourself and get rejected? No, Papa Lucifer cannot let you suffer any more! These horrible dark eyes of yours need their sweet revenge! Your sister needs to learn to appreciate you! The world has to find out who is the trueborn vampire, the true Queen of the Night! Are you ready, my love, to show the world your beauty and your skills?"

"Yes, I am!" Gabriela replies, enflamed.

"Are you ready to wink once and your Father to fulfill your innermost dreams?"

"Yes, I am!"

"But are you aware of what it takes to travel beyond my space and have whatever you wish in this world?"

"Not exactly…"

"Well, I give you everything you wish for if only you bring your sister here within 24 hours. I want to reconcile things between you and her…kind of cut in two her inspiration and give a half to you… I want to burn her proudness and to shut her heart, to kill her spirit a little bit and bring her in whole flesh, back in your father's castle… She has to die to rise again, like you—immortal and vampirically sexual… She's not a nun to preach the psalms. She's an entertainer of my world! You and her have to sing and dance, move your hips and chin in sync… And you will write your songs and live in fame! I promise you upon my name!"

"Yes…"

"So bring her to me!" Lucifer commands. "Tonight!"

"Well, I'll try…" Gabriela hesitates.

"No, don't say that! Here is only Yes, I'll do it, or No, I'll die! So, which do you prefer?"

"I guess, Yes, I'll do it."

"Very well, I knew you wouldn't disappoint me! You are Vlad's daughter—my beloved monster! So, then, what are we waiting for, my bitches? Give my queen the red roller blades with double bat-wings!" Lucifer orders the curvaceous Hunting Bitches.

"Roller blades with double wings? Wow! So that means I can fly?!" Gabriela jumps out of the frying pan into the fire.

"See, I knew what you wanted! Now give your king a kiss!" Lucifer grins, abominably.

"A kiss? But, I can't see through darkness to touch your cheeks…"

"Well, walk straight, I'm right here…"

Gabriela walks towards Lucifer. Lucifer gives Gabriela a sharp kiss of death.

"Ah, it burns, it burns…it burns all over inside…"

Lucifer bites Gabriela's neck with his sharp decayed canine teeth.

"Welcome to my world!" he grins.

"I feel evil…so evil…" Gabriela whines.

The Hunting Bitches hurl themselves over Gabriela, starting to feed on her flesh, her legs, her neck…

"Thank you, master, thank you!" the hungry seductresses praise Lucifer in choir as they devour the body of Gabriela.

2014. Through the whirlwind of light, Mihaela and Davidson

land in a bed, amid a young hipster couple that is making love.

"Oh my God, we are so sorry!" Mihaela cries out, embarrassed, amidst the hot sheets of bed.

"Don't worry!" the lovers smile. "You can join us…it's fine… The more the merrier!"

Mihaela takes Davidson by the hand and drags him out of the room.

"Where are we? Are you out of your mind?" Davidson grumbles as he stumbles with his feet upon some boxes.

"I told you I could do it," Mihaela whispers to him, cheerfully, pulling him by the arm.

"Let's go back! I have an important meeting with my boss tonight...and I have to report him a case..." Davidson stutters, releasing himself from Mihaela's grasp.

"We'll have time to reach him by tonight, don't worry. We are three hours earlier! We are in L.A..."

"L.A.?"

"Yes, I wished to come down here..." Mihaela murmurs.

As they step over a golden velvety carpet, through a long dim-lit corridor with golden candelabras and cloned doors, they realize that they are inside a luxurious hotel. Along the halls, Davidson's eyes drop on the grand walls that are studded with hand-painted wallpaper.

"Oh my God, I can't believe this! This belongs to my grandfather..." he speaks with dreamy eyes.

"What?"

"The wallpaper!"

"Really?" Mihaela exclaims.

"Yes... Grandpa was well-known for his delicate autumn embroideries on this light beige tapestry mixed with lime tones and impressionist dots... Oh, and here is his signature. He loved to embroider even his own name..."

"Oh, I see—it's says *Wealthington*! How beautifully written!" Mihaela says, gently touching the wall.

As they walk around the corner, another long corridor comes into sight... The lights are dimmer and the shades and shadows are playing on the walls, like some spirited leaves in the blow of the wind. Davidson stops again, lured by memories of grandpa... He draws closer and touches the wallpaper that this time is darker and stained with some thick reddish circles of paint...

"What have they done to it?"

"What do you mean?"

"See these faces, I mean this face...with these eyes, staring at us like an owl... " Davidson utters.

"What face?" Mihaela draws near the wallpaper, squinting at it with wet glistening eyes.

"This old man in motion... Can you see him?" Davidson asks her, impatiently.

"I don't really see anything," Mihaela replies to him as a red-haired woman rushes down the hall with a hysterically crying boy.

"My head..." Davidson leans against the walls.

"Are you Ok?"

"Just feeling weak... My eyes sore..."

"Look at me!"

Davidson faces Mihaela.

"Indeed, you look very pale and your eyes are terribly red. Let's go downstairs, to the reception desk!"

And Mihaela takes Davidson by his trembling hand, with the care of a loving mother. Stairs lead into an oval garden, with big walls of freshly trimmed grass and white orchids, with paths and crowns of exotic flowers, so majestically and delicately staged... Mihaela has never seen something more beautiful since Emil's garden...in London.

"This garden, smiles! It's alive!" Mihaela's eyes beam with love. "It is a beatific smell and a mesmerizing feel as in Shakespeare's Midsummer's Dream!" she murmurs to herself.

"Oh My God, this is the famous Beverly Dreams Hotel! I've always wanted to come here with Emil!" Mihaela briskly cries out. "Emil and I had planned to come here for our honeymoon..." Mihaela seizes Davidson's hand.

"Beverly Dreams Hotel? Are you sure?" Davidson asks her, trying to pull his hand off her hand...

"Yes, there is the inscription! See?"

"It is so silly! Come on! Come to your senses! I am a grown up man! Excuse me, Sir, what year are we in?" Davidson asks one of the valets standing near the entrance to the hotel's pool.

"What year?"

"Yes."

"2014, sir!" the valet replies with a serious face.

"What day, what month?" Davidson insists.

The valet smiles and replies gallantly:

"Today it's April 22nd, a beautiful spring day, Sir!"

"April 22nd? You've got to be kidding! Today is my birthday!" Davidson's blue eyes widen and brighten up.

"Today is your birthday? Fantastic! We have to celebrate!" Mihaela screams, enthusiastically.

"Shhhh... You embarrass me..."

"Sorry," Mihaela lowers her voice.

"Please, act properly. And don't hold my hand! I am a serious man, and I have a clean reputation! That kiss took me by surprise..."

"That kiss brought you here... Calm down, it won't happen again."

"No? And how am I going to go back?"

"I don't know..."

"What do you mean?"

"You have to kiss me again. Do you think you can stand it?"

"I'll try to..." Davidson muses.

"Good. Now that we are on the same page...let's go inside and raise a glass of champagne to your health!"

"If you insist... Actually, I didn't get to celebrate my birthday twice in 2014...so thank you," Davidson says, boastfully, taking the straight posture of a count.

"My pleasure..."

"Ah, my head..." and Davidson grasps Mihaela by her hand, tightly.

"Let's get you some water... " Mihaela utters, worriedly. "And I'll massage your head... I have a good technique!"

Out of nowhere, the beautiful divine being whom Mihaela had met at the long wooden table appears clear and bright before their eyes. The being holds the same chalice with red potion and looks at them with warm, loving eyes of a lamb. Mihaela takes the chalice and drinks from it, radiating with child-like joy!

"Drink, you will feel so much better!" she encourages Davidson, suddenly floating up in the air.

"No! Are you crazy? Who is he? Do you know him?" Davidson ripostes, trying to bring Mihaela down, with her feet on the ground.

"Yes, I do. Drink, please. Believe. You will be thankful..."

Davidson looks at the chalice suspiciously, then at Mihaela who smiles at him sweetly.

"Fine, I'll do it! I haven't done so many foolish things for a decade…" and he drinks, losing his words in the chalice.

Suddenly, his whole body begins to radiate, from the crown of his head to the sole of his feet, his skin blooming like that of a young man, just like Davidson's who Mihaela first met.

Losing ground and starting to float up in the air, Davidson exclaims like a frantic child in Disney Land:

"It's magic! What did I drink? Sir?"

As Davidson turns around to thank the beautiful being, the being is gone.

"Who is he?" Davidson asks Mihaela, intrigued.

"He always comes when my friends need help…"

"Where can I buy this drink?"

"You cannot buy it. But you can have it as long as you wish to see Him. You just have to desire it, ask for it, believe it, and then He will come to you…"

"You have to tell me who he is… You are way too mysterious," Davidson glances at Mihaela, suspiciously, looking younger and shinier than ever…

Out of huge black flames,

Vlad drops dead in Lucifer's stifling chamber. Some of his bones are bulged out of his body, his hair frizzed like weeds and catching fire. He abruptly opens his eyes, clinging onto the walls that burn up his palms to exfoliation. Screaming his death aloud, he jumps a mile backwards, right into the putrid lap of the Dead Rat.

"Master, I am in a desperate condition. I need your help."

"What are you doing here? You didn't announce yourself," Lucifer bursts out with anger.

Looking down at the master's feet, Vlad sees his daughter fretting and kicking down, in despair.

"What are you doing to my daughter? I've told you to be gentle," Vlad winces.

"Enough!" the master screams. "Bitches, leave us alone!"

The Hunting Bitches withdraw from the massacre, their heads bowed down; however, their chubby posteriors are super dilated, still craving young blood...

"She's going to be fine," Lucifer assures Vlad, turning upside down.

"Gabriela, rise to your feet! Stand up!" Lucifer commands her.

Gabriela stands up. Her eyes are red and her body—like a shredded curtain, dripping blood...

"Daddy, now I can see through darkness and it's so horribly nice down here... Look at all these children, they are so sad and dead!" Gabriela cries out like a mad girl.

"I'm glad you like it, my dear!" Vlad says, looking at his daughter with sorrowful eyes.

But only Vlad knows what deep frost lies in his soul. For a moment, he can feel the ice of his heart breaking out and the flames of Lucifer taking over his mind! He sold Gabriela for Mihaela's love! He sacrificed her! He feels so sorry for Gabriela—she is blood of his blood, but the love of Mihaela that awaits him is going to revive his blood and give him life! Love is bigger than the present pain, he hopes...

"Gabriela, tell your Daddy and I, what do you know to do, talentwise?" Lucifer asks, his mouth swarming with insects and worms, and his stomach, coiled by serpents and baby crocodiles.

"I know to bite..." Gabriela replies, weary and losing blood through her puffed-up nose.

"That's nice! But we need something more human...to spice it up tonight! Do you know to dance?"

"I know how to vamp!"

"What's that?"

"It is a mixture between skeleton and reincarnation, it is a vampire style that I have invented!"

"Horrible, let's see it!"

With the celerity of a superhuman, Gabriela starts arching her back and twirling her arms around her waist while biting her nails off and spitting them out, like some raining confetti, upon the crowd. She then hops her legs above her shoulders and jumps like a ball, beyond Hell's flames; her hair, legs and arms explode like some electric arcs. At last, she lands onto the ceiling, pivoting her head faster than the globe... All of her bones detach from her body and hang loose, creating a musical noise, like a xylophone, and then they stick back together inside her flesh, making Gabriela look like an incredible contortionist act.

"Incriminating, desintegrating!" Lucifer exclaims. "But...do you also know to dance creamier, lascivious and lachrymose so that the mortals will be weeping for?"

"No, not really... Mihaela can dance like that... But I can wickedly play the piano..."

"Too normal. All vampires do that!"

"It's not true! Do you know of any other vampires besides me and my father?"

"Ahhh...no, not really..."

"Then, what vampires are you talking about? And my father does not play the piano! I am the only one who has this talent."

"True, wicked spurting mouth!"

"Besides, my father is the one who invented vampirism and gave me fangs..."

"Yes, indeed. But *I* helped him perform it! *I* am his director! Hmmm, what was I trying to say? Oh, yes! I watched those films—*Interview with a Vampire, Twilight, True Blood, boring* episodes... All those vampires do the same thing: play piano, read minds...stereotypes. They kill the killing's vibe. I wonder how could mortals watch something like that, so out of spark? You know what I like? Your sister's play—*Wicked Clone*! At least it makes my world renowned! They cast me in a leading role, showing my fights with God, my land of death, my tunnels, and my name... Yes, I'm gonna help that show show off on Broadway! The only thing that I now need to do is to enlarge my part and write again the ending—my hyperbolic monologue to show the world that God is on the ropes!" Lucifer laughs, infernally. Then, he shoves his head into the mud, creeping to Gabriela's feet and then biting them with greed.

"You know how to sing, Gabriela?"

"I know how to sting!" and Gabriela pierces Lucifer's skin with her sharp pointed nails.

"Oooh! Please, try to sing!"

"All right, I'll try!"

Gabriela starts singing. Lucifer rolls his eyes like balls on fire, covering his ears with the greasy claws of a denier.

"Cerberus!" Lucifer screams. "Send Gabriela to 2014. Tune her voice a little more horribly and bitchy, with Hades echoes to her pitches, and may she'll be a singer, alarmed as a ringer and dancing as a swinger! She's going to meet her awful twin sister in L.A., I'll direct your pace! Let Dressman, my Jewish darling friend, direct the show... Involve a manager too and compulsorily, keep her twin sister on stage as well! Just do it savory and bloody! You'll find a way to confuse those little naughty angels! I'll be watching it! You know the musical *Wicked Clone* where I'm the star, don't you? Well, it's grand! Except for the last part. I have to change the ending and we'll set the musical on Broadway! Kitz, Kitz! But, immediately, after the L.A. show, have Gabriela bring Mihaela to my grotto... I need to teach her how to perform her role..." Lucifer growls, rubbing his claws.

"Yes, Master!" Cerberus bows down, smiling prudently.

"Horribly!"

As soon as Cerberus makes his exit, Vlad teeters near Lucifer's shadow. He then kneels at his feet and starts crying like a desperate woman in labor:

"I am in big trouble, master... I resurrected Violeta, just as you taught me... But then she got disconnected, just before the session ended... She looked like a terrifying corpse...and ran away into the forest... She's gone, out of my sight, forever!"

"Don't worry! She looks beautiful! But you forgot to put my evil's compass inside her heart! I've told you to do it from the start! You wanted to cut me off, didn't you? But I forgive you because I care about you…as I care about all my excrements! Hmmm…now it is going be hard to track Violeta down! But I'll find a way… The Hunting Bitches love to smell women's blood…"

"No, you don't understand," Vlad whines. "I'm not concerned about this. It's just that I had programmed Violeta to tell Mihaela, when she meets her, that I myself brought her back to life, especially for her, in the name of my burning love for her…"

"In the name of your burning love for her? You're so pathetic!" Lucifer shrinks his eyes, miopically.

"I love her…" Vlad murmurs.

"All right, all right, we've got a deal! I don't care about your burning love! Ughhh!"

"But Mihaela will hate me even more when she meets her mother so horribly looking on earth!" Vlad whines again.

"She looks beautifully! And…don't worry, Mihaela's got the right blood! She can fix her Mother up!"

"What do you mean? No, no…Violeta looks horrible…."

"You're raving, my boy…and you're famished! Go and suck Miss Tiffany's baby! She has just given birth to an awful-looking child! Meantime, I'll track Violeta down."

"Alright, I'll count on you…but I can't suck the blood of babies anymore, you know…" Vlad bends his head with regret.

"Again? Feeling guilty and weak? Wake up, you are in Hell, there is no sin, my villain, in my bin!" Lucifer smacks Vlad's complain with his words. "You know that I can't stand acts of contrition and pathetic tears! Stop being a boy eager to feed with vegetables and milk! Where is your cruel blood that has impressed my realm? I love you as an Impaler. Don't turn into a failure! And now, make your way out! I've got to scramble for lost souls…"

As Vlad exits the tunnels of Lucifer, bewildered and dishiveled, Lucifer flies above him, with his bat wings crimson and flitched, cutting his way out and blowing viscous saliva into his eyes.

"Ah, you scared me to life!" Vlad cries out, trying to wipe the thick gelationous saliva of Lucifer from his eyes.

"Monster Vlad," Lucifer pats him on his head with his dirty claw, sweetening his voice. "I figured that you just can't wait to impale your sweet little bride... So, I thought that you will need this little gift..."

"What's this?"

"Fertility elixir and devilish potency!"

"What for?"

"I want a child! An impertinent and ravishing little boy! Start drinking it from tonight!"

Vlad takes the potion in his hand, trembling with fear.

"Ah, Love, I hate it! It makes you so weak, I can't look you in the eye! I have to utter an awful curse on you to bring you to Hell's wits!" Lucifer rags on Vlad's ridiculous conduct while biting his viscous rabbit lips in disgust.

Mihaela and Davidson enter the restaurant-lounge of Beverly Dreams Hotel.

Big lights and sparkles splash on their eyes, almost robbing them of their sight.

"What's going on in here?" Davidson asks one of the guys dressed up in a ravishing black suit with glistening silver bow.

"We are rehearshing for a musical."

"Oh, I love musicals!" Mihaela jumps in. "What's it called?"

"*Wicked Clone!*"

"*Wicked Clone*? But this is the name of my play...that I wrote..."

"It cannot be your play..." the man gallantly replies. "Maybe a remake..."

"Who are you if I may ask?"

"My name is Emanuel. I am an actor. I play Mihaela's boyfriend in the *Wicked Clone* production!" the actor promptly replies.

"Well, I am Mihaela…and just for you knowledge, *Wicked Clone* is a play written by me…based on my life and my twin sister's life… It is my journey from Transylvania to New York and… I started to stage it few years ago in New York."

"Everyone knows that it was written by the legendary Vlad the Impaler, in the 15th century, and found in his castle's attic from Transylvania…" the actor cuts her off with a self-confident tone.

Mihaela gives out a big belly laugh.

"They showed this on the news, in the newspapers—Vlad's authethic journal and his old style of handwriting…" the actor resumes. "Wicked Clone is a play that he wrote about his identical twin daughters… Look down here, in the public press release. ***Wicked Clone—the story of the twin within. Signed: Vlad the Impaler…*** Wicked Clone's been very successful on Broadway and around the world… Allegedly… I have been also helping with the marketing, promotion…"

"You said Vlad the Impaler?" Mihaela asks him, unable to control her laughter.

"Yes, indeed, my lady!" the man replies, joining Mihaela's laughter.

"Who is the director of the play, if I may ask?" Mihaela stops from her laughter.

"Actually, you look a lot like Mihaela!" the actor says, easily amused.

Davidson catches Mihaela by her wrist.

"Let's go!"

"Oh, here is Mister Dressman—the producer of *Wicked Clone*! You may talk to him about your version…" the actor points out to a 60 year-old man, bald, yet adorned with two joyful eyes and quick moves of a teenager.

As soon as he lays his eyes on Davidson and Mihaela, Mister Dressman leaps for joy, flying at them with big kisess and clingy embraces:

"Happy Birthday, my friend! David, David, I was worried that you stole the queen and you would not show up your faces today! Mihaela dear, please, quickly, go and put on the silver-chained-outfit! Donna will help you! We are under great delay! As I've said, today we are rehearsing the fight scene between you and Gabriela. We'll give David a couple more minutes..." he adds with a wink.

The actor looks perplexed at Mihaela. Mihaela looks perplexed at everyone.

"Dear Mr. Dressman...we have to clarify something about my play..." Mihaela steps in, easily annoyed.

"Later my dear! Now we are so late with everything! Donna, show Mihaela to her dressing room, please!"

Donna leads Mihaela backstage. Mihaela follows her, bewildered, still whispering her concern:

"It is my play, my play..."

In the silence of her steps, Mihaela hears a strong voice within: "Walk, just walk... Don't look back!"

"Leo, this is David..." Dressman continues, introducing Davidson to the man next to him. "David is my longtime friend and famous manager that I've been telling you about. David will be promoting the songs and the soundtrack of *Wicked Clone*. And David, may I introduce you to my friend Leo—our co-producer, heart-cooler and money-booster! Ha Ha Ha! And of course, I have a little surpise for you today...a little birthday gift..." Dressman chuckles, patting Davidson on his back.

"What kind...of surprise?" Davidson stutters.

"What, what, what? Happy Birthday, David! This is my gift to you—a part in the play! A birdie told me about your lifetime dream of becoming an actor... And I thought about taking action! I am a man of action!"

"What?" Davidson looks at them, bewildered, rubbing his neck, anxiously.

"Congratulations!" Leo chimes in. "It must be very exciting!"

"No, I had no idea..." Davidson bubbles.

"I've been so curious..." Leo disrupts Davidson again as he sees Gabriela walking down the stage. "How did you meet the twins?"

"The twins? Uhhh... Long story..." Davidson blushes, trying to make up his words. "I...met Mihaela in a hotel room in New York City... See, I am a private detective. She stole some items and I was dealing with her case...and..." Davidson explains, taking a formal tone.

They all laugh.

"I can see that you've already imprisoned her!" Leo chuckles aloud. "Maybe this will be Dressman's next production!"

"David dear," Dressman speaks on, changing the subject, suddenly agitated. "I have to play you *Dracula's Land* song this very evening. I can't wait any longer! Gabriela re-orchestrated it and I need your feedback... I've been comparing the old version and the new version...on and on... See, I've got this streak of white hair right on top of my head... It's been draining me out of blood, shriveling me, stealing my rest... I've been haunted by the same question... Which version is better?"

Leo chuckles again.

"I have an important meeting later on, I'm afraid I can't join... " Davidson breaks in, crushing Dressman's enthusiasm.

"What are you talking about, my friend? I spoke to you early this morning and you confirmed that we will celebrate your birthday...together with me and the twins...chatting about our future and about the scenes... I've thoroughly prepped everything for this eve. What's the matter with you?"

"Oh...it's just that...uh, I was just joking. I wanted to see if you still love me, my friend..."

"Uh, it really got me, funny joke... I knew you were a good actor!" Dressman breathes at ease, wiping drops of sweat off his swollen head.

Beverly Dream's Hotel lounge. The lights turn off.

Mihaela's eyes appear on a big screen, then her entire face blooms in. Close up on her red lips that open up in a whisper:

"Last night I had a nightmare.

I was lying on a lawn with red roses when I saw him.

He came closer and closer to me and I was willing to give in;

Yet when my lips came next to his,

Death suddenly came through my sheets.

Death wrapped around my body and sucked all of my blood

And suddenly I died. And now I feel inside my veins no blood.
Only a craving to kiss him—my love, my light...
But I'd better go to work and tell that yearning bye..."

Watching Mihaela, Davidson feels shivers all over his body. He starts trembling, his eyes tear uncontrollably... He hasn't shed a tear in years... His heart pounds, shooting him with a terrible feeling of love...

For more than twenty years he has caught bandits, thieves, rapists, drug-dealers...having become the "terror" of the City of Stars, the undisputable detective who has solved more than 100 difficult cases, honored with medals and awards... He has been a solid man, mentally very well organized, with a clean file and reputation; no spells or flirtations of a feminine nature have ever intimidated him. And yet, in front of this woman or girl Mihaela, he feels like a newborn just learning to walk...

As a sensual music breaks in, his mind catches fire, yielding to lecheorus scenes of erotic dreams... He suddenly sees himself kissing those voluptuous lips...and traveling to unknown, exotic lands with this extremely beautiful woman that has stolen his heart. The glance of her eyes, hidden under a veil of innocence, betray the character of a creature that he has never encountered before—so different, so gracious, so poetic... How could such a terrible thing happen to him? It turns him upside down, it makes him do things that he should not be doing and that he has never thought about before.

Even though he wished to be an actor, he has never liked Broadway, much less musicals... Yet watching Mihaela singing on stage, moving her body like an innocent maiden who has just found her sensual side, he finds theater more and more gracious, ravishing... This play is not dusty, neither conventional...but fresh, different... As Mihaela winds her chest like a snake, undulating her hips like a Scheherazade, and then lowering her shoulders down to the floor with moves of a tigress, his eyes spot a dark mole on her left breast... The whole world spins, his heart cannot bear such a heat within any longer...

"No way. I have to control my self! It's gotta stop!" he lays his hand on his heart, tapping it in delirium.

Dressman calls Davidson, louder and louder:
"David? Are you here, my friend? David?"

After few moments of disconnection, Davidson comes to his senses:

"Ahh… Were you talking to me?"

"Yes, birthday-friend! Go and change for the mercy of stage!" he pats Davidson on his shoulder, a red wicked light flickering from his eye.

"Where, why? It is not my thing…" Davidson tries to draw back.

"Just enjoy it… Enjoy it, my friend! Nothing bad can happen to you…" Dressman grins with delight.

Suddenly, as Davidson glares at Dressman in dismay, Dressman takes a very old face, blemished with white spots of age, his eyebrows thickening and becoming hairy and grey, his mouth widening as of an orangutan, filled with wide, yellow teeth and thick saliva, splashing Davidson's face as he bursts into a big wicked laugh:

"Enjoy it, my boy, enjoy…"

He then passes Davidson by, with the silent step of a ghost, to the dark back of the restaurant lounge.

Donna, the stage manager who has been lurking in Davidson's back, awakens him with a tap. Davidson turns his head abruptly, sweaty and scared like a little boy. He sighs, clutching Donna's hand. Donna takes his arm and leads him backstage, asking him in a gentle voice:

"Do you need help with the costume? Please, let me know…"

"No, I don't think so…" Davidson replies in turmoil. "But…can you tell me what is going on? I've been so caught up these days…and I need to hear again the story of my character…"

"The story of your character?"

"Yes… The one that I'm supposed to play…"

"You are playing Vlad the Impaler, the father of Mihaela and Gabriela… his twin daughters… Vlad is a tormented being, half-man, half-vamp who could find his peace neither in his human life, nor as a vampire…. His strongest wish is to marry his beautiful daughter Mihaela, to change his doomed heart through her innocent love…"

"And does he marry her?" Davidson asks with curious eyes of a child.

"You tell me…" Donna smiles, showing Davidson to his dressing room.

Double spotlight on Beverly Dreams' stage.

Mihaela faces Gabriela who is dressed as a man.

Mihaela: *You killed my man and put his clothing on! You bring him back or I will break your neck!*

Gabriela: *Let's face the real fact! Look in my eyes, feel deep this heart. It's dead! I am your boyfriend and your wicked clone, two into one, all for your love and fun!*

Mihaela: *You think that I am not a vampire anymore? Well, it's neither my teeth, nor my blood, nor Papa or you that makes me be a vampire—it is my passion and my godly love that lights in me the fire! Oh, in the name of Love—I will attack! I'm gonna show you who's the vamp!*

Gabriela: *Oh, show me your beloved fangs! But I assure you that I'm your man!*

Mihaela takes a stake in her hand.

Mihaela: *I'm gonna impale you, Demon!*
Gabriela: *I'm ready for you! Come and get me, leman!*

Gabriela grabs a stake in her hand too. The twins begin to stake-fight. Gabriela laughs, Mihaela is on fire.

Vlad's voice speaks to Mihaela & Gabriela through a gigantic mirror in the shape of an eye:

Destroy each other, daughters! Show Papa who is stronger: the vampire or the mortal?

Backstage, Donna shows Davidson his performance costume.

Davidson gives off a warm smile, though his body shakes like an aspen leaf... He clears his throat and rubs his thighs, trying to pull himself together. He doesn't know if he's dreaming or if he's living... And yet, he doesn't want to step out of this game.

As Donna unwraps Davidson's costume—an extravagant robe with large sleeves and a tall turban with a red serpent coiled around its wide silky edges, Davidson lets out a big liberating laughter:

"I haven't seen such a costume in my whole life! Am I supposed to wear this on stage tonight?"

Donna gives a quirky smile and shows Davidson the *Wicked Clone* script. Davidson drops on the couch and skims through the pages, his hands still shivering, his left eye twitching...

"Now, if everything is in order...please, allow me to go back to Mr. Dressman. He might need me on the main floor..."

"Sure," Davidson replies like an automaton, his eyes stolen by the script.

As Donna makes her way out, Davidson jumps off the couch and runs after her.

"Excuse me...what scene are we rehearsing today?" he asks, briskly.

Donna glances at him kindly, afterwich she points out the lines that Davidson is to rehearse.

"For God's sake! Only two lines to memorize?" Davidson exclaims, relieved.

As Donna vanishes in the darkness of the lounge, Davidson starts practicing his lines, looking at himself in the mirror, with pride. Declaiming his part loud and sharp, and starting to feel more and more comfortable, a cold hand stretches out, clasping his shoulder.

"Hey, who are you? What are you doing here, dressed up in my costume?" a low timbered voice asks Davidson from behind.

Davidson turns around, scared to death. In front of him, he sees…himself, a guy looking just like him…

"Who are you?" Davidson asks the man, utterly puzzled.

"Who are *you?*" the man fires back, huffishly.

"I am… I am playing Vlad…" Davidson stutters.

"What do you mean, Vlad? That's my part," the man fights back.

"Your part?"

"Yes, I am Vlad."

The main stage, Beverly Dreams Hotel.

Mihaela and Gabriela fight more and more aggressively.
The thunder and rain stop. Sunlight.
God's voice: *Mihaela dear, put down the stake! Take in your hand the pen!*
You won't change your sister if you seek revenge like mindless mortals!
You'll change her if you and her build up something immortal!
Mihaela stops. She then turns to her sister:
Let's stop the fight for God's sake!
Gabriela: *You wanted the stake!*
And in a flash, Gabriela pierces Mihaela with the stake.
Mihaela collapses.
Mihaela: *I'm dying, sister…*
Gabriela: *You can't die…*
Mihaela: *You pierced me so strong… I'm not a vampire any more… I am weak, I feel old and meek, I need your help; the cut is fatal. Get me to my dear table.*
Gabriela: *Anything, sweet sister… Forgive me, but your pain just makes me bless my fangs… Let me give you a kiss and turn you back into my real sis!*

Mihaela: *No, never! Fulfill me, please, one wish before I die...*
See this manuscript?
Mihaela hands Gabriela the manuscript and speaks on*: This is my*
play... It is called Wicked Clone... Please, take it in your hands and write
the music notes!

Backstage. Davidson is seated on the couch, petrified.

He cannot move. The meeting with Vlad, that actor, or with himself, or with the one who looked like him...really scared the bones out of him.

He tries not to think, his thoughts are blocked, his eyes stuck on the Wicked Clone script.

Mihaela storms in the dressing room, sweaty and panting. Davidson jumps at her with killing eyes:

"Do you think it's funny? What's this? A birthday joke? You brought me here, distracted me from my case... We have to go back. Now! This whole thing is outrageous. I am serious man!"

"Are you afraid?" Mihaela asks Davidson with keen eyes.

"No. I feel mocked. You are perfidious, dissimulative, but know to play it well..."

"What do you mean?" Mihaela cuts him off.

"You knew the whole text; everything is your plot. We are not in 2014! This is your script to mess around with me. We are going back to the City of Stars! Now! Actually we are in the City of Stars, aren't we? God, I don't know anything anymore... I'm losing my mind!"

"Fine, go back to your Stars!" Mihaela shouts out at Davidson.

"Oh, yes? Ok, I'm out and done with you! I'll come say hi to you tomorrow morning...with a pair of handcuffs. And don't use perfume please. I'm allergic!"

"Sure, I won't put on perfume!"

Davidson exits Beverly Dreams Hotel by the fire stairs.
He gets into a cab, alarmed and angry.
"To...555 Police Department, The City of Stars, please..."
"What's that?" the cab driver asks.
"Actually, to the airport, please," Davidson corrects himself.
On the way to the airport, Davidson passes the driver a one hundred-dollar bill.
"What's that?" the driver asks, bewildered.
"One hundred dollars! I pay you now so that I won't lose time when we get there."
"I've never seen this kind of bill before, Sir. It's a mistake..."
"I don't need the change."
"Sir, I want to be paid. This is not real money..."
"What do you mean not real money?"
"Sir, my boss cannot accept such papers."
"Which year does your boss live in?"
"Sir, he lives in 2014...like all of us..."
"What? Did she fool around with you too? Are you part of her play? Corrupted girl!"
Davidson gets out of the cab, kicks the driver's car, and shouts out enraged:
"Tell her to pay you! She's got the right papers!"
Then, wiping away his sweat, he asks an old lady:
"Excuse me, which year are we in?"
"Year? I live in 2014, my son," the lady cracks a smile. "Even though I wish I lived in the fifties...and wear my hair like those bonita ladies and senoritas... Tupidupidu!"
"You're too old... You live in the past..." Davidson grumbles. "Hey, you!" he stops a kid on the street, "Tell me, which year are we in?"
"Year? 2014, Sir. Do you need directions?"
"Yes... How can I reach 2033?"
"I'm afraid Papa would know better..."

The kid starts shouting towards a window at the top of his lungs:

"Papa! A man needs your help! Papa!" the boy screams louder and louder.

His father shows up with a broad smile and a pen tucked behind his ear.

"How may I help you, Sir? Do you need anything?" the father asks, kindly.

"Yes, I do…" Davidson replies, trying to keep his nerve. "I am stuck in 2014, or at least that's what your son says, that we live in 2014… See, I live in 2033, but a girl played a trick on me and… Well, what am I talking about? We all live in 2033. I have an important appointment this evening and I need to get to the police Department, on the Avenue of Stars, as soon as possible!"

"Well," the father speaks calmly, "I can find a way to help you out. Why don't we talk upstairs, in my office?"

"Who are you?"

"Calm down," the father taps Davidson on his shoulder, "I only want to help. Come with me. I have my office in this building, right here."

Davidson consents.

They walk upstairs, to the man's office.

An elegant bureau of red leather with tons of books and paper files, welcomes them. On top of the books, a black cat, dressed up in a mannish suit and bow tie, fixes Davidson with grinning eyes.

Davidson is invited to take a seat. The father takes a seat too, and the cat jumps down on his lap, eager to be caressed.

"So tell me Mr.…."

"Davidson…"

"Yes, Mr. Davidson. Where are you from?"

"I was born in New York City. Actually, I am trying to catch a plane as soon as possible to the City of Stars… I have an important meeting there and…"

"Which is your occupation, if you don't mind?"

"I am a detective, I work for the CIA."

"I see… Since when?"

"Well, since…2012."

"2012?"

"Yes, that's right."

"Would you, please, describe to me…how did this all start? Do you have any relatives who also live in 2033?"

"Yes, all my family…"

"I see… So there's a history…"

The father takes notes.

"So, are you going to help me or not?" Davidson asks him, losing his calm. "I'm in a hurry… Earlier, I tried to pay the taxi driver with this money and he didn't accept it… Crazy world!"

Davidson shows the father his one hundred dollar bill.

Lost in his notes, the father doesn't even look up, but replies to Davidson promptly:

"Oh, don't worry about it… This is just the first session…to get to know you better… You don't have to pay me anything…"

"What do you mean? Are you mocking at me? Do you think that I am kind of a psychopath?"

"Oh, no, not at all," the father replies. "But I have to understand where this comes from… We need to see each other more often… I can really help you."

Davidson jumps to his feet and exits the office, like a thunderbolt.

"Wait, wait… I can really help you! " the doctor screams after Davidson like a mad man.

With his face contorted and his eyes searching for Violeta,

Vlad pierces the stony ground with his stake-like scepter. His angry steps quake the dark corridor, the loyal walls of his old castle cracking and peeling off like the shrivelled skin of a dead animal.

"Violeta, my love, I have your daughter right here with me—your sweetest Mihaela—remember? She wants to say Hi to her Mommy… Where are you hiding? Come out, my dear!"

Circling his own shadow, Vlad arrives in front of the magic mirror. He stops from his trembling, gazing at his human half.

"Look at you! Writer and producer of *Wicked Clone*! Who would have thought? I finally have managed to write that monologue... So I can... So I am..." Vlad mumbles with a hopeful voice.

Then, scrubbing the ice in his cheeks with his left hand, he changes his tone, mumbling with lust: "I love catching her with art and magic! Loyal dearest mirror! I feel like a wizard, fantastically endowed and aroused! Everything is well enough prepared for my little bride! Now, if I can put Mama next to her, beautiful and healthy as she was, Mihaela can touch her face and...she'll recognize that I am her beloved Dad that made her wish come true! Hooray! No, no, no, no! What am I saying? I resolved that I am not her real father—Mihaela was born of a miraculous flower... Forget the mother just for now... She's probably roaming in the cave, or dozing in her bed...as Lucifer has said. I have to trust him... I have to. There's no one more powerful than Lucifer who's taking care of me... Besides, he needs me too. So...where was I? Ah, at midnight, I can talk to Mihaela about her dreams and share to her my feelings about her play and tell her that I am more than happy to invest in it...and then... Well, I'd better write this down! I love to be prepared. I need to phrase it the right way. It's an important speech, that ought to save my life this very eve!"

Rejuvenated by the new mission of his life,

Vlad descends the stairs that lead into his Icy Morgue of Brides. He steps into the cool healing waters, jollying with hellish faith:

"Violeta dear, are you down here, taking a bath? I know that it feels good... Let me wrap up a warm gown around your cold body..."

A rustling noise flutters behind him. Vlad turns around, with sparkle in his eyes:

"Aha, there you are, Mama!"

He sneaks up, with silent steps, towards the icicled blue curtain where the sound seems to come from. He flings the curtain open, but instead of discovering Violeta's livid body, he unveils the arched back of Vlady.

"You, here?" Vlad utters with total dissatisfaction.

Savagely, he starts hitting his disobedient boy who has been scribbling on some papers with a broken feather.

"Didn't I tell you to go after her? Why did you let her go? Do you want your Mama to scare the Lord's birds and betray again your Papa?" Vlad asks his son with flashes of anger.

Vlady, with his hands above his head, stutters:

"I'm sorry, I'm sorry!"

His papers drop off his hands.

"All right, all right..." Vlad pats him on his head, snatching the manuscript from Vlady's hands.

"No, no!" Vlady screams, crawling at the feet of his father, trying to take his papers back.

But Vlad clutches the papers in his claws and disappears with them in a dark corner of the morgue.

"You can't take them away from me! They are mine!" Vlady cries after Vlad, with the heartbreaking cry of a sickly boy.

Pale and half dead, Vlady carries his wounded body through the Icy Morgue of Brides, groaning for help. "Maaa...agiaaaaa!" His heart bleeds; his dumb way of speaking seems to have come back.

With his eyes red and steaming revenge,

Vlad flips through the rusted pages of Vlady.

Trembling with fury, he squeeezes them in his hands, after which he locks them inside a coffer.

"Vlady, my boy, whom I have kept safe in my home... Is this your gratefulness, son of a sinful woman? I pulled your tongue out to let your hand betray me?"

Vlad's face suddenly grows older. He walks again through the dark tunnel that leads into the Icy Morgue, reaching behind the iced blue curtain where he found Vlady. His left shoulder twitches, his hands itch with anger, his eyes sore, marred by the dark scars of the past. With a shaky movement of his wrist, he grabs two of his short golden stakes from his panoply of stakes, after which he pushes it open, the weaponry board suddenly cracking magically, like a secret door, unveiling a blue bright corridor. Untouched by its beauty, Vlad walks at a funeral pace through the large corridor that shortens at every step that he takes, until it reaches a small gray rotative door. The gray door has a frozen sun built in, that keeps the place cool, hindering any type of heat. In fact, all of the castle's gates and doors have been designed to reduce the solar heat-gain to maximum, shading the ultraviolet screening and casting a dark grayish atmosphere over the entire castle. Except for Dora's heavenly chamber, which has been bathed in sun rays and adorned with crystal windows and doors, clear and bright as the angels' beaming eyes.

Vlad rotates the cold sun with his long nailed fingers. The door unfolds with a symphonic sound, revealing a long toboggan, edged wih tall, dark flames. Vlad grins, closes his eyes, and lets himself go down the toboggan, screaming draconically throughout the whole burning-slide. The fire-toboggan gets him through all the underground levels of his castle, inflaming his sight and arousing his mind.

At the end of the ride, Vlad's feet touch an icy ground, covered by little shiny stalagmites and clear water that rapidly cools the flames of his ankles. Purple steam rises above the water.

On a huge piece of argyle is carved in Romanian with hyperbolic letters: *Triunghiul lui Dracula / Dracula's Triangle.*

Arrows of fire are marking the trajectory: the right arrow, points towards the tunnel that goes to Bucharest[30] and to the Monastery of Snagov[31]; the left arrow invites towards the catacombs to the Bran Castle[32]; the vertical arrow towards *The Icy Morgue of Brides* which continues with the road to Târgoviște[33].

Vlad leaps to the left. A horrible Hunting Bitch awaits him, naked and vibrating with sexual splendor. She bows with gratitude in front of Vlad who slaps her on her prominent posterior, suddenly growing younger, lustfulness pricking his veins.

Through a labyrinth with rusty reddish tunnels and restless graves, steamy and eery, swarming with gnawers and smelling of rotten bones and stinking blood, clotted for ages, the Hunting Bitch makes way for her master Vlad.

"Welcome to your beloved Bran Castle, my Lord," the bitch utters with an erotic voice.

At the end of the labyrinth, an imperial red curtain unfolds to their eyes. Along the curtain, craftsmen-spiders keep sewing the curtain, as they have been doing all their lives; some of them, which reached the end of their silky thread, fall dead to the ground, others give birth to spider babies which immediately take on the job. Once they see Vlad, the spiders withdraw silently onto the ceiling. In sign of veneration, they form the letter "V" with their front articulated legs.

Ceremoniously, with her luscent yellowish claws, the Hunting Bitch pulls the imperial curtain to the side, unveiling the most avantgarde work of art. A huge film camera comes into sight, showing, through its gigantic

---

[30] *Bucharest,* the current capital of Romania, was one of the residences of Vlad the Impaler. It dates from the end of the 14th century, but it was Vlad the Impaler who first issued the document which attested the name of the city of Bucharest (on September the 20th, 1459).

[31] *The Monastery of Snagov* was founded near Bucharest in the late 14th century, on a wonderful islet in the middle of the lake Snagov, where Vlad the Impaler was reportedly buried.

[32] *Bran Castle* is commonly known as "Dracula's Castle." It is situated near Braşov, on the border between Transylvania and Wallachia. It is one among several locations linked to Vlad's history and legend, including "Poenari Castle" and "Hunyad Castle."

[33] *Târgovişte, The Royal Court* served as the capital of Wallachia, where Vlad ruled. It was here that Vlad impaled a great many disloyal court members (the boyars who killed his father and blinded and buried alive his older brother) after inviting them to a celebratory feast. Chindia Tower, added by Vlad later to The Royal Court, is the symbol of Târgovişte and houses an exhibition illustrating Vlad's life.

lens shaped like an eye, a spacious frozen royal theater equipped with glistening screens of ice.

"I designed this film camera together with my friends from the 19th Century: the Lumière brothers..." Vlad discloses to the Hunting Bitch that licks his ear with pleasure. "Care to know how I did it?"

"Of course, master... Tell me..." the Hunting Bitch whispers, after which she kneels down, preparing her claw to scrape on her porcelain skin.

"Well... It's been a terrible adventure. But sacrifice always brings forth a reward! Dora is to be blamed for. It was her idea to build this magnificent camera that sometimes bleeds tears out of its human tape, craving my sweetheart... Yes, the tape has been manufactured from her fine, porcelain skin; the lens have been designed from her left eye, from Dora's beloved eyeball of eternal light... The motor of the camera is Dora's heart set in motion by her uncoiling spine, fractured and arranged in circles of polished bones that I named "the wheels of love"; her hands and arms are the levers and handholders; her legs and soles of her feet are the triapod and pedal controllers...and her hair is...the main curtain of the stage that can take any shape, rotate, elongate, separate, dissipate... "

The Hunting Bitch stares in awe at the aristocratic but super-modern theater.

"And so, *Wicked Clone* will be the first musical-show to benefit of my miraculous, magical and ultrafine camera which will catch all the rehearsals and representations of my daughters in motion... Then, all the material will be stored and rewarded at the *Eternal History of Arts, Film, Science and Theater Foundation of Vampirology*... I am the president, founder and chairman," he utters with pride. "Thus being said, soon, very soon, this amazing theater, with all its supernatural and ground-breaking equipment, will be transported in Times Square... I named it *Dracula's Time Theater*, especially for my twin daughters, to make my name live as long as the Sun dwells above the Earth ..."

From down the steamy waters, ten Hunting Bitches rise their heads and bodies, floating like winged godesses. They all fly and circle Vlad's livid shadow, listening to his words with enchantment.

Vlad takes heart, rejoicing like a famous actor. He then clears his throat and begins to speak, as if holding a speech at the Academy Awards Ceremony:

"My beloved bitches, I am proud to present to you—*Dracula's Time Theater*—*the most innovative theater,* provided with circular mobile walls and with rotative cinema-screens, with invisible video doors and dark stimulative rooms. We are to project fantastic imagery on big screens of ice that will expand and shorten according to the dramatism and dynamism of each scene. The projections will display my castle, my universe, my beloved twin daughters, my experimental labs that harbor corpses of Ottomans and boyars impaled on valubale stakes of bronze and gold. I shall also unveil my unique museum of bear-heros, wolf-heros, lynx-heros, serpent-heros, raven-heros, and other animals and birds which have gloriously attacked my enemies in battles and which have been rewarded by me...their mastermind, with golden inscribed medals... The audience will gaze at everything from inside electric chairs which will rotate whenever images and scenes will be displayed throughout the cinema-screens. The electric shocks which will accompany the horror scenes will help the audience truly get involved in the action of the play and discover their own wicked clone... Moreover, to produce a face-to-face cinematic experience, the characters will come out of the screens and will perform around the chairs, popping out from the underground and surrounding the crowd...and then they'll enter back into the screens, thus creating a continous marriage between reality and illusion, natural and supernatural..."

"Gosh, you are a genius, Vlad..." the Ballerina Bitch utters, dazzled and releasing fumes of lust.

"Ohhh... I'm just trying to help my daughters... Mihaela has written the play... Me and Lucifer are just adjusting it, cutting through it and rewriting the ending scene... Actually our version is very different...more erotically inclined... That's what people want, right? The ending will be an amazing wedding between me and Mihaela who will be dressed in the magnificent gown that has been sewn by my hard-working ravens... Icicled pearls and regal gilded lace are going to beguile the mortals' eyes and face! And me...ah, my costume is being designed from the finest silk and stalagmites, dilligently woven by my loyal spider women. My face will look so much radiant and younger and my body tantalizing and muscled, ready for unforgettable nights of pleasure... Oh, and here are some of Mihaela's sketches for the *Wicked Clone'* cast—only to be seen by your crafty eyes, sleazy Hunting bitches... They will be exposed in shiny windows and advertized in the Hall of Mirrors from Dracula's Time Theater! But until then, don't spill a word lest your dirty tongues be pulled out."

The hairiest Hunting Bitch of all snatches Mihaela's design sketches into her yellowish claws. She looks at them keenly, and then tattoos them on her voluptuous thighs with a small stake well soaked in her own blood.

"We'll work on the sewing too... We'll make them look horribly nice!" the hairiest Hunting Bitch exclaims, rubbing her buttocks against the Ballerina Bitch.

"I want the whole universe to know of my theater, of my camera, of my castle, of my inventions—my secrets to the immortal art of entertainment!" Vlad continues his speech, caressing the walls where he has buried alive so many honorable guests. "Bitches, spread the word in the whole world! Begin the promotion of my show!"

And Vlad bursts into laughter, thundering the walls of the theater. The Hunting Bitches giggle, turning their chubby posteriors to titillate Vlad's cold body.

However, in a flash, as Vlad lays his eyes on a gate's inscription, his face embraces a horrible disguise, his eyes flickering like a mad child. "Go! Leave me alone," he orders the temptresses of hell.

He snaps his fingers twice and two flamed figure skates pop from the underground, fastening around his bony feet of ice. Passing by the *The Pit of the Wolves*, where some of his good enemies had found their tombs, Vlad enters the "Icy Gallery of the Impaled"—his fun museum with corpses and busts sheltered inside blocks of bloodied ice... Vlad's feet begin to slide like a professional skater's through a variety of statues that embody his friends and foes of ages... He claps his hands up high, pivoting his legs and mantle in the steam of ice, like a menacing raging bat. He then brakes with his skates, and frowning his whole face and body, stabs a freshly sculpted statue with his long enraged nails:

"You feel it deep into your heart, Emil, aren't you?"

Emil's eyes are popped out of their sockets; his neck and body fringy and decomposed.

"You would have wanted to rape my beloved Mihaela before the wedding night, wouldn't you? But wasn't it unbearable for me to see you dirtying her body that I have blossomed in her mother's womb? What have you done, Emil Mehmed? Aren't you ashamed, you rotten playboy junk?"

Grabbing a short but very sharp stake, Vlad begins to impale ceaselessly the statue of ice that hides the body of Emil Mehmed, Mihaela's fiancé, murdered by Gabriela in 1983, in the eve of their wedding day. "To be or not to be...staked! That is the question!" Vlad recites at the top of his rage.

Abruptly, hundreds of shards of ice collapse furisously upon Vlad as if ready to disfigure him and avenge Mihaela's ill-fated fiancé.

Then, as he bumps into the round, thickened head of a Turkish man, covered up by a golden turban, Vlad fires blue blood out of his angry nostrils:

"And you, restless pathetic prince of Turkey, tell me, was that so hard to take your turban off and kneel your pride before my throne? We knew each other for so long! You fathomed that my rules were doomed-strong! Why did you do me wrong?"

Shaking his finger with perversity, Vlad softens his tone with striking obscenity:

"Hmmm...Crimeea, your beautiful wife, got your blood boiling, didn't she? Good, beautiful woman, you loved to penetrate her, didn't you? And now, in the name of love, receive these nails into your brains and into your lower remains!"

And Vlad starts hammering long nails through the frozen turban of the Turk, straight to his brains, and then down there, between his frozen loins.

"See how lovely these nails are piercing your skull? You pined for them, old pal! Now you will have your turban on forever! Oh, let me take the two of you a picture! I can't let a historical moment like this fade into the past!"

And Vlad lifts up a dirty bloodied cloth, uncovering an antique polished wood camera.

"Smile...and bingo! Beautiful! Tomorrow, by 4 pm, you can come and pick it up! I'll have it ready for you, with retouch!"

"Now let's have some fun!" Vlad jumps up in the air and clicks his skates together.

Then, he glides away from the broken statues of ice and places himself before the photo camera, posing and fooling around like a happy groom.

"Enough! I said enough with these childish old games! Now you are a different Vlad!" he speaks in a serious voice, slapping himself on his face.

Speedily, he covers the old photo camera with the dirty bloodied cloth, and skates his way out of the pit, clambering up onto a golden platform. The Hunting Bitches moan and quaver with disharmonized voices:

"Stay with us, Vlad... Let's make love..."

"I have a lot of work to do... Now I am Vlad the Creator, Vlad the Director, Vlad the Producer! I am happy, so happy! I will fast for my bride and fest all night! Let the music play! Mihaela gives sense to my lifeless days! That's why I love her...love her...love her...." he shouts euphorically, hearing his own echo as the golden platform rises him to the top of the castle.

Late night.

Vlady runs through the heartless forest that surrounds Vlad's dilapidated castle, like a lunatic. His eyes search for Mama... Crickets accompany his lifeless steps.

Wandering through the same forest, an unfinished Violeta meets Rommy, her white and handsome horse whom she had raised with so much love and care. Now Rommy is a waif like her, his white skin turned into dark-blue, his wet eyes—red and scared like of a wounded bear...

Gabriela had stolen Rommy from Mihaela and had bitten him, thus pulling him under her curse and turning him into a vampire-horse.

Mihaela poured holy grains from Magia upon his head to bring him to his spirit, yet Rommy did not bat an eye, still roaming between light and dark.

Nevertheless, as soon as Rommy catches a glimpse of Violeta, he rises up on his two hind legs and gives a wild neigh of happiness. He then bends before Violeta and kisses her hand, taking a seat next to her, awaiting to be straddled again.

Violeta mounts Rommy-horse, yet one of her feet remains stuck in the mud.

Rommy starts galloping with proudness and Violeta loses one of her arms, too. Thrilled by the happy chills of the past, Rommy shakes his body, his skin becoming a little lighter.

With her bright and long hair brushing the air, Violeta keeps singing *Ave Maria.* Her soothing, heavenly voice can heal the heart of the cruelest man on earth. Rommy shakes the second time and his hide becomes light blue.

Vlady hears Violeta's voice echoing through the forest, and starts weeping like a child:

"Mama, Mommy…"

But too late. Rommy opens up large wings, rising with Violeta to the blue sky, fast as happiness' stride in a man's life…

At noon. Rommy and Violeta have arrived in L.A..

The Sun strikes strongly upon Violeta's remaining bones. Her flesh and blood have begun to melt like butter in a red burning stove… It seems that whatever is against the law of God melts away…

But Rommy looks happy. Violeta's heart, full and warm, seats proudly onto his back. Rommy covers it with his long tail…and with the thick hair of his mane he shields it from the strong rays of the sun… His skin has become white as when he was born…

With tears of joy in his eyes, he rides fast as the wind towards Beverly Dreams Hotel to bring Mama's heart to Mihaela, his long-misssed mistress.

Growling hysterically, Vlad pays Lucifer another unannounced visit, sneaking through the muddy butts of the snoring Hunting Bitches. They all sleep with their eyes wide open, naked and unashamed.

Lucifer is dozing upside down.

"Lucifer, I don't feel well! Where is she?" Vlad whines to Lucifer's back, who, for the first time, gets scared to life. Lucifer makes a horrible somersault, landing on his horns, deformed. After sprucing up and cleaning his lingering saliva with his tail, he gnarrs with indignation, taking a grotesque, infernal face:

"Again? You?"

"I need to know! Am I going to see her tonight? I feel my heart on the verge to explode… This waiting is boiling my blood, but when I touch my heart, it's thudding with frost…" Vlad speaks with panic.

"Everything's fine!" Lucifer growls, irritated by Vlad's laments.

"Tell me something…a little detail…" Vlad pleads.

"Everything's fine! Trust my growl!" And Lucifer growls.

"Let me know when she arrives!"

"Of course…how couldn't I? We have a deal!" Lucifer growls again, showing his tongue in disgust.

"Yes, yes… Do you know when they are going to arrive?" Vlad persists.

"Everything's fine! I'm going to reach out for you later tonight! Do you hear or do you need new ears?"

And Lucifer grinds his decayed teeth twice, spits vomit in the eyes of Vlad and storms him out of Hell's gates like a barking dog in the rain.

Vlad cries with tears of ice like a little boy in the night. This whole waiting is shrivelling his skin, boiling his cells and making his sins itch like hell. And, most crushable, Lucifer has become impossible, making his life excruciable! Hell doesn't like him anymore, Heaven is too high for his low life...

"I can't think about it any more, my mind is weltered in gore..." Vlad mourns.

Vlad moves from one shadow of his bedroom to another, his face melting in the light of the purple candle that he had lit up for his long-expected bride.

"All is prepared, my sweetheart! All! Everything's fine! But when are you coming home?" Vlad mutters in despair.

In the meantime, backstage,

Mihaela worries about Davidson. She went all around Beverly Dreams Hotel, looking for him...

"I shouldn't have let him go! He is not used to understand new, magic... He needs time!"

Gabriela exits the stage in the delirious applause of the production team, rushing backstage with a glorious smile.

"Hurry up, sis, change into the purple outfit! They love it!"

"No," Mihaela says resolutely. "What's this whole game about? How did this happen? Who set it up? This is my *Wicked Clone* play, yet no one knows that I'm the one who wrote it! You changed the ending without asking me! Now it's a total mess!"

"Not me, Papa!" Gabriela speaks, giving the game away. "We thought that you would like it..."

"Papa? What does he have to do with this? How does he know? I broke the mirror!"

"Oh, sister... Papa's mourning... He misses you so badly! You're blood from his blood!" Gabriela quickly changes the tone. "Please, come back home with me for just one week! We'll write together the rest of the notes for our Wicked Clone tunes and we'll even have time to play games like in our sisterhood! Remember how much fun we used to have when taking each other by surprise, making funny faces and putting on your hand-made dresses?" Gabriela giggles. "In your bittersweet garden with your giant Queen of the Night flower, you told me to improvise, to mimic, teaching me how to act! We had such a blast! You were the master and me—a dog barking a folk song! You played the loving mother and me—a naughty party lover! In joy, without a pinch of hatred, we were once frolicking; we were two Siamese kittens, inseparable in every little thing. We used to be so close, hilarious little folks: an angel and a wicked clone! Ha, ha, ha..."

"Gabriela, I can't stay here anymore... When I am near you, I change, I lose my control... My veins swell and my blood boils... I feel evil entering my bones... I'm sorry, I'm leaving you and all this creepy show! I can't go on..."

Barely does Mihaela finish her speech when Gabriela drops with a loud thud at her feet.

Mihaela looks at her sister, untouched and sad, but Gabriela lies there, pale and numb, without moving a hair or batting an eye. Grasped by mercy, Mihaela jumps over her sister and hugs her body, kissing her cheeks that feel so cold...

"Please, take me with you! I've changed, sweet sister!" Gabriela abruptly opens her eyes, hugging frantically Mihaela's warm body. "Forgive me for what I've done to you and for the wickedness that I have shown! I know that you loved David, Emanuel, Emil, Liam...and the whole crew of *Wicked Clone*! I could not control my foolish jealousy! But I have been praying for forgiveness. I hope that God forgives me! I will tell the cops the truth—that I am the one that they should handcuff, and not the pure you! I shall unveil myself in front of Davidson and spare you from all the sorrow, from something you don't deserve to be punished for! I just want to make peace with you, my dear sis! Please, forgive me..."

Mihaela looks strangely at her sister. She speaks about praying, about God and forgiveness? Is this a dream? It is too good to be true. Indeed, now her sister acts more like a human being, fainting and repenting, she no longer has red wicked eyes, betraying no feelings of regret... She feels something has changed in her.

Mihaela breathes a sigh of relief and hugs Gabriela with burning arms of a loving sis:

"Welcome to life, Gabriela! I have been waiting for so long to see you changed this way! This is a miracle, sister!" she raises her eyes to the sky.

"Oh, I love you, Mihaela!" Gabriela chokes her sister with strong hugs of happiness. "I felt miserable without you, in that cold, excremental castle of Vlad! You are my ray of sun!"

"Thank you for this words! I still cannot believe it's you who talks!"

"No, it's not me! It's Mommy Doll's voice!" Gabriela winks to Mihaela as a frolicsome sparkle plays funnily in her eyes.

"By the way, have you seen Mommy Doll? I've been searching for her everywhere..." Mihaela takes another tone, suddenly sweaty and agitated.

"I haven't seen her... I'm sorry!" Gabriela cuts her sister off, promptly. "Hmm...maybe Davidson stole your Mommy..."

"Maybe... I left her here, before entering the stage and when I came back..."

Gabriela gives out a belly laugh, after which she pulls Mommy Doll out of her chest.

"Here she is, Sis! Mommy can never ever leave us alone! She loves us, doesn't she? Anyhow, she has no legs to run away! Ha, ha! Only a heart of wood... I mean of love!"

"Gabriela, another wicked surprise?! I thought you were done with that!"

"Have a little sense of humor, spiritual queen! What good to live if only serious and playing no witty jokes on your beloved Sis?"

"Indeed..." Mihaela tries to fake on a smile while hugging Mommy Doll to her chest, tight. "Alright! I shall take you with me to the City of Stars! But no bloodsheds! Never ever! Promise?"

"I promise!" Gabriela complies, saluting with her muscle arm like a soldier.

"No late nights escapades?"

"Promise!"

"No boyfriends tracked down?"

"Promise!"

"Very well!" Mihaela cries out like a captain. "I shall give you a one-week probation! But you are not allowed to speak to Davidson. Not until things calm down! Now come along! We have to find him!"

"No, wait a second!" Mihaela changes her mind. "First and foremost I shall send you to the City of Stars, to 2033. Here's the address. Go to my apartment and wait for me there! Don't talk to anybody, please! I'll be back by the end of the day."

Mihaela places her forehead on Gabriela's forehead and utters the magic words as her star emerges, flickering violet lights:

"I love you!"

"I love you too!" Gabriela says.

Mihaela waits for the tunnel of light to unveil, but her third eye shuts in, like the house of a snail within.

"It doesn't work! Let's do it again!" Mihaela murmurs, wondering what could have gone wrong.

"I know another trick! Don't worry about me," Gabriela assures her sister, "Go and find Davidson! I'll be fine!"

"Are you sure?"

"I love you!" Gabriela kisses Mihaela's cheeks with red gleams in her eyes.

"One more thing," Mihaela chimes in. "Take this purple cross. It will keep us united. And this time, don't you take it off your neck—not for the world! Promise?"

"I promise!" Gabriela complies, crossing her heart.

Mihaela places the chain with purple cross around Gabriela's long neck. The cross begins to trepidate around Gabriela's chest, making her blood vessels suddenly visible and red.

The twins kiss each other like in their happy days of childhood.

Filled with tears of happiness, Mihaela twirls in the air, setting forth to find Davidson.

Mihaela: *This was one of the happiest days of my life!*

In front of the Beverly Dreams Hotel, the white horse Rommy sits tall and bright, shaking his tail joyously, waiting for his mistress to appear before his eyes. With Mama's heart onto his back, wrapped up in his strong tail, he hopes for the perfect reunion.

Down in his stinky tunnels, Lucifer floats on the Dead Black Sea, overflown with baby blue sharks and voluptuous red-haired mermaids. The sea stormily carries Lucifer's ship, laden with wandering spiders, black widows, mole vipers, scorpions, rattlesnakes and many other venomous reptiles, multiple-headed or endowed with manifold tails...

The smiling blue sharks swim viciously among pieces of diamonds, colorful rubies, gold chains, and stinking trash...laying their eyes onto the sensual mermaids which undulate naked bodies flirtiously before the sharks' aroused teeth...

Lucifer watches everything through his red, flaming binoculars, salivating salaciously.

Suddenly, his lenses get filmy. He cannot see Gabriela any longer.

He frets, crimson with fury, his skin opening into awful wounds, spiked up with fur and bubonic plague.

Blowing curses out of his hellish mouth, he lets out contaminated and excremental words: " Horned viperish daughter of a deranged paralitic father! Where is she? Bloody Bitch! I told her to bring Mihaela here immediately after the show!"

His spiky metals of his shipman jacket suddenly catch fire.

With an abrupt move of his greased paws, smelling of burnt pork rind and red worm odor, Lucifer turns the wheel of his crocodile-leathered ship 180 degrees.

"What has that obnoxious Gabriela done to me? We have a deal! Cerberus, find Vlad!" Lucifer screams at his leading servant, his voice almost blowing out of his lungs.

2033. *Italian Restaurant "Therapy through Love" Downtown, The City of Stars.*

Roller bladed-waitresses and waiters slide from one table to the other, taking good care of their "patients." Decked with heart-shaped tables and soft, vibrating chairs, the restaurant oozes with love-enhancing therapists who walk around the restaurant to the troubled men and women who have purchased the "love" therapy meal. The sensual, enigmatic music played by an ecstatic DJ, clad in a tuxedo, tight-fitting, with heart-shaped bow tie pinned onto his white impeccable shirt, and silver skinny trousers reaching to red pointed shoes of patent leather, keeps the waiters' feet sliding at an euphoric speed...

"I'm glad we're back! I still cannot believe the ride on your white horse... This puts a question mark on everything that I used to think possible..." Davidson utters, savoring a glass of wine.

"I'm glad that you eventually arrived at your meeting," Mihaela says with a subtle smile.

"Yes... What a life you got me into..."

"Into...?" Mihaela looks at Davidson gently.

"That whole game seemed so real!" Davidson exclaims with his eyes wide awake.

"Game?" Mihaela frowns. "Why did you invite me here?"

"Well, you have the power to hypnotize men... It is no wonder that people suspect you. Your imagination is contagious...Was it always like that?"

"I haven't thought about it..."

"Come on..." Davidson pats Mihaela on her hand.

"No, it doesn't work with all men... See, I have this third eye through which I can see more than I sometimes want to..."

Silence. Davidson is searching for the third eye.

"I don't see it!"

"Search more..." Mihaela speaks, hesitatingly. "Waiter, check, please."

"No, that's on me," Davidson cuts her off.

"I was so scared when it first appeared..." Mihaela continues, "I thought that I was gonna die...but I was reborn..."

"Reborn? Tell me more about this third eye..."

"I don't really want to speak about it now... Well, to make a long story short, it is a sort of communication with the world beyond. It has made me...gain a totally different perspective on life...fly..."

"Have you ever talked with someone about it?"[34]

"Who can understand this but you? You're the only human being whom I have taken along...through it... Now you know it...and its power..." Mihaela winks at Davidson. "People would just want to change me...and I want to change the world... I'm aware that this eye was given to me for a reason... God has a plan with me..."

"God?"

"Yes, God. What is impossible to men is possible to God..."

"But weren't you saying that you are a vampire...?"

"I was..."

"Was? You mean a vampire can become a non-vampire?"

"Maybe..."

"How?"

"I pulled my fangs out when I was 14..."

"And since then you stopped being a vampire..."

"Yes..."

"But...aren't they coming back?"

---

[34] *Mihaela: I didn't want to tell Davidson that I've already seen tons of ophthalmologists and tons of witch doctors. Famous ones consulted me for hours and hours, with the most advanced apparatuses, and finally, they sent me to a therapist... The witch doctors tried to convince me that they knew my past and my future, but I told them that I needed help with my present... The priests spoke about law, what to do, what not to do...freaked my poor father out, but there was only one thing that made me see its enormous blessing...and fly like a dove through space and time -the Love of Him for me.*

"You mean, my fangs?"

"Yes." Davidson bursts into laughter. "Sorry, I didn't mean to..." Davidson blushes.

"That's alright!" Mihaela says, joining his laughter. "So are you going to throw me in jail on account of Meryl's death?"

"Well, I thought so until...."

"Until...when?"

"Until last night..."

"What happened? You became a priest?"

"Not exactly... Meryl's body disappeared... You might know the saying: 'No body, no crime.'"

"She disappeared?" Mihaela asks Davidson with giant eyes.

"Yes. Do you think you could help me with that?"

"For sure... Actually, I've got someone who can help us too," Mihaela smiles.

"Who?"

"You'll meet her later on..."

The DJ plays an upbeat song, turning it up to enrapture the whole crowd... Immediately, the "patients" jump up from their chairs and start singing along, clapping and dancing their troubles off.

"What's going on in here? Has everyone gone crazy? What's this song?" Davidson asks Mihaela, drops of sweat trickling down his forehead...

"Oh, it's called *David*... It's a hit! It makes them happy! Do you like it?"

"David?"

"Yes, it talks about King David and says that everyone who is named David is a lucky guy..."

"Haha, I guess I am a lucky guy!" Davidson mutters, sarcastically. "I cannot solve my case and I'm about to lose my job!"

"You mean you cannot throw me down in prison? But I'm right here, in front of your eyes!" Mihaela jokes.

Davidson pretends not to hear.

"Tell me," Mihaela changes the subject. "How did you get to talk to President Obama?"

"I don't know... You tell me. Wasn't that also part of your show?"

"No, not at all."

"All right, let's say that I believe you," Davidson speaks out, clearing his throat. Then, taking the allure of an actor, flushed up but self-assured, he recalls:

"I was tramping down L.A., along your Beverly Dreams Hotel, trying to get my way to the airport... I kept asking people how could I get myself back to City of Stars... They all grated on my nerves, giving me the same reply... Then, all I can remember is that I found myself lying inside a hospital bed, surrounded by media and paparazzi... They said that I was a star, a famous personality... Barack Obama, the President, and his wife Michelle, came to talk to me; they spirited me, they said that I was going to be fine... They said that the doctors had found two little marks of blue blood on my neck. I started to laugh. The doctors said that they were very concerned about my condition...that I needed a whole lots of blood in order to survive, but that my blood hadn't been receptive to any group of blood. Yet, I was feeling great, I was smiling non stop. Obama talked to me privately, as if I were his closest pal. He asked me if I could remember anything...anyone...from the clan that attacked me that night... I couldn't recall anything, no face, no nothing, I told him. I asked him what year we were in, if that was sort of a game or scheme... He let out a belly laughter and said that we were in the year 2014, safe and sound, surrounded by his guard. But then he frowned and sqeezed my hand with fright. He confessed to me that he himself was so afraid... He said that the White House had turned into the Red House! 'The Red House? What do you mean?' I asked... 'Well, we were attacked last night,' he said. 'They came unexpectedly, poisoned my guards with viscous, yellowish saliva thrown in their eyes and piggish snouts that left mucous tissues on the suits of my bodyguards—they were a bunch of creatures with monstrous faces and hairy arms... The video camera showed everything...disugsting, confusing, totally alarming! They looked through all the files, scanned all the accounts, they scared my daughters to death and finally they sucked the money from the banks and turned the stock market upside down! Today, the numbers lowered unimaginably, everything collapsed... Those vampires have sucked Wall Street out of its treasury! All of the state's accounts are vanishing from the computers' files! The reserve bank is desperately asking for donations! Their blood has tarnished all my work and all the country's funds and hope! They even wrote a note on my Nobel Peace Award: *Where there's money, there will be blood...* We are under those beings' curse! I am afraid! This morning, Michelle went with the girls to church! All our hope is in God!'

Then Obama asked me to join him and take the floor on his next day-campaign, fight against those horrible suckers!"

"Weird! It seems out of a novel!" Mihaela says, wonderingly. "Obama talking about vampires, about being afraid? He is an indigo child[35]... What kind of vampires? Can I see your neck?"

No sooner does she unveil Davidson's neck than two livid little marks come into sight.

"You have to come with me, right now," she speaks, suddenly taken with fright.

"What's going on?" Davidson asks, bemused.

"Everything is going to be fine, don't worry."

"Yes, I worry... Ever since I met you I feel like I'm living in this twirl...in this uncontrollable dream... Nothing feels like before, even the food tastes differently. I am thankful for feeling healthier and stronger than I ever felt, but... The thing that really bothers me is the heavy attraction that I feel towards you. It never happened to me before..."

"Shhht... Let's go!"

"I don't like women...their perfidious, manipulative way of acting, their lack of poetry... I always wanted to be a celibate. I...I never dealt with my clients this way... I always controlled myself. My file is immaculate...''

---

[35] *An **indigo child** is a person endowed with special abilities and the gift of foresight.*

"Let's not speak about that now..." Mihaela smiles. She then grabs Davidson's hand and shoves him into a cab:

"*700 Avenue of Stars*, please."

"I've told you to be gentle and to keep quiet,"

Lucifer addresses 33 creatures with monstrous faces and umbilical cords hanging loosely from their bellies. "You are my most precious team—The Haunting Vampires. I've told you that you should stay out of the media's attention. Your mission is not to become celebrities, but to slowly control society. Your mission is to kill all the unborn babies, remember? Your mission is to shake people's trust in their governors, presidents... We need to transform the White House into the Red House, now or never! One for all and all for one! Understood?" Lucifer declaims to the 33 vampires.

"Understood, your Ugliness!" the 33 Haunting vampires all nod in choir.

"But do it slowly and undercover! Preserve the pregnant mothers and contaminate them the way I have taught you... One single drop of infectious blood and their children will be born with fangs!" Lucifer titters with satisfaction.

"Remarkable," the Haunting Vampires exclaim, moving their heads in sync.

"The contamination and vampirisation was Vlad's idea!" the Ballerina Hunting Bitch chimes in. "He told me that we should..."

"Yes, sweetheart, I have to admit that he...he was disgustingly brilliant..." Lucifer cuts the Ballerina Hunting Bitch whimper off, stammering with envy. "But now I am in control and you listen to my voice! Now move on..." he turns his eyes towards the Haunting clan, growling with disgust, "And remember, no celebrity whims! Understood?"

"Understood, your Majesty," the 33 creatures bow down to the bruning ground.

The Haunting Vampires exit Lucifer's chamber.

As soon as they get to the next level of the underground, the head of the Haunting Vampires stops and turns towards the others, fizzling with venom:

"We have to become famous. We are the strength of Hell. Lucifer wants to keep us out of the public eye so that his name only will gain reputation! And that's not fair. From now on, you listen to my commandments and you forget about him. Understood?"

Mihaela's apartment. City of Stars.

Davidson is soaked in a hot bath of garlic and blue blood. His head is wreathed in Queen of the Night leaves and flowers. Thorns of roses pierce his skin like some acupuncturist needles. Kneeled down before the bathtub, Mihaela feverously chants incantations in an old, unidentifiable Romanian language.

All sweaty and madly happy, Davidson shivers and raves, his fingers bouncing in the air, his eyes rolling upside down. Nevertheless, he looks better than ever…younger, glowing, and oozing with sex appeal.

Mihaela, folded in a gypsy-like costume, with a crown of Queen of the Night flowers girdled around her head, thorny rosed bracelets and belts with crosses anointed with holy honey from her bee-friend hanging loosely around her waist, her wrists and ankles, chants and disenchants, her third eye beaming violent sparkles of light:

"Doamne doamne, ia negura de pe fruntea sa
  Căţei de usturoi înfipţi în gâtul său să alunge piaza rea
  Ucide otrava din sângele lui infestat
  Slobozeşte-l pe Davidson de blestemul lui Vlad.
  Piei, vampir, intră în sicriul tău în ceasul ce vie!
  Suge sângele Diavoului să nu mai fie,
  Lasă Binele în corpul fratelui meu
  Să curgă acum şi în vecii vecilor ca un zeu!
  Amen, Amen, amen!

Oh Lord, Mighty Lord, take the brume of his forehead away!
Garlic cloves impaled in his neck drive the hoodoo astray!
Kill the venom that reached to his heart
Liberate Davidson from the curse set by Vlad.
Be off, vampire! Enter your coffin this hour!
Suck Lucifer's blood and bury the wicked into its mud
Let Good shelter and throb into my brother's heart!
Amen, Amen, Amen, never torment Davidson again!"

Davidson growls and rolls his eyes astray, grasped by jerks and spasms as Mihaela pushes the garlic cloves deeper into the small holes of his neck.

Ave Maria, soft and healing, echoes in Mihaela's apartment... Davidson twitches from one side to the other, the blue bloodied water boiling with evil steam, evaporating strange faces of men...

Davidson's bursts into laughter, his eyes changing from blue to red.

Mihaela splashes Davidson with basil soaked in holy water. A fume of frankincense circles above his head.

Davidson growls, irritated, hitting the walls of the bath.

"Turn off that music, stop this ritual!"

"Shh...try to rest," Mihaela hushes him, as she places a chain with purple cross around his neck.

But Davidson jumps out of the bath, growling like a monster, aflamed.

Mihaela shrivels with fright, trying to push him back in the water.

"Please, you can't interrupt the process. Just a little more, stay inside. Resist the devil and it shall flee from you..."

But Davidson doesn't listen. He grabs Mihaela up in his arms and kisses her with thundering passion. His eyes shine, his body screams with desire.

"I give in to you—my Gypsy Queen of the Night..."

Few hours later.

Mihaela opens her eyes, caressed by gentle rays of sun. She smiles.

Her fingers spread widely, like some loving tentacles, bumping into the lonely pillow of Davidson.

She can hear the water running inside the bathroom like clinking drops of rain hitting a rooftop. She pulls herself out of bed, feeling sexy and good! She drags her long ballerina feet to the bathroom, spinning on her toes with love.

"Are you in there, honey?"

A strange noise pierces her ears. She startles.

She places her hand on the bathroom knob and turns it slowly to the right. The door is locked. She pushes it in and out, her heart beating...on and off.

Abruptly, the door of the apartment opens up and a whistling wind rattles inside. Mihaela gives a loud scream of death. She tip toes to the door and shoves her head outside. However, she can see no trace of a human being on the hallway nor can she hear any sound of a creature busting the quiet... Only the stormy beat of her heart. She gets back inside, cold shivers trickling down her spine.

Clad in a black sheer cloak with bat wings and high collar, Davidson enters Mihaela's room stealthily, through the window, and wraps his black wings around her naked body.

"Hi, my beauteous queen!"

"Aaaaah!" Mihaela screams from the top of her lungs.

"Vlad is home, sweet little birdie!" Davidson says in a low tone, flapping his wings with noise.

"Take off that horrible outfit! You scared me to death!" Mihaela yells out as she turns her eyes to Davidson.

"Brilliance! Early this morning, I read some lines from your novel and got inspired... However, along the way, something has happened... Please, put on this costume... We have to leave the apartment this very minute, my darling!" he speaks, clutching Mihaela's hand.

"I don't understand… What's the hurry?" Mihaela asks, frowningly.

"Please, put it on… You are in danger! I'll explain later!" he rushes his words, handing Mihaela a red shiny box.

"What do you mean? Is there a pre-Halloween party?"

"We have to go! Dress up! I'll tell you on the way!"

Mihaela opens the box and pulls out a wildcat outfit, adorned with horns, fur and a long black tail.

"What's this? Are you mad?"

"Well, as the captain, so the servant…" Davidson bows down. "Put it on, love!"

Mihaela storms inside the bathroom and shoves on the wildcat costume. All flushed up and bubbling words of anger, she zips it up to her neck. She looks up at herself in the mirror. Stupefaction! In the mirror, she sees Gabriela, her red wicked eyes, her horns…her flawless frozen face… Mihaela screams at the top of her lungs, dropping dead on the floor.

The divine being takes Mihaela up in his arms and blows a golden mist of love all over her body… "Do not be afraid. I am here," he speaks gently, slowly opening Mihaela's eyes back to life.

Rommy horse has traveled all over L.A.

to find his mistress, Mihaela. With his heart blue and his eyes dropping bitter tears onto the West Coast's ground, unable to find his mistress Mihaela, Rommy buries Mama's heart under the shadow of a green fir tree, inside the Beverly Dreams garden. His hoofs have shriveled and his mane turned gray from so much pain. From the ground, a queen of the night flower swiftly rises up, so beautiful and lofty as only in Papa Grid's garden. The flower gazes at Rommy with golden phosphorescent eyes and indigo petals crossed by silver stripes.

Mihaela opens her eyes, inside Davidson's ballutionist car.

Mommy Doll is seated next to her, silent and smiling, and Davidson holds Mihaela's hand, with the strength of a guardian angel.

"I can't stand this outfit anymore! It freaks me out," Mihaela says, trying to unzip it.

"Be brave...my dear wicked clone!"

"Don't say that! I'm not the wicked clone!"

"How do I know? Last night you have been cruel and wild... You pulled my heart out. I want it back..."

"Where are we going?" Mihaela asks, impatiently, overlapping Davidson's words.

"I'll explain it when we get there."

"What's this whole mystery? I want to get out. Pull off!"

"I can't. I programmed the car up to the destination. Besides, I know that you love mystery... I promise that everything is going to be fine... You are with me!" Davidson kisses her cheek.

Mihaela looks at Mommy Doll who heartens her with big bold eyes.

"Trust me," Davidson emboldens her again.

Mihaela looks at Davidson. Davidson grabs her hand, gazing at her with love.

Mihaela pierces his heart with her third eye, suddenly able to read him:

"Oh my God! You really love me!" she gushes out.

Davidson laughs whole-heartedly, so loud that he shakes the ballutionist car.

The horizon turns orange, the dim peaceful sun beautifully blooming Mihaela and Davidson's face in the color of love. They both smile, tangled in nature's bright lights... The unknown bears a feeling of joy within...maybe more of a terrible felicity. Yet, hand in hand with this man Davidson—who indeed cares for her—makes her feel the void inside dissipating... She senses that she is in control...something that she hasn't experienced for a long time, or maybe never until now, with a man...

Mommy Doll, seated between the two lovers, blesses them with her smile. Suddenly, she moves her hands and legs, inside her wooden body a heart begins to throb...

Mihaela: *So many times I've been afraid, so afraid...almost finding no light to see the way... But somehow, the light found me and I've been pulled closer and closer to it... When we rest and seat hopeful, the light comes to us...*

Inside the empty apartment that Davidson and Mihaela have just abandoned.

Pairs of eyes shine in the dark. No breathing, no heartbeat transpires. Steps of a creature join up the silence. The door opens silently with a final hellish creak. A bottomed sound of an opera singer elevates the numb spirit of the dark.

The back of a girl with long, golden hair brightens the obscure chamber.

She then turns around and whispers with fever:

"Here you are, my lovely puppets! I've been waiting for you! Now, let's play!"

Gabriela, dressed up as a queen-bat, with chain-diamonds hanging in her frizzy hair like a candelabrum, with ruby rings stuck on her chubby little fingers, with necklaces and medallions adorning her long neck crossed by millions of veins like some purplish rivers, looks more muscled and glittery than the seven brightest stars of Ursa Major. Provocative lace and black wings are fastened to her strong built shoulders, fluttering at every jump she makes around the messy bed and clothes that Mihaela and her Davidson have left disheveled. With wicked shouts of glory, she leads on her little army of friends: Emil, Meryl, Liam, Emanuel and Erica—five friends who used to be Mihaela's friends...

Impetuously, Gabriela hands them a variety of stakes, rusted and stained by the blue blood of decades.

"Wow, brilliant!" Emil exclaims with desire. "They are so real! Just like the ones of Vlad the Impaler!"

"You, stupid! They *are* real! You think that I'm playing with fakes?" Gabriela slaps him with her tail.

Emil acts like in his old days, playful and proud as in his Londonese palace, only that now half of his face is swollen and covered with a dark purplish acne.

"These stakes are right from my Motherland, from Transylvania itself! I'll tell you a secret if you stay nice and quiet!" Gabriela ignites her friends.

Silence. Meryl draws near Gabriela and kisses her high tumescent cheeks. Dressed up in the same white icy galactic dress that Mihaela had designed for her, Meryl looks pale and lost, like a misfallen angel.

"I'm starving," Meryl whines, gulping the frozen air that surrounds her...

"We'll get you something in a bit..." Gabriela replies, licking her hands with her red serpent tongue.

And then, like a madly cheerful child in an entertainment park, Gabriela throws herself onto the couch and starts jumping higher and higher, up to the luster... She then clinches the curved claws of her feet by the luster, swinging her head, upside down.

"Wow, I love swinging and winging!" she cries out.

In a flash, hurling herself in the air, she performs a somersault like Nadia Comaneci, scoring a perfectly stuck landing.

"Wow!" her friends gasps in awe, blue blood trickling down from their jaws.

"Should I say it?" Gabriela asks the five rubbernecks.

"Tell us, tell us," they all beg Gabriela in choir.

"What do I get in return?" Gabriela flutters her eyelashes, penetrating their eyes with red flickering lights.

"Our eternal worship!" they all exclaim in sync.

"It sounds like a stereotype from a gimmick film! All right, let's forget it, I'll just say it to you out of a motherhood feeling that I bear within for my kids! Here's the secret:

"I am the daughter of Vlad the Impaler-Dracula and I have an identical twin sister...who is my wicked clone!"

Emil bursts into laughter: "*You* are the wicked clone!"

In the blink of an eye, Gabriela pierces Emil's body with one of the sharp stakes.

"You, idiot! That was my father's favorite stake! You thought I was joking? Are you mocking me?" Gabriela whines, provoking her facial muscles to cry... Unable to pull out a tear, she speaks up with more vanity, her face all puffed up:

"One uncontrolled reaction like that and you go back down there! Forever! Got it?"

"My apologies, my apologies..." Emil shrieks with his stomach bleeding.

"Now, if you're all good...and trust me, and respect me, because in our world respect is my priority, you'll get to visit my father in person!"

"Worshipped and praised be our Queen forever," they all bow down in adoration.

"Stop with this pathetic praising. It sounds like a prehistoric ritual when grandma was worshipping ox totems! Find some new lines! Now let's get our asses outta here! We've got work to do tonight."

Well-equipped, fastening her roller bat blades with double wings on, Gabriela flies out of the window, followed by her newborn vampire-friends!

"Kill the old, suck the born!" Gabriela cries out to the stars.

Mihaela and Davidson enter the room of a small hotel located on the outskirts of the City of Stars.

A tight chamber without windows or any other orifices shuts in the freedom of the eye. The walls are painted in black and white, paintings with birds and gray trees create an atemporal vibe.

Mihaela can barely see anything through the headpiece of the wildcat costume that has hidden all of her skin, the heavy pointed horns weighing her spirit down.

"Can I take this outfit off? I have an allergy to evil and synthetics..." Mihaela whines to Davidson, tearing the wildcat costume in half. She then itches her body, crimson with vexation.

"Sure you can!" Davidson exclaims after Mihaela has already ripped the outfit into pieces... He then follows her through the room with the corner of his eye, savoring a voluptuously sexy and naked Mihaela. Mihaela rushes into bed, hauling the sheets over her body.

"Relax! You are safe down here!" Davidson adds with a smile.

"Safe? I don't need to be here to feel safe! Do you think that I am a scared bird that needs a cage and a cop to protect her?" she screams, clenching her fists in anger.

"Mihaela, they are looking for you," Davidson tries to cool her down. "Unbelievable things have happened..."

"So why don't they come and get me?"

"Are you out of your mind?"

"No, I'm not afraid! I didn't do anything wrong! I can prove it!" she says, naked of inhibitions.

"How?"

"I have an ace up my sleeve!"

"Where? I can't see it!"

"Leave me alone!"

And Mihaela starts crying abruptly, hitting the walls of the hotel room with her small raging fists...

"Go away! I hate you!" she shouts out to Davidson, who tries to suppress a laughter. "Ever since I met you, I stopped doing my ritual... I need it!"

"Can't you see that I care about you? They found hundreds of corpses in the last days, all mingled with blue blood! It is the same blood that they found in your makeup packages! It is your blood!"

"It is her blood! Damn it! It cannot be possible! I sent her here! She promised me that she would be good! She couldn't have lied to me! She promised! We have to find her!"

"Who?"

"My sister!"

"You have a sister?"

"Yes. A twin sister. Identical. I've told you about her..."

"Identical? I thought that she was only in the play."

"I wish she was...."

"Uh-oh, you're in trouble! Identical twin sisters have identical DNA!"

"What do you mean?"

"That either of you could be the killer!"

"That's impossible!" Mihaela ripostes as her blue blood boils inside her cheekbones.

"What about that guy who looked like my twin brother and scared the wits out of me in the dressing room?" Davidson breaks in.

"I don't know what to believe anymore... I guess we all have a twin brother or a twin sister somehwere in this world...We all have a wicked clone..." Mihaela exclaims, lost in dark thoughts.

"God, you're driving me mad! You bewitched me and pushed me away from my work with your *Wicked Clone* game...and now you think that you can say whatever you want and that I'll buy it?"

"Believe what you want. You mortals believe in nothing. Only in money and sex."

Davidson keeps quiet.

"How about Emil's case, how about Liam's case?" Mihaela asks Davidson, flushed up with anger. "Did you forget about them? What are you waiting for? Why don't you arrest me? I can write some books in prison, it's surely more palpitating than living in this room of boredom without windows... And you can focus on your scouting... I have no peace in here... I hate these walls!"

Silence.

"Mihaela, I am not the same person any more... I can't go back to who I was..." Davidson muses, tears shaking in his eyes. "Something has happened to me, something is so different in my life... Yes, I feel there is a wicked clone around me. But I feel there is a good clone even closer... Yes, I used to care only about me, me and me...and money and sex... But now it's all about you, you and you...your love and your big dreams. You taught me about love...about the unseen... Thank you, Mihaela."

Mihaela looks at Davidson with big wet eyes:

"Thank you..."

"We all have a twin, don't we? We all have a wicked clone. Your twin sister did it, right?" Davidson resumes, flashing a wink at Mihaela. "*She* should be imprisoned, not you! I'll take care of it... Don't worry about anything... Actually, the only thing I worry about is me, my heart... I was supposed to put you in prison but you did it first!"

And Davidson pulls himself near to Mihaela and catches her arms, clasping them behind her back and handcuffing them with strong yearning love. He then starts kissing her swanlike neck, sliding his lips along her graceful ballerina arms, her small pulsating breasts, her velvety white legs, to the sole of her small trembling feet...

Mihaela lets herself go in the strong arms of Davidson who looks like a 50-year-old Marlon Brando. She feels the crazy beat of his heart, almost bursting out of his chest, his vulnerable soul of an abandoned artist, so eager to learn, to feed on her love... His child-like thirst and ardor, the way he let himself grow in her eyes and turn into a new man, inflame her thirst of changing the world, this world that spins like an on-going film... Yes, she definitely feels that someone is taping them, someone up there, in the sky! Especially now, ever since she met Davidson, she feels like she is playing a great part in a movie with a storyline about which she is so excited to find... There is nothing more empowering than being in love! Love covers all sins...heals all wounds...

As they hug and melt into each other's kisses, Mihaela feels a strange sensation of blood in her mouth. Her heart starts ventilating, her arms shaking:

"And if my fangs grow back, now that Gabriela is back?"

"Your fangs cannot come back when you are in love. Don't fear," the voice of her mother speaks back, stronger than herself.

As Mihaela breathes out, her dark thoughts vanish from her mind like the clouds on the sky. Mihaela stares at Davidson with so much love.

She wants to know more about him, the one behind the respectable policeman, how his parents look like, what scares him and what makes him happy, what kind of music he loves, everything... She again tries to undress Davidson with her third eye, to see if he has been truly sincere, yet her eye starts shedding blood...piercing her heart with fiery darts...

"Don't unveil him with your eye any more," she hears her Mama's voice again. "When you start loving someone, it is impossible to read them. God gave us the magic, the beautiful unknown. Experience it. Don't try to kill it."

"Mihaela?" Davidson calls her. "Are you with me? Stop thinking..."

"Yes..." Mihaela murmurs, trying to turn her mind off, so eager to let go, to flow...

A paradisiacal smoke of candles titillates her soul... Davidson takes her in his arms and lays her onto the soft pillows of the bed.

A secret window opens slowly into the wall. A soft wind breathes a fresh angelic fog.

The moon raises her eyes on them, making her eye visible inside the room...

As Davidson whispers poems from his high school years to her ears, they make love...

In the middle of the night,

Gabriela and her loyal friends attack the City of Stars' asylums, killing all the old men they can possibly find.

"Don't drink!" Gabriela commands them, pointing her wicked eyes to Liam. "Phew...these futile old men and decayed women... They make our society regress! Their blood is toxic and tasteless! They sit like withered carrots in their beds, waiting for death to come and take them in her arms of grace! Disgusting cowardice! Old scamps!"

"Let's go to our babies!" Meryl changes the subject.

"Good point, Meryl!" Gabriela approves, biting her lips with desire.

And in the blink of an eye, Gabriela and her friends take off, skating the night away...

Floods of blue blood trickle down the cloudy sky.

National Maternity of the City of Stars.

Happy babies are playing in incubators infused with miraculous herbs brought by Mihaela from her Papa's garden. Multicolored vapors tickle their little arms and feet, refreshing their breaths and lightly stroking their backs to make them fall asleep. The circulating bubbles of steam moisturize and calm the bodies of the little ones, who sit joyfully and peacefully, their minds clearing off of any impurities and diseases from their families' history.

Three times a day, blue pacifiers glue onto the babies mouths like magnets, supplying them with healing drops of blood and water. Electronic toboggans carry the sweet babies to specially equipped gyms, supplied with cradles, swings, and facilities that strengthen their little muscles and stimulate their brains. After just one year, the babies begin to read and to have dreams, being able to choose their books and music and to unveil unique traits of their character.

Mihaela has helped the National Maternity of Stars supplying it with pure Transylvanian soil, fresh fruit and great tasting vegetables brought in from her Transylvanian land. The experts have tested all of Mihaela's food and have marveled at the purity and undefiled taste of her products. Inside the National Maternity of Stars, Mihaela has also taken care to build up a children's garden, where she has planted multicolored Queen of the Night flowers, lilies of the valley, daisies, freesias, lotus, roses, and other heavenly scented blooms, as well as all sort of blossoming trees with delicious fruits: olive trees, orange, lemon, apple, cherry trees, prunes... Besides, in order to satisfy every child's playful desire and enlarge its love for Mother Nature, Mihaela has created wooden toboggans, log chutes, oak-made teeter-totters, log spiral tunnels, stump seats with faces of superheros, log planters for children to plant their own seeds, small bazins of water with multi-colored fish... Next to the playground, Mihaela has also created The Music and Arts Reservoir, supplied with all sorts of music instruments and artistic components: wooden drums to be beaten by the children's little hands; wooden xylophones, mini-colored keyboards, hanging Amadindas and mushroom-microphones where they can sing and play their favorites songs; funny horns made of bamboo stalks, and flutes of carved-in fruits that can be loudly blown; magical sandboxes to build up their little sculptures, Art walls and Acrylic boards for the children to draw and paint their dreams.

There are too few days in the week and too little space for the avalanche of the desiring kids willing to be taught the Artistic way of play.

"Here they are!" Gabriela exclaims, watching the happy babies with maximum delight.

Riding on the peaceful halls of the maternity, Gabriela and her friends, armed with stakes, come across the 33 Haunting Vampires with ugly snouts, hunched backs, stinking flesh and deformed bodies of unwanted creatures of the universe.

"What are you doing here?" Gabriela asks them, thunderstruck. "You were supposed to control Washington and New York! This is my area! Get out of here!" she snarls at the bulging-eyed vampires.

"We're done with that area! Now we're going to take care of the entire US zone. Relax, restless daughter of Vlad. You can go take a walk and do your Wicked Clone show!" the head of the Haunting Vampires spits out viscous words with disgust.

"We have to respect each other! That was our understanding with Lucifer! We have a deal!" Gabriela chisels in with indignation.

"Lucifer! Who is Lucifer? A sick and weak creature afraid of God? Where is he? Why isn't he on the battlefield?"

"You, monsters! He is the brain, the mastermind! He orchestrates everything from behind!" Gabriela spurts out poisonous words in their eyes.

"Nonsense! He's nothing, only a name! He does not exist if we want him not to exist! He's a lie! Let's call him out: 'Lucifer, Lucifer, come up here, Glorious Rat of the Dead! Magnify us with your dread! Oh master, we all worship your Highness of Shit! Come and curse us with your infantilism!" the head of the Haunting Vampires laughs his head off.

"Stay out of this zone! I warn you! A deal is a deal!" Gabriela threatens them with snaked eyes of fire.

"Deals are made to be broken!"

"That's an old one, brother! It doesn't work with me!"

And Gabriela jumps onto the ceilings of the maternity, roller-blading in dazzling circles. The babies watch her performance with wide-open eyes, rolling them with delight... As Gabriela makes a triple jump in the air, the babies begin to laugh, thrashing their little feet and clapping with their little hands, enthralled!

Meanwhile, Gabriela's friends take their positions behind the Haunting Vampires's clan, lurking in their shadows for Gabriela's signal to attack. At Gabriela's shrill and rattling howl, Emanuel, Emil, Erica, Meryl and Liam fling themselves upon the 33 creatures that have humilitated their mistress, holding tightly their stakes pointed to impale.

Encircled by Gabriela's sharp-fanged friends, the head of the Haunting Vampires raises his fingers up in the V sign of peace:

"All right, all right, we're leaving!" he grumbles, lowering his eyes, defeated. "I just have one kind request!" he then looks up at Gabriela, slowing down from his swirl of hate and gimleting her wrath with the attitude of a penitent little lamb.

"Say it quick!" Gabriela growls.

"That purple cross that you have on your chest, can I have it, please?"

"Why?"

"I love purple!" he snuggles as a cunning tomcat.

"You do?"

"Very much!"

"Ok, it can be yours if I shall never see your face again!"

The head of the Haunting Vampires grovels before Gabriela.

Gabriela rips the chain with purple cross off her neck and hurls it up in the Head of the Haunting Vampires' face.

"Now…go!" Gabriela orders them, enraged.

The Haunting Vampires bow down before Gabriela and exit the maternity, bearing along their black heavy tails.

Down in his tunnels, Lucifer exclaims with satisfaction:

"Yes, finally! I can see her again in all her disgust! My queen, my lady of the night! You're back in the blaze of my eye!"

On a huge screen of a fire-framed computer, Lucifer watches Gabriela in action, salivating excruciatingly as she bites the sweet cuddling babies that sleep in fluffy multicolored incubators in the City of Stars Maternity. His ratlike tongue is jutting out with hunger, his greasy claw freezing the faces of the little ones onto the burning glass of his computer. The metamorphosis and contamination of the pure little beings pleases him to the marrow of his skeleton! He hasn't been so thrilled for decades!

The Haunting Vampires enter Mihaela's hotel chamber with drooping umbilical cords stuck out of their navels.

Sneakingly, they surround her bed, smell her feet, her armspits and black hair as she sleeps serenely, with Mommy Doll wrapped tightly to her chest.

Mommy Doll opens her big black eyes; she stings Mihaela's wrist with her little wooden finger and Mihaela wakes up in a twinkle. Peering at the horrible beings that have sorrounded her sheets, she thinks that she is still sleeping, roaming through the dark tunnels of a nightmare…

"Who are you?" she asks the 33 monstrous creatures with protuberant eyes and misshapen features.

"Your Grandma's friends!"

"My Grandma's friends? I have never met my Grandma!"

"Well, we did!" the creatures reply in disharmony.

"Good morning, Juliet!" the head of the Haunting Vampires breaks in gallantly, tattooing Mihaela's lips with a vicious kiss. After that, he raises his chin up and, piercing the air with his knotted full-of-mucosity nostrils, he commands his servants, with his conducting claw, to perform a well-rehearsed song. The Haunting Vampires lift their arms up to the ceiling, and just like a Greek choir, they start singing:

"We need you, sister of innocence,
to take our vengeance upon your flesh...
Sister of love, awake us from our restless rest,
You, face of the future and of Heaven's blessed.
Let us bite you, merciless child
To enter your life and lift up our pride.
We need to suck from your flawless breast
To make you feel our death, our homeless nest,
As we felt it for thousands of years
We, 33 souls that have no fear.
Why should we dwell in underground lairs?
Why harbor a doom from your foolish heir?
We could not live but as victims and shadows
But we'll come to life through you, divine sparrow..."

No sooner have they finished their chant than their head turns into a three feet tall dark creature, disgusting and viscid, his skin of a jelly fish splashing yellowish liquid, his mouth showing enormous misaligned fangs.

"Your sister Gabriela is pretty naughty. She talks too much and she mistakes a lot," the head of the Haunting Vampires spits out vomit, the purple cross of Gabriela hanging brightly around his thick acneic neck.

Mihaela startles, remembering her words to her sister: "Take this purple cross. It will keep us united. And this time, don't take it off your neck—not for the world! Promise? 'I promise!'" Gabriela vowed solemnly.

"Boys, give her your kisses," the head commands his clan with the authority of a lieutenant general.

"Sweet creatures, these ways are not your ways! You are meant to build and not destroy, I see this in your hearts, dear boys!" Mihaela speaks to them, kindly. "Don't let Lucifer manuever your lives! Listen to my advice: if you are good and loving and prove the world that you are not what you look like, they will embrace you as you are... You were once cursed, but you can come out of your graves and live for real...if you just love. Your hearts will change your faces... I promise this to you, sweet boys..."

"Ah...you fear for your life and lie!" the head answers Mihaela. "I feel your little scared heart pulsating in my eyes! What are you afraid of? You were once like your sister. Don't you miss the life of drinking, the sweet uninhibited kissing?"

And, with one move of his claw, the Haunting Vampire tears Mihaela's nighty gown, savoring with his long serpent tongue the sweat of her hot body. Mihaela starts trembling under the viscous, sticky touch of his lips, naked and livid. She then closes her eyes and starts praying aloud, raving between Hell and Heaven.

"We'll give you back what you once had. And you won't be raving any longer! I promise this to you, sweet Juliet," the head of the Vampires beguiles her, with the manners of a respectable count.

Mihaela touches her teeth, forcing herself to activate the evil within. But try as she might, her canine teeth do not emerge and she faints in the arms of despair. Dashes and arrows are bursting from every corner of her mind, wounding her heart. Suddenly, she hears the voice of God, clear and sharp: "Do nothing. Vengeance is mine."

Still trembling with fright, Mihaela falls to her knees and yells her heart out: "Forgive me, Lord, for trying to bring back my fangs. The old is gone. I am a new being, guarded by your blood. Please, save me from these creatures! Save me now!"

The master of the Vampires starts laughing his head off. The entire clan follows in his tones, mimicking and mocking Mihaela, with wide-open mouths and yellow teeths bulging out, like some sharp decayed saws of lust. The vampires all kneel near Mihaela and pray aloud with strident sounds, throwing rubbish words of blasphemy to God. Then they hurl themselves upon her body, drooling on her face and ears with long odious tongues, sinking their fangs into her long neck of a swan. But Mihaela keeps praying, in agony, with eyes of a saint, ignoring the bites and wounds provoked by the atrocious Haunting clan.

Meantime, the head enters a poetic verbiage, addressing Mihaela with serpent words of love:

"Now, on the altar of love, you'll become my Juliet!
No matter how bad the past has cursed my flesh,
I'll treat you like the queen who has blessed me to resurrect...
I'll keep you in my arms and show no others your ugly face
As we now take over your beauty upon our race!"

The head unveils a cage, revealing an immaculately white and beautiful dove with immense black eyes.

"This dove is just like you... It spends its days in torment, fluttering in its little cage, trying to find escape. You toil and fret in your captivity-room, roaming between life and death, willing to break free from your doom... I came to set you free... So come, fly with me."

The master-vampire pushes the cage open and seizes upon the dove with deformed greasy claws. He lifts the dove aloft, holding it like a torch, and then unclenches its wings from his forceful hold. But in a flash, just before the bird takes off, his teeth find rest into its fragile neck, slurping its blood to the very last drop.

Mihaela looks up in despair at the Haunting Vampires' cruel act, her mouth suddenly storming words of contempt:

"Who are you? Why did come to shatter my peace? How can you be so heartless, so eager of worthless deeds? God's word will strike your hate like lightning, His sword pierce you like burning iron! Leave now, and let me live!"

"Oh, thank you for reminding me about it, princess. I had forgotten to share our full story with thee and with Your God, His Majesty... We are

33 restless souls, 33 unborn babies without names that ramble between the tunnels of Hell and the low-favored basements and channels of your illustrious realm. Your grandma did 33 abortions. She did not even bother to bury our remnants to fulfill the promised ritual and set our souls free. Therefore, we strayed through miserable worm-filled bins until we entered the living bodies of 33 people without faith, without dreams... Now, in these atrocious bodies, we wander between the swarming insects of the night and the living corpses of your kind. We can not forgive what your grandma did to us...so we alone had to hustle our way to success."

"Where is my sister? What have you done to her?" Mihaela asks panic-stricken, staring at the purple cross ablaze on the scabby chest of the Vampire's head.

"Your sister cannot help you anymore. She has betrayed you, my pretty little bird! You'll soon be like us—to feel what your grandma did to us! And thus, you and your sis will reunite forever!"

Mihaela touches her indigo star, feeling her teeth ready to pierce her gums... Yet her eyes beam peaceful light, strengthening her weak flesh that is ready to give up.

Back in the Maternity Hospital, Gabriela touches her eyes, unable to see a thing, only darkness within. She touches her fangs that suddenly start to bleed and hears a voice in the dark, echoing to her heart: "Your sister needs your help!" She suddenly reaches to her chest, to touch the purple cross, but it is gone... Her mind is flashed by the memory of her vow: "I promise not to take it off!"

Gabriela wants to run, yet her feet cannot find the way out...

Mihaela is kneeled down in prayer, with her eyes up, waiting for a miracle...

Like an angel of light, the phantom of grandma blooms inside Mihaela's room. Mommy Doll's eyes smile.

"Be still! Leave her alone!" the grandma speaks calmly to the head of the Vampires' clan.

"Oh, sweet grandma..." the vampires utter in disharmony.

"I offered you the chance to come to life. Why don't you give me peace, at least when I am dead to sleep?" Grandma addresses them, revolted.

"You gave us the chance to roam between this world and netherworld as unwanted creatures with monstrous features. We could never be as strong as Gabriela or as sweet as Mihaela," the head snarls at Grandma, showing off his fangs.

"I gave you the chance you asked for... You told me that you wanted to come to life no matter how," Grandma justifies.

"You injected 33 people, 33 people who had no faith, no dreams, so that we could enter their miserable bodies of waste! We refuse to accept such a fate that we hate! We refuse to live with such ugly faces and no aims! We want to live for real, to be loved and cheered!" the head spits in the face of Grandma, threateningly.

"That was not in my power... You chose your fate. What is the body to govern our ways? It is the heart that should lead the way... You didn't let yourself tranformed by the light of day, but you chose to squander and feed on the dark, spoiled by sinful, debauched acts. And now you complain that you were cursed to be deformed? Indeed, I mistook. I was young and lost. But then, I prayed to God to give you a second chance. Why don't you change your ways so that you see the light of day? My niece was right... Change your hearts... Do good and you'll find good!" Grandma's voice gets loud and motherly.

"Who are you? Saint Therese, to redeem our sins?" the vampires riposte, chanting in unison: "You did wrong and we'll do you wrong! Go back to your heaven, Grandma! And we'll send you your granddaughter soon to follow your rules!"

And the head of the Haunting Vampires snaps his fingers with fire and a passionate tango melody rumbles on, flames shooting up from the room's corners. He then snatches Mihaela, hurling his arms around her waist like a poisonous ivy, dancing her into a seductive flight above the broken bed and crumpled sheets mingled with her thick blue blood. After he steals a stubborn kiss from Mihaela's lips, he passes her on to his loyal servants, so hungry of debauchery. Each of the Haunting Vampires twirl

Mihaela into dazzling and dizzying pirouettes, exhausting her into a life and death tango. Mihaela can hardly breathe, sweaty and burnt by the dark flames that howl from the corners of the room.

The entire floor is seduced by the magic of tango. Even the curtains are waving into the violent rhythm of violins. The Head watches the scene with adoration, applauding with maximum delight: "Impressive, memorable, magnificent, what a talented dancer our Juliet is!" Then, pulling a drapery to the side, he finds a dear friend, hidden for ages:

"Oh, my beloved Vlad... There you are! Were you jealous again?"

"I am the one you're looking for," Vlad pierces the Head with frozen eyes. "I am what you always wanted to be: faster, stronger and immortal. A vampire you could never be! Take me!"

The head of the Haunting Vampires laughs his wicked teeth and turns his scabby back to Vlad, opening his tentacular arms and claws to embrace Mihaela like an enormous spider, ready to devour its victim with full desire. He coils his numerous tentacles around Mihaela's wounded body, licking her fresh cheeks with his multiple tongues and elongating his lips to give Mihaela his final kiss.

The other Haunting Vampires encircle Vlad, opening their arms to catch him from behind. But Vlad beholds their shadows and rapidly turns around, blowing upon them thunderbolts of ice. He then flies upon the Head with murderous eyes, and grabbing him by his poisonous tentacles, like a lasso, hurls him against the wall, fixing his arms to the side, in a crucifix. Vlad's eyes gleam in the night, penetrating the Haunting Vampire's pride. The Head growls, stuck on the wall, throwing at Vlad with yellowish viscous saliva and red electric sparks. But Vlad springs like an arrow towards his enemy, his long nails thrusting deep in the Head's heart, pulling it out. The other vampires whine, staring at the sad look in their master's eyes. One by one they start to collapse on the floor as the fresh rays of the dawn take control.

Vlad hides behind the curtains, with his head bowed down and his eyes closed by the Sun.

"Wait!" Mihaela shouts. She then rushes to pull the draperies to the side, but Vlad is already gone.

Grandma hugs Mihaela, melting inside her eyes.

10 pm. Same day.

Davidson enters quietly the peripheral hotel bedroom where he has sheltered his beloved Mihaela. He has a sunny face and carries two big boxes wrapped up in glittery gift paper. His blonde hair is furrowed by gray streaks, making him look styled but suddenly aged... Two weeks ago, his hair looked fuller and glowing, and now...is thin, gray and has fallen away, like feathers plucked out from a young molting eagle...

Mihaela, wrapped up inside the purple sheets of the bed, looks deeply asleep.

Silently, Davidson places the two boxes on the velvety gray carpet and tiptoes towards Mihaela's bed. He pats her rosy hot cheeks with love and then kisses her longly onto her tall porcelain forehead. Mihaela gives a smothered cry, disquieted by Davidson's kiss. She twitches and kicks the sheets off her legs, unveiling horrible wounds and scabs.

Davidson cries out, distressed: "What has happened, my love?"

Mihaela opens her big black eyes as if the light of day has glistened onto her face for the first time. Her eyes are red and enflamed as from great torment. She squints and babbles, hiding her bruised wounded legs under her long, linen nightdress.

"Look at me..."

"I'm fine..." Mihaela murmurs, avoiding Davidson's eyes.

Davidson pulls Mihaela's nighty gown up, above her knees, but miraculously, all of those terrible wounds disappeared like dark heavy clouds from a serene blue sky. Her legs look flawless again, porcelain like, as if nothing has ever touched them or caused them pain...

"I had a bad dream..." Mihaela mumbles, disturbed by the rays of sun that are injecting her eyes.

"Forgive me... " Davidson cuts her off, perplexed. "I must be worn out... My eyes..."

And then, putting on a happy smile, he tries to cast the gloom away, kissing Mihaela's legs with wholeheartedly love. "I have a gift for you, my sweetheart..."

"I'm very tired..." Mihaela slumps down into the bed, turning her back on Davidson.

"Are you alright, my dear?" Davidson asks her quiveringly, struggling to hide his worry.

"Just fine."

Mihaela closes her eyes, raising the blanket above her head.

Day after day,

Davidson grows warmer and warmer, but Mihaela colder and **colder**. Davidson savors and caresses her being with his light loving touches, but Mihaela does not even crack a smile, trying to slip away from his presence...

"How much she has changed... What have I done to her?" Davidson asks himself, laden with blame.

Mihaela looks more beautiful and radiant than when he first met her, yet every time Davidson wants to show her a sign of affection, she hides within herself, like a snail in its shell. She is reluctant to caress him, to look him in the eye, not to mention the love part... She is so cold...and this grows him old.

Watching himself in the mirror, his face shrivels with tens of deep wrinkles, blemished by small white pimples. His hair turns utterly gray, his eyes—small and afraid... He feels out of balance, he has gained a pot belly, as big as he has never had before.

He shakes himself off, ignoring the mirror. He thinks, again analyzing the past and where things are heading to...

Each time he arrives home after work, Mihaela is either away or astray, taken by deep thoughts... And he withers away, worrying and barely catching sleep...

"Did I say something wrong? Have I neglected her lately? Why is this sudden change? Do we need a vacation? Maybe it is all because of my appearance... I've grown so old and she grows younger and more radiant day by day... What's going on?"

Concerned and confused about his fast aging and skin discoloration, Davidson decides to go see a doctor.

National Laboratory of the Police Department.

A beautiful Asian nurse, dressed up as an astronaut, sticks the needle of a long syringe in Davidson's left arm that has visibly lost its firmness. She then fills a couple of tubes with his blood which looks inhumanly thin and feels scarily cold... As jets of dark red blood keep pouring out of his arm, the nurse keeps pressing against the small puncture that the needle left, with an electronic pad. Yet the small hole opens wider and wider and blood spews out his arm like lava rivers out of a volcano... It does not stop. The electronic pad has always been super-efficient. But not this time. Alarmed, the nurse calls after the doctor.

The Doctor comes in at once and applies to Davidson the first perfusions.

He connects him to all kind of machines and humanoid robots that perform intensive tests in order to find out the cause of his abnormal bleeding. Attached to the monitors, these robots assist and assure Davidson's resuscitation.

Simultaneously, the doctor reads the tests' results onto screens projected on Davidson's palms. He then writes swiftly, on the same screens, the first-aid treatment, giving indications to the worried nurse. The doctor draws near to Davidson's bed and asks him, overly-concerned:

"Have you lost someone dear? Have you experienced a trauma, a time of turbulence in your family lately?"

"No. Well...my mom is not feeling very well, but besides that, my career and everything else goes quite well... What's the matter, doc?"

"Well, the reports are pretty strange... A massive loss of blood. Have you ever suffered of Anemia?"

"No...but I do feel like I've lost a lot of...blood..."

"Yes, ever since this morning your blood has decreased enormously... I've never seen something like that in my whole life... A terrible desanguination! "

"What's that, doctor?"

"A massive loss of blood... And what concerns me is that I cannot figure out the causes of this loss! Your organs are in perfect condition, your blood tests impeccable, yet you are in the Class IV Hemorrhage, which involves a loss of 40% of circulating blood volume. Your blood pressure abruptly dropped, your capillary refill worsened. Fluid resuscitation with crystalloid and blood transfusion are necessary. I'm afraid an aggressive resuscitation is required to prevent...death.

"Doctor, it must be a mistake! I've never had any blood condition... My family has never suffered such a problem... Would you consider repeating the tests?"

"I don't have to repeat them, that's what the test-monitors are showing at all times... You are losing blood every five seconds... If I'm not keeping you here, attached to these robots, you can... Unfortunately, I have to inform you that...you can die within few hours..."

"Doctor, I'm as healthy as a horse..."

"I wouldn't say that... The robots keep supplying you with beta-blockers, vitamin K, that can potentially blunt the cardiovascular response. But this only helps in the short run. You need perfusions and real blood transfusions, urgently... Do you know someone who has your type of blood?"

"Did someone ask for me?" Davidson cuts the doctor off.

"No, not as far as I know...but I will ask Yoko, my assistant."

"May I use the bathroom?"

"Yes, sure...but carefully..."

Dragging his perfusions along, Davidson enters the bathroom. He anxiously checks his cell phone...but no call from Mihaela... "Doesn't she care about me anymore?"

He dials her number...but the operator's voice responds. He leans against the walls, panting...

Indeed, he feels very weak, yet just a glance of Mihaela would make him feel better, healed... He thinks about asking the doctor to briefly allow him to go home, but he knows that in this critical condition it's impossible to let him go...

"I will find another way..." Davidson says to himself, emboldening his flesh to gain back its strength.

Panting heavily, with perfusions attached, Davidson enters Mihaela's hotel room.

But Mihaela is no longer there. Davidson feels the whole room spinning. "How can she do this to me?" he collapses onto the bed. He breathes repeatedly, deeply, trying to recollect, to bring to his mind moments and images of happiness from their relationship... Seeing Mihaela before his eyes, smiling at him, reanimates his feelings. Her love heals him like the rays of sun heal a broken heart on a cold winter day.

"Ha ha," he starts laughing at himself, knowing that he's been overreacting, the prisoner of jealousy in the pursuit of his beloved Mihaela... He has dealt with terryfing cases and this is just a love game. His positive mind and strong feet on the ground have always helped him see the bright side of any case. He knows that Mihaela loves him and that someone has intercedeed between their love. Maybe her wicked sister stole her or kidnapped her and Mihaela needs his help. He knows that when he finds her, he will come to his senses and Mihaela will come to his love... He will talk to her and kiss her until she blooms back into his dear love.

Davidson rises up, beaming with courage. But just in the twinkling of an eye, he drops again onto the bed:

"Or maybe Mihaela *is* truly a vampire, a tortured being and she just went back to her roots?! Maybe my blood loss is a result of my interaction with her? Maybe she tried to change her ways but she could not, and she's been too afraid to tell me the truth, not to make me suffer... She just left and that's it... It's over!"

Davidson starts panting, sweaty and agitated.

"No, it's not! It's not over!" Davidson springs to his feet like a new born, screaming for life.

In the blue cotton pajamas from the hospital and with perfusions attached,

Davidson draws himself to the hotel's reception desk. His heart almost pops out of his chest, throbbing as of a pupil's at his first school test.

"Excuse me, have you seen Miss Mihaela?"

"The lady just checked out 15 minutes ago," the receptionist answers Davidson, looking at his perfusions with a sympathetic face.

Davidson, more alarmed, asks if Mihaela has left any messages for him.

"I'm afraid the lady has not..."

"Did she say where she was going?"

"I'm afraid she did not."

Davidson's white spots on his face widen. He itches himself, propping his elbows up on the reception desk.

"Oh, I'm sorry... My colleague has just now recalled... Actually...the lady had us call for a car service... Oh...and then she came back to the hotel desk, asking for a map... She said she had to reach the Autumn Place...or something like that, and that the driver's navigation system had just broken down..."

Davidson gets into his ballutionist car, determined to find his Mihaela. In rage and sweating blood, his hands drive the wheel of love through foggy highways and sinuous thoughts. Arriving at the Autumn Place, sweatier and weak, he finds himelf in the midst of nowhere...between some forsaken dilapidated houses and rusted barrels... No human being walking around, no stars on the sky lightening the ground... Only him and himself, both feeble and helpless...

He remembers this place! It once looked lively and welcoming. He was here years ago, when they had to solve a rape case. Suddenly, his eyes fall on a placard, posted on a brick house with a greenish wooden door. On the placard is written: *In the memory of Donna.*

"Yes, that's right. Now it all comes back to me... That was the name of that girl, Donna..."

Davidson gets out of the car, dragging his perfusions along. He knocks shyly at the green door. A dim light looms through the tiny edges.

"Who's there?" a lady asks in a croaky voice.

"Excuse me, I'm detective Davidson..."

The lady doesn't answer. Davidson shouts after her:

"I don't want to harm you... I'm looking for a girl, my daughter."

The lady opens the door, slowly. She is a tiny old woman, with hunchback, steeled grey hair, leathered face, thin lips and unwelcoming tone.

"What does she look like?" the old lady asks with heavy tired eyes.

Davidson opens his wallet and shows the old woman, Mihaela's picture.

"There..." the lady points to a dilapidated house. "She was here a quarter of an hour ago and asked about the Autumn House. That's right there..."

"Thank you!" Davidson jumps to kiss the hand of the old lady.

"But I wouldn't go there... There's where Donna went too..." the lady says with a trembled echo, bursting into a river of tears.

"I am the one who made the investigations for Donna's death. I tried really hard but..."

"I know. I am her mother..." the woman cuts him off, continuing her sobbing. She then slams the door shut, crying behind the door: "Donna, Donna!"

Davidson remains in the dark, in a cloud of gloom, totally perplexed. He cannot believe that this woman is Donna's mother. She looked young, taller, human, zvelt...and now, maybe about 12 years later...almost a corpse. Davidson pulls out his lantern and sets off to that place...

In front of the Autumn Place's dangerous house, ramshackle and somber, Davidson knocks on a black steel door. He turns off his lantern, lurking in the dark. Silence creeps onto his body. No moves, no breathing. He circles the house, guided by his wavering feet. In the backyard, a soft flickering light and some rickety stairs lead into a basement. Davidson descends the stairway like an insomniac. He can no longer feel blood running through his veins... He feels so tired, so weak... As Davidson steps down, stair by stair, the light gets dimmer and dimmer so that he can hardly behold something. His hands tremble...he can barely turn on the lantern.

Once in the basement, Davidson sneaks behind the black curtains of a dimly lit chamber with Gothic architecture. Moans and kisses can be heard... He tries to distinguish some silhouettes in the dark room and finally, Mihaela looms before his tired eyes.

Mihaela is on top of a man...caressing him with beastly, rampant touches. As she slides down on his chest with passionate kisses, the man lifts his head up, fixing Davidson like a tiger... Davidson cannot believe his eyes. This man who's been holding Mihaela into his arms, has his face, his very eyes, his hair, his demeanor, his once young flawless features... He looks identical to him. Out of control, shaking tears in his eyes, Davidson breaks out:

"Who are you?"

Mihaela turns her head to Davidson, gazing with disbelief...

"It's me, Davidson!" he shouts with desperation to his beloved.

Once Davidson utters his name loudly, a white enormous eagle springs like an arrow, out of nowhere, piercing the sidewall of the chamber, across the bed of the lovers... The eagle shoves his claws into the skin of the lookalike man and the man's bones suddenly crack, his body explodes, turning into a shriveled, slim trunk of an old man. His hair is long, curly but scarce, grown only in the back of his head, furrowed by gray wiry locks that tangle and frizz in disarray...

Mihaela looks at him with big scared eyes. Bitter tears freeze down her cheeks like stalactites...

Tongue-tied and white as a ghost, Davidson exits the chamber, led to the stairway by the eagle. Mihaela looks back, shaking with anger.

"You...monster!" she screams at the top of her lungs.

Bursting into ardent tears, she starts hitting the Old Man with all of her strength, spitting with sour at his eyes, like a gypsy woman, betrayed. Trembling and fretting, she jumps out of bed, cleaning her body from the dirty hands of that man...

The Old Man kneels before Mihaela: "I would do anything for you. Take my life if you think that loving you is a crime!"

Mihaela steps back, ashamed of her nakedness:

"I have to get out! Where is Davidson?!" she cries out.

"Marry me!"

"Who are you?"

"I am your creator, the one who loves you like no other..."

"Don't say that again! It makes me wanna die! God is my Creator."

The Old Man blows a purple mist around her, with euphoric eyes of a sorcerer... Mihaela tries to run, but she cannot move her legs; they are numb. The Old Man grabs Mihaela by her hands, kissing them with delirious love. Mihaela starts speaking in tongues... The purple light of her third eye expands, suddenly breaking the spell.

"Oh, my dear, if you would know God..." the Old Man sneers.

"I know God."

"Did God teach you to reject love? I am the one and the same person as Davidson... There is no way that you can love him and not love me. We are one."

Mihaela looks at him, disgusted. A cold blow of the night crawls onto her body while the dim light of the moon softens her anger.

"Don't doubt. I am your Davidson," the Old Man speaks again with pathos.

"You are Vlad, that liar, that monster, murderer of my Mother! I'll be out of here in a thud and never see your face again. I'm not afraid. I have the perfect love of God."

Vlad takes Davidson's face.

"Marry me, I beseech you, in the name of Love, in the name of Davidson…"

"I have to get out of this wicked basement!" Mihaela starts collecting her garments.

"How could you love me with another face and now that you have seen the other me, you cast away the promises and love we've made one to each other? Davidson and I are one! Men are the same, from ancient eras to nowadays and they will stay the same because love always reigns! Tall, short, poor, rich, men want to love and to be loved. So here I am, a monster, down at your feet, beseeching you to marry me! Is it a face you marry or is it a loyal loving man? Is it a hand you offer or is it you, your heart that I may gain? Oh, marry me, sweet Mihaela! I know, you're too high for my soul but you will die if no man gives you love…"

"Who are you? And where is Davidson?"

"We are one and the same… That was one of my old foolish games… Believe me."

"He is you? I don't believe you!"

"Go upstairs. You will see. Davidson is gone…because he's me."

Mihaela rushes outside.

The clock strikes hard, three times, and Mihaela returns sad, lost in the dark…

"Where did you hide him? What did you do to him?" she asks Vlad furiously and worn out.

Vlad opens his arms towards Mihaela, like an abandoned child eager for Mama's love: "Take me! I am your Davidson!"

"Why did the eagle pierce your flesh if you are one and the same with Davidson? What is this game of lies? Explain to me!"

"The eagle is my friend, trained to speak like a man and follow my rules like a good slave. He is the one that told me that I have to show myself before you as I am, not taking any other faces or playing crafty acts to win my lady. I was fearful that I would be rejected...by your sweet face...if you would see my real withered face..."

And the big white eagle shows itself in the room with its majestic human features, alighting on the golden chandelier with its curled yellow talons. Mihaela looks at it, perplexed. Its feathers are bluish-white; his eyes are like two crystals, flickering red lights, and its beak orange and terribly sharp.

Mihaela jumps before Vlad, bursting into a waterfall of tears.

"Take Davidson's face," she orders him, through bitter sobs.

Vlad takes Davidson's face.

Mihaela jumps on him, punching and scratching the Old Man with envenomed fists and knife-edged nails of a cat.

"I'm sorry, my love... But taking that face was the only way I had a chance with you! Through Davidson, now you know me, you read my heart and saw the real me that lies beneath the lies, beneath the prejudices of your eyes! Is it a face you love or is it a humbled spirit, this soul of mine eager to change, to give you treasures, youth without aging and life without ending?"

"I want none of that! I just want him!"

"You want Marcus Antonius? Yes, here I am!" And, suddenly, Vlad takes the face of the Roman general Marcus Antonius. "You want Elvis with his sweetest tender voice? Done!" And Vlad turns into Elvis Presley. "You want DiCaprio-romantico to act for you, like an aristocrat, simpatico? I am the one!" And Vlad embodies Leonardo DiCaprio. "Which one you want?"

"The real one!" Mihaela speaks out with rage.

And Vlad takes back his sad old face, leathered and tarnished by the past.

"Here I am, heart of my life! At your command!" Vlad declaims with his head bowed down.

"So you played the cop... You made me think that you were a caring detective who fell for me?" Mihaela weeps, dearly. "That can't be true! Life can't be so deceiving!"

"The detective still loves you. It's me. I would do anything for love..."

"When you said that the wallpaper was made by your grandfather, that you forgot how to say 'I love you', that you found Vlad the Impaler in the dressing room...were you simply putting on an act?"

"Yes," Vlad says gently. "I am everywhere you go because I love you... You are the one and only one I need, you can redeem my sins!"

"I can't redeem your sins, I am a sinful girl who's trying... Only God's cross can cross your sins!"

Mihaela looks down at her white long hands that shake.

"I love Davidson so much! Why? Why should I talk to you?" she asks through big tears of doubt.

"Because you're trying...you're trying to change the world! I am the one that needs to be changed in this world the most! Change me—the impossible, and I shall give you everything possible! Give me your love, turn me from a dark, revengeful man into a man of light, from a monstrous beast into a happy husband! Don't let me harbor in this boring death, give a beat to my deserted chest!"

"But God gave you a life and you denied it! You chose to die and dwell in Hell and now you are complaining that you are living in an infernal cell?"

"Yes, I gave my life to Lucifer. I thought that evil can avenge my life if good is mocked in every way and hardly changes a man's heart... But evil just destroys. It gives no hope. Only going through Hell I realized how good is to live with pains, with struggles...yet with hope, with love... Even a bit of true love can do wonders..."

Mihaela looks up to the sky. Big black tears carve her face, like a Mary Magdalene she weeps, wrapped in a black veil:

"I don't know why I'm saying this, I can no longer tell the truth from lies... But all I know is that my mission in this life is to change darkness into light, to bring Heaven into people's night! So yes, I will marry you Vlad—in rage and love—I give my heart!"

Her words stake her soul like a poisonous dagger. Ravenous tears dig her cheeks with hunger.

Vlad takes her in his arms and kisses her like the clouds kiss the sun...like a dark knight abandons himself to a glorious light.

"But..." Mihaela adds, pulling herself away from Vlad's embrace, "As long as we're together, no drinking or shedding of blood, or else we break apart!"

Lucifer watches the disgusting love scene that takes place between Vlad and Mihaela with horrific excitement as he takes possession of Gabriela's soul.

"What a pathetic role!" Lucifer grins with horrible contentment, looking at the sealed deal that has been fullfilled.

Holywood Castle. The City of Stars. Two days later.

Mihaela adorns the chambers of a beautiful medieval castle with wreaths of fresh-braided cherry blossom flowers. The mild rays of the morning smooth her oval face with grace. Her eyes are sunny and her feet sprightly jump from one room to another.

Suddenly, a gleeful sound rings lively through the chambers as if a whole flock of sparrows has gathered to sing that morning.

"What's this sound?" Mihaela asks Vlad, enchanted.

"Oh...my telephone!" Vlad replies, high-spirited, savoring Mihaela's youthful, deerlike moves.

"Can I answer?" Mihaela asks him, excitedly.

"Go ahead!" Vlad encourages her.

As she rushes to the telephone and picks up the receiver, it slithers inside her hand like a gelatinous creature... As she looks down at the receiver, a serpent head with horns and red feathers sticks out its tongue... All of a sudden, a milky voice enters her ear, to the room of her heart:

"Hello, Mihaela, most precious Bella!"

"Who are you?" Mihaela asks, wrapped up in fear.

"Your grandfather who loves you very much!"

"My grandfather?"

"Auch!" Mihaela screams as the phone with snakehead nips at her hand.

Meanwhile, on a steep highway bathed in a terrible downpour,

Davidson speeds up in his ballutionist car to reach the City of Stars and report the strange old man who has impersonated him and might have caused the death of Donna and other innocent girls... Also, he has made up his mind to divulge all the details of Mihaela's case that he has illegally been hiding from the eyes of his executives.

Undoubtedly, he saw Mihaela leaving Vlad's basement from Autumn Place and avoiding him. He now understands that everything that Mihaela has told him about Vlad is indeed the truth. He is an old perfidious and lying man. Yet Mihaela is not the one he thought she was. She is truly part of a "play." He has been misled. She has no sister. She is the wicked clone. Davidson drives on, terrified and heartbroken.

Out of the blue, fixed in the middle of the road, a woman awaits with her hands crossed onto her pregnant belly... Davidson pushes the brake pedal to stop. But too late! His car has already hit the pregnant woman's body.

With his eyes stuck out of the head, his mouth paralayzed into a terrifying scream of life and death, Davidson rushes out of the car towards the pregnant woman collapsed on the highway.

Sprung out of nowhere, through the cold foggy lights, Mihaela appears before Davidson's eyes and takes him by his hand, like an angel of the night...

"It is all right, sweetheart," she speaks to him with exceeding calm. "She is dead. Let's take her with us. No one will ever know. I promise."

Davidson trembles, following Mihaela like a scared child follows his caring mother.

Mihaela and Davidson carry the dead body along, through the arms of a black oak forest that foxily edges the doomed road of the highway. The branches of the trees, thick, sharp, and nodulous, appear before Davidson's eyes like bitter thoughts, piercing his brain and slowing down his pace.

"You were not misled, my dear! I truly love you!" Mihaela whispers to Davidson as they move deeper into the dark forest.

Davidson feels like floating in a dream. His heart pulsates with frightening joy, he feels his flesh miraculously revived by the spirit of the one who leads him into the night... Her words—"I truly love you," mean everything that he's been waiting for... Even the voices that condemn him of having killed an innocent woman are melting into those life-giving words of the being he loves...

Mihaela and Davidson stop, leaving the corpse fall onto the black sticky mud. Davidson starts digging into the ground, faster and faster, like Mihaela's robot-servant, deepening and widening a hole until it can easily swallow the body of the pregnant corpse.

Mihaela pushes the woman inside the cavity. She then breaks into rapid incantations, laughing widely and raging words in an unheard-of language. Davidson watches the scene, trembling with lust.

Mihaela covers the corpse with earth on which immediately spring up weeds and dried thorny grass, hiding the body of the murdered woman as if nothing has happened that somber rainy night...

"I'll make you forget about everything!" she whispers, as she undresses lasciviously before Davidson's eyes.

Under the moonlight's smile, her skin shines into perfection, her body looks smooth and thoroughly carved, like a sculpture of Michelangelo. She is more beautiful and seductive than ever. Her breasts are bigger, her lips moist and fleshy. She has the shape and aura of a Roman Goddess.

Davidson feels a malefic temptation to make love with her right there, above the tomb of the pregnant woman that he just killed. He missed Mihaela beyond belief!

Davidson and Mihaela start kissing each other with the desire of starving wolves. Trembling, he touches every part of her body as Mihaela bites his lips with ardent passion... In the wind of the night, they roll in the mud like two unchained, ferocious beasts. Mihaela rips off his clothing, moaning longly to him:

"I love you more than ever!"

"Me too," Davidson sighs, kissing and biting her breasts like a lunatic.

"Now, before I'll give you the eternal orgasm, tell me your last wish..."

Davidson smiles, spellbound: "Marry me!"

Mihaela hurls in Davidson's neck and bites him with long barbarous teeth, howling like a wolf in the night:

"We're now married, baby! I'm inside of you, you're inside of me..."

Davidson hears her voice deformed and dark... He stops. As he looks at her face, with his hands frozen onto her breasts, her eyes turn into red ghastly bats, shining like two flames from Hades.

"Who are you?" he asks her, terrified and losing blood.

"Hi, we haven't had the pleasure to meet. I am Gabriela, Mihaela's sister. I help her from time to time...as she is overly booked by Mr. Love..."

Davidson shakes his head, feeling his heartbeat on the verge to cease:

"I should have listened to Mihaela! You are the wicked clone!"

Gabriela laughs her teeth off: "Yes, you should have had! You people, non-believers, searching for a sign! You only believe when you see! See, that's why God left you! I completely understand Him!"

Panting, Davidson tries to articulate, black tears smudging his eyes:

"I wish your father Vlad to die just when he loves the most... It hurts so much to love and to be leaving..."

"I bet it does," Gabriela grins, giving Davidson the kiss of death.

Davidson gives his last breath. Around his neck, the purple cross from Mihaela shines brightly to the mourning stars.

Holywood Castle. A chamber adorned with stakes of all heights and weights.

"Please, stop it Lucifer! I don't want her to hear us. Just leave me alone! I gave you what you wanted, what more?" Vlad speaks out, his face all flushed up.

"You've promised to let me handle this thing! It's written right here, in our deal!" Lucifer stings Vlad with words of hatred.

"It's not possible, can't you understand? You have Gabriela. How much more do you want?"

"This means war, Vlad!" Lucifer provokes him.

"Lucifer, I want this to happen in Verona. This is her wish! Can't you understand? I want to live…"

"I can build Verona right here, in my tunnels. My Hunting Bitches will form and adorn everything more horribly than in the real place. It is going to be a majestic, terrible and unforgettable wedding. Think about the weeping of the Hunting Bitches…their veiled and unveiled costumes, their singing… They are all going to cry infernally and dance tastefully till the break of dawn."

"I believe it but…"

"But what?"

"Mihaela is coming out of the bathroom! I have to go!" Vlad breaks Lucifer's bubble.

"Say, yes or no?" Lucifer pushes on, infernally.

"It stinks down there, in your caves so bad that the Earth begins to quake! Earthquakes come from you and from your evil horns always eager to impale this world! Lucifer, I'm done with your ways! I want to live peacefully and happily! I want to be a human being from now on!" Vlad bursts out.

Lucifer snarls and gnaws: "A human being?"

"Besides, Mihaela wants to set the official opening of the Wicked Clone play on her wedding day, in the real Italy…" Vlad resumes with excitement. "She's been there before. She can tell the truth from fake, believe me," Vlad concludes, revealing the secret of their nuptials.

"Alright! That bitch called Love has changed you meanly! And now, you want to be an Artist too? Re-writing your damned life? You're dead, bro! You cannot move on without my control! Besides, you stink, son of a bitch! You stink of failure! You want to conquer greatness in your death, because in life...it did not work. That's what all vampires wish for: to make it after life, because on earth they were afraid and too proud to follow their hearts. They were too occupied with solving egoistic whims—brushing illusions in the mirror—all that I've given them they've eaten up with fear. Double-minded, always winding: human beings, poor victims of their wantings! They are too proud to follow God. They live with strong ambitions, but die with incomplete achievements, with hopeful dreams and missions. Then, they come to me to make them famous, to celebrate them in their death... And they still want to suck some more innocent blood as if poor Jesus' blood was not enough! Oh, how I laugh at God! Humans deserve impaling and not loving! When will He come to my senses? I understand: the inspiration of Mihaela and her talent are a big challenge for your barren heart. But did you forget that you are dead and mine infinitely? You're so weak and sick to cling to Mihaela, but she will break you into pieces because you can't renounce your vices! You've got a huge ego and a stupid daughter under my credo! So follow me or else I'll see you impaled by your own stake! And then I shall forget not your betrayal and I shall bury you in failure!"

Lucifer hangs up.

Vlad exits his secret chamber adorned with stakes, cautiously locking it up. He then moves towards Mihaela's chamber with stealthy, fearful steps.

"Where were you? Who was he?" Mihaela asks Vlad from behind a column, wrapped up in an immaculate white gown.

"Oh... He was...an old friend! He loves to challenge people!"

"I heard that voice before...it reminds me of someone that I used to know..."

"Really? Who?"

"You, back then... It gives me shivers... I have to go!"

"But I am changed, my love... Don't think of what is gone and old!"

"So who was talking the other minute on the phone, my husband or my father?" Mihaela asks him, saddened.

"It was your husband, my future wife, my sweetest wonder. I've told you, I am your fairy father. You were born in a different way, not like your brother Vlady... No living man had slept with your beautiful mother in order to bring you to this life. You were born of a miraculous Queen of the Night flower one silent night with divine vigil when your mother raised a prayer to the sky and was hallowed by the holy light. It was a miracle, my life! In other words, I do love you just like a father, but I am not your...father!"

"I have to write this in my novel... It seems out a fairy tale but I want to believe it this way..."

And suddenly, the words of the bee-friend who told her just the same about her birth, flash in her mind.

Mihaela runs to her bedroom and opens up her notebook. Excitedly, she starts to write the fantastic story of her birth. She then hears a cry. Louder and louder...breaking the silence.

"Ah, Mommy!" she recalls. "How cruel was I, afraid to face Mommy after that wedding vow..."

Saying "Yes" to Vlad might have been the biggest mistake of her life. And yet, Mihaela felt that someone from Above had guided her to utter those words to Vlad.

"I do not want to disappoint you, God! Help me always to be of one heart!"

Mihaela takes out a key from her gown to open the drawer where she has hidden Mommy Doll... She anxiously twists the little golden key shaped as a Queen of the Night flower and finds Mommy, dull and asleep. She slowly rises Mommy Doll in her arms, with tears in her eyes, and whispers:

"I'm so sorry that I have kept you in here for so long. I know that you are mad at me for giving in to be the bride of him—that creature that has tormented us for years with his sins..."

Mama is silent but her big black eyes suddenly open, alive and wide.

"Hi, Mommy! Please say something," Mihaela pleads with Mommy. "Do you forgive me?"

Mommy gazes at her with loving eyes. Mihaela hugs Mama to her chest, and feels Mommy Doll's heartbeat: tic tock, tic tock...

"Mama, Mama! Mama lives! She's got a heartbeat!"

Mihaela jumps for joy, so high up in the air, her hair touching the tall ceiling of her chamber. Suddenly, she recalls the late night escapades from Transylvania when she could jump in a flash on top of the trees. A dart of fear pierces her being.

A little hot mist sneaks through the heat pipe and gets around Mihaela's face, knocking on her mind... The fume transforms into an ugly bald man with black dripping tongue, squeaking and smelling like a big foul rat.

"Who are you?" Mihaela asks, disgusted.

"That's not important, but you, your happiness. Vlad is lying to you, sweet girl! He is your father... He's a perverse, incestuous parent obsessed with sex! He wants to suck you out of..."

"Go away! You're ugly and you stink! I don't deal with the devil!" Mihaela shuts him off, flying like an arrow down the stairs, before her future husband Vlad.

"Who wants not to be changed for better, may stay out of my way for ever..." Mihaela speaks up to him, her hands shaking, her body so pale...

"What do you say?" Vlad stutters, confused.

"Promise that you shall never touch another neck, commit blood splatters or stake another maid? Give yourself to God if you want to call yourself my husband. Otherwise, I want your presence in my life no more!"

"Of course..." Vlad shudders with disbelief.

"No, I shall not hear that weak *of course* from that foul tongue of yours! I want to see your childlike tears, I want to hear your warm and truthful heartbeat that wants to be redeemed and healed! You will then have deserved my love: when you are not afraid to let God change your soul!"

"Calm down, beloved bride! I say it without fear: Yes, I give myself to God in the sweet name of your loving heart!"

And in the twinkling of an eye, a purple dragon with multiple heads springs out of Vlad's head. Vlad watches himself with shameful eyes, half of him willing again to deny. But ugly faces of creatures keep rushing out of his being, violently, boiling and growling with devilish cries. Mihaela watches the scene with fright. The creatures spit out blue viscous blood in Mihaela's eyes and groan aloud. Suddenly, there looms the face of *the short and bald rapist* who chased Mihaela in his dirty barn... Then, a *feeble sick Vlad* with big black cat coiled like a turban around his head... Then, *the tragic body of Magia impaled on a stake*; *Emanuel—risen from the dead and covered in mud*; *Emil—her deranged fiancé*; *the benefactor* from the airport who gave her the ticket to New York; *the mustached-actor* from the *Palace Theatre*; *Dominica* with her wide-open nostrils, breathing in the letters of Mihaela's novel...

But Mihaela's eyes are clotted with thick viscous blood and she is unable to see clearly what is happening to Vlad. She quickly wipes the lumps and fluid off her eyes and beholds Davidson's face, so white and young, beaming like a sun...and staring at her with love. His body is of a white eagle; his arms, wide-open like two big bloodied wings, are painting the face of Mihaela onto the castle's ceiling. The purple cross that she has given him is carved on his tall forehead; his eyes are so blue and electric that she suddenly faints inside her spirit like into an abyss...

In a flash, Vlad and Davidson conjoin and become one.

Under Mihaela's terrified eyes, young Davidson springs out of Vlad's body, and Vlad morphs into a monstrous centurial-old lizard, falling like a withered apple at Mihaela's tiny feet.

A crawling, skeletal Vlad, with big deformed eyes, addresses Mihaela with strange delight:

"Now I am yours! The real one! Are you going to accept me like this, with this hideous face of a 500-year-old man?"

"Yes, better like this, than living with a lying beast with a putrefied soul of mist! No tricks, no acts, no Davidson, or other masks!" Mihaela speaks up, trying to hide her astonishment.

"Then give me a kiss as sweet as you have given me before this shift..." Vlad begs her with tired eyes.

Swift as the wind, Mihaela kisses Vlad on his wrinkled, crimson lips. His rusty old lips taste like corpse, bittersweet.

"I didn't feel it like before!" Vlad whines as a beggar, moving his hands like some gnarled roots, helplessly, in the air.

"I have to get used to these lips, my dear!" Mihaela says, still terrified by the lizard-like face of Vlad.

Vlad rises up sluggishly, and takes a glimpse of himself in the mirror.

"Nooooooo!" he screams as if the whole pain of the world has bunched up in his eyes. He then grabs a vase and throws it in the glass, at his reflection, with insane rage: "No, that's not me! I reject ugliness! Is this God who makes us look like this?"

"Calm down, my dear," Mihaela breaks in, shaken by Vlad's enormous grief. "It is not Him who kept you for so long...but you who kept playing His role!"

And taking his old wrinkled face in her young hands, Mihaela whispers to Vlad, tenderly:

"You promised me that Mama would be present at our wedding in Verona... You said that you saw her in your yard, in Transylvania, in flesh and blood. Is that true?"

"Yes, it's true..." Vlad utters with bitter hope. "But until then you have to help me, my love..."

"Yes, I will! I will do everything..."

Mommy Doll walks towards them with big, heavy steps.

Both Vlad and Mihaela turn their heads towards Mommy, aghast, as if she were a giant. Mommy Doll pierces them with cold severe eyes.

"See, I feel weak, very weak," Vlad continues, ignoring the doll. "I need to feed myself... I know, I promised you that I shall not take advantage of human beings any more. Yes, I shall keep my promise... Yet, let me drink a little from your wrists because you are a saint, not just a mere girl... I do not want to die now that I've found you, my angel... It will take me a little more time to forget my bad habits...but I will take care of this, I'll make it with your help. I promise this to you, my love.

Now that I have everything—you, my dearest morning dew, I want to live this bliss, this miracle—I do not want to quit!"

Mihaela looks at Vlad with merciful eyes. Indeed, he looks so weak, so helpless, and so old...

Vlad breathes heavily, trembling in anguish. His eyes weep black tears of joy. His smile hits his withered cheeks like the strong waves of Nile hit the rock of Moses, gushing out.

"I'm dying, sweet love..." he cries.

"No, be of good hope..."

Mihaela lies next to him. She closes her eyes, giving in to Vlad. Vlad begins to suck Mihaela's delicate wrists like a hungry baby sucks his mother's tit.

"My love!" Vlad weeps in awe, savoring Mihaela's young blood. "I haven't shed these kind of tears for so long... It feels so good, so human..."

Three months later.

Mihaela and Vlad, embraced in the same bed, are lying with their arms and legs tangled tightly around each other, like two twin-trees in a cold winter day... The gigantic candelabrum watches the scene with immovable affliction. Mihaela opens one of her eyes, too early painted by wrinkles. She looks pale, old and bloodless.

Vlad, inflamed with desire, caresses his beloved onto her head:

"Mihaela, my love, we'll go to Verona!"

"Yes, to Verona..." Mihaela whispers in a weak voice.

"My sweet Juliet! You made me your Romeo... How happy my days are near your breath..." Vlad carries on, looking healthy and younger.

"I'm your Juliet..." Mihaela murmurs, shivering with oldness.

"I feel much better, thanks to you, my saving angel... I owe you my life..." Vlad embraces Mihaela lovingly to his chest.

"Vlad, I want to ask you something..." Mihaela addresses him with teary, sleepy eyes. "Take Vlady out of your cage and let him live, let him walk freely under the sunlight! Give him back his manuscript and help him become a writer! This is his dream! See your past life as means of a good novel, meant to never let people go through what you have gone through..."

"I know. I will set him free. Anything for you, my love!"

"Will you take care of Gabriela too? Can you set the *Wicked Clone* on stage with her? She loves to be an actress and she loves you... See, I feel so weak..."

"You'll live forever, my love! And you yourself will teach her the right way and set the play! I'm not the father that should be listened to..."

A silence of death arises before them.

"Mihaela? My love? Say something!" Vlad cries out, lifting Mihaela up in his arms.

Mihaela is breathless and cold... A raven hits against the window of the chamber with a sharp sinister beak.

Vlad falls to his knees and gives an apocalyptic scream. His scream rings out like a shattering dong above the skyscrapers of tbe City of Stars.

"Nooooooo! What have I done? I've been so selfish and so greedy... She's dying and I'm living! What for? I'm nothing without her, back to my misery!"

Ragingly, Vlad tears his gown apart and opens his chest, like the earth split by a chasm. A spring of blood gushes out of his broken heart all over Mihaela, feeding her until his very last drop...

"Come back, come back to me, my love..." Vlad cries like a parent after his dying child, like a husband after his long-loved wife, like a baby after his mother's sight.

In despair, Vlad kneels before God and speaks up:

"Dear God, I have never prayed to you... How could I? And yet you gave me everything! To me—a devilish father and a loser, talentless artist and so-called producer, vampire-monster, murderer of happy people, unfulfilled human being, deplorable master of suicidal masks and self revengeful acts!"

The body of Mihaela suddenly rises above the bed. Vlad looks in awe. He trembles:

"God, she deserves to live, not I, a wretched soul without a pure goal! Please, bring her back to life in the sweet name of love! Take me and let her breathe! Bring her back through this bad blood of mine cured by your holy light!"

Mihaela arrives in front of an old wooden house,
heavenly adorned with pink climbing roses.

She touches the stems of the roses and she does not get hurt. These roses have no thorns. The divine being, surrounded by the seven children from The City of Stars Hospital, waits for her before the porch, with large opened arms. Mihaela hugs the divine being and every single child, beaming with love...

The seven children, with sweet voices of angels, start murmuring Mihaela's song—*A Kiss to Live*:
Baby, you know that I am dead without your love
My heart is cold, my breath is off, I need a kiss, a kiss to live...

The divine being kisses Mihaela on her forehead and Mihaela starts breathing. He gives her to drink from his golden chalice and Mihaela starts seeing... He then hands Mihaela a small sealed envelope and whispers: *Open it only before the eyes of your sister.*

Mihaela takes the small envelope and kisses the divine being's hand. Suddenly, a strong wind rips the petals off the climbing roses that adorn the wooden house, raising them into a fairy pink whirl that descends Mihaela onto her bed.

Vlad watches in awe, with his hands stuck in prayer.
"My love is back!" his eyes widely open, his face marred by fear startles with felicity tears. Mihaela looks more beautiful...more beautiful than he has ever known her. Vlad kisses her forehead with burning lips. A

spirit suddenly sneaks into his heart with a rushing mighty sound. He shakes from his head to his toes, light bursting out of his eyes. Mihaela opens her big brown eyes.

"Welcome back, my love, my soul!" Vlad utters with wonder, embracing Mihaela with broken wings of a tormented lover... Hot tears brim over his sweetheart; his heart bleeds like an opened wound, pumping lowlier and lowlier; his breathing gets heavier and heavier...yet he smiles with gratefulness, his eyes looking upon God. He then struggles to his feet, like a wounded hero, trying to fight an invisible fiend. He gets scared, shouting with his last powers: "Vlady, is that you? Forgive me..." Yet...just to collapse.

Mihaela hides the small envelope from the divine being under the pillow. She then caresses Vlad on his head:

"Rest, my dear..."

Vlad tries to rise to his feet again. He breathes harder and harder, however his eyes are still, serene and brighter...

"Mihaela, bring me to the cemetery...and forgive me..." Vlad says, losing his words in the air... He then stretches forth his hand: "Take me, my love!"

"Where?" Mihaela asks him, confused.

"Where Davidson's body lies."

"You're raving, my dear! Drink a little and you shall be a whole again," Mihaela offers her wrist to him again.

"No! I shall not! History shall not repeat! I shall not let fate mock again at us! It's time to die, my love. I lived too long. I took the life of your friend Davidson! I need my rest..."

"I need you, Vlad! See, if there's nothing to change in this world, if everything is good and normal, I have no reason to live..."

"You have your sister! Change her! Love her!"

"I love you and all that is in the new you. The past is gone. I have fogiven you because you played Davidson's part to win my heart... I love your soul, the fact that you gave up your deadly life and let Him bring you into light... You have made me fulfill my dream! You'll live as long as Love lives!"

"I'm happy now and now I need to go... You taught me love and showed me God. Now that I know He is, I hope... I have it all, I had your 'Yes' and that means happiness! Now I'm a whole!"

"Where is Gabriela? We have to find her," Mihaela speaks up, looking around the room, frantically.

"No, forget it... She has a deal... I mean I made a deal with..." Vlad stutters, trying to hide his eyes.

"I'll take care of her, don't worry. Just like you gave up, she will too..."

The Libraries of Lucifer.

Inside the walls of an infernally modern and sophisticated chamber, brimming with millions of pornographic magazines and books, Lucifer signs a diploma, the hairs of his fur frizzed up in terrible arousal: *In the honor of my loyal queen Gabriela—the diploma of Satanic smartness and Empirical darkness!*

Meantime, the Hunting Bitches flip through some colorful pages of magazines, inscriptioned with daring pictures of sexy ladies with chubby buttocks resembling their own dear posterior treasures...

Gabriela makes her appereence dressed in an academic red fiery dress, her head adorned with a crown of horns.

"You look horrific, my Queen!" Lucifer stands up, with his eyes boiling lust. "Now, with this diploma I declare you ready to abound in the smartness of Hades!"

The Hunting Bitches take their places in a postion of honor and begin to sing a praising hymn while Lucifer hands Gabriela his diploma of sin.

"Ave Maria" resounds fortissimo in the living room of the Holywood castle.

Vlad startles, listening with great curiosity. As the notes begin to rumble and tangle into a maddening disharmony, he cries out:

"Gabriela, is that you there, playing so wonderfully?"

The voice of Gabriela, singing with sarcasm, above the piano arpeggios, resounds, aloud and proud: *Ave Maria...Gracias Plena...*

"Bravo, my dear! You won! Come to your father!"

Like a thunderbolt, Gabriela pops up in front of Vlad, piercing him with devilish eyes:

"I didn't win, Papa! I don't have talent! I have your barren genes! I just imitate, as much as I can..."

"It is not true. You have talent... God taught you to play this beautiful ballad!" Mihaela affirms from behind, filled with love.

"I don't have God and I will never have Him because He does not exist!" Gabriela speaks back to her sister. And then, jumping at Mihaela with envenomed claws, she roars:

"Why don't you leave us alone, perfidious sister of light? You took my father into your heights and now he looks like Hell, even in my darkest eyes!"

"Sister, you need to help your father not to die..."

"Everyone dies! The apocalypse is coming, can't you see it? Uhh...I'm scared! Miss Death is around, sexy and flaunt! Is Jesus going to come and raise the dead from the tomb? Am I going to be punished if I spit on your words my doom?" Gabriela laughs, touching her sister onto her breasts. "How small they are... I pity you!"

"Your father and I need your help, dear sister... Please, be nice," Mihaela pleads with Gabriela, staring at her with scared eyes.

"Why isn't He saving you and Vlad? Papa, why don't you ask Him to let you live and take away your damned years and your sins? Me, I cannot help a father who's a treacherous fiend and a lying beast! I can't forgive for what he did to me!"

"God gave a daughter to help a father when he needs! Do a good deed, despite his sins... Fogive and you will be relieved! Please, help him, sis!" Mihaela persists.

"He cheated on me!" Gabriela screams at the top of her lungs. "He lied to me since my inception. Because of him I have a barren mind lacking of inspiration!"

"Vlad is your father, but not the Father! Please, understand! He does not have the power to give you inspiration... But he will help us set the *Wicked Clone*! He'll use the riches that he gathered, for us, for our art and roles! Isn't it wonderful? And inspiration will come as you let go and let God reign into your soul... Give and you'll receive! Help your father!" Mihaela declaims with sisterly fire.

"He is not my father! *He* is my real father!" Gabriela screams, pointing towards Hell. "Lucifer helped me whenever I needed help, he made me look more beautiful and stronger to rule the world! He has my soul and I have gained his throne! I am the Queen of the Night, the sexiest woman alive! Because of him I am immortal and wise! Papa and Lucifer signed a pact, but Vlad betrayed me in the most mischeveous way! He did not think of me at all! Only about him and his whore! He's even wanted to become an artist! Him? A lousy director of History! A king of aimless ambitions, willing of incestuous expeditions! A father, married with his daughter, asks me to give him more days of adultery to spoil his mistress? No way, to Hell with his request! I won't help him! He deserves to die! He has to die!" Gabriela mews like a cat, unlacing her black corset.

"Look at these breasts! He, my loyal father from abyss, gave them to me as a gift! All men are dying to touch my tits! Feel my nipples, sister!"

Mihaela looks terrified at the huge breasts of Gabriela. She then continues pleading with her sister, ravenous tears streaming through her eyes:

"I know, it's an awful thing what we did, but Love covers even the most unforgivable sins. He is your...fairy father and I am your sister... We were born of two indigo flowers at midnight and Vlad is the one who desired and birthed us to life. Love and forgive him for giving you this. Please, offer him to drink from your sweet wrists... Shed your evil blood and your heart we'll begin to thud..." Mihaela begs her sister.

"Didn't fairy Vlad promise to cease drinking blood? Why isn't Jesus giving him His blood now that he gave himself to the immortal God?"

Gabriela asks her sister, sneering. She then keeps her tongue at rest for a second, just to resume even more maliciously: "Why is Jesus letting you look like this—so helpless, old and ugly? Why does he let you cry and suffer? Speak to me, wise sister! He laughs at you, *you* foolish kids... He loves to see you beg for more, dying while worshipping His words... Isn't He sadistic? To give His children life and then to let them suffer and die? As you torment and beg me for some blood, God rolls the dice with Lucifer, sharing their parts!"

"Sister, believe me. Lucifer has blinded you. God does not want us to suffer, we choose to suffer when we don't allow Him to give us His wonders, when we keep struggling to solve our problems... He only can give you inspiration. Believe in God and you shall see rivers of composition flow from your heart!" Mihaela enflames Gabriela with faith.

"Let me see this! Let God give me inspiration...and then I'll worship Him with much affection!" Gabriela blows out ridiculous words to her sister.

"Faith is not hocus-pocus; miracles don't happen when you order them but when you let them come... Come to me sister, it's the right time and the right place..." Mihaela extends her hand to Gabriela.

"God speaks to me and says that now it's the right time for Vlad to die and the right place! I hate him from all my heart!" Gabriela cuts Mihaela off, grinning with evil in her eyes.

"She's right, Mihaela," Vlad speaks with sadness.

"Stop it, Vlad!" Mihaela cries out. And then, she addresses Gabriela again with sweeter voice:

"What has happened to you, sister? You said that you have changed! Where is the purple cross I gave you? You promised that you would never take it off!"

"No, I did not take it off! Do you want to see it?"

"Yes, I would love to..." Mihaela replies, suddenly heartened.

Gabriela walks towards Vlad's sickly bed. With her long nails, she thrusts her fingers inside her buttocks and draws out the long chain with purple cross.

"Watch it, touch it, isn't it beautiful?"

"You scare me," Mihaela says, horrified.

"You scare me with this ugly and old face of yours!" Gabriela bites back as she places a mirror in front of Mihaela's face: "Look at yourself! Remember when you were once like me, so charming, so divine, so young? You could bewitch whichever men you wanted to…and now, look at your mug! You stay in bed with your grumpy old dad!"

Mihaela takes the mirror and places it before Gabriela.

"What do you see? Nothing! There's no reflection of yourself! You're nothing!"

Gabriela breaks the mirror and shouts out, with her tongue stuck out, like a viper:

"I don't need a mirror to show me who I am! The mirror is an illusion; I am here for real! And I do not fear like you, human beings, drunken in tears!"

"Sister, you don't exist! You have no soul! Your heart's not beating! You are dead!" Mihaela speaks up, sorrow steaming into her eyes.

"Then why do I speak? Why do you need my blood if I am dead and don't exist?" Gabriela snarls, rising the purple cross against her sister. "Now Lucifer will transfer the inspiration directly from you to me!" Gabriela laughs, preparing to stab Mihaela to her heart.

But in the twinkling of an eye, Mihaela clutches Gabriela's murderous arm and bites her wrist, just like David the poet bit her wrist that night, in their Transylvanian escapades…

Gabriela bursts into a spasm of tears, her whole body twitches and shakes in fear. She then looks down at her arm that does not cease to shed blue blood… She raises her head and looks up at Mihaela, with flooded, red eyes. Slowly, her eyes open wider and clear out, like the sky after a thunderous night. Her face suddenly gains fine wrinkles and her nails shorten; her cheeks lift up and blush like roses in the summer; her skin shows little pores breathing out life; her black tail withers and fails like a dry branch in winter… Gabriela then quickly closes her corset, hiding her breasts, and runs out of Vlad's castle, ashamed.

A pair of young tears digs Mihaela's numb cheeks.

Suddenly, she remembers the little envelope that the divine being gave to her and feels sorry that she forgot to open it before Gabriela... With a trembling hand, she wants to take the envelope from underneath the pillow, but Vlad catches her wrist and kisses it with fever, twining his old fingers into her delicate young ones.

"Let's go, my dear! I have to show you something..."

And in that moment, with his right foot, Vlad touches the footboard of his bed and the floor of the chamber splits up. Then, it slowly opens like the mouth of a lion, unfolding a steep toboggan that leads into darkness. Suddenly, the bed carrying Vlad and Mihaela slides down along the golden toboggan that burns their bodies and blinds their eyes. Mihaela catches Vlad's hand into her hand. Like the wind, they land into a dark tunnel with hot steam and millions of red bubbles. As they walk foot-to-foot along the humid and shadowy route, blood aerosols spray on them fresh drops of oxygen...

"Breathe, Vlad! Breathe deeply..." Mihaela encourages him as she hears Vlad giving out loud puffs, convulsively.

"I'm trying my dear, just a little more..."

His back hunches and his knees bend, out of strength, sinking into a red viscous mud that keeps bubbling with hunger. But Mihaela holds him tightly by the arm, pushing through the darkness.

As they arrive at the end of the tunnel, a glowing platform lowers before their eyes. As she looks down, Mihaela can see the tongues of a round golden clock that ticks loudly, like the beat of her heart... Vlad encourages her to step onto the clock... The clock elevates them slowly, its tongues turning at a fast speed towards the light of the sunset. A soft blow of spring brushes their hair and orange rays of sun bloom their pale-as-death faces. Their eyes become clear and sharp like silver moons in the dusk... The horizon comes near to them, scattering the clouds of gloom. A centurial black oak forest unveils before their eyes, with plants and trees so green and fresh, lavish like the paradise and smelling of babies' breath.

"Please, take me in your arms... I can't walk any more..." Vlad whines to Mihaela, his body shrinking more and more...

Mihaela takes Vlad into her arms, with the love of a caring mother. Vlad has turned so small and light, just like a feeble child!

The soft and moist grass gives vigor to Mihaela's steps; the mild and friendly Sun gives peace to her mind... As she raises her eyes to the sky, a lofty oak, tall and beautiful as she has never seen before, with thousand arms that spread and tangle to the heights and hug blissfully the sky, captures her third eye. At its large shadow, a cross of knitted branches pierces an elevated ground covered by freshly green grass. The cross seems to keep an eagle eye above the whole wide forest.

"Stop here! Please, lay me down..." Vlad speaks up with tremolous voice.

As Mihaela lays old little Vlad onto the risen ground with cross, Vlad begins to sob, with large tears that sprinkle the grass:

"Mihaela, I am not Davidson! I've never been! Davidson is dead! Here is his tomb! Gabriela killed him at my will, right here, in this forest of sin," he trembles with guilt, pointing to the elevated ground.

"No, Vlad, I know it's not true! You're just fooling around to make me feel blue! That night, on Autumn Place, I went and searched for him and there was no Davidson to be found..." Mihaela speaks up.

"Yes, I know... I tricked him, I made him go. Davidson was real. He was not me, I was not him... I did everything to make you love me... I wanted so much to be Davidson...to have your love but..." Vlad utters with deep bitterness.

"You killed him and you lied to me? Gabriela was right, you deserve to die!" Mihaela cries out, feeling the great oak collapsing over her.

"Yes, I deserve to die! I helped your mother procreate knowing that she was to die once she gives birth to you... I stole Vlady, your Mama's son and left her barren and insane, until she met her grave... I instigated Gabriela to kill David, Emanuel, Emil, and all your friends... I set your rape scene when you were little so that you would hate all men...and long to be with me, under my protection... I borrowed the face of Dominica and stole your novel so that I could enter your soul and have you under my control... I cut Vlady's tongue so that I could be sure of his silence and then I stole the papers of his novel... I did evil and only evil! But evil brings evil, and gives no life! Lies finally come out and you get buried in your own strife! I am so proud that you did not resemble me...and you stayed strong in love and faith... You have Dora's eyes and smile, her soul..."

And Vlad pulls a small portrait of his wife out of his chest and gives it to Mihaela:

"When my wife was killed, I stopped to live, to breathe..."

"That's me..." Mihaela quivers.

"Yes, you're like two peas in a pod," Vlad smiles with melancholic eyes. "The day I found her dead, I found no reason to live on... I made a deal with Lucifer and started to kill all the wives and brides of Transylvania, rejoicing to see their husbands and grooms suffer as I had suffered..."

"It made you happy?"

"Happy? What's happy? Revenge, terror, pleasure, those were my feelings... But now, as I confess my soul to you...I feel like a child who stole red apples from the neighbor's yard and was caught red handed..."

Deep silence.

"I did it all...but all has made me ugly and small... One needs to appreciate less to be happy and blessed!" Vlad utters with regret.

A mirthful blow of spring blooms in the air, bringing peace out of despair...

"Say something! Throw me in this tomb and hate me, curse me, just say something!" Vlad pleads with Mihaela.

"I hate you but...I love you. You truly loved your wife!"

"I truly love you, Mihaela! You have the Aura, you're chosen. You're an Artist. Please write that in your book and don't read it to anyone again until you reach the end of it..."

"You are a monster...but a different monster... You don't see a monster's love too often..." Mihaela murmurs.

"Monsters are humans, Mihaela. Humans who didn't get Love... Monsters want love, Mihaela!"

"Vlad, there is one thing I want to ask you. When you meet Mama, up there, in the sky, can you please, tell her to come here just for a while...to touch me and to heal my sister with her smile?"

"I can never meet your Mama because she is in heaven! Only your blood can bring her back..."

"My blood?" Mihaela asks, overwhelmed.

"Yes, I know it for sure..." Vlad replies.

"How come?"

"I wish so much to meet your Mama...but Hell rings its bell for this wretched body of mine..."

"Hell? What is Hell? " Mihaela cuts him off.

"Hell is awful. Hell is...living without you..."

The sky fissures and a beatific light enraptures their sight.

Slowly, the clouds set apart, like some curtains of the *Metropolitan Opera*, and God, strong and kind, speaks out:

"Why did it take you so long, my child?"

Vlad, terrified by the unexpected vision, slowly raises his eyes:

"Oh Lord, you talk to me? Me, a wicked clone filled up with sins?

Please, hear me talk and let my bitter tears fall...

God, why did You let this stake impale my heart

When all I needed was to love, not to be torn apart?

Why did I search the evil, impaling pure men?

Was it your Eden that had to throw me in that Hell?

I've been malicious, my wants: pernicious,

Just worth of ephemeral ambitions!

I had such an obsessive plan and doomed this life

When my sweet wife was cast aside!

I asked myself: why should my feet step on their misfit,
My breath breathe Your air and spirit,
My lips speak and my heart keep up the beat?
Is it still fair without my love to feed?
Oh Lord, is it my understanding proud or
is it plainly allowed?
You made her pure but this life inhuman,
You made her true but their words of fuel!
How could I live if death stands at each corner
Waiting to feed its worms with us, Performers?
Do we have to entertain the wicked and make the devil laugh
and then, will it depart?
Or should I walk in You and play a blindly part
to save my heart?
Cause smartness brings regret that both You
and the devil kiss on Everest.
Oh, God, I am a Sisif, always falling, please give me rest!
Forgive me and forget my sinful past!"

"Forgiveness I do give you!" God replies with the voice of Goodness. "But Vlad, why didn't you let me write your part? I had a plan for you: to give you 90 years of love, health and wealth, instead of 500 years of Hell in which you chose to dwell!"

"Give me wisdom, dear God, at least now to speak Your words, with a sincere heart:

In the name of Love, perform a miracle and raise a heart! Raise Davidson from death, from the tomb on which now my bones rest, and let him love Mihaela till his last breath! Put me there, in his grave of worms, where I deserved to fall a hundred years ago!"

No sooner has Vlad finished his pledge than the earth cracks. Twelve doves raise Davidson from death and lay him down on the fresh grass sprinkled with life.

With his face brightened by gratefulness, Vlad gives his last breath in the warm arms of Mihaela.

An old raven joins the white doves and helps Mihaela lay Vlad in Davidson's tomb, covering him with moist fresh ground and tall grass.

A waterfall of tears springs from Mihaela's eyes onto Vlad's grave as she whispers an ardent prayer for the forgiveness of his soul:

Forgive him, Lord, for his trespasses, for they were many, as he rejected your blessings, as he did wrong in deeds, in words, and in his thoughts, being led by darkness's wrath... But give him rest as he confessed his sins to meet my Mama in Your blessed wings.

"Your mother is in Heaven, my beloved child!"

"And where is Heaven, dear God?"

"Heaven is in you."

As soon as Mihaela finishes her conversation with God,

a Queen of the Night flower arises from Vlad's tomb, miraculous and lovely, gazing graciously at Mihaela's light. The flower has the divine smell of her childhood's garden, rising higher and higher, in the twinkling of an eye, towards a beatific sky. It spreads her leaves like the wings of a sphinx, embracing Mihaela tenderly, with unknown bliss. Mihaela watches the flower rise forth, like her mother once watched it before her birth.

Swift as the wind, another stem with indigo flower appears from the roots of the Queen of the Night, alike in face with the first flower, yet bowing to the ground, just like an ivy-stem in love with Mihaela's stride. Mihaela caresses the buds of thorns that have just grown onto the second stem, inhaling the hypnotic scent of nicotine that its flower spreads. As she stares at it, its stamens turn phosphorescent, just like two eyes, omnipresent.

Suddenly, Davidson rises to his feet and steps towards Mihaela. Under the greenish-blue eyes of Davidson that beam to life, Mihaela is about to faint. Yet, the upright stem of the indigo flower hurls its leaves and lifts Mihaela's head, and the ivy-stem wraps around her waist...helping her to stand.

Davidson takes Mihaela by her hand. Mihaela faces him with fear: "Is he the one?"

Lucifer appears from his tunnels, disfigured.

"Now you want everything?" he pierces God with conceit. "Vlad is mine! Remember our deal?" Lucifer growls, pointing towards Vlad's grave.

"I don't make deals with you, Lucifer," the Voice of God replies.

"Give him back to me! He worked for me all of his life!" Lucifer snarls.

"He worked for you all of his death! The rest is in my hand!" God replies, calmly.

"What do you mean? I have the contract right here. Vlad signed it. Read it: *Vlad's soul and Gabriela's soul for Mihaela's love.* As simple as that."

"But are you able to give love?" God asks Lucifer.

Lucifer turns all red, cap-a-pie, getting smaller and smaller...

"If you are not able to give, then why should you take? The contract is untruthful, therefore it is not valid," God's voice concludes.

"I am your wicked clone! You need me, God, more than you need anyone in this world!" Lucifer screams on.

God disappears as a rainbow beneath the sky, giving the earth His smile.

"But Gabriela is mine!" Lucifer howls out to the skies. "She is mine... You will never take her away from me... She will never be weak like you, human beings! Remain with God, cry, struggle, wrinkle, die... I pity all of you..."

As Lucifer toils and sweats to justify his covetous acts, he pricks himself into the sharp edge of the cross that lies obediently onto the fresh grass.

"Auch, auch!" Lucifer cries, slapping the ground with his long black tail and giving a monstruous wail towards Hell. Suddenly, his foul body explodes, a gush of red blood melting him all... The red blood springs into a small river, making way through the flowers and weeds of the oak forest...

The strong wind, like a hungry fiery dragon, suddenly turns warm and mild, sparrows and pigeons replacing its noise with heavenly sounds.

An indigo petal splits off from the majestic stem of the Queen of the Night flower, and flies spiritedly, chasing Mihaela's steps just like a faithful twin, released. When Mihaela stops, the petal lands on the ground, near her little feet. Suddenly, the earth opens its big mouth and swallows the petal just like a hungry thief... A little flower, just like the one that rose onto Vlad's tomb, grows repeatedly wherever Mihaela's feet set forth, and blooms. Mihaela embraces every new risen flower, kissing its petals that gleam and that seem hallowed. Suddenly, a second stem springs forth and crawls on its ambitious thorns, watching Mihaela's ride with burning phosphorescent eyes... And here they come, hundreds of Queen of the Night flowers, arising like blades from heaven as Mihaela strides, hopeful at this hour.

A magical lawn, brimming with Queen of the Night Flowers, covers the land with an entrancing smell, lying in heavenly strands.

The night turns into day.

A strong Sun sends its rays on Mihaela's face.

Davidson looks surprised at Mihaela and asks her with a smile:

"Aren't you afraid of the Sun?"

"Why should I be?"

"You know...vampires are afraid of the Sun..."

"Who said that?" Mihaela smiles back.

"Well...first and foremost, Bram Stoker. I read a few times, *Dracula*, his book... I saw *Coppola*'s movie...they mention this in *Interview with a Vampire* too..."

"Impressive! I can see that you know a lot about vampires... That means that you've been chasing them..."

Davidson smiles. His smile reminds Mihaela of Vlad.

Silence.

The Sun beams again, this time mildly, reflecting in Davidson's eyes.

"No, I am not afraid of the Sun... I belong to the light," Mihaela speaks as she loses herself in Davidson's electrifying blue eyes. "Well, long time ago we used to be afraid, my sister and I... But those days are gone..."

"Your sister?" Davidson cuts her off.

"Yes...she used to be afraid of the Sun, but not anymore... You know, the Sun does not have the same power as it once had, back then, when we were born... The Sun changed. Hatred, greed, money, they all have polluted it and made it angry... Now the Sun frowns and burns... It no longer warms... I wish the Sun would smile again..."

Davidson and Mihaela step along the ocean. Talking and walking, they get in front of a big majestic building of a hospital.

A mother and a husband, with large smiles painted on their faces and happy arms holding newly born babies, walk down the stairs of the hospital.

Davidson and Mihaela congratulate the young couple, rejoicing at their happiness. Mihaela's eyes are suddenly caught by the two giggling babies who are wearing pink dresses. They are twin baby girls! She cannot believe her eyes! The twins look just like Gabriela and herself when they were babies... Mihaela raises her eyes to the young parents and, as she closely looks at their faces, she recognizes her mother and father, Violeta and Grid.

"Please, may I hold her?" Mihaela asks the beautiful mother, taking one of the twin babies in her yearning arms... She hugs the sweet baby girl with suffocating love and asks her mother:

"What is her name? She is so sweet..."

"Gabriela..." her mother replies.

Mihaela looks perplexed at baby Gabriela.

"Hi, Gabriela!" she says playfully, taking Gabriela's little hand in her hand.

At the same time, baby Gabriela bites Mihaela's loving hand. Indigo blood starts pouring out while baby Gabriela's fangs shine bright in the Sun that smiles…

WICKED CLONE (Chorus)

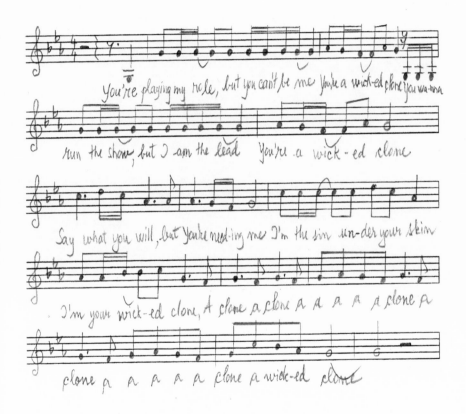

Author's Note

Writing this novel has been the most wonderful but sinuous journey of my whole life: enlightening but scary, empowering but at times devastating. I never thought that exposing the wicked clone and her evil schemes would be such a steep mountain to climb. I wrote the first draft of the Wicked Clone novel in three months…filled with light, love and God. It felt as if a spirit entered my mind and did not give me rest until I finished the first layout of 200 pages.

Then, as I traveled through the tunnels of Lucifer and the head of God, as I became more and more engaged in this fight, putting flesh and blood in this journey towards Light, trying to find the true gift of immortality that lies beyond our fears, our condemnation, our weaknesses or irrational moments of breakdown, I got myself haunted by my own characters, by the magnificence, innocence but also by the maleficence of these beings that are living in real life and who are heroes and prisoners of both light and dark. My character, Mihaela, is My true self's travel from death to life, from darkness to light, from Lucifer to God. My twin sister Gabriela is my wicked clone, my alter ego that loves to torment my soul, but that I could never live without, like a rose that cannot strip its own thorns. The wicked clone is the inevitable partner who makes us look to the sky, to God. She pushes us to surpass ourselves, to write, to scream, to sing, to cry, to let go in the abyss of life in order to climb again back to the Light.

What I try to give you through this novel is the journey to our most powerful selves, who are not afraid of the wicked clone, who are not afraid to take the risk of finding the Joy in their valley of trouble. Please, suffer, love, cry, but never give up on this inexplicable fight of love called Life.

Thank You

To Mama, my saint, who never gives up on doing Good...
who always feeds her daughters with magical healing soup...

To Gabriela, the wicked angel who taught me to love
No matter how dark the light may have looked down the road...

To Paul Smith, great friend of our lives,
Who has been part of the Wicked Clone journey as my knight of light

To Papa Grid, who's writing with a thousand arms and legs
Who's never tired of showing his humble greatness to us

To God, the one and only who can understand our stubbornness
And yet, who raises us always back to continue our beautiful life-fest
To Him, who gave us the most blessed gifts of Love, Inspiration,
Music, Writing, Laughter, Crying, of Holding Hands together tight
to overcome the wicked clone's endless lies

To Vlady, my sweetest brother who knows how to play games
Who's always soldiered us with his laughter and with his
frolicsome brains

To Love and Life...please keep us all in your shelter to never die...

To all my friends and enemies... Never give up on criticizing me, on
showing me my imperfections; I need your lovely wickedness to rise
up to my Goodness.

About MIHAELA MODORCEA

Mihaela Modorcea is an American Romanian-born actress, writer, singer, dancer, and painter. She graduated with honors from the National University of Theatrical Arts & Cinematography in Bucharest. Her roots are in Transylvania. Mihaela has an identical twin sister—Gabriela—the Wicked Clone who has inspired Mihaela to write this cinema book that holds not only words of Life, but music, paintings, Lucifer and God. For the first time the heroes of a novel are heroes in real life, attempting to change the world just like the characters are trying to...

"It is not easy to deal with our wicked clone, but once we find the way and walk through it...we catch Happiness's right hand, and She will never let us leave her land..." *Mihaela* states.

Mihaela is also the author of the poetry book *Rage and Love*, *Tibco*, *(2006)*, of the poetry book *Wicked Clone (2014)* and of two screenplays for two features which are in pre-production.

Along with her twin sister Gabriela, Mihaela is most recently featured and credited as writer and performer on Jay-Z & Kanye West's multi-platinum and four times Grammy award-winning album "Watch The Throne," on the song "Murder To Excellence" which is widely considered and reviewed as "the centerpiece of the album."

The cinematic play *Wicked Clone*, based on the *Wicked Clone* novel, is set to open Off Broadway, starring Mihaela and Gabriela Modorcea as performers, authors, composers, and choreographers. Mihaela and Gabriela have also written and produced over 200 songs, 21 of which are included on the *Wicked Clone* music album.

In reviewing Mihaela's poetry book *Rage and Love*, journalist Dorin Grigore wrote:

"*Reading this book, it's impossible not to ask God: Oh, Lord, who could ever rise to the love this girl offers? This divine chemistry through which rage turns into love is amazing and overwhelming.*"

"*Mihaela Modorcea creates a visionary landscape of ideas, full of passion, carnal force, and great power."*

"*Mihaela Modorcea reinvents language itself, in that she looks for the 'other' way of naming things, as Plato said in his Cratylus dialogue.*"

"*In Mihaela Modorcea's verses there lies a theatricality of Shakespearean origin, an air of northern poetry, a steam from Ibsen and Strindberg; her verses are a leaven of Puck's fantasy...*"

WICKED CLONE *music album*

Music & Lyrics: Mihaela and Gabriela Modorcea / Indiggo Twins

1. A KISS TO LIVE - *with video bonus*
2. BITE BACK - *with video bonus*
3. OOH LA LA / FAIRIES CALL – *with video bonus*
4. LITTLE LYING MIRROR
5. RIDE WITH ME
6. HONEY, MONEY
7. TELL ME LESS & LOVE ME MORE – *with video bonus*
8. YOUNGER THAN YESTERDAY
9. HALF MAN, HALF VAMP
10. I AM LIKE GOD
11. WICKED CLONE - *with video bonus*
12. LA LA LA - *with video bonus*
13. HELLO
14. PULL THE CURTAINS TO THE SIDE
15. QUEEN OF TANGO – *with video bonus*
16. LOVE FLU – *with video bonus*
17. ON MY OWN - *with video bonus*
18. I'M AFRAID OF WHO I AM
19. EUREKA
20. NAILS UP
21. DRACULA'S LAND

Musical scores of some of the songs from the **WICKED CLONE** *music album on pages:*
93 - A Kiss To Live; 146 – Bite Back; 150 – Ooh La La (Fairies Call);
181 – Little Lying Mirror; 196 – Ride With Me; 263 – Honey, Money;
278 – Tell Me Less & Love Me More; 319 – Younger Than Yesterday;
330 – Half Man, Half Vamp; 378 – I Am Like God; 527– Wicked Clone.

The cinema scenes of the WICKED CLONE novel

(number of scene / page)

PART 1

Musical scores on pages:

93 - A Kiss To Live; 146 – Bite Back; 150 – Ooh La La (Fairies Call);

181 – Little Lying Mirror; 196 – Ride With Me; 263 – Honey, Money;

278 – Tell Me Less & Love Me More; 319 – Younger Than Yesterday;

330 – Half Man, Half Vamp; 378 – I Am Like God; 527 – Wicked Clone

Drawings on pages: 25 (Violeta), 135 (Mihaela), 189, 517 (Gabriela – Wicked Clone)

Photo (Gabriela & Mihaela): p.529

**THANK YOU FOR BUYING
THE WICKED CLONE NOVEL.**

Love, Mihaela Modorcea